Seeking Hades' Ember

Vera Foxx

If you would like to read the
Female Main Character's Parents,
you can find their story in the
Under the Moon main series *The Alpha's Kitten.*

This story can be read as a stand-alone.

Table of Contents

$\mathscr{P}rologue$

Under The Moon

Hades sat upon his throne, sulking while drinking the amber liquid in his hand. It no longer had a taste, the ice cubes having long dissipated as he sat watching the liquid swirl within. He tilted his head and sat in wonder at how things can be taken for granted. Just like the ice cube: once precious to his alcohol, to keep it cool and collected, had now disappeared from his cup, just like his Persephone.

That damn goddess Selene had ruined his life. His one true love was ripped from his grasp and was destined to be with another, some damn messenger angel that he has no care to know the name of. Persephone was his. He had specifically picked her out of all the goddesses because of her beauty and grace. He held her in his palace for more than 1000 years; she never faltered in her reluctance towards him, and he never forced her to love him, just to give him time to show how much he cared. Once he thought there would be a breakthrough, only to find out that she had been matched with a messenger angel passing through hell.

She danced into his arms like a sailor to a siren, never looking back at his heartbroken self. Before he could intervene, Zeus and

1

Selene came down stopping the altercation. "She is mine! I have a deal in place!" he spat as he tried to walk through the god wall before him.

"Look at her, Hades. She is happy now. Be honest. Was she ever happy with you?" Zeus spoke in all seriousness. Hades growled and tried to pass but was blasted away by a large bolt of lightning. "That's enough, Hades. You can never break the soul bond that now binds them. It's time to let go." Persephone grabbed onto the angel as he flew her out of hell, leaving Hades to wallow in the darkness alone.

"Hades," Selene spoke in her serene voice. It was her that had caused this, the cause of his love to leave him. Selene had ruined everything, all the work he had tried to win her heart. All for naught.

"It is your fault!" he roared, and Selene stepped back from his fierce anger. "It is your fault she left. Why could you not have paired her with me!?" Growling, the underworld began to shake and crumble under their feet. Demons ran from the scene to seek shelter.

Selene composed herself, letting her light blue robes dance across the crumbled ground. "She was not your match. Your souls did not complement each other. You have a soulmate to complete yourself. I promise you; you will be happier with your mate than you ever were with Persephone." The scowl on Hades' face remained as he walked away from his brother and niece. He was tired and fed up with the world going up against him.

That was nearly 1500 years ago. Another drink of the warm liquid went down his throat. It continued to refill as he wallowed in self-pity. The great idea to create his own mate went down horribly. Trixen, the supposed perfect mate he created ended up a complete disaster, wreaking havoc in both the human and supernatural realms.

Hades sighed once again as one of his servants graced his presence.

"What?" he snapped.

"Most benevolent, the Goddess Selene is here to see you." The servant bowed reverently at the stewing god. Hades' jaw ticked at the thought of that monstrosity gracing his presence.

"What does she want?" he whispered.

"For an audience with you, regarding your mate." Hades' head turned slowly. His permanent frown that sat on his face since the day Persephone left only deepened.

"Bring her in."

Selene briskly walked through the large throne room as many servants bowed before the Moon Goddess. She smiled as she stood before the God of the Underworld. "Greetings Hades. I bring you good news."

Chapter 1

Hades

I rolled my eyes in frustration. What the hell does this woman want? The first time she visited me in her entire existence was only to tell me that Persephone was not to be mine. Now, she comes to the underworld for a second time, to brag about it. The nerve of the damn woman.

For years I have heard of the 'wonders' that this woman has done to the supernatural world as well as the Olympian gods. She was granted the gift of finding the missing piece of every supernatural, and it was working so well, that she decided to expand her prospects into her own world with the gods. In my opinion, everyone was damn well happy before her. Zeus had his whores, Poseidon had his conquests, and I had Persephone. The one thing I ever fought over in this dull, rancid life that I had for my own.

Even though I was the oldest of the three major gods, I chose to be down here. To live in my own world away from Earth, the humans, and the Celestial glory of all the other gods. It was quiet down here when I wanted it to be. Now mostly you can hear screams in the night of those left in Tartarus.

"What do you want, Selene?" I spat out her name with venom. The woman better hurry up; I had better things to do than listen to the shit she has to say. She doesn't even have her own mate.

"As I said, I've come to bring you good news." She took a few steps forward and a poof of a cloud popped up behind her as she sat down. She laid on it and plucked a grape from a small bowl that had appeared.

My jaw ticked. "What of it? Speak up so you can show yourself out."

Selene groaned in frustration as she sat back up and dusted off the invisible dirt from her hand. "Fine, you are no fun." Selene stood up again and started walking up the steps to my throne. The demons beside me began to cower and back away, knowing I wasn't in the mood to tolerate such insolence.

Once she stood beside me, she leaned over to whisper in my ear. "Your mate has been born!" Selene stood up happily and clapped her hands in excitement. The giddy cheerleader gig was not something I was a fan of. Gripping my glass tightly, I drank the whisky in one shot and put it down lightly on the throne. Servants continued to back away, knowing this was the calm before the storm.

"What. Of. It." I growled each word individually.

"I just thought you should know! We got off on the wrong foot, and I wanted to make sure you knew so you could search for her. I can even show you who she is now." She lifted her hand to make a magical portal appear, but I slammed my glass to the floor as I stood up.

"I'll have NOTHING to do with you and your mate shit." The castle grounds shook, and the servant demons ran in fear. Selene frowned and waved her hand, making sure I couldn't see the child that was destined to be my soulmate.

Selene showed no fear because she was protected, protected by most of the gods on Olympus due to most of them have found their mates. I knew my outburst wouldn't do anything to her, but my temper had grown throughout the years and even the concubines had grown fearful of me. No one had the aura of my Persephone.

Selene walked back down the throne stairs and tutted when I sat back down. "Do what you will Hades. You only get one soul mate." I gripped my fist in anger, feeling my claws scraping against the palm of my hand. I could love no one more than I could have loved Persephone, of that I was sure.

As Selene neared the exit of the throne room, she grabbed the door and looked back at me. There was sympathy in her eyes, but I dared not look into her eyes any longer as she spoke. "The longer you take to accept that you have a mate to claim, the harder it will be for her to accept you." With that, Selene walked out the door like she was never there.

20 years later...

Jillian

"Dammit girls, hurry up!" the pungently large man spoke as he continued to prod us like cattle. His name was Teddy Johnson, or 'master' as he liked us to call him. "This is getting ridiculous; how long does it take for you filthy whores to shower?!" Another smack was heard with his wooden police stick on the wall of our communal showers.

The new girls that had come in last week. They were scared, beaten, and broken, much like how I was when I arrived here at just nine years old, at least I think I was nine. Before that, I don't remember much. When I woke up, I had lost all memories of who I was with no clothing or possessions to remind me of my past or where I came from. Just me, sitting in an empty cell with a large t-shirt that said, "*Cheaters Anonymous, Gentleman's Club.*"

I was the youngest one of the entire group of women and did a lot of physical labor. Cleaning the cells, making food that I couldn't eat, making beds that had been used in ways a nine-year-old should know nothing about.

From that age on, I was just a slave to Master. The large man with a gut that overflows the buckle of his pants. He is overweight, smells, and has a ridiculous bow tie he likes to wear on work nights and has a ridiculous fascination with me and hasn't sold me to the highest bidder just yet. I keep wondering when he is going to finally get rid of me because I am not the most obedient slave he would want.

There were a few times he put me up on the auction stand in the back of his strip club. The area was for strict VIP members that wanted a taste of the merchandise on the poles. The people that lived outside the club didn't know the difference. They thought it was a regular strip club with regular people. Even the town cops would come in when they were off duty to gawk at the girls.

Little did they know they were all stolen from their homes, their families, and their lives.

When I was up on the stand to be sold, I always threw a fit. I acted rabid, biting when he tried to touch me, slapping his hand away. He loved to slap, hit and punch my body when the buyers weren't around. He often says that my skin was my best feature, with his bloody red handprints on it. My skin was alabaster white, mainly because I hadn't seen the sun in God knows how long. My hair was long, blonde with a hit of red. The perfect strawberry blonde highlighted girl. Yes, girl. I looked no older than fifteen.

Since I was so young arriving at the club, I never got a proper meal. I was lucky to get the pizza crusts off the patrons' plates as they left at 5 a.m. every morning. If I was lucky, someone left a fry our two along with half of a hamburger. Dancers always got a bit more food than me, because Master said he had to keep their tits 'perky.'

I'm not sure what my true height would have been if I got the proper nutrition, but I'm close to 5'2" and far too skinny with breasts that finally came in the past year. Now, he has really been pushing me to be sold. Saying I'm the oldest virgin he has ever kept at twenty. "You'll fetch a pretty penny," he would say.

"Time's up! Get out!" The water turned cold and all of us girls huddled together as we went back into the large common cell that held us. There were cots on the floor. Everything was completely minimal, no personal effects, a small blanket, and barely-there stripper attire or waitressing uniforms.

Since I was considered the senior, I helped the new girls get ready. Some were crying, some praying. I didn't dare tell them I stopped praying five years ago because no help was going to come. Now, I was just in survival mode and helping those cope with what cards that we have been dealt with.

Some nights I would sit with the new girls, petting their hair, and singing some sort of lullaby. If I didn't, their cries would call for unwanted attention which could lead to beatings, rape and other sadistic things.

Once the girls were dressed, Master's men led them out one by one as they went for training. I was the last in the cell, getting ready to walk out. I had on my waitressing uniform, which was extremely revealing, just a bit more than those poor dancers. My breasts were exposed and pushed up high, and my tiny skirt barely covered my rear end. "Hold on, there Jillian," Master spoke quietly as he rolled his cigar in his mouth. He let out a puff of smoke in my face and I turned my head in disgust.

"You listen here, and you listen well. Be a good girl tonight, show some smiles or that gorgeous alabaster skin will be slapped by yours truly." He chuckled as another puff of smoke left his mouth. It wasn't a threat; it was a promise. "One more thing, you act up, I'll break you in your first time if you get my drift." Master gave an evil smirk and walked away.

The nights he tried to sell me and failed, he would paddle my butt, thighs, and stomach, all of which could be hidden under my uniform. He didn't beat the other girls like me because they had to perform. The cops would question why some little girl was up on stage, so thankfully I never had to grace the stage. Now he was threatening something completely new. Have him take the one thing left of me or have someone else do it.

"Yes, Master." I kept my head low, not daring to look him in the eye. I knew his limit, and tonight was it.

By the time I got to the floor, the male patrons were already seated at tables. Girls that I helped dress were dancing, sitting, and talking with some rich male businessmen. They all acted so pleasantly when they sat on some of their laps. Even though they sit there with a smile on their faces, their insides had already died knowing that their lives were ruined.

Gracefully walking to the kitchen, I picked up my small apron and the notepad and headed to a few tables. Many were regulars and knew my name which they call for me constantly. "Jillian!" Loukas called me over. He and his crew came in every Friday night like clockwork. However, this night he had different friends with him. "How is my favorite waitress?" Loukas held out his arm for a side hug.

"I'm well, thank you." I gave a genuine smile. Loukas could always make me laugh and his commentary on the new girls' dancing was unexpectedly hilarious.

Loukas was Greek and had the beautiful, tanned skin that every man should be jealous of. His dark stubble on his strong jawline lined up well with his strong cheekbones I'm sure he was a lucky catch for some lady if he would get out of a strip club.

"Guys, I want you to meet Jillian! She started working here a year ago and we've become best mates!" All the men looked over at me and gave me a friendly smile. Some looked like they were out of place, unsure how they should be acting but Loukas quickly gave me their names. "Hermes, Ares, and Vulcan," Loukas said with pride as he sat. "We have one more coming. He'll be here in a few."

The men were like Loukas, tall, strong-looking, and handsome. Vulcan had a bit of twitch in his left eye, but he could easily get anyone he wanted.

"Pleasure to meet you." I nodded at them.

The three stared at me until Vulcan spoke up. "Aren't you a little young to be working here?"

I blushed scarlet, knowing I look extremely young. "I'm actually 20," I said meekly. "Good genes I guess." I shrugged my shoulders.

Loukas's lips were pressed in a thin line and looked at his friends. After a few moments, they gave me their drink orders and I went to the bar to have them prepared. Looking back, I saw the small group talking in hushed tones, arguing, and throwing napkins in each other's faces.

My hope was they never get on the VIP list. They all seemed good-natured, and it would be a shame to see the reputation I have of them tarnished. Especially if I am to be auctioned off tonight. Letting a large sigh escape my lips, I grabbed the tray to head back to their table.

A cold chill surrounded me as I started handing them their drinks. The music was blaring, and the lights were flashing, but as I stood up after handing Vulcan his drink, I felt a large shadow engulf my body.

Chapter 2

Loukas

"Have you gathered enough information about this strip club?" There was a pause from Vulcan. *"Cheaters Anonymous?"* He laughed at the name.

"Yeah, I have." I threw the paperwork on his desk. I had everything, down to the last picture of girls entering the club, bagged, and gagged, and often leaving the club with different men. They never return when they leave and where they go was a mystery since I haven't been given enough personnel to follow. I'd help, but Hades was only willing to give so many resources.

I was Hades' 3rd-degree bitch. Anytime he felt like something needed to be investigated when regarding a high-class, low-class demon, or even a demigod, I had to step in and check it out. Hades doesn't leave the Underworld much, ever since Persephone left.

All and all, it was a good thing for me. I could spend more time on Earth in his penthouse he never uses and have a little fun with the willing girls. A vacation from hell, not bad if you ask me.

"All right," Vulcan spoke, "I'll contact Hermes so he will be the witness and Ares for the manpower. Do you really think a god is involved in this though? Seems a bit like human activity to me."

Vulcan rubbed his eyes. He had spent way too much time forging relics for the higher-ups, so now he transferred out so he could do something different along with taking on his nickname- Vulcan. It took a lot of pleading from Hera since she was her son and her favorite. Vulcan was one of the and kinder gods, even though he was not considered the most beautiful. To any human, he would still be a catch.

"That's what I thought too." I pulled out a folder and opened it up to page 87. "This here gives me a feeling in my gut." I had circled an item that was being held by the owner of the club, Teddy Johnson. It was a large helmet, one that could have been easily mistaken for just an acting prop, but it wasn't.

"This isn't," Vulcan spoke in shock.

"It is!" I said with excitement. "The Helm of Darkness."

"Hades needs to know about this." Vulcan stared at the picture in disbelief. The Helm of Darkness was Hades' way of making himself invisible. Only a few had dared to wear it. Those that wore it without permission became dark from the inside out and their only hope would be to gain mercy back from the gods.

"I agree. Will you call him?" I begged.

"The fuck, no!" Vulcan said, exacerbated. "We have been friends for ages but each day he gets worse and worse. I can hardly keep my own calm demeanor around him. He just reeks of hatred. I don't like to associate myself with that." Vulcan sat back and drank a sip of his coke. "I love the guy, but it isn't healthy for me, even my therapist said so."

"Therapist?" I said sarcastically. "You are such a pussy."

"I have a lot on my plate right now. You leave my therapist out of this!" he yelled as he pointed his worn finger at me.

Just then, Hermes and Ares walked through the door. Hermes' blond shaggy hair was unkempt as always. His boyish features were evident, and he pranced over and hopped in the chair. Ares looked stoic; only his close friends like us knew his playful nature.

"Good of you all to show up," I spat playfully and gave them pats on the back.

"We'd been here sooner but Hermes has started to lose his touch." Ares' eyes lingered on Hermes.

Hermes held his hand to his chest. "I can't help it that you weigh 300 some pounds of muscle. I'm not meant to carry that much. Messages, people, messages. I am the MESSENGER. Not a freaking taxi." Ares laughed out loud as he slapped his leg.

"All right, enough, down to business. The club we are going to open in a few and we need to give you the rundown of what's going to happen." I quickly explained to Hermes and Ares the background on how the Helm of Darkness was being used in a human trafficking/strip club. They were shocked. They had frequented the club many times and never caught a thing. I was to only monitor several strip clubs in my region for any fishy behavior of gods or demigods taking advantage of female humans. I never thought I would stumble on this.

"I have contacted Hade's assistant and he will meet us at the club at 10."

"Couldn't talk to him directly, could Vulcan?" Ares teased.

"Fuck off man."

All four of us entered the club and sat down at my usual spot. I was waiting for my favorite waitress to show up. I knew the girls here were being forced to use their bodies but I knew this girl was different. There was something about her that kept me coming back to make sure she was all right, and she didn't get sold off. There were nights I would sit outside the club at the back, waiting for them to take the girls out and made sure she wasn't one of them.

"I want you guys to meet this girl. She's sweet, kindhearted even. Not an evil bone in her body." Hermes laughed in his new body form. Ares, Vulcan, and Hermes always changed their form since they were the more popular gods. We couldn't afford anyone to take notice of us and blow our cover.

"Sounds like a crush," Hermes teased.

"No, no, more like a sisterly thing. She's real timid though. Took me months to get her to open up a bit." I scanned the lounge waiting to see her, and there she was. Her light hair and her short stature were easy to pick out of a crowd. She really was a woman in a teenager's body. "Hey, Jillian! Over here!" Jillian waved and held up a finger to let me know she was coming.

"Be nice, guys, she's shy. She's been here for a while. I'm not sure why, but she's held out long enough. This all ends tonight when Hades gets here."

"Maybe Hades will just blow the place up and we don't have to deal with it at all." Ares propped his leg up on his thigh.

"The least amount of blood the better, brother," Hermes said as he straightened up as Jillian came over.

Once I introduced her to the guys, Vulcan had to ask the dumbest question. "Aren't you a little young to be working here?" Jillian's face flushed bright red as she looked down at her notepad.

"Oh, I'm 20, I just have good genes I guess." She tapped her foot a few times before she excused herself to get our drinks.

Vulcan straightened his posture, a frown on his face. "She's twenty years old. Underfed. Her growth was stunted," he growled. "Her eyes are sunken in, and I could even see a faint mark of a handprint on her upper arm! You let this go on for months?"

"What the hell was I supposed to do? We can't interfere with humans. Now that I have my reason to intervene, we can get all the girls rescued, even her. I'm going to help her get a fresh start. I've got an apartment close to the penthouse."

"Why do you care about that one?" Ares pointed as Jillian put in our drink orders. "Why not get all the girls' apartments?" I shook my head back and forth and rubbed my stubble.

"I just have a strong urge to protect her. I don't know why." I looked to the door, waiting for Hades.

"Is she your mate?" Hermes leaned in to listen.

"No, definitely not. I wouldn't have minded one bit if she was though." I smiled. Jillian was gorgeous, her long locks of blonde hair, her green eyes, and her dark lashes. She was certainly grateful and kindhearted, a bit skittish but considering her circumstances I wouldn't expect anything less.

Jillian came back over and began to lay our drinks down as the front door opened. A dark god-like cloud descended on the whole club. The aura that Hades was giving off was scaring the lesser demons to their knees as he walked in. Luckily, humans wouldn't know the stifling atmosphere, but it worried me that whatever being we were searching for would notice. As Hades walked closer, he felt my fear of being given away and quickly reeled in his oozing authority. Now he just gave off an expensive CEO that doesn't take shit vibe.

His steps were slow as he fixed the cuffs on his suit. The music was now only in the background because his shoes were the only noise we could hear. The coldness rushed in as he finally reached our table and stopped immediately and stared down at Jillian as she placed the last drink on the table. She smiled but stiffened when she turned around and strained her neck to look at the God of the Underworld.

Both locked eyes while me and the men just sat there, barely breathing. Was he going to push her to the side for getting in his way? Turn her into some hog-like creature? I've seen it too many times and I worried for the innocent child in front of me. Before I could speak, the owner of the club, Teddy Johnson came by, breaking the long eye contact.

Hermes was whispering to Ares and my heart finally started beating again. "Jillian! What did I tell you about getting in the

customer's way! Mike, take her back to get her ready for the VIPs."
Jillian's face fell and looked at me and gave me a small wave goodbye
as the tears started to well up in her eyes.

She was getting sold tonight, and she had no idea that I knew.

"Ah, gentleman." Teddy rubbed his hands together. "I heard you
were wanting more of a 'hands-on' experience." Teddy sat down
without asking and Hades continued to stand. His eyes were still
staring at the spot where Jillian was standing.

Hermes cleared his throat. "Yes, we were. When does it start and
where? Money isn't an option; we want the best," Hermes said
smugly. Teddy's eyes twinkled in excitement and Hades finally sat
down beside Hermes.

"Tonight, is your lucky night, gentleman. I have nothing but the
best, especially tonight. In fact, I have a 20-year-old virgin that looks
like she barely graduated high school. Fair skin, long hair, and great
tolerance to pain." My heart hitched thinking he was talking about
Jillian; she fit the description perfectly. Before speaking, I could hear
Hades' growl beside Hermes.

"Ah ha ha! That's the spirit. The auction is in," he glanced at his
watch, "20 minutes. I suggest you head over there now for a good
seat. A lot of men are coming tonight so have your wallets ready."
Teddy left the table and we all stared at Hades.

The god was good at keeping his emotions in check but the way
he growled at a human was unlike him. "You all right, brother?"
Vulcan asked in concern. "Would you like me to get you a drink?"
Hades shook his head in response and leaned back and pulled out a
cigar to light. Taking a long drag, he looked at the cigar and looked
back at us.

"Let's get to work," he growled and headed back to the VIP
section of the club.

Vera Foxx

Chapter 3

Hades

Cheaters Anonymous, the bane of my existence. I had heard of many demons and demigods running in and out of this run-down shack. The strippers were somewhat appealing if you were into that sort of thing. I've never been one to enjoy watching a naked woman dancing on a pole in public. Why the hell would you want to watch that and have a permanent set of blue balls in the club is beyond me.

The only reason I was here was that The Helm of Darkness was indeed missing. Someone swapped a fake in my trophy room which now must be redone. Fire exploded from my body when I realized someone had broken in. This caused me to turn some demons into a fiery crisp. The smell is what bothered me, the burned flesh and hair. That smell will never leave my nostrils and I'll have to resurrect the damned souls because they couldn't keep their distance. It isn't that hard, stay out of my fucking way.

I willed myself into the Earth realm and appeared in the alleyway in the back to avoid any suspicion. The Armani suit I wore today was tight because some idiot can't do measurements correctly. My biceps were going to practically rip out of it. I look like a damn fool.

Walking inside you could smell the sweat, the pheromones, and smoke wafting in the air. A smell that utterly disgusts me. I find more strippers and their clients washed up on some of the shores around the underworld; many of the men that end up in Tartarus. I understood that many women had no choice, which apparently these women don't. This was why Loukas was dead set on finishing this tonight. The Helm of Darkness was the icing on the cake.

As I neared Loukas's table with his three musketeers and my once close friends, I saw the backside of a tiny thing. She was small and delicate, and her movements were graceful. She had a slight smile that I saw on the side of her face, a face that didn't look like it belonged here. When I mean here, I mean here on Earth.

It was angelic.

Walking up close behind her, I feel her stiffen. Her body slowly turns, and her gorgeous emerald eyes meet mine. An electric current ran through my body. The depths of the meadows of her eyes were deep. I could almost see the flowers blooming in her eyes. A version of herself was running and looking back, holding out her hand for me to grasp. She's laughing, smiling, begging me to come with her.

Before I could say another word, the owner of the club walks up and reprimands her for bothering his customers. My fists tighten, ready to burst him into flames but he has all the information I need to find my helm. I hold back and sit in the booth with Hermes. His body has hardened, looking at me warily.

As the idiot begins talking, my mind begins to drift. How could this girl have such a hold on my cold heart? I haven't felt any emotion in so long and just looking into her eyes gave me the peace that I have craved for so many years. I felt rested and, rejuvenated, and I needed to know more about this girl. I had to find her and figure out what she was doing to me.

"Tonight, is your lucky night, gentleman. I have nothing but the best, especially tonight. In fact, I have a 20-year-old virgin that looks like she barely graduated high school. Fair skin, long hair, and great tolerance to pain," Teddy said as he puffed out his cigarette.

Right, Loukas said Teddy was into sex trafficking but what it sounds like is that my mystery girl will be put up for auction. I tightened my grip on the table; the thought of anything happening to her brought my blood to a rage. I could feel the fire in me coming forth. If I didn't get it under control, I would set the damn place ablaze.

Once Teddy left, everyone looked at me for leadership. Uneasiness at the table was apparent as I lit my cigar with the pad of my thumb. I had to play things nice until I figured out what this girl means to me. Sure, she took my breath away, and made me feel calm but what of it? She could be some siren-granted legs for a few years before she rips some poor unsuspecting soul to pieces.

Taking a few puffs, I get up. "Let's get to work." I don't look back and head to the back of the VIP section of the club.

The room wasn't that large and held several small tables where two people at a time could sit. Small candles lit the table with a single short, stemmed rose sitting in water. At the front of the room was a small black stage with a pole in the center with lights pointed at it. Me and my men sat down. Vulcan looked extremely uncomfortable and out of his element. He has always had a soft spot for humans and knowing these girls have been through the wringer had him riling underneath.

Hermes and Ares continued to have small conversations, playing the part that they were meant to do. The outward appearances they have chosen did not match their personalities. They all looked like they came from the Jersey Shore, wearing suits.

I rubbed my dark hair back and crossed my legs in anticipation. This was going to be a long night; I could hear some of the men in the room talking about the "small girl waitress" being up for action. They were talking about my girl.

Fuck.

My girl? I barely knew her. I just needed to see if there was something more. If not, I'd have Teddy Johnson keel over with a heart attack and grab the Helm.

"Gentleman, gentleman, pipe down," Teddy smirked as he saw the men reaching for their wallets. "Tonight, we have some special girls up and they are ready to meet their new homes with all of you. Just remember, no refunds. Once she is sold, she is out of my hands and into your beds." Men snickered and cheered while I sat in disgust.

Can't even get a girl willing to get in their beds so they must buy them.

Loukas nudged me and I nodded at him to continue. "Once the auction is over, he goes to his office. Until then he is busy dealing with the girls. That is when we can head back and discuss the helm." I looked back to the stage as they brought out the first few girls.

Random descriptions were thrown out about their likes and dislikes. Many of them are shivering in fear, while some look like they wanted to be sold. Probably a fear tactic. Anything was better than staying here, I was sure of it.

We had been here for over an hour, over 20 girls had sold, and he had made a killing. The girls were sitting on their new owners' laps; some men were already undressing them and feeling their bodies with no shame. Here I thought the gods were ruthless, but most humans were animals. Their torture will be the most pleasant to deliver. I felt the fire on my fingertips until Ares nudged me. I growled, sending out a warning.

"Sorry, your hands were on fire. Just one more girl and we can head back." I waved my hand to extinguish the fire and looked to the stage. I hadn't seen my mystery waitress girl and hoped she just got sent home and not get into this tangled mess. Luck wasn't with me tonight as I saw her step out.

They had her in white stilettos and baby pink doll lingerie. Her golden hair was curled and pulled back halfway to show off her slender neck. Her skin was white as the lights shone brightly on her push-up bra. Her underwear was also baby pink, hugging her hips and showing her ass cheeks. The fury I was feeling as the men looked at her body had me seething.

Teddy made her walk up and down the stage so every man could get a good look. There were whistles and jokes made. Once Teddy said his piece about her, she was cuffed to the pole, so he could use his cane to point out the finer qualities she had. The fire in my hand was starting to ignite and the darkness of my power was flowing outward. Loukas pulled me back. "Just hang on. We are so close." I gripped my fists; the hell is wrong with me?

"Gentleman, don't let this act of submission fool you." He smirked. "She can be a bit feisty when she wants to be. She did have to have a few spankings before she came out here tonight." He winked and had her turn her back to the audience and lifted part of her flowy lingerie to show three bright red handprints.

More men let out jokes. "Oh, she's a little! I'll be your daddy!" one man yelled.

"Let me give you a spankin' doll!" another chipped in.

As she turned back around, I saw the defeated look on her face. Her head was down, and tears were running down her face. Teddy grabbed her face and looked into her eyes. Human ears couldn't hear, but I could hear what he told her. "You better perk up or I'll deflower you tonight myself." He pushed her cheek away, and when he did, she saw Loukas. If I thought her heart couldn't break anymore, it was completely shattered now. I'm sure she thought that Loukas was different but the look she had at Loukas crushed anything left she had.

Loukas stared back at her with a small smile, unable to give away our cover. I could feel his guilt rack through his body. Why did he care about the waitress so much? He wasn't in love with her, was he? A growl left my throat and I tried to cover it with a cough.

Ares glanced at me questioningly and Hermes smirked like he knew something. Ares and Hermes began whispering again. Before I could ask, Teddy started speaking.

"We start the bidding off at $20,000. Who will take the virgin doll Jillian home?" Teddy announced playfully.

Jillian, that was her name. Warmth filled me knowing her name. I whispered it silently to myself as I savored it on my tongue.

Men started throwing out numbers. "$50,000!"

"$80,000!"

I couldn't let her be sold.

"$90,000!"

I wanted to know more about her.

"$115,000!"

Her eyes investigated mine again and this time we didn't look away. Did she feel it too? What was I feeling?

"$500,000," I said sternly. I was done with the bidding; it was time to get this shit done. Get the helm and get Jillian out of here with me. While I was at it, I'd burn this mother fucker down.

Teddy Johnson clapped excitedly and yelled out, "Any takers? 500,000 going once!"

Before he got to twice another man stepped up. "600,000." Teddy's eyes saw dollar signs. Who the hell is bidding now? I jumped up and looked over at my victim. It was that fucking angel, Malachi. My jaw ticked.

"The hell is he doing here?" Ares said out loud.

"700,000," I spat.

"750,000." He smirked. Little does he know; money runs out for a damn angel. They mainly stay in the Celestial Heavens while most of my work is done on Earth. I've got business on Earth he doesn't know about. I could go all day.

"Two fucking million," I roared. The room went silent, and Malachi's eyebrows furrowed. His mouth was pressed in a fine line and stomped out the door. Fuckin' pussy. The rest of the men sat quietly with their girls. I glanced back at the stage. Jillian was on the floor, tears streaming down her face, while Teddy is gloating with his men about big paychecks for everyone.

Loukas went to the stage to help Jillian up, but she pulled her arms away from him. Hurt was in his eyes as he tried to help her up. "You are just like them," she sobbed.

Teddy unlocked the cuffs and gave them to Loukas. "She's yours now. Have to say I was a little disappointed, doll. I was looking forward to a good lay tonight if you didn't sell." He licked his bottom lip, trailing his finger down her cleavage and that was when all mother fucking hell broke loose.

Chapter 4

Hades

Once his finger grazed her skin, I saw red. Anger flew through my veins as I snapped my fingers. Darkness fell upon the entire club and a three-block radius. Darkness was something that I was accustomed to. It was where I worked, where I thrived. In the darkness, I could accomplish the most abhorrent things. Take life from one of the living souls that tainted the Earth. I was the only god granted this power; the power of death and the Underworld demanded it. Not even Zeus himself could take life. Many could say I was the stronger god, and indeed I was. I just didn't let it be known to all.

There were screams as the club was in darkness; with the snap of my fingers, Jillian fell asleep, falling into Loukas's arms. My body was repulsed that he would hold her to his chest. I slowly walked up the steps, the emergency lights guiding me to the stage. Every soul stood in fear, along with my gods and demon. Loukas looked up to me in fear, fear that I was going to put harm upon this innocent woman. My jaw ticked, and I held my arms out to pick her up.

Teddy Johnson stood barely to my shoulders as he stood quietly as I carried her with one arm under her legs and the other behind her back. She was cradled into my chest, her light breaths brushing my neck. Feeling an instant calm come over me, I knew I had to complete the mission as set out originally to do.

"Mr. Johnson, I need a word with you. Immediately." My voice was low and thick. If it weren't for finding the Helm, he would have been dead the moment he thought about touching her.

"Y-yes sir, this way."

Loukas, Hermes, Ares, and Vulcan stood in surprise as I took Jillian with me to the back. I looked back at them and nodded. That was their cue to free the girls from their bondage while Loukas followed me to the back to carry on with our plan. There was going to be a bonfire tonight.

Teddy led us to his office, covered in papers, stains, and food. The man had no pride in his things; all he saw were dollar signs. Loukas walked into the room and took off his jacket and laid it on the couch. I gently laid Jillian on it while I laid my own jacket on top of her naked skin.

She looked so peaceful sleeping; small puffs of breath came from her lips, and her eyelashes twitched in movement. Moving a piece of stray hair from her face, I felt a warm tingle go through my fingers. She was breath-taking, and I wanted her.

I wanted her to be mine.

Standing up, I unbuttoned my cuff links and rolled up my sleeves. Teddy was looking rather disheveled as he sat behind his desk. The worry lines on his face made him look older and his face larger, if possible. The lights were flickering on and off from the emergency lights. No doubt because he never has them serviced.

Loukas stood by Jillian, protecting her. Still not aware of his intentions, I gave him a low growl in warning, and he took steps away from her. His head was bowed, and a smirk played on his lips. Brushing my hair back, the clicking of my Italian leather shoes stopped at the front of Teddy's desk. Leaning over with my hands as a support, I spoke to the snake in front of me. "Where. Is. The. Helm," I said deeply, low. His shaking became worst as I spoke of the relic.

"I-I don't know what you are talking about," he sputtered like the pussy he was.

I chuckled darkly and ripped the fake hair from his head. "Oh, but you do. I have on good account you do know where it is, Teddy Johnson." Teddy winced and rubbed his head.

"Do you know who I am?" I raised to a standing position, crossing my arms. My eyes were ablaze, my eyes immediately turning into a glowing red. Dark smoke was falling from my 6'7" frame. The fire in my fingertips were oozing, setting small pieces of his paperwork ablaze.

"A-a demon?" he cried, almost wetting himself. His body was shaking uncontrollably.

"No, no, no…" I rounded the desk, taunting him. "I am the King of the Demons." I elongated a claw and scratched the hardwood finish off his desk as I neared. Teddy's breath became harsh, his heart beating quickly. It was only a matter of time before he had a heart attack, just as the fates had predicted before arriving here.

"I'm mother fucking Hades." I smiled. "Now, where is the Helm? Don't lie to me," I growled out warningly.

"It's here. It is here. Please don't kill me!" He opened the drawer, and my helm was sitting in the lower part of the desk. I ripped it from his hands and threw it at Loukas.

"Now about that not killing you," I said quietly. "I won't personally kill you." Teddy grabbed his chest and started coughing. "No, your time was up anyway. However, I don't think your time is over with me yet. The fun," I leaned into where our noses were touching, "has just begun."

I slammed my fist on the desk, causing it to break into two and burst into flames. The loud noise didn't even wake the angel on the couch. Teddy was sputtering, holding his chest, and falling quickly to the floor. My flames quickly engulfed him while he screamed for mercy. If only he knew what was really coming. Wrapping my jacket around Jillian, I picked her up again and led her to the outside of the club. It was completely dark, except for the emergency lights. The women had left, and cops were on the outside taking statements from the stolen girls.

Many of them crying, wrapped in blankets. The men who bought the girls were sitting in police cars. Hermes and Ares stood by our black limo and opened the door. Sitting inside the limo and holding her close, the rest of my men came in with me to head back to my penthouse suite in town. Loukas had been staying there. He better not have fucked anything up.

"What's the plan, My Lord?" Loukas asked as I pet Jillian's hair. Sitting up straighter and closing my eyes, a loud explosion came from *Cheaters Anonymous*. People were screaming in fear, running away from the flames. Buildings beside it were now on fire as the fire burned hot.

Opening my eyes again, Loukas and his friends looked on in worry. "Back to the penthouse," I whispered.

"Hades, what is it with this girl?" Hermes spoke softly, not to anger me. "What do you feel for her?" I continued to look at her face, and small, tiny freckles danced on her skin. She was as light as a feather, obviously malnourished. Her body spread warmth within mine just by holding her.

"I don't know," I whispered again as my thumb went across her cheek. "…but I'm going to find out."

Jillian

Feeling something plush underneath me, I gave a slight moan. It felt so good, and it even smelled good. I was able to stretch my body like a starfish, I had so much room, and I didn't even feel like I was close to falling off the cot. A few bones in my back popped as a faint smile fell on my face. I must be dreaming, and I don't want to wake up.

The haze was leaving me, the place where you are half asleep and half-dreaming. Coming to, I realized that I wasn't on my old, broken cot that slightly leaned to the left. In fact, it felt too good to be that cot. Blinking my eyes a few times and keeping them open, I notice the room I was in is not anything I have ever seen before.

The room was dim, the lamps only providing minimal light. Enough to look around the room but have difficulty reading. The walls were a deep blue, and the sheets on my body were a silver color. They felt so smooth against my skin as I played with the hem on the top of the sheet. The bed was larger than ten of my cots alone. All this room for me?

My thoughts of last night started rushing back. The auction, standing in front of all those men, being called horrible names such as slut and whore. Someone had bought me and bought me for more money than Master had ever received.

It was that same man I saw when I left my last table of the night. His face was handsome, and he looked older with dark stubble on his jawline. His hair was unkempt like he ran his fingers through his hair one too many times. There were worry lines or possibly angry lines that made him much older than he probably was. Once I glanced into his dark eyes that were hard and stoic, they softened. This man had been through a lot, that was for sure.

His eyes were deep pools of darkness, ones that I could easily drown in. My own soul continued to be pulled by him and pointed right into the blackness. *Him,* my soul continued to whisper. The more I stared, the more questions I had; he was just a customer of a *strip club*. Nothing good could come from a man like that, especially since he *bought* me. In that stupid VIP room, along with his friend Loukas.

God, Loukas.

I thought he was my friend, but it all ended up for naught. He was just like the rest of them, getting his in with Master so he could buy one of us. My heart hitched as a faint sob left my lips. I had felt alone before. I've always been alone, but I thought Loukas was different. He never hit on me or slapped my rear end as I walked by. He was honestly nice and tipped well. Probably thought I was able to keep it.

But now, now I was more alone than ever. He was just there to enjoy the spoils of his own friend. Did they buy me together? They all seemed close before I passed out. What kind of sick world is this? If only it would end for me. That's all I want right now. I haven't been able to catch a break in so long, and now I was going to become a sex doll and give up the last part of me that I held onto.

Before I could continue with my pity party, there was a knock at the door. I jumped and tried to scoot my body to the furthest side of the bed but quickly stopped when I felt a pull on my hand. There was a needle in my arm along with a plastic tube.

Are they drugging me?

"Hello," the deep velvet voice spoke at the door. There was light pouring in the door, and with the darkness that was surrounding me, I could only see the outline of his body against the light. His hands were in his pockets, standing there, waiting patiently.

I pulled my legs up and wrapped my arms around me. Only to notice I was wearing a large black t-shirt that swallowed my whole body. A few tears left my eyes as he began to walk closer. His hands were still in his pockets, but you could hear the clicking of his shoes.

"I'm sorry if I startled you," his baritone voice spoke. "How are you feeling?" The voice held concern, but I knew not to trust it. Men liked to play with women's emotions, and I knew he would be just the same.

"Fine," I whispered. Even though it was just a faint sound, he heard it and came more into the light so I could see his face. It was Loukas's mystery friend. His eyes were still dark and didn't hold onto the stoic face he had earlier. There was a faint smile on his lips as he sat down at the end of the bed. I jumped a bit and slid back farther into the headboard.

"I'm not here to hurt you," he said slowly. "I wanted to get you out of there, and I'm not going to do anything you don't want." My heart was beating rapidly; my breathing was a bit unstable. I don't know how long I was out, but I was certainly feeling dizzy.

"Jillian," my name rolled off his tongue. "It's all right. No one will hurt you now," he continues to coo at me. More tears escaped my eyes. That is the only action I could let out. The tears.

"That's what they all say," I whispered again as I hugged my legs tighter. The man's hand balled into a fist and a few deep breaths were blown in and out of his nose. His strong features softened again, and he rolled his shoulders.

"I'll be sure that it doesn't happen again." He paused. "I'm sure you are hungry. Loukas will bring in your food in a moment." His voice was rougher than earlier. The man stood up, buttoned his suit jacket and walked to the door without saying another word and shut the door.

Chapter 5

Jillian

Hushed whispers on the other side of the door. My heart continued to beat wildly in my chest. My hand was still attached to an IV pole, complete with clear fluids and another bag being mixed in with the tubing. I wanted to pull it out but was stopped by a hand.

Loukas's warm hand touched my knuckles. "I wouldn't do that, love. It's giving you some nutrients you need." His voice was soft and delicate, but it didn't relieve the gasp that fell from my lips. He had come into the room so quickly and quietly; was my mind that foggy? Growing up with Master, I had to be quick-thinking and listen well. If I didn't, it could mean punishment or facing the wrath of one of his men. I always had been on alert and now I wasn't.

"Are you drugging me?" I whispered almost silently. Loukas furrowed his brows and sat on the bed next to me. Even though he hurt me emotionally, I still felt comfortable around him.

"No, Jillian, we would never do that. You were extremely dehydrated, and we did some blood tests. You are extremely malnourished." Loukas looked over my form as I continued to shake out of fear and the coldness of the room.

"Are you cold? Do you need another blanket?" A blanket, I would have done almost anything to get a blanket over the years. Winters were rough at the club. Master didn't want to pay for extra heating in the basement, saying a bit of shivering would keep us from getting too fat. Without saying a word, Loukas rose from the bed and grabbed a blanket hanging over a decorative chair and wrapped it around me.

"Thank you," I murmured, and he just nodded.

"I'm sure you have questions," Loukas rubbed his hands together between his legs, "but first you need to eat." Loukas had a tray full of food that sat on a nearby dresser. It was complete with spaghetti noodles with meat sauce, garlic bread, a small salad, and a large glass of water. My mouth watered looking at it. That must be the most food ever to be presented in front of me. Loukas chuckled as he flipped the tray's legs out and sat it in front of me on the bed. "Come on now, dig in."

Loukas didn't have to tell me twice as I untangled myself from wrapping my arms around me. I twirled my fork in the noodles and gathered as much sauce as I could. Once it dropped on my tongue, I was in instant heaven. I continued to eat like it was my last meal, but it wasn't long until my stomach churned in protest. I had barely eaten five bites and I was already full.

Loukas had been watching me as I ate and noticed immediately stopping. "Jillian what's wrong? Do you not like it?"

I shook my head as I bit my lip. "No, I'm just full. I don't think I can eat another bite."

"What? That's impossible. You've barely eaten anything. Come on, you must eat more." Loukas took my fork to put another large amount in my mouth, but I protested.

"That is the most I've ever eaten in a single day," I whimpered. "I feel sick being this full."

Loukas nodded with a sour expression and put the tray back on the dresser. "I know you are upset with me but let me tell you that our friendship is true and I was not there to buy you or anyone else in that hell hole." I sat silently while I continued to look in my lap. "The club was under an investigation for certain criminal activities, and I noticed things not looking legit my first time being there. That first thing was you." Tears welled up in my eyes as he talked about our first-time meeting.

"The first time I saw you, Jillian, you were eating off leftovers in the back alley." I sobbed at how embarrassing it sounded. "I thought maybe you were homeless, but you walked back into the back entrance to the strip club, and low and behold you worked there!"

Loukas threw his hands up. "In the line of work I'm in, I had to dig and find out more than just the human trafficking to save you. You won't understand now, but later you will." Loukas handed me a few tissues as my body began to shake. He sat beside me and put me into a side hug.

"Just know we are here now; we are going to keep you safe." After a few moments and several hiccups later, things became quiet, and you could only hear the small drips from the IV still invading my system.

"Who is we?" I asked. My mind was racing a million miles a minute, albeit it was still foggy. Loukas admitted he tried to get me out, but couldn't he have called the police and let them know about the trafficking? Maybe the authorities were in on it too, more so than I thought. There were cops that came to the club daily.

"Do you remember my friends from the club last night?" I nodded. Ares, Hermes, and Vulcan, were able to get all the girls out of there and back to their homes. They even found the transactions of where the other girls had gone as well. Hopefully, the FBI can find them."

"What about your o-other friend?" The man that had come into my room only minutes ago was still sitting in the back of my mind.

"That was Hades," Loukas said calmly. "He's the one that really saved you." I looked up at Loukas and gave a small smile.

"Tell him I said, 'thank you,' then."

Loukas stood up and fixed his dress shirt. "How about, you tell him yourself? He is right outside the door." My breath caught a little. The only guy I was comfortable with was Loukas. I hadn't known Hades that long.

"Hey, hey, listen," Loukas cooed. "I promise you, none of my friends would ever hurt you. Do you trust me?" I raised my knees to my chin and kept the blanket wrapped around me as I sniffed my nose in agreement. Loukas let out a big smile showing his teeth. "Hades, come in."

Hades opened the door; the light wasn't as bright in the hallway as it was before, so I was able to adjust my eyes to see his face. He looked tired and worried as he stepped into the room. His first three buttons on his shirt were unbuttoned. His black shirt was wrinkled, and his sleeves were rolled up to his forearms. He pulled up a chair at the end of the bed and leaned on it, looking at me with uncertainty and vulnerability.

"Hi," I whispered and buried my nose into my knees so he could only see my eyes. Hades gave a small smile.

"Hey there." His voice was like hearing gravel rumble in his chest.

"T-thank you. F-for saving me." I gave a small smile back, hugging my knees tightly again.

"You are most welcome." Hades held out his hand for me to take, I was still unsure of this man. He did buy me, but he hasn't hurt me yet. Loukas gave an encouraging nudge when I glanced at him. I unwrapped one of my arms and placed my hand in Hades'.

Hades

"Are you done yet?" I snapped. The doctor had poked and prodded Jillian for more than an hour. I made sure she stayed asleep as one of the female maids changed her into a large shirt that engulfed her small body. Her bones stuck out more than I originally thought. The uniform hid them well and I'm sure that was the purpose.

"Yes, My Lord. She is finished. I'll be sure to run these blood vials quickly. She is receiving fluids and a few rounds of antibiotics and vitamins to held with any deficiencies she may have." The doctor bowed and left the room. I wanted to be alone with her, to figure out what this woman was to me. Her eyes were an entrapment that captured my soul far too quickly in the short amount of time I was with her.

Her green eyes had their own vocabulary, and it was a beautiful language I wanted to learn.

She was so scared, submissive, and meek. My own anger and frustration turned into nothing but worry as she shivered in my arms as we brought her up to the penthouse. Touching her as I had laid her down, I felt small tingles throughout my fingers, and my desire to keep her near me had strengthened tenfold since I was in the auction room.

My need to protect and care for her was strong, but what of it?

I wanted to keep her close to my body, to keep her warm. My mind was consumed by her, and my heavy heart had lightened considerably at just a few words that I had exchanged with her. I was becoming obsessed with her, more so than I ever felt with Persephone.

Her skin was soft and glowed even in the dimly lit room. I wanted to be here when she woke up and to see her open her eyes again so I could stare into them, but she didn't know me. She knew me as the man who bought her.

Loukas knocked lightly on the door and walked in. "How is she?" His hand went to touch her foot which was covered by a blanket, but I let out a growl in warning. His hands rose in surrender and backed away. "My Lord, what is it?" he inquired as I continued to hold her hand. My face contorted to anger; what was I feeling? Standing up quickly, I headed to the door. I needed some air.

I left Loukas to his own devices to watch over her. She knew him best; she would be more comfortable with him and that infuriated me more. Grabbing the nearest vase, I threw it against the wall, smashing it into hundreds of pieces.

"What's got his panties in a twist?" Ares whispered to Hermes while he snickered. I whipped my head around and glared at them as they mocked me.

"Say it to my face," I yelled. "I don't need your damn whispering. I can hear it all. I will burn you to a damn crisp, help you heal, and do it again." My breath was staggering, my veins protruding from my neck like a mad man. I had become this in the past thousand or so years, so it was natural for me to be pissed off. My friends no longer wanted to be around me because of my damn attitude but it was better that way.

"Hades, you must calm down or you will wake the girl. She's already scared. Do you want her even more afraid?" Hermes smirked and rose from his seat. He walked over to the liquor bar and poured himself a glass of whisky.

"You are awfully confident," I growled. "What do you know?"

Hermes, even though he wasn't a trickster god, knew how to have fun at other people's expense. He would hold secrets and let them out at just the right time to anger and piss off some demi-god. "I do not know what you mean." He sipped on his drink as the ice clinked into the glass. Ares had his arms spread across the back of the sofa; his lips pressed into a line trying to hold in a laugh.

"You overgrown carrier pigeon, spit it out!" I stomped to the other side of the room and gripped Hermes's neck and lifted him in the air. His glass dropped and pieces of glass scattered on the floor. Vulcan had just walked into the room and looked on in bewilderment. "The fuck?" he whispered to Ares who only shrugged his shoulders.

"Put me down, you overgrown firecracker, and I'll tell you." Hermes sneered as he started to turn blue. Even though gods couldn't die, they could still experience pain and pleasure as well as try to heal from other misfortunes on each other's bodies.

Dropping him to the ground, he let out a cough and rubbed his neck. "All right then." He straightened his suit jacket and sat back on the couch. "Let's begin with a story..."

Ares began humming and started to sing, "A tale as old as timeeee,..."

I arose from my seat and punched Ares' nose so hard it immediately bled while he laughed hysterically. Vulcan gathered some towels and started to help Ares clean up the blood while Hermes looked at the scene unamused. Rubbing his eyes with his thumb and index finger, he sighed and looked back to me. "Really? Do you want to know or not?" I sat back down and waved my hand to continue. "Do you remember, some fifteen hundred years or so ago when Persephone left?"

"Bad call, Hermes," Vulcan interrupted. Hermes narrowed his eyes and continued while I scowled at him.

"Selene has slowly given gods, angels, and demons mates to help the supernatural balance. I've seen it firsthand when she pairs souls, and let me tell you, it's a beautiful thing." I scoffed, hearing about Selene. She was just a dark goddess hell-bent on making my life miserable. I laid my head in my hands as my elbows rested on my legs.

"And 20 years ago, Selene visited our dark lord over here with a message." Vulcan and Ares leaned in to listen better while I sluggishly lifted my head. My eyes weren't concentrating on anything, just playing the memories in the back of my mind.

"Your mate has been born!" Selene stood up happily and clapped her hands in excitement.

"What. Of. It," I growled each word individually.

"I just thought you should know! We got off on such a bad foot and I wanted to make sure you knew so you could search for her. I can even show you who and where she is now." She lifted her hand to make a magical portal appear, but I slammed my glass to the floor as I stood up.

"I'll have NOTHING to do with you and your mate shit."

"The longer you take to accept that you have a mate to claim, the harder it will be for her to accept you."

Chapter 6

Hades

"Fuck." I fell back onto the couch. My fists were again in their tightened grip, a debilitating headache was coming on and it was all due to my insolence.

I had just come back from talking to Jillian; she had just woken up from her slumber. I was hoping she would be more accepting of me but of course, the fates were not on my side. Jillian was petrified. Once I left the room and had Loukas explain what was going on, she wasn't *as* scared of me. Her heart was at a steadier pace. Her innocent eyes looked up at me in question and wonder as I kept my hand held out to her.

She didn't want to touch me, and I didn't blame her.

My face has had a permanent scowl fixed on it since Persephone left me, but now she was starting to become a fleeting memory. My heart didn't ache for her, it ached for Jillian. Damn Selene, what have you done?

Jillian reached out her tiny hand to shake mine and the warmth radiating from such a small person gave me something I had longed for, *feeling*. Deep in my soul, I felt her. The end of my lips began to tilt upward, causing Loukas to smile like a damn fool. Even though he was a demon, he certainly had his own personality that was brighter than the rest of them. Some days I wonder if I accidentally created an angel half-breed.

Small sparks could be felt on my fingertips. I wonder if she felt them too. Her hand was still cupped in mine as she continued to stare at our hands. Maybe she did feel it.

"Jillian? Do you feel up to a shower? Get cleaned up?" Loukas interrupted our moment. I gave him a glare in which he rolled his lips into his mouth realizing his mistake.

Jillian looked between me and Loukas, unsure of what to say. "I- is that alright?" She finally looked at me.

"Of course, it is. I clasped my other hand on top of hers. "Whatever you need, say the word. I'll personally see to it," my voice was still low and gruff, but she gave a small smile. We certainly had a long way to go but since we have eternity, which didn't seem to be a problem.

Jillian

After much deliberation if I needed a maid to assist me in showering, it was decided I could do it on my own. After I mentioned I had never taken a shower by myself without people watching, Hades stormed off while Loukas showed me how to work the controls. Usually, it was just a spicket of cold water that would rush down our bodies; it was all I really knew. The warm water was refreshing, and I never wanted to leave.

Drying off, I came out of the shower and wrapped a large fluffy towel around me. It was so large it wrapped around almost three times. The floor rugs were equally squishy and soft, it brought a smile to my lips. Even if I could sleep on this fluffy rug, I would be forever grateful.

Loukas continued to talk about how they rescued me, how the strip club was burned down and that even Master- I mean Teddy Johnson died of a heart attack during the raid. I was happy that the girls were all free, but where did that leave me? Why did they take me and leave the rest?

Given the run around for the past fifteen minutes of why they picked me to stay with them, Loukas had me come out to meet the rest of the men that helped shut down the club. All I was wearing was one of Hades' large black shirts that I easily could swim in. The shirt touched my knees while his boxers continued to fall. Luckily my hairband was still tied to my wrist, and I was able to tie them tight.

The penthouse we were staying in was massive. We were on the top floor overlooking the brightly lit city. It was far from the strip club, on the upper east side of town. This was where the high rollers lived as the girls would say.

The main living room was bright, the floors a light marble and sparsely furnished. The open concept kitchen had black granite tops and stainless-steel appliances. My mouth must have dropped at looking at it all because I heard Hermes laughing. "There's the angel! It's good to see you standing there. The doctor said you wouldn't be walking for a few days due to lack of food in your system." Hermes patted my shoulder. Little did everyone know; I could go for days and days without food. My body had just grown accustomed to it.

"Don't make her stand there. Offer her a seat." Ares pointed to the couch, and I quickly sat on my knees to keep my legs covered. Loukas grabbed the blanket off the couch and quickly wrapped me up. I'm so used to moving around and when I stay still, I ended up getting cold.

"Where's Hades?" I asked curiously.

They all looked back and forth at each other. "Why? Do you feel a pull towards him?" Hermes asked and Ares slapped his head. Not understanding what he meant, I tilted my head to the side and looked at Loukas, who in turn shrugged his shoulders.

"You all are here. I was just wondering," I mumbled. Hades was a different kind of man. Brooding, mysterious, and powerful. I could feel the power in his stare or when he enters a room. I wasn't sure how I felt about him, I knew I was curious about him, and he intrigued me. He and his friends were different than any other men I've met.

"So why do some of you have Greek mythology names? Are you all of the Greek descent?"

Ares scoffed and Hermes laughed. "Something like that." Their answers were vague, and I was getting tired of making conversation. My body was still tired and would probably be for the rest of my life. I laid my head on the arm of the couch and let out a sigh.

Hades walked into the room, his fists clenched and jaw ticking. Infuriated was the only word that came to mind when his face scowled like that. Everyone flinched but after holding his hand that one time, I didn't feel scared around him. There was something cloaking me, warming me when I was in his presence. Hades was the bad guy of the group, the one in charge, the one that protects everyone else.

Before I touched him, I didn't know any of that, I feared him. Thoughts of him betting two million dollars on me and then falling to the floor in fear crossed my mind. My heart clenched remembering the god-awful memory. *He hasn't touched me; he's only helped me.*

Hades sits down while Hermes pulls out a notepad filled with scribbles. "Jillian, I would like to ask you a few questions about how you came to the club. It would really help us out on our investigation, maybe help other girls like you to see how they were targets." I wasn't too keen on the idea of reliving old memories but helping other girls might let my mind rest a bit.

"All right," I murmured.

"Can you tell us when you came to the club and how you got there?" Hermes as well as the rest looked at me, concerned. Wrapping the blanket tighter, I recalled my memory that even the men at the club couldn't believe. They thought I had become mentally deranged from being kidnapped.

"I don't remember anything about my past before I got to the cage they put me in. The first thing I remember was being put in the cage, with a new shirt on me that bared the strip club's logo. There was a man in a gladiator-type helmet that stared at me for the longest time." Hades stiffened and Loukas leaned closer. "I asked him where I was, what was I doing there. I wanted to get out, but I didn't know where I would go. There were no memories," I sniffed.

"Then Teddy Johnson came up to the cage and yelled at his men asking where I had come from. They didn't know and started yelling some more. He banged on the cage and asked me who brought me in. The man in the helmet was standing right beside him, so I pointed to him and screamed he was right beside him."

Ares appeared shocked as I continued my story. I dared not look at the others, feeling the heat of their stares.

"The gladiator stood there, arms crossed, and then walked away and into Teddy Johnson's office. Teddy started throwing his hands in the air and stomped off and went to his office as well. A long time had passed, and he was grinning like he won the lottery. He came up to my cage and banged on it with his cane and said, 'We are going to make tons of money and it all starts with you, Jillian'." I sobbed.

Loukas came over and gave me a hug while Vulcan kept his mouth covered with one of his hands. Tears welled up in his eyes. Hades' eyes were red, not just figuratively. They burned like a lake of everlasting fire.

"Fuck!" Hades got up and pushed the couch backward, causing Vulcan to fall with a crash. Loukas got up to help restrain Hades and talk him down, but Hades was having none of it. He stormed the kitchen, throwing things, banging on the table like a mad man. Each time a loud noise would drop to the floor, I would flinch, thinking it was heading toward me.

Somehow, he caught some of the appliances on fire and I closed my eyes and covered my ears. It was too much noise, and I had nowhere to run. He was screaming and yelling in another language, possibly Greek or Italian. Ares, Loukas, Hermes, and Vulcan backed up and let Hades have his way with the penthouse. Tables overturned, chairs broken, and fine China spilled to the floor. A few tears escaped my eyes seeing the rage he had.

What had this man been through to cause him so much pain? His inner demons were suffocating him, and he had no way to control them. The men stood and looked on in pity as he continued the rampage. They knew not to mess with him but the aching in my heart couldn't let him continue.

With shaky legs, I stood up. If he hadn't hit me by now, then I don't think he would hit me in the future. He pushed his men away harshly, but I couldn't see him doing that to a woman. The urge to touch him was strong and I couldn't help but take those steps toward him. I could hear Loukas whispering for me to come back, afraid to have his voice above a whisper. Hermes just told him to stop and see what I could do.

Hades was staring out the window, a half-torn desk chair in his hand. His shoulders showed his ragged breathing rising and falling. I walked on the balls of my feet, closer still trying not to disturb what memories or demons were plaguing his mind. My small hand searched for his large one that was balled into a fist.

My small hand touched his knuckles as I finally whispered out, "Hades?" His eyes bolted to mine so fast it made me jump. His breathing slowed down, and his fist began to unfold. "Hades, are you all right?" My voice was small compared to this giant man and he took it in gladly. His eyes closed and I slipped my hand into his and he held it tightly. "I'm sorry," he whispered.

Giving him a small smile and a gentle squeeze, I said, "It's all right. We all have our bad days."

Chapter 7

Hades

Jillian's big emerald eyes investigated my fire and instantly melted it away. Only steam remained as I breathed in her scent. She smells of cinnamon and a warm fire, it comforted me to no end. Her angelic voice, her first real sentence to me, had my rage extinguished to just a mere smolder.

Her hand in mine squeezed me so gently it was barely noticeable. My hand could easily crush her and yet she continued to bring me reassurance that everyone had bad days. She was becoming the light of my darkness and she didn't know the effect she has on me.

Jillian's small grin started to fade and the small grip she had on my hand began to fall. "I'm…" she spoke but didn't have time to finish because her eyes instantly closed and she fell. I quickly grabbed her and pull her into my arms as we sit on the floor by the massive window. The sounds of clacking Italian shoes enter the room along with heavy breathing.

"The fuck did you do?" Ares yelled. I didn't look at him as I held her, stroking her hair as her heartbeat continued at a steady pace.

"She passed out, her body is weak," I growled. I didn't want to acknowledge it but in my cold heart I knew all of this, all her suffering was my fault. If I had only listened to Selene, I could have protected her, saved her from the life she has been living but my blackened heart failed to see reason. At the time I thought I didn't need her, but now I do.

Picking her up gently, cradling her head into my chest, her arm was dangling at her side, I walked through the crowded doorway. "Where are you taking her, Hades?" Loukas spoke harshly. Stopping me in my tracks, I turned my head over my shoulder and glared at him.

Loukas was my demon; he may be one of the best demons I've ever created but he was crossing a line. He has had explicit instructions to never use my name in front of others. "The fuck you call me?" Black smoke started to fizzle around my body. Loukas step back and got on his knees and fell to the floor.

"I'm sorry, My Lord, please forgive me. I'm only thinking of Jillian." I growled so loudly the windows shook along with broken China on the floor.

"If you have any value in your life, you will stop your obsession with her." I grasped onto her tightly. "She is my mate and your future Queen. Do you understand me, demon?" Loukas continued to shake in panic. I'd gotten rid of his best friend only a few hundred years ago for calling out my name in public.

"Yes, yes, I'm sorry. Thank you for your mercy," he begged. I continued to walk up the stairs and into the master bedroom. I didn't want to let her out of my sight right now. She calms me and I'm sure our bond will only grow stronger when we stay close. However, duty calls and a plan to take her back with me needs to be in place.

Laying her on the bed, I put the covers over her to make sure she was comfortable before I headed back down the stairs. Loukas was sitting on the couch with his hands on his head while Ares, Hermes and Vulcan were talking in hushed tones.

"Meeting, now," I demanded as we headed to the dining room. The dining room doubled as a conference room since I never had guests to dine with anyway. "Sit," I commanded as they entered.

I leaned back in my chair; feet propped up on the table looking over the lighted city before me. Rubbing the stubble on my chin, I let out a large sigh while feeling the heated gaze of my 'friends.'

"We leave back for the Underworld tomorrow; I'm taking Jillian with me." Hermes stands to protest but I throw up my hand. "She will be safer with me than on Earth."

"You're right," Hermes says, and I raise a brow. Is he fucking with me? "There has been a disturbance in the Celestial Kingdom." Ares bangs the table.

"'Bout time! I've been itchin' for a war!" Ares stands up and strips himself of his human form, now daunting his pelt and armor. His sword was at his side as he unsheathed it and banged his chest like a damn baboon.

"Down boy!" Hermes laughs. "There's no war yet. I don't even know what the disturbance is about, but I'm hell-bent on finding out." Hermes was a messenger god, but he was also a spy. He never took sides unless completely necessary and even then, he tried to stay neutral.

"If you hear anything, let us know," Vulcan speaks up. "Especially since the Helm has been gone for years. Who knows how long someone has been planning for a power struggle?" Hermes nodded to Vulcan.

"What of Jillian? She is your mate, isn't she?" Ares sat down, throwing his sword on the table. I began to stew; they may have known that Selene had told me about my mate being born but they didn't know that I had the chance to see her birth, to know who she was, and follow her to protect her.

The guilt was eating me away. One day I'll have to tell her, and I pray that day doesn't come too quickly.

"She is." I willed a glass of whisky in my hand.

"And human," Vulcan added. "Has that been done before for the gods?"

"For demi-gods but none of the original twelve have been mated with a human," Hermes spoke. "Selene has been hunting souls for the perfect matches for the big 12 and usually they are paired with other gods."

A loud scream came from upstairs and before it stopped, I was transported to the middle of the room. My fists were ready to fight off whatever was on Jillian only to find her in the middle of the bed, back to the headboard, shaking. "What's wrong!?" I run to her, forgetting I could be the one she could be afraid of.

"H-how'd you get in here?!" she sobbed with a hand over her mouth.

"I was sleeping on the floor," I lied. My voice as was as calm as I could make it. "What's wrong?" The room was dark as night with no moon, but my vision was perfect. Her eyes were glassy, fingers shaking as she kept her hand over her mouth like she was going to scream again.

"I'm sorry," she hiccuped. "It was dark, I had a nightmare, and I didn't know where I was. I didn't mean to, I swear..." her voice trailed off and I rushed to her side. Her body flinched at my sudden burst of movement and my aching heart broke. She was so damaged, and I did this to her. I stopped right in front of her and held out my hand. She took a moment but put her hand in mine. Progress.

I sat next to her, my eyes begging to ask if it was all right and she nodded slowly. Taking another step, I wrap my arms around her shoulders. They were stiff but relaxed promptly. "I won't let anything ever happen to you again, Jillian, I promise." Her green eyes again melted into mine. "Sleep, I'll keep your nightmares away," I whispered.

"Can I have the light on?" she whispered to me. I snapped my fingers, and a low glow of a lamp illuminated the room. She was able to see everything if she wanted. Taking a deep breath, Jillian not realizing I didn't have a sound activating for lamps, her head fell on my chest, both of us still sitting up on the headboard. As soon as she was asleep, I could tuck her in, but I don't know if I would ever be able to let go.

Jillian

The room was still lit lightly, just as I fell asleep from the night before. Hades was kind enough to see me through a horrible panic attack. I should be afraid of him, to run away and cower in fear. Of all the men I've met in my life, he looks the most dangerous, yet he has been nothing but gentle with me.

The nightmares have been with me all my life, or at least my first night in a cell back with Teddy. The haunting of that man in the helmet, my fingers always working to the bone cleaning and cooking for Teddy's men. Slaps, punches, and even those degrading hits to my thigh were common before he could no longer mar my skin since I was in public.

The man knew how to cover his tracks, that was for sure. I'm guessing that is why it took Loukas so long to gain some evidence, any sort of evidence of human trafficking, and whatever else he was looking for.

As I contemplated my pathetic use of a life, I realize I'm not alone. There was soft breathing, and my body was molded into the perfect position for me to relax. I wasn't laying on a broken cot, freezing in the night, but I was rather warm, and a blanket of safety was wrapped around me. I let out a large sigh and snuggled into the blankets more, relishing in the warmth.

My eyes popped open. Someone else breathing beside me. Looking through my eyelashes, I see Hades' sleeping. The scowl that is permanently on his face was now soft, his eyebrows weren't angry, and his lips were gently parted. For once in a long while he looked relaxed. Not wanting to wake him, I closed my eyes and laid in the arms of a man I knew nothing about.

All logic had flown out the window but the feeling in my gut had overpowered my mind. For once I felt safe, and I was going to lay here and relish it.

***

Movement on the bed roused me and the warm blanket that covered me was no longer there. Hades had stood up and was unbuttoning his shirt. Without turning around, Hades let out his gruff voice, "Jillian, are you hungry?"

Hungry, I know that word.

"Yes." Honestly, I could go until dinner, but I didn't want to upset him.

"Good. Would you like to eat here or in the dining room?" Not wanting to be a burden, I told him the dining room would be fine. He nods and walks to the bathroom and shuts the door.

This isn't my room, so I get out of bed and immediately go to the kitchen and let Hades have time to get ready for the day. The clothes I was wearing were still clean; I could wear them for a few more days. Which reminds me, I'm not sure where I will go. I've got no money to my name, but these people helped me so much, I can't ask for more. I'll have to see if I can find a homeless shelter and see if I can start from scratch there. I've always been good at cleaning and cooking; I'm sure someone would want a maid.

Humming my way through the kitchen, I pull out a few pots and pans ready to make breakfast for everyone. The kitchen only had a few places where burn marks were left on the cabinets and was overall clean after Hades being upset.

The fridge was fully stocked, filled with eggs, fruits, bacon, sausage, and my mouth began to water at being able to finally eat a breakfast that I have made. Deciding on French toast, eggs, and sausage, I got to work. The smells from the kitchen were filling the air and my mind had wandered into maybe feeling the grass beneath my feet one day. I don't even remember touching the grass, but my heart beating light and free gives me excitement. Maybe they would let me go out today if they liked their breakfast.

I had stacked the last pieces of French toast on the table. The fruits were cut, glasses were out, and the table was set. Everything was to perfection, just like Mast- I mean Teddy liked it. For a crusty old man, he liked the finer things. I remember him smacking my fingers with rulers to set tables correctly at the club's restaurant before opening time. Only to be thrown into the kitchen to then cook for those I had made placemats for.

"Where is she!?" A manic roar came from upstairs. Thundering footsteps coming from upstairs as well as the main floor. Hermes, Ares, and Vulcan were practically nude wearing just boxers or boxer briefs, showing their ripped bodies as they were looking around the area until their eyes glanced over to me. The look in their eyes held rage as their muscles flexed.

Out of instinct, my body started shaking. My hands came up to shield me from them trying to hurt me as I backed up into the wall. "The fuck is she?!" I heard the roar again; Hades was standing on the balcony looking down at all of us. I leaned back into the wall, falling slowly and wrapping my arms around my legs. My eyes shot up to him, his lower body was wrapped in a towel and if I wasn't so scared, I would think he was the most handsome angel I had ever seen.

But I was scared because the look in his eyes was nothing but rage.

Chapter 8

Jillian

He was so angry I almost saw steam come off his body. His friends went from a fighting stance to the defensive as he took the stairs two, three, and four at a time. His strides were long, and his team almost shuddered in fear. One hand was on his towel, so it didn't fall, and his eyebrows furrowed in confusion.

"Did you tell her to make this?" He slung his hand at the table, veins protruding from his neck. They all shook their heads but Hades advanced, getting ready to grab Hermes by his neck.

"Stop!" I screamed. "I-I made it. I'm sorry." I kept my arms up so no one would hit me in the head. I've seen Teddy angry, and when he got angry, he would hurt me or someone else.

Hades' fury was halted as his eyes softened. The veins in his neck retracted and his muscles were no longer bulging out of his body. "Jillian," he whispered. "I-I'm sorry. I didn't mean." His fists balled up again and he turned around to storm up the stairs while holding his towel and slammed the door.

My body was still shaking on the floor until Loukas ran into the room, hair wet and clad only in a bathrobe. "What happened?" Loukas frantically looked around the room and saw me on the floor.

Running to me, he grabbed me and pulled me up. My eyes were threatening to let the tears fall but once Loukas sat me in the chair, I felt much calmer since Hades' glare was no longer on me.

"Hades blew a gasket." Hermes came to the table to sit down. "Don't worry Jillian, he would never hurt you. He's just angry you made breakfast."

"But why? I was trying to be nice," I muttered.

"Doesn't matter. He doesn't want you working." Ares poured himself some juice. "You have worked all your life and he wants you resting, not trying to tend to us fools even though your breakfast looks fucking amazing. The hell? Is that French toast?" Ares grabs a few and piles them on his plate. I smile genuinely for the first time in ages and Loukas catches it.

"You all right there, Princess?" I wiped my mouth from the orange juice.

"Yeah, I've just never seen someone so excited over French toast." I chuckle.

"Shit, I hardly ever eat carbs, not good for the bod." Ares starts to rub his abs and begins to flex while chewing with his mouth open. He was the most muscular out of the group, but far too much for my taste. I could see him working out all hours of the day to maintain his bulk.

"Do you think I could go outside today, Loukas?" Loukas rubs his chin and thinks.

"I'll need to ask boss man, but I'm sure he would love to take you out, but I think he was wanting to make the trip home today."

Home, that means he was leaving. My heart hurt to hear that. Hades had saved me from the worst place and now he had to go back to his own life. He seems so successful especially if his clothes said anything about him. A high-class job, family, maybe even a wife, a dog or two to go back home. If anything, I should be grateful. I was selfish to think that he would let me stay as long as he did.

I don't know why I was attached to him. He comforted me last night; that was the first comfort I have ever felt in a long time. In fact, I don't remember anyone ever comforting me before. The adrenaline of my nightmare, the fear that is still within me fueled my need to be held by him and his warm embrace. It was nothing more, nothing more than someone there that allowed me to latch on to have one night of peace.

"Oh, well I am most appreciative of what he has done for me. I'm really indebted to all of you. I hope to pay you all back someday once I get a job."

"There will be no job, Jillian." Hades was in his full suit, walking down the stairs. His brows were still bunched up in anger, but the permanent frown was now just a thin line. "You are coming back with me, to my home."

"Oh?"

"Wow, Hades, way to ease her into that statement," Hermes joked.

"What I mean, Jillian is that I want to take care of you." Hades kneeled on the floor next to my chair. He looked up at me with his dark eyes, pleading. "We still think there are more people like Teddy Johnson out there and they may be looking for you. I think it would be safer if you came with me."

My heart was beating erratically. I couldn't go back to that place, not now that I just got out. A wave of pain engulfed my body, and I was struggling to breathe. "Jillian, breathe," Loukas muttered from the other side of the table.

In one swift motion, Hades lifted me up in his arms and cradled me to his chest like a child. He held me tightly until I started to breathe again. "Follow how I'm breathing, concentrate," he cooed in my ear. "In and out, that's it." My breathing became normal, but a few stray tears fell across my cheeks and onto my lap. How embarrassing was that?

"I'm sorry," I whispered. Not even sure that he heard me.

He tightened his grip and ran his fingers through my hair. "I'm the one that is sorry," he spoke lowly.

With his steady breathing and his heavy heart beating in my ear, my eyes drifted slowly closed. I've never felt so safe in a person's embrace but here is where I hope to stay, at least for a little while.

✳✳✳

The next time I woke up, I was in an even larger bed than what I woke from previously. The whole room didn't even look familiar. This was something I had never seen before. Dark red carpets with dark wood accents adorned the dressers and nightstands. Several low-lighted lamps were scattered across the room. I blush thinking if he left those on for me, knowing I'm scared of the dark.

The bed's comforter is silky black along with dark color sheets that warm my body just right. I no longer felt cold like I did back in the other bedrooms. A small fire also glowed in the far corner of the room next to a door that leads to the bathroom.

Sitting up, I dared to get out of bed only to be stopped by something around my waist. Hades' arm was wrapped around my waist tightly. I dared not move; I was afraid that he would get angry again. He's never hit me, but I've seen plenty of angry men hit only when the time was right. Laying back down, he nuzzled me closer, and instead of being repulsed by it, I leaned into it.

It felt nice, to have someone hold you and keep your nightmares away. For the first time in two sleeping sessions, my own demons didn't come to haunt me. They only held Hades and some woman in a long light blue robe smiling at us both. Before I was ever able to speak to her, I wake up.

Hades starts to stir, and I watch him as he starts to wake. He gently unfolds himself from me and lets out a large yawn. He looked like a predatory cat ready to go hunting for his meal of the day.

"Afternoon, how did you sleep?" Hades spoke in a rough voice. The voice was heavenly, and I wished he would talk like that more often.

"Very well, thank you." I pulled the sheets up close as he exited the bed.

"When you passed out, we decided to bring you back to my home. I hope you don't mind." I shook my head no.

"We have the best doctors here and our goal is to get you healthy, Jillian. I need to see you eat and rest more. Is that understood?" I hummed yes as he patted my head. "This is my room; it is one of the more comfortable rooms. You looked so comfortable in my arms; I didn't have the heart to move you to another room once we arrived upstairs." Hades rubbed the back of his neck and was he blushing? One of the most good-looking men I've ever seen was blushing!

I whined. "Sorry about that. I guess you were comfortable, and I felt safe." I looked down and played with the comforter.

He beamed and gave a swift kiss to my knuckles. "The same goes for me. I've enjoyed our naps. They fill me with comfort." I grinned back at him, and he gave me a smile for the first time that showed his teeth.

"I do have a room for you. It's across the hall. It wasn't ready when we arrived, but it is now. It is filled with clothes your size, a bathroom, and if you think of anything you may need, you let me know." My lip wobbled a bit. Hades was the kindest person I have ever known.

"Jillian, what is wrong?" Hades came and kneeled beside the bed. Something I've noticed he likes to do when getting my attention. He makes me feel like I was so important.

"You are just so nice to me; I don't know what I did to deserve this. I can never repay you." My heart clenched. One day I'll have to leave, and when that day comes, I would have to pay him back.

"Jillian, you are to never repay me, do you understand?" His look was hard as he held my hand. "I did this for you. You are a wonderful woman that has dealt with some shit and I'm going to make sure you get treated like the princess you are."

My heart swelled three times the size, but I couldn't help to think that he wanted something in return. Nothing in life is free and everything comes with a price, that is what Teddy taught me. You want to eat, you work, and some girls had to pleasure men to even get a safe place to sleep at night. I'll still have to be wary, even though he makes me feel safer than I have ever felt.

"Thank you," is all I say, and try to keep the tears at bay.

"Now come, let me show you to your room." I scooted to the end of the bed and had to jump off. The bed was tall and I'm hoping my bed isn't as such. I would need a ladder to get in it. Hades chuckled as he took my hand and lead me across the hall.

The double doors opened to show a lightly colored room with beautiful Southern plantation-style windows. The light was streaming in brightly, showing the soft glow of the setting sun. A white goose-down comforter laid on the bed; it looked so fluffy I could melt into it. The bathroom was large with white marble and a large jacuzzi tub and shower. I don't remember if I have ever had a bath before, so I looked over to see how deep it was.

"I could do the backstroke in this thing," I muttered back at Hades. He gave a side smirk and opened a cabinet with many products that any woman would adore. Makeup, perfumes, lotions, razors, shampoos, oils, bath bombs, the list went on and I stood in shock. "All for you, Jillian. If you need something else let me know." I stood with my mouth hanging open; my voice was still faint around him.

Hades was large and in charge and I'm this meek little thing trying not to get hit. Who knows when he'll get angry again?

"My Lord?" I heard a voice coming from the bedroom. It was a woman with dark raven hair that was as tall as Hades. Her long legs and short skirt were accentuated by her high stiletto heels. She was beautiful, all the things I wasn't.

"What is it, Magna?" Hades huffed in irritation.

"The head maid said you needed some assistance." Magna unbuttoned two buttons on her top, unbothered that I was in the room. My eyes grew wide as I looked at Hades and his playful look turned deadly.

"Get out," he growled. Magna stood confused and quickly buttoned her top and left. I knew that look, the hired help to help him with any 'problems' he might have. My heart stung. He may have said he rescued me, but what did I get thrown into now?

After all, he did buy me.

"I'll have a maid come and help you with the bath and get dressed. I'll come get you for dinner," Hades spoke grumbling, and stomped out of the room, slamming the door shut.

Chapter 9

Hades

"You bitch!!" I yelled into the hall as Magna ran down the hallway. Teleporting to the end of the hall before she could reach the corner, I gripped her neck roughly and squeezed. Her hands automatically went to her neck as she tried to scratch at my hands.

I am the King of Pain, think that is going to do anything to me? I threw her up against the wall, and she winces at the contact. Breaking her neck would be so easy. Just one flick of my finger and her spine would be disconnected with her head. "The fuck do you think you are doing, Magna?" I growled out, frustrated. Jillian could have read so much into those few words that the whore said. Hell, she probably thinks I'm trying to get her well to treat her like one of the maids.

"I'm... s-orry, My... King, I was just...thought..." she sputtered. I slammed her head back into the wall, leaving an indentation.

"That's the thing though, Magna, you DON'T THINK!" Footsteps were running down the hall the greet us. If they knew what was best, they would back off. My mood was already sour, and the time had come to teach this bitch a lesson.

"My Lord." It was Loukas. "Jillian is requesting you."

"Jillian," I whispered as I let the name roll over my tongue. Even her name soothes my anger. The rage building inside me became just a dull rumble.

I let go of Magna who fell to the floor, her high stiletto shoes causing her to grimace as she tried to stand up. She fell twice more before she was able to gain her footing.

"Let this be a lesson to you. I don't want any whores in my palace any longer. Pack your stuff and head to the village." Magna bowed her head respectfully and ran off down the hall. "Did you hear that, Loukas? Make sure all of them are gone, every single one. Even the ones you have fucked. I don't want them here." Loukas nodded and I headed back down the hallway to her room, Loukas trotting behind me.

Knocking a few times, I opened the door to see Jillian pacing back and forth. "Jillian, what's wrong?" My voice went from raging fury to calm and relaxing in a matter of seconds. Is that what it is like when you are so enthralled with someone?

"I heard screaming. Are you all right?" Her emerald eyes looked up at me with worry. I couldn't help the small smile on my face. "Of course, Jillian. Just some servants getting into a bit of a brawl." I could feel Loukas's eyes roll behind me. He's lucky that Jillian has taken a liking to him.

"Has a maid tended to you to help you with the shower?" Jillian blushed and moved her foot around like she was being scolded. Damn, she's adorable.

"N-no, I was just going to have Loukas show me how to work the shower. I can get ready on my own." I held back a growl as I fixed my collar. Loukas took a steps back and left the room. He shouldn't be anywhere near her.

"Here, Jillian, I can show you." I walk into the bathroom with my hand on the small of her back and show her how to use the knobs as I did at the penthouse. How sad it is to take the small things for granted. I'm sure she has never watched a day of television in her life let alone listened to music that isn't for strippers.

Once settled, I headed back into the hallway to speak with the servants of the palace.

Jillian passing out in my arms was both a blessing and a burden. A blessing so I was able to have us all transported here instead of making her fall asleep myself. I don't want to have to use my power on my mate. She should have free agency to fall asleep when and where she wants. It still pained me to see her pass out so quickly as she did.

Her body stayed dormant, and I held her for as long as I could until we arrived at the palace. The doctor made sure to take note of how bad off her bones and body are. She may be close to twenty years old, but her body is small, and her bones are soft. There will be many medications including IV therapy to get her back to a normal state. Not to mention the amount of food she is going to have to ingest.

Most demons around the castle stay in their demon form, so upon arrival I had to have Loukas arrange a mandatory meeting to let everyone know to stay in their human forms until Jillian has been told. Many demons were not happy, but my wrath is what scares them the most so they will comply. It takes quite a bit of their stamina to remain in human form so shifts will have to be cut shorter and new help will be needed until Jillian's transition here will be deemed all right.

I don't think she could handle another shock of new information. The fact alone that someone could be after her scared her. However, if I leave it too long then she will think I am keeping things from her. A delicate line has been set here and I must know when it will be safe to tell her.

Another doctor will be coming in to assess her mental capacity. It is strange she doesn't remember anything from her early childhood and could be the result of foul play since The Helm of Darkness was being used while taking her to the club. I let out a growl that doesn't go unnoticed by the servants cleaning the hallway. Many scattered and ran away in panic.

Rounding the corner, I finally find the old concubine room. I haven't used the willing women for a thousand years and the thought of even seeing one repulsed me. They were all afraid now. They were afraid when one of them came back with bruises on their arms and legs because the damn thing wouldn't sit still. Not that it mattered; it never filled the hole in my heart back then.

Now the maids think they can have a go with me. After today they won't even try again. I don't know what the hell came over Magna but I'm glad she's gone.

"Listen here," I roared as the girls looked at me in surprise. Many of them sat on their beds, some combing their hair and some laying back and enjoying the piles of food and heated pools. A lot of my friends come by and use the room, saying they needed to be 'broken in,' since I was too much of a ticking time bomb to give them pleasure. The newer concubines didn't know my wrath or my anger problems, so they looked at me seductively. "Get. Out," I roared.

Girls screamed and some were grabbing their bags as I walk past the door.

"Aw man!!" Hermes appears. "This is the whole reason why I visit! Guess I'll need to give them the proper send off." He winked. I glared at him. I don't need them. If they want a good time with my friend, sure why not? They like to go after Ares but he's too busy working out in the gym.

Ares isn't liked by the other gods on Olympus or in the Celestial Kingdom, he stays down here with me. The God of War and the God of the Underworld make a good match when trying to get shit done.

My office sat at the far west wing of the castle. I hadn't been there in few days since I was with Jillian so budgets, Under World Census, the comings and goings of souls were all scattered across my desk. I sat in my chair and sighed.

I have got to get my anger under control.

"*Yeah, no shit,*" Cerberus growled in my mind. The three headed mutt comes up from his resting place beside the desk. His large paws hit the ground with a loud thud as he stretched. Cerberus was my first companion when I descended to the Underworld, creating him the day I entered, and he has yet to leave my side even with giving him many outs.

"*What's all the excitement about? I heard your whores running around clacking their heels like someone offered them some good dick.*" I chuckled as I scratched under his maw.

"Close, Cerberus. I've found my mate." I smiled.

"*Damn, is your face broken? I haven't seen your teeth in ages,*" he snorted. I pushed him playfully away as I get up from my chair and walked to the window. I had to will the sky to be blue and the grass to be green. It isn't always dark down here, just deeper shades of the colors of the Earth. The sky remains a red due to the flames of fire lakes and Tartarus. That took quite a bit of my power to block all of it out, but it was worth it.

"*I'm guessing that's why it looks extra cheery down here then?*" Cerberus nudged my leg for a pet.

"Yes, she is human, and she's been through a lot. I don't want to burden her with who I really am until I find her healthy." Cerberus sat on his hind legs while one of his three heads continued to nuzzle my leg. "That is why I need to ask you a favor…" I started but was quickly cut off to Cerberus cracking his bones and two of his heads instantly retracted into his body.

"*Yeah, I got it. Just for her though.*"

"Thank you, my friend." Walking back to the desk and pouring a glass of whisky, I tell Cerberus her story. How she was abused, beaten, and broken and about to be sold into sex trafficking until I came along. Repeatedly, Cerberus growled and often bared his teeth. Even the small bit of information about Jillian and he was already protective. It might be best to have him as her permanent guardian until she has been shown the truth around her.

"You need to work on counting to ten, make sure you don't blow up around her. You have to show her the soft side to the Dark Lord of the Underworld." I rolled my eyes as I took another sip from my glass. Cerberus was known for giving his 'life' advice, and he was the only one I would take it from.

"Thanks, I think I know that." In retrospect, I wasn't throwing things like I normally do. Anything could set me off, a sound, a wrinkle in my clothes, hell even Cerberus snoring would piss me off. Now I was calm and sated, for now. If someone touches her or upsets her, I cannot guarantee I can reign it in.

When she made breakfast this morning, I thought one of my friends asked her too. I was livid and that was putting it lightly. She had worked every day for so many years and here she was making breakfast to 'be nice.' I sighed heavily again, thinking how scared she must have been. I didn't think. I just acted. A terrible pattern that I will need to break quickly. *Think first, you damn fool.*

"My King." One of the maids knocked on the door. "Dinner is served." With a curt nod from me and an impatient Cerberus trotted to the door, we walked out to pick up my beautiful mate from her room.

Chapter 10

Jillian

After a long bath, which I wasn't sure I was going to climb out of, I wrapped myself in a warm fluffy towel that made me giggle. I couldn't get over that I was in the largest bathtub in a giant bathroom that was larger than the room I slept in with thirty girls. My giggles were short lived as I turned to the mirror. You could easily see my bony shoulders, my gaunt face, and large bags under my eyes. My hair was dull and lifeless and I'm sure I weighed a hundred pounds wet.

A large sigh escaped my lips. How Loukas and Hades brought the girls and I to freedom and kept me was beyond a miracle. Then they pick me out of all the girls and bring me here, to this beautiful home. The other girls were prettier, fed better and had curves in all the right places. Me? They purposefully had me malnourished, to keep me small and have a pretty price over my head.

Walking out of the bathroom, I headed to the closet. I really didn't want a maid to come in and dress me. I helped too many girls get ready out of pity. I didn't need any of that since my body was so disgusting. Hunting through the closet I found an abundance of clothes. Dresses, skirts, pants, jeans, shirts, just about anything a girl could want. Did he know my size? *Weird.*

Thumbing through the rack I found a pretty plum colored dress that covered up my bony shoulders and stitched at the waist. I still had plenty of room to go in the waist area, but the way Loukas had been forcing food the past two meals, I knew I would gain it fast.

My hair was dry and with a bit of concealer to cover the bags under my eyes, I was ready for someone to retrieve me. Part of me wanted to venture out on my own but with a room as big as this only made me worry how big it was on the outside. I wasn't one to get lost or get into some sort of confrontation with some maids since there was a fight earlier between them.

Before I could let my mind wander into thinking of all the things that could go wrong, there was a knock on the door. Jerking my head up and walking to the door, I cracked it open to see who it was on the other side. It was Hades and my smile widened on its own accord.

"Hello Hades," I muttered. Hades' smile widened as he took in my appearance. I haven't even opened the door and he was looking at me like I was the light of his world. His eyes looked happier than what they were the first time we met. The dark shadow had left him and was looking more, dare I say, human?

There was no mistaking he looked like a god carved from stone. His body towered over mine easily and the recently shaven face made me want to touch it. It only makes me question more of his name, of his friends' names. I was lucky to have something to read at night. The history books were a favorite and Greek mythology always fascinated me. I would read about them over and over until I fell asleep at night. Wouldn't that be amazing if he was the real Hades, God of the Underworld? He certainly had the looks for it. *Ha, is it hot in here?*

I bet they are in the Mafia and those were the names they picked for themselves. Don't they use code names? Teddy's men used code names, but they weren't as cool as Hermes and Ares. Their names were Spike, Rage or Rogue. *Could they be into something illegal then?*

My imagination was running away from me as I continued to look up into his dark eyes.

"Are you ready?" His smile widened even more. I blushed looking down at my feet. "You might want to open the door a bit more if you plan on coming out." He grinned.

"Oh, right," I muttered again and opened the door.

"You look beautiful, Jillian." His hand brushed a piece of my hair away. I gave a tiny smile, looking away. I felt anything but beautiful. The bruises are still fresh, and the lifelessness of my face will tell me otherwise. "Look at me." He put his finger under my chin and ever so gently lifted my head. My eyes burned with unshed tears.

"If all the painters of the world tried to recreate your beauty on canvas for a thousand years, they still would come up short because no one can recreate your perfection." I looked at him in awe as my mouth parted. No one has ever told me such words or attempted to say anything kind to me and this man, the one who bought me, made my heart melt.

We stood in silence, looking at one another. His hand never left my chin as we stared into each other's eyes once again. He glanced at my lips, and I hate to admit, I looked at his too. Hades began to lean in until I heard a loud bark that made me jump.

"A dog!" I squealed. Beside Hades was a giant dog that reminded me of a bulldog but much larger. His jaws are massive and his teeth even longer. This animal may not even be a dog for how ferocious he looked but it didn't scare me. The body was large and full of powerful muscles. He had black sleek fur and had a twinkle in his eye.

"Can I pet him, please?" I almost started jumping up and down and Hades chuckled.

"Of course, you can. This is Cerberus." I didn't have to even bend down to pet him, he easily reached my mid-torso. I hadn't petted an animal in all my life and the large canine didn't even frighten me. He felt familiar. Reaching out, he automatically leaned into my touch. His breathing was heavy, and his head rubbed into my palm.

"Aren't you a good boy! You are so sweet!" I smiled widely at him. He jumped a little to lick my cheek. "What kind of dog is he? I didn't know dogs could get this big."

"They definitely can. This is a specially bred dog. There isn't really a name for him, one of a kind." I continued to pet him until I found a sweet spot on his chest and started scratching. His foot banged harshly against the floor, and he finally rolled over onto his back. I started laughing, continuing my assault.

"Does my big boy like that? Do you like that?" I cooed at the large dog as it groaned in delight.

"All right, that is enough of that. You are going to make me jealous." He laughed again. It was a wonderful deep laugh that I'm sure rumbled in his chest. His hand took mine to lift me from the floor and he put it in the crook of his arm.

"Come on, Cerberus, you attention hog," he growled out playfully. Hades walked down the large hallways. This wasn't a mansion; this was a palace or a castle! The statues, the paintings, portraits, there was one we passed by that caught my attention and made me stop. It was a picture of Hades in a long dark robe with a dark crown on his head. He looked angry as he sat on a throne full of thorns and skulls, a scepter in one hand and another hand gripping the arm of the throne.

A small gasp left my lips and Hades gripped my arm tighter while he cleared his throat. "Uh, that was a bit of a gag gift." He laughed lightly. "My family has a sick sense of humor." He cleared his throat again. "Anyway." He continued to walk me down the hall. "It was great seeing you laughing with Cerberus."

I hummed in response. "Yeah, I don't remember the last time I laughed that hard." Hades patted my hand that was still around his arm. His touch was warm and inviting, something I wouldn't expect of a man of his beauty. At first glance, he's cold and desolate. When I am around him though, my heart flutters violently like it never has before, and I doubt it is because my blood sugar is low.

Cerberus takes a giant leap ahead of us, shaking me from my thoughts again as we entered the enormous dining room. Hermes, Ares, and Vulcan were talking and sipping on glasses of wine until we approached the table. Hades pulled out my chair and I muttered a quick 'thank you.'

"You look ravishing, Jillian. Who knew you would clean up so well?" Hermes gave a wink as he drank another sip. "I'm sure Hades told you all about how gorgeous you look tonight."

I pursed my lips to try and hide a smile. "I take that as a yes," Vulcan added.

Hades kept piling food on my dinner plate while everyone talked. I kept mostly quiet, tasting every bit of food that was on my plate. Turkey, rolls, stuffing, potatoes with gravy, every bit of a Thanksgiving meal I had always dreamed of. I ate as much as I could, which wasn't much but Hades kept insisting on one more bite. I felt like a child, but I didn't mind it. I've never had someone to fuss over me, so I just laughed it off and tried just one more bite, for *him*.

Hades' friends felt more at ease talking with him than the first two days I spent with them. He was more relaxed and carefree and even laughed at a few jokes Ares threw at him.

"Jillian, are you all right?" He asked me for the tenth time.

"Yes." I smiled back up at him. "I do have a question though."

"Ask away then." Hades gleamed. *Wow, that smile.*

"Um, I was wondering if you guys were in the mafia or something?" Ares stared at me for a few seconds until he burst into laughter, pounding the table. I inched lower into my seat at his boisterous noise as he continued his ministrations. With one quick glare from Hades, Ares cleared his throat.

"No, we are not," Ares said. "But it would be fucking awesome if we were!" The table laughed again as I fiddled with my fork.

"What's on your mind? I see you deep in thought," Vulcan asked. He was certainly more in-tune with emotions and less on the talking.

"It's just, this place, it's huge. I would think someone from the mafia would have a place like this with all the servants. Some of them look dangerous like they are going to pull out a gun or something... and, and your names!" The servants here were not normal, not one bit. They were all tall, bulky, and wearing clothes I wasn't familiar with. They didn't look they fit them properly, some being too small.

"I will explain everything to you soon," Hades spoke. I'd like to get you to settled in and work on your health before we get into that."

Dear heavens, they are doing something illegal. My eyes widened.

"Jillian, it's fine. We are not doing anything wrong," Hermes said seriously. "You are safe here, more so than anywhere else."

His word didn't comfort me like Hades did. I was still in unknown territory. My purpose for being here was yet unknown. *Everything has a price* continued to ring through my head.

Hades

Jillian was able to stomach a normal sized plate of food, much to my persistent pushing. I could tell I was pushing her too hard when she kept putting smaller and smaller pieces of food in her mouth. Vulcan had to reprimand me in front of her for pushing. Lucky for him, since my mate was there, he didn't get a fork in his eye.

Jillian had only been up for a couple of hours, but it was apparent she was already tired, rubbing her eyes like a small child. "Jillian, would you like me to take you back to your room?" I reached for her hand that was on the table and gave her a little squeeze.

"I'm not sure why I'm so tired," she yawned. "I slept all day, and really well too." My idiot-self gleamed with pride. She slept well because of *me,* the bond that we share. She felt safe and secure with me and hopefully I would be able to sleep with her more often.

Cerberus licked his jaws several times as he came out from under the table and let out a yawn himself. *"What did you eat?"* I spoke to him through my mind. Looking from Jillian to Cerberus, I could see the guilty look on Jillian's face. She couldn't lie; the small innocent smile that played on her lips was so damn adorable. I wanted to nuzzle into her neck and give her a playful nip to show her who's boss.

"I don't know what you are talking about." Cerberus turned and gave Jillian a good lick on her hand as she giggled playfully.

"Who's a good boy?" Jillian cooed.

"I'm a damn good boy," he announced while I rolled my eyes.

"There is something about her. I don't know, Master. I feel so comfortable with her," he purred. Can I possibly be any more jealous her petting his damn head? A small growl came from my lips and Hermes threw a roll at my head.

"The fuck?" I growled out and Hermes played innocent. Jillian looked between the both of us and gave a laugh. Damn that laugh was sexy. It was playful, innocent, and I wanted to hear more of it.

After taking her to her room, she requested that Cerberus stay with her for the night. The puppy eyes she gave me was enough for me to bend over backwards and give her whatever she wanted. I would hunt down her enemies, kill my friends and go to war with the gods if it would make her happy. Damn, and I was so close to kissing those perfect lips earlier except Cerberus had to be a cock block.

The day I kiss her, hell will freeze over. I will plan a festival in her honor for just letting my lips grace hers.

"I guess it's all right," I said playfully. Turning to leave, she jumped towards me and gave me a large hug. Her head barely reached the top of my chest as she buried herself deep within it. Not taking any time for granted, I wrapped my hands around her waist and bent down so I could breathe in her scent. Kronos, she smelled like a perfect cinnamon roll. She laughed again and pulled away. My body ached to hold her more, but I couldn't push her, not yet.

"Thank you, Hades!" And she pranced off with a smirk of a smile on Cerberus' face.

"Protect her," I growled at him.

"With my life, Master."

Chapter 11

Hades

"All right, men, let's get down to business," I spoke as I poured myself a glass of scotch. The dinner went well, and Jillian wasn't as terrified of me as she was the past few days. I felt relaxed and was able to enjoy the company of others rather than wallow in self-loathing.

"Right," Loukas spoke rubbing his brow. He had been staying away from Jillian as per my request, hell, demand is more like it, but I still didn't trust the little bastard. She saw him as a friend, and I had to respect that eventually. Once she was officially mine and bonded to me then she could have him as a friend. Maybe. "As far as I could tell from the torture demons, Teddy Johnson never used the Helm. After some research I realized no human can wear the Helm without becoming completely dark and eventually dying by suicide due to the magical qualities of the metal. He just always kept it in his desk, per request of the man who used it."

I rubbed my chin while Hermes jumped his leg up and down on the chair. "What about Malachi?" His eyes went to the window. "Malachi is an angel. What the Tartarus was he doing there at the strip club trying to buy Jillian? That isn't his jurisdiction." Hermes shook his head.

"Maybe he was trying to rescue her, saw us as a threat. You know Angels don't trust demons and, sorry no offence, the God of the Underworld," Vulcan added.

"Then why didn't he save any of the other girls?" Ares flexed his muscles as he played with his dagger. "It doesn't make sense; he was going after Jillian for a reason."

"We should check into Malachi then first," I quipped. "He is our prime suspect. The Helm and Jillian are linked, and I want to know why."

Loukas clicked his pen then wrote a few notes on the paper. "I'll get on that, my Lord. I will have to go back to Earth and get permission to question a few angels."

"Do what you must, Loukas. Be discreet, I don't want people knowing what we are doing right now. She's still in danger being here." Loukas nodded and left the room.

Hermes, Ares, and Vulcan fell into casual conversation, speaking of any demons they took a liking to as they had officially returned to the Underworld since my unbearable attitude has changed. We had all been great friends before Persephone and during the time I tried to court her, but once she was gone, my life was meaningless. To fill the void, I worked out in a gym that Ares frequented but he became too scared of me to even work out with me. Vulcan, the calmer of us, moved to Earth along with Hermes to deal with our interactions with demi-gods that get out of line.

"Master," I heard through the link that Cerberus and I share.

"Is Jillian all right?" I panicked.

"Oh, she is great all right," Cerberus chuckled. *"She just came out of the shower in a damn towel, holy shit."*

"Cerberus," I growled. *"You do not look at her."*

"She's gonna drop it, holy Kronos. She's changing in front of me. Those milky legs, that round ass, Zeus all mighty," he sang.

"CEREBRUS!" I couldn't take it anymore. I willed myself into Cerberus' body to find that Jillian was asleep with her arm around him.

"Master, that was too easy." I let out a heavy sigh.

"If she didn't like you so much, I'd make you stand at the gates of the Underworld again."

"But you won't, because she loves me," Cerberus snickered. *"That's not all she said though."* I nudged him while he paused, and he chuckled at me. *"She thinks you are devilishly handsome and has warm feelings toward you even though she thinks she shouldn't."* My smile widened. She thought I

was handsome. Thank Kronos because I was getting worried. Women would bow at my feet, but she never did.

"What else did she say?" I mused. I needed to feed my pride right now.

"That she's scared. She doesn't understand her purpose here. I think she is worried what everyone's intentions are." I sighed heavily. I knew she would think that. More time, time that I don't have.

"Thank you, Cerberus. I'm quite jealous of you right now." Jillian held onto Cerberus tighter, and he purred into her touch.

"You'll have your time, I'm sure of it Master."

Cerberus would be the perfect companion for her until we had the thief who stole the Helm. It makes me wonder if he or she knew all along that Jillian was my mate and made sure that I would never find her. Mates make you stronger; once intertwined during a bonding, you are considered one. I may be a selfish bastard and didn't want a mate at first but after seeing her I realized I was a fool.

Fool to believe I didn't need her, and now I had to deal with the guilt from almost rejecting her and putting her through hell. She doesn't know her own birth parents; this horrible life was all that she knew. I was going to have to ask Hecate for her help in finding out if she had an enchantment put on her. Writing down a note on my desk to send to my assistant in the morning, I carried myself to my room and left my friends to bicker and drink.

They would be staying here permanently, and it only made me smile that after all these years they would willingly come back. However, I don't think it was just for me they were staying; they had taken a little interest in my mate. Not in a romantic way but a protective way. She was a light that this darkness needed, and I was going to continue to make sure her soul continued to shine.

Jillian

My head was resting on a beautiful silk pillow. My arm held a large stuffed calico cat and I nuzzled into it deeper as I tried to sleep. The thunder outside rolled through the room as I shuffled under the sheets more. I was going to be a big girl and not get my parents. I told them just today how big I've grown, and I wasn't scared of anything. What a bad impression it would be if I ran to them now.

The window blew open with a force. The rain started to pour in as I rushed to the large windows and I shut it tight, being sure to set the latch so it wouldn't happen again. Several of my drawings scattered across the floor. The paint was now smudged and ruined. I was going to give it to Mom for her birthday tomorrow.

I sighed and tried to flatten out the crumpled wet paper. Maybe I could fix it later.

I jumped back into bed; my daddy's shirt hung all the way to my ankles. He said he liked giving his shirts to me and Mom; he said it makes us smell more like him. He has a nice forest smell to him. I wonder what I smell like to him when he Eskimo kisses me. It's his favorite thing to do with his favorite girls he says.

Sitting back into bed, taking my stuffy, Macaroni, back with me, I curled up but felt uncomfortable. Someone was watching me. Sitting up, I glanced around the room to see no one. I was big and strong, so I would check every space. Under the bed, the closet, even in the toy box, there was nothing there. With a huff, I get back into bed.

"Are you finished looking for me?" the voice called to me. I stilled, not wanting to look behind me. The voice was coming from my bedroom door, the only escape I had.

"W-who are you?" My voice shook as I began to hold back tears. It couldn't possibly be the boogieman, daddy said they aren't real.

"I'm not the boogie man, if that is what you are thinking." I gasped loudly as I turned around. It was a man, not overly muscular, but enough to show his strength. He wore a large helmet on his head while wearing all black clothing. His hands were also covered in black gloves with a white handkerchief in his hand.

How did he get here? I need Daddy and Grandpa! They will save me when I'm in trouble. Before I let out a loud scream, he lunged at me while I tried to get away. Kicking and screaming I pulled down lamps, toys, and pictures across the room. My voice continued to wail until he finally caught up with me. His arms pulled my weak body down on the floor and shoved the handkerchief to my face. I tried to stay awake, I did. "Please let me go!" Mommy will be so upset if I'm not at her party. "Please let me go!"

"Please let me go!" I screamed out loud. "Please, don't take me away from them!" I cried out into the dark. It was so dark in this room as I started sobbing. "Please don't take me back there, please!" My voice was already scratched and hoarse when I suddenly felt a pair of large arms come around my body.

My body began to still as I heard encouraging words whispering in my ear. "My little angel, you are all right, it was just a dream." My ugly sobs become more of a whimper, feeling the warmth of his body against mine. The soothing touch caused me to relax almost instantly. Who else would have those strong arms to protect me, the one who saved me from those predators? *Hades.*

The voice was soothing and strong as he spoke with a rattle in his chest. I must have woken the whole mansion. The warmth of his body relaxed my muscles and I molded into him. I felt safe, for once I felt like this is where I belonged but the thought of all of it being false hope made me tense.

"Shh, Jillian it is all right," he cooed as he petted my hair. My face was now in his bare chest as he continued to stroke my messy strands. "I'm here and nothing will ever happen to you." The husky voice had me hypnotized as my hiccups began to subside. I take a large sigh and I gripped onto his waist tighter as I recalled the horrible dream. It felt so real, like I was there.

"Are you all right?" he whispered in the shell of my ear. The heat of his breath sent chills down my body. Was I all right? No, I wasn't, and I gave him an honest answer because I couldn't lie to my rescuer.

"No," I whispered. "It was so real." My voice shook. Hades kissed the top of my head.

"Would you like to talk about it?" I gripped him tighter and shook my head no, while closing my eyes. Somehow it didn't seem so dark with him in the room.

"How about we try and get some sleep? Do you want me to stay?" My mind replays all the dirty men I've ever met. They use women, abuse, rape and hurt them but I could never see Hades doing that to me. He makes me feel safe. He gives me a reassuring feeling.

"Please," I whispered to him. I felt the smile grace his perfect lips while they sat on the top of my head from his reassuring pecks. Hades slid down and fluffed the pillow and laid back without letting me go. My face was tickled by the small amount of hair on his perfectly toned chest. If I wasn't so scared, I would have taken the time to admire it because what can I say, he was attractive.

"Get some sleep, my little angel." He gave a reassuring squeeze and rubbed circles on my shoulders until I finally did drift off to sleep.

Vera Foxx

Chapter 12

Jillian

The bed was warm, just like the previous night when I woke up with a nightmare. Hades' lips were gently parted as he slept. He looked at peace while his worry lines had ironed out in the night. His breath smelled like a hint of mint and whisky; a very manly smell that made me want to purr in contentment. If we could stay like this all day, I wouldn't complain. It was safe here in this bed with him.

I should have reservations, but I don't. My gut had never steered me wrong before while working at the club. Hades leaned back to stretch, and I watched his rippling torso move with his body. Hades was certainly built, and it brought a blush to my cheeks as I looked away quickly. His smirk let me know he saw me ogling him, but he didn't say anything. He was too much of a gentleman for that.

"You are hungry. Let's get you fed." His voice was demanding yet gentle at the same time. "Come on, little angel. Get ready for the day and I will meet you back here."

I thought the dream last night would escape me the longer I was awake. That was what my other dreams did. Dreams of running outside being free as a child should be. By mid-afternoon I would have forgotten all about my dreams the night before. This dream was printed in my mind. It wasn't a dream; it felt like it was a reality.

Could it have been? The man in the gladiator mask seemed real enough. I could feel the claws from his hands gripping my ankle as he pulled me from the room. The coldness of the air as it slipped in when I put my drawings and paintings away. Too real. I shivered and shut the shower head off to get dressed.

Hades was leaning up against the door frame when I opened the door. He was wearing a tight black shirt with black dress pants. His muscular arms flinched as he uncrossed his arms and held out his hand. "Ready?" He smiled and I took his hand gladly. He intertwined our fingers, and I couldn't help but blush. I had no reason to; he slept in my bed last night and that was intimate enough.

"I want to show you around today. Loukas said you wanted to go outside." I smiled a genuine smile.

"I would love that. I don't remember the last time I felt the grass beneath my feet." Hades' large smile turned smaller at the mention of that. I would have to remember to not bring up such silly things.

"Angel." He had me look at him. "Don't be sorry. I want you to tell me these things. I want to give you new memories, happy ones." I couldn't help myself as I stood on my tip-toes and placed a kiss on his cheek. Sparks flew across my lips and Hades stood in shock. Looking down at me, he leaned closer and gave me the exact same kiss on the cheek. "You can do that all you want, angel." I giggled as he led me to the dining room.

Hades made sure to fill my plate again and the doctor was also at breakfast. He watched what food I ate and how much and gave me several vitamins. Along with that he had me sit for IV therapy that included some steroids to help me feel even hungrier. "You are very underweight. We need you gaining quicker. Your stress levels have decreased so you will feel more fatigue. Be sure to take naps and get plenty of rest," he lectured while Hades crossed his arms and scowled.

"Don't lecture her, Aramose, or you will be the one with the lecture," Hades growled out in irritation and Aramose looked like he just wet himself.

"Hades, it's all right. He is just concerned." Looking back at the doctor, I patted his hand. "It's alright, he is just worried. Hades will take good care of me." Aramose looked back and forth between the two of us and his eyebrows rose to the top of his head.

"My apologies My Lord." He bowed to the ground at my feet. "I did not mean it, Mistress. Please forgive me."

Looking up at Hades in question, he grabbed my wrist and led me out of the room. "He's an idiot," Hades ruffed. I laughed at his childish behavior as he led me to the front doors of the mansion.

As quick as Hades had taken me outside, I couldn't help but slow down to where he was practically pulling me. His pace slowed and turned back. I could feel him watching from my peripheral vision. He couldn't possibly know what was going through my head right now.

The sun felt warm. It was a natural light that tickled my skin as it shone down on me. Letting go of Hades' hand, I stepped off the sidewalk he was leading me down and into the grass. It was a lush, emerald green, much brighter than in pictures that I had seen. Each blade of grass had its own look, small, jagged pieces where it had been cut on each blade of grass. I threw my shoes off quickly and felt it between my toes. Refreshing, like it was always meant to be here. My body wanted to sink into the ground and feel the warmth the Earth was giving. The urge to run through the grass, through a forest and dive into a lake was strong. I wanted it all; I wanted to spend the rest of my days outdoors. My eyes teared up as I looked to Hades, standing with an expression I had never seen before until this moment. Sorrow.

Hades

I tend to forget how I take things for granted. I don't remember the last time I looked at a flower to smell its aroma or look on its beauty. Jillian stood there, standing in the grass of the well-manicured lawn. She didn't care for the carefully placed stones that you could walk to the nearby fountain; she didn't care about the statues that decorated the entire yard. Jillian was happy because she was touching the soil, the dirt and it wasn't even Earth like she thought.

I will keep our home like this, in its tiny bubble if I must. One day soon I will have to tell her the truth. The sun she looks at and the blue sky she adores is just a haze of power cloaking her from the true look of the Underworld. What would she say when I show her our true world, that she is meant to be down here with me? The sky would be tinted red, and the colors of Earth were just darker down here. An orb of light will light the day and a moon like orb to brighten the night but nothing of what Earth is.

The Underworld is its own place. Not as depressing as one may make it to be, but it's still different.

Lost in thoughts, I find her with a stray tear flowing down her cheek, not of sadness but of happiness. Jillian is happy to be standing in a pile of grass meant to be pleasing to the eye. Jillian should have never had to cry over grass or the sun shining in her face; she should have never dealt with the suffering because of me.

Jillian will never accept me, and I don't know if I can ever let her go.

She walks up to me, bare feet, and all, and puts her dainty hand on my rough face. "What's going on in that mind of yours?" Her head tilts to the side and gives a smile. I touch her hand with mine, not wanting her to take her hand away from my cheek.

"Nothing. Come, let me show you around."

I led her to the garden, thinking she would appreciate that most, in which she did. Each type of flower she wanted to inspect, asking its name and where they normally reside in nature. Taking her time, she touched at least one petal and smelled its sweet aroma. As we continued, she immediately grabbed my hand and pulled me to where the large fountain sat in the middle of the courtyard.

She grabbed my hand all on her own.

"Is this a wishing fountain?" she asked curiously. I laughed at her innocence. "What?" She chuckled. "It isn't?"

I held he hand and kissed it. "It can be if you want it to be. Are you wanting to wish for something?"

Jillian pursed her pouty lips together and wiggled them back and forth on her face. "I do, but I don't have any coins," she sighed. Reaching into my pocket, I pulled out two coins after I willed them to be there.

"Here, take these and make some wishes." Jillian smiled up at me and took them quickly and muttered a quick, 'thank you." She closed her eyes and threw both coins in the water. Jumping up and down and grabbing my hand again, which I fucking loved, I asked her, "What did you wish for?"

Gasping, she shook her head. "No, I can't tell you! It won't come true." Her emerald eyes looked up at me and squinted, accusing me of breaking the wishing fountain tradition.

"Fine, fine." I faked hurt, putting my hand to my chest. "How can I make them come true if you don't tell me?"

"You don't make them come true, the fate of the fountain does!" she explained. "Now show me more!" she begged and pulled me away.

Little does she know I could touch her forehead with my thumb and see what she has seen, I could feel her feelings and her sins but of course she would have no sins. I can even hear the two wishes she thought in her head, but to claim those from her would be wrong. I'll have to keep guessing and maybe, one day she would tell me what her heart really wishes for.

The thought briefly crossed my mind to try and dive into her mind, to see her past and see through her eyes what parents she had, but if she can't remember it herself, her mind wouldn't have the memory either.

I took her through the rest of the garden that had various statues of the gods. It intrigued her more as she asked about each one and their powers. Her smile would brighten when she heard stories she had never heard of before from her textbooks she was sometimes given. Such as how Aphrodite may be the goddess of love but has a secret love of miniature animals such as goats and ponies. Jillian's eyes would squint to check for the slightest hint of a joke but gave a soft smile when she figured out she wasn't being tricked.

The end of the garden of statues were coming and I knew this statue would hurt the worst. It was of Selene, one of the new gods from the past 3,000 years. Looking on her face, even in stone made my stomach churned in painful ways.

"She's so beautiful. Who is she?" The statue had her in a simple garb that covered her breasts and wrapped behind her back and holding onto her hips tightly covering parts of her she would never want to be seen. Her hair was let loose and went to her waist, unlike most of the other goddesses who had their hair up. The necklace she wore was a crescent of the moon that was a broken sapphire to make it stand out amongst the granite. Looking down, she is petting a large wolf at her side and smiling widely. Her first species she granted to have mates.

Jillian walked up to the wolf and put her hand on it, staring at the wolf first that was staring adoringly at Selene. "This wolf is huge," she whispered as she looked up. From the looks of the scene before me it looked like Selene was looking at her. Jillian's innocent eyes traced Selene's soft features

"Who is she, Hades?" She snapped me out of my stupor as I watched her. I felt the fire rise within me; this was my fault. I could have stopped all of this and protected her. Selene gave me a choice and I slapped her in the face.

"Let's leave this story for another day," I huffed while I shoved my hands in my pockets. Turning around I heard the small padding of her bare feet trying to keep up with my long strides. I needed to leave. I couldn't let her see me angry. We had come so far.

Mind-linking Cerberus, I told him to keep her outside so I could blow off some steam.

"Jillian, I must make a phone call. Cerberus will keep you company." I left without telling her goodbye or telling her when I would come back. Kronos, I didn't know when I would be able to come back, if at all today. Glancing back, I saw a worried Jillian with both hands clasped together and a disturbed look on her face.

We've both got some internal battles to go through for this to work but right now I needed to torture something, kill, spill blood to make this rage in me die right now.

Bursting in the doors I see an anxious Hermes writing at his own private desk in the main entrance of the hallway. He throws his pen down and stands up to follow me. "Hades? What's wrong?" I didn't answer and began stripping out of my shirt. I liked to feel the warm blood hit my bare body as I torture souls that deserve it. I needed to feel Teddy Johnson's fear radiates off him, fuel my power within me as I suck him dry of his aura. I'll take my time with him, pulling out his fingernails one at a time, pluck out his eyes, do the little things that will build until I finally have the final finale with him: pulling his beating heart out of his chest and let him feel the life squeeze out of his soul. Only for him to regenerate and start all over the next hour.

I can't do anything to fix Jillian's past but being sure I torture the soul for all eternity will have to do.

"Shit, well you lasted five days without having to go to Tartarus. What do I tell Jillian? She will be looking for you." I stopped, gripping my fists tightly and then relaxed.

"I'll be back when I can," I spoke harshly as I calmed my breathing. "In time to help her sleep." I sighed as I left Hermes to his devices.

Once in my room, I threw on my black cloak and transported directly to the Tartarus gates. As far as the Underworld was to the heavens, Tartarus was as equally lower than the Underworld. It takes great attempts to come here and only my most evil demons come to play in this playground.

Titans are still imprisoned here, and we no longer hear their pleas for help. Some 15000 years could do that to even the evilest of creatures. Now we have sections and stations of different men and women we torture based on the evil they had conducted in their previous life.

The man I was looking for was strapped to a pole that looked like a stripper pole. He was being beaten with paddles on his naked body as some demons took it on themselves to have him watch all the poor souls he tortured. Instead of watching in glee, he would feel their pain 100-fold. His eyes were full of tears of the physical and mental burden he was now carrying. As I walked up, I saw the picture of Jillian flash before his eyes.

It was recent; in fact, it was the night we saved her. She was wearing her pink outfit with her high heeled shoes. Silent tears dropped from her cheeks as she looked in the mirror. "Now, here's your punishment, doll." He took his hand and slapped her outer thigh harshly.

"Thank you, Master." Her lip quivered, and he led her out of the room.

Thunder rolled through me as I cracked my knuckles and the tortured demons looked up. They were the worst looking ones of them all. Their skin was practically eaten away, only bone and muscle remained. Their skin was charred black from the flames of Tartus that flare during the afternoon shipment of new souls. Claws slowly retreated and their tails let go of his limbs as I approached, knowing I could blink and have them gone in an instant.

Teddy Johnson looked up at the sudden break he was receiving only to have his heart smashed again. "Y-you," he whispered.

"Me," I growled.

Chapter 13

Jillian

He just left. Hades looked so angry, and I didn't know what to do; there was a glimpse of sadness in his eyes and in my gut, I knew I needed to stay away. Cerberus came out looking happy while I stooped down to give him all the cuddles.

He groaned and whined when I found his spot as I beamed at him. Hermes came out with his hands in his pockets and a cigarette in his mouth. "Look what we have here, beauty and the beast." Cerberus huffed as he gave a playful nip at his ankles. "Easy their boy, remember who feeds you!" I chuckled while standing to my feet.

"Hades is going to be out of the house today; he needs to go to the office to take care of some business." I nodded as I fiddled with my fingers. "And you, young miss, need to get inside for your IV therapy." I groaned out loud and did a little foot stomp.

"I'm doing fine; I haven't gotten weak in a few days!"

"That's because the therapy is working." Hermes looked me up and down and flicked the butt out of his mouth. "How about this, stay outside for a bit while I work here in the garden. You can go as far as the fence but don't go past it. Do you understand?" The fence was a long way off, and I wasn't planning on straying too far anyway. There was too much to look around just on the grounds.

"Yup, you can go inside. Cerberus is with me."

"I don't think Hades would like that, and he wants to make sure you are always safe. Go on," Hermes said in a no-nonsense tone as I walked away from the cobble-stoned path.

The large lake on the back-side of the house looked interesting so walking over, I went to put my feet in it; it was cool and refreshing as I walked around the edge. Small fish swam around. Cerberus looked on questioningly, so I put my hand in the water and splashed him, causing him to yip and run away. Laughing, I got out and went to sit under the willow tree.

Being outside was heaven. I could see myself sleeping under the stars every night if Hades would let me, but I doubt he would do that. Being in nature was calming and brought a whole new sense of peace. The grass, the dirt, and the smell of the flowers and trees were how I dreamt it would be. I wanted to engulf the earthy scent all over my body.

Cerberus came behind me and let me lay my head on his stomach while he purred. It was lulling me to sleep. I wasn't planning on sleeping, but he curled up around me since he was so large. I tried to get up, but he huffed at my wiggling, so I stayed still. He could still chew me to pieces if he wanted.

"You're no fun, CC." Another huff, and he laid his head in the grass as I curled up close. I suppose a small nap wouldn't hurt.

Howls from the moon woke up. "I must have slept late," I muttered to myself. The moon was full, and the small town was just a few feet away from the treehouse I was sleeping in. The lights were flickering on and off, and several other children laughing and giggling as they ran around a large mansion.

"Ember!!" I heard a woman yell. "Ember! Where are you? You are going to miss the party!" It was completely dark outside, but I could see perfectly. The woman had long golden locks of hair with a smile on her face. She was holding a small bundle in her arms, a baby that couldn't be but a few weeks old. Two other small boys are flanking her sides; one looks to be close to my age.

"Ember!" she yelled again, and I jumped out of the tree. I felt drawn to them, so I followed her voice. "There you are. Where have you been?" Confused, I looked at her and pointed to myself. "Yes, you! Were you in the treehouse again?" I nodded, still wondering why this woman thinks I'm this Ember girl. She smiles again at me, and the eldest boy grabs my hand. "Make sure she doesn't get away, Dante." The boy held my hand and gave me a look of mischief in his eyes that looked like his mother's. Was she my mother too?

Her green eyes looked into mine. "I don't know why you don't like listening to the story about Hades visiting our pack. It was a great honor to help him."

Again, I looked at her confused as Dante pulled me along to sit next to the roaring fire.

"That's because she likes Hades, Mom; I've seen her read those books. She doesn't think he's mean." The mother scowled at the boy. "Enough, Hunter. Hades is a force to be reckoned with, but he protects this pack as he promised us years ago as thanks for ridding him of that horrible demon creation. He gives us the extra assurance that none of our own will get hurt by any other demons with his special powers. We would know immediately if something was amiss."

"What about your cameras, Mom?" Dante asked. "Those help too."

The woman laughed. "Only so much. It is more so for unwanted humans because cameras don't work in use of magic. The only way someone could get in would be a god-like being, and we don't have any threats from them." Dante nodded, and the woman handed me the baby. I panicked, having never held a baby before I tried to pass him off to Dante.

"What? You always like to hold Steven. Mother gave him to you." Dante pushed the baby back into my arms. He was sleeping peacefully as the woman approached a gigantic man with dirty blonde hair in a man bun. He kissed her lightly on the lips as they both looked down on us.

"Alright, gather 'round. It's time to hear the story of Hades' visit twelve years ago." Children ran to the fire while the adults laughed and found a seat. Many kids were murmuring how scary Hades was, and he could turn the entire pack house into a raging inferno. My heart hurt at the jokes they made, and I wanted to go push them off their stupid log.

"The day was much like this one, a cold, and winter snow started to approach. Your Luna was preparing herself for the Luna and Mating Ceremony when Trixen the demoness came to put an end to your Luna's life. She was an evil demon created by Hades, and he had lost control over her. Luckily, our strong Luna was able to destroy her, and with that came a great gift from Hades. The protection barrier."

A little pup started waving his hand around frantically while the large man chuckled as he held onto his wife. "Yes, pup?"

The little pup stood up to ask his question. "Why did he create that demon? Why would anyone want to hurt Luna?"

The big man's smile dropped, and he took a large breath. "We can't go into much detail. We can tell you she was created for a good purpose, but all that went awry, and she took it upon herself to destroy mate bonds or give hope to others that she could create a stronger bond with someone, not their mate." Gasps from the crowd lingered as I sat confused.

What is a mate bond?

Steven sputtered, and the mother came over to pick him up. "Thank you, Ember," she whispered to me. Ember? Am I Ember in this dream?

A dark silence fell on the crowd, and the fire slowly faded into darkness. Looking around, I was the only one left at the now-dead fire. In the woods, I saw a twinkle of reflecting light from the moon. My eyesight could no longer see well in the dark as I squinted to see better, only to have the figure right in front of me with a blink.

The man in the gladiator helmet bent his body low and looked into my eyes. "Forget," he growled, and I screamed to getaway. Yelling, crying, and pawing at the dirt, I tried to hold onto the logs for my life. I couldn't be taken away, not again! My hands drew blood as dirt and rock scraped my fingers.

Tears dripped down my face as I continued to forget what the kind couple and familiar children looked like. "Help! Dante!" A flash of his body, looking back at me into the darkness, was seen, but he didn't move. His eyes held tears and looked away, **leaving me alone to be dragged into the darkness of the forest.**

"No! No! Let me go!!" I could hear my voice become louder as I thrashed around the tight embrace on my body. Pushing and shoving, I tried to get away, but I was too afraid to open my eyes. That gladiator helmet mask did nothing but bring forth the nightmares, and I dared not look him in the eyes. There were several coming from my attacker until I heard a voice.

"Jillian! It's me! It's Hermes!" His voice and my body couldn't register it. I was still in the fight or flight mode, and right now, I wanted nothing more than to not to feel restrained. The grip became tighter as I yelped out, and I felt my body being lifted from the ground.

He was going to take me, and *he* was going to send me back to Master. I'd rather die than go back there, and I would not subject myself to that kind of emotional and physical torture any longer! Twisting my body, I heard another grunt as another pair of arms gripped hold of me, holding me impossibly tighter. I couldn't move. My body was completely immobile.

As I tried to wiggle free, I could hear Cerberus barking and Loukas stroking my hair. "That's it, princess, wake up now." Blinking my eyes a few times, my lashes were drenched in tears as I began to move my eyes around my surroundings. I was in a brightly lit room with lights shining down. Squinting my eyes, I could see the outline of Loukas, Hermes, and Ares.

"Are you done thrashing around?" Ares was still holding onto me tightly into a cocoon as my face looked right at him. Nodding embarrassingly, he laid me gently on the hospital bed of crisp white sheets.

"You gave us quite a scare, little one," Hermes whispered. "Hades isn't going to like this," he murmured to himself.

"You shouldn't have left her alone!" Loukas yelled, rubbing his forehead. "She's fragile, and she needs to be looked after!"

Ares pushed Loukas to the side forcefully, and he hit the instruments table. "She isn't weak. Hell, I had to use some force to keep her wrapped up like that to keep her from hurting herself. Stop babying her." Loukas growled back, Ares puffed up his chest in defiance.

"Please stop," I muttered. "I'm fine now; I'm sorry, was trouble." Hermes knelt beside the table and laid his head down.

"Jillian, you have nothing to be sorry for. Now can you tell us what you have been dreaming that keeps giving you nightmares?" I shook my head 'no' as I crawled up into the fetal position. I lived these dreams every time Hades was away, and I didn't want to relive them while I was awake. A few stray tears left my eyes again while Hermes blew out some air in frustration.

"We can't help unless you tell us what's going on, princess." Loukas patted my head and played with my hair while I sighed.

"Just not right now, please." Loukas tisked his lips. Hermes went to the door and let in the doctor; he was wearing his pristine white lab coat with a stethoscope around his neck.

"Mistress, I heard you were having some night terrors." The doctor saw all the men in the room and made a motion for them to leave. However, they all just stood there with their arms crossed.

"Patient confidentiality, men. I need you to leave so I can examine her."

Hermes shook his head, "No, by order of Lord Hades, we cannot leave her."

"And yet you still subjected her to a night terror. If you had woken her sooner, it wouldn't have escalated this far." His eyes narrowed at Hermes, who looked hurt as he uncrossed his arms. I pulled my arm out from my knees and put it on Hermes'.

"It's all right, and you didn't know. Don't worry about it, and Hades won't get mad." Hermes gave a sly smile and patted my head.

"Doctor, they can stay." Giving him a reassuring glance. The doctor sat down and pulled out his stethoscope to listen to my heart, check my blood pressure and oxygen levels, and even take a few blood samples after checking me over for bruises. The boys continued to stare the doctor down like he would do something horrible or unpredictable. Everyone was staring, and I was starting to get uncomfortable.

Clearing my throat, I asked "Are we done here, doctor?"

"Almost." He grabbed another needle and put it into my arm. The tube was then hooked up to an IV pole. I groaned. "Yup, I got you now!" He chuckled while I flung my body back onto the bed.

"I don't wanna," I whined. The men chuckled at my childishness. Now I was stuck here for at least an hour, and taking a nap was out of the question, not without Hades. Without another word, the doctor left, and I was left with a dog and three heavy breathing men in the room.

"When is Hades coming back?" I thought I would ask again. Even though these men were protecting me and doing it well, I couldn't help but crave Hades. I felt this strong connection to him, and I couldn't figure out what it was. Thinking back to the dream, the girl, Ember, had a strong link to the Hades story. It almost pained her to hear the other children complain about the King of the Underworld.

Could this girl be me? The Dante boy felt so close to me; I could almost feel his touch when he dragged me to the bonfire. What could it all mean? Were the two dreams connected? It all ended up the same though, me being dragged away by the terrible masked villain.

Hermes looked to Ares. "Soon, little one, soon."

Chapter 14

Jillian

After the slowest IV drip on the planet dripped the last bit of fluid in me, I quickly ripped it off and jumped off the table. There was a new energy in me that I hadn't noticed before and I was ready to prance off down the hall until the doctor held out his arm. "Hold on there. Where do you think you are going?" Hades' men came up behind me and Loukas put his hand on my shoulder.

"You can't be running around the house like that. The IV drip had some caffeine in it to help with the few headaches you said you get. Once it wears off in about an hour, I don't want you to have a crash and feel groggy again."

"Right." I nodded trying to compose myself. I couldn't help it. I was feeling lighter than ever. "We have scheduled a few other," he cleared his throat, "specialists to come in and check on you in the next few days." Loukas patted my shoulder in understanding like he knew what he meant.

"When they are here you need to be able to tell them what was in your dream. I want you to be prepared to tell us that." My fist clenched. I didn't want to repeat the nightmares again. Loukas rubbed my back.

"I'm sure she will be ready. Hades will be back and I'm sure she will cooperate." I crossed my arms, already worried about the next few days. They need to just let it go. I don't want to think about it and I'm going to be stubborn.

"Aw come on." Ares ruffled my hair as he walked in front of me. "Let's do something fun. How about order take out and a movie?" My eyes lit up.

"Yeah! What can we watch?!" I jumped in excitement as the guys walked down the hallway.

Ares kept asking what kind of pizza I wanted, but the only thing I could come up with was cheese. I've only eaten crusts of pizza, not the actual cheesy topping part and of course, they all gasped and threw a few swear words around and said they were going to get a variety.

Thirty minutes later, Ares burst through the door with over fifty boxes of pizza. My mouth hung open as servants looked on in awe as the boxes towered over their heads and I couldn't help my laughter as Cerberus started jumping trying to get a few.

I had a whole box of pizza to myself. I chose pepperoni with mushrooms along with some garlic dipping sauce and a large milkshake. I knew I couldn't eat it all, but I was going to try my best. They were all doing so well trying to cheer me up from my embarrassing dream and assault on Hermes and Ares.

"What movie should we watch?" Vulcan spoke up. He had spent most of the time in Hades' office yelling at someone, but I dared not ask. Vulcan was such a sweet and kind soul, so if he was yelling, I'm sure something was wrong.

I sucked on my milkshake, trying to think of some movies I always wanted to watch but nothing came to my head. It wasn't like I could sit and watch commercials while the TVs were playing at the bar.

My silence got to Ares as he jumped up and said he had the perfect movie. He grabbed the remote and immediately typed in the movie, 300. "Dude, no!" Hermes jumped to grab the remote. "She can't watch that shit. Are you that much of an idiot?" Ares feigned innocence as he held onto it as he sunk into the couch.

"It's a great movie! They did a great job historically. Except they forgot to put how Ares showed up and helped kick some ass!" They continued to argue back and forth about the movie, and I sat there just munching on my pizza. I was used to men fighting at the club and that part didn't bother me. It was them coming after me and needy hands and I knew these guys wouldn't lay a finger on me.

Boxes scattered on the floor and a tired Loukas walked out of the office, shutting the door behind him. He watched me as I sipped more of my milkshake and watched Hermes and Ares continue their fighting over a remote. The two large men who could pass off as brothers were starting to get heated and Vulcan was over on the other side of the room making a call to his therapist.

"Sit the fuck down!" Loukas yelled, upset.

Ares didn't like it one bit and stomped over to him and grabbed him by the throat. "You have no dominion over us, demon," he spat.

Demon?

I cleared my throat to try and break the tension. "Hey guys, 300 is fine. I read the description. A bunch of topless guys fighting, I'm down." Vulcan laughed in the corner while I snuggled into the blanket fort I created around me. On either side of me there was Loukas and Hermes as we hunkered down to watch.

Blood, so much blood.

It was all just a movie, but the blood would splatter even on the television screen. Ares was bouncing his head while eating some popcorn that Vulcan went to pop for us. How could he eat like that? Loukas's head had lulled to the side; he looked exhausted. During the day, he had been out of the house going to town, running errands for the company while Hermes has to babysit.

The credits started rolling and it was already 11 pm. I was tired but not *that* tried to sleep into a sleep full of nightmares. Where was Hades?

Vulcan got up to switch off the TV and stretched his body letting out a loud gruff. "Well guys," Vulcan looked over at me and bowed, "my lady, it's time for bed." Everyone got up from their spot and the servants came in to clean up after us. I stayed in my blanket fort staring at the ground. I was *not* going to bed. They would have to inject me with something if they wanted me to sleep and I know they would never do that.

"Come on, little one, off to bed. I'll walk you there." Hermes went to grab my hand, but I buried myself it farther into the blankets.

"I'll just wait until Hades' gets home thanks." Nope, no bed for me.

Ares and Hermes had a little stand-off, probably thinking it was the movie. "It wasn't the movie," I blurted out. "I just can't go to sleep until he gets back," I murmured and hugged my legs. How could I get so dependent on Hades so fast? He had inched his way into my heart. I wanted nothing more to be around him and I couldn't understand why. I did know he took the nightmares away.

Loukas came to sit beside me to console me, but I shook my head. "You guys go ahead. I'll be all right." I tried to give them some reassurance, but they weren't having it.

"I don't think he's coming home tonight. It's late. Come on, I'll sit with you while you sleep and wake you up if you start having a nightmare."

Ares knocked Loukas in the shoulder. "Not a good idea. Let's just watch another movie. Less blood huh?" I nodded, and he went and picked out another movie, Beauty and the Beast. Vulcan put a pillow on his lap and beckoned me to lay down. My legs were across Ares and Hermes as we all began to watch.

I fell in love with the music, the actors and the actresses. How a simple girl changed the heart of a beast entranced me. By the time we got to the end, I felt my eyes flutter. Trying to defy gravity, I shook my head to wake up. Only I couldn't shake my head again because Vulcan was playing with my hair.

Cerberus had his head on the couch, watching me as I finally shut my eyes.

Hades

I had spent 12 hours in Tartarus, beating, torturing, and making that pathetic waste of soul wish he had never thought about hurting her or anything else. The evilest, vile, and pathetic demons that live here on the outskirts of the pit were even threatened by my own ministrations of abuse. They fed from him, the pain and the suffering. Some of them won't have to feed for days; they love it when I grace their presence.

Many demons came to watch, the walking corpses they were didn't even startle me anymore. The first few times I saw these demons that I created I was appalled at how they would suck the life out of the tortured souls.

It was getting late, around midnight back at home, and I needed to be back and see the light that gives me hope that we would be happy again. Wrapping up the last session with Teddy Johnson, I threw my robe back on, the blood still stained my skin as I slipped it on.

"When will you be back, My Lord? You were gone for five days. We had missed you," Orpho, the leader of the torture demons, asked as I washed my hands in the basin. Red blood dripped into the water as I smirked.

"I'm not sure. I've found my mate. If I find out more about this Teddy Johnson and what he did to her, I will come back." Orpho bowed and had Teddy thrown into a cage. He would get to rest for an hour before the next shift of demons came in.

With a flash of smoke and lightning, I reappeared in front of the palace estate, not wanting to startle Jillian if she somehow left her room in the night. Opening the door, I could see the flickering of the television in the main living room next to the kitchen. Walking slowly in my bare feet, my black robe trailed behind as I saw Ares slumped in the recliner with a beer in his hand.

Jillian's head was resting on Vulcan's lap with a pillow propping her head slightly up. My fists tightened, still not over my high of inflicting pain. Right now, I could take all the gods and the demon holding Jillian's feet and make them turn to dust.

"What. Is. The. Meaning. Of. This." My voice was low, but immediately the men perked up. The rage in my eyes couldn't compare to the fear they were having now. I felt in the pit of my belly as the smoke started to rise from my body.

"Wait, Hades, let us explain!" Hermes laid Jillian's feet back down gently on the couch as she to stirred.

"Why are you touching my mate?" I seethed and walked forward, ready to grab Hermes until I heard a small cry coming from the couch.

"No, please don't take me," she whimpered. Immediately Vulcan shook her arm to wake her.

"She wasn't sleeping too hard. I think it was just the start of her dream," Vulcan said.

Jillian sat up and started rubbing her eyes. "Hades?" she whispered as she looked around. Before she could get a good look at me, I willed a suit over my body to cover up the dried blood. "Hades, you're home!" She got up from Vulcan quickly and ran to give me a hug. I grabbed her, shocked she would run to me so quickly.

"You worked too late. I waited up on you." She looked up at me and smiled, and I couldn't help but smile back. Brushing her blonde hair out of her face, she then buried her face back into my chest.

She waited up for me.

"Hades," Hermes spoke to break the spell I was completely under.

"What?" I snapped, causing Jillian to appear concerned. I held onto her tighter and she immediately went back into my embrace. Loukas kept weaving side to side with his feet, not sure what to say.

"Out with it." I kept my voice even not to disturb Jillian.

"There was an incident today. We tried to get ahold of you," Vulcan spoke up and straightened out his suit. "She fell asleep and had one of those night terrors and we had a hard time waking her up. Jillian had to visit the infirmary." Letting out a growl, Jillian held onto me tighter.

"She's tired. We will talk about this in the morning. You all are dismissed." I glared at each of them as I picked her up, one arm under her legs and one behind her back. She giggled and smiled at me as she wrapped her arms around my neck. Giving her a kiss on the forehead, she stopped giggling and nuzzled into my neck.

"I'm Okay now that you are here. You make me feel safe. Sorry I'm so clingy." A light tint of pink kissed her cheeks as I just gave her a little squeeze.

I felt instantly hard. This whole time I was worried about her never having feelings for me and here she was openly attaching herself. I needed to tell the truth. She was strong enough now and the bond has really taken ahold of her and I'm sure she has questions.

Tomorrow. Tomorrow, I'll tell her who we really are.

Taking the stairs two and three at a time I gently put her down on the floor as we reached my room. "You are staying with me tonight." Jillian beamed up happily and I gave her one of my shirts to wear. Ever since the first night she wore one of my shirts, which was all I wanted her to wear. Maybe one day, nothing would be underneath it.

I internally groaned. *One step at a time, Hades, one step at a time.* I knew the bond was working her to trust me, to be attached to me, but for me, I was already attached to her and only wanted to get closer. Tasting those lips, that's all I want to do right now, but not until the truth. I can't betray her, not again.

Chapter 15

Hades

The next morning, I found Jillian's legs intertwined with mine. Her head was buried in my bare chest as I saw her slightly parted lips take a breath. Kronos, she was captivating. If I had taken just one look at her as a baby, I would have instantly fallen for her. Not in a sexual way but in a loving protective way. My stubborn ass had to go screw it all up, and now I am faced with if she will even stay once she knows the truth.

I was going to do it. I was going to start telling her piece by piece the truth if everything checked out well today. Today, we had Witches, Shamans and Sorcerers coming that deal with memory magic. If I could have found a Vampire that has experience in compulsion, I would have called for them, but the one I was thinking about was actually suffering in Tartarus for the overuse.

The artificial sun had broken through the small crack in the window that let the fresh air in. Jillian told me how much she enjoyed the fresh air, and I would open the whole damn window if she really wanted. The thought of an open window scared her at first, worried someone would crawl through I'm guessing.

Constantly reminding her that I would never let anything happen to her was going to be rough, but I'll do it for as long as she needs me to. Her eyelashes tickled my chest as she looked up to me with the cutest smile as she rubbed the sleep from her eyes. "Did you sleep better?" She hummed as she sat up to stretch her arms. The shirt road up, exposing her milky legs, and I had to pull back before I let out an involuntary groan of approval.

"I'm going to get dressed. There are several doctors coming in today to check on you. Is that all right?" Jillian gave a little pout and I wanted to suck that lip right into my mouth. Gods I want to take things farther with her. I just didn't know if she would let me.

"Do I need to tell them about the dreams?" she whimpered and my dead heart just about damn broke. Sitting back on the bed and putting my arm back around her, she promptly curled up in my lap. Jillian wasn't scared of me as she wrapped her arms around my waist.

"It would really help them figure out what's wrong." She sniffed and hid in my chest. "What if I was there? Holding your hand through everything? Would that make it better?" She gripped my waist tighter and mumbled she would try. "Good." I kissed her forehead as she hopped off my lap and headed to her room.

She was still a quiet little thing, but we have all eternity to get to know each other and start new memories because she was *mine*.

Once dressed, I came out of my room and instantly went to hers. The door was open, and she had just put on some pink ballet flats. Wearing a plaid pink and navy skirt with a white top, she looked damn sexy. When I had sent out a demoness to retrieve clothing for her, I didn't realize she would pick things Jillian would wear. Some of it looked downright ridiculous, but Jillian paired things nicely.

The skirt made her short legs look long, licking my lips I wiped my hands down chest. I didn't want anyone to look at her right now because the crazy thoughts in my head were getting more risqué by the minute. Jillian's tucked-in white shirt outlined her breasts and you could see them bounce in them when she pranced over to me to take my hand. Fuck, this was going to be hard.

Taking her down to the infirmary, the whole damn squad was in there. Loukas, Ares, Hermes, and Vulcan all sat in the corner like helpless puppies while Cerberus whined at the door. Jillian stepped towards me and gave everyone a wave as she sat on the bench.

"I think it is best for fewer people in here, don't you guys think?" I growled out as Loukas shivered at my command. *Yeah, you sick fuck, I know what you are doing.* "Besides, Loukas, how is that assignment I gave you?" *Remember you are supposed to be interviewing angels and about why Malachi was at the club the night we saved my mate?*

"Yes, Sir. The interviews were concluded. When you have availability, we can go over them." I nodded but gave a death glare while I folded my arms. If they made me ask twice, I was going to drag them out by their dicks. One by one they left the infirmary while Jillian tried to hide her giggles. She thought the whole thing was amusing. If I wasn't so damn stressed about what was wrong with her memory, I might have laughed too.

"My Lord, I have great news!" The doctor smiled as he walked in the room. He better have a cure, or I'll toast him right here. "Um, Dr. Hecate is here!" I let out a little breath I didn't know that I was holding. This would be the second-best thing to happen. Hecate was the goddess of witchcraft and sorcery. If she couldn't help then no one really could.

Hecate walked into the room with a white doctor's coat. She must have been informed that my mate wasn't aware of our kind. She had also changed her appearance to be more human-like, adding a few flaws in her face and hair but overall, still looked like Hecate.

"Wow, she's beautiful," Jillian whispered as Hecate came up to her.

"I think you are the beautiful one, Jillian." Hecate used the back of her hand to touch Jillian's cheek.

"Now, I heard you were having some nightmares. Could you tell me about them?" Jillian immediately stiffened, I grabbed her hand and gave her a kiss on her knuckles.

"It's all right. Hecate and I have been friends for a long time. She will help, trust me." Jillian still didn't like the idea, but with my touch, she calmed herself.

"Why don't you sit down Hades and let Jillian sit in your lap? That can make her feel more comfortable." Not wavering, I picked Jillian up and sat in the chair across the room while Hecate brought the wheeled chair closer to us. Jillian leaned her head on my chest as she took deep breaths. Hecate grabbed both of her hands and began to massage them.

"Go slow and from the beginning, all right? We can stop and take a break anytime you want."

With a shaky voice, Jillian spoke of her first dream. The open window, the pictures flying to the floor during a storm, the smell of pine on her father's shirt she wore to bed. Everything was in vivid detail until the man in the 'gladiator helmet' comes into view. She said he clawed at her, wrestled her to the ground. She had never dreamed this prior to the times she had been with me. It was the same exact helmet she saw bring her to the club.

The second dream caught my attention more. It sounded like she was part of a small neighborhood that held a party at a bonfire. As she tried to continue to tell me what they had gathered for, the tears rolled down her cheeks. Her breathing became erratic, I grabbed her tight and buried her into my chest. I couldn't bear to listen anymore; she was my frightened angel that had been ruined by some sick fuck that took my damn helmet. Once I find out who took it, I will make them pay.

"Did the man in the helmet come back, Jillian? Is that what happened at the end?" Her grip became tight around my shirt as I cooed her to calm down.

"It's all right, I'm here." I kissed the temple of her head as she came to. I rocked her back and forth like a child. Hell, she probably didn't get this as a child for all I knew. The dreams she was having made me think she did have a childhood with her own room, a caring community, but how does it compare to the last ten years?

"Hades?" Hecate spoke through to my mind. Hecate being the god of witchcraft could do many things such as mind-linking someone who they have no affiliations with. However, even her being the god of witchcraft, she had her limitations. I looked up at her as Jillian dozed off. Jillian was still physically weak and now mentally. Every time she dreamed; she would wake up more exhausted.

"Jillian has been tainted with a type of grey magic. It is a mixture of both light and dark. Usually, one practices either light or dark but this, this is different." Hecate stroked Jillian's hair as she slowly went to sleep. *"There are not one but several spells on her that include both and are intertwined with one another. I'm guessing that is why I am feeling this grey magic she has. One is memory loss which is black. The next is the white which is a suppressant. Someone is suppressing her strength, her body. It is usually used on cancers of the body for humans but whoever cast this spell didn't concentrate on one part like you would cancer, but the whole body."*

"So, someone just wanted to make my mate even weaker?" I growled. Hecate didn't look to me, her throat bobbed as she wrote several notes on a clipboard.

"Unfortunately, I can't say for sure Hades. Again, there is a mixture of other magics inside her that I can't pull from her. Magic evolves every day, and this is the first time I have witnessed this many spells on one person. Who have you wronged lately that is powerful enough to cast so many spells?"

"No one new that I can think of. You know where I have been the past 1000 years. Hecate nodded. *"Should I contact Selene, see if she can help and if a bond can take care of this, since it doesn't look like you can help?"*

Hecate shook her head as she pressed her thumb to Jillian's head. *"I'm sorry, she won't be able to help either. Jillian's best bet is to ride it out. I could try and rid her of every individual spell separately, but the consequences would be far worse in her weakened state. Jillian being with you has already awoken some of her memory. The bond is helping just enough, be patient."* Hecate put an invisible cross on Jillian's head and touched the stone around her neck, one to have said to hold most of her power.

"I've blessed her that no other spell would ever touch her with any magic... Once she comes out of these spells no one will be able to cast a single thing on her head. A gift only precious enough for the future Queen of the Underworld."

"Thank you, Hecate. I appreciate your efforts."

Hecate instantly vanished as I continued to hold Jillian in my arms.

✳✳✳

I still needed to talk to Loukas about the new knowledge he had on the angels he spoke to but right now, I just wanted to concentrate on her. It was all my damn fault and stewing over it wasn't helping one fucking bit.

Carrying her out of the infirmary, I took her with me to my office. She has nightmares without me so I'm going to have her with me the entire time she naps. I don't give a flying bat out of hell if anyone gives me shit about it.

My office was filled with papers. Male servants were dusting but scurried out the door when they saw me enter with Jillian. Looks like my friends must have done every cunt in the damn place since I haven't seen any maids around here. That's how it should be. My woman was the only one I needed under this roof.

I took a long drag of her smell. She still smelled like gardenias on a crisp, spring morning with a hint of cinnamon. Her golden hair had become lighter, not as dull as when she arrived, and the color on her face was showing that pinkish hue when she would get embarrassed. Sneaking one kiss wouldn't hurt, would it?

The cheek and forehead kisses were great, don't get me wrong, but I wanted those pouty lips of hers. They were calling me like a fucking siren and if I didn't have a taste I think I would drown. Pulling her closer to me, I tickled her cheek once more to see if she would open her eyes. Leaning in, my nose grazed hers as my lips were mere centimeters away before her eyes fluttered open.

Vera Foxx

Chapter 16

Jillian

I felt nothing but good dreams as I felt Hades' arms wrapped around me tightly. Once I had explained all those horrible nightmares, my body instantly felt weak. I was tired of being the weak one. I wanted to be strong, but my body felt like large weights were pulling my body to the center of the Earth.

Hades and all his friends were these strong and ruthless people. They could rip people in half with just their bodies and I'm this dainty girl that can barely hold her eyes open. It made me mad but what else could I do?

Take the IV therapy, the medicines, and hope for the best? Ugh, the thought infuriated me. If Hades was around, I felt much better. The pull to him was strong, like I was meant to be with him, or was it just because I saw him as my rescuer?

Every kiss on the cheek or on the forehead threw sparks across my skin and I craved for more, I just didn't know what. Just being with him was enough but there was always that next step my body wanted to take.

Slowly coming out of my dream state, I could feel Hades cradling me in his arms. All I could hear was his deep breathing and maybe the faint hint of his heart. I instantly wanted to wrap my arms around his neck until I felt those familiar sparks touch my forehead. My inner girl screamed violently as I felt the sparks spread through my body.

The faint hint of someone tickling my cheek did the same as I laid completely still until I felt the heat of his face so close to mine. Fear of missing anything more, I fluttered my eyes open to see a startled Hades as his face hovered mere centimeters from my face.

I didn't feel uncomfortable or disheartened at the proximity of his face. In fact, I enjoyed it. Smiling at him, I cupped his cheek with my hand, and he closed his eyes and gave a large sigh. I'd never been kissed before, and I wasn't sure if I was even doing any of this right.

Wait, did he want to kiss me? Maybe he didn't and was checking to see if I was breathing? Heaven's what do I do? I should go bold, lean in a bit? Is that right?

I leaned in just a little. His lips lightly touched mine as I closed my eyes. I knew that much, keep your eyes closed to savor it and not look completely weird. However, this felt more natural than I thought; it wasn't clumsy at all.

Hades leaned in further, planting his lips on me. A whole firework show was happening on my lips, and it tingled all the way to my toes. I raised my other hand to cup the other side of his face while he held me up by my back. His other hand went around the back of my neck. There was no backing out now; he had full control of the kiss.

It was slow, tedious as he pecked my lips a few times. As he eased off, I looked at him with half hooded eyes. "Just follow me," he whispered as he went in again. His lips began to move as I followed his lead. They danced across each other. His lips were warm and began to press mine harder. I couldn't help but let out a little sigh until he had me straddle him in his chair.

My breath hitched at our seating position, but he kept a firm hand on my neck keeping me in place. His tongue tickled my lip and I leaned back to catch a breath. "Part your lips for me, angel." Hades' breath was husky as his other hand rubbed my back. Leaning back in, he tickled my lip again as I opened my mouth to feel his tongue slide in.

The sparks made tingles dip between my thighs, a feeling of excitement I had never felt before as he continued to explore my mouth with his. A louder sigh, more like a moan, escaped me and it only encouraged Hades' grip on me to tighten. A growl rumbled in his chest as the kiss deepened. It was passionate and hungry, and I didn't know which one I wanted more.

Melting into him felt like heaven. My body instinctively pushed into his chest as my arms went around his neck and he pulled me closer. There was no space between us, and I still craved for more. I had never taken drugs, but he was quickly becoming my addiction, my drug. "Jillian," he whispered as I felt his chest muscles harden.

There was a subtle knock at the door that burst open, and I tore my lips from Hades. Turning around revealed Hermes and Ares both with their mouths open. My face flushed with embarrassment as I tried to turn around, but Hades gripped my thighs tighter to keep me in place. Looking at him, he could see I was extremely uncomfortable, and he pulled my head to the crook of his neck.

"What do you two idiots want?" Hades strained his voice. If I wasn't in the room, he surely would have gone nuclear.

"Loukas said to meet here and discuss what he found." Hades' jaw ticked as his hand went to cup my face.

"Angel, I have to work on some things," he spoke gently, looking into my eyes. "I would very much like to continue this later." I bashfully smiled and looked away. Pulling my chin back to look at him, he pecked my lips. "Cerberus should just be outside the door. How about you go wander around the house? The library isn't far." I grinned and gave him another peck on the lips and did a walk of shame around Ares and Hermes, both still staring at me like I had another head poking out of my shoulder.

Hades

Jillian shut the door behind her and scurried off with Cerberus. My eyes glared harshly as these two idiots before me. They should be punished for their misdeed of interrupting something so precious.

Her mouth, Kronos, it was amazing. Warm, pleasing and every cliche thing I could think of. I wanted to suck that bottom lip until it bled, it tasted so good. Ice cream, she tasted like strawberry and vanilla ice cream. It was her first kiss, it had to be. Jillian was so shocked when I finally pecked her lips; she didn't know what to do.

Massaging her lips with mine, she got the idea quickly and she was a damn pro. Made just for me she was, Selene was right. As much as I didn't want to admit it, she was a matchmaker, and a pro at that.

Growling, I let them know my disproval again as they both slowly sat down. Waiting to see if I destroy the room, which has happened way too many times recently. I ran my hand through my hair roughly as I slammed my hand down.

"Well, get on with it!" The quicker this is done, the quicker I could go back to my mate. Jillian, my mate.

Loukas hustled into the room, feeling the looming darkness. I could feel the smoke leaking from my pores. Loukas came to the desk and threw down a picture of Selene. Everyone in the room looked at each other in confusion as I raised a brow.

"She's missing," Loukas breathed out heavily. Hermes jolted us. He was the messenger god, the god of rumors; how the hell didn't he know?

"I'll be back!" Hermes was gone in a blink of an eye. Ares continued to look like a damn baboon looking between Loukas and me.

"This is what you wanted to tell me?" Loukas furiously shook his head.

"No, I just found this out, but Selene hasn't been seen in over a week and it isn't like her. She always has meetings with demi-gods and Zeus. No one is supposed to know. The angel Irine told me she had missed a series of meetings with Hera over the past few days. It accidentally slipped while I was interviewing her about Malachi as to why he was even at the club. The warrior angels as well as Werewolf trackers are now involved in the search. They have teamed up to find her, reporting foul play. Her home was ransacked, and her Sphere of Souls has been taken."

The Sphere of Souls was Selene's way of pinpointing certain characteristics of souls that would make a good match. Selene has the final say if souls should be matched, but the Sphere of Souls cut her time in half. No one can even use the sphere without Selene. She created it herself and can only be unlocked by her own heart's rhythmic patterns. The kidnapper must have realized this and grabbed Selene along with it.

"As much as this is upsetting about Selene, I'm worried about Malachi. What did Irine say about Malachi being on Earth and in that club?" Loukas stood back up and pulled on his collar.

"I know you don't want to hear this, My Lord. But..." Loukas paused again and slowly back up as I stood up.

"Spit. It. Out," I growled.

"Malachi is Persephone's mate. He wanted to buy your mate to make sure you never saw her so you could be alone through eternity." Loukas's face paled as my human complexion melted from my face. Losing complete and utter control wasn't something I did very often but the words slipping from this demon's mouth had me seething. I could feel my black hair slip and my bright blonde hair flow to my shoulders. The darkened skin complexion lightened instantly, and the imperfections slid from my body.

My tattoos stayed in place, as I pulled Loukas by the throat. Ares came to me but backed up as soon as I held up my hand to stop him. My black robes pooled around me as my bare feet gripped the floor.

"Explain," I hissed.

"Malachi wanted to teach you a l-lesson," Loukas started to gasp. "He wanted to keep Jillian away from you for 1000 years so you would feel his pain as he longed for P-Persephone." Loukas gasped for air as I let him go. The selfish bastard. It had been 1000 years since she had left, and he is still hell bent on revenge.

"Does anyone other than Irine know about this?"

"I-I don't know." Loukas continued to rub his throat while he was piled on the floor. There may be a connection here.

"How did Malachi know that Jillian was your mate? Did he kidnap Selene?" Ares stood with his fists clenched. "I'll kill him. Selene is one of the most precious gods and he dare mess with the mating processes. We are all still waiting for our mates!" Ares walk to the wall, easily punching a hole. There was too much testosterone in this room.

I needed Jillian, and I needed her now. Just her presence would help me calm the demon inside me. Taking a large breath, my hair quickly returned to black, my skin tanned, and my clothing turned to its proper attire of dark jeans and a black shirt.

"Loukas, you need to go back. Put some feelers out on Malachi again. I'll have my secretary set up a meeting with Zeus. I don't care if we aren't supposed to know; it now has us involved with too many connections pointing to Malachi and now my mate is involved." Loukas nodded quickly and exited the room as I was left with Ares, staring at a damn hole in the wall.

"Are you done, Ares?" Ares could be a monkey at times, hell even like a gorilla. He wanted to smash, break, kill and rage war on any country or person that looked at him funny but there was one thing about him that not many knew. He had a heart, and he wanted a mate. Doing every woman that graced his presence over the centuries had torn him inside out. Now he just lifts and answers the prayers to wolf packs for strength, often joining them.

Ares tutted and turned, his scarred face on display. No longer the playboy smirk that laid on his lips, just his true form of battle reminders. "We'll get to the bottom of this, Ares." I patted his shoulder in comfort, something I normally didn't do, and he gave a twitch of a smile. Walking out the door to find Jillian, I hear Cerberus in my head.

"Master, pool, NOW!"

Chapter 17

Jillian

I closed the door quietly as I did a mental fist pump in the air. We kissed! I wanted to swoon all over the floor. The thought crossed my mind if I did it right. I mean, he did show me how, but I hope he wasn't repulsed. I wouldn't know how to do such things sitting in a cage. I was twenty years old and had yet to have a first kiss. I'm sure due to my circumstances, he was all right with it? Hades did say he wanted to do it again. I'm going for a win on this one.

Cerberus was tilting his head in that puppy dog manner, and it made me recoil my emotions. I wished he could talk; it would be nice to have more friends around here. There were no other girls around this palace at all since my first night. All of them had been male and they wouldn't even look at me and be friendly. They did their duty and left, no room for conversation.

Taking off down the hallway at an almost skipping pace, we headed to the south side of the mansion of this palace. The slick floors and beautiful paintings of fairies, flowers, cherubs, angels, and demons decorated each hallway. I found them fascinating as I tried to look at every single one down the hall. I approached one that had a half man, half beast. They were transforming from human into a wolf.

A human was standing next to the wolf, almost bare apart from leaves covering his privates. It hit me it was a Werewolf. Out of all the paintings it stuck out the most. The dark fur, the elongated teeth, the muscle beneath the fur. It was fascinating. Blinking my eyes a few times I saw blonde fur, rushing through a forest. The green eyes stood out to me as its large tongue lopped to the side in playfulness. Blinking a few more times I could feel the fur on my fingers as it was hanging on while the rushing wind blew passed my hair.

Laughing, giggling, screaming in delight were other children on other animals, Wolves. These large Wolves were darting through trees and under logs as the children laughed and egged them to go faster. The Wolf I was riding was the largest of them all and let out an enormous amount of strength for a bellow of a howl.

As quickly as these daydreams started, they stopped. It felt real as if one of my nightmares. I could almost taste the forest pine on my lips zipping through trees. "Ember," escaped my lips as I remembered that name. The name I was being called only last night. "Ember." Cerberus looked to me like I grew two heads, so I shrugged my shoulders and continued to walk down the hallway that led to a large atrium like room. I'll have to continue thinking about it another day. Now was my time to explore and check out the home I had been living in.

The sun shone brightly as I made my way into the glassed room. It was warmer than most rooms of the palace-like home. Instead of the darker furniture I would normally see, this furniture was light and crisp, all equipped for a perfect sunroom. Blue light reflected in the windows as I walked closer. Knowing I shouldn't, I put my hands on the glass, and looked through the windows only to see a large pool.

I let out a quick squeak of delight only to have Cerberus whine and shake his ears. "Sorry, baby." I pat his head and ran for the nearest door that led outside. Cerberus trotted behind me as I walked outside to the pool area. It was the bluest water I had ever seen. Of course, it was due to the blue elaborate tiles on the bottom of the pool, but it looked beautiful anyway. I took off my shoes and dipped my toes into the warm waters. I don't know if I really knew how to swim but I really wanted to try. I'm sure with all the clothes that Hades had provided me with, there would be a swimming suit in there somewhere. Getting lost in my thoughts, I heard two women talking.

"Oh, there it is," I heard a woman's voice come from beyond the fence. Looking up, curious I saw two women jump the fence. Their legs were long, and their skirts were short. Beautiful features adorned their faces that looked nothing short of a model. They both strolled towards me barefoot while their tops were just a colored bikini top.

"This is what has the Lord all up in a fuss?" one of the women motioned to me while I looked at Cerberus. He growled at them in warning, but they just huffed in annoyance.

"Yes, her, she made me lose the perfect job because the Lord didn't want any distractions," she air quoted as I stood there like a small child.

"What's your name, human?" the first woman spoke while jutting out her chin at me.

"I'm Jillian, it's um, nice to meet you?" It wasn't nice to meet them, and calling me human? Did he really get rid of the women that worked here because of me?

"Sure, sure." They came closer. Cerberus comes closer to block them from getting near me. His jaws snapped and the second woman used her hand to act as a battering ram and pushed Cerberus without even touching him. I gasped as he yelped when he hit the pool fence.

"You can't do that!" I yelled, still in shock as they walked closer. The closer they got, the closer the pool became and the initial worry about knowing how to swim was growing on me.

"We should just kill her now. Then we can go back to our everyday lives," the first woman spoke while picking her now elongated nails. "Her newness will wear off but who knows how long that will be."

"You can't do that. We have Hades' blood. He would know it was you."

What is going onnnnnn? Panic rose in my throat as I eased my way away from the edge of the pool. I wanted to run but the fear climbing up my spine forbade it.

"Right." Her nails retracted as I stood in surprise. "How about we take her to the village, let an Incubus take care of her, and then suck her dry of her aura? They don't know who she is, and the blame won't be on us." The other one nodded and approached.

Turning to run, I heard Cerberus' battle cry as he bit one of the women on the leg while I tried to run. Keyword was tried because my leg was swiftly caught as her claws grew scraped down my leg. Letting out a blood-curdling scream while shaking my leg, the strength behind the claws grew bigger. Looking behind me I no longer saw the woman that had grabbed me but a red-skinned, raven-haired woman with hooves for feet and small horns that protruded out of her head.

Never in my wildest dreams would I have thought to see that sight. It was worse than the gladiator helmet guy! My fingernails clawed at the concrete, leaving bloody fingerprints in my wake. Cerberus was still ripping his head back and forth at the other woman that had transformed. One arm left my leg and a ripe pain hit the back of my head. The shock of the hit had me stop fighting to rub it with my hands and I was swiftly thrown over a shoulder.

Screaming again, all I could see was Cerberus grow four times the size of his original self along with two other heads protruding his body. The shock was scary but now I was being carried away on a large creature running, no, galloping through the yard of Hades. Once we breached the far fence that was specifically told not to go past the world became a deeper red.

Sniffing I could smell embers and the dark earth being kicked up by her hooves. She was laughing maniacally as she continued to gallop through the trees. My breathing became haggard as I felt myself become weak. I had still not recovered from my years of being deprived of food and I knew I was no match for what was about to happen.

One thing was for certain; I was not on Earth. I was in some alternate dimension, and I had a terrible hunch that all the names such as Hades, Hermes and Ares were real. I'm in the Underworld. The whole idea of thinking how amazing it would be if Hades was a god had worn off its appeal. Now I was riding the back of some demon woman that was about to shove me in some room with an Incubus demon I know nothing about.

I kept praying this was just a dream, a dream that felt more real than all the others, but the blood dripping down my leg was telling me different. I could feel the chunks of meat flapping as the wind rushed by.

Focus, I had to focus. "Where are you taking me?" I yelled over the wind brushing my face. The smell of sulfur continued to infiltrate my nose, making me sick. Trying to get a sense of my surroundings so I could run back to the only safe place I know, the demon chuckled wildly as we entered a small village. Her gallop became a canter and eventually a walk and I heard several hooves hit the cobblestone path.

"Put me down!" I yelled and with one forceful swing, I landed on my rear, instantly hearing a snap. Pretty sure I just broke my butt.

"Ouch! What is your problem?" Several of the beasts looked on in curiosity and even what looked to be small children came and joined the crowd.

"This whore made us lose our jobs, so we are going to have her taught a lesson!" Several other women looked on at me with disgust and whispered.

"I didn't do anything! Hades brought me to the house and that's it!" Many gasped

"The Lord brought a human whore? Surely, she won't last. He'll break her." I held back a sob. Are they serious? Surely not, Hades had been nothing but kind to me. "And she uses his name like he is some commoner, such disrespect!"

"Hades is kind and gentle. He would never hurt me." I gave a scornful look while everyone laughed. Another demon pulled me from the floor and gripped my arm tightly.

"The Incubus House it is then for the whore!" They all cheered while I tried to pull away only to become exhausted. Some of the beasts were hooting and hollering while others looked on in horror with whisperings. I knew one thing was certain, not one beast stood up for me. They let them take me to a black building with triple x's on the front.

Flashbacks of what I went through spun through my memory. Trying to scratch the beast holding me, I screamed for Hades. Hades was the only one who could save me. Even though he kept a huge secret from me, I held onto hope that he wasn't lying about his affections. That might break me to pieces right there.

The door opened as I stood in front while the two beasts held me in place. Feeling like a sacrifice, I tried to step back only to be greeted by a tall, darker skinned man. He was attractive and looked as human as could be except for the two small black horns coming out of his head. Many women would find him attractive and maybe spread their legs on purpose for him because I was sure he was packing. His bare torso and the sweats he wore indicated how confident he was in bed.

Gulping in a large swallow of air, I tried to wiggle free again until he grabbed my wrist. It burned at the touch of this new beast as he pulled me in. "She will be taken care of." He smirked as I got pulled further into the darkness. *I am going to be raped.*

"Mmhmm, a fresh one. A pure one," I heard a male purr as it brushed my ear with its lips. I could feel them all around me, breathing, tickling my skin with their breaths. My own breathing picked up as I felt the tears stinging in my eyes.

"Oh, do not cry, it isn't fun when you cry. We will make you feel pleasure," one purred as it kissed my open wrist. I already felt dirty as the warmth around my body made me stiffen.

"H-hades wouldn't like this," I managed to say. "He will come for me, and you will all get in trouble." They laughed in the dark while my eyes continued to adjust.

"Why would he come for his little whore? He has better things to do." The words clicked in my head as I repeated them to myself. *Whore?* I couldn't be, not after the way he treated me. Then again, he may want a willing one. Pain seared through my chest at the thought of him using me.

Why would he come? He was the King of the Underworld. He could have anyone, anybody, and he of all people took me in? My heart clenched at the thought of the kiss. I had poured what little I had into that simple action and to him it may have meant nothing.

"That's it," one stranger cooed in my ear. "Doubting him, you can put your faith in us. We can make you feel good." A lone tear dropped on my cheek.

"Please let me go. I just want to leave," I begged.

"And go where? Who would want you, especially now that you are in the house of the incubus? Your body might as well be tainted already." Another sob ripped from me until I heard a large crash at the door I had originally walked through. The light poured through the doorway and feeling hands grip my arms.

It's *him*.

Chapter 18

Hades

Fury.

Rage.

Blood.

Cerberus showed me his sight as he was grinding on the bones of a demoness that had breached the fence line. She was no longer in human form, now donned in her red skin and onyx hair. Cerberus was not known for violence. He may show his dominance and stature, but he almost flat out refuses to spill blood. I created him in a time where darkness did not loom in my heart.

Ares felt my aura leak into the office outside the door; on alert, he waited for me to motion him to follow. I could no longer feel her on the palace grounds. As I mentally searched the area, she was gone. A large growl ripped through me as Ares followed. We transported to the backyard. Blood and parts of the demoness were strung across the grounds and nearby statues. Her torso laid on the cement, dripping into the now tainted pool water. Cerberus continued to growl, showing his complete form as well as his height.

The demoness was gurgling, coughing up the blood that had drenched her lungs. Pulling her up by her neck, I held her over the water. "What happened?!" I yelled, Cerberus tried to speak to me, but I shut him out. I wanted to hear from this demoness before me. She wouldn't talk, so I stuck my thumb into her forehead with my free hand, pushing hard enough to penetrate her skull. The shrills didn't keep me out as I watched their plans for Jillian from start to finish.

I lost my form as I felt my ink-black hair dissolve and my skin brighten. I have had many names throughout history, Lucifer, Beelzebub, and Dark One, but the human favorite was the Fallen Angel. Fallen from the grace of God. The God humans referred to was actually Zeus. There was no such fall; it was me who took shelter into the Earth to make sure our own father didn't return to attempt to kill us all again.

Gritting my teeth, my hair waved in front of my face, mocking me that I can't keep control, I threw her remains aside, scattering to dust. She won't regenerate; I won't allow it. She has forfeited her right as a demon for touching and even thinking about hurting my mate. Ares puffed up his chest and asked for direction.

Cerberus was already on the trail, and we head to the village not far from here. The demoness is taking her to the worst place for a human. It is a place of nightmares for those who sleep. Incubi are only used when summoned to curse a human or supernatural. They are hard to control, and only the best witches and sorcerers can tame them. There have been several times throughout history I have unleashed them, such as the dark ages in the human world. Many political leaders, royals, and bluebloods tried to drain their people of money, leaving them in poverty while they suffered.

The church that was established by humans claiming I was the Fallen Angel, Morning Star, and now devil declared that one must pay for their sins through money. The only way for humans to pull a family member's soul from the holes of hell was through payment. Not one dime was received, and I would never agree to such a tragedy. If they were in hell, they deserved it. If they lived a good life, they would spend their time in the Asphodel Fields.

Jillian would be thrown into the Incubus lair; none have been released in many years and will be hungry, thirsty to drain an aura and eventually a soul. They don't care if the soul is evil or good. However, a virgin soul will be sucked dry in a matter of seconds.

With a snap of my fingers as we continued to run, I folded the Underworld, so now our feet hit the cobblestone path of the village. If it weren't for the red-skinned demons, this village could house many humans. Many stop to stare and fall to the ground for mercy. I never graced the village unless I came to destroy those who did an unworthy job. The smaller demon children kiss the ground and dare not look on my bare face.

"Where is she!?!" I roared as I stomped to the building. The ground shook as several more demons realized who I was and fell to the ground from afar. "Get that demon," I whispered to Cerberus. I flashed a picture in his mind, and he smirked as he ran off. Ares had already reached the Incubus house, and with one push, he knocked down the door. Ares stood to the side, arms crossed, daring for anyone to pass. No one would, but you could never be too sure. Everyone seemed to be an idiot today.

Jillian was in the middle of the room, hands clutching her chest, pleading for them not to touch her. Several hands were grabbing her upper arms while I could see the hint of someone whispering in her ear.

Doubt. They were spreading doubt through her mind that no one would come for her, to give up and relent her soul. I could hear Jillian whispering to herself, "He will come for me, he will, he will come for me." If I weren't so damn furious, I'd swell with pride.

The Incubi's heads all darted to the door. The light was trailing behind me, and the front of my body was darkened. They didn't need to see; they knew who I was. Taking slow, calculating steps and reeking my dominating presence, they all slowly backed away. "My Lord." One bowed to kiss my feet. I pushed him back with one foot as he fell to the ground.

These Incubi may look intense to a human, even dashing and attractive, but they were nothing but a pebble in my shoe. A worthless demon that only comes in handy once a thousand years. The worst part, these demons were the worst of them all. They were locked away for sucking the life of too many beings at once.

They will all pay.

Dearly.

Jillian opens her eyes, and even with my blonde hair, she realizes who I am. Running to me, she latches on to my torso and buries her face into my robes. I hold her tight, checking for bruises until I see the long claw marks down her leg. A growl escapes me, but she continues to hold onto me. Flicking my head up, I see the faces of five Incubi with horrified looks.

"You came, you came," Jillian sobbed as I wrapped her in my robes. Waving my hand, I had every single demon chained from the ceiling of the house. I gave a glare at them as another chain ripped around their heads, choking them so they couldn't speak while another chain with a heavy metal ball hung from the appendage between their legs. Their groans filled the room as I kept Jillian's face buried into my robes.

Walking out with Jillian in my arms, Ares does a once-over to see blood from her leg. His face reddened as he tried to go into the room. Holding him back, I shook my head. We would deal with them later. There would be no traces of the incubus house.

Cerberus comes back, dragging the demoness from one of the apartments; many demons have gathered in the square to witness the punishment. I put one arm under Jillian's legs and another behind her back as her thick lashes look up at me. She knows what I am now, and even under terrible circumstances, she isn't afraid. Clutching my cloak, she lays her head in the crook of my neck.

"My Angel, I'm going to put you to sleep and take the pain away. When you wake, we will be home, all right?" Not saying a word, she nodded her head in confirmation as her body finally slumped into my grasp. Leaving a gentle kiss on her forehead, I handed her to Ares, who took her gladly. He wrapped her up in his arms and stood as the war general he was.

"Listen here!" I yelled as the buildings trembled. The whispers quieted as all the demons stood in distress. "You all stood by and watched as your future Queen was handled poorly and thrown into the damn Incubus House. The fuck is wrong with you?!" There were cries from the crowd, knowing my fury was building. Smoke had begun to flow beneath my robes and cover the path. Several demons started screaming as they felt the smoke hit their feet and the acid ate away at their skin.

"You left her there to die; you let an innocent human in there to die. You all can sense an innocent! I CREATED YOU! I can DESTROY YOU!" The whites of my eyes turned blood red; I felt the pressure as I did the day I lost someone I thought I loved, Persephone. Now I almost lost the only one that truly mattered, my Jillian, my mate.

Screams and smoke began to cover the ground in its entirety, but their feet remained planted to the ground. I wanted them to feel the burn in their walk as they worked the bowels of hell. They will feel the pain for weeks if not months for betraying their Queen, an innocent.

The strangled screams became quiet as they tried to listen to my quiet words. "If I find anyone dares hurt the future queen of the Underworld or did not try to help fight for her safety, so help me Rhea, I will drown you in an everlasting fire and listen to your screams as I fall asleep at night throughout eternity."

Demons cried out in pain as I let the smoke retract from them, their feet bloody, sore, and raw from ripping their skin. The Incubus House was next; they would suffer something entirely worse.

Staying on the outside of the home, I snapped my fingers and let the weights grow heavier until they dropped to the floor. Their members were now ripped from their bodies. Screams of agony and pain filtered through the broken doorway. It was music to my ears.

They will hang there until I decide what to do with them. My glare to the demons surrounding us know they cannot help or face my wrath even further.

Cerberus held the one that scratched my mate's leg, and an evil glint came to my eye. She will not survive this day; her soul will be ripped from the demon's soul pool, never to regenerate and never to have a chance to find her own mate. Ares looks at me, pleading. He dances on the balls of his feet; he wants in on the fun, and I had taken most of it.

"Ares, is there something you would like to ask?" I joked mockingly.

"Can I have her? I've got new stuff to try." The fact his itty bitty brain had come up with something new to torture people gave me a chuckle.

"Sure, why not?" It was sometimes fun to share with Ares; he appreciated my lust for blood and pain for those that deserved it. Taking Jillian back into my arms, he started rubbing the palms of his hands together, chuckling darkly to himself.

"Come, Cerberus, this involves you too." Cerberus huffed and continued to drag the demoness who was clawing the ground to get away.

Jillian did not stir in my arms; she lay almost lifeless as I cuddled her to my chest. She was small, delicate like the flowers she loved to smell in our garden. More demon warriors will be brought to the palace; now that Jillian knows what I am and who we all are, this will help in the transition for her to become my mate.

Knowing the truth of just of who I am is just the beginning. I have many more secrets to spill, and Jillian still has to find herself. Granting my lips to touch hers, I groan into her mouth. The sparks fly as her eyelashes flutter gently while her face continues to nuzzle into my smell. My heart instantly calms as we begin our walk back to the palace. Her leg needs tending to, and I need to be with her until she wakes.

I will not let her have another nightmare.

Jillian saw me in my correct form and did not seem bothered by it. The adrenaline and the bond rushing through her may have had something to do with it. I was too late to tell her on my own; I needed to be forward with her on other things in the future.

But she is healing. Her mind is still healing.

I shook my head. She is stronger than she appears. I'm foolish, but I can't help but worry.

The servants will now be in their proper form and no longer hiding. Many are excited for her to know who we are; others are wary. They think my mate may not be strong enough, but little did they know she was a fighter. She had fought her way into my heart like I never thought anyone could. I just hope she will accept her surroundings once I show her what the palace really looks like.

If she hates it, I'll change it. I'll keep the bubble around the palace, so she never has to see the reddened sky. I'll do what it takes to keep her because she is supposed to be *mine.*

Chapter 19

Under the Moon

The rain came down in heavy sheets as the thunderous Alpha Werewolf trudged through the mud. Training had been demanding that morning due to the warm nor'easter that had come the previous night. The Alpha thanked the goddess that it wasn't yet cold. This would have easily been several feet of snow.

Wolves began running to their small cabins, away from the packhouse. The packhouse now only housed visiting wolves and single wolves waiting to be mated. Alpha Wesley had promised his mate, Charlotte, that he would make her the perfect small plantation home on their territory after their mating. He kept that promise, and Charlotte kept the house a safe haven until that one unfortunate night.

Wesley took the key and opened the door to the dimly lit home. His three sons were in bed, but the faint light from the stairway indicated his mate was still awake. Wesley sighed heavily, knowing precisely what she was doing on a night like this.

Trudging the stairs one by one, hoping that his mate would leave the room, he slowly gazed at the pictures on the walls. His three boys were growing to be strong wolves, and Dante proved that he would be a strong Alpha once Wesley relinquished the title, which still would not be for a long time, his mate would tell him.

Charlotte had an extreme attachment to all her children ever since that night that haunts her memories. The night before her birthday will remain a stain on a usually happy occasion. She will wait until her daughter is brought back home if she ever wants to celebrate another birthday.

It had been eleven years since their daughter, Ember, was taken. It was on a night like this. The storm raged on the outside of their two-story home, and Charlotte often thought to check on her first-born daughter, Ember. However, Ember told her before she went to bed she was a 'big girl' now and that the future Alpha female could handle a little rain. Charlotte smiled at the thought of her baby girl, thinking Ember was an actual significant Alpha. She had yet to gain her Wolf, which wouldn't be for another two years and then a few years after that until her first shift.

Charlotte, never growing up a Werewolf, had to learn the hard way when her eldest son, Dante, started yelling to his mother someone was talking in his head. Immediately, she called Wesley, who only laughed and playfully added he forgot to tell her about Wolves waking up at the age of thirteen. Charlotte gave an excellent scolding to Wesley, who only had to give her extra pleasure in bed that night as punishment.

Wesley stood at the top of the stairs; he could hear Charlotte humming in the rocking chair in the lavender-painted room. Holding onto the overly stuffed calico cat, she pets it lovingly while staring at the bed. Giant sighs, and a few tears fell down her face as she clutched it tightly.

Leaning up against the doorframe with his hands in his pockets, he stared at his beautiful mate. Charlotte took it the hardest, saying she was a mother, and a mother should always protect her babies. She continued to rock into the chair, holding the stuffed cat while silent tears tickled her face. She began singing Ember's favorite lullaby.

"*Lavender's blue,*
Dilly dilly, Lavender's green.
Let the birds sing,
Dilly dilly,
Let the lambs play.
We shall be safe,
Dilly dilly,
Out of harm's way.
I love to dance,

Dilly dilly,
I love to sing.
When I am Queen,
Dilly dilly,
You'll be my King."

Wesley's emotions got the best of him, and he let out a light sniff and rumble in his chest. Charlotte didn't turn as she knew he was there the entire time.

"Do you think she is still alive?" Charlotte whimpered as her tears soaked the stuffed animal.

"Of course, she is I haven't felt our bond break from her. Wolves know when they have lost a pup; it is painful as the connection breaks. I've told you this." Wesley squatted down beside Charlotte and brushed her hair back. Charlotte had been a strong Luna, even with the loss of a child. She made sure her sadness never got in the way of raising her three boys, but in private and often away from Wesley, she would sit in Ember's room and stare at the window. Charlotte felt weak once in her life before she met Wesley, and she wasn't going to let anyone else see it.

Wesley worried for his Kitten. He loved her more than life itself, and it killed him to watch her slip away as the years went on. Her birthday was the worst, and the entire pack made sure that they never mentioned or celebrated. They would leave gifts by the door for their Alpha to pick up and give to her at a later time.

"But my heart continues to break, my Alpha. It breaks every morning when I wake up and every sunset that she isn't here. She should be training to be the next Alpha if she wanted it." Her breath heaved as she leaned her head to Wesley's chest.

"Kitten, Dante was made to be an Alpha. He has also drawn up plans to have our bodyguard and security business include private investigators. We have hired ten new supernatural detectives to find her. There is still hope." Wesley nuzzled into Charlotte's hair while she dried her tears.

"I certainly hope so. I want to apologize for every-"

"No," Wesley growled as he lifted her up. With one hand behind her back and the other under her knees, he took her to their room. Charlotte had decorated it with bright, airy colors, and the large picture of their combined Luna and Mating ceremony hung over the bed.

"You have nothing to apologize for." Wesley towered over her as each elbow flanked her sides. Wesley kissed Charlotte's forehead longingly. "Ember is strong. Do you forget who her mother is? You survived through the worst, and yet here you stand with three sons who adore you. Ember would never blame you; if anything, she would blame the pack warriors." Charlotte took a large, heavy sigh.

Wesley went on a rampage the night Ember was taken. Warriors were beaten to a bloody pulp, that his little princess of the pack was taken out from their own home. It was later found that the use of solid magic had infiltrated the ward that Hades had created.

Wesley fell to the side as Charlotte curled up into Wesley's arms. His thumb continued to draw patterns in her arms as she cried silently for their daughter. Each storm brought new pain to Charlotte, and each spring and summer seem to make it worst.

"I've contacted Sorceress Cyrene and her coven. They plan on coming to visit in the next couple of weeks." Charlotte sniffed while looking up at her mate. "I'm going to try and have her test the wards again to make sure they are still standing strong and maybe contact Hades." Charlotte's eyes widened at the realization that the King of the Underworld may come. "Don't get your hopes up, Kitten. He's a busy god, and I don't think he would want to come to visit a measly pack."

"But we helped him! Trixen could still be running around it if it weren't for us! He has to help." Wesley petted Charlotte's head and pulled her to his neck. "Ember would have loved it," Charlotte whispered as she tickled Wesley's chest. "Ember loved all the stories about the gods, especially Hades."

"I'll have Cyrene bring that up; maybe that will make his head swell and want to visit. Not many find the God of the Underworld that interesting other than just being fearful of him."

Charlotte hummed as they both drifted off to sleep dreaming for their one and only daughter to come home.

Jillian

My eyes fluttered open, and I sprung up to a sitting position. I had immediately started breathing heavily, placing a hand over my chest as my heart began to slow again. The smokey s'mores smell calmed me now that I noticed I was in Hades' bedroom.

Had it all been a dream? The pain in my rear and the large bandage on my leg told me otherwise. It stung as I traced it with my fingertips. The blood had seeped through on the bandages. It was old blood that had turned dark, so I had to be sleeping for a while.

All of this wasn't a dream. The demon ladies, Hades actually being THE HADES. I gasped and slapped my hands to my face. Gods were real; what of Hermes, Loukas, Vulcan, and Ares? They all were too!? The excitement in me wasn't of fear but pure admiration. Hades was not the evil guy everyone thought he was. He was so nice and sweet to me, but he did seem pretty pissed when he came to my rescue.

Hades rescued me, again! I could squeal at how exciting this was. I heard a groan on the floor, only to be met with large yellow eyes. Cerberus purred as he stood up and gave me a quick lick on my cheek as my head leaned over the bed.

"That's my good puppy," I cooed, scratching his ear. "You ate that big 'ole demon, didn't you? Just for me!" Cerberus continued to purr in his throat as I hit his spot on his chest, giggling and leaning a bit too far; I caught myself and sat back on the bed. My leg was still stinging in pain as I groaned while Cerberus put his paws on the bed to look. "Just hurts a little, big boy. Now, where is Hades? I think he has some explaining to do." I gave a pointed look at him as he looked sheepish.

Not ten seconds had passed until Hades was standing at the front of my bed. I yelled loudly and threw the bed sheets over my head. "Don't do that!" I squealed. Hades gave that wonderful low laugh as he sat on the bed and pulled the sheet down. He was no longer with his bright blonde hair and skin but his tan and dark hair that I was so used to.

I folded my arms and tried to act angry while I squinted my eyes at him. "Explain." I held back a smile. At first, Hades looked worried until that devilish smirk came into view. He touched my uninjured leg, and I instantly melted at his touch.

"How much do you remember, my angel?" I tilted my head to the side, licking my lips.

"All of it, from the kiss to those red demon women to that weird house where those things touched me." My lip quivered, remembering that part. I could deal with the scratches and being dragged, but that Incubus House was downright frightening. Hades got up and pulled me to his lap, being careful of the bandages on my leg. There was a low growl in his chest as he held me tight.

"I'm sorry. That will never happen again." I looked up at the towering god and gave a small smile, knowing his words were valid, even though he withheld that he was a god. I mean, I get it. If he had told me that from the very beginning that he was a god, I would have laughed at him and then died of a brain aneurism.

"So, you are THE Hades?" I questioned.

"Unless there is another God of the Underworld that I don't know about, yes I am." I giggled as I held him tight. As I was getting comfortable, my body stiffened. If that was true, then Persephone should be down here. I mean, he stole her, brought her here, and she ate that pomegranate. I sat up straight, startling him as I looked at him in the eye.

"W-what about Persephone?" If he has her somewhere and has me as some side chick, I will walk right out of this room and go find a job. I'm not staying down here to be used; I'm better than that. I'm thankful he and the rest of them saved me, but that doesn't mean I deserved to be second best and a side piece. I felt the anger well up in me as Hades gave an amused look.

"She isn't here; she hasn't lived down here for over a thousand years. She is with some angel now. Malachi?" he questioned himself. "I'm not really sure who she's mated to." Hades' rubbed his chin with a bit of stubble that started growing. The questioning looks on his face was cute when he thought, but I still had a lot of questions. Like mated? What does that mean?

"Mated? Like animals? Did you mate with her?" I could feel the jealousy rising in my stomach. I didn't like that word; the only thing I could think of was terrible animalistic tendencies between people taking their sexual frustrations out on each other. I've seen it in the club, and it was disgusting.

Hades gave another amused look and that sexy smirk showing his perfect white teeth. "Are you jealous?" I glared at him, huffing while crossing my arms. I was getting mad, dang it, and it was darn frustrating. He's older, of course; he had a life before me and I'm sure lovers. All right, that hurt. That overwhelming feeling of jealousness was fading into sadness until Hades made me straddle his waist.

"Hey, hey, hey, angel," he cooed. His knuckles ran across my cheeks. "I have been an absolute ass before you, but I did not touch Persephone." My heart skipped a bit hearing that; he was supposed to be so in love with her. "I thought it was love; it wasn't. She didn't care about me as I did with her, and I was bitter about it for a long time. Not once did I touch her, force her into anything. Except to live in the Underworld," he whispered that last bit. "I was an angry person because I was alone and no one wanted me, and I had no one to love until you."

My breath hitched as he squeezed my waist. Hades and I just kissed, and he already loved me? It hasn't been that long; we had only known each other for such a small amount of time. How could he have feelings like that? Then again, he was the only one that gave me the wonderful warm fuzzies I get just mentioning his name. My body heats at his touch, and I crave him like a kid wanting an ice cream cone on a sweltering hot day. I sighed into him, holding him tight.

"I think I love you too, Hades," I whispered, barely audible, but he heard it. "I'm scared I don't know what love is though. What if I am wrong?" Hades pulled my head back and looked into my eyes while the pads of his thumbs rubbed over my cheeks.

"I can't know everything of what you are feeling, but I have an idea." My questioning look gave way to his following statement that left me stunned.

"You are my mate, Angel. My soulmate."

Chapter 20

Jillian

My mouth couldn't move. I'm Hades' soulmate? What is a soul mate? It sounded serious, but I wasn't sure what it could all entail. I haven't been taught about love, just the world of men pawing all over women in a strip club. There was no love involved at all. Just the mindless touching, watching, and sometimes the sex.

Hades' knuckles brushed my cheeks again, something he really liked to do, which I didn't mind because I felt the sparks fly through my cheeks. "Do you feel that?" he mumbled while I tilted my head into his palm. "The sparks, do you feel them?" I nodded my head in understanding while he continued.

"Every soul that is created is not complete; it is missing something. It is missing a vital part that could make them whole. I never really understood what all that meant, and I didn't care about it at all until you." Warmth surged through my body that he would think of me this way. Was I his missing piece? I was just the disposable extra help for most of my life, and he was this god that could control everything in the underworld. I couldn't be that special.

I was mortal, I was meant to die in time, and he would live on forever. Does this mean he would have to live on without his soul mate?

"You will live with me, forever." His voice was stern as he lifted my chin. His eyes were dark as his gaze bore into me. "Once we complete our bond to one another, you will stay with me, and we will forever be together."

This was some fairy tale stuff going on right here. Was he pulling my leg? Do guys do that? Boyfriends, I mean? Make these promises and then not deliver? I've only seen a couple movies, and so far, there is always a guy making promises he doesn't keep. My throat felt constricted as I felt the weight of my questions pounding me lower into the ground.

"Hades?" I gazed into his eyes while he held me to him close. "This all seems so… unreal."

He hummed, "It does, doesn't it?" His hand ran through my now thickening hair and held the back of my neck. "I know you have questions and a lot of them. Let's leave the soul mate part out of it right now and get used to where we live, hm?"

That sounded like a good plan, one step at a time.

Hades

Jillian's beautiful eyes held so much confusion, questions, and doubt. I wanted to tell her everything, every last detail that led me to her, but we would get to all that information in time. Jillian is my soul mate, and that brief explanation left her speechless. She doesn't have a full grasp on love, and I was forcing her to accept a bond she would have no clue about.

Fucking idiot.

"How about we start with the beginning?" Jillian nodded as I gently picked her up, making sure not to touch her bandages. The physician was able to stitch her up nicely, repeating that it would hardly scar. He had already noticed that they had begun to heal, which he found strange but then again, he wasn't used to dealing with humans much. My mate was a fighter.

Taking Jillian to the living room, we walked past the large portrait of me on that damn throne. Jillian's eyes sat on the portrait as we walked by.

"Hades, that wasn't a joke gift, was it?" she inquired.

"No, it wasn't," I sighed as I held her close.

"So, have you always been grumpy then?" She giggled while I gave a chuckle. Her laugh was addicting.

"Yes, I suppose I have. For most of my life. Wouldn't you be grumpy too if your own father ate you?" Jillian gasped as she gripped my shirt.

"It's true then? He ate you and the rest of the gods?" I nodded while I came to the living room and sat on the couch. Several servants brought in a variety of dishes ranging from kinds of pasta, hamburgers, steak, fries, salads, and fruits. I made a small plate for Jillian to munch on as Vulcan came into view.

Vulcan had been extremely upset over Jillian's kidnapping; I felt terrible for the poor mate he will have one day. He would worry his ass off, making sure she was always comfortable. Jillian's eyes lit up as she saw Vulcan; he was still in his human form as he sat in the chair across from us to grab a hamburger.

"You are THE Vulcan, I mean, Hephaestus?" Vulcan smiled as she said his real name.

"Excellent pronunciation. Not many humans can pronounce it." Jillian beamed as she held her hands together. I nudged her to continue her eating, but she quickly started the conversation.

"Not to be rude, but can I see your true form? That isn't rude to ask, is it?"

We both laughed. "Yes, of course. I actually prefer my true form. I stayed this way to carry on our façade until you were ready to accept us. Good thing you took it well from the looks of it."

"I find it all fascinating!" I stuffed a strawberry into her mouth while she gave me an 'are you kidding?' look. Vulcan threw his head back and laughed.

"It's the bond; you are ready to accept your mate for who he is, and so you will with his friends." I shook my head, letting him know not to bring it up. His eyebrows went up in understanding as he stood. Straightening his shirt and running his hand through his hair, it instantly grew. Instead of looking like a Greek descendent, he was now sporting shoulder-length brown hair and a burly beard that reached the top of his chest. His muscles were significant and veiny from having to wield so many weapons for the gods.

"Woah," she breathed. "You're big." Vulcan was large and could be quite intimidating, but he was as gentle as a mouse. He never wished to hurt anyone and had one of the kindest hearts. I still couldn't understand what Zeus had planned when he paired him with Aphrodite. She could be a straight-up bitch, and no one could handle her.

Vulcan let out a hardy laugh as he sat back down to throw more food on his plate. Jillian continued to ask him questions animatedly. She wanted to know the types of things he forged and if he continued his trade. Vulcan stayed away from the topic of the Helm, a smart move on his part because I didn't need Jillian having another breakdown anytime soon. She was taking all of this like a true queen could have with this much information.

We heard the front door slam, and I immediately knew it was Ares. Kronos, he better have hosed off the blood before he came waltzing in here. Jillian perked up at the sight of Ares; he was clean thankfully and showed no signs of any pent-up anger and frustration. Ares had his release.

"Fuck, I'm starving." Ares sat down and pulled a giant steak and a twice-baked potatoes to his plate. Jillian sat at the edge of my lap, leaning forward, looking at Ares like he was a damn unicorn. Ares's jaw slacked as he was chewing with his mouth half open and saw Jillian bright-eyed and bushy-tailed.

Sitting back, Ares chewed slowly as he glanced across the room, seeing Vulcan smirking and me with an unamused face. "What?"

"Can I see!!" Jillian wailed about ready to fall to the floor. I scooped her back up and sat her on my lap again, but her eyes were on Ares. Jealousy was welling inside me as I gripped her tighter. She didn't budge and continued to look at Ares.

"I don't think Hades would like that...." Ares spoke on the side of caution. "You probably need to see Hades' first." Jillian gave her puppy dog face of confusion while I growled at Ares.

"Your true form, you bastard," I snapped. "Not your damn dick! And she will never see THAT!" Jillian turned around and scowled.

"Hades, that wasn't nice." Vulcan snickered again in the corner while Jillian patted my cheek.

"I was talking about what you really look like!" Jillian snubbed her nose. "And not anything else. Yuck."

"I'll have you know-" Ares started before I cut him off.

"Show her your form," I spoke lowly before Ares finally stood up. He did one massive shake like a dog and burst into his casual god-like form in his battle pelt. Ares' muscles were large, enough to make all the human girls squeal, but Jillian shrunk back into my chest. Ares' hair was pulled around tight in a Viking braid that hung over his shoulder. He kept his face clean-shaven and didn't pull out his weapons to show. Damn good thing, too, because if he was going to peacock his way into my Jillian's heart, he had another thing coming.

"You are kinda scary," Jillian whispered.

"Yeah, you should see what the women say about my-"

"ARES!" Vulcan finally spoke up. "My man, give the girl a break. Besides, Hades could toast you now; he's only getting stronger by the day." Ares finally kept his mouth shut and shoved food in his mouth.

Jillian stopped eating and yawned and cuddled closer to my body. She still couldn't hold a full plate in her stomach, but she was doing well otherwise. The bruises left by the idiot Teddy Johnson had faded. The doctor even said her bones were getting stronger, almost at an alarming rate. The bond was working for both of us, and I was ready for her to be well.

Loukas came out of the office with a briefcase in hand, no doubt to let me know what else he had heard from his assistant friend that worked with Zeus. It was time to get to the bottom of this Malachi business which I had a bad feeling about.

"Jillian, you look well!" His smile brightened. Jillian saw him as her friend and trusted him more than the rest; he found her, so letting them be friends was a given. I still didn't have to like it.

"Yes! Much better! And I know…" She winked while Loukas's eyes darted around the room.

"You know what?"

"What everyone is, so can I see what you really look like?" Her eyes fluttered at him. My body stiffened as she looked at him; I only wanted her to look at me, damn it. I curved her legs back around to me and tried to give her a sip of milkshake, but she shook her head. "I'm so full, Hades. I couldn't eat anymore!" The whine had my heartstrings pulled. I've heard other humans use the whiny voice, and I hated it, but I loved it when she did it. It made her sound needy, and I really did need her.

Loukas perked up when Jillian started to lean in to kiss me and threw his shirt on the couch beside us. I growled as his smell wafted near my nose. "Sure, Jillian, I'll show you." This is not good; he fucking has a crush on her. His heart was racing, palms sweaty. I could smell his want.

"Show me, show me!" Jillian was absolutely oblivious.

Loukas didn't look like the rest of my demons; he was indeed red-skinned but had no hooves, and his horns were not as large. Some demonesses called him the "tamed one," but he had more power than the rest of them. He could seduce, destroy and sniff out the things I desired, which were traitor deities and supernaturals.

Loukas's hair was tossed to the side in short waves, and his body's torso was lean with a good bit of muscle.

Nothing compared to me.

I should have made him fat.

"What do you think?" Loukas turned around like a damn model to show off, holding his arms out like he was some demon god.

"Awesome!" she stared. "You can go back and forth between human and demon form then?" I'm going to rot one day in Tartarus for this, but I'm doing it anyway. "All you change just like that?" We all nodded while Loukas looked at her longingly.

"Jillian." My index finger glided across the tip of her jawline. My lips parted, and I tried to give her the most seductive look that I could. Her eyes investigated my dark ones as she smiled. "Who do you think looks the best?"

Me Damnit.

"Oh, that is easy!" she declared while looking around the room. "Cerberus! That's who!" she cooed as she petted him under his chin.

"*Fuck yes, I am I'm a damn good boy,*" he purred in my head.

Jillian started laughing hysterically as my mouth dropped. Her hands came on either side of my head as she pecked my lips. "You are the most handsome, my silly devil." My smile brightened as Loukas grabbed his shirt, obviously trying to ruin the moment. I could feel Ares' eyes glare at Loukas as he walked out of the room.

"*But I looked the best,*" Cerberus whined again while I gripped my mate around her waist a little harder.

Chapter 21

Jillian

Hades had work to do in his large office. I didn't get a great look the last time I was in there because of my nerves. Now that the truth has come out about him being the actual Hades and the weird statues, paintings, and a mansion that had no other homes for miles gave me a little room to breathe.

I knew something was different about this place; I just couldn't put my finger on it.

The walls were lined with an enormous number of books. On one section, there was nothing, but scrolls piled on top of each other in neat piles. The papers looked old and could have been original copies of some famous texts. As I trailed my finger deeper down the bookshelves, I caught a glimpse of books varying in sizes about different animals and species. Most of them were animals I had never heard of: Silent Tarsiers, Abyssinian-Bat, Zorse-Ram, Wilk Markhor, and Snow Faerie Fox. I was about to learn more about the Faerie Fox when my eye caught another book, Werewolves.

That name piqued my interest more, so I grabbed it and limped over to the couch. Hades was nose deep in an e-mail, wearing some reading glasses absorbing the light from the screen. How could anyone be so scared of him? He doesn't scare me at all, and to think I was, in the beginning, was stupid. Of course, at the time, he was kind of grouchy and angry all the time.

Hades didn't shave this morning; he had dark stubble that he continually scratched while reading. On occasion, he would write a few notes on paper and move his mouth to the side while he thought. He was devilishly handsome, even if he wouldn't switch back to his proper form often.

Everyone showed me what they looked like last night, yet he didn't offer to show his. I barely got a glimpse of him when he saved me from the incubus house. Does he not like his own form? My continuous stare alerted Hades as he looked up through his glasses. He gave me a toothy grin while I blushed down to my neck.

"What do you have there? Something to read?" His voice was amused as I flipped through the pages.

"Yeah, I saw this book on Werewolves. I guess I didn't realize that since you are real, all these other species were real too, so I wanted to look." My eyes glanced back at Hades; he was staring at me intently. The thought ran through my mind again of the steamy kiss we shared a few days ago in that very chair. I longed to do it again. Was it because of that bond we have for each other?

I felt my heart flip as he stood up and walked to the couch next to me and sat down. "Werewolves are mighty creatures. I've worked with them several times. They aren't as strong as gods, but they are certainly resourceful and can put up quite a fight. I feel they are stronger than Vampires and Witches, to be honest." Hades flipped the page open, showing a female and the different stages of their transformation.

"When do you have to interact with Werewolves? I thought you stay down here mostly." Hades let out a large sigh and rubbed his eyes with his thumb and index finger. His head laid back on the couch as he closed the book.

"There will be a time I need to explain some mistakes that I have made. I just fear you won't want to be with me once I told you." My heart pained to see him have this internal battle with himself; he's kept it locked up for so long.

Hades has rescued me twice in my life; if there was one thing he did wrong that he regrets, then I think I owe him that much. Besides, it was before me anyway; he's lived for so long he would have to have a ton of mistakes.

"You can tell me. I won't leave you," I whispered as I ran my fingers through his hair. "Everyone makes mistakes; it is just best we learn from them, right?" He let out a little scoff as he pulled his head back from the couch.

"I'll tell you, but let's take a field trip first. I know you are dying to get outside." I felt my face light up as I stood up to walk out the door. He caught my hand and pulled me to his lap.

"I can walk more now," I protested, but he put his finger to my lips.

"I know, but where we are going, you can't walk there. Now, wrap your arms around my neck." Obeying reluctantly, I did what I was told, feeling the sparks travel up my arms as they rubbed his neck. Our faces were close, nose to nose. His s'mores and campfire smell filled me as his lips brushed mine.

Closing our eyes, our lips met, and immediately sparks flew. I felt tremendous air rush around us as his arms encased my body in his. My hair whipped around us as it danced with the wind. My one hand slid down from around his neck and touched his cheek. I wanted to feel as much surface area I could; the pure pleasure at my fingertips had me going insane.

The kiss had become heated as Hades' hand trailed down to my rear, gently cupping and squeezing. A small whimper left my lips as I fisted his shirt. Groans left his throat as he sucked my bottom lip. Pulling back, still feeling his hot lips on mine, I took a breath.

"Wow, I don't think I will get used to that," I breathed, looking into his eyes.

"It gets better, trust me." He smirked as he pulled away. My face was going to be a permanent shade of red.

Crickets singing caught my attention as I looked at our surroundings. We were in the middle of a forest, sitting on a large blanket with a lantern in the middle. A small basket of food sat beside us. The god is going to make me fat. I just stinkin' ate.

He's super sweet, though, my big evil devil.

"This place... it's beautiful." Hades held on to me as I looked at our surroundings. We were on top of a mountain right at the cliff. Large trees were behind us and a bright open sky in front. The stars twinkled in the sky as I smelled the fresh air. It felt clean, full of pine. A smell that reminded me of the man in my dream. Could it be real? If I am Ember in real life, then he would be my father.

"Everything all right? I thought I lost you there." Hades pet my cheeks as I cuddled closer. The air was fantastic as the wind gently blew by.

"I'm just speechless; it's so beautiful. This isn't the Underworld anymore, is it?"

"It's not, but I could create something like this for you. I'll create anything you wish." His words fell out of his mouth like a velvet ribbon, entrapping me with his soft words. Hades lifted my hand from my lap and brushed his lips across my knuckles. "Anything at all."

"As long as you are there, that is all I need." I smiled back at him. Forgetting the whole field trip, I shuffled myself more comfortably in his arms as we began to kiss again until he held his head back to shake.

"What's wrong?" I asked worriedly. Hades put a hand up to his temple with his eyes closed. Growling, he let out a frustrated sigh.

"A powerful coven is trying to contact me. They will keep pestering me until I answer."

"Well, go answer them. Don't be rude!" I chided as I let him sit away from me. Hades set me down on the blanket, covering me with another as he scooted the basket over for me to eat.

"Stay out of view; I don't want them to see you." I nodded my head, half paying attention as I looked for any chocolate at the bottom of the basket.

"Hades we call upon you-" A bright orb shown in front of Hades that had a picture of a woman on the front. She looked worried as she and several other women around her were chanting.

"What is it?" Hades snapped as he continued to rub his temples. The woman stared at him, almost shocked that it worked.

"My Lord, thank you for answering us; it has been many years-"

"Yes, Cyrene, I know. Now get on with it." Hades waved his hand, but I put mine on his knee and gave him a calming look. He has got to get his anger under control around other people. His eyes softened, and he even gave a smile to me.

"The Lord is smiling," a witch spoke to Cyrene's left. Hades' smile faded, and the scornful one returned.

"What is it you called me for?"

"My Lord, the ward you have placed on the Black Claws Pack has been weakened for many years. This is the first time we've been able to reach you." Hades' eyebrows rose in question. "We tried contacting you for some ten or so years but not once you answered."

"I've never received a summons from you in all this time. This is the first. Are you sure you practiced the spell correctly?"

"Yes, My Lord. We have done it every year around this time for your help." Hades rubbed his stubble on his chin.

"Something is amiss," he stated. "I will talk to Hecate and come by the Black Claw Pack in one week. Is Alpha Wesley Hale still the Alpha?" Cyrene nodded as she began to look around the orb.

"What is it?" Hades snapped again, more harshly. His eyes glowed, and his fist tightened.

"Hades," I cooed at him. I put my hand to his cheek as he forgot about Cyrene staring at him from the orb. I made sure to keep my face away as he held he had to keep my own next to him.

"Goddess, he found his mate," Cyrene whispered as the Witches all talked excitedly. Hades glared at the orb.

"One week, Cyrene. Let them know." Hades waved his hand as the orb vanished.

I had more questions after his talk with this sorceress named Cyrene and about the Werewolf group, but I knew not to ask with the mood he was in. Hades had been really working hard all day today on something. The few pieces of information I could hear him talking to Loukas about were about someone named Selene missing and Hermes having trouble coming back.

Knowing that Hermes is a Messenger God, he must have a busy job running around gathering information. I hoped he comes back soon. I was really enjoying having all the men in my life; they made it fun and exciting. The male servants not so much; they dared not to look at me, let alone breathe or talk. It was tough to ask for things when all they did was nod and shake their head.

"Hades? Why don't the servants talk to me? Why aren't there any women either?" Hades stiffened as he took a sip of his wine. Cleaning his throat, he put down the glass as we witnessed a shooting star overhead.

"I kicked out all of the female servants and maids after that incident the first day you were here," he said, pulling his collar.

Oh, snap. That was the day the woman was basically taking off her clothes in front of him. Gah, that whore. I squinted my eyes and folded my arms. I had forgotten that little detail.

"Good choice; they seemed slutty." Hades gave a glorious laugh. "I mean, her boobs were practically falling out of her top, to begin with. You didn't sleep with her, did you?" Hades' face became stern.

"I don't fraternize with the help, angel. I won't lie, I did have a, uh, harem, so to speak." I gasped and slapped his shoulder.

"And you knew you were going to have a mate?" My voice flew a few octaves higher. "How dare you!" I stood up to look over the cliff. "I know I wasn't around, and you may have relationships, but having a bunch of concubines at your disposal is rather terrible!"

"Angel," he pleaded, trying to wrap his arms around me.

"You better get checked for diseases. I've seen things; I know what kind of yucky stuff you can get." I waved my finger in his face. "I never thought I would get so mad at you!"

Hades' face grew miserable. I swore I saw his eyes water, but I held firm. He went down to his knees and wrapped his arms around me, his head in my stomach as I let out a little grunt from the pressure.

"My angel, I am so sorry. I am full of mistakes." I could barely hear his voice as he spoke into my torso. The vibrations made me want to giggle, but I held back. I was flippin' angry!

"They meant nothing to me, as terrible as it sounds. They didn't. They were gifts from other gods and supernaturals, and I hardly even touched any of them. I swear this to you, Angel." His grip grew tighter, and my resolve grew weaker.

"The last time I even touched a woman was thousands of years ago, right before I met Persephone, and even then, she wouldn't let me touch her."

"Smart woman," I spat. "But thanks for being honest. I guess I can't fault you if it has been so long. Maybe all those diseases washed out of your system by now," I half-joked. "Maybe that's why you have been crabby for so long because you haven't gotten laid," I snickered.

Hades whipped his head up to look up at me, arms still wrapped around my torso. "You have been talking to Ares too much."

"What about the male servants? Why won't they talk to me?" I raised a brow.

"Because no one talks or touches what is *mine*."

Chapter 22

Hades

Jillian was mine, and I wasn't going to let anyone have her. If I had my way, I wouldn't let Loukas or my friends talk to her, so I drew the line at the servants. They will bow before her and grovel at her feet and nothing else. They cannot speak to such a precious jewel; she is the brightest diamond amongst the polished obsidian stones of the Underworld. I wasn't going to have anyone lustfully look at her.

Jillian gave off her captivating giggle as I stood up to wrap my arms around her. My heart about burned in the fiery pits of hell, thinking that my mate was angry with me. My soul can't take it; I'll give her whatever she wants and spoil her throughout eternity.

"Was that what you wanted to tell me earlier when we were in your office?' Letting out a frustrating sigh, I glanced at Jillian, who had not stopped looking at me since I begged for forgiveness for even having a harem. Her soothing voice almost made my body go slack but hearing that she still wanted to know what evil sin I had created to cause much despair to the supernatural realm and Earth gave me fear.

Trixen was given immense power because of my stupid decisions, thinking I could create my own mate. Even in my stupidity, I knew it was a bad idea to keep many women locked away, yet there I was. The God of the Idiots.

"I'll tell you, just please don't leave me." Jillian's eyes softened, and her hands came up to my chest.

"As long as you are honest with me, I won't leave," she whispered. I wanted to believe her words, but the thought of telling her everything made my stomach tie up in knots. I still had much to say to her, and I didn't want to do it all at once.

We both sat back down on the blanket; our lantern still shone brightly in the evening sky. The sun had made its descent as I had her lay down with me. Her legs automatically curled around mine, and she nuzzled into my chest while gazing over the beautiful view.

"I was an angry god," I started as her head shifted to look at the side of my face. Her finger traced my jawline, and I let out a breath. "I wanted Persephone; at the time, she was the most beautiful goddess I had ever laid eyes on. She played in a meadow with her mother on Earth, and the moment her mother looked away, I dragged her down to the Underworld. As time continued on, I tried to woo her; I fed her the most elaborate foods, gave her flowers and gifts that Aphrodite herself would be jealous over. Not once did she show any interest."

Jillian shifted closer and pecked me on the cheek. Biting my bottom lip, I tried to resist the urge to stick my tongue in her mouth and have my way with her.

"I was stubborn; I didn't want to let her go; I promised her that one day she would fall for me, that was until Selene, the Moon Goddess started pairing off souls."

"Go on," she whispered quietly as the crickets started chirping louder.

"First, Selene started off with the Werewolves; Ares had created the race to help humans fight gods that had created other species based on human anatomy. Ares took the strongest warriors and gave them the gift of shifting into Wolves. They were ferocious beasts and could take down many of the evil Vampires, Witches, and other types of Shifters. Once most of the evil, the defective ones, were disposed of, the years went by, and there was nothing for the Werewolves to do. When they are not fighting, they are restless, so Selene stepped in and realized they were not a whole person; they were missing an important part of themselves. Their other half."

I shifted my body, so Jillian lay on top of me, her head resting on my chest.

"Now all Werewolves were destined to find their someone, and their beasts were then satisfied and didn't hunt for blood. It worked so well, other creatures were allowed to have a soul mate. Vampires call them beloveds, Faes their destined one or mate. It wasn't until I had Persephone in the Underworld for a thousand-years when Selene and Zeus stepped in with some angel. I didn't get a good look at him because I was distracted, but he grabbed Persephone and slipped away. I was livid; I destroyed half of the Underworld in one blow. The fire burned the villages; Hermes and Vulcan left the Underworld to stay elsewhere." I grabbed Jillian a little tighter as she glanced into my eyes.

"That is so sad, Hades. I'm sorry." My fucking mate felt sorry that I lost someone I thought I loved? Kronos, it made my chest hurt. She was damn fucking perfect.

"Years later, I created a demoness, Trixen. When I create a demon, I put one drop of blood into their bodies to have almost complete control. I can know where they are, control their desires to a certain degree and make sure they cannot leave the Underworld. With Trixen, I didn't because I wanted her to have her agency, to be able to choose me. I created her to be my mate."

Jillian went to sit up, but I held her back down as I sat up. She squirmed a bit and grunted when she realized she wasn't going anywhere.

"But Selene was giving everyone mates. Why couldn't you wait for me?" Holy fucking damn shit, her lip went into the most prominent pout. Jillian could be so childish and innocent sometimes; it made my cock want to do nasty things to her sweet body.

"I told you, I was an idiot!" I threw my hands up in defeat. "I was so mad at Selene; I didn't want her help. I wanted to make things on my own, but it blew up in my stubborn ass face." I twisted Jillian, so she straddled me while she still kept her arms folded around her body. I couldn't force her to hold onto me, but I was losing control of her not wanting to touch me.

"I put too much of my anger and frustration about bonds into her. Some of my aura slipped. It was a foolish thing on my part, but her brain didn't let it go. She rejected me the moment she opened her eyes and sought out nothing but revenge. Her power was incomparable to most demons and what was worse was she possessed a strong magical Witch with a blasé attitude about herself. Trixen easily took over her body so she could roam Earth and cause nothing but pain to humans and supernaturals for no reason at all."

Jillian held back a sob as I further explained. The Werewolf pack that I need to see was the pack that stopped Trixen. I could not reach

Trixen each time they delayed her, and a tiny human turned Werewolf who is now the Luna saved the world from the demoness' wrath. Luna Charlotte suffered the most for years dealing with the bitch. Trixen practiced bonding brands on her skin and told the vampire he had to check her blood for the right time of ripening until he could forcibly bond with her." Jillian gripped me tighter.

"Charlotte had proved strong once she met her mate, Wesley Hale, and proved that a true bond was more potent than a fake one. It couldn't be erased, and it only pissed off Trixen more. Charlotte was able to slaughter her the first time she shifted, proving again how strong a Werewolf bond really was.

"That poor woman." Jillian let a single teardrop. "And to think she was human and didn't know how to fight or control her Wolf." I smiled as I tilted her head to kiss her cheek.

"A Wolf is a special bond between the human side and the animal side. They were made for each other just as soul mates were made for each other. They complement."

Jillian gave a small smile and wrapped her arms around my neck. "But she is OK now, right? She lived through it?"

"She did; unfortunately, she and many others suffered for my mistake. Those who died by Trixen's hands have been given a second chance and reborn. They won't know of their past sufferings. It still lingers on in my own guilt." Jillian put her fingers through my hair, tilting her head as she kissed my forehead.

"See, I didn't leave. You gave those who suffered a second chance. You made a mistake, and it's over now. Even if it did make me angry that you would try and replace me." Jillian stuck out her tongue, and I leaned in to try and suck it in my mouth. Sticking her tongue back in, she slumped her shoulders. "What do you have to do with that 'pack' of Wolves?" Jillian threw up air quotations with her fingers.

"I put up a barrier to help protect them against rogues and magic. They have been trying to contact me for years, and since they haven't been able to, I wonder if someone else is using a magical ward to prevent them from summoning me. If this is the case, we need to go investigate."

Jillian gasped as she pounced on my lap a bit too hard, "I get to go too?!" she squealed.

My hardened dick was now lip as noodle as I tried to adjust myself. "Yes," I grunted. "You get to go too; you can't leave my sight." I gritted my teeth. Jillian got the idea and got up from my lap. Her hands cupped her face as her eyes blinked with worry.

"I'm so sorry. Did I hurt the little devil?" Looking at her bewildered, I tried to hide my hurt.

"Little devil?" I scoffed. "It isn't... fuck." Jillian ran over to the basket and got the icepacks and tried to hand them to me.

"I'll be all right, angel, just no bouncing." Her face was full of concern; I reached out my hand and pulled her back into my lap. "I'm all right, trust me." Kissing her forehead, she melted into me. I could never get over how she felt.

We wrapped up our basket with half-eaten food, and I placed the blanket over Jillian's shoulders. She gave me that smile that could make my cold heart melt. "Are you ready to head back?" I asked.

"I guess." She pouted again. I gripped her chin and sucked on her bottom lip. Her tiny gasp made me hard as I pulled her waist closer. I wanted her to feel what she does to me, the days have been long, and my body was aching to take her and claim her body and soul.

Her eyes widened at our kiss, and she stepped back, cupping her mouth with her hand. "Hades," she whispered while a blush dusted her cheeks.

"What's wrong?" I smirked. "You see what you do to me?" I pulled her back into my arms, rubbing my length across her stomach. My pants were painfully tight. Jillian kept her hand over her mouth as I leaned in to kiss her ear. Her eyes closed and melted right back into my arms. Holding the basket in one hand and my other hand reaching the small of her back, we transported back into the bedroom.

Our bedroom.

I continued to trace kisses down her neck; the sparks entered my mouth as I let open kisses trail down her neck. Jillian's eyes remained closed, leaning into me. I dropped the basket and made a thud on the floor. It didn't wake Jillian from her trance.

Picking her up, I had her straddle me with both of her legs wrapped around my torso. My lips never left the bottom part of her neck. The top she was wearing was low but not low enough. I took several strides to the bed as I laid her down gently, kissing the top of her chest. Her hands threaded through my hair as she took my lips back to hers.

Sticking my tongue in her mouth, she met mine with such passion. One of my hands traced the bottom hem of her shirt, sneaking my hand up her sides. I couldn't get enough; I wanted to taste every bit of her body while she let me. My cock was ridiculously hard as it pressed into her inner thigh.

First, my hand went over her breast as I gave it a gentle squeeze. My fingertips felt the underside of her bra. Jillian hummed into my mouth as I felt her nipple pebble underneath my touch. Pulling away, she gasped for air.

"Hades," she breathed.

I was filled with lust for her. I wanted to take her and make her entirely mine, but I wasn't sure how far her limit was. "You taste divine, angel." The hunger in her eyes and the scratches on my scalp gave me the go-ahead to lift her shirt. Closing her eyes, she moaned as my head pressed to her chest. I could sleep here throughout eternity and never wake up.

Jillian pushed her chest up as I felt one of her arms go under her back; a small click sounded through my ears. Dear Kronos, she unlatched the one piece of fabric that kept her breasts confined. Lifting my head up, I pulled her bra away; her breasts were perky as they stared right back at me.

"Angel, you are gorgeous." They were glorious, perfect, and any other word that would describe the heavens. Jillian was damn excellent. Groaning, I rubbed my cock on her thigh again as she gasped. My hand instantly grabbed a large handful on the right while my mouth reached for the left. I sucked and licked her perked nipple; she tasted of sweet honey and cinnamon.

Jillian brought her arms around my head, pushing me more into her breasts. Fuck I'm definitely a breast man. As I engorged myself on my mate, leaving bite marks all over her porcelain skin, there was a knock at the door. I would burn whoever was on the other side of the door for a thousand lifetimes. I had every damn intention of continuing my pursuit of my mate and ignoring it entirely, but Jillian stilled.

"A-are you g-going to get that?" she whispered, disappointed. I pulled her to my lips, sucking until I let it go leaving a loud smack.

"They know I'm here." I kissed under her ear.

"Then go get it, so they don't think we are..." She looked towards the door. "You know," she whispered. Even though I was sporting a raging boner and blue balls were in my future, I gave a chuckle.

"To be continued then?" Her eyes were hopeful as the blush painted her cheeks.

"To be continued," I growled.

Now it was time for me to burn the mother fucker on the other side.

Chapter 23

Jillian

Oh. My. Gosh.

Hades was giving me that smile, but I saw the fire in his eyes. He was not happy about the interruption, and I feared for the entity on the other side of the door. I've been lucky they haven't been towards me, but others need to watch out. I've seen a little bit of what Hades can do, and he does have some anger issues.

I pulled my shirt down over my exposed chest, and he slid down my body and gave a quick nip at my hip. A shot of sparks ran straight between my thighs. I squeezed them shut while the pink tint of my cheeks covered me all the way down to my chest. Hades groaned and adjusted himself as he finally slid off the bed. Before he left, he covered me with a blanket, wrapped me up, and kissed my temple.

"Don't move; I don't need anyone seeing or smelling your arousal," his raspy voice invaded my ears as my heart leaped out of my chest.

"Smell?!" I squealed.

"Your mate is a god, so of course we have heightened senses, and let me tell you, Angel, you smell divine." He bit the side of his mouth and strode over to the door. Hades' gait was powerful as his back muscles tensed as he approached the door.

I couldn't believe we went as far as we did. The ember of lust I had for him had exploded into a blaze only meant for two really in love. Could it be love? I'm beginning to think so. I don't want him just for his looks, but the way he treats me, makes me feel, protects me, and cares for me. It is like no other feeling I've ever had or remember. Love is what I am describing, isn't it? To care for someone unconditionally?

Hades was so worried I would leave him that it made my stomach hurt when he gave me a look of defeat. With the mistakes he had made, I felt the desire to comfort him. He continues to put himself down and hold onto the sins he had created for himself, yet he still continues to rectify his wrongs.

Being in the underworld and watching those with horrible crimes themselves be punished and never forgiven has made Hades sit in his own sins of guilt. He must learn to forgive himself on his own time, just like anyone else.

A small smile came across my face as I realized he was mine and I was his. It made the overwhelming feelings a little less scary. We both had to get to know each other; he's lived for so long, and he has wants and desires, and I would love to know what makes him tick. He claims Persephone made his life spiral down, but there is something else. Even when I continue to tell him I won't leave if he is honest, I fear he is holding something back. If I had secrets to tell, I would tell him. I just don't have anything to give.

I must be patient and continue to reassure him that I'm not leaving. With a new set of determined goals, I cringed as the sound of the door knocked again.

Hades growled which only made me shiver. Every sound this manmade was so sexy. I rolled myself into a burrito as he looked back at me and raised his brow. "Don't smell me, don't smell me," I chanted.

Hades opened the door to be greeted by Loukas.

Uh oh.

Hades gripped his neck as he stepped into the hallway while he shut the door behind him. This wasn't good; I owed Loukas for saving me. He was a great friend the past year while I worked at the strip club. He was the only one who made me smile and made my shift a little shorter.

My body was wrapped up like a burrito as I tried to wiggle free. Rolling back and forth on the bed, I landed on the floor with a large thump and landed on my bad leg.

"Owie!" I slowly rolled out of the blanket only to find Hades and Loukas looking at me, confused. "I fell, I'm fine! But please don't fight!" I pouted my lip, knowing Hades would do anything for me when I did that.

"Don't do that, angel," he growled. I fluttered my eyes at him, begging him not to hurt Loukas.

"Please don't hurt him; he didn't know. When the door is shut, don't knock on it, OK Loukas?" Loukas looked between Hades and me and gave a slight nod. He looked hurt, and I couldn't understand why. Did he like me? I'm supposed to be Hades' mate; he will get his own mate, too, right?

With the tension in the room thickening, Hades continued to stare down Loukas for looking at me. I wrapped the blanket back around and stood next to Hades. "I'm pretty tired," I yawned. Hades immediately scooped me up in his arms and deposited me in the bathroom.

"Get ready for bed; I'll be back in a moment." The quick peck on my lips left too soon as he turned his back to me to talk to Loukas. Grabbing his hand, I pulled him to me, flush against my body. My hand immediately caressed his face.

"Please don't hurt him. I'm sure he has something important to say since he came to your room." Hades let out a sigh and a slight nod before walking out of the bedroom and shutting the door.

Now that the tension was gone, I opted for a bath since I was all hot and bothered. Filling the large bath with oils and bath salts, I waited for the water to warm. My clothes were peeled off me in an instant as I squealed internally at the bath before me. Unwrapping the bandage, expecting to still see a few slash marks, I was pleasantly surprised that there was hardly any. Only a few light scratches remained that looked it could be nothing more than a cat's claws. Whatever they were putting in those IV mineral nutrient bags was working. I've never healed so fast in my life.

Wanting nothing more than to ease my aching muscles, I slid into the tub until my entire body was submerged. The aroma from the lavender helped me calm myself, and I shut my eyes. The bubbles kept my body hidden like a blanket as I heard slight popping from the tiny globes.

As I grew comfortable, I fell in and out of consciousness. The water became cold, and I was no longer comfortable and thought about getting out until I heard a chitter. It sounded like a squirrel but in a bathroom? My eyes fluttered open to see a bright red and orange fox with little wings on its back. It was small, small enough to fit in the palm of your hand. Its tail was aflame while the tips of its wings were black and charred. The tips of his ears and paws were also black, which made me wonder if it got too excited, would it just burst into flames? I started giggling at the thought of the entire fox on fire which only made him cock his head in confusion.

It chittered again at me, its head looking down as it stared at me in the water. It would glance at the water, then at me. Chattering again, almost scolding the water and myself so I went ahead and stood up and reached for a towel. The poor thing was in distress as it hopped off the tub and flew up on the counter. I wrapped the towel around my body, and the cute little thing looked me up and down, somewhat satisfied. It chittered again, using its paw to show me what it wanted next.

Hairdryer.

Did it want me to dry off? Bossy little thing. I reached for it as he chittered again for me to start it up, and I dried my hair while it patiently waited and watched. Its eyes never left me once as I brushed and dried it, which did take a bit. Once my hair was dry, it looked me up and down with a satisfied look and used its paw again, pointing to the door.

Opening the door, it flew out faster than I was expecting and flew right into the closet that Hades had my clothes put in. On the left were suits, shirts and pants and all of them were in black of course. On the right side of the closet, there were dresses, shirts, skirts, jeans, and anything I could think of. Every day the closet continued to grow, and I wondered where all these clothes were even coming from.

I went to a large chest of drawers and shuffled through each one until I found something to wear to bed. All of it was lacy, barely-there or silk. I curled my nose up, not wanting to even think about putting that on after the steamy session we had earlier. I shut the drawers quickly until the little fox animal started chittering again. It was scolding me! It hopped up and down and pawed at the drawer until I finally stomped my foot.

"Excuse me, would you cut it out?!" It sat back on its hindquarters and let out a little huff. I turned to the opposite side of the closet and found Hades' plain black knit shirts and boxers. Being a creep, I smelled in his scent. Mmm, smores. I wonder if I have a smell too?

I put on a shirt that reached me mid-thigh and decided to forgo the boxers. The little fox scurried out right as the bedroom door opened. Hades had a scowl on his face only to have it lightened when he saw me.

Did I really bring that much happiness to him? "Hades!" I jumped across the room and gave him a hug. He pulled me in and rubbed my back. "There is this cute little creature thing that has been bossing me around. Is he your pet too?" Hades pulled back from me.

"Pet?" he questioned. The chittering started again, and it flew up and landed on my shoulder. The fire on its tail extinguished, and only bits of smoke rose from its rear.

"This thing..." I pointed at the little critter. Its nose was pointed and full of sharp little teeth that hung over its maw. If the thing was bigger, he could really do some damage. Hades looked at the fire hamster and back at me.

"It's a Phantomtail." Hades took his finger to pet its head but it only snapped at him. It growled and started chittering again like Hades could understand every word it was saying. It continued chittering while Hades began smiling. The little Phantomtail stuck out its tongue and flew into the closet.

"What is a Phantomtail exactly, and why did he try to bite you?" I stared into the closet, waiting for the creature to come out, only to hear light snores coming from the dirty laundry. "What the?"

"Phantomtails roam around the underworld. Their primary job is to help lost animal spirits back to their humans. Shifter spirits sometimes get separated from their human counterparts and need to be led back to the Asphodel Fields to be with their humans. Phantomtails can be very protective over the animals they protect. I have known a few Phantomtails to find a human they like and treat them like their own little kit." I giggled.

"So, it thinks I'm its kit?" Hades nodded.

"What were you doing when he found you?"

"I was in the tub, but I kept falling asleep until it started to chatter at me to get out." I scratched my head while Hades folded his arms.

"That's why, you can't take care of yourself," he chided while I scoffed. "I leave for just a little over an hour, and you are falling asleep in the tub. Maybe he should follow you around. Better pick a name for him." I gasped.

"I can keep him!? Yay!!!" Cerberus walked into the room and put his nose in the air. He started growling and headed over to the closet. The chattering soon became tiny screams as I ran inside the closet to save the Phantomtail. "No, Cerberus! Don't hurt him!" I picked the Phantomtail up and pulled him to my chest while I petted his head. It purred contentedly while glaring at Cerberus.

Cerberus looked to Hades, who only shrugged his shoulders at him and started to whine. "Oh, Cerberus, you are still the bestest boy!" I scratched his belly while he groaned, but my new bestie didn't like that; he started chatting with me again. "Oh, this is going to be hard!" Hades laughed while my heart felt so warm about all of us being in the same room.

It felt like a real family, a real home to be in. I never wanted it to end, and I couldn't imagine life getting much better.

Chapter 24

Hades

Do I want sweet and tangy BBQ sauce or savor the meat as is? Toasted? Roasted?

I could smell the fear on the other side of the door; it was Loukas. He should be scared. He ruined a moment I had been craving since I met Jillian, and something tells me he is doing it on purpose. The large dark wooden door slung open as I gripped the handle. Loukas's head was bowed and cowering in fear. Good, he should be.

Gripping his neck, he let out a gulp as I closed the door behind me, so my mate didn't have to witness such violence. She didn't deserve that. Slamming Loukas on the other side of the wall, a few pictures of demonic entities fell to the floor with a thump. "What do you want, Loukas?" I spat out as I tightened my grip.

"My Lord, there is news about Selene-" he tried to breathe "-H-Hermes is back!" There was a loud thump on the floor of my room; dropping Loukas to the floor, I opened the door to find Jillian tangled up in the blankets. She was rolling around on the floor, looking completely helpless.

"Please don't hurt him; he didn't know. When the door is shut, don't knock on it, OK Loukas?" Jillian's lip sat out in a pout that made me groan internally. Her wide eyes looked up and gave a confused look.

Fuck, does she know that works too well on me? I wanted to kiss her senselessly when it was out because it was too damn adorable. Loukas looked distant as he stared at her; too many thoughts were running through his mind, and I didn't like it. Not one damn bit.

"I'm pretty tired," she yawned, and I scooped her up and put her in the bathroom. Once more, she begged me not to hurt Loukas, but I really fucking wanted to. I wanted to see the light leave his eyes so he could no longer glance at my angel. She was mine, and no one could take her from me.

However, I would keep my word, just for her.

I motioned for Loukas to leave the room, and we walked in silence down to my office. The halls were dimly lit, and only a few servants were about the palace. Ares was waiting by the door with his arms crossed as he nodded for us to come in. Hermes stood in the corner near my desk; his eyes were looking out in the Demon Forest. The moon cast a dark red glow across the land as I sat in my chair, ready to hear news from the Celestial World.

"Give me what you can, Hermes." Hermes rubbed his chin as he sat beside Ares on the couch. Vulcan just walked in with a tray that held numerous cups of coffee. Vulcan sat across the other two and flexed his hands several times before leaning back into the black leather couch.

"Do you want the bad news or the worst news?" he scoffed. He looked towards the door. We left the office door open with Loukas standing by, listening so we would be aware of any unwanted ears.

"Just give it to me," I spat as I slapped my hand on the table. I still had a raging set of blue balls that were killing me, so no matter what, my night would get worse.

"Selene was indeed kidnapped; I saw her wrecked home myself." Hermes let out a sigh. "There were angels there and a lot of them. They were checking the place for magic, curses, wards, and barriers, but they have found nothing, not even a trace of hair." Hermes scoffed as he picked up his mug. "Selene was taken along with her Sphere of Souls, this could be bad news. If someone tries to control her pairing, it could end up disastrous. Supernaturals and even deities will be paired with the wrong soul, almost causing an involuntary rejection and possible death. Millions could die."

Vulcan took a breath from the news. If anyone deserved a mate, it was him, and I've said it too many times I lost count. "What is the plan then, Hermes?" I said, breaking the silence.

"Right now, there is none because some other shit has hit the fan..." We all waited for his dramatic pause before glancing back at me. "Hecate has gone missing too."

"The fuck? Who can kidnap her? She is the goddess of all witchcraft; she would see anyone coming a mile away!" Ares stood up from the couch and started throwing his hands in the air. He's always had a thing for her, but she never did budge on any of his advances. She played cat and mouse with Ares for a long time until Selene announced the paring of souls; now, she waits for her soul mate to appear.

"I just spoke with her a few days ago about Jillian; how long has she been missing?"

"Around thirty-six hours, it hasn't been released yet to the other gods. Zeus is trying to keep this under wraps before he has more information." I stood up and started pacing. So far, Malachi had no connection to Selene other than taking Persephone as a mate; it had to be a coincidence he was there that day when I came to retrieve Jillian.

The room fell silent again as I paced to the window. Phantom tails were running around the forest edge. An animal must be lost but coming this far into the palace grounds was a bit of a stretch.

I needed to get back to Jillian; I wanted to go to Tartarus, but now that I have had a taste of Jillian, which sounded more appealing. Having her in my arms would be better.

"There's one more thing," Hermes spoke quietly. All of our attention adverted to him as he faced one of the many bookshelves cluttering the room. "Malachi is not Persephone's mate."

"What?" Vulcan stood up. "I saw it with my own eyes while Hades was being distracted." Hell, I was worried. I didn't see who came for Persephone; I just knew she was gone. "Malachi was the one who came down for Persephone!" Vulcan's voice stressed.

"Gabriel is her mate," Hermes spoke with conviction. "All of the supernatural world says this to be so. However, when you talk to any gods and demi-gods, we all say it is Malachi. Now, there is something fishy with that, don't you think?" I scoffed while Hermes put his lips to a thin line.

"Humans get our history wrong all the time; what makes you think the supernatural world is any better?" I went to the liquor cabinet for a scotch and poured it over ice. "I had to correct numerous things Jillian has asked me; humans have it almost completely wrong."

Hermes pulled a large book from the library shelf. It was dusty, old, and ragged, and he placed it on the coffee table in the middle of the room. Hermes took a big breath in and blew. Years of dust and dried bugs fell to the floor. Vulcan's eyes scowled as he looked at the dirt littering the floor.

He always was a clean freak.

"The Muse of History," Hermes read aloud. "The God of the Sky and the God of the Underworld have been given this book by Clio, and you have yet to open it," Hermes teased as he flipped the pages.

"And what would I do with it? It is just a book of the history of our kind, more like a gossip column. Why would I want to read…"?

Ares and I ran to the book as Hermes flipped to my page. In bold letters, **Hades God of the Underworld** column stood. It had everything that had ever happened to me over the years. When the Underworld was established, significant events and even when I stole Persephone from her mother. As I scrolled down the page, there was a picture of Persephone in the background holding onto a bright angel. Zeus and Selene were standing in front of me, holding me back.

Instead of focusing on my utter embarrassment, I looked to the angel. Gabriel. "This isn't Malachi," I said out loud while we all looked at each other.

"Why do I remember Malachi as her mate?" Vulcan spoke, confused. Loukas stood quiet in the corner; his expressions changed with the rest of us talking. He started to rub his head as he was thinking.

"Speak up, Loukas." I walked towards him. Loukas backed away slightly as he realized I was walking towards him. He was still scared shitless.

"I had a terrible thought." His voice shook. "What if Malachi had a spell set to make everyone believe that he was Persephone's mate? The spell could be breaking, and that is why he needs Hecate."

"If the spell has lasted this long, I doubt the spell is breaking. Malachi wants to do something else," Hermes spoke up again. "Gabriel has been walking around the heavens all this time and doesn't have a clue Persephone is his. Malachi and Gabriel even act like good 'ole pals."

"Whatever this is, it hasn't lasted for long," Ares interrupted. "Why would he have taken Selene and Hecate now? Whatever was cast on the gods has only recently changed our thoughts of who

Persephone's mate really is. No one has seen Persephone either, have they, Hermes?

Hermes shook his head. "Nothing out of the ordinary; she stays to herself anyway. The last sighting of her was a few weeks ago with Malachi. So, she isn't being held captive. I can follow up and see where she is."

"What do we do now?" Vulcan gathered the coffee mugs from the table. No one touched a thing; we were too busy in our own thoughts and the desires to figure out why two goddesses could be missing.

"We can watch Malachi's patterns, see what he's after. I have a feeling Jillian somehow ties into this, and I want to know why," Hermes pulled out a small black notebook and started to thumb through the pages.

"Jillian stays out of this," I growled. "I don't want her near the bastard, and she can't leave to go anywhere without me." Hermes paid no mind to my threat and ripped part of the parchment.

"Here, Malachi and several angels frequent this club on Friday nights. We should all go, disguised completely different than our strip club cover." I gritted my teeth. Did he not just hear what I fucking said?

Loukas's back straightened as he looked down the hallway.

"My Lord, there is a chattering noise going on in Jillian's room." I pushed past Loukas and practically ran down the hallway, only to be greeted by Jillian staring up at me with her beautiful green eyes.

"Hades!" she squealed as she pounced on me. Jillian introduced me to her little friend, a Phantomtail known for its disappearing tails and taking care of lost spirit animals and humans. Cerberus had joined us, and he hates those fuckers.

"*They go around lighting shit on fire, emotionally attaching themselves to certain souls.*" Cerberus could go on for days how annoying they are, but I could already tell Jillian had an emotional attachment to the little guy. He was cute in some girly sort of way.

Cerberus whimpered as Jillian cradled the Phantomtail to her chest, cooing at it like it was a little baby.

"*But I'm the best boy. I'm the baby,*" he whined while Jillian huffed at her horrible predicament. All these males were around, biding for her attention, and she still didn't understand any of it. Jillian continued to pet the little rat that I told her she could keep. Let's be honest, though, he wasn't going to leave her side; he had already grown his attachment to her, and I couldn't zap him into dust because it would upset her.

"What should we call him?" she quipped as she hopped on the bed. My shirt rode up her thighs, so she was barely covered. Just a little more, and I would be able to see the lips I was really after. My heated stare was caught on quickly as she pulled down the shirt more.

"Sorry, I got so excited I didn't finish dressing," she blushed as she nuzzled the Phantom tail. I'm getting jealous over a damn squirrel. Can't she pet me like that? Fuck, it is getting me hard already.

"Now you know how I feel," Cerberus whined again as he put his paws over two of his heads.

"We?" I asked. "It is your animal."

"But he's our baby. We have to take care of him together." Cerberus started laughing in my head as I held back a laugh.

"Our baby?"

"Yup, we take care of Cerberus together, and now this guy, so we name him together," she spoke confidently. I leaned my head back on the bed and threw my arm over my stomach while Jillian sat thoughtfully. "How about Fluffy?" Cerberus started laughing out loud but covered it with a choking sound. The little Phantomtail didn't look amused and glared at her.

Stretching my chin and sitting forward, I pulled Jillian to my lap, and the little Phantomtail sat in her hands, glaring at me. I could feel the soft skin beneath my hands as I trailed my finger over her thighs. "What about Blaze?" Jillian gasped and nodded her head enthusiastically.

"That sounds so much better. Fits his surroundings too!" Jillian pecked me on the cheek while Blaze puffed out his chest.

"You are great at naming our animals. I bet you would be great at naming babies too!" Jillian blushed as she kissed my neck. I stiffened as she spoke about children. Part of me wanted to roar out in triumph that she would think of me naming children, our children.

Then the other part of me slumped in defeat. "Angel, did you know that the God of the Underworld is infertile?"

Chapter 25

Jillian

"Angel, did you know that the god of the Underworld is infertile?" Hades' voice sank and gave me a sad smile while petting Blaze. "I'm the God of Death, not of life, so why would I be able to give life even if it was in my mate's womb?"

"Hades," I whispered as I straddled his lap. Blaze jumped off and hid in the closet while Cerberus left the room.

"If you want children someday, children that would come from here," Hades' hands caressed my stomach lovingly, "that is the one thing I cannot give you."

Hades' eyes looked so broken; I could feel his heartache as he confessed this truth. He was just so handsome, loving, and caring I could never leave him for something like this, not ever. Hades may see himself as something dark and sinister, but I could see the light inside him when he looked at me.

I've never thought about having children; I was a child myself when I was taken away and practically forced to be a slave in the adult entertainment world. Honestly, I didn't know how to even interact with children. My days were limited, or so I thought. I would be eventually sold and killed so I wouldn't be another mouth to feed and dreaming of children was so far-fetched.

Would I like to have children? Maybe, someday if I had escaped but as selfish as it may be, I didn't want to share Hades right now. If we really wanted children, we could adopt. I'm sure we could find some demi-god that isn't enjoyed by either parent. We had options, but Hades was dead-set on the nightmare of not having our own. Hades needed to know I was all right with not having children. If having Hades meant no children, there would be no children because why would I deprive him and myself of each other's love? I could never see myself with anyone else for the sake of children. Children should be brought up in love, and Hades would be the only person I ever wanted to do that with.

"That's all right," I said softly as I touched his face with my hand. "We can have tons of fur babies like Cerberus and Blaze!" I giggled, but Hades didn't laugh with me. Squeezing me tighter, his head fell on my shoulder, and I returned his embrace.

"Don't you want someone that could give you children?" he mumbled on my shoulder. I rubbed his back with one hand and played with his hair in the other.

"Of course not; why would I want anyone else? You are my savior, my rescuer, and you stole my heart. I don't think I could bear to be without you. The thought has me tied up in knots if I never got to see you again. We are supposed to be soul mates, right? That's why I feel like this? This need to be with you?"

Hades' head pulled from my shoulder; his eyes were red around the edges. "You won't leave then? Even if I can't give you children?" I shook my head and smiled.

"No, never. You are stuck with me. We need each other. I was feeling all antsy when you were gone earlier while I took a bath; I didn't like it." Hades gave a sigh, and his hand came up to cradle my face.

"Jillian, will you be with me forever?" His voice was pleading and longing for my answer. As crazy as it sounded, I wanted to spend forever with him; I wanted to be with him every waking moment. He kept me safe, he was patient and loving, and that nagging part of my chest kept pulling me closer to him, not just physically but emotionally as well.

"Of course, I will be with you forever. I couldn't imagine anything else," I replied. Hades engulfed me in the biggest hug as I wrapped my arms around his neck. Big sighs and almost sobs left him as he held me. I continued to hold him close and swayed us back and forth as he calmed down.

"There is still so much more I need to tell you about what this means, but I'm dying to kiss you," he rasped.

"Well, what's stopping you?" I shot back as his million-dollar smile embraced my lips. One arm held my back in place while the other dug into my hair. Sitting up on my knees, I made myself taller than him, pressing my chest to his. Groans left him as I pulled at his hair.

Hades tugged at my lips with his teeth as his tongue slipped into my mouth. Sparks flew across us as one of his hands went lower on my back and onto the outside of my thigh. A soft moan left me as I felt him go under the back of my shirt as he cupped my bare rear-end. "Hades," I whispered in his mouth. He pulled away, letting me catch my breath. Tiny chills erupted on my skin as he pecked my shoulder.

"I make you feel good here." He put his hand in the middle of my chest. "Let me make you feel good in another way." My heart spiked as he rolled me onto my back. His hand reached up my shirt and he kissed my breasts. Letting out small pants as my hands trailed through his hair. The small nips on my nipples made me rub my thighs together on their own accord.

A low devilish laugh left Hades' throat. His hand traveled down my waist and to my hips as he continued sucking on my body, leaving marks in his wake.

A warm hand parted my thighs as my breath hitched. It burned and ached in my lower region, and I was dying to know what he was doing. Would he take care of it or make it worse? "I want you to relax." His finger dipped between my folds as I gripped his shoulders. Fingers felt so foreign down there; his callous fingers felt good as he parted the folds. Ever so slowly, he began to circle his fingers around my clit, and I immediately moved my hips to get more friction. The girls at the club were not kidding; this could feel really good with the right person.

His finger continued to rub in circles, sometimes stopping to dip into my cavern to fill his finger with more of my moisture. I thought this would be dirty and disgusting, but it all felt like heaven in hell.

The pressure began building in the pit of my stomach as I rose to a peak and shattered to pieces as he continued to rub the little nub of nerves. I sighed out his name, and his kisses on my breast were now on my lips. My pants became calmer as I gazed into his eyes. They were pitch black full of lust.

His finger still lingered on my clit but started slipping lower into me, going farther into my hole. His finger felt unbearably tight as he rubbed my walls. "Damn Angel, we have work to do," he husked as he tried to add another. I whimpered; it felt good, but it was almost too much.

In and out, he thrust his fingers inside me; the wetness I was creating made a suctioning sound as again I came undone by his hands. "Hades," I whined as he picked me up gently.

"Shh," he kissed my forehead and took me to the bathroom. Taking a warm cloth, he wiped me clean between my thighs, but I saw a raging problem he had of his own.

"Um," I blushed, not sure how to bring it up.

"Tonight, was about you, Angel. I know you aren't ready for this." Hades moved his member to make himself more comfortable. It was large. I had nothing to compare it to, but it was bigger than I thought one could be. Yeah, that was going to be a scary thing.

Hades carried me to the bed. Hades was so tall and muscular; I just couldn't handle how sweet he was taking care of me. God of the Underworld pampering a hopeless human. I internally swooned and melted into him. "I'm taking a shower; I'll be back. Try and sleep." Leaving a kiss on my forehead, I wrapped myself up in the blanket and waited, knowing I would not be going to sleep until he returned.

***

Waking up the following day, I kept hearing mumbling. It was growing louder and was starting to wake me up. I tried concentrating on the sound, but it was hard to make out until it came in loud and clear.

Ember!

I stuck my finger in my ear to shake it while Hades was lying next to me. He had no shirt on, and I was too nervous to check underneath. Too caught up looking at Hades' body, I forgot about all the mumbling.

The sheets were so low I could see the perfect V-line. My heart skipped a beat as I felt warm arms wrap around my waist. His abs flexed, only making me giddy.

"You know, it isn't polite to stare." Covering my face with my hands, I made a little squeal until he threw me back on the bed. His face went into my neck, and he planted warm, wet kisses. A little bite almost had me mewling. "Let's get you fed; I don't need you getting weak on me again." Hades climbed over me and got out of the bed. IN THE NUDE.

His glorious butt was on display, and I just got an eyeful! My virgin eyes!

I gasped loudly, picked up the pillow, and shoved my face in it. "You can't do that!" I yelled into it while I heard him laughing. Hades tried to come take the pillow, but I shook my head along with it. "Pants, pants!" I mumbled, and his laughter got louder.

"You will see it sooner or later," he chided as I heard him walk into the bathroom. With a click of the door, I jumped out of bed and got dressed quickly, making sure to put on a set of good underwear and pants. I can't make it so easy for him, I giggled as I forced a pair of skinny jeans on.

Putting on a pair of sandals and a mint-green shirt, I saw Blaze sleeping in the laundry basket with his tail smoking where his flame should be. That's going to make everything stink! "Blaze!" I sang, trying to wake him up, but he wouldn't budge. Picking him up, I cradled him to my chest until he started to stir. "Did you sleep well, my little flame?" I cooed as his eyes lit up.

Hopping on my shoulder, Blaze got comfortable and curled up in my neck. I left the closet, and Hades was standing in his black boxer briefs heading straight towards me after leaving the bathroom. I stopped and stared a bit too long, and his deep chuckle reverberated between my thighs. "I'm going to go brush my teeth!" I squeaked as I ran to the bathroom to shut the door. His laugh could be heard in the bathroom, and it made me smile that much more. Hades could be such a wonderfully happy person, and I was excited to see more of him as we grew closer.

Brushing my teeth, I felt a cramp coming from my stomach; it had me double over for a moment. I grunted as the pain subsided and continued to brush. Blaze poked my cheek with his little paw to question me. "I'm just hungry, fella. I'm used to eating bigger meals now."

Cleaning up, I headed back out of the bathroom for a waiting Hades to escort me to the dining room.

As we began eating, Hades started talking business with Ares and Vulcan; since Hades hasn't been tending to his duties, he had to appoint several demons to do some of his jobs. Two were taking his place, one that would handle Tartarus and the other would be at the Fields. I couldn't imagine working in Tartarus, but Hades said it wasn't where he needed to go often unless to blow off steam or punish someone who hurt me. My eyes grew wide, and he grabbed my hand to kiss it.

"No one will ever touch what is mine, may it be before me or right now, never." I hid the blush by turning away, but he grabbed my waist to have me turn and kiss him. "Stop, people are staring!" Several male demons looked on with amusement until Hades sent off a glare that could set them ablaze.

He continued talking in some sort of code; let's face it, I'm not stupid. Something was going on in some Celestial Kingdom, and people were missing. I didn't know who or why but I'm sure I could figure it out when I give him an excellent pouty lip later.

Picking up my fork to shove another mouthful of eggs in my mouth, I felt the awful cramp again. It singed my insides as I started to rub my stomach feverishly. Trying to be discreet, I put the eggs in my mouth and concentrated on the intricate pattern on the plate. A demon walked up to fill my glass with more apple juice and stopped abruptly and didn't move. I looked at him, knowing this might be a mistake because Hades does not like demons looking at me. I braced for him to burst into flames.

Hades, however, was still talking, but the demon's eyes met mine. Fire blazed in them as he dropped the glass pitcher to the floor. I stood up to back away, bumping into Hades. "What's the meaning of this?" Hades barked at the demon.

"M-my Lord!" he bowed, but sweat was beading between his horns. He took a knee and placed his head on the floor.

"Spit it out!" Hades snapped again as I put my hand on his shoulder.

"I smell fresh blood, My Lord." Hades' head whipped to me and started lifting my shirt for signs of damage.

"Stop!" I yelled, frustrated, but my stomach began to hurt again. Hades was becoming furious as he flung his chair back with a loud crash to the ground.

"You are bleeding!" he spoke, concerned as I shook my head.

"N-no," I faltered. "I didn't cut myself." Hades continued to look at my hands and arms when the worst thing possible popped into my head.

"Oh, dear," I whispered as I bolted from the room. Hades was yelling for me to come back, and dishes were breaking on the floor. I wouldn't be surprised if the whole table was broken right now. All I could think about was getting out of there and hiding in the nearest bathroom.

Hades

"Jillian! Come back!" I yelled too harshly. I took our plates and threw them on the floor. Fuck, seeing her back running away from me hit me like an arrow to the heart. Why the hell was she running? I gripped the table and threw one more pitcher of apple juice on the floor, something that was Jillian's favorite but fuck she isn't here to drink it!

Ares had his hands back away from the table, mouth agape with a large amount of food. The god acted like he is a damn barbarian. He should be off parading around some war than keep his sorry ass here. Vulcan had his elbow propping up his head while snickering.

"Care to enlighten us?"

Vulcan sat up and pushed his chair away from the table. "Sure! But you aren't gonna like it." Vulcan walked out of the room and grabbed the first aid kit in the kitchen he had installed for Jillian. I would have never thought of it if it weren't for him. "You are going to need this." He pushed it to my chest.

"The fuck is wrong with her, you prick?" I growled.

"Something all human women do; they menstruate." I lifted my eyebrow and looked at the contents of the first aid kit.

"Why would she be embarrassed about that?" I asked softly as I picked up some of the items in the kit.

"It's probably her first one. If you don't have enough fat or meat on your bones, a women's body wouldn't be able to support a child anyway. Jillian has been skinny for so long, and now that she is getting her figure and being healthy, her body decided to 'woman up'." I rubbed my hand through my hair and grunted. I should go torture Teddy Johnson some more.

Stupid fucker.

"You don't think I have to explain…" I waved my hand around the items in the box while Vulcan shook his head.

"She grew up around a bunch of women; I'm sure she picked up on it or was explained to her. She isn't dumb, Hades. She is just embarrassed." Vulcan went back to his seat while Ares was dry-heaving, listening to our conversation.

"That's so gross!" he whined. "I can't even look at my bloody steak right now!" Vulcan slapped him upside the head giving him a few choice words. "It's normal, nimrod. Now you get to go do a chocolate and ice cream run after breakfast." Ares whined again, but Vulcan gave him a dirty look.

I closed the box, waved for a few demons to pick up the mess, and then ordered them to leave the palace. Demons have a high sense of smell, and most of my demons crave blood because it usually leads to death. It's like a damn homing beacon for sharks. Once the demons leave, I'll keep her locked up in the palace with us or maybe take her to Earth for a short vacation.

Chapter 26

Jillian

My breaths were quick as I slid my bare feet on the marbled floor and reached for the door of the bedroom. I was running so fast I lost my sandals somewhere between Hades' portrait and the dancing witch sculpture around the corner. Poor Blaze was hanging on for dear life on my hair, growling at me for trying to run away from my little protector.

Pouncing into the bedroom, I untangled him from my hair and placed him on the bed. The chattering and hisses leave his lips were adorable, but I had more significant problems to worry about.

Hearing his soft flutters trying to catch up, I slammed the door shut and locked it. Not it could keep the God of the Underworld out. Another cramp ripped through me, and I pulled all the drawers out, hoping to find what I needed. Why Hades would keep some sort of pad in here was beyond me, but a girl could dream, and I mean, really dream.

Nothing, absolutely nothing. I ran to sit on my royal throne only to groan, realizing my once perfect pair of jeans was probably ruined.

Growling and pulling at my hair, frustrated, I slapped my hands on my thighs. How could I not have known this was going to happen? How many years has it been since I learned about this situation that happens to all women?

"You know, she is of that age where she should be getting her period," one of the long-standing strippers spoke as she powdered her nose. "Do you think she's been told about the birds and the bees?" Anna stood up and started to walk towards me. I had just finished a load of laundry that held all of their outfits, and my job was to hang them up, making sure they were wrinkle-free and ready for wear.

"Well, ask her," Jane spoke. "I'm sure she knows what the act is but isn't sure what all comes with it. She's only what 11 and workin' here?"

"I'm 16," I whispered. I pulled down my sleeves to cover up the bruises. I knew the other strippers talked about me. I help them when they first arrive, but I'm gone to help the newer ones get settled once they understand their role. I knew what made Teddy Johnson tick, and if they wanted to not get beat, they would listen to my words.

Several of the strippers grew accustomed to the job and started to enjoy it, supposedly. Really, they were scared for their lives and what would happen next. If they made enough money, then they wouldn't be sold; they would collect the money and give it all to Teddy.

"Sixteen? Child, you are so young looking." Anna came in and pulled my hair back. "Thank you for the clothes." She looked at me in pity. "You looked out for me when I first came here three years ago, and I never really thanked you. I've been too scared to talk to you, worried you or I would get beaten again." Anna's eyes watered. "But I want you to know, if you have questions about things, things a mother would tell you, I am happy to help." I nodded.

"I know you understand this place and what it's for, but do you understand how a woman's body works?" I shrugged my shoulders. I had seen some women carrying small tube like products but never really asked. Thought it was for aftercare from having to deal with customers.

"That women are for men's pleasure; that's all I really know," I whispered. Jane's eyes watered as she watched Anna interact with me.

"Not all men are like that, I assure you. This is just a bad place with a bunch of evil people," she whispered.

So, Anna told me the birds and the bees and how a man should treat a woman. We sat in the chair talking until the club opened, and once the cage doors creaked, Teddy Johnson glared daggers at Anna. The rest of the strippers stood in fear as he walked in, holding the cane he used to beat me with. "Enjoy your talk?" he rasped. "Jillian won't be able to experience any of that because she will be long dead before I let it happen. Now get out there."

That night I scrubbed the bathroom floors at the club with a toothbrush while Anna was sold off to the highest bidder.

I groaned again, wondering where Anna could have gone. It was nice to have a friend, even if it was for a good hour. She taught me enough to help me, but she also told me what to fear the most and put even more fear in my heart.

Gentle knocks were at the door while I continued to sit on the toilet. Groaning, I put my face in my hands. "Go away!" I pleaded, but the knocks only grew louder.

"Please, angel, come on, please. I can help," he said calmly.

"No, it's embarrassing. Please just let me be." My heart began to ache that didn't feel like my own. Rubbing my chest to relieve the pain, it didn't stop. "Hades? My chest hurts."

"You feel me; you feel our bond and how I'm worried about you. Now, can I come in?" I didn't want to let him; this was such an intimate thing. Men aren't supposed to be comfortable with this, right? Not answering, I heard the door unlock, and it crept open, and I saw a sheepish-looking Hades close the door behind him.

I hid my face with my hands and held my thighs tight; wanting to curl up in a ball, I let out a small whimper. This is racking up to be the most embarrassing moment of my life. Hades knelt down and tried to pull my hands away, but I wouldn't let him. Pulling my hands back, he let out a chuckle.

"Angel, it's completely normal. Why are you so embarrassed? We knew you were getting healthy, and this might happen. Come on, let me help." I sniffed and let my hands drop to my lap.

"Let me take care of you, please?" I nodded my head silently while he took the bottom half of my clothes and left the room. I sat here, bottom half-naked, until he returned with some of his joggers and a fresh pair of black undies. Leaving the box he brought in on my lap, he kissed my forehead and left the room.

I think I just swooned.

***

Hades carried me into the living room next to the office he works in. The couch was massive and had a huge flat-screen TV that was loaded with tons of movie channels. I couldn't understand how to work the remote. I let Ares take over most of the time, and we would watch the action and war movies; I didn't mind it too much.

Ares would be so intense as he would watch them; watching blood spatter on the camera lens was almost comical as Ares' smile would creep up his cheeks.

When Hades was with me, he would lay on the couch and spoon me from behind and have his arm draped over me while we watched random shows. Hades asked what I would like to watch, and the only thing I could say was "something happy" or "something funny." He always delivered and would bury his nose into my shoulder and sleep.

I never thought gods would sleep, I thought of them as all-powerful beings, but it looks like everyone needs their rest. The way Vulcan would talk, Hades barely rested, and since I've been here, he has had the most sleep in a long time. I was happy that I could help him in some way, even though it was something small.

I had finished off a small tub of Ben and Jerry's ice cream, triple the chocolate with a fudge core, and I was stuffed. Who knew eating your way through some hormonal embarrassment from your soulmate would make you feel so much better?

We were in our usual position, but this time Hades and his hand was at the top of the joggers, palm down at the seam. They were loose and easy for him to get his hand into. All he did was lay the palm of his hand on my stomach, and I felt heat radiate from his palm. I instantly melted and let out a slight hum of enjoyment.

"Vulcan said that might make you feel better." He kissed the back of my head.

"Mhmm, it really does. You can leave it there as long as you want." I laughed as he stopped on a movie channel. It was called 'Hercules', and the character Hades was grey and had bright blue hair. I started laughing, and Hades was growling behind me.

"Who comes up with this shit?" he scoffed as he turned the channel. "Of all things, why would I have blue hair? It's insulting!" I continued to laugh as I gripped his hand on my stomach.

"You think that's just hilarious, don't you?" he joked as he turned my face. Tears were in my eyes at the harmonious laughter I was emitting. Hades showed his pearly whites and leaned in to kiss me, but there was a ring at the door.

The servants had been ordered away, so it was only Hades, Vulcan, and Ares. I couldn't see Ares opening the door, and I heard Vulcan calling for Hades. Hades growled in his throat and held onto my arm tightly. "Don't leave Blaze or Cerberus, do you understand?" I nodded worriedly as I watched him stand from the couch and walk out the entryway. Turning back, "If Cerberus tries to lead you somewhere, you go."

"What's going on-?" Hades cut me off.

"I mean it. It's to keep you safe." His voice was low as I heard his bare feet smack across the floor. Cerberus growled, hopped on the couch, and snuggled next to me while Blaze started chittering at Cerberus to let go. I continued to pet the both of them to sate their inner beasts while I waited.

I would just stay here on the couch and do what I was told, but the curiosity was getting the best of me. "Come on, let's see what they are doing." Cerberus whined and pulled on my shirt. "I won't be seen, come on." Cerberus hopped off the couch as I stood in the entryway to the living room. I had one hall to walk down, and I would be able to peer behind a giant statue of Aphrodite. It would be the perfect place not to be seen.

Tiptoeing and grabbing my stomach from another cramp, I made my way down the dark hall. I heard talking, some shouting as I reached the doorway before the statue. Before I had my chance to get closer, I realized I didn't need to because now they were full-blown yelling at one another.

"She is to come with us; she cannot stay here," the angel boomed. He was dressed in white robes, chest shining in pure porcelain skin. I recognized him from the club; he was the one that tried to buy me! I squatted down lower to the ground because my legs began to shake. Cerberus sat in front of me, so if the angel-like creatures looked over, they would see him instead.

"Jillian is my damn mate; of course, she can stay! She's human but she's mine!"

"Rules are rules. Hades, only gods and spirits can remain in the Underworld, and she is obviously living. Hand her over, and she can stay in the Celestial Kingdom while we wait for trial."

"Never," Hades growled, and wisps of black smoke began to travel from his body. Cerberus barked and pushed me to the floor. Nodding his head in the direction we came; I ran down the hall.

"She is here; go search for her!" I heard the familiar voice say. Running back to the living room, Cerberus grew to the size of a large Clydesdale horse. Jumping in front of me, he knelt for me to climb. Blaze tried to help by pushing on my rear, but his small stature couldn't do anything. Holding onto Cerberus' collar, he let out a large howl as he reached the far west end of the palace.

The large windows I had looked out over the pool just a week ago stood staring down at Cerberus as he ran towards it. "Cerberus!" I shouted, but he continued on, huffing while gripping the floor with his padded paws. In one swift movement, he jumped and crashed through the window.

Thousands of shards of glass rained down on us. I could feel it nick parts of my skin as he leapt one more time to jump over the massive pool. It proved to be no obstacle for Cerberus. The men or angels were shouting behind us as we ran. I dared not look back because falling off was not an option. My legs gripped Cerberus tighter as I saw dozens more of Blaze's kind emerge from the forest.

Cerberus grunted in disgust but continued ripping the soil under his claws.

At least fifty Phantomtails were flying towards us. They came in an array of colors, blues, purples, yellows, and reds, and they talked to Blaze. Blaze flew ahead of them all and in front of Cerberus, who continued to chatter in his ear. In a language I didn't know, they ran faster and in a slightly southwest position. The sun was still high in the sky as we ran, but it became darker as we went deeper into the forest. The trees lost their green, the dirt became black, and ash had begun to rain down on us.

Tartarus? I wondered, but then I remembered it was far beneath Hades' Underworld. For hours we traveled until no sunlight was left, the moon had not risen, and there were no signs of stopping. The Phantom tails begun to land on Cerberus and chatting to him to get him to go to a slow canter and eventually stop at a large lake.

With no moon, it looked black as tar, and even though my thirst for water had started not long ago, I dared not take a drink. Sliding off Cerberus, I got a better look at my surroundings. Rocky cliffs were to the right of us, just where the lake meets the sand; it would be an excellent place to stay for the night. The trees were straight out of a horror movie. Finger-like branches blew in the wind, and I couldn't help but squeeze my arms to my body.

The large crowd of Phantomtails gathered around and started pulling at my joggers to walk there. Looking at Cerberus for confirmation, he shrank back down to the size I was used to and pushed me along with one of his heads.

This was getting stranger by the minute. I never knew the Underworld could be so large and vast. Not once did I see another person, demon, or soul encounter us along the way. My heart started to ache to be away from Hades. It had only been this morning since I saw him, but my worry was only growing that he hadn't come to find me.

Who do you pray to when you are mated to a god? Zeus wanted me to come to the Celestial Kingdom, so I doubt he would be the right choice. What about Selene? The mating god? Remembering her glorious statue in the garden with a wolf beneath her fingertips gave me a glimpse of hope.

I'll take what I can get. Once we were settled, I could pray for guidance on what to do next.

Chapter 27

Hades

"What do the fuck do you mean Jillian can't stay here?" I growled out. I could feel my black knit shirt ripping from my slow, heavy breathing. After sitting behind Jillian, my joggers weren't much better for wear, and her delicious ass kept rubbing up against it. She was innocent to the whole thing but damn, she gave me blue balls like a mother fucker.

"I mean what I said," Malachi spoke cockily. "Part of the Underworld guidelines is that you bring no living soul here into your domain. You are breaking code written by the gods, you being one of them. You need to put her back on Earth or let her come with me, and I can bring her to Zeus. We can figure a way to keep her safe until your trial." Malachi looked at his fingers as he picked the dirt underneath.

"Shit," Vulcan whispered as Ares walked up. I heard the nails of Cerberus tap across the floor behind me. Jillian is starting to become bratty if she thinks she can come in here. "Cerberus, get her out of here. Go to the Darkened Forest and keep running. I'll find you when I'm done. Protect her." Cerberus didn't respond, but I heard him pulling at Jillian's shirt, who now was running down the hallway.

Now that Jillian was going to be safe, I could unleash something more lethal. "Tell me why you are here, Malachi. I'm not in the mood for games." Angels spread about the room, some ducking into nearby hallways to look for Jillian. "Run, Cerberus." I beckoned him, and a loud howl left his jaws. No angel would be able to keep up with his proper complete form.

"I don't know what you could possibly mean, Hades," Malachi mocked. "I'm just doing my duty as an angel and making sure laws are abided by."

"That law hasn't been enforced in thousands of years, and you know it." I stepped forward, leaking my wisping smoke on the floor. "If we summoned Zeus right now, what would he tell me about this little act you are doing?"

As much as Zeus got on my last cranial nerve, he was an overall good god. He was just and did things fairly amongst us. A god-whore he was but weren't the lot of them? He was younger than me and took place in the sky that I could have quickly taken, but I preferred to be away from the chaos. Zeus took pride in his work. If Zeus knew that Jillian, a human, was my mate, he would have never summoned Malachi to take away something so precious. Especially when he had not been granted one.

"Go ahead." Malachi crossed his arms. "I have time." I felt Malachi's heart-pounding; for being such a lowly enforcer angel, he certainly was putting up a fight. Vulcan, who could sense it as well, smirked as he willed a glass of scotch from his hand.

"Drink?" Vulcan offered. Malachi looked between the drink and me, warily weighing his options, when we heard a loud crash at the far end of the palace. I chuckled darkly and grabbed Malachi by the neck with one quick swipe. Other angels enter the room in a rush as they watch me slowly choke the life out of Malachi. His hands gripped my clawed hands as the nails pierced his neck.

"Lord Hades, please!" the angels pleaded. Many went on their knees as their wings touched the floor. A sign of total respect to a god. Malachi's light that embodied him begun to fade, now looking nothing more than mortal.

"Please, my Lord!" an angel known as Thebes spoke. This had always been a follower, a sheep that would follow a wolf into its den.

"Speak, Thebes, because Malachi has a short time to live." My smoke started to go through his nostrils, stealing the light inside of him.

"Malachi told us to come here, that Jillian was in horrible danger being in the Underworld. She would lose her life here as the fumes of Tartarus slowly suffocate her until she would no longer wake from sleep."

Ares snorted in laughter while Vulcan elbowed him in the ribs. I sighed heavily. "And you believed the shit that he spewed?"

All the angels nodded their heads. "Malachi said you wouldn't understand because you never have humans come down here. A god that doesn't spend much time with human mortals would have surely forgotten the harmful effects it could have for anyone that visited." Thebes looked around as the other angels nodded. "Plus, it is in the great law book."

Sure, it was in the Law Book of the Gods. I put it there to keep all those damn heroes out. Hercules is one of them, the cocky bastard. Give him a bit of strength, and he thinks he owns both heaven and hell. Deities couldn't even step foot down here; I'd burn them alive and feed their carcass to Cerberus if I wanted. I was the enforcer; I was there when it was written. If Malachi had read the fine print beneath it, he would realize I could have anyone down here that I wanted. No other god had dominion over overruling or carrying out such discrepancies over my world.

I gave an evil grin and threw my head back and laughed. It was not a laugh that I would have with my mate, but a laugh of the ridiculousness that Malachi would instill in a bunch of weak, pathetic angels. "I guess the rumors are true; angels will believe in anything some higher being will spout!" Turning to Vulcan, I said, "I guess I need to stop calling Jillian my angel; it is, in fact, an insult!"

Tossing Malachi to the floor, he sputtered as the outside light covering his celestial body began to glow again. As he rubbed his neck, I waved my hand, setting fire to his wings, turning them to a charred black. His screams only fuel my fire of revenge for him, especially for looking at my sweet mate the night of the auction. I wanted him to remember never to look or touch what was mine.

Other angels go to his aid, but I waved my hand for them to fall on the floor like a bunch of bowling pins. Once the fire had consumed, which was rather quickly, he was left charred wings of black soot. It would take time for him to heal from this one. My darkness beckoned me to finish him off, but there is a chance he may know where Selene and Hecate are. Call it intuition, but I can't rule out all options.

Summoning my torture demons from beneath the palace, they immediately came forth. Their bodies were full of black tar, hunched shoulders, and two large ram horns on either side of their heads. Malachi continued to wallow in pain as the other angels sat in shock.

"Take Malachi, put him in some…comfortable quarters," I spoke lowly.

The torture demons bowed as each one grabbed a limb, tugging and pulling at his wings all the while. "Hades! You will regret this! You are making a mistake!" I hummed while rubbing my thumb to my lips.

"I'm sure I am," I whispered, be he heard me. "Ares? Ready to have some fun?"

"With pleasure." He rubbed his hands together.

✷✷✷

We traveled down to the deepest part of the dungeon. Down deeper in the cold, wet walls, we found Malachi chained and defeated. His legs were spread as his wings drooped. Malachi's fellow angels were sent back with a message of staying the fuck away from me and my mate, or inevitable repercussions will be handled forthwith. They will learn from their grave mistake of trusting in an old senile angel.

"I've got some questions, Malachi, and I need them answered swiftly. Otherwise,…" Ares stood tall with a metal ball with spikes on a chain. His beefy, macho self-stood tall. If I didn't know any better, you would have thought he was on steroids, but no, it was all him. Probably had a small dick too.

"You get the idea; he's become quite a big help around here." Dragging the chair in front of the bastard, I turned it so I was straddling it. My arms were resting on the chair while I tilted my head innocently. Learning a few tricks from Jillian might pay off.

"So, why do you really want my mate?"

Malachi scoffed and looked away. A few feathers fell to the ground. "I ain't telling you shit," he spat at the dirt before me. Ares came over and slammed his mallet on one of the damaged wings with a light gruff. Malachi screamed while I willed myself a latte and sipped it like some elegant aristocrat.

"It's starting to smell like fried chicken in here, isn't it, Ares?" I cleared my throat as my miniature dragon, Hellbones, slithered to me up. Ares was in his battle mode, so getting a response from him was slim. Hellbones was the runt of his nest, and I didn't have the heart to send him away and be tormented by his siblings. The rest flew to an island in the land called Bergarian. The island was home to all dragons, but they only nested in the Underworld.

"What do you think, Hellbones? Does he smell like chicken?" He licked his lips as he went to smell Malachi. His tiny teeth were razor-sharp, but his mouth wasn't big enough to swallow him whole. He would have to eat him piece by piece. Malachi backed away as his bleeding wing shuttered.

"No wonder everyone hates you. You're a sadistic fuck," he rasped.

"Only to those that deserve it." I placed my latte on the saucer and willed it away. "Now, give me answers."

Malachi looked to Hellbones and back to me. "I don't think you want to do that." My dragon licked his lips. "In fact, I think you should let me go." Raising my eyebrows, I paced around him while Hellbones waited for the snap of my fingers. One snap was all it takes.

"And why is that?"

"Because Persephone might be sore with you if you end up hurting her mate. You do know she can feel every bit of pain you inflict on me, right?" I twisted my fist and heard the knuckles pop. Even though the infatuation I had with Persephone was not love, I didn't want her to suffer more than she did. Knowing what it is to have a mate and that power of emotion and attraction towards another soul made me guilty for holding her so long. However, I was intrigued at him still using his own mate as an excuse.

"Rumor has it, you aren't even Persephone's mate at all," I taunted as I bent down to remove a feather that landed on his head. "That it is, in fact, Gabriel." Malachi's eyes dilated, but the rest of his body showed no signs of faltering. "Now, why would that be?"

"What the hell are you talking about? Persephone is my mate! I came to hell while you threw your hissy fit and took her with me. You are out of your damn mind!" Malachi's teeth gritted. Hellbones started to get antsy.

"Hades, I need you to feel," Vulcan spoke as he put his hand on my shoulder. I had been so caught up in my interrogation that I didn't feel his presence.

"All I feel is anger and rage, Vulcan I suggest you-"

"Feel with your heart, Hades," I growled out and ripped my shoulder from his grasp. I was about to slice up Malachi's torso when I felt it. The pang of worry. This worry wasn't of my own but of someone else's, Jillian.

Fuck. I got so caught up in rage that I forgot. "It's passed sundown; the threat is gone. You need to get Jillian wherever they may be. They could still be running." I growled as I pushed the chair away.

"Give him something to think about, Ares, and call it a night." Ares cracked his knuckles as I ran up the stairs.

Jillian

My bare feet felt the old broken leaves. They crunched softly until I hit the smooth sand. One hand was on Cerberus, and the Phantomtails tails glowed for a perfect path for us to follow. The cave was dry and dark, but it was engulfed in the light once our friends flew in. Tiny water drops would fall to the rocks, but it wasn't wet enough to be uncomfortable.

Starting a fire would be nice, but the nagging in the back of my head said it might not be wise. I wasn't sure what animals were out in this wilderness, and Cerberus was huffing out all the lights of the Phantomtails. They chittered at him, almost arguing that it was okay, but he wasn't convinced.

I never thought the Underworld would be cold. The talk of fire, brimstone, lakes of fire, and overall heat that tried to consume your sins is what I thought it to feel like. Here, it was cold and lonely, even with all my furry friends around.

Sensing my distress, Cerberus came and curled around me. He was in a larger form as I leaned my head on his torso while he laid down. His face wrapped around me, and his tail tucked my legs into the fetal position. The rest of the Phantomtails came to sit on me like a blanket, covering me with their balls of warmth. It worked; it kept me warm, but my heart felt empty with Hades not around.

I hadn't slept without him since he charged into my life. Anytime I did sleep, I was haunted by nightmares. I forced my eyes to stay open as I remembered the promise to myself outside the cave. To pray, pray to a god for help.

I had prayed long before I came to the Underworld; I prayed for salvation, a hero to save me from the nightmare I lived. It never came, and a nagging feeling always told me that I should have never been there in the first place.

Closing my eyes, I put my cold hands together like I had seen the little children do on television when their parents put them to bed. In my mind, I called out to the one person I didn't know much about, the Goddess Selene, the goddess of mates. If she was listening, surely she would help, right?

I called out to her, begging for Hades to be all right. My worried soul was restless as I prayed, begging for him to be safe from any harm. He may be a god, the God of the Underworld, but sometimes even a god needs saving.

As I continued to pray, my thoughts started to haze, and my consciousness faded out.

Chapter 28

Jillian

I was nestled softly, feeling warmth instead of the cold that I fell asleep in. The Phantomtails had either lit their tails back to life while Cerberus was sleeping, or Hades had found me, and I was at home in bed. I preferred the latter but I'm not that lucky.

Opening my eyes, I was in a small log cabin with a fire roaring at the hearth. I was sleeping in a pile of hay with large blankets on top; it was literally a nest I was sleeping on, and I didn't mind. The smell of the fresh forest floated in through the window, and small chatting could be heard outside the large wooden door. The area around me felt so real, I wondered if this was a dream at all.

"It's a dream," a voice spoke with a hint of a melody in her voice. It was quiet, barely audible but I noticed it. Turning my head to my right, next to the fire was a woman with a beautiful face. Her bright blue eyes shone like the moon. Her glowing hand came from the rags she wore. The hood covered most of her dirtied face as she touched my hand.

Speechless, I let her touch me as she pulled me from the nest-like bed. "We don't have much time," she whispered. "Just know your mate is just fine," she smiled.

"S-Selene? The Goddess Selene?" I tried to kneel in front of her, but she just made a little laugh.

"No, child no need for that." The other hand appeared, now holding my palm close to her.

"I'm happy that Hades finally woke up and claimed you. I was getting worried." Confused I sat on my knees to kneel at her to listen. "I don't have much time, I've been captured, and I cannot match souls, and if I don't find my way out quickly, I may not be able to reverse what Malachi is planning to do."

"Malachi? Who is Malachi?" I whispered. The whispers became yells and cheers outside as she gripped me tighter. "He has us both, Hecate and I, but I fear he is working for another."

"Another? Who is the other person?" The scene around us started to blur and the hard thuds at the door became louder.

"Ember!" Selene grabbed me harshly and had me investigate her blue spheres. "Find the Sphere of Souls," she rushed, panicking. "It is at your favorite spot as a child. Listen to the voice inside you!" Selene hissed. My head started pounding. *You are Ember!* Selene's voice faded as my body rocked back and forth. A loud whooshing howl swept the room, and the fire was extinguished. I was left in the dark with the moon rising above the window as the shaking became gentler. The bed faded along with the other furniture in the room. The chair where Selene sat left nothing but a crescent moon on her seat.

My eyes instantly closed and fluttered open again to be welcomed by the cold cave. Hades was knelt, stroking my shoulder gently. "There's my beautiful soul mate," he purred as I jumped from Cerberus. His clothes had changed, he had a dark pair of slacks on along with a crimson dress shirt that was rolled up his forearms. Black flame tattoos traveled up his arm while a few rings tinkled as Blaze sat with his tail bright.

"You're Okay!" I wrapped my arms around his neck as he chuckled into my hair.

"Of course, I'm Okay, I'm the King of the Underworld!" Hades pulled me back and swept a thumb pad over my cheek. "I'm sorry if that scared you, I wasn't expecting company. It's been taken care of, and you will not see them again." Hades smoothed out my hair as I held onto him tightly.

Hades had a been working tirelessly on that missing person report that Loukas kept bringing up this week. Now there wasn't one but two people, and with a dream I just had, at least I thought it was a dream, I knew that they were connected. I'm dealing with gods and goddesses; I'm sure some magic is coming into play here because I'm not just an ignorant human anymore.

"Selene and Hecate are the ones missing, aren't they?" I blurted at him as Hades eyes widened.

"How did you know those names?"

"I've read about Selene and the other gods in books while you work in your office. That's beside the point," I rushed while waving my hands about. "Selene visited me just now! I prayed for her to help you and she came to me in a dream!" I gushed. Even the rags couldn't disguise her beauty. I couldn't imagine Aphrodite could be more beautiful.

"W-what did she say? This is important, Jillian." Hades held onto my shoulders.

"First of all, my name isn't Jillian, it is Ember! That name I keep hearing from my dreams, it is my name!" My excitement woke up the Phantomtails that were all growling in annoyance while Cerberus stood up and shook them off.

Little chatters filled the room as Hades pulled me to his chest. "Ember," he whispered.

I felt a shiver run through me; it sounded right. This was my name. Jillian always felt foreign on my tongue but truly saying that Ember was my name felt good. It felt like home. Now that I knew it was my name, I wanted him to say it all the time. "Ember." He titled my head back and planted a kiss. "Forever my burning Ember."

✳✳✳

It took us just a blink of an eye to return to Hades' palace. Next time he should just blink me to the cave instead of making me ride Cerberus. No offence to my doggy friend but my riding a galloping canine while dealing with your lady time wasn't fun.

Ares and Vulcan joined us in the office as I spilled my guts about the dream I had. I spent more time describing her and how beautiful she was. Her blue moon eyes and light hair covered by nothing but rags were still stunning. Vulcan continued to smile as I spoke once she vanished a crescent moon was left on her seat.

"We need to find the Sphere of Souls, correct?" Vulcan interjected. "Not only that, Jillian-I mean Ember is the only one that can do that." My heart sank. How was I to remember my past when I couldn't even remember my name?

"It will be fine, Ember. One day at a time." Hades tucked my hair behind my ear as I sat on his lap. Pulling me to his chest, he had me listen to the steady beat of his heart. "It looks like Ember is more tangled up in this mess than we thought. Selene has her involvement in it and now I wonder if that is the reason Hecate wouldn't remove some of the spells cast on her. Hecate must have foreseen this and needed to buy time, but time for what?"

Ares had his dagger out, sharpening it on the couch. Every once in a while he would spit on the rock as he sharpened it more. Vulcan stood in deep thought how all these pieces of the puzzle were going to fit together.

"Who has a vendetta against you?" Vulcan finally broke the silence. Hades smirked while he chuckled.

"In my wild and free days, plenty. I've been quiet the past 1500 years, you know this." Vulcan hummed.

"Make a list, no matter how big or small. We can start there and go one by one. Loukas can visit them unannounced and see if we find anything. We aren't just dealing with Malachi, like you said, Ember. Someone is the head of the operation and Malachi was just stupid enough to go to the front lines."

Loukas walked in the room, popping a sandwich in his mouth. "What did I miss?" I waved at Loukas brightly who gave a gleaming smile in return as he sat down.

"Her name is no longer Jillian. Her true name is Ember." Hades growled. Loukas jumped back up from the couch.

"What! You remember!" Loukas came running up to the desk to congratulate me, but Hades let out a loud growl.

"Know your place, demon."

I tapped Hades on his hand. "He's just excited like me, you need to lighten up a little." I kissed his cheek, but he still wouldn't let me get down from his lap. Grunting I folded my arms while pouting.

"Not going to work." Hades pulled my lip with his and I flushed in embarrassment.

"Stooop," I whined. "Demons and gods are watching," I said whispering in his ear. Vulcan chuckled while Loukas sulked back to the couch. Getting ready to explain to Loukas how I figured out my name, a large knock came to the door. Ares stood up, baring his large chest, and holding his dagger he was playing with.

"Enter," Hades spoke loudly, and the pit of my stomach dropped.

Creatures, no, monsters walked through the double doors. They needed both doors wide open for their massive bodies. Their red skin had boils and blisters while some oozed a terrible stench. Black tar covered their backs and it dripped onto the floor, only to disappear after they had moved a few steps away. Large fangs protruded from their bottom jaw, curling upward just enough to touch their high cheekbones. The black hair on their heads ranged from short to long and their horns were large, almost too big for their heads.

I literally stopped breathing in fear.

Hades

Ember was paralyzed in fear so much that she stopped breathing. My torture demons stood up straighter from their natural hunch over forms and grinned ear to ear. "She is impressed," one of them spoke as he flipped his hair back.

"Yes, look how repulsed she is of our form."

Rolling my eyes, I slammed my hand on the desk. "Go to your human forms, NOW!" The demons shook as their backs and bones began to break. Ember shivered into my hold as she threw her face into my neck.

"W-what are those things?" Her voice shook so much I barely understood her.

"Demons who manage the dungeons here in the palace. I have them here for special treatment of gods and deities if they piss me off." Ember's hand clutched my shirt as I cupped her face. "They won't look like that anymore around you."

"We impressed her so much she is shaking," one of them whispered as they gave each other high-fives.

Ares grunted as he went to the three demons and punched them each square in the jaw respectively. "And everyone thinks I'm the dense one around here," he spat as he turned to sit on the couch.

The demons sat up straight, placing their jaws back in place. "The Queen of the Underworld is not who you should be scaring half to death. It is my damn prisoners. She is not of this world," I yelled. "Do not make the same mistake again."

The demons trembled at my voice as they stood in their human forms. They now looked like average human men, not at all appealing to even the most beautiful of women of Earth. "We apologize for our insolence," the leader said as they all put their foreheads to the ground. "We did not understand. We are sorry if we caused too much disturbance to our future queen."

Ember peeked out of my neck to see the three humans. She dared not let go but was able to look at them in the eyes. "Now speak why you are here. You are tracking tar on my floors."

They all stood up with heads bowed. "We are sorry, our Lord of Darkness." Shit, when they pull that line it means they did a major fuck up.

"What. Is. It." I gritted my teeth while pulling Ember back into my hold.

"M-Malachi has escaped." The whole room went into slow motion as Ares and Vulcan stood to rush towards me, but it was too late. With one wave of my hand the demon in front of me burst into ash while the other two began to hug each other for a lifeline.

"Explain," I growled. Vulcan and Ares stood beside me as I held Ember's head to my neck. I didn't need her witnessing any of the destruction I was about to unfold.

"He just vanished! After you had brought our queen back, we searched the entire palace and there was left over magic residue in the cell. It was foreign and powerful, a type we have not been trained on. It was that of a god, a god must have set them free!" A deep rumble went through my chest as Ember held me tighter.

"Hades?" Her voice rode my anger like a gentle song.

"I'm sending you to our room. Do not leave until I come to fetch you." Ember opened her mouth to protest but she was gone in an instant. Cerberus was already there watching her, and Blaze wouldn't be far. They were both more trustworthy than anyone else.

"I'll go guard her room," Loukas announced as he headed to the door.

"No, you stay," I demanded as he stopped his skip to the door. Damn idiot.

"There is something else you are not telling me." Standing up from the desk, I let my fingertips trail the hard wood. Passing the lamp, I swatted it to the floor as my Italian leather shoes clicked on the floor towards them. Both dropped to their knees, shaking. "What. Is. It? What is it that still has your disgusting hearts still beating so rapidly?" Licking my lips, I grabbed the one on the left by the collar, pulling him up with one arm above my head. His dark eyes looked down as his hands tried to scrape away the rings that dug into his throat.

"My Lord," the other one pleaded. "Malachi, he took, he took the Helm."

Chapter 29

Ember

One moment I was sitting in Hades' lap, and the next, I plopped down right in the middle of our bed. Shaking my head and getting over the dizziness, I tried to recount what had happened. Was that a dream? Did someone just puff into nothing but ash and dust? A gasp left my lips as I covered my mouth with both my hands.

It DID happen! Hades just waved his hand, then "poof!" That horrible beast was gone! Granted, he *was* a terrible beast, but they did look like an average human at that moment.

What the heck is going on with all this magic! Snickerdoodles, this was getting exhausting. I needed a break, a nap, or something, but I seriously doubt I would get any rest if I tried to sleep.

The door burst open, and Cerberus came trotting in with Blaze on top of his head. I perked my head up to watch the two interact, but from the looks of it, Cerberus was annoyed. "*Stupid damn, hamster,*" I heard as Cerberus walked by. My eyes widened, swearing I could hear that he was talking.

"*Well, I don't like you either. The whole three heads thing doesn't even make sense. You aren't even a dog.*"

I gasped loudly as I pounded my fists into the mattress. "YOU BOTH TALK?!" I squealed as they watched me. Both tilted their heads to the sides like little puppies. "Say something," I begged as I crawled to the edge of the bed. Both were staring; Blaze's mouth hung open.

"Did she say she could hear us?" Blaze's voice was unbearably cute. It was squeaky but not too terribly high since he was a boy. His tail flickered a bit of smoke from his tail as I started blinking my eyes rapidly.

"Say my name," I whispered.

Cerberus didn't even open his maw, and I heard it as clear as day in my mind. *"Ember? I hope her name doesn't change again. This is all getting confusing."*

I screamed out loud and jumped on the bed. Pointing down at them. "You both can talk! I can hear you in my head! Snakes! This is insane!!!"

"You can really hear us? How can she do that?" Cerberus snorted as Blaze jumped off him and crawled to the bed.

"I don't see why she can; she's human," Blaze huffed. Blaze crawled up my arm to sniff in my ear. *"The only way she could hear me is if she was an animal. What about you, Cerberus?"*

"Hades is the only one that can hear me. Then again, I've never left the Underworld or talked to any other humans."

Blaze hummed while my mouth hung open. "I can talk to animals. Do you know what that means?" A grin popped on my face as I did a little squeal and butt wiggle on the bed. *"I must be a Disney princess,"* I whispered. Watching TV has paid off; I knew what I was now.

Cerberus growled, *"No, you are not; those movies aren't real. I'd like to know why you can hear us."*

"I think my memory is slowly coming back. I hope once I remember where I came from, it will give some answers. Maybe that will tell me why I can hear you."

Blaze scratched his fur while staring at my head. His nose started to twitch as he neared my head again. Licking my ear and burying his nose inside, I squealed in laughter. "Stop, stop! What are you doing?"

"Just... just trying to test a theory. It's too faint to be sure, but there might be something more to you. Just keep resting like you've been doing. I knew when I sensed you, you were special. Just didn't know what," Blaze mused.

"Special?" I questioned.

"Yeah, some Phantomtails like me get hooked on certain animals and people for some reason or another, and I got hooked on you. It is like a deeper connection we are supposed to figure out. You are a puzzle, and I need to figure you out.

Until then, you are stuck with me." Blaze puffed out his chest while Cerberus huffed.

"*Then you will go back, right? Wherever you came from once you figure it out?*" Cerberus popped his head up, hopefully.

I pushed Cerberus in the shoulder. "That's mean." I pointed my finger at him.

"*I just want you back to myself, and I don't need some fire hamster taking away all my scratches.*" Cerberus sat back on his butt.

"*I'm a Phantomtail, not a damn hamster! I will also stay as long as I want, you mutant dog!*" Blaze hissed.

Before they could start their fighting again, I silenced them quickly. "So, since I can hear you both, want to tell me what is going on in the other room? Hades kicked me out, and I landed in here," I huffed, crossing my arms. "He's never kicked me out before. He usually lets me stay on his lap and... -" Cerberus nudged my hand with his nose.

"*Hades just popped off one of his demons. He didn't want you to watch anything more. You were scared stiff in there.*" Cerberus licked my hand for me to scratch his head.

I gasped. "The demon really is gone? Dead? Where does he go?"

Cerberus sat back down on his hindquarters and scratched one of his three sets of ears. "*The demon will be put back into the demon soul pool. Hades will revive him once he gets over his anger with him. If he's super pissed, they will be cast out and go live in the River of Styx.*"

I gulped. "Does he do stuff like that a lot? Wave his hand and 'poof' they are gone?" Cerberus shook his fur.

"*I'm sorry, what?*" he acted innocent.

"I said-" Before I could grab Cerberus' collar, a warm hand engulfed my wrists. Hades was back.

Cerberus took this as his cue to leave, and Blazed followed by blowing me a kiss with his tail. "Are you all right?" Hades pulled me close to him. Did he just hear me talking to Cerberus? He didn't look too surprised.

"You turned someone into dust!" Hades eyes lowered.

"I did; it was punishment." His mouth was in a thin line. "He didn't do his job. Don't worry; I'll bring him back and give him a less...favorable job later." Hades paused for a brief second. "It is just the way things have to be run around here."

I wanted to snap at him, but I kept it to myself. As long as his demon was given another chance, I would allow it. I didn't know how things ran around here and until I knew I couldn't do anything. He's older than dirt, and he may have a sound system going.

"Alright, fine." I took my hand away and marched towards the bathroom.

"Where are you going?" he questioned while following me like a puppy.

"To shower, I reek of cave, and now I probably have demon dust on me."

"You are sore with me," he mused. I stopped to turn around in the doorway.

"How so?"

"You want to yell at me. Your anger is coming off of you in waves, yet you do not wish to speak; why?" Hades came closer; the heat of his body wrapped me in a blanket. It soothed me, but not enough to shake a heavy feeling.

My stomach turned up in knots; the uneasy feeling washed over me. Was it because I didn't want to argue with him because I didn't understand Hades' world yet? Or was it that he could wave his hand and kill anything at will?

"Come here, Ember." My mind screamed one thing, and my body did another. I let him engulf me in his arms while I nuzzled into his chest. "He is not completely dead. His soul is now in purgatory, where he will wait until I summon him again. It's like a prison, a punishment. I don't do that with any other living being except for my demons, who deserve it. I would never, ever do that to you or anyone you cared about. Do you understand?" I nodded my head into his clothes, taking in his scent.

His smell had become stronger to me than it was earlier, and I let myself enjoy the warmth.

Hades

"He. Took. What?" I must articulate my words around these demons because it seems they do not fucking understand my questions. Both sat on the floor in shock as they tried to crawl away from me.

"We are sorry! We went to check the rest of the dungeon, and the door to your trophy room was open. The chains were gone, the enchantments expelled. When we walked in, the Helm was gone along with the Demon Sword." The one laying on his back trembled as he put his hands up to cover himself.

"Anything else?" I gritted.

"No, my Lord."

"Good." I waved my hand as both shrank to nothing but a pile of ash. "Vulcan, can you see what you can come up with regarding the dungeon? Check for traces of witchcraft, possibly Hecate? It isn't a coincidence that Hecate, the most powerful witch goddess, and Malachi disappearing from the Underworld is a coincidence now, is it?" Vulcan shook his head 'no' as he trudged through the door.

"Ares, what do you think we should do?" I tightened my knuckles as I played with the rings on my fingers as I stared mindlessly at the bookshelf. The only thing not causing me to burn down the entire palace was Ember. She already saw me lose it with one demon; I didn't need her despising me from ruining our home.

"You ask for my opinion?" he questions, raising a brow.

"Time for you to step up to your god-like status and take responsibility, hmm? I think a war is brewing," I spoke darkly. "We best prepare." Ares took hold of the butt of his ax and did a bow and left the room with a skip in his step. Ares and I understood one another. We combined our armies, and together we have become powerful. If we wanted, we could conquer the heavens, but it was something we did not want. We wanted peace to live out our own lives and keep gods and deities out of human business.

Walking back to my room, I could hear faint talking from the other side of the door. Ember was talking, assumably to be Cerberus. I found it endearing she would speak to him like a person until she started saying she was a Disney princess. Cerberus started rambling she wasn't a princess. Fuck that; she was my queen.

Sneaking into the door, I tried to work my brain on why Ember could hear both animals. She was having an actual conversation with them like she would a person. I created Phantomtails and Cerberus in the Underworld, so I don't see why she shouldn't communicate with them. This bond must be taking hold of her more rapidly than I expected for her race. I know I haven't paid attention to supernatural bonds, and I haven't studied it at all in angels, demons, and gods. There just wasn't *enough* information on the subject. Ember and I are going to have to take it slow and be the guinea pigs for Selene.

Cerberus was asked if I liked to poof my demons into ash regularly, but I gave him an evil eye. Pretending not to know what was happening, he scratched his fur until I took hold of Ember's arm.

Fuck, she was beautiful; I could hardly concentrate. Just in the past twenty-four hours, her beauty has bloomed into my heart. Her physical strength was making leaps and bounds, and I could only contribute that to the bond.

Answering her questions and rushing her into the bathroom, I quickly changed into grey sweatpants and got on the bed. My arm was thrown over my eyes as I contemplated what my next move was.

Hermes hadn't been heard from in a while, meaning he is still questioning angels, demons, hell, anyone for that matter, trying to figure out any leads. Loukas was preparing the list of all the gods or deities I've pissed off.

And Kronos, I still had to go to the Black Claw Pack and check their wards. It will have to be postponed; Ember's safety is more important.

Feeling a dip in the bed, I grabbed her, and she let out a squeal of giggles. "Easy, handsome," she cooed at me while I nipped at her neck. Fucking blue balls, I was rock solid for her, and I was damn near hoping she was about done with this human woman shit.

"How are you feeling?" I pried a little as she traced a tattoo on my arm.

"Much better, actually." She smiled. "Vulcan had a pamphlet in that first aid kit; the first one isn't supposed to be so bad. I even took some medicine that was inside."

"That's good to hear," I hummed while I pulled her to lay on top of me. Her legs straddled the upper part of my waist as her face buried itself within my chest. I was glad she wasn't in any pain and was even happier that it wouldn't last long because I needed to taste her. I needed to put my fingers in her; hell, I wanted my cock to bury itself in her and finally mark her as mine.

Unlike supernaturals who bite, gods could descend their souls onto their mate. It was like dipping your body into the water and coming back up again. You would be drenched in each other's spirit, and forever, it will stay. Once it is said and done and we both feel the pleasure take over our bodies, I would dip my soul into her body, causing her to latch onto mine, and her chest will bear my scepter, which is my mark.

It is a cross with an upside-down crescent moon with a jewel in the middle. It will look beautiful on her white skin. Ember is now sleeping soundly in my arms as I feel her breathing has evened out. Taking a deep breath, I can only imagine how wonderful it will be once we bond. My feelings for her have grown substantially, and when we are both are bonded to each other, it will become almost unbreakable. We will be stronger ourselves as well.

Brushing her hair behind her ear, I put my chin on top of her head. Listening to her slow breaths.

"Hades..." a voice keeps calling to me. "Hades..." I sit up from the bed to look for Ember, who is missing. "Hades, over here!" Her small playful voice

comes from the door. Her little head pokes out behind it as her strawberry blonde hair falls to her side.

"Hades, come here," Ember giggles as I hear her feet running across the floor. I'm still donned in my sweatpants, too lazy to care about anything except to catch my escaping mate.

I threw the covers off, feeling the cold floor beneath my feet as I ran down the hallway. Her laughs fill the end of the hall as I see wisps of her hair fly around the corner. I smile at the game she's playing; I was going to be the hunter and claim my prize.

"Hades! You are too slow!" I hear her running again; this time, I cheat and start imagining where she is and transporting there. Each time she deters me and laughs around another corner. Biting my lip, I take one more chance and appear inside the relic room. Ember is staring at the Helm with a look of horror on her face.

"Hades?" Tears brimmed her eyes as she saw the Helm sitting in its rightful case like it was never stolen.

"Was it you? Did you take me?" Ember's hands were trembling as she backed away from me. Walking forward, my hands low in surrender,

"I would never, ever do that! It was taken from me! I found it the night I found you. I punished who took it!" The stress in my voice barely pulled at her heart as she continued to step away.

"You hid this from me." Her breathing became rapid. We both looked back at the Helm only to see it was gone, and Ember started to scream.

"No! No!" Ember begins to pull her hair. "Don't get me again, please no!" Her body crumples to the floor, and I go to catch her. Only when I do, her body isn't there. My arms were empty, void, and even cold.

"See what happens when you don't claim your mate, Hades?" Selene's voice appeared behind me. Selene was standing in rags, just as Ember described. Her glow still lit up the entire room beneath the dirt on her face. Standing up, I marched over to her to grab her, but she was only air. "You certainly made a mess of things, didn't you, Hades?" Selene tsks as she reappeared in the same spot. She was no longer the joking self she once was when I met her. "You've altered the future by refusing your mate from the beginning, and not only is your mate in danger but others as well. Do you think Vulcan will forgive you if Malachi gets away with finding the Sphere of Souls and halting all soul pairings?" Selene then glances to the floor, saying with barely a whisper, "And even break mate bonds?"

I grit my teeth. "But I found her. I want her," I pressed. "She's mine, and no one will have her."

"So you say, but you will have to fight for her to keep her and protect future mates as well. Good luck, Hades." Selene turned around and disappeared into the darkness that once was my relic room.

Chapter 30

Ember

It had been several days since Malachi made his escape and Hades has been hard at work sending Loukas and other messengers throughout Earth. Hades had a hunch that Selene was either on Earth or a place called Bergarian, a place where most supernaturals lived.

Hades gave me a book to read regarding the place, saying it was far more beautiful than Earth and meant to bless the creatures the gods had created. Like Earth however, they had their problems like any other. There was a nation called 'The Cerulean Moon Kingdom' that housed most of the shifters. Werewolves, lions, panthers and even dragons were littered about the land, and it only urged me to want to visit more. "Can we go please!" I begged. I even tried doing the pout which I have figured out only works when he is on the fence about something.

"Not yet. Let the threat pass and I will take you wherever you want." Hades had gotten in the habit of pecking me on the lips each time I didn't get my way and I'd in turn, I melted. Anytime I was getting upset about something he would do it; it was like he knew it would sate me to where I would be quiet. I bet it has something to do with that bond.

I continued reading, eating and being a slob. I haven't rested so much in all my life. I was getting restless having to sit around all the time, so I started bugging Ares and Hermes more.

Hermes had come back with no new information. Selene and Hecate were still missing and there were no traces of them, barely any magic to even track. Zeus was getting more frantic by the day. Sometimes you could hear a thunderstorm down in the Underworld as he rumbled above Earth. I was glad I wasn't on Earth for once, people were thinking the apocalypse was coming.

Hermes was sitting in the game room, flipping through some magazine when I entered. Hades had finally let me go out of his sight as long as Cerberus and Blaze were with me. I could still hear them talking at times but at others it sounded like static. Hades commented it was strange, but he wasn't concerned because he would say, "You were made for me, and I to you. You would have to gain some of my power to help me rule." I would shrug my shoulders and just continue. No use in worrying about it.

"There's my little flame," Hermes joked as he threw the magazine to the other side of the couch. "What has you looking all glum?" I went over and plopped myself right on the couch and let out a large, annoyed sigh.

"I'm bored," I mused as I stared at the high ceilings. This ceiling had demons and angels fighting with each other. Did Hades higher a decorator or did he just 'poof' everything into existence?

"You are?" Hermes rubbed his chin as he leaned back. "Well, how long have you been living down here with us?" I counted on my fingers as I finally got an exact number.

"Two weeks give or take?" I questioned, still looking around the room. Hermes chuckled.

"He's lasted this long, that's strange." My head whipped back to Hermes who had a glint of sparkle in his eye.

"What do you mean?"

"Well, you are mates," he deadpanned. My mouth hung open; I waited for myself to come up with a question, but I just sat there.

"Mates are supposed to be, well, mated." I blushed as my eyes darted to the now interesting rug on the floor.

"Well, I've been… not my best." I scratched my head.

"I'm just kidding with you, flame. In fact, I think we should go do something while Hades is working." I perked up at the idea.

"What are we going to do?!" Cerberus growled but I hushed him. Hermes smiled again and rubbed his dirty blonde curls from his face.

Hermes was definitely more of a feminine looking god. He was tall, lean and didn't have a scar on his body. He wasn't made for fighting; he was made for speed and agility. Hermes' long fingers traced the couch as he continued hum and chuckle to himself.

"Go get a swimsuit on. We are going swimming." I jumped up from the couch, excitedly.

"Will Ares come too!?" I headed for the door, turning around while my hair whipped into my face. Hermes continued to sit, tracing an invisible pattern on the couch.

"Of course, he will; he wouldn't miss it," he whispered as he started laughing to himself.

Running up the stairs and into our room, I dashed for the closet. Blaze sat on my shoulder while chittering something. "Can't understand you right now, Blaze. Not sure why." I shuffled through the drawers finding some swimsuits.

"Oh my." I gazed at a black two piece. The bottom was cut out, so it looked like a thong. "That's too much," I mused and continued to dig. All of the swimsuits I looked at were two pieces, not a single one piece. I growled at the lack of style choices and ended up pulling out a dark crimson one. It had jewels outlining the hems. There were so many strings, it reminded my times back at the club. I would be tying for days and my fingers would get sore. This time I was the one tying an outfit for me.

This was a swimsuit though; it was technically different. Right? Nah, not really but this was Hades and his friends. They wouldn't think anything of it. I mean, these things were here to be used and it was kinda pretty.

Many times I thought the things that the strippers wore were beautiful. I just thought it was sad they couldn't go and use it on someone they really cared about. Instead, dirty old men would rub up on them. I internally shudder as I ran to the bathroom to change.

I didn't look half bad in it, I thought. My bruises were gone, and my skin had a healthy glow to it. The extra calorie shakes that Ares had prepared for me were doing wonders. I didn't look as gaunt as I did before. My hips had widened, and my chest totally filled out. My goods were actually looking like goods! Some of my friends back at the club might even be jealous of these! Adjusting my top one more time to pull them up a bit higher, I walked out of the bathroom and put on one of Hades' shirts.

Walking around half naked in front of the servants might not be good. I didn't need to see another puff of ash pile on the floor.

Screaming outside caught my attention as I approached the opened patio door. Loukas was in a black swimsuit, his tail waving back and forth in a crouched position ready to attack Ares. Ares, being much larger than Loukas, didn't even have to crouch; he just had his hands out ready to just jump on Loukas.

Hermes was in the pool, lounging on a blow up mattress reading another magazine. The man likes to read gossip columns that's for sure.

"Flame!" Hermes waved as he pulled down his sunglasses. "Glad to see you have joined us, get in! Water's warm… just like everything else in the Underworld," he muttered. I smiled and waved as Loukas turned around, but Ares took it as his time to strike, letting out a mighty roar and threw Loukas in the pool.

The splash got water all over the deck while everyone was laughing as Loukas swam to the surface. Ares jumped and with his large form, more water ended up splashing out as well as getting Hermes wet. He wasn't amused.

Grabbing Hades' large shirt and pulling it over my head before throwing it on a nearby chair, I was left in my bathing suit. The water was extra blue, and I took my foot and dipped it into the water. Hermes was right, it was warm. It occurred to me that I wasn't sure if I knew how to swim. I scratched my cheek to figure out where the shallow end of the pool was until I noticed it was eerily quiet. Moving my head slowly, I glanced to the right side of the pool where the boys were.

"Shit," Loukas whispered while Hermes snickered into his magazine. I looked down to make sure a boob wasn't hanging out and all my parts were covered but everything was in order.

"What?" I shrugged my shoulders, still leaning over to test the water.

"Does Hades know she's out here?" Ares punched Hermes in the shoulder.

"Ow, and no. It is more interesting this way."

"What is more interesting?" I questioned as Ares gave a disapproving look.

"Let's play a game," Hermes announced as he got off his floating mattress. "How about chicken?" Loukas jumped up and started heading to the shallow end of the pool.

"Ember is my partner!" Loukas swam towards the end of the pool, and I took the main stairs to enter. The water felt fantastic, not cold enough to cause a chill but not warm enough to make it feel too hot once we started swimming. I tickled my fingers on the surface of the water and Loukas stood up beside me.

"I don't know how to play chicken. How do you play?" I asked.

"Oh, it's easy. I'll get under the water, and you climb on my shoulders. Lifting you up, you are to battle against Hermes with your hands and try and push each other off into the water. Not unless Ares wants to be on the top."

"Screw that!" Hermes waved his hands. "I can't lift 300 pounds of muscle!" Cerberus growled at Loukas, but I couldn't understand what Cerberus wanted me to do. "Calm down, Cerberus. They won't let me drown," I laughed. Hermes laughed as well. Cerberus took a sharp look at Hermes who only nodded his head and Cerberus ran off.

"Why is he being a grump?" Loukas had put himself under the water and I climbed on his shoulders. Loukas's hands grabbed onto the front of my legs as Hermes was on Ares' shoulders. "Wait, this isn't fair. Ares is way taller than Loukas!" I whined. "Plus, you guys are gods. You'll cheat!"

"Oh, come on, let's just play a little bit." Hermes kicked Ares in the ribs to move forward.

"I'm not a damn horse, Hermes, watch it," Ares growled as he leaned backwards and dunked Hermes in the water. I started laughing and had to hold Loukas's head so I didn't fall back into the water.

Ares pulled Hermes back up just in time to for us to see smoke trickling into the pool.

Hades

My head was pounding.

The dream from the other night was still haunting me. It was on constant repeat to tell Ember about the Helm. There just wasn't an easy way to tell her. I can't just 'word vomit,' like she says, to tell her this. Ember has had nightmares about this damn helmet since she met me; what if she thinks I was the one who took her!

I buried myself in work, trying to figure out where the missing gods were but I was coming up at a dead end each time. My next step was to meet with Zeus, someone that Loukas couldn't go and get an audience with. I needed to know if Zeus did in fact put the order in for Malachi to grab Ember from me. If he did, then I'm going to have to re-evaluate my whole plan about Malachi and turn it onto Zeus. The only problem, would I bring Ember with me because she was not leaving my sight. I didn't trust my own men and demons for her protection.

The pounding in my head continued and I rubbed my temples in a clockwise position. I told Ember she could leave the office; she was becoming restless since she had been healing so well. I could also sense that her monthly was completed but I dared not touch her. I was too afraid to do anything; I had to tell her the truth first.

Kronos, I needed her now. Her presence calmed me and abated all the fears I had as strange as it sounded. She kept me grounded while I worked but it was selfish to keep her in here. If Cerberus watched her, she would be fine.

"Master," Cerberus called to me. "Master, you need to come to the pool area." Cerberus trotted in and Ember was nowhere in sight.

"Where is Ember?" I growled at him. Pushing away from the desk, I began stomping out of the room. Cerberus was trotting alongside me as his head began to survey the area. He does this when he's nervous. "What is wrong? Where is she? Why did you leave her?!"

"Relax." He picked up the pace. "She's in safe hands, almost literally," he mumbled. We approached the patio at the back of the palace; they were wide open leading to the pool. The water was moving about, causing waves. I heard Ember's laughter penetrate me as I walked out.

"Fuck," I whispered. She was going to be wearing a swimsuit if she is out here. Damn, and they are all skimpy ones. "Fuuuuuuuuck," I cursed myself again as I walked out.

Ember was wearing a red suit with diamonds sparkling the front. Her breasts were almost pouring out of her top and my dick instantly went to attention. Before I could appreciate the view before me, I noticed Loukas's head was smack dab in the middle of her thighs.

Feeling my eyes glow red and the smoke tendrils leaving my limbs, the fire in me started to blanket the pool. Ember's laughter halted as she looked around and Loukas's smug face fell to a worried one.

"Better be worried, you piece of shit," I growled out and I could feel my claws extending, wanting to slit the little bastard's throat.

"Hades!" Ember squealed as she waved her hand at me. Her breasts jiggled back and forth and that only made things worse for my temper. I wanted them, damnit, and Loukas's head was also next to her damn cunt. My head is the only one that should be there.

"Put me down, Loukas," Ember chirped, and he obeyed. She had no damn clue what was going on.

"Are you mad that I came swimming?" Her big eyes looked into mine as she walked to the side of the pool. Her body was dripping with water and one droplet ran down her breasts. I wanted to be that droplet.

"I'm fine," I lied as the smoke continued to pour from me. Ember tilted her head and raised a brow. I bent down to get a better look at her breasts, I mean her.

"You're mad at me. I'm sorry, I should have invited you too." Hermes was cackling in the background and Ares had his arms up in surrender.

"It was all Hermes. I voted my displeasure for this." Ares began to get out of the pool while Loukas stood completely still.

"Wanna come in?" Ember pulled on my shirt to get my attention. For a second I thought about it, and then maybe drown Loukas during the process so he could feel the breath of life leave his lungs, but I couldn't. Not with Ember here.

"How about you come with me? I have a surprise for you." My husky breath left chills on her arms while I glanced over at Loukas. His fear was still there but I could feel his anger.

"Yay! A surprise!" Ember used her feet to jump from the bottom of the pool and lifted herself up with her arms. Her breasts were bouncing as she finally stood up. Kronos, I'd do her here to show everyone she was mine. But she wasn't ready for that.

I willed my cloak around me as I pulled her in. I didn't need anyone staring at her ass while we walked back into the house.

"So, what is my surprise?!" Ember jumped again as well as my cock.

"You'll see." I kissed the temple of her forehead as we walked back to our room.

Vera Foxx

Chapter 31

Hades

I led her down the hallway, and I could feel her excitement through the bond. We haven't even done many things on the physical side, and I was about to rectify that. Just knowing she was wet and naked under my cloak made me painfully hard as she continued to squeeze my hand as we walked.

"What is it?" Her excitement couldn't handle the surprise as she jumped in front of me. The cloak fell down part of her shoulder and she didn't even try to cover it back up. Her pale skin against the red string that barely held her breasts in her suit was going to drive me mad.

"Fates," I swore under my breath as I pulled her to me and just transported us to our room.

"I'll never get used to that; you gotta warn me! I get all dizzy." The cloak dropped to the floor, and I was able to drink her body in. Her suit was slowly creeping up her ass, giving me that perfect view of that crease under her rear that drove me mad. Ember started to wander around the room, looking behind curtains, under the bed, and each movement she made, it took all the strength in my body not to put my hands on her.

"I don't see anything different…" she wondered aloud. I stalked towards her; her thoughts were clearly not on me but that was about to change. I could feel my eyes darken as her eyes were everywhere but me. I was getting jealous of the entire room. I wanted her undivided attention.

Letting out a growl of disapproval, her body snapped back to face me. Her hair was the only thing still wet on her, her suit had mostly dried but the water droplets from her hair skimmed down her chest.

"Hades," she spoke breathlessly. In an instant I had snapped my shirt off my body as I pulled her in by her waist. Lowering my nose to the side of her neck, I tickled her in that one spot under her ear. Chills erupted across her skin, and her breathing became slower as she held in a whimper. Ember's hands went straight to my chest as her fingertips tickled my chest muscles.

"I am going to give you a surprise." I brushed her hair to her back. I was going to give her pleasure she has never had. My lips traced hers; she leaned in closer, wanting to get closer to me. I felt the heat coming from her body. Her arousal was no question, but the fear was still there.

This is uncharted territory for her, so I had to play this right. Unfortunately, I was no stranger to the opposite gender, but I can give her one thing my tongue had never touched. The soft, tight cavern of her pussy. I will dive in and savor her flavor and feel her spasm against me.

While my hand reached around her back, I untied her top. It dropped to the floor effortlessly as she gripped hold of my shoulders. Chuckling, I led her to the bed until her knees felt the back of the mattress. Making sure not to let her fall, I eased her down and we both crawled to the middle. The movement of her breasts made me groan, and I swear they had gotten bigger in just a few days. My dick rubbed my jeans harshly; the pain of the material was too much. I willed them off, leaving me just in my black boxer briefs.

Her breath shook as she looked down my torso. I was no stranger to the gym, and it was a good thing because her arousal just filled the entire room.

Hearing footsteps nearing the door, I closed my eyes to put a barrier around the room. Not this time, fuckers. Hearing struggling by the door and a few obvious curses, I continued my seduction on Ember.

Ember gasped as I started kissing her nipples; they felt cool against my tongue as I warmed them with my mouth. Her hands ran through my hair and my dick immediately rubbed against her leg. It was involuntary, my hips wanted the movement and damn it felt good. "Hades," she breathed again as my other hand that was kneading her breast traveled down to pull on the tiny string holding her bikini. Her hand movements stopped in my hair, and she held a breath.

"I'll go slow, my beautiful flower, don't be afraid." Ember's body was tense, but the lust flowed through the bond. The hesitant worry was there but once my eyes glanced into hers, she melted back into me and nodded her head. Kissing her, trailing down to the small of her waist, to her bellybutton and to her hips, she began to wiggle her hips.

The itch, the pull, the burn and tingle she was feeling was surely driving her crazy. Fates, she has never felt this before and the excitement rolling in my body told me I haven't felt true pleasure until now. Too late to ask if she has ever had an orgasm. I was down at her shaven pussy. Smooth skin found my face as I rubbed and bathe myself in her scent. It was overpowering to me, and it was the sweetest scent I ever had the ability to describe.

Placing open mouth kisses to her inner thighs, I sucked them lightly leaving tiny love bites along the way. Finally parting her lower lips with my tongue, an instant growl escaped my chest. Ember was insanely wet, and my tongue slid into her with ease tasting the honey of her body.

"Oh!" Ember moaned as she moved her hips. Grabbing them for her to hold still, she put her fingers into my dark hair and started pulling me closer. Gladly I rubbed my tongue over her bundle of nerves, and she let out a squeal. "What is that?" she breathed. I swear I was going to lose my hair how tight it was but it turned me on even more.

Taking my rough tongue, I continued to flick, pull, tug and massage her clit as her little moans filled the room. Her high continued until she shattered around me and her cum filled my mouth. Her essence filled me, and I wanted more but I had to take this slow. To savor her like a fine wine or scotch, spread out her pleasure.

Ember was panting as she let go of my hair, her cheeks tainted pink from her release. "Oh, my gosh," she continued to whisper, not looking me directly in the eye. I chuckled darkly as I continued to trail up her torso and kiss each breast lightly.

"Look at me, Ember." Ember covered her face and shook her head while I put my hand around one wrist. "It isn't anything to be embarrassed about. I enjoyed your noises, feel how much I liked them." Ember let me take one of her hands as she looked with one eye. I had her bare hand trail down my torso until she felt my raging erection.

"Oh," she spoke a little loudly while I kissed her cheek. Trailing kisses to her mouth, I let my hand go, only to have her grip me tighter. Fuck, she wasn't scared. Ember moved from the tip of my length down to the base and just through my damn boxer briefs I thought I would cum right there.

"Ember." I leaned my head back while gripping her breasts. She was biting her bottom lip as she continued.

"Is this right?" she purred into my neck, leaving butterfly kisses.

"Yes," I rasped, feeling my Adam's apple bob. She took my mouth and kissed it as I began to swallow. "Oh, Ember." Ember stopped tugging on my cock as her fingers trailed around the top of my briefs. My body wanted the contact again and thank the fates she had the decency to move into that unbearable piece of clothing. Ember's small hand wrapped around the middle, not even able to make it around its circumference. "Yes, that," I whispered as she began to pump me up and down. The precum was almost as much as me getting my release. The tingles of her touch were driving me mad.

Stopping, she pulled down my briefs to get a better grip and she gasped. It was the same face she had when she saw the demons that lost Malachi. Grabbing her hand, I brought it to my face and kissed her palm. "I would never hurt you," I kissed it again. "I will never do anything you are uncomfortable with. We can stop if you want." Ember contemplated my question, glancing back from my cock to my face, and she gave a bright blushed smile.

"Maybe not all the way right now." I nodded and tangled my fingers in her hair as I kissed her, laying her back on the bed. My cock brushed her pussy as I laid on top of her. Fucking heaven, it was fucking heaven as I moved it across her wet core. I growled and got off her; if I kept doing that I'd go back on my word and fuck her world up.

Breathing heavy, worried I had scared her, she kissed my neck and down my chest. Ember's kissed either the side of my hips and looked directly at my cock. I wasn't small by any means; I was a damn god, of course I would be bigger than any human. The sexiest part of all, her scared face became one of lust as a drop of cum pearled at the tip.

Licking her lips, I held back a stifled groan as she licked the tip.

For. The. Love. Of. Rhea.

Ember sucked the tip with her mouth while holding the base. She bobbed up and down a few times and looked up at me with those big doe eyes. "Like this?" She stopped, seeking approval.

"Kronos, yes." I struggled to not force her head back on my cock. Her head bobbed again; in no way, I wanted to force her any lower but damn she did. She went lower and lower until she gagged. I sat up worried even though it was the sexiest thing I heard. It let me know I was big enough to please her later.

Ember continued and my dirty hands couldn't help but tangle in her hair. My hips flexed and pushed up as it hit the back of her throat. I groaned as my muscles tightened as she continued to suck. Fuck she just felt so damn good.

Hearing her groan, I hissed, "Ember get up." I gritted my teeth, pulling her up. Confused, she stopped, and her innocent eyes grabbed my attention. Flipping her over I smashed my lips to hers and felt the warm spit still on my cock. I pumped it only a few times to release myself on her stomach.

Our foreheads touched as we were both breathing heavy. "Ember," I breathed while she smiled.

"Did I do okay?" she whispered and I couldn't help but let a small laugh come out.

"More than Okay." Brushing her hair out of the way, I kissed her lips and told her to wait there until I returned. Grabbing a damp towel from the bathroom and coming back, I saw she hadn't even made an effort to move as my seed was still spilled on her stomach. I couldn't help but have guilt fill the pit of my stomach. All of that goes to waste because Hades couldn't give life.

The pained looked must have shown because Ember sat up and motioned for me to come over. Cleaning her gently and throwing the towel on the floor, I curled up in bed with her. "What is my mate thinking about?" she whispered.

"I think you know." I touched her face. Everything about her, I was so in love with. I don't think I could ever bare to part with her, not one single day. I would give anything to give her what she desires, hell even me. A little part of each of us to make a child in both our images. Would she want just one or would she want many? The small jab in my heart made my breath hitch and Ember pulled herself closer to me.

"I don't need anything else, Hades," she hummed in my ear while tickling the hair on my scalp. Her arm was wrapped around the back of my head, skimming the top. It was soothing, the gentle strokes of my hair moving along with each of her fingers. I could feel myself almost purring. "You are enough."

Vera Foxx

Chapter 32

Ember

I felt so confused. My heart was telling me what Hades was feeling. It was the strangest thing. Without even looking into his actions, I could feel the internal struggle he was having. I wasn't sure if it was the bond that we shared or something different entirely. I wasn't an expert, and Hades wasn't either. His mouth was telling me one thing, but it was his aura telling me another.

He was feeling inadequate for sure; any man would if he couldn't give someone he loved a child, but there was an overwhelming feeling of guilt and regret tied along with it. The emotion was building with each passing second as we sat there in silence as I ran my fingers through his hair. Trying to be calm and not prying too much, I pulled his mouth towards mine and kissed him lightly.

"Tell me what is wrong, Hades? I thought we were supposed to be in this together?" Hades closed his eyes and heaved a heavy sigh as his head went straight for my lap. Sitting up, I rubbed his bareback, which was full of ridges of muscle and tanned skin. My heart skipped a beat, and my mind started drifting elsewhere. Hades was noticing my reaction, but I coughed to break it.

"No secrets, Hades, I feel guilt all over you, and I know it isn't about the baby thing." I talked more sternly. Hades stiffened and stopped stroking his thumb on my thigh.

"How would you know?" he accused but not in such a manner of throwing it in my face. His expression was of pure interest.

"I feel it, in here." I pointed to my heart. "I feel your guilt weigh on you like bricks. It is like part of me is feeling something that isn't mine," I trailed off. "Is it the bond?" Hades sat up on his forearms and kissed the top of my thigh.

"Part of it? It shouldn't be so strong," he mused. "You know it isn't your feeling?" I nodded. What would I have to feel guilty about anyway?

"It's like I can just look at you, and when I take in your eyes, I feel the overwhelming feeling of guilt and fear." Hades' breath caught as he sat up in the bed and put his legs over the side. His hands immediately went to his face.

"I do have guilt, and I am afraid," he stated. "It is strange you can feel it so strongly since we aren't bonded but we are a different of a human and a god being together," he chuckled. "Anyway, there is something I need to tell you."

I scooted closer to him as I pulled the bed sheet around me. "Then tell me," I whispered while putting my cheek to his shoulder. Hades growled out in frustration and pulled his hair.

"I can't," he breathed. "I'm too afraid you will leave." Letting out a breath, he stood up in his completely naked form. His butt was nothing but muscle and I could see the indentions and smooth lines that covered him. My heart caught up in my throat, and I couldn't swallow. Looking away, concentrating on the carpet, I forced down the spit in my mouth.

"Hades, I told you I wouldn't leave. I'm scared you will leave me. I'm not that much of a-" I was stopped by Hades smashing his lips to mine. It was rough but ended gently as he continued to peck my lips.

"You are my everything," he whispered in my mouth. "Don't think anything else otherwise." I nodded. I pulled him in for one more kiss.

"All right, I'll tell you." Hades walked away and put on a pair of black joggers; thank heavens because he was way too distracting. Sitting his knees on the floor in front of me, he held my hands; he closed his eyes and looked into mine.

"Do you remember the masked gladiator that took you from your home?" My heart stopped, and Hades squeezed my hands tight.

"No, no, you wouldn't." The tears were pooling. Hades would never do such a thing; he would never take a young girl and sell her off. Hades started shaking his head.

"I didn't do it; someone stole that helmet from me. It is my helmet, but I swear to you it was stolen. You can ask any of our friends. I swear to you, I didn't take you. You have to believe me." Hades' head rested in my lap as my heart continued to be at a standstill.

I felt the honesty, and guilt that rode his heart like an earthquake was slowly fading. In my mind, I felt a small whisper as I concentrated, and the breath of wind spoke, "*Truth, he's telling the truth.*" It was the same voice that spoke my name just a week ago.

"*Who are you?*" I tried to ask, only to hear Hades' sob. My heart broke in an instant. The King of the Underworld was crying into my lap. "I'm not leaving," I whispered as I continued to pet him. Hades gripped my thighs tighter like I was going to float away and never return. It was tight enough to form bruises, but I said nothing; if he needed security, I would give it to him.

The helmet, the bane of my existence, and the object that haunted my dreams was something that Hades owned. Many nights I cursed the helmet, but it should have been the man behind it. I saw nothing but the object that hid the villain from the world. The coward that couldn't show his face. "Is the helmet still out there?" I gulped, and Hades' dark eyes met mine.

"I had it, the night we took you from the club. It was in my possession, and now it is gone again. When Malachi escaped, he took it." My mouth was set open as a tiny squeak fell out.

"Was it M-Malachi who took me?" My hands fell into a ball, tightening my hands around each other. My breath became quick and lean, and Hades immediately sat down on the bed and pulled me to his chest.

"They will pay. They will pay dearly." The voice was dark and almost made me feel scared. The once crying god was now angered as he held me. Feeling the revenge and hate in his heart, I knew he would protect me. "I will make sure they suffer a fate worse than death and torture. He will face the Titans and their hunger for violence. He will spawn over and over and deal with the pain you and many other women had to endure a thousand times over."

My breathing slowed, feeling the warmth from his chest. "I swear to you. I will get the helmet back. I will fight for you and my mistake." A hint of guilt crossed his heart, but it faded far too quickly to read it. The bond was a strange thing. One minute overwhelming emotions came from him, and it was gone just as quickly. Hades' chest continued to rise and fall as we sat in each other's presence. My finger trailed around his chest tattoo, and his skin shivered.

Earlier, he gave me the greatest pleasure I had ever felt, and it felt even more amazing that he did it. His hands, his tongue, the way he spoke to me took me places in my mind and body I wanted to explore more. I didn't want to seem overly greedy, but after our talk about him giving up one of his dark secrets he held from me, even though he shouldn't have, it made me want to share more of myself.

"So, you aren't mad at me?" He kissed my forehead.

"No, you had no control over Malachi, who stole something from you. You had no way to prevent it! I just hope I don't see it again; will you destroy it when you get it back?" Anything that led back to him and caused me discomfort he would be upset over.

"Anything for you."

We sat in each other's presence as we both calmed down from the sincere confession. Hades' burden was lifted, but I feel like it wasn't everything in my own heart. He was just now calming down, so I would bring it up another time. Every time I asked him a serious question, he would always give me an honest answer.

"I have another surprise for you." His voice was a bit raspy from being silent. My ears perked up as I bit my lip.

"Oh? Just like the one I just had?" I tried to keep my excitement to a minimum but failed miserably. His smile became a side one. Hades pulled down the sheet with which I had covered my breasts.

"It was something else, but I don't mind another surprise like this one." My nipples instantly hardened as he made me straddle my naked form across his lap. My face flushing red, he grabbed my bruised bottom lip with his teeth and tugged while he groaned.

"My flower wants to give me her aroma, does she?" His fingers lightly touched my thighs as he danced around to the innermost part. "I want to do something different than before." Hades' kisses nipped at my chest and right back up to my neck.

His fingers trailed closer to my core and parted my lower lips. My heart jumped as I felt him rub a finger close to my clit. My hands immediately went to his shoulders and around his neck. "I want to see how tight you are." He kissed my neck as he pried my lips open. "I want to see how much stretching I'll have to do to you." Letting out a moan, I felt one finger slip inside.

"Fuck, so wet." He took a large inhale. His finger curled inside, and I gripped him closer. His one finger began to pump inside me as I started riding his finger. "One more, flower. One more inside you." Hades slipped in one more, and it was undoubtedly tighter. A good, slightly painful tight. My back arched backward as his finger thrusts went faster.

I really liked it as he pumped faster, and I buried my head in his neck. Nipping it, biting it, I felt like an animal. "Do you feel this?" His finger grazed my inner wall, deep inside. "I will take that from you and make you mine forever when I bury myself into your body." The dominance he radiated went through me as I felt the pressure build. Hades held me closer as his one hand thrust into me harshly. My teeth began to itch; I had an overwhelming feeling of biting him.

The orgasm shattered me as I threw my head back and his mouth immediately went to my breasts, sucking my nipples harshly. He groaned as I felt my teeth itch again, throwing myself into his neck and grazing his shoulder. His body trembled at the scratch I left him with my teeth, and my body collapsed. Hades was breathing hard, my juices were left all over his pants, and my teeth's itch went away.

Both sets of my canines were elongated, I could feel them with my tongue. Feeling them, I felt a sharp point on one of them. I glanced at the dresser mirror. I slapped my hand over my mouth, and Hades pulled away with worry. "Ember? Ember, what's wrong?"

I pointed to my mouth and his shoulder; there were two long scratches left with blood beading in places. Hades' laughed instead of getting angry. "That was the hottest thing I had ever felt. This is a bit embarrassing, but I cummed without you touching me." He let out a chuckle. My hand was still on my mouth as he tried to pull it away. "Ember, it's Okay." Reluctantly letting go, I touched my teeth again only to feel their normal bluntness.

"I, I thought I had fangs," I rushed out. "I looked over at the mirror; they looked like fangs!" Panicking, I go to get off his lap, but Hades' holds me down.

"You must have thought that after you bit me. There are no fangs in your mouth, and damn, you can bite me all you want."

Hades' smile led me to laugh as he pecked me on the forehead. I swore I saw some fangs. They looked so real. Unlike the demon fangs that I had seen, these were thicker, but they were undoubtedly sharp. Patting them a few times in my mouth and glancing back at Hades' shoulder, I couldn't understand how my blunt teeth could have done that.

"Now, uh, I do have a surprise for you, really," Hades spoke up. I wiggled my eyebrows, and he playfully nuzzled into my neck. "What the hell am I going to do with you!?" He gave a heartfelt laugh as I wrapped my arms around him again.

"The rate you are going...." I teased while he put a finger up to my mouth to silence me. Hades was so playful when he wanted to be. Not being worried or upset about things, I was ready to see Selene and Hecate back, and he wouldn't have to be too engrossed in work all the time.

"No, really. I have to go to the Celestial Kingdom and visit with my brother." Hades' tone went serious, and I stopped laughing. "He will be a deciding factor in how I want to proceed with this investigation on finding Selene and the Helm. I believe Malachi took it, but I also believe that someone is coaxing him to commit the crimes."

"Tell me what to do then; I want to help!" Hades shook his head and pulled me close.

"I want you to stay close to me, never leave my side, so I know you are protected." I wasn't about to go wander around some heaven area with a bunch of crazy mythical creatures anyway. "Do you understand?" I nodded into his chest.

"Go get dressed; we are going to arrive in style." Hades gave a mega-watt smile as he patted my butt to go wash up.

Chapter 33

Ember

Standing in front of the mirror, I wiped my dress down again for any signs of wrinkles. It was a black, floor-length dress with lace across the chest that laid perfectly around my shoulders. My shoulders were bare, just for the small number of love bites that Hades had left earlier. While I was in the bathroom, trying to cover them up, he swatted my hand away and carefully wiped the barely-there makeup.

"I want everyone to know you're mine," he growled in my ear as he tickled my waistline with his fingers.

My hair was slightly curled at the bottom, black heels to match, not an inch of color. My strawberry blonde hair was a sharp contrast as I compared the two. "I have one last thing," Hades announced as he walked up behind me. Through the window, I could see his crisp black three-piece suit. A small gold chain dipped on his right pelt, meant for a pocket watch. Did gods really need to tell time?

The smell of his musky cologne danced around me as he held my hair back and draped a red ruby necklace around my neck. I gasped at how beautiful it looked. It sparkled even in the window on a tiny silver chain. Shaped like a crescent, I stared in awe.

"In honor of Selene for bringing us together. I had to do red, not her signature blue color. I have to show who you really belong to." Turning around to scold him that he was mine too, he held up his cuff links. "And to show I am yours; I need your help to put these on." Smiling, I helped him put on his red cuff links, and he pulled me to the door. "You look ravishing." Hades dipped down to capture my nude pink lips as he tried to close the door. Blaze hopped into the air and set out his wings to glide and sit on my shoulder before the bedroom door shut behind us.

Walking outside, six-midnight black horses were hitched up to a large black carriage with hints of gold trimming around it. The footman as well as the driver were both cloaked in dark robes and had their faces hidden. The door was opened, and as we stepped inside, the blood-red velvet seats came into view, and I sat on the opposite side of the open door.

Hades didn't waste time and sat right beside me as he put his arm around me. Black and reds, that's what all I was seeing. Everything was dark and dreary. As much as I loved Hades, the color scheme was going to get old and fast. "Hades? Have you ever thought about switching up your color pallet?" Hades held a deep chuckle in his throat as he adjusted his tie.

"I'll change anything for you, Ember. Do you want a white horse and carriage?" I looked at him dumbly as he nodded to the window. Sure enough, the horses and the carriage had turned white. The inside red velvet cushions were now a light tan with gold and silver trimmings. I laughed out loud as my fingers traced on the soft, plush seating.

"No, silly, we don't need it all white. I'm just asking for a healthy medium." Hades squeezed my hip, and the now white carriage turned brown while the horses remained black.

"Better," I mused as I nuzzled into his chest. "Do you feel like you have to maintain a reputation? Is that why everything is black?" Letting out a sigh, Hades sat up straight and unbuttoned his jacket.

"Somewhat." He adjusted his rings on each of his fingers. "I am supposed to represent death. Why not have everything black and red? I never minded the colors before because they matched what I felt. Now, I'm not so sure." Hades winked at me while I giggled. "I'll change whatever colors you want as long as you are by my side." His kiss lingered on my forehead as I heard the driver slap the reigns.

The carriage ascended into the sky. No jerks or uncomfortable bumps or jostles rattled the carriage as we reached higher into the Underworld's red-tinted clouds. Blaze curled up and sat on the opposite side of the carriage. My hand went to Hades' thigh as we climbed higher and gave it a gentle squeeze.

"Is that why you always stay in your darker form and not with how you really look?" Hades put his hand on mine, rubbing it gently with his thumb.

"Yes," he trailed off as he looked out the window. The sky became dark, and we were no longer in the land of the Underworld. The air grew cold; Hades' arm came around me again as he felt my shiver. My black dress was beautiful, but not so for the vast darkness outside the carriage. It was bone-chilling. Little candle lights flickered on, and my body was now perched on Hades' lap.

"I have a reputation to maintain. I was once told I wasn't scary or intimidating once, so I changed my look. It was hard to keep it like this for extended periods, but now my body has grown used to it. I now have to concentrate on what I truly look like. I almost forget until I lose control and look at myself in a mirror."

My heart broke. "Hades, that is terrible! You shouldn't have to change how you look because of that stupid comment! You look handsome and intimidating in both forms! Didn't you see those Incubus guys shaking when you rescued me? They were paralyzed in fear!" Hades let out a loud growl and held me tighter while I squeaked.

"What I'm trying to say, Hades, why don't you try and be in your regular, normal form?" I tilted my head and gave my famous pout. Yes, I have now named it my secret weapon, even though it doesn't work all the time.

"Maybe," Hades mused. "Just when we are alone for right now, how about that?" Kissing his lips, I whispered, "Perfect. In fact, when we become bonded, will you be your true self?" Hades leaned back to take in my entire face. I could feel the internal struggle he was having. Why does he feel so insecure about this?

"You really want that?" I nodded my head again excitedly.

Hades' lips capture mine. His tongue seeped in as I groaned into his mouth. Fingers entangled into my hair, and his hand cupped my breasts. Giving them a gentle squeeze, he nipped my lip playfully. "These are fantastic. I just want to bury my face in them." His face immediately went to my chest while I started laughing. He could play with them all day long if he wanted; he knew how to make them feel really, really nice!

As we traveled in darkness for a few more minutes, I became antsy. Where was this place? You couldn't see up nor down, and you certainly couldn't see anything in front of you. "This is between worlds or realms," Hades answered my internal question. "The journey to the Celestial Kingdom is a long one from the Underworld. First, you have the Underworld, then Earth who is also parallel to a land called, Bergarian. To continue onward and upward, you have the Celestial Kingdom. No one from Earth or Bergarian is allowed to travel between the Underworld and the Upper Kingdom; that is why it seems far. While we travel through this darkness, it seems long, but in reality, when we arrive, it only takes seconds.

"I don't even want to know how this stuff works." Hades laughed as the darkness started to turn to light. The candles flickered off as the wheels of the carriage took a light tap to the ground.

So, we know the Celestial Kingdom is solid, so far so good. The door was opened, and a bright light filtered in as Hades stepped out. The lone hand that was left waiting for me to take was hovering mid-air as I took a deep breath. My heart was racing, my fingers were tingling, and my nerves were through the roof. Hades did nothing to rush me as I bent down so my head wouldn't hit the top of the carriage. The bright light blinded my eyes as I put my hand up to shade them. Looking back in the carriage, Blaze continued to sleep.

"Let him sleep," Hades whispered as I put my foot down on the solid ground.

Light murmurs were heard far from me. Hades pulled me to his side. Once my eyes adjusted, the whole world was ten times brighter than that of the Underworld. Light green grass, lightly cemented walkways with gems embedded within blinded me as the sun hit.

Hades and I were standing in front of gold-colored gates with large stone columns; instantly, they were opened for us as our heels clicked on the stones. Clouds that you would typically see in the sky were floating closer to the ground and all around us. They weren't just puffs of precipitation clouds that you could swipe your hand through but had a more material touch to them. Several glowing figures were sitting on them, I'm guessing minor deities because they weren't the most beautiful, especially comparing them to Hades.

Their eyes lingered on us as we walked by; their bare chests reflected the sun with either sweat or oil covering their bodies. One male hopped off the cloud structure and was strutting around naked. Grabbing Hades' arm, I tugged on it and had my eyes making a wiggling motion to look behind us. Hades rolled his eyes and pulled me along.

I thought it was the end of it, but the crowd behind us began to grow. Some had togas, robes, and some sort of linen trousers, but many people, which were just men, were naked. "They are naked, Hades! Why didn't you warn me?" I whispered. The men behind us started laughing and elbowing each other.

"Those are angels. Ignore them; maybe they will go away if they know what's good for them." Hades stopped abruptly and stared down the group of men and pulled me to his waist. "She's mine, now begone." Hades' eyes glowed red, and numerous angels left while a few stayed. "Is there a problem?" Hades' rigid body became relaxed, and I had a terrible feeling something was going to happen.

"Just seeing what all the fuss is about...." one of them mused. He was tall, almost as tall as Hades, with orange locks that trailed to his eyes. "Pretty little thing, no mark on her at all, huh? You haven't claimed her yet." Hades grit his teeth as his smoke tendrils begin to crawl out of his body.

"Watch it, Gabriel." Wait, Gabriel? THE Gabriel?

"Woah," I whispered as I held tight to Hades' hand. Vulcan had given me a summary of how Gabriel was supposed to be mated with Persephone, but now he had forgotten or was made to forget by some force of magic.

"Someone is impressed." Gabriel waved white robes over his body as I began to back up. He strutted over and stood next to Hades. "Better claim her before someone else does. You know mates are supposed to be a gift, not that you deserve one," Gabriel hissed.

Hades' fingers grew claws as he gripped Gabriel's neck.

Immediately, the other angels came to the rescue but were stopped by Hades' other hand, who had them frozen. The loud growl from Hades' throat was interrupted by a booming voice that could only be described as thunder.

"HADES! BROTHER! Finally, you come to visit!" White robes trailed behind the man with a short blonde beard. His hair was to his shoulders, and his arms opened wide. "It's been centuries!" Hades quickly dropped Gabriel, who slinked away from the scene and gave a pity glance towards me.

Shaking it off, I stayed near Hades as both brothers hugged each other. "Finally! Come, come, I've been expecting you!" Several deities or fairies came forth and ushered us in. They only reminded me of tiny fairies I had seen in storybooks, but I dared not speak what I thought. I didn't want anyone angered at me for voicing my opinions, yet.

"Zeus, we don't have much time." Hades' voice was rushed. Zeus! This man was Zeus? He looked so young! Then again, Hades was older than Zeus, and he looked young too. I couldn't wait until I didn't age, not that I had wrinkles to worry about yet.

"Nonsense, come in!" Zeus led us into a giant palace. White, everything was white, cream and gold. The chandelier was full of diamonds that decorated the slightly patterned floor of Greek decorations. The palace reminded me a lot of Hades' home except with tons of light. Almost too much; I was blinded.

Zeus led us to a large sitting room with a large white marbled hearth with the twelve original gods on pink quartz pedestals. Zeus went to the hearth and stoked the fire, causing small flames to ignite. Several of the fairy creatures bowed as we walked by, all of them staring at Hades and me once we had passed.

"Hades! As much as I want to catch up, I must know this beauty before me. Is this your mate?" Zeus' eyes were full of mischief as he walked over to shake my hand. Hades immediately stood in front of me.

"That's enough, Zeus. I need to speak with you first." Zeus frowned and let out a grunt of disapproval.

"You wound me." Zeus willed a drinking glass that filled up on its own. "I'm just curious about the woman that finally ignited a fire in your stone heart." Zeus motioned for us to sit down, and Hades pulled me closer to him on the white-colored couches. Sensing my discomfort, Hades rubbed his thumb over my knuckles, but his eyes never left Zeus'.

"Drink?" Hades' eyes narrowed.

"Did you send Malachi to collect Ember?" Zeus' head tilted in confusion.

"No, but I did send Malachi to collect someone called Jillian." Hades stood up, and the dark smoke leaked again, but I grabbed his hand. His breathing slowed as I put another hand on top of his.

Zeus glanced between the both of us as the realization dawned on him. "You are Jillian?" I shook my head no as Hades stood frozen in time.

"My name is Ember, formally Jillian. My memories have been taken away from me, but I did come to remember my name." Zeus sent someone after me, so I didn't want to spill all the information we had about Selene. He was looking for her, as well as the rest of the gods. If he found out that Selene had visited me, he might try to keep me or use me for his own personal use. Hades squeezed his hand with mine, recognizing I wasn't divulging into giving important information away.

"I see." Zeus tapped his glass with his finger. "I did send Malachi to collect you." Zeus paused. "Ember. Selene had told me that a woman named Jillian would need to be saved from an untimely death that would have happened the night of the auction at a strip club. Malachi was to save you and take you to a secure location here in the Celestial Kingdom. He hasn't returned, so I thought he was finishing up his orders." Zeus tapped the glass again as he waved his hands for one of the small fairy-like women approaches.

"You're lying," Hades growled.

The fairy's wings were gold, and the slight drapery of cloth covered her chest and privates as she fluttered close to him. Nodding her head, she zipped out of the room quickly.

"What do you mean I'm lying?" Zeus looked up at his outraged brother, who was oozing his smoke.

"You are just now following up on it? It's been two weeks since the auction!" Hades yelled. "If this was the case, then you would have known Ember was missing, and Malachi had something to do with it!"

"I've been a bit distracted, if you haven't noticed," Zeus gritted his teeth. I've got the rest of the gods figuring out that Selene, as well as Hecate, is missing; sorry if I don't follow up on every human girl on Earth."

Hades slammed his hand on the glass table in front of us, causing it to shatter. "Selene told you Ember was in danger that night!"

"Selene went missing the night of the auction! It slipped my mind!" Zeus lost his calm, playful demeanor as Hades stalked forward. I sat on the couch, feeling as small as a rabbit watching two gods come head to head. Zeus had tiny bits of static electricity buzzing around his head as he stood up.

"Zeus is telling the truth," I heard a whisper. Looking around, I realized it came within me. "Feel it, I feel his honesty." Concentrating on Zeus, looking past the anger he was feeling for his brother, he had no guilt on his soul. He had nothing to hide. The only thing that Zeus was feeling was the overwhelming burden of finding the two missing gods.

"He's telling the truth," I whispered, aloud again. No one paid attention as Hades began yelling.

"What if I had lost your mate if she was to be protected by me?" Hades' spat. Loud thunder rolled through the room, and lightning struck the lamp table.

"If you had accepted Ember when you knew she was your mate as a baby, she wouldn't have been kidnapped and dragged to that club in the first place! YOU could have protected her!"

Chapter 34

Ember

The sharp pain in my heart came suddenly as I gripped my chest. My other handheld tightly to the white cushion. If my nails were any longer, then I was sure to pierce the skin. Hades stood frozen, and his eyes softened as he looked back at me sitting on the couch.

"*Truth,*" the voice began to whisper over and over. The voice in my head was unreasonable. Hades could never do such a thing, to reject the idea that his mate could be found as just a baby. "Hades?" I whispered quietly, daring not to let go of the couch. My body might have floated away and mixed with the horrible sound of Zeus' words if I had. Hades' silence only confirmed that Zeus had spoken the truth and the voice in my head was indeed correct. A fire burned my eyes as Hades rushed to my side.

"Ember, let me explain..." he started, but I just moved my knees away from his kneeling form. Hades had the chance to know who I was when I was born, and he rejected the idea?

"Then explain." I dared not look at him. I would lose all my composure if I had. I'd run back into his arms and tell him it was all right and forgive him on the spot. I gave him so many times to come clean and told him his sins were okay. That I would forgive him. Not once did he bring this up. The guilt still lingered on his heart from just earlier today; he could have spilled onto me, and I would have still given him my heart.

This, I had to learn that THIS was the last bit of the guilt that sat on him. The burden I would have overlooked if he had just told me himself. But no, he hid this from me. Now he is slowly leaking all his regrets and sorrows. Time after time, I forgave him. Time after time, I showed that I was understanding.

I would rather live in the club for another five years than deal with the pain I felt inside me. The blood that flowed through my arteries around my heart even hurt; could that be such a thing? Each passing platelet felt tight, flowing through my body.

Many feel physical pain is the worst kind of pain, but that is far from the truth. This emotional pain of rejection felt far worse. The fact that he hid this instead of telling me was far, far worse than anything I felt at the club. I could live with the bruises on my skin; however, the bruises that now lay on my heart were another matter.

"Selene came to me, the day you were born." Hades' throat bobbed as he pulled at his tie. "She gave me an option to see you, but I rejected her." Hades' breath was heaving, but I remained still, not going to comfort the soulmate that I was to love unconditionally.

"I said I didn't need a mate and that I didn't want her help. I made her leave, and I never saw you. I swear, if I looked at you, I would have jumped at the chance..."

"But you didn't," I interrupted. "You didn't even give me a chance. But that isn't what I'm so mad about, Hades. I mean, you wouldn't tell me. When did you ever think I would reject you after all the things you have confessed to me?" I held in a sob. "Sure, this was a big deal, hell it should be a reason I should walk out those palace doors if I was anyone else, but I'm not." Hades took a step towards me, but I got up and stepped back. Defeated was the only word I could describe him. His shoulders were slumped over, and his eyes glassy.

"I've been really understanding; it's an insult and downright hurtful for you to think I wouldn't forgive you." My heart ached as I heard howling in my head. The waterworks could no longer be held as the once burning eyes filled to the brim with a gushing waterfall. I wanted to scratch my chest and my head at the same time until it bled.

The pain came in waves as my knees fell to the floor. There were hushed and hurried whispers around me, but the scream in my head was far louder. A gentle hand that was not of Hades pulled me to their side and rushed me out the door.

My legs pulled me along as the arm around me held me tightly, whispering encouraging words of, "We are almost there, keep walking. We will fix you right up." A warm tapping on my shoulder was felt on the opposite side of me, nuzzling my cheek. Looking past the tears, Blaze chittered, and his voice became clear.

"It will be all right, Ember. It will be all right; the pain will subside."

Not only do I feel my own despair, hurt, and disappointment but the guilt, depression, and sadness from Hades weighed on me as well. Doubling these intense emotions pushed me further and further to the ground until I collapsed.

"Michael, pick her up, bring her here." A set of muscular arms lifted me into the air and placed me gently on something I could only, in short, be described as a cloud.

"Pasithea, can you help?" My eyes still closed, I felt a wave of calm work its way from my toes up to my neck.

"I can only help so much; she has a strong empath ability." The lulling deep feminine voice soothed my raging headache as I felt Blaze nuzzle into my ear on the pillow under me.

"An animal," he whispered. *"There is a spirit animal attached to you. I just don't know what."* Blaze continued to chitter something in my ear as his voice faded away. The overwhelming emotions lifted as I barely felt my own.

"There she is," the first voice that had taken me out of the living space spoke as I slowly opened my eyes. Her face became familiar, and realization struck me. Hera. "You gave quite a scare back there. You held your own in front of two gods and gave one a personal beating; you did well." Hera chuckled as she petted my forehead with a white cloth. The other woman on the opposite side of the bed must have been Pasithea. She continued to wave her hands over my body and mostly my heart.

"Did you know you were an empath, Ember?" I shook my head as she smiled. "I'm the goddess of relaxation, calmness, and meditation. I hope it is all right, I put your body in a meditative state. I let your mind alone because it is too strong for me. Which I find odd." Pasithea pondered as her hand left my chest. "As I was trying to calm you, I felt many emotions in your body and mind that were not your own. There were two others you were feeling inside of you, causing me not to calm you as well. One I assume to be Hades, and the other, I'm not sure. You are an empath though, very rare to be a true empath for a human."

Hera's eyes narrowed as she heard Pasithea speak. "What do you mean? You said you felt two in her body?"

"Yes," Pasithea confirmed. "Her body radiated sadness, and other emotions that did not line up with her body. There was guilt, depression, and regret, along with another entity inside her. Rage and vulnerability. She was, in a sense, holding three entities' emotions in her body. Something that no human or even god should want or be able to handle."

Blaze started chittering at me again and nodded his head. "Just a few moments ago," I pointed to Blaze. "He told me there was an animal inside me." Hera looked at Blaze while thinking.

"A Phantomtail. They help the animal spirits cross over." Hera let out a sigh and dampened another cloth on my head. "Who are your parents? Do you know?" I shook my head, only for a few tears to fall.

"Someone cast a spell on me, and I don't remember anything before I was sent to a terrible place." I sniffed while Pasithea gave me a tissue. "I just found out my real name not long ago, and memories are slowly coming back, but it is a process. Hecate said she couldn't take any spells off because they were intertwined so much it would hurt me in the long run." I wiped my nose.

"This is becoming more complicated, and Hades has certainly made a mess of it," Hera grunted as she sat back in her chair. Taking in the room, it was much more of a homelier room than that of the palace. It had beautiful tan walls, with paintings of men or women doing various activities like reading or swimming. The bookshelves were lined with ancient books, couches, and seating areas littered the room for a lot of company.

As much as I wanted to think about what was wrong with me, my mind and heart drifted to Hades. My emotions may be in check for a moment, but my heart still wanted him. My mind not so much. I should be exceedingly angry and upset. I spent most of my life locked away, and he could have prevented it all. However, I was angrier he didn't tell me. In a way, the hardships I had gone through shaped me into who I was today after the little time I have spent away from the club.

I've proven myself strong. I had proven myself to be a fighter even in the lowest points of my life. I would turn it to make it for the better. Hades' holding information from me hurt the most. Feeling my fists tighten, I let out a growl.

Why would he think I would leave? Why hold it from me? I accepted he was a god, there were demons, we were mates without question. More than accommodating I have been! Folding my arms while I argued with myself, Hera laughed.

"Relationship trouble, huh? It's all right to be mad and upset. He deserves it. I'm surprised you aren't throwing something." A frustrated tear fell again as both Hera and Pasithea laughed.

"He should have told me." I rubbed my nose. "He's done more than make up for it. He saved me, has tried to write the wrongs, but he wouldn't even entertain the idea of telling me." Blaze growled at me, sensing that I should be even angrier than I was. I was hurt; that's all there was to it. You can't change the past, but he could have built our relationship stronger by telling me rather than having people pity me as I walk into the Celestial Kingdom.

Embarrassment flooded my cheeks as I put my hands to my face. "Does everyone else know?" Hera rushed to my side. "Oh no, dear, no. Zeus and I knew only because we rule together. Selene told us just a few weeks ago before she disappeared." I thought back to Gabriel; he looked like he knew, though.

"Let's get you something to eat." A large man walked into the room with giant white wings. He was shirtless but had on a long white skirt and held a tray full of food. His hair was as gold as wheat and touched just the tip of his ears. "I'm Michael, Hera's bodyguard and slave. Nice to meet you." He smiled while Hera slapped his arm.

"You are not a slave, you big oaf," Hera giggled.

"Well, in bed maybe." He winked as he set the tray down beside the bed. My eyes widened as everyone in the room started laughing.

"Unlike Hades, the rest of the original twelve gods haven't been given a mate yet. We have very open relationships." Hera traced her finger down Michael's torso, and his feathered wings shivered.

"You have guests. I'll visit with you later." Michael took her hand and kissed each finger as he left. Hera's eyes lingered as he shut the door.

"I do hope he is my mate. If not, he will make a woman very happy." The sadness in her eyes spilled into me as she longed after him. There has to be a way to turn off this empath thing. If I feel everyone's emotions now, it is going to get overwhelming.

"Do you think Athena could help her, Hera?" Pasithea continued to hover her hand over my heart. "Dear Ember, your mind wanders, and sucks in every emotion you can find. Hades did a number on you to make you feel this overwhelmed."

"An excellent idea; I'll have one of the servants bring her." Several Fairy creatures came in with a wave of Hera's hand. My spark of interest helped me to sit up as I saw them up close. "These are a type of Fairy, Ember."

"I'm sorry, I didn't mean to stare." I lowered my head while the Fairies laughed. Their voices reminded me of those musical bells you could hear at Christmas times on the streets. Sometimes if I had listened really hard, I could make out some sort of song.

"It's all right; we don't get to see many mortals either. We both can be intrigued." With a brief order from Hera, the Celestial Fairies left in a hurry while both beautiful goddesses helped me up.

My body felt weak as I put my feet on the floor. "Even though you were only feeling their emotions for a short time, your body wasn't used to it. You will feel weak, and on top of your condition of years of malnourishment, it will feel double. Don't worry, you will heal." Pasithea stroked my hair that was surely a mess, and waved a few men in white robes in.

"Hades has sent us to check on you. You were given a strict medication through IV that we are supposed to administer; however, Asklepios has made you something in pill form that will help you much more substantially." Hera held her hand to hold the pill and grabbed a glass of water from the tray.

"Asklepios is a friend of mine; he is the god of medicine and healing. If anyone can help you with your ailment of fatigue and nourishment, it would be him. Plus, no more pokes and prods," she laughed. Taking the pill and not thinking twice, I took it in one large gulp. I was tired of thinking, tired of feeling.

"Hades would wish to speak with you," one of the robed men spoke up from the doorway. "He's very concerned about your well-being." The man shook as he spoke; Hades must be throwing a tantrum.

Hera stroked my hair one more time. "You can do as you wish. We will take care of Hades for you."

"I'd like to be alone," I whispered. "Just somewhere where I can gather my thoughts."

Hera took my hand and helped guide me to a room with a canopied bed. She had me lay down and pulled a giant plush, white-down comforter over me. "Just rest, try not to think. Things will work out. I know it. Hades does care for you. He's just not used to even friendships, let alone having a mate." I nodded as she walked out of the now darkened room with a single low-dim lamp.

Rolling to my side, I let the tears flow. I let out my frustration and Hades' complex emotions that were brewing just down the hall. The tears flowed, my hand banged the pillow, and I pulled at my hair just so I could feel something physical instead of feeling it internally.

Chapter 35

Hades

I watched as Ember fell to the floor. Her body shook as she held her head and her heart. I had absolutely done a royal fuck up, and I knew this was coming. I was being a fool and blindly shutting it away. If Zeus wasn't a complete prick, I could have had a few more days to break the news to her. Telling her the moment I was spilling my heart out about the Helm should have been my first clue she would have accepted what had happened. She believed and accepted the truth with ease.

Ember would have been hurt, undoubtedly so. Now, I had made it ten times worse by having her hear it from my younger brother, who has absolutely no filter and no damn soul as far as I thought. How Hera puts up with his shit is beyond me. Then again, they were only an item in the eyes of humans.

"You are a piece of shit." I stood as Ember was being led away by Hera. The goddess of marriage and relationships would be the best comfort for her. Maybe she could talk to Ember and calm her down. Unfortunately, that is wishful thinking because I knew Hera would come back to chew my fiery ass out.

"I spoke the truth. I have no regrets." Zeus waved his hand to sit down, but I lunged forward, pulling at his white robes.

"You have already interfered in my life before involving my relationships, and here you are at it again. I believe you should be the one in the Underworld having no regard for your family's feelings," I hissed as I knocked his drink from his hand. "You are a complete ass, I've known her for several weeks, and the bond is still forming. I wanted to break it to her gently, and you go and blurt out a sentence that will now haunt her the rest of our immortal lives. She will doubt me, she will...." Zeus cut me off with a stiff blow to my jaw.

Stumbling back, I put my hand on my jaw to lock it back in place. The static electricity was sparkling above his head as well as his fingers as he tightened his fists. "You have just a little under a month with a mate is enough time to tell her the truth and why she is with you now..." Zeus growled as he started to circle me. Just because he was the god of the heavens, he believed he was more superior. "...Is beyond a reason of a miracle."

Sure, Zeus defeated Kronos but only because Rhea had enough of him swallowing her children. Zeus was hidden, and once finally raised to maturity, he was ready to fight and ultimately defeat Kronos. I was the firstborn. I was not given the luxury of killing the monster. In fact, I suffered the worse since my fertility had been taken away from me being in Kronos' stomach acid too long.

Now, trying to be high and mighty, Zeus lectures me on relationships when he couldn't keep his dick in his pants for Hera. For a few thousand years before learning of Selene's new attempt to make mates for the gods, he cheated on her constantly.

Talk about a hypocrite. Giving out advice, my ass.

"Out of all the gods, you shouldn't have been allowed to be the first to receive one." Zeus yelled. I growled as my fangs descended, ready to rip his damn head off. "You work in the Underworld, away from the light, away from the normalcy. What mate would want to live in a dark hovel of death and destruction? I live in the sky, where it is bright, and I see the happiness in every face I pass. Bringing joy to those who are saddened, having the angels help those who are of pure of heart and in need." Zeus smiled as he approached the hearth with each original god in place. He walked to the very end, where should be the first god born, which was me. Tapping the base with his finger, he moved it back behind the rest of them.

"You bring death. Your body even knows this, so why were you the first to gain a mate?" Zeus' tone went sarcastic. I stood in silence, waiting for his answer before I strangled the lightning from his body.

"Because Selene wanted to see your mate reject you because you can't give what most women want... a child."

That did it.

Zeus swatted my statue from the hearth to the floor and put up his hands to crack the lightning at my torso. I felt nothing. I was pain and suffering, so why would I falter at just the tickle of a bit of static? The heated punch of my fist singed his hipster beard, bringing the scent burning hair and flesh into the air. Gaining his composure, he stood up to crack his neck as a few bolts ran through the palm of his hands.

Easily dodged, I crouched forward and aimed for his legs. His screams felt music to my ears as he grabbed his leg and tried to use his head to push me away. Putting him in an easy headlock, I took my knee and smashed his nose. The touch of death that I left for the vilest of humans was activated, and the skin began to melt.

"Had enough, little brother?" I laughed darkly just as Hera walked into the room. Celestial Fairies flew around in shock in the state of the room, not paying much attention to their master.

"Hades, it is enough. Now let him go." Hera waved her hand as Fairies cleaned the mess. Couches had been pushed over, and a few stray lightning bolts had set fire to the curtains around the windows. Out of the chaos, I caused the least amount of damage. Not unless you counted Zeus. I damaged all of that piece of shit.

Straightening my suit, which had nothing but a few pieces of rubble, I walked to Hera closely to speak privately. "Is she all right? Is Ember all right?" My voice came out more panicked than I wanted, but Hera, being the loving sister she was, cupped my cheek.

"She is fine and overwhelmed. She's relaxing with Pasithea, and Athena is on her way. There are a lot of questionable things going on with her body," Hera spoke thoughtfully.

"You mean the magic?"

"No, something else. Pasithea said she has the gift of empathy, almost unheard of for a human. Ember can feel and suck in the feelings of those around her so strongly it triggered her body to shut down. On top of it all, she has magical wards and supposedly another entity in her body." Hera spoke in hushed tones as she explained.

An Elven woman walked into the room and rushed to Zeus' side. That was probably his side piece of the decade. Her long brown hair was braided and swept the floor. Her purple robes and golden ropes that tightened and accentuated her assets sparkled in the sun.

"Your Majesty," the Elven woman bowed to Hera. "Is it all right if I take Zeus away to help with his wounds?" Hera nodded. Zeus and Hera hadn't shared a bed in centuries, but both remained the

King and Queen of the Celestial Kingdom. Once they both gain their mates, I'm not sure how that would work out. Not my problem.

"Ember has also been given her nutritional supplement in pill form; Asklepios already had such a pill ready for her. Why didn't you bring her here before?" Hera didn't understand my concerns. I thought and still think Zeus was part of the conspiracy. "He would have healed her body more quickly if you had."

"I didn't want to subject her to more stress. What was working in the Underworld was fine. Hecate said slow and steadily with Ember, that there is much for Ember to figure out independently. Her memories, her dreams, I wanted her relaxed and not deal with that asshole." I glanced to where Zeus stood. His gold metallic blood still staining the floor.

"You both have your ways, but you know why he is this way, don't you?" Hera wrapped her arm around my own as I led her to the couch. Willing a pot of tea, she poured us both a cup and dripped the honey into the cup without asking.

Ignoring the question, I asked, "Vulcan made you this set, didn't he?" Hera smiled as she looked at the intricate gold designs.

"He did. I miss him."

"All you need do is ask, and he will come." I took a sip and set it back down on the cracked table.

"He is my son, and he feels he needs to find his own place in this world. Zeus hid him far too long, and I did not fight hard enough for him. If my time comes to find a mate, I will ask Selene to pass my gift to him if he doesn't already have one." Hera's eyes drifted to the large bay windows, where she saw Michael sparring with other angels. Her love for him had only grown, and since the announcement of mates, she thought of ending it with him. Her passion for her mate would cloud over her love for Michael, and it would only break his heart if they were not together.

"You shouldn't blame yourself. Rhea did the same to us. I do not hold her accountable." Rhea had taken her place in the stars after Kronos chained. Quickly changing the subject, Hera spoke about how Ember took the news. Ember was more angered that I didn't tell her, not the fact she suffered all those years. A strong, capable woman I had for a mate, and I overlooked it all. "She loves you, Hades. Ember takes truth as more important than anything. She doesn't want the information to be hidden from her most of her life was hidden."

"I must see her." Hera looked warily at me as I gave her pleading eyes.

"She told the servants she wanted to be left alone to think. I think that is for the best." Hera put her small cup back on the saucer and went to stand up. "If she asks the truth from you again, even if you are not ready to give it...." Hera glanced down at me. "You give her the truth. She has been hidden from her own past and now just wants answers for the future."

Resting my forearms on my legs and my thumbs rubbing my eyes, Hera patted my shoulder. "Leave Zeus alone. I can tell you now that he has been busy with Selene and Hecate missing. I was there when Selene asked he take care of Ember that night if you had decided not to rescue her."

"Where is Malachi then? Where is he?" I growled, and Hera scowled.

"I do not know, Hades, but I will find out. Mark my words."

Hera stilled at the door, her back still facing me. Her hand touched the handle and glanced back. "Zeus only wishes to have a mate. He craves it and is jealous that his brother, who cried he didn't want Selene's help, was granted one. Try not to be too hard on him."

***

Hera told me that I should not find Ember and leave her be, but I didn't listen. My heart was beating for her, I could feel her sadness through the bond, and I wanted nothing more than to hold her tight and beg for her forgiveness.

Following the bond, I walked down the brightly lit hallways. The cold, white marble was blinding and not warm like the palace where we lived. Carpets of white and gold were few and far between, and I swear I could feel the cold go through the soles of my shoes. The pull in my chest became strong as I came across the golden door with tiny cherubs painted on the doorway. Light pinks, blues, and purple flowers laid over the door.

Does Ember like these colors? Does she like it here better than our own home? I'd change anything she wanted if it meant to keep her with me. Where it's safe.

I willed myself to the other side to see the room dimly lit and a small figure on the bed. The curtains were drawn, and the darkness felt more familiar than the light. Ember's form was small; her cheeks still held the light pinkness to them. Her eyes were puffy, her lashes still wet from her crying. I wanted to reverse time and kiss every single tear that trailed down her face.

Ember sniffed a few times, and I grabbed a nearby tissue to dab her nose. The strawberry blonde hair was sprawled across the pillow, and her pink lips puckered as if she was thinking. Her green eyes I longed to look into were sitting in darkness. Ember's fingers began to twitch as she held onto the sheets, a habit she had right before she has a bad dream.

Not heeding Hera's warning of leaving my mate alone, I took off my suit jacket, shirt, shoes, and pants and left myself in nothing but my boxers. Crawling into the bed with her, I pulled her back to my front and felt the warmth radiate. Immediately, she moved her body, facing me, and her face was directly to my chest. Skin to skin now and ultimately relaxed, she took long breaths of my scent. I had wished she was a supernatural so she could smell me like I could smell her. The aroma she gives off calms me when she is near, and I crave it like a drug she truly is.

My arms wrapped around her tiny waist. Hera had her dressed in a plain white lace gown that went just to the top of her knees. I'm sure it would just cover Hera's rear if it was her nightgown. My mate was small and fragile, and I had to get clothes personally made for her. I was fine with that. I was fine with everything.

How stupid could I be? Most of my existence was made making mistakes, running from them, being angry at the people trying to help me. Ember was doing what a mate is supposed to do, feel. She felt me, and I took it as the bond, but no, she has something more. Now there was something else inside of her, and Athena was going to be our only hope to figure out what it was.

How can she pull in emotions so well? It explained how much information she had pulled from me when she did ask about my past or why I was feeling the way I was. Ember could feel the guilt and the burden on my heart.

Fuck.

I had inadvertently made her suffer as well. Blaze was sitting on the bedpost, watching me with anger. His tail went ablaze as he saw me staring at him. "Fuck off," I whisper yelled as I nuzzled into Ember's hair. Stupid judgmental squirrel.

I would make it all up to her. Hell, I'll let her look into my mind so she can see every bit of my past. My mood brightened instantly. That is what I would do, let her know of all my history. Something that should terrify me, but knowing she was my mate, she was here to stay even if she did see the worst in me. Numerous times she said she would stay, and I had to trust her.

I had long lost my trust when I tried to take Persephone. She was wonderful in the beginning, just asking for time. Time turned to days, weeks, and then years of nothing until she despised me. I tried to give her everything. No love was returned. Meaningless gifts she had asked for collected in her room. What brought her happiness for a few days only made her hate me more.

The day she said I didn't even look like a God of the Underworld was what cut me to the core. I changed the very person I was and became bitter along with her. I should have let Persephone go. We were never a match.

Now I do not have to hide. I will bear my soul to her to make her happy. She has not once asked for shiny jewels or lavish gifts. She asked for the true person that I really am. Rest my little mate, for I will show you every part of me when you wake up.

Chapter 36

Ember

I groaned, rolling over in the bed. The heaviness of my head continued to move around the pillow as I opened my eyes. Waiting for the bright light to stain my pupils, I opened them slowly. I saw deep reds and black instead of the bright white that I knew of the Celestial Kingdom.

There was a lit fireplace on the opposite wall in the room. The bedposts were a deep cherry redwood, and only a deep red sheet covered my body. White candles in various candelabras littered the room on bedside tables, dressers, and free-floating shelves.

Slinging off the single red sheet covering my body, I glanced at the black lingerie set that I was wearing. I swore I went to bed in one of Hera's nightgowns as I patted the leathery brasier and crotchless panties.

Oh, my gosh. What in heavens name am I wearing!?

My lady bits were out in the open for all to see, yet the leather surrounding my butt was more like straps, only to push my bum cheeks up and make them plump in the back. All I was missing were some garters. The sight had me red with embarrassment.

What. The. Heck.

"Ember," a husky voice vibrated through my chest, down to my thighs. Squeezing them tightly, I looked around the room as I crossed my arms to cover my naked body.

"Ember," he spoke again as I saw two glowing red eyes in the dark part of the room corner. As he walked forward and into the dim light, I saw it was none other than Hades. My heart jumped as his black, unbuttoned shirt flowed effortlessly as he walked. His movements were slow as his confident barefooted strides went to the bed. Curling my legs up to hide my body, I realized my bits were going to hang out. I had nothing to help hide my body. Scanning my hand around on the mattress, I tried to find the silk sheet for nothing to be there.

"Looking for this?" The grinding of stones in his voice only made me sweat as he pulled up the sheet with his right hand. "You won't need it." The feelings of confusion bubbled down into my belly as the anger rose like nasty heartburn.

"I'm mad at you!" I growled out while I pointed at him. "You lied to me! You kept things from me! You-." Hades' lips attacked mine as I tried to speak to him. His opened mouth kisses trailed my neck as I moaned into him. His touch was cooling the fire that had lit just before he pounced on me. The anger subsided and the hunger for his body on me grew bright.

The suckles he brought to my skin; the marks he was leaving on my body set me in a trance. Soon I was no longer conscious in my body. I was watching and feeling from the inside. Another being had taken over me.

"Yes," the voice inside my head spoke for me. "Touch me, quench this fire in my body." I no longer fought as Hades growled back and nipped his lips along my hips. Long claw-like nails grew from my fingers and ripped Hades' black dress shirt down the middle of his back. Hades groaned and attacked my breasts, pulling the leather bra from my body. My nipples sprung free as he tugged on them harshly. My breasts chilled into the dark air, even with the roaring fire.

My fingers embedded into his hair as he assaulted my chest with his mouth. Feeling every crevice, pulling with his lips, gripping as much as he could with his hands. I mewled into the air handling his touches.

"Fuck," he growled as his hand pulled at my other breast. The voice coming out of me wasn't my own, and I didn't want to question it.

"I need your tongue," my body growled like an animal. "I need you to taste me." My hips bucked as I threw my head back. Hades' fingers swiftly plunged into my core as his tongue sucked on my bundle of nerves. Everything was happening so fast I felt my body trying to push it over the edge.

Hades left a hefty slap on the outside of my thigh that made me tumble over. The groans my throat was making were loud and unrecognizable to me. My body grabbed my breast with one hand, and another tangled into Hades' hair. Tugging him, pushing my core right back into his mouth. He drank my essence like I was the fountain of youth. His face covered with wetness as I cummed over and over as his finger pumped into me religiously. From time to time, he would pull his fingers to examine the drips flowing down onto his arm, licking the remnants.

Adding another finger, I winced. "Mate, I need you," *my voice purred as the hand retreated from his hair. Hades' red eyes glowed as he glanced at me.*

"Then let me claim you, make you mine." *He pulled my hips closer to his. Willing his pants off in an instant, I ripped off my own crotchless leather underwear in an instant as his dick brushed my core as he hovered over me. The heat from his cock burned into my cavern as he had me taste myself on his lips.*

The tip was right there, right there for my body to suck him in.

"Are you sure?" *He placed another kiss on my lips. My nipples puckered again as his hot chest heaved up and down on my body. Hades' member rubbed my core again, deliberately making me wrap my legs around his waist. More friction. I needed more.*

I couldn't understand who was in control anymore. One moment I'm watching from the sidelines, and the next, I'm being thrown back into the ring, and I am the one in control now. All my anger of his lie left me, and my heart wanted nothing more than to have him dip himself into me, mate with me, make me his.

Nothing felt more right than right here.

With the lie and all, I still wanted him. It scared him to lose me, but it doesn't excuse it. All relationships have flaws, and that makes them grow stronger. He wouldn't be out of the woods yet after this was over. Right now, I needed this.

"I just need one word." *Hades' red eyes glowed with lust. My hands came to Hades' face while he lined the tip of himself to me.*

"Yes."

Hades' hips tried to thrust forward, but the warmth of his body vanished into thin air. I left my hands where I was holding his biceps, and my body was completely naked. My eyes wide, I looked around the room. It was cold again, and the fire at the hearth was nothing but smoke.

Blue vagina, I have blue vagina. I kept thinking to myself as I thought of those terrible men at the club that often left with "blue balls."

"Hades?" *I whispered quietly. This was so incredibly awkward.*

A chuckle came from the same darkened corner of the room, and my head whipped to see who it was. A wolf came prancing out and sat on her rump on the carpeted floor. She was beautiful, white, and almost glowing as she sniffed the air at me.

"Hello, Ember." *The voice came into my head again, and I knew exactly whose voice it was. This wolf, even when her lips didn't move, I knew it was her.*

"Y-you have been trying to talk to me?" *I questioned,* "Are you in my head?" *My hand came down to my mouth to close my gaping mouth. The wolf looked on curiously while she licked her lips.*

"I have. You've been through a lot. I've been hibernating for far too long. I was supposed to appear right before you hit puberty, but the past few weeks watching from the inside, I think you are way past that," *she huffed.* "I also can't *see your early childhood. Why is that?"* She tilted her head as she pranced over to the bed.

"Um," I tried to find the words. There is a dog in front of me, asking me questions like I know the answers. I had NO answers, and I didn't know if I was dreaming or wide awake! My head had the dull pain again, and the wolf instantly put her nose in my hand.

"Hey, I'm here. Don't worry. I'm your Wolf. Don't you know that?" I shook my head no.

Pretty sure if I had a wolf, I would know about it. Especially one that lived in my head. Rubbing my cheek, trying to calm the panic, I tried to think of something to say.

"Oh, I guess if you can't remember your adolescent life, I guess you wouldn't know about me," she mused. *"You are a Werewolf, Ember. I'm your wolf!"* My brain needed a reboot because only one sound came out of my mouth, and it was a continuous, *"uhhhh."*

"There you go! I help you shift, heal you, and all that jazz. You read about Wolves the other week in Hades' office! Let me tell you, he is a hottie. We really lucked out in the mate department; don't you think? Selene really did a good job!" The wolf rushed her words quickly. *"That scene we just experienced; I came up with all on my own. I think he would like leather; don't you think?"*

The continuous *"uhh,"* sound I was making was now silent as I continued to stare at her. My mouth was still open, unable to speak.

Sure, I read all about Werewolves while Hades worked but now experiencing it gave me panic. Wolves were social creatures; they lived with each other and comforted one another. I never lived in such a place. Or did I? The dreams of the bonfire with so many people sitting around it and listening to a large man's story started to make sense. He was, 'the Alpha," the man in charge and the woman? Was the Luna? Possibly my parents? A gasp left my lips.

I was part of a pack that was my home. The wolf continued to stare at me, reading me like an open book. Her eyebrows widened, and she nudged my knee with her snout.

"Well, say something. We got to figure some stuff out before we get mated. I mean, a god, right? How cool is that? A Werewolf and a god together; we will be the Queen of the Underworld. Our parents and pack will be so proud! Wait…" The wolf lowered her head. *"Where is our pack?"* I shrugged my shoulders and fiddled with a sheet that was magically back on the bed.

"You know what I know if you can see in my memories. That dream that I just thought of, that's all I know about any sort of pack. Someone took me to that terrible club-" My breath hitched. The wolf put her paw on my knee.

"Hey, it's all right. I was lucky that Selene visited me and told me your name. She said that was the first step. To know your name. The rest would be up to us as we stay with our mate." I gripped the sheets beside me still shaking at this Wolf's words.

"*We had a lot of spells cast on us. Memory, body weakening, barrier spells, you name it. Things are slowly piecing together, but it is taking time.*" I spoke. She nodded her head again and looked at the floor.

"*That explains why I fade in and out with you. I can see what you see, but sometimes the light goes off, and I miss things. There are other times I can see, but you can't hear me. It's frustrating.*" The wolf huffed as I laughed. "*I've cried MATE so many times, but you just keep going on with life like nothing is happening. I'm glad Hades recognized it.*"

This Wolf was going to be the death of me if she kept talking. I couldn't keep up with her half the time. Getting used to her being in my head was going to be a significant change. At least I'd always have a friend.

"*What's your name?*" I petted under her chin.

"*Elea,*" she purred.

A Werewolf. I was a dang Werewolf. It explained a lot, and now I know I wasn't going crazy. The fangs, the claws, and my sensitive nose. I touched my teeth and felt them descend a little when I thought about them coming out. Gasping, I touched them, and Elea laughed at my reaction.

"*That reminds me.*" Elea jumped on the bed to get at eye level with me. "*As this spell keeps breaking, we might shift, and that will be bad news if we don't have a pack.*"

"*How so?*"

"*Well, Werewolves are social creatures, you know, and when a pup first shifts, they need the help of the pack and their parents. A mate can help with the pain, but Hades isn't a Wolf, so he won't be much help coaching you through it. I have never been around any other Werewolves. I haven't talked to anyone about how it works. I don't want to break the wrong bone on your body when my body emerges.*"

"*Woah, Woah, woah.*" I held my hands up. "*Break my bones?!*"

"*How else would you shift, duh?*" Elea rolled her eyes. "*Anyway, we need to find a pack that would take us in before we shift. Once we have our shifting under control, we can go back home with Hades.*" I sighed heavily and fell back onto the mattress.

"*Hades won't let us go alone. He will come with us.*" I didn't want to be without Hades, anyway. Hades was my protector, even if he withheld the truth from me. "*He's angry with me right now because I won't see him.*"

"*I don't think he got that memo…*" Elea snickered.

"*What do you mean?*" I asked her as I sat back up on the bed.

"*He's cuddling with us right now. You're sleeping, and he snuck into your room. You had that hot, steamy dream before I showed up because the bond is trying to get you to hurry it up, and I enhanced it a bit. He probably smelled your cummies in the sheets,*" She snorted a laugh and rolled on the bed. "*I had so much fun taking control. I knew you would be too pissed, but once you let go, boy! Over and over….*"

"Okay, stop!" I squealed and put my hands over my ears.

"He's even poking you with his magic scepter right now..." she whispered, and I leaned into smack her, but I woke up with my body sitting up straight in the bed. Hades was snoring lightly beside me.

Was that dream real? I was in-between consciousness and dreamland, so I wasn't sure.

"Nope, still here!" Elea barked as I shook my head.

"Don't do that," I whispered.

"You can talk to me in your head. You don't need to wake up Mr. Sex God. Just let him know you are still mad, but get some romping done. I'm horny in here too." I slapped my face and pulled down my cheek. I have a horny wolf that wants to forgive too quickly.

Hades looked peaceful again as he grabbed my waist. Falling back into the covers, I put my head right under his chin and kissed his Adam's apple that I found so incredibly sexy. A small thought ran through my head to just start kissing him up and down his neck until I heard my own devil in my head.

"Do it..."

"You are a bad influence, you know that?" I spoke back to her.

"That's what I'm here for and for you. We've got our mate and each other. We will figure all this out together, even finding our parents," she cooed into my ear.

"Thanks for not giving up on me, Elea." Elea hummed, and I swore I could see her curl up in the back of my head. *"And Elea, thank you for working so hard to get through the barriers."* Elea nodded her head as she curled into a comfortable ball and soft snores took over us both.

Chapter 37

Hades

"Wake up! You are in some serious trouble!" Hearing the harsh words of a whisper and poking my on my head, I slapped the hand that dared to touch me. Rubbing my forehead and opening my eyes, I see none other than Hera's hands on her hips. "Get up!" she mouthed as Ember was curled up in my arms. I didn't have to get away from her if I didn't want to. I don't care if Hera helped yesterday. Ember is nuzzled up in the crook of my neck; why the hell should I move?

"No," I deadpanned. "She's sleeping; let her sleep." Hera stomped her foot again like a scolding mother.

"We have things to discuss, not just you sneaking into her bed and using the bond against her. Now get up; Athena is here to speak with us." Before I think about letting go, Athena walks in wearing light blue robes and gold ropes wrapped around her body. Her burgundy hair was wrapped tightly in braids around her head as she held a white book that looked too heavy to carry. Gracefully gliding through the room, she placed it on a nearby table. "He won't let go of her," Hera accused me while pointing her manicured finger. "He's being as stubborn as Zeus, and I can't seduce him out of bed. He is almost bonded to his mate."

I shivered. I would never do it with Hera; that sounded repulsive. "Shut up," Hera immediately read my thoughts as I chuckled into Ember's hair. She stirred for a moment but immediately sighed.

"It's all right, Hera. We can talk from here. Ember needs all the rest she can." Athena elegantly sat on the bed next to Ember. Taking Ember's hand, she recorded her resting heartbeat and checked her skin, nails, and hair. Ember did not move once as I held her in place.

"Hecate was right; she does have a lot of barriers on her. Luckily Hecate was able to briefly tell me how deep they were in her soul before she left." Athena grabbed the book from the table and laid it out on the bed. Symbols decorated the page where she had bookmarked that would be familiar to a coven Witch. A Celestial Fairy came into the room with a tray full of different powders. Green, gold, blue, and words of ancient Greek and Latin were written underneath each. Athena took her index finger and dipped it into the gold powder twice and once in the blue.

Touching Ember's head, she drew a crescent moon on her forehead with three dots on the underside. Whispering the ancient Greek to herself, Ember stirred, and her eyes flew open. Ember's nails grew and sliced my right peck muscle with three distinct scratches. I hissed at the sudden pain but felt myself already healing.

"I'm so sorry!" Ember darted her head around the room, stunned to see women and servants standing around her. Her breath picked up, and she began to look back at her hand and to my chest.

"It's all right, it was an accident." I tried to comfort her, but she pulled away.

"I didn't, I don't know…" Her breathing went to full-blown pants, and she grabbed her head. Her claws retracted, but her whimpers came loudly. "What the hell did you do to her?" I growled at Athena, but her face was impassive. Her hand went to Ember, but I swatted it away. "Answer me, what did you do? You are hurting her!" I pulled Ember back into my arms as her body went limp. "Ember!" I gently shook her as Hera looked on in horror, and Athena continued to look as if nothing was wrong. The smoke tendrils seeped through the sheets, and Hera called in for Vulcan and Ares. Both prominent men burst into the room as I held Ember close and fire sparks began to light at the end of the smoke, fingers grabbing at the sheets.

"Hey man, calm down." Ares held up his hands. "Athena is trying to help Ember. She told me all about it. Athena has to remain calm to help her breakthrough a barrier."

"Can you women not talk outright and tell me this shit?" I yelled. "Quit all this deceptive shit, now what the hell is wrong!" Ember stirred again, and Vulcan went to grab a glass of water.

"Hades." Ember's voice was groggy and low, not sounding like her sweet self. "Hades," she repeated as her eyes popped open. Blackness stared back into my eyes. Ember was no longer Ember; there was something else, and I knew it wasn't a demon. Blaze jumped onto the bed to get between us, but I swatted him off the bed. Chatting away again, he hopped back on the bed, rushing to my mate. Growling at him, he stopped to argue, but my eyes went back to Ember.

"Mine!" she growled and pushed all her strength on me. I was pinned back on the bed with her thighs tightly around my torso. My hands dared not touch her as they stayed hovered over her back. Ember growled into my neck as she began to smell into my hair.

"Fuck, that was hot." Ares rubbed his chin as he set down his sword.

"That is why I couldn't speak," Athena painfully spoke as she rose from the bed. Closing the book, she put it on the nightstand table and pushed people away from the bed. "Ember isn't human, not even part human." Athena's hands were put together as her lips formed a thin line. Ember's body gripped me tighter as she nipped and nibbled my neck. Would it be wrong if I had a raging boner in front of everyone?

"What do you mean?" Vulcan stepped towards her. "She heals at a human pace. Her body even ages as a human who is nutrient deficient. I've seen her lab results."

"She is a full-blooded Alpha Werewolf," Athena interrupted. Hera sat down by a nearby chair as one of the servant Fairies helped her. Fanning herself, she looked at Ember's body attached to mine. Ares gave a smirk and slapped Vulcan's chest.

"Badass, our girl is a complete badass. She'll be able to spar with me now!" Giving Ares a glare, I sat up from the bed with Ember still attached.

"Mine," she growled again, and a purring noise came from her chest. Her Wolf must be present because the Ember I know wouldn't be so bold.

"Ember?"

"Not Ember; I'm Elea." Elea sat back. Her crotch was directly above my dick, and she moved her hips, giving me an evil smirk.

"Mate," she purred as she leaned forward and kissed up my neck. "I've got Ember loosened up a bit for you. She won't be so mad now but don't screw it up anymore!" A swift slap to my chest had me jump as well as everyone else in the room.

"No more hiding things. We hate that. We can feel when you keep things from us!" Growling again, her head came to my chest, and Elea started rubbing her face thoroughly all over me.

"W-what is she doing?" I laughed as I pulled her off. "She's a Werewolf; she is marking you as hers. Elea wants her scent on you to warn off any females that might take you before you are both mated." Athena sat on a nearby couch, grabbing a cup of tea that Vulcan had made for her. Vulcan glanced at Hera, his mother, and made one for her as well.

Hera stood as Vulcan approached, took the teacup and saucer from him, and put it on the table next to her. "Vulcan," she sniffed, and Vulcan engulfed her in an enormous embrace.

"I'm so sorry how you were treated here." Hera gripped on Vulcan. Vulcan rubbed his mother's back lovingly and kissed her cheek.
"All is forgiven, Mother. Hades has taken good care of me. We will rebuild what we have together. We should concentrate on Ember now." Vulcan looked at the both of us and smiled. Hera nodded as a Celestial Fairy stared too closely at us.

"Mine," Elea growled again, looking at one of the Fairies. Hera made the extra women leave the room while Elea continued to hold onto me tight. Once the threat was alleviated, Elea instantly calmed. I was the possessive one, and now Ember will have a possessive side too. This could be good or bad, but right now, it is a damn turn-on. I felt myself growl lowly as I kissed her ear.

"You are so damn sexy," Elea whispered. "I told Ember I was mad at her for not bonding with you yet. I'll get her warmed up to the idea. Then we can do it all night long, all sorts of ways." Elea winked at me while tickling my shoulder, a Werewolf's claiming spot. Fuck, having Ember leaving a mark on me would be sexy as hell.

Athena cleared her throat, causing Elea to glare at her. "Oh, sorry," Elea relaxed slightly. "Thank you for helping. That barrier has been difficult to pull down."

"Not a problem; I'm glad you have been working so hard to help Ember. She's been through a lot." Elea nodded solemnly.

"I don't know our parents, and we need them. We need a pack and soon," Elea rushed. "I don't think I'm supposed to even come forward yet and take Ember's body. This all feels so backward." Athena pondered as she got up to walk to a nearby shelf. Finding a large black book with a moon engraved on the front, I knew what it was right away. It was a Werewolf bible or manual. It held more information than any of the smaller books I had on the shifters. I never came across them until my run-in with them some twenty three some years ago when they helped me get rid of my rogue demon.

"You will need a pack, whether your birthing pack or not. It says that other wolves need to help bring you forth while someone close to your human side stays close. Since Hades is the only one close to you, he would be the best option to help you both shift. It will be... disastrous if you don't find a willing pack to take you during the change." Elea whimpered in my arms while I held her close.

"What will happen?" Vulcan stepped forward, worried for Ember. He had become attached to her in a sisterly way, and that I was grateful, unlike Loukas, who was treading on the tight ropes on the fire lake. Blaze started yelling in his own chattering language, and Elea just waved at him with a smile. Blaze calmed and sat on the side of the bed, making sure he was away from me, to keep me from smacking him across the room. "Ember and Elea will both die."

"She will not!" I snapped as I picked her off the bed. "We will find a pack, and everything will be fine." Elea looked up at me longingly and nuzzled her head into my neck. "I know of a friendly pack that will help her; they have a powerful sorceress there too. It will be fine." Elea held me tightly and whispered a small thank you in my ear.

"Hold on a second," Ares spoke up. "I've seen pups go through their shifts on their own in the woods when I worked with them during the shifter wars. Why is Ember any different? Why can't she do it on her own?"

"She's lost her memory of her early years living in a pack, and her wolf wasn't even present during this time. Most adolescents get their wolves at twelve but don't shift until 16 or 17. Ember is almost 21 and has spent no time with wolves. Werewolves learned by example and each other. Elea could break the wrong bones, shift too fast or too slow. Only those that have been changed from human to werewolf have been given the knowledge to shift correctly, and even that is a rare occurrence."

"She's so smart," I heard the sweet voice of my Ember whisper in my ear. Turning her head, I saw her beautiful green eyes. Hugging her close, I kissed her forehead.

"You're back," I breathed.

"I was always here." Ember petted my cheek. "I've just got a little bit more of me now, I guess. Sorry she attacked you. She's been wanting to say 'mine; for ages." She rolled her eyes as she pulled me in for a peck on the lips. "No more lying and keeping stuff from me!" Great, I get scolded twice.

"I swear, tonight I'll let you see everything about me. With one touch, you can see everything from my birth to where we are now." Ember scrunched up her nose.

"I don't think I wanna do that. That'd take forever. Just don't lie anymore." My forehead touched hers as I stood standing in the middle of the room.

"Everyone is staring," she whispered shyly. The vast amount of personality changes that Ember and Elea have was enough to give a whiplash.

"Right," Hera spoke. "Anyway, Ember, there is something else about you besides your Wolf that I wanted Athena to check on."

"The empathy gift?" Hera nodded.

"Elea acted like she didn't know what it was either," Ember said sadly. Athena walked closer to touch Ember's cheek.

"We will work on it together to block out the different emotions you feel." Athena backed away and looked both of us up and down. "Right now, however, I think you both need pants." All I had on was a pair of black boxer briefs which was sporting a big boner, and Ember's ass was almost hanging out.

"Damn, he got lucky," Ares grunted as he stomped out the door. "I need some Werewolf ass, too," he mumbled while Vulcan smacked him upside the head. Ember's legs tightened as her face grew red, as they walked out the door.

"Hera, a word?" Zeus walked in, still sporting a black eye. Getting carried away last night was good for him. He needed to remember who the firstborn was. Hera nodded and waved gently to Ember. Hera had turned the guest quarters into our room since we wouldn't be leaving right away. Ember had to learn to control her abilities, and Athena was the only one that would be able to help. Hecate would be the better choice, but we will have to make do.

"I'm going to go shower." Ember let her legs unhinged from my body as she stepped on the carpeted floor. My arms didn't let go, however, and she laughed. "Hades, I'm gross. I didn't even shower before bed." An evil idea popped in my head as she pushed me away again. "I'll only be a minute." Ember picked up her clothes from a nearby table and closed the door behind her. I wasn't waiting a minute. Not after her and Elea rubbing their sweet core all over my dick. Adjusting myself, I waited until the shower ran, and I heard her close the glass doors.

Sure, the bathrooms in my palace were great. Fireplaces, deep pools for a tub, steam showers, but there was one significant difference. The Celestial Kingdom had nothing but bright bathrooms, while mine was lower on the light. The Celestial Kingdom didn't cut any corners. I'll be able to see every damn thing on her body, down to the last freckle.

I pulled my shorts down before I even opened the door and snuck in. Ember's body was facing the opposite direction, so I got the perfect look at her pear bottom ass. Her breasts were large, so I could even see the outline of them as she showered. I didn't need any foreplay. I was going to explode just from looking at her.

Ember took the shaving cream and rubbed it down her leg. Each time she swiped the razor up her leg, her ass would be in the perfect position for me to fuck. The water dripped down her back as she finished and then began to wash her hair. The soap fell in chunks down her sweet body. The slight hum leaving her throat drew me near like a damn siren. Opening the glass door, I walked in. I had watched for far too long. Ember had teased me, and she didn't even know it. Grabbing my dick and giving myself a few pulls to calm myself, I stood right behind her. My dick immediately grazed the top part of her ass as I slid my right hand around her waist and palmed her stomach.

"Hades?"

Chapter 38

Ember

I could feel Hades' eyes on me as he entered the shower. How long he had stood outside the glass doors, I wasn't so sure, but I could smell his campfire smell as soon as he opened the door. I continued washing the soap out of my hair. I was nervous, and I didn't know how to react. Now, I was standing, butt naked, in the shower with the hottest thing on two legs.

Hades' rough hand trailed my hips as the palm of his hand hit my stomach. Stepping closer, I felt himself touch my upper back. He was big, and I knew I was going to be in trouble.

"Hades?" I questioned, knowing very well it was him. The tingles couldn't lie. The hot touches he left on my skin were a fire burning through me until it settled between my thighs.

"Yes?" his velvet voice tickled the shell of my ear. A feat for him to have to bend over and still have his cock pressed up against me. I was short, but we always fit so well together like a puzzle.

"Am I taking too long?" I whispered as his other hand came up my waist to grab onto my breast. My head immediately leaned back to his rock-hard chest as I breathed heavily in his scent.

"No, just the right amount of time." My butt immediately rubbed against him, only managing to graze his balls. Even those were huge; the panic I was feeling inside me started to heighten as I only felt Hades' lust through our bond and my ability to read emotions.

"Don't be scared; we aren't going to bond yet." My shoulders slumped, maybe not in relief, perhaps disappointment. I wanted to have himself buried inside me; I wanted to feel more connected with our bond, now that I know I could feel everything he feels. Elea was at the back of my head scratching incessantly, begging for me to make a move. She was more like my little cheerleader, rooting me on to do the things I had only thought of doing with Hades.

"I- I just haven't seen…that with all this light," I stuttered. Hades, who was open-mouth kissing my shoulders, paused, and I felt the grin. His emotion was elated as his hand continued to roam my body.

"You haven't?" His voice was full of mischief. He chuckled into my ear. I gasped, feeling his fingers trail lower to the apex of my thighs. "Are you scared to see it in all its glory?"

"N-no," I stuttered, and Elea just laughed in the back of my head.

"*Ask him to touch it first,*" Elea rooted me on. Taking a large swallow of spit that had gathered in my mouth, I searched for the courage to ask.

"C-can I touch you first?" Hades' emotions heightened into excitement as he rubbed his dick harder on my back.

"Anything for you, flower." Turning around, only looking up to see Hades' face, his eyes were dark with red in his pupils. I should be scared. The demon-like eyes would scare any human. Then again, I wasn't human, and he was my mate. My mate, mine.

Hades went from my eyes to my breasts as he held one hand behind my back to keep me close and the other on my chest. "Touch it," he growled, "Feel how I want you." I bit my lip, the excitement building in me. My hand tickled his hip bone, and Hades' closed his eyes as the sparks only intensified. Using one hand, I felt his shaft. It was like velvet, slick with the water running down our bodies. His girth was significant, and my small hands couldn't go around it entirely.

Gasping, he took my other hand to cup his balls. "All for you," he breathed heavily. I stopped breathing as he placed my hand around the tip. "All for you," he whispered again. The tip was wet; whether it was from him or the shower, I wasn't sure. When I used my thumb to rub around the knot, it was definitely slicker.

Hades eyes were still closed as I held him, all of him, in just my two hands. Relief, excitement, and lust flooded through him as I continued to manhandle him. My confidence began to grow as Elea whispered to me to take him into my mouth. Hades had done the same to me. He made me feel things I wanted him to feel. As Hades leaned his head back and hit the shower wall, I took this as my chance to look.

It wasn't as scary as I thought seeing it in the full light; feeling him, knowing he loved me, gave me the extra push. I pulled out of Hades' grasp quickly as I got on my knees. "What are you-" Hades stopped as he felt me licking the tip of his cock. "Oh, fuck."

My tongue licked him a few times like a sucker, and I took him in my mouth as I became comfortable. The saltiness of his fluid made me want more of him, but I put as much as I could in my mouth. I hummed as I reached the back of my throat. I couldn't take any more. Pulling my head out and back down slowly, Hades groaned and gripped my hair.

I felt myself getting wetter by the minute. I wanted nothing more for him to touch me there too. "Ember." He pulled me off of him and picked me up, and I squeaked.

"Did I do something wrong?" I gripped my lip with my teeth, and he burst out of the shower.

"No, it was right, so right, Fuck." Both completely wet, he carried me to the bed while he laid down. "I want you to straddle my face while I eat you. Suck me at the same time." Elea howled in my head and almost took control when I hesitated. Hades' cock was bobbing in the air, waiting for me to sink my mouth over him. Hades' sensing my hesitation, pulled me over his lap.

"We don't have to." His hand cupped my cheek, but I shook my head.

"I want to," I whispered and turned around. Gripping my hips harshly, he pushed my core into his mouth. Immediately moaning, I grabbed his cock and sucked. Both of us were moaning as we pleasured each other. My hips started to grind his face, and his lust only thickened the air. His fingers buried deep into my butt cheeks, which stirred my courage. Being bold, I pushed his dick farther into my mouth only to gag, but I opened my throat the best I could.

My body shook as I felt him sucking on my clit. His tongue would flick it intermittently as I squirmed in his hold. Hades' balls began to retract as I continued to massage them. One last flick to my clit, I fell over while I sucked, and his thick liquid filled my mouth. Hades had swallowed mine, so I swallowed his. There was much more than I thought there would be. Some dribbled out of my mouth, and I went down to lick the remnants as Hades' licked my inner thighs.

Hades moved my hips and turned me around as he had me lay on his chest. "Holy Kronos," he breathed.

"Yeah, what he said," Elea groaned in my head. Glad she enjoyed it.

"That was, wow." Glancing up at Hades, he looked like he was on another level of heaven far greater than that of the Celestial Kingdom.

Zeus

Athena was in the room behind me as I leaned up against the wall. Last night, Hera had asked for Athena and her knowledge to help Ember. Little did I know that Ember would have a history far more significant than just some human mate to my brother.

A damn Werewolf, I sighed as I ran my hands through my thick beard. Of course, Hades would get a Werewolf, a beautiful one, and on top of it, she was his mate. The first of the original twelve gods to be granted such a gift.

Why the hell wasn't it me? I've done nothing but help sustain the gods in proper order. We help those who we can without ruining the fates decisions on human lives. With my help, we created a world full of supernaturals so they wouldn't be hunted by misunderstanding humans. I had done my part and paid my good deeds, and here we have Hades, the god who stole a goddess for a thousand years, get his greedy little hands on a mate.

Tightening my fists, I felt the sparks electrify my skin. I wanted my touch alone to do that to a woman. I wouldn't need to feel the electricity of my own self. I wanted my mate. Damn it, Hades.

Fine, in all seriousness, Hades did deserve this. He was the firstborn, suffered the most, and only chose the Underworld as his domain because he knew how much I didn't want it. Hades had shied away from the light, feeling like darkness was his own friend. Then as time went by, he found no one to love because he was stuck with death and darkness all around him. When someone did catch his eye, Persephone, he did the most outrageous thing and kidnapped her.

I beg to differ from that story. It was fishy all around. There was more to the report. I think Persephone wanted him to take her because her mother Demeter was an overbearing mother and Hades was the only way out. Once the deal was struck and the seasons were created, Persephone was happy to get away, but her company with Hades was not. Hades doted on her, gave her everything she wanted but only grabbed and asked for more.

When Hades started to ask for the damn relationship, she shunned the idea. It was completely one-sided, and her anger for him grew. Persephone grew tired of being in the Underworld; she wanted to be free. Still, with Demeter's deal with Hades, she was only allowed to be in the Underworld. I heard her prayers, prayers for me to get her out of the deal, but the deal was solid. The only thing that would break it was Selene's new promise to have every god meet their matching soul.

Lucky for her, she got out. Malachi grabbed her and took her up to the Celestial Heavens, and they reside on a hill not too far away from the palace grounds. Their relationship is different, more so than I thought a mated pair would be.

Hades always grabs Ember, touches her, holds her, and gives her looks of complete adoration, all to be reciprocated by Ember. However, Malachi doesn't get the reciprocation that Persephone should give back.

I had enough listening to Athena speak of the Wolf and mighty empathy power inside of Ember. I needed to talk to Hera. We've got some problems that needed to be dealt with, and I didn't want to discuss it with Hades until the time was right.

Being a dick to Hades wasn't the smartest thing to do. Who are we kidding here? I should be the god of unfortunate decisions. Hades had given me much, but my jealousy over his mate put me over. The tension of finding two missing gods was doing me in, no sleeping, no sexcapades, and hardly eating.

"Hera." I broke the intimate moment that Hades and Ember were sharing. "I need to speak with you." Hera looked at the loving couple and back to me and gave the nod to Ember. Ember was the tiniest human I had come in contact with, I guess now a Werewolf. I never spent the time getting to know any supernatural, but I'd take the time if they were all like her.

"Come with me," I gently spoke to her. Hera and I have an interesting relationship. She's the goddess of marriage and relationships, so she took it to heart when we decided to be together as a couple. My cheating didn't help her, and she stopped coming to our room, now my room. That was several thousand years ago, and now that Selene has promised mates, she is even more reluctant to be in the same room as me.

I was a fool back then. Being the high god and giving orders to others. Gods, deities, and other creatures looked up to me. Women threw themselves at me, and being an idiot, I accepted. I thought I could get away with anything, but not in Hera's eyes. She found me with some Light Fairy the night she was supposed to be spending with Athena. No words from her once she saw the sight. Hera just bowed and left, never to return.

Hera was the perfect companion and I fucked it up. Hera cared what I thought and did everything to keep our relationship afloat. I turned around and made her look like an idiot. A marriage god that couldn't keep her partner from wandering astray. That didn't stop me, though, from embarrassing her further. I continued to bed more women than I could count and sometimes two, three times over. I tried to fuck her out of my system. Never worked, never will.

I wanted her back but have no clue how. My current Elven woman that is with me I don't even sleep with. She was just for appearances, so the gods wouldn't think anything different. Gods are gossiping pieces of shit.

Michael has captured Hera's heart. I'd seen the way she looked at him. Part of me was jealous, and a fit of heated anger would run through my veins, seeing them look into each other's eyes. Michael cared for her as well. He doted on her. Brings her flowers from the Olympian fields and takes her to exotic isles of Earth. I'd watch them make love to each other on the sands of Tahiti. I could be a sick bastard.

Hera used to look at me that way. She used to give me the adoring look she gives Michael, but no more.

"What do we need to discuss?" she spoke, breaking my thoughts.

"Yes, about Malachi. He is indeed missing, along with Persephone. They are not in their home, and their belongings along with them." I pulled my hands behind my back as we continued walking. Angels bowed as we walked to my office.

"What do you make of it?" Hera mused.

"Hades' helm is missing. Loukas spoke to me a while ago. Hades currently thinks I am a prime suspect and has not divulged any information to me. Loukas has been helpful. He says he cares for Ember and believes she is in great danger being separated from Hades again."

"Should we be wary of Loukas?" Hera opened the door to my office, and we both walked in. Closing the door, Hera sat on the sofa next to me with her hands folded in her lap.

"I do not know. He has been loyal to Hades, so Loukas coming to me to give information willingly is a concern. We will have to pay close attention to him."

"Hades created him. He should be able to sift through Loukas's thoughts and desires," Hera argued.

"Loukas is different than other demons. You've noticed when he isn't in human form. Hades has given him more agency, but why he hasn't confronted Loukas, I'm not sure." I scratched my beard.

"Ember must have said or done something. Ember is a soft-spoken person, and she may see him as a friend." I hummed at the idea.

"Either way, he needs to be looked over. He could play a part in all of this. I don't see Malachi being the one pulling all the strings here. He may be one of my more cunning angels, but he isn't the strongest. Do you think Michael could get closer to him?" It was a selfish thing to ask for, but I must. Michael was strong, and his mind wasn't made of bricks.

"I suppose." Hera fiddled with her tassels.

"Hera," I whispered. "I am truly sorry how I treated you." Hera looked away at the window, watching the angels on the field talking and sparing.

"You hurt me, Zeus, but I will always do my duty. I will help you rule here as long as you don't have a mate. Once you find her, you will make her your queen, and I will move away so I can find mine." Hera's voice was soft, no longer harsh like she had been all these years.

"I know I wronged you, but I do hope you will become my mate." Hera's eyes darted to me as she scooted down the sofa, appalled at the idea.

"You don't mean that." I sat closer to her.

"I do, Hera. No other woman can hold a candle to you." Hera's breath hitched.

"Don't say such things. You will have your mate, and I will have mine. We would never work, Zeus. You've hurt me too badly." Hera stood up from the couch and darted to the door. I was quicker and slammed it shut before she could leave. "Let me go." She stood still.

"No, I want you to know how sorry I am." Letting go of the door and falling to my knees, I grabbed her hands and kissed them. My cheek held her hand, and I whispered into them. "I was a fool for losing you. Pushing you away and letting the power of being a Celestial King get to my head. Getting away with such impurities was wrong. Please, Hera, will you please forgive me one day." Hera's eyes pooled little stars as she took her hand away.

"I forgive you, but that doesn't mean I want you as a mate if it came down to it." She turned and walked out of the office, slamming the door in my face.

Chapter 39

Ember

Hades laced our fingers together as we left the guestroom. I was able to get a better look at the hallways as we walked down the long corridors to Athena's study. Athena and most of the original gods were able to stay here in the Celestial Palace, each having a wing of their own and can be called upon by Zeus if needed.

Athena was one of the favored by Zeus, meaning she would help him with decisions involving the fate of the gods and how to deal with certain situations in feuds. Who knew the gods would be angered with each other so much that Zeus would have to be in the middle of it? The way Zeus handled himself with Hades proved he wasn't the most emotionally stable kind of guy.

We passed several naked statues of women, Fairies, Sirens, and even a few Wolves along the way. Each Wolf had dazzling eye colors such as blue, green, and even gold. "Zeus tries to have all the creations created by gods represented with their own statues; Ares helped create the Werewolves, so there are plenty of Wolves down his wing to commemorate them.

"Huh, I wonder why Ares couldn't sense something in me since he is so connected with Wolves?" Hades chuckled and squeezed my hand again.

"Ares may be strong, but he isn't the most intuitive. He's nothing but beef and brawn, not much upstairs." Hades pointed to his temple while I laughed.

"I heard that! You are flaming pile of shit!" Ares came around the corner, strapping his ax on his side. He was in his original attire: a battle skirt of leathers, straps for holding weapons, and his gladiator sandals. Hades laughed and smacked him on the back.

"I'm only joking. Where are you headed?" Ares tightened his belt as he puffed out his chest.

"To the sparring grounds. Those angels look pretty weak; I might have a talk with Gabriel too." Hades narrowed his eyes and gave a curt nod as he left.

Hades' mind was still drifting to why Persephone's mate Gabriel had no remembrance of their meeting. It is supposed to be memorable, enjoyable, something you would never forget. While Hades thought I was sleeping, I could feel his worry through the emotions. Anxiety, fear, determination, it was there like a smoldering pile of ash that hovered over my heart.

After several winding and twisting turns, we reached Athena's wing of the palace. On two pillars held massive owls that were sitting on olive branches filled with gold. The eyes of the owls had black onyx stones, and the wings were dipped in glowing amber. As we entered the wing, there were rows of books on either side. Not one wall was clear; all of them had some sort of picture or map.

Athena was a regular librarian or bookworm. Beside several doors there were glass boxes sitting on pedestals of stuffed animals and beasts with their claws and jaws hinged open. I shivered to look at one of the serpents striking a helpless rabbit.

"She's great at battle strategies," Hades mused. "Athena also has her very own helm; instead of becoming invisible like mine does, her helmet provides her alertness and strength. Pretty handy when battling unruly supernatural beings."

The last door on the right held floor-to-ceiling doors. Two angels perched on either side of the door bowed their heads and removed their spears that had a cross next to the front. "Athena is expecting you," one grunted and opened the door. I gave a small thank you, but his face remained that of displeasure.

Who peed in his cornflakes?

"You're late." The door slammed open, and Athena rose from her seat behind the desk. "I do have other duties to attend to, you know. Like finding who is responsible for your helm disappearance and a missing Malachi and his mate." Hades gritted his teeth.

"So, he's missing. Zeus knows?"

Athena nodded. "I assure you, Zeus had nothing to do with trying to get rid of your mate. He was just following Selene's orders before her disappearance." Athena walked to the couch in front of her desk and motioned for us to sit down.

"We aren't here to talk about that. We have more pressing matters." I didn't know that it could even be possible to be more critical than finding missing gods? Gods were more substantial than regular immortal supernaturals; whoever took them must have something powerful on their side. What could be more pressing than finding two missing gods?

As I go to sit down, Hades pulls me to his lap. "Hades," I started to complain, but he gripped me tighter.

"It makes me more at ease knowing you are here." His nose ran up my neck as I shivered.

"That's enough," Athena snapped. "Time is of the essence here!" Athena grabbed her large book, one of many, and dropped it on the table. The table shook, and the few cups of tea clinked. Athena licked her fingers as she flipped through and danced her index finger across the page.

"Hades, do you think you could let go of your mate for ten minutes?" Athena let out an exasperated sigh as I tried to get up.

"Nope." He prolonged the p and gave her a wink. Athena growled put both her hands out for me to grab hers.

Ten minutes went to three hours, I was exhausted at all the techniques she taught me to control my empathy power. By the end of it, I could block out everyone in the room and home in on one person at a time. My range was twenty feet, and Athena wanted to write everything I felt down in her white notebook. "This is so interesting," she mused as she flipped to another page. Hades' head was dropped back on the couch, and his mouth was slightly open. Little snores left his lips, and I couldn't help but giggle and not pay attention to my tutor.

"There is no recorded record of this other than a god," she babbled, "that can project and read emotions from that distance." Hades let out a louder snort/snore, and I laughed hysterically until he woke up.

"Yeah, of course," Hades coughed as he tried to look like he was paying attention. As I was about to tell him how adorable he was, there was a scratching at the door to the library's entry. The angels outside were arguing, and smoke and entered under the door while the screams of: 'put it out,' and 'get that thing away from me,' got louder.

"Kronos, is it Blaze?" Hades questioned. I projected my empathy towards the door, and sure enough, it was Blaze, and he was worried and upset. "It is. Let him in!" I shouted, and the angels screamed for him to back up, but snarls and roars burst through the door. The front of the door was charred and black, and Athena scoffed.

"What did you do to my door, you little-" But before Athena could finish, we saw Blaze, the size of a lion, enter. His nails clicked on the floor as he approached, and Hades only scowled.

"Ember," Blaze spoke through to me; his voice was considerably more profound than his usual chattering.

"Yes, Blaze?" I stuttered as he sat in front of me, destroying the coffee table and knocking Athena's book off the table. Hades gripped me tighter, ready to stand, but I pat his chest, my eyes never leaving Blaze.

"You cannot put this off anymore; you need a pack. Elea demands it. Do you not feel her?"

I managed to draw out long stutter before lifting the block that Athena taught me just hours before. *"We have just days before we shift, Ember. Don't block me out. If I shift without you with me, we are both as good as dead!"* I gasped as everyone sat looking at me.

"Blaze said I will be shifting soon. That block you taught me kept Elea out; she couldn't reach me."

Athena nodded. "Be sure to only always let her in then. You both need to leave and take her to a pack. Elea will need to speak with a few of the other wolves and become acquainted. I'll let Hera know of your departure."

Hades stood up with me in his arms and took me past the charred doorway. The angels' robes were still on fire as they tried to extinguish them. The grumpy cornflakes guy was even more grumpy as he ripped his clothes off, and his undergarments looked like a diaper. I snorted in laughter, and he gave me a pressing look.

"Aw, is the baby grumpier?" I whispered only for Hades to hear, but angels have good hearing too, as he swore under his breath. I gasped. "He can't say that can he? That's so naughty for an angel to do!" I giggled.

"I didn't know my mate could make an angel curse. If there was any doubt in my mind before it is gone now. Well done," Hades smirked.

Ares was in the fields, along with Vulcan, having a heated discussion with the angel called Gabriel. I remembered him from the first day here and the haunting look he gave me. "Can you find out his emotions, Ember?" Hades put me on the ground as I concentrated.

"Now see here." Gabriel pointed his finger at Ares. "I know nothing about Persephone; she's Malachi's mate. I can't touch her!"

"But you like her! I've heard the other angels talking. They say you stare at her while she is making flowers in her garden; you try and talk to her every chance you get!" Ares pressed.

"She has a mate! I cannot pursue her!" he growled out as he pulled his hand through his hair. "End of discussion." Gabriel went to walk away, but Hades grabbed his shoulder. "What if I was to tell you, you should have feelings for her?" Hope flowed through Gabriel as his heart filled with delight. Gabriel wanted that more than anything, but he was thoroughly denied it because of Malachi.

"What if I told you, you are her mate. That it was written in the ultimate history books of our kind?"

Gabriel was instantly saddened. "You shouldn't joke about this; this is even lower than I ever expected you would be, Hades." Gabriel's eyes glistened as he looked away. Anger flowed through him as he stretched his wings and took off into the sky.

"He loves her," I whispered. "He cares for her, but he thinks Malachi is really her mate. I don't know about you guys, but I think Persephone is involved in this." Hades eyes didn't leave the sky as Gabriel continued to get smaller as the distance grew between us.

"I agree with you," Vulcan spoke. "Gabriel isn't part of this fiasco, but I believe that Persephone and Malachi are. Now to find them is the question." Vulcan wrote down on a pad and paper.

"No, we have to find the Sphere of Souls," I corrected. "Selene said to find that first. The only way to do that is for me to get my memory back," I sighed, irritated. Hades held me in his arms and stroked my hair.

"One step at a time, let's get you shifted first. Maybe that will trigger something." Hades turned to Vulcan and Ares. "We leave for the Black Claw Pack this evening. I will warn their sorceress, Cyrene, that we are coming."

Both of our friends muttered in agreement as Blaze continued to walk with us in his larger form. Many angels stared at us while we retreated to the main living space of the Celestial Palace.

"Where is Hermes?" I asked curiously. "We haven't seen him in forever!" It has only been two days, but that was a long time for Hermes. He would always come back to let us know if he found something or nothing at all.

"Good question, he should be around here," Vulcan mused as he looked out over the vast window that held the kingdom. Zeus came barreling into the room along with Hera, who was beside him clutching his hand.

"Hermes has been taken!" Zeus shouted. The room grew silent as Vulcan and Ares growled.

"How do you know this?" Hades roared as he stomped to Zeus. Zeus held out a note that had been ripped from a dagger.

"I found this on his home door in the city. I had sent angels to retrieve him so I could send a message to Poseidon, and when the angels returned, they brought me this."

Hades,
Revenge is the acceptance of pain.
Accept the fate that the fates themselves
Are too scared to give you.
Malachi

Hades crumpled the paper and lit it on fire in an instant. "They want to play games?" he growled out. His dark hair turned to his beautiful white-blonde hair, and his attire shifted from his Armani suit to his devilish robes. His strides were long as he reached me, not being scared in the slightest, and gripped me by my hips and wrapped his cloak around me. Smoke had covered the once white floor entirely while Zeus and Hera looked on in bewilderment.

"Then we will play games." Hades' body stiffened as fire engulfed all around us. A stream of a fire beacon came from our bodies, shooting upward, causing the glass ceiling to break into a million pieces and spread out across the sky. Dark clouds now covered the kingdom as it rained drops of fire.

Hades' voice changed to a deep baritone with a rumble in his chest. "Now hear this," his voice spoke for all to hear. Looking over my shoulder, I saw angels and Celestial Fairies stop in their tracks, listening to his voice. Many angels and Fairies grew panicked but stopped to hear Hades' message.

"Anyone lays a hand on my mate, Ember, they will seek certain death. There will be no forgiveness." Hades paused for effect. Vulcan and Ares stood with stern faces while Hera and Zeus remained panicked. Loukas just walked into the room, watching the scene unfold. He was in his demon attire, looking on in horror. His face darted from Zeus to Vulcan to figure out what was going on.

"Turn over the missing gods within twenty four hours, or you have sealed your own damn fate. The real fun will begin once your body rots into the ground." Shivers went up my spine as he announced his threat. The sky continued to stay dark as his words seeped into the ground of this holy place.

The smoke seeped into my hair, causing it to fly upwards as my fingers gripped Hades' cloak tightly. Not once did the fire come too close, so I never felt its warmth; instead, I still felt the cold darkness of Hades' words.

"Hang on," he whispered as he wrapped me in his cloak before Hades, Blaze, and I were engulfed in flames.

Chapter 40

Loukas

Hades knows how to make a statement.

Hades engulfed the room in flames, setting couches, furniture, and even the drapes ablaze as Hera starts ordered Celestial fairies and Angels to come to douse the room with water. Rubbing my forehead, I step towards Zeus, who looked like he pissed himself.

Zeus could be completely oblivious of Hades' power. It is only by Hades' good graces Zeus is in the position he is holding. I knew that Hades didn't trust Zeus. Still, with the political advancements and knowledge he had regarding the whereabouts of gods and their businesses, I had to take the opportunity to discuss the helm and the situation at hand.

Was I going against Hades' wishes? Yeah, sure, I was. Only a fool would think that Zeus could devise a plan of this magnitude, to take away Hades' mate and steal a bunch of gods to do it. He isn't that what could you say, tactful? Why do you think Athena has to hang around him in his war room all the damn time? Zeus is just dense. What sweet justice it would be if Athena ended up being his mate. Her being asexual, he wouldn't be able to do a thing.

Laughing internally, I walked up to the King and Queen of the Celestial Kingdom, both still in shock of Hades' outburst. I've seen explosions like these before, this one is a bit more on the extreme side, and I was dying to know why.

"Your Majesties." I bowed while my tail caught a falling vase. Hera looked me up and down and scowled as she crossed her arms. "Loukas, what are you doing here? Trying to play both sides?" Zeus started choking on his own spit, staring at Hera like she had lost her head.

"Hera." He went to help retract her statement, but she just held her hand up at him. I smirked as Zeus backed down immediately. He was still in deep shit from when he went on a power trip so many years ago. Zeus is still in the doghouse. Everyone in the damn palace knew he hadn't gotten anything in well over 300 years once he realized no one could compare to Hera. She should have been the goddess of beauty, her elegance, grace, and poise. Hell, her bravery standing up to a pathetic god that cheated on her and didn't bat an eyelash as she walked out of his bed chambers, never to look back.

She got herself a good angel, Michael. I would bet my soul that he was her mate. "Well," she drawled. "What is the meaning of this? Playing both sides will get you nowhere. You better not be trying to double-cross someone." I held my hands up in defense.

"Hey now, I'm the one that helped rescue Ember from the very beginning! Even before Zeus executed the order to have her brought here! Which he forgot about, by the way." Bam, threw him under the bus just like he did me. Zeus' eyebrows narrowed as he whispered some profanities under his breath.

"Now, I don't like Ember in that way," I defended. "She's the first person that showed interest in friendship to me since the first day I was created." Hera rolled her eyes as she flicked some rubble from her shoulder.

"Not buying it." Zeus was nodding his head, agreeing with me until Hera denounced my confession. Now he is back to deciding with Hera. Really Hades? You gave this guy the head job?

"It's true. Hades is my creator and master. His friends are gods who hold closer status to him. I'm his damn errand boy and private investigator. He nor his friends would call me a friend. I am beneath them, but Ember doesn't see me that way! So, what I want to be close to her. Gain a little attention. I was friends with her first! It isn't any of your business anyway."

"Watch your language. You are speaking with the high gods, you know." Zeus snapped. I backed up and bowed my head.

"I apologize. I am being true to you with my words and intentions. I am very concerned about Ember's safety." Hera's face softened, and Zeus looked at her as if what to do. Gods, Zeus is such a suck-up. How can the gods not see through this bullshit?

"What has happened that has him all in a fuss?" I asked. Hera turned to Zeus, and he nodded for confirmation.

"Hermes has been taken, and there was a note on the door of his home threatening Hades and his mate." Anger pulled into me as my powers sizzled. Hades was more lenient when he created me, giving me powers more than of an ordinary demon. I felt my horns grow longer at the thought of Ember being stolen. This time they had been far too careful to hide themselves. They almost got away with it the first time.

"Loukas, Malachi is the one that left the note." Hera huffed. I scoffed as I rubbed my chin. He's an idiot too, he couldn't have possibly come up with a plan like this. Could it be Persephone herself? Getting revenge from staying down in the Underworld too long? She always enjoyed herself when she received gifts from Hades but not once displayed any affection towards him. She had grown quite hostile towards the end of her stay but was always compliant staying in the Underworld.

Persephone could have planned this, gotten revenge on Hades by stealing his mate. But why? She was saved by Gabriel in the end. She should be head over heels in love and not want to get revenge. And why the hell is Malachi involved?! Fuck, my head began to hurt.

"They have gone to the Black Claw Pack in the Earth Realm." Athena walked into the catastrophic scene. Bits of fire still being put out while Fairies were ordering new furniture to be brought in. "I suggest you go in your human form. Wolves are superstitious creatures and finding out that a demon and three gods entering their territory undetected would cause problems. Not only that, but they will also be helping the God of the Underworld with his mate. Tread lightly, gentleman."

Ares and Vulcan looked at me with disappointed faces. They were angry that I had divulged such information to Zeus, but I had no choice. I knew he wasn't involved. If he was, he would have been more assertive checking on Ember's status of her being retrieved. Now that Zeus knows, he can find some high ranking Witches to make a potion to help find the invisible perpetrator. The angry gods walked towards me, changing into their human appearance, and I did the same.

Ares grabbed hold of my upper arm. "You've got a lot of explaining to do," he growled. "You broke his trust; don't expect to live for long. Ember can't even save you from this." Vulcan nodded to his mother and held on to me as well.

"Let's go."

Ember

The wind rushed around us and my hair tangled into the wind. It was a large cyclone being thrust into a void of nothing as Hades held me close. This was far worse than when he transported me from room to room in his palace. This was long-distance and made me sick. Clutching tightly to his cloak, I could still feel the anger rolling off him in waves.

Sure, I'd be ticked too, Malachi took our friend! Hermes had played some jokes, sure, but he was always loyal to Hades. Hermes stuck around even after Hades PMSed for a thousand some years. We had to find the Sphere of Souls and fast. I wanted to bang my head up against a brick wall to shake any sort of memories that might be lodged in my brain, but it would be useless.

Talking to Elea to see if she could break open some doors in my head would be useless. She would probably suggest we go mate, and everything would wake me up. It wasn't a bad idea, but how horny she is, I wasn't sure if she would stop and make sweet love to him all night.

I guess it wouldn't be so bad.

Holding my breath so I wouldn't breathe in the stagnant air, we dropped to the ground, and I put all my weight on Hades. The cloak was still engulfed around me, Hades' head out the top looking around before he let go for me to gain my balance. The ground was littered with leaves, and the forest around us was naked of any type of vegetation. We must be in the middle of fall. There was a crisp chill in the air as I rubbed my arm. Being still dressed in a white tunic dress with robes wrapped around my body to keep it in place, this wasn't the best idea for the weather.

Hades pulled me back in and wrapped his cloak around me. "We will have to wait for them," he ruffed. "I've sent word to their Sorceress that we are here." Hades still had his original form, and he closed his eyes, and I saw the dark hair envelope his hair.

"Please no," I whispered as I pulled his face to mine. "Just be with me, stay with me. The real Hades." Hades sighed deeply as the black hair receded.

"I thought we promised when we are alone."

"You are still the God of the Underworld, no matter what your hair color is, but I do love seeing this face rather than the other one." I kissed his nose as his shoulders slumped.

"You know how to vex me, woman." I put my arms around his torso and breathed in his scent.

"Mmhm, you always smell so good to me." Hades laughed.

"You always smell good to me too, Ember." We waited only a few moments before he heard the rustling of the leaves and heavy pants. Three wolves came to our tiny spot in the woods as they looked us over. Two were deep grey, while one was a sandy color. He was more significant than the two grey ones and stood at the front of the group. His head cocked to the side and barked.

Elea barked in my head, but I was confused. "Elea is barking, and I have no idea what's going on," whispered to Hades. Elea stopped barking and finally spoke. "*He wants us to follow them back. He's acting strange.*"

I hummed and told Hades what we were to do. "The Alpha and Luna couldn't come to greet us? What a shame," Hades tsked as we walked. Elea relayed another message that their youngest child fell out of a treehouse at the last minute, and Luna was detained. She would be with us in a moment. Hades ran his hands through his hair. "Maybe we should find another pack if this one is going to give us trouble."

I shook my head no. "Elea seems excited she's all jumpy. Maybe things will be fine." I rubbed his arms as we walked towards the light in the distance. We made it through the last line of trees. A giant treehouse, two stories with a rope, that went up stood before us. I stopped while everyone kept walking and stared at it. It looked so familiar to me, and I couldn't place it where I had seen it before.

"This treehouse." I touched the tree as flashes of light went through my vision. "I've seen it before." I squinted my eyes to get a better look. It had a few letters that had been rubbed out. The treehouse didn't look like it had been used in ages. Boards were falling, and the name E. H. Club House was on the side.

I gasped involuntarily. "My dream," I whispered to Hades. I think I think I saw this in my dream. My heart pounded as a group of men and women began to gather. Some looked afraid. Others were curious about the God of the Underworld present in their territory.

Hades grabbed my hand tightly and held me back as a large man with blonde hair and green eyes approached. His hair was pulled back into a ponytail, and the woman beside him had strawberry blonde hair just like me. She was considerably shorter than him, maybe my own height.

"Gods," the woman whispered as she cupped both hands to her face. Immediately tears ran down her face. I felt joy, sadness, guilt all into one, and her emotions kept changing, so I had to block her out. Hades stood dumbfounded, not sure what was going on.

The large man stood stoically still as he grabbed his wife. The entire crowd stood still as I held onto Hades for dear life peeking my head around Hades' muscular body.

"Ember?" the woman squeaked. The tone, the way my name hit my ear, was like a train hitting a wall at 100 miles an hour. Flashes of light went through my eyes as my knees grew weak. Visions of this woman singing me lullabies in bed while the storm raged outside.

Kissing me goodnight and to make sure the Sprites don't bite. The large man shifted right before my eyes, becoming a sizeable sandy wolf beckoning me to ride on his back. We ran through the trees while the pine needles entangled in my hair, and I screamed for joy watching my brother on my mother's back.

"You are going to make a great Alpha one day," my father spoke while we sat by the lake. Every Sunday, he would take me to the pack lake and give me words of wisdom. He told me great Alpha stories about how to protect a pack, the pack comes first, and it isn't always strength that takes care of a complete whole. Honesty, integrity, grit was what made a great pack, what made our pack the greatest in all North America. "You will always have your grandfather and me. Once you turn 25, you will have it all. The greatest responsibility a Wolf could have." The lake water rippled, and another scene fell before me.

"I would make a great Beta!" the boy said as he held up a stick. "I'll be the master of the weaponry while I stay by your side if you have me, great Alpha," Dante bowed as he held onto his twiddled weapon.

"But of course!" I chided back as I stood next to him. Our heights were the same, me being just a year older than him. "And Hunter will be our Gamma!" We both laughed as we wrestled with each other on the ground. The pool ripped one more time, and a baby was put in my arms.

"This is Steven." I sat beside my mother in a hospital. He was so small, but his grip was firm as he held onto my finger. "See, he likes you already."

"At least this one likes me. The others didn't like me that much." Mother laughed as she petted my hair.

"That's because you weren't too happy to see them either. Babies can sense fear and intimidation, you know." I tilted my head at her.

"They can?" Mother nodded while kissing Steven's forehead.

"How can you know they can feel that?" My heart skipped a beat as Steven nuzzled closer to me.

"It's a feeling, something you can feel with your heart. When they are born, babies have this intuition, and then it fades because no one tries to listen. If you pay attention to those around you, you can unlock how people feel not just by their

actions but by their aura. That's something I learned from a few Fae back in Bergarian."

The white light pulled back to me as we all still stood between the tree and the clearing. The small town had already gathered in a large group; it was massive as Hades and I looked on. Blaze chittered in my ear, but I couldn't pay attention because I was too transfixed on my father and mother before me.

My father, my mother. Oh, my gods, my family. My heartbeat is quick as I let go of Hades' hand. He felt my excitement through the bond and nodded. I took one giant step forward and held my dress with my fists until finally, I dared to call out to the two people I'd missed the most while being gone.

"Mom? Dad?"

Chapter 41

Charlotte

Today was not a good day. I had many emotions running through my head as I tried to prepare lunch for my family. Ember has been gone for over 11 years and the storm last night blew my memories to the forefront of my mind.

I sat in her room again last night as I heard the rain pattering on the window. That same window that my oldest daughter was taken. The dark shadow that withdrew from the room and the footprint left on the windowsill haunts me every storm and every birthday. Pictures that Ember had drawn just the day before my birthday flew around the room in my visions. Wet papers, ruined cards, markers dripping their ink into the carpet. I saved it all. All of them sat in a box on her desk, where she sat for hours to make them.

Wesley found and rescued me when I was just nineteen years old, living in a run-down apartment running away from an abusive foster father. The mate bond he couldn't deny, so he did everything in his power to get me to his pack to keep me as his. Wesley is the Alpha of the Black Claw and the strongest in North America. I'll never forget the day I found out about this life after I came here to work for him as a computer security specialist.

I had come to work for him. That was all the intention was to be his employee, but the tingles he left on my skin told me there was something else. His kindness overshadowed anyone else that tried to become my friend, and he made me fall for him hard. Despite my battle scars, both physically and mentally, he waited for me, nursed me back to health.

Deciding to become like Wesley, a Werewolf, was a no-brainer. I was to become Luna, to help the pack grow and, most of all, take care of our own family one day. Who knew that once I changed that I would literally fight a demon, Trixen, from one of Hades' horrible experiments of trying to find love on his own?

"Ember, where are you?" Regret filled me. I changed to become stronger, a better warrior; I became something I only read about in fairytales to protect my children from ever facing any sort of torment I went through as a child. I gave extra care, attention, and love that I never received so my family would grow up an average family. A typical Werewolf family.

Even with the ward that Hades had provided us, saying it could keep out unwanted humans, rogues, and deities on the territory was a blessing. When there is a will, a motive, there is a way to break even a god's protection. Our warriors never found a lick of evidence, and our trackers couldn't find our daughter, an alpha, whose smell was strong enough in itself.

Cyrene, our new resident Witch, and her coven had merged with us after Trixen was killed but would often go on expeditions to other covens across the country. They wanted to practice their magic in peace, which they have. They had become most helpful in keeping in touch with Wesley's distant family in Bergarian. The only person we had wished to call for the past eleven or twelve years was Hades though. No summoning could call him to ask why the ward didn't work or who broke through.

Days turned into weeks, weeks into years, the Witches had tried to contact Hades daily. In the confines of our territory and in Bergarian, no one was able to contact him. Cyrene came back with terrible news each time when she returned from Bergarian. "No one can summon the God of the Underworld."

No one, not one living creature, had been able to reach him. Cyrene researched through thousands of spell books only to come up with one conclusion, someone had put a barrier around the Underworld. Hades never leaves the Underworld, and if he did and you were not summoning him, then you were out of luck.

The day that Cyrene was able to reach him gave us hope. We were to see him in a week, but he never showed and never contacted us back. Again, our hearts sank, thinking it was all just a mirage.

A giant yell came through the mind-link, and I dropped the ceramic plate to the floor. Scattering in a thousand pieces, I reached down to pick it up. *"Mom! Steven fell out of the treehouse north of the territory."* Dante's wolf could be a bit loud when reporting when he was on duty. Dante had been the most helpful when it came to my days or nights when I lost sleep. He stood up like the Alpha he would become if we didn't find our dear Ember.

"Thank you, Dante. Mind-link your father and have him pick him up. I'm guessing he broke his leg again, and he is having trouble healing it?" Dante grunted as I heard him tell Steven to sit by the tree.

"Yes, he's fine. Wait, Cyrene is here! Cyrene just teleported and said that Hades is coming and needed help. I will lead him to Ember's old treehouse!" Dante rushed through his words as I dropped every last piece of ceramic.

"What?" I breathed

"I'm going to lead them here now; I'll tell Father to meet us near her treehouse! Hurry, Mom!" I dashed out the door quicker than the lightning that took Ember. No shoes, just the long maxi dress I wore.

"Hunter!" I screamed as I saw him at the end of the porch. He was chopping wood, getting ready for the winter storm the elders had predicted in a few days' time. "Hades is coming! We need to go." Hunter threw his ax back on the stump and ran with me holding my hand. My sons had become everything I had hoped for, even if I was a little overbearing. My hand started to heal. I didn't realize I had cut it on the way out.

Hunter grabbed my hand but didn't question. He knew I was careless when there was any possible news of his sister. Licking my hand, so the wound shut completely with his Alpha-strengthening saliva, we dashed to the tree line.

A girl, no taller than me with strawberry blonde hair, stood, holding hands with the God of the Underworld. He was just as I remembered him. Blonde hair, deep dark eyes, and his intimidating aura. Underneath it all, I knew he wanted to be loved, and this girl that had her hands intertwined with his, I knew he found the one. I smiled, knowing what happiness he must have found, but my heart told me not to be so excited.

Our Ember was still missing, and this was my chance to have him help us. The girl turned from facing Hades, and her green eyes investigated Wesley's and mine. Wesley held me tightly to his chest as both of our hearts stopped.

The other Wolves around us faded into the distance. Dante brushed his fur up against my leg in comfort. "*Daughter*," Victoria, my wolf, cried. The howl in my head rang clear as I felt the wetness of my cheeks. Wesley's grip tightened. Remus, his Wolf, was speechless like he usually was, but the whimpers were loud and clear.

"Mom, Dad?" Ember took a step away from Hades as he held her hand in confusion. Ember looked back, being just as emotional as I, nodded at him as he gently smiled and let go of her hand.

Another giant step towards us, and I couldn't hold back anymore. I let go of Wesley as we ran into each other's arms. Wails left my mouth as Ember cried in my arms. Not long after, I felt Wesley run-up to the both of us, squeezing us making sure we never left. "Gods, Ember," he heaved a sob. Wesley's hand ran through Ember's hair while I continued to kiss her cheeks.

All of us were in the dirt, clothes muddy from the rain the night before, but I didn't care. I would roll in it all day to have this moment repeat itself.

"Ember!" Hunter yelled as he came tumbling in. His dark blonde hair, down to his shoulders like his father, whipped Ember in the face as she laughed. Dante had returned, shorts in hand, and flew to us in an instant. The large dog pile left in the middle of the pack grounds was a sight, I was sure.

Cheers, applause, and howls lit the entire territory. Wolves patrolling came to a screeching halt as they saw the whole Alpha family hugging each other. Steven, the youngest who would not remember Ember stood beside the dogpile while limping. His leg was healing but not fast enough to join the fun.

Ember stilled as she saw Steven. "Steven?" Her lip wobbled. "You grew up to be so big," she whispered. Steven limped towards her, and Ember gave him an enormous hug. "Last time I held you like this, you were only days old," she sniffed. Steven was now eleven, and she had missed his first steps and words. I knew that Ember had a strong connection with him, and the emotion I felt in her was intense. We all felt it. She had missed us as much as we had missed her.

A loud growl cut through our thoughts as Wesley stood up menacingly. His back was ridged as he marched halfway over to Hades. Fur was coming over his arms, Remus was coming out, and now was not the time.

"You took my daughter?!" Remus heaved a breath as his claws came forth. I ran to him to pull his arm. "You broke the ward. You took Ember!" Hades stood with his arms crossed as he narrowed his eyes.

"You dare talk to me that way?" Hades smirked as Ember let go of Steven.

"Stop! Dad, stop!" Ember ran past Wesley, and Hades opened his arms. Ember buried her head in his chest as the onlookers stood in amusement. "He's my mate. He saved me! He saved me!"

Remus retracted his claws and retreated. Wesley shook his head and grabbed my arm for comfort. "He saved me," Ember breathed again as she attached herself to his cloak. "He took me out of that terrible place and took care of me. I lost my memory... I." Hades put his finger on her lips and gently brushed back her now dirty hair.

"I think it is best if we take this inside." Hades' voice wasn't loud. It was low and possibly more dominating.

"Let's go to our home, in the study," I cooed at Wesley. He was still on edge, and I knew I had to calm him before anything else was said. "Let's go, come on. I've got lunch in the oven too." Our family all huddled around Ember, giving plenty of room to stay away from Hades and his touch. The Wolves were mind-linked to prepare a large feast for dinner in celebration of Ember's return home.

Victoria paced in my head and nudged me. "*I think there is a lot more happening than Ember returning home.*" I nodded silently.

"*That, I would have to agree with you, Victoria.*"

Hades

Ember was back in my arms, where she should be. Her family found their lost daughter, and I had wished I had put the pieces to the puzzle together sooner. Ember was gone for eleven years; Cyrene has tried to contact me for the same amount of time. My mind was too busy wondering about the missing gods to even think of this coincidence.

We entered a large home, a little smaller than you would see as a southern plantation house. It was white with shutters on the outside, and the inside was clean, bright, and light with green plants. There was a roaring fireplace in the middle of the living room, but instead of the brightness of the main room, we went to the study. A small wandering orange tabby cat hissed as it scampered away.

The study was just as significant but darker in wood than the rest of the house. I felt more comfortable here, and I had wondered if Luna Charlotte would have picked up on that. The large couches and chairs were scattered around a large desk, and I had Ember sit with me, despite just finding her parents.

Ember would glance between her mother and father. Wesley glared at me, unbelieving that I did not have taken his daughter. Charlotte's eyes continued to brighten as time went on. How depressed she could have been? I knew her past. It was dark and full of terrible memories caused mainly by my demon. Ember would soon put the pieces to that mess of a puzzle together, and I wasn't looking forward to that.

"How did you find her?" Wesley's voice boomed. He wasn't scared of me when it came to his daughter. Cyrene had warned him countless times before to be careful and tread lightly, but that was thrown out. The thought must have triggered Cyrene because she came in barreling in the room.

"My Lord!" She bowed down and touched her face to the dark wooded floors. "We are so grate-"

"Get up, Cyrene. No time for formalities. Just sit." I waved my hand as Ember scowled at me.

"That's not nice," she whispered, but they all heard it. Charlotte giggled and nudged her mate.

"Sound familiar, Alpha?" She nuzzled into his neck. Wesley continued to glare at me, waiting for me to speak. Her brothers were sitting on the long couch, and my mind continued to play scenarios of how this will go.

"I found Ember at a human trafficking club disguised as a strip club." Gasps went around the room while Wesley slammed his fists into the mahogany desk. It broke in two, and Charlotte just glared at Wesley.

"Babe, that is number twenty four since you have known me. You need to chill!" The boys snickered, but Dante's guilty look caught my eye. He rubbed his hands together, and a trickle of sweat filled his brow.

Interesting.

After another hour of explaining where Ember was and how she was my mate, the room was silent. I told them how I found her, the helm, the immediate threat of her being taken away from me, and how three gods were now missing. I trusted this pack more than my brother, and they had helped me before. They could do it again and help protect their daughter. It was my fault that she was taken; if I had just listened to Selene, none of this would have happened. I dare not tell Wesley this could have been prevented, and Ember seemed to understand.

"We don't need to tell them everything," Ember winked. "Some things are better left unsaid," she spoke to her parents while they nodded reluctantly. Now that the Alpha and Luna know of Ember's hardships, the real issue arises. Her shift.

"You haven't shifted yet?" Wesley asked concerned. Ember shook her head 'no' as she twiddled her thumb. Pulling her close, I kissed her temple while Wesley scowled.

"She was weak, remember? All the spells on her made her human, maybe even weaker. They are slowly going away and Ember being able to remember you all is a miracle. We just have this hurdle to face." I kissed Embers' knuckles as she leaned into me.

Wesley rubbed his chin. "We need to get the elders in here. I haven't heard of an adult wolf going through a shift."

"Hey, I did it." Charlotte pushed Wesley in the shoulder.

"That's different, baby." He pulled her to his lap. "You were human turning into a Wolf. Ember is a Werewolf that has been suppressed from her Wolf side for far too long. With her being weak for so many years, she will have difficulties." Wesley looked at me pointedly. I knew what he was talking about. There was a chance she might not make it if her bones hadn't become strong enough. Charlotte looked between the both of us to try and read our thoughts but came up blank.

"How about lunch then?" she asked as we all let out a huge sigh.

Chapter 42

Ember

My dad's stare continued to bore into Hades as we held our hands above the table. I'm sure seeing his daughter that was once a small thing the last time he saw her and now brings home a mate disturbed him. Then again, Hades was my mate so he couldn't disapprove could he?

Mom had made Monti Cristo sandwiches, a fried ham and cheese sandwich that I remember that used to be my favorite. I patiently waited until she put the large pan on the table until reaching for one quickly and scarfing it down. I didn't realize how hungry I was until I started eating.

"I'll have Ashley come over and make us more. She'll be so happy to see you too, Ember," Mom said as she went back to the kitchen. "I can't believe she's back," she whispered to herself as she held back a sob. Going to stand to go comfort her, my dad grabs my hand.

"Give her time, she's been through a lot. She blames herself for you being gone. Please sit, this would make her happy, you eating your favorite." Giving small smile I grabbed my second sandwich and watch my older brothers look at me in disbelief.

"I can't believe you are here." Hunter put down his fork. "We thought about you every day and where you went. Mom and dad tried their hardest, even we started going on hunting trips to look for you." Hunter chuckled. "Who knew you would be rescued by your own fascination." I tilted my head in confusion and Dante laughed.

"You mean, you don't remember reading all about Greek Mythology as a kid? We used to make fun of you all the time about it. You were so fascinated with Hades and saying he was a nice god even though all of our literature said otherwise. No offence." Dante nodded at Hades who waved his hand. "We should have spotted it sooner that it could be a possibility especially with mom's relationship with all that demon stuff."

My mind went blank as I put my sandwich down. "Huh?"

Hades squeezed my hand and rubbed his beard. "Remember the story about Trixen I've told you about?" I nodded my head quickly which ended up slowing down as the memory of the story flowed. A new Luna had destroyed Trixen against all odds. Mom did that?

"Oh, my gosh," I whispered. "Mom destroyed your demon?"

Hades kissed my cheeks as they blushed pink. "She did. I owed her, so I put up the ward that was supposed to keep her and your entire pack free of danger. Even there I failed her too, just as you." Hades eyes drifted to me, and I didn't need my empathic abilities to know his guilt.

"Not your fault," I mouthed as I hugged him. His grip was tight as he stroked my back with his thumb. My dad cleared his throat and Hades grunted at disapproval.

"You haven't been mated and marked yet. I still have some say." He pulled at the collar of his shirt and went back to eating. The joy that was under my dad's heavy exterior was overpowering. He was happy I was home and his reluctance to show it in front of Hades was deafening. Power hungry males, I shook my head.

Squeals came from the kitchen as I heard the door open with a loud bang. "My fire is back!?" Ashley or Aunt Ashley came bursting through the doorway with an excited look. Jumping from the chair, we collided with each other as her excitement tackled me to the ground. "Aunt Ashley!" I squealed.

"Look at you! You are so tiny, just like your Mom! And mated to a god! Oh, my stars what a banging mating ceremony we are going to have! I can't wait to get started!" Dad stiffened and rubbed his temples.

"No mating ceremony until she shifts. That is the first priority." His excitement for me being in is presence wavered and his worry and dread hung over him like a storm cloud. "We also need to make sure she is healthy enough. I'm having the pack doctor come in, along with Cyrene before dinner to take a look at her." Cyrene bowed her head at the end of the table.

"That reminds me." Hades pulled out a pill bottle and handed me a pill. "Swallow this, remember?" I nodded and drunk it down.

"The God of Health and Medicine constructed a pill to aide in her healing. Her bones have been considerably strengthened and should have no problems shifting. It's the mentality I worry about." Hades stroked my back and led me back to the table to eat. Dad didn't look convinced.

"She will still see the doctor, and I'll have my Wolf speak with, Elea is it?" I nodded my head in confirmation. Elea and my dad's wolf Remus were already talking. It was in hushed murmurs, but I could feel Remus and his possessiveness of me being his daughter. Feeling the love from just my dad's Wolf was enough to make me excited for the next part of my life.

"Once she has shifted and deemed healthy, I would like to bond with her," Hades interrupted the silence. My dad and brothers growled as mom entered the room with another tray of sandwiches. My body stiffened once Hades made the announcement. He just told everyone we were going to do it!

"That's enough!" Mom barked and all the men held their heads down, including Hades.

"I think that is a lovely idea. Ember, we can plan a perfect ceremony for you! Great bonding time with you me and Ashley. She's the party planner; Beta Evan's mate is about to give birth any day and needs her rest." Mom giggled as she sat the tray down.

"Yeah, because Beta Evan always is fucking her." Hunter nudged Dante and Mom threw a sandwich at him.

"That is enough! Do not use such words around the table especially with our special guest!" Dad snickered and Mom hissed at him.

"You think it's funny, but you do the same thing. When I wasn't in my depressing moods, he's have me locked up in our bed-"

"Ew mom," Steven spoke up as he put his hands on his ears. "That's gross."

"A bond is a powerful thing. Once you find your mate you will feel the same." Dad pointed his fork at my brothers. "You will be head over heels and will do anything for her, and I mean anything." Daddy looked at Hades while he nodded. The tension slowly dried up as conversations went to casual mumbling.

A lot had changed since I left. My treehouse, which was centered just on the edge of town, was still there so I could watch Wolves go by. It was considered taboo to go anywhere near it, like preserving it for when I came back. Instead, Dad built another one, not as large, on the northern part of the territory near the lake. Dante had taken up Dad's fishing time and was learning all the secrets to be an alpha.

I could remember bits and pieces of my childhood, but I felt a lot was missing. I remembered the important things such as conversations at the lake and where we went to school in the human town over. The day I was taken and the days leading to it was a blur. The only memory I had was the dream where the masked man came in to take me.

The one thing I needed to find was my favorite spot, my favorite place to play as a child. Sure, the tree house was a fun spot and my favorite, but I vaguely remember having "the spot." This spot no one knew about, and I was certain that was where it was held. The problem is, I didn't know where it was, what was around it or anything. I just knew the treehouse wasn't THE spot. I would check anyway because I was curious if my treasure chest was still there.

"Maybe we could show Hades around?" My mom spoke up as we heard a knock at the door. Dad stood up and wiped his mouth. "Who is it?" Mom went to stand up, but Dad waved for her to sit down.

"I'll check, Kitten just wait."

Before Daddy got to the door, it opened, and three men showed up. Looking all like their Greek selves, our friends walked through the door. "Loukas! Ares! Vulcan!" I jumped up to run and give them a hug, but Hades was quick and pulled me back. My hips rubbed up against his groin and he growled.

"Don't move, or I'll go find your room right now." The vibrations in his chest set me off as I started giggling and my brothers groaned.

"Wait! The Ares!?" Dante jumped up along with Steven and Hunter and rushed towards the entrance.

"Loukas is in deep shit," Ares growled as he pushed him to the floor. "Tell us every bit you told Zeus." Hades' anger built but I grabbed his hand.

"Tell. Me. What." My family slinked back, and my father looked between Loukas and Hades.

"Loukas's a demon," I whispered, "He's my good friend." Loukas's head jerked to me and smiled but that did not make Hades any happier.

"You told him" Hades pulled him up by his collar. "You told Zeus what we know!" Hades' smoke leaked from his robes again and

I sighed exasperatedly. I was just glad it didn't leave a permanent mess anywhere.

"Hades, just wait, let's hear his story," I begged but Hades growled and didn't let his eyes veer away from Loukas.

"Can't do that, Flower. He betrayed me, his master." I looked at Loukas and tilted my head in confusion. Loukas only nodded in confirmation slowly as he gripped Hades' hand to steady himself.

"Loukas told Zeus that my mate would find the Spere of Souls. Do you know what kind of danger that puts her in, you fool? We don't know if we can trust Zeus! He could be lying!" Loukas's face turned purple as he lost the air from his lungs. Panicking, I knew what Loukas did was wrong, but I didn't want him to kill him!

Pulling on Hades' arm, my family watched in horror as their daughter dared to defy the God of the Underworld. "Wait Hades." Hades eyes softened as he looked at me.

"I cannot let this rest; he will be punished."

"Just hear me out! Before you had your temper tantrum with Zeus, he said he didn't do it. I felt it, Hades. He was telling the truth. He had no idea that Malachi was after me and was only following Selene's orders. I felt his emotions and he spoke the truth!" Hades gripped loosened but not enough to drop Loukas.

Hades glared at Loukas and dropped him to the floor, harshly, causing a hole to erupt in the middle. "You have to fix that, that doesn't look good bashing your in-laws' home." I whispered. Hades chuckled and pulled me to him for a brief kiss.

"Loukas, you are sentenced to the dungeons of the Underworld Palace until we have things resolved. Your judgement will be decided from there." With a wave of his hand, Loukas had vanished before our eyes. My family stood in awe while I just giggled how utterly normal this was to me now.

Vulcan came to my mother and bowed, giving her a kiss. "It is an honor to meet the woman who destroyed Trixen."

My dad growled as he pulled mom back into his embrace. "Um, t-thank you," she stuttered as she blushed.

"I think this has been enough excitement. How about Ember getss some rest before her appointment? Cyrene, be ready at 4pm sharp at the medical clinic with your best healers." Dad ordered as Cyrene agreed and left the house. Cyrene looked at Hades with such adoring feelings of my Hades. My throat growled as she left and mom only giggled as she elbowed dad.

Taking Hades' hand, I led him up the stairs. It was amazing how I remembered the exact layout of the house. The bedrooms were all upstairs so Mom and Dad could watch us closely, which didn't help one bit. My door was the furthest down the hall because I was the oldest. The pink and purple letters on the outside of the door remained, Alpha Ember.

A little smirk played on my lips as I traced it with my hand. Hades was pensive as he studied the door, but I opened it before he could speak. I felt his confusion, his wonderings of what I was going to say in regard to the Alpha title. I had never trained for it, other than the supporting words from dad. Age ten was when I would start training and I never made it.

My room was left the same, besides the mess that was left behind. A wooden rocking chair was beside the bed and a calico overstuffed cat sat on it. Picking it up I smelled it and it all smelled of my mom. Dried tearstains laid on the white portions of the fabric as I petted it. "Mom really did spend some time in here huh?" Hades nodded as he walked around the room looking at pictures.

The entire left side wall was covered in colorful drawings and random polaroid pictures. Mostly my brother Dante and I and one special one that sat in the middle. It was the last picture taken before I was taken. Steven was holding onto my hand as I kissed him on the forehead.

"I'm sorry you missed your youth." Hades frowned as he sat on the bed, holding a framed picture of my family. "I'm sorry I messed up and didn't see you when I could." I sat beside him and put my head on the side of his arm. I wasn't tall enough to even reach his shoulder.

"I'm happy that you told me the truth. Yeah, it sucks I was away from them, but it made me stronger in other ways. It's in the past but you must learn not to be so hot headed and not listen to people. I hope you learned your lesson?" I giggled as I elbowed him. Hades continued to stare down at the picture frame.

"When this is all over, I can see if Hecate could conjure spell to reverse time?" I raised an eyebrow questioningly. "It hasn't' been done but with magic, anything is possible I suppose. We could rewind and you could stay with your family, and I would watch over you." I scoffed and threw my hands down on my lap. Standing up I went to the large window that now had bars covering them.

"Ok, Hades. One, we don't know if you can change time to do something different. There must be a law against that, otherwise time and space would be so screwed up!" I waved my hands around. "Two, you have to forgive yourself since I have forgiven you." Hades glanced at me again with those dark eyes. I wanted to kiss him until he believed me. "And three, I wouldn't change anything that has happened to me. Look who I am now!" My hands fell to my sides.

"I went through some hardship, but a lot of girls had worse and continue to do so. Once this is over, I want to be the protector of those girls. If I didn't go through what I did, I never would have known of such a crime being trapped here in a Werewolf community. I wouldn't have become as strong mentally either. Look what I can do now! I can read people's emotions, tell if they are lying. How cool is that?"

Hades smiled while he bit that thin bottom lip of his. "I don't know if I would have gained that power before being magically experimented on, but I have it now and it gets stronger every day when another barrier breaks. I'm here now, today because of you. You saved me, you gave me a love story I will never forget, and it will be written down in history books to come how the God of the Underworld swooped in and saved his mate from certain death and misfortune. You will be written in a new light just because of that. You don't have to be portrayed as some evil god. You will be the one in the light."

I threw the picture frame from his hands onto the bed and straddled his lap. "You, my Hades, my mate are perfect just the way you are. Blonde hair, dark eyes, sweet, talented, powerful, indescribable hunk of a god that deserves so much more than this self-loathing guilt eating your soul shit."

I kissed his forehead. "We're in this together. In the end you saved me and I'm gonna save you."

Chapter 43

Ember

I put my hands on either side of his face while I continued to straddle him. His deep dark eyes bore into mine so fierce that I swore I saw the constellations of Orion. "Now kiss me damnit."

Hades didn't falter and slammed his lips into mine while his arms wrapped around my waist. If there was a doubt in my mind that there was space between us, that all had dissolved away because our bodies themselves almost became one.

I pulled at his hair as his nails dug into my dress, holes ripping through the silky fabric of my tunic dress. The ropes were torn away harshly as I clawed at the buttons of his shirt. The small bed squeaked as Hades hovered over my body. My head tilted up, exposing my neck, and Hades placed opened mouthed kisses, sucked, and pulled on my delicate skin.

"I want to make you mine," he growled. "I want to take what was given to me, and I want you to bite into my skin and let every soul know you accept me." I moaned as I pulled his hair again, and Elea howled in joy.

Mouth trailing to my nipples, I heard stomping coming up the stairs, but Hades waved his hand at the doorway. "Someone is coming," I whispered as he continued to pull at my tits.

"They can't come in, and they can't hear us," he mumbled. Lost in the pleasure of his mouth, I reached for his cock that was already dripping. I wanted him to claim me right there, but it wouldn't be wise with my parents just downstairs.

"Hades," I whispered as he pulled off his pants. His dick sprung free as I felt it slap my naked leg.

"Just a touch, I won't enter your flower yet." He chuckled darkly as I felt his shaft rub on my clit.

"Kitty whiskers," I breathed as he pushed his dick hard into my bundle of nerves. It was warm, hot, and the tingles ran up inside me. Hades was dangerously close, too close. One little slip and the head of his giant cock would enter me, and we would be done for.

"If you think this feels good, wait until I buried deep inside your pussy. I'll make love to you, and my balls slap your inner thighs." I wanted to come undone right there. His dirty words were a turn-on I never knew I would like. I wanted him so badly, but the thought of bonding with my mate was quickly making me think of my parents downstairs.

"Don't think." I felt Hades get frustrated. "I want you to just feel me. Feel how much I want you to cum in you. Spill myself into your cavern and watch you suck me in your body." That did it. I heaved out his name as his dick rubbed my core as I felt my own essence coat onto his cock. I felt his dick pulsing on my pubic bone, where he spilled his load on me a heavy grunt later. The waterfall of emotions wracked me as he held me.

"What am I going to do with you?" Hades panted as his thumb caressed my cheek. "I don't think I can hold back anymore; I just about took you right there." I giggled as I grabbed his hand.

"Next time then." I lowered my lashes to get a look at his still throbbing member. "Again?" I grinned mischievously.

"I would," he nipped my ear, "but your parents and Cyrene are just outside the door screaming." My ears perked up to hear as Hades waved the ward from the door. Shouting continued as my dad banged on the door excessively.

"Get this ward off, she isn't home an hour, and someone has her already!?" Mom was hysterically crying, and Cyrene was chanting in Latin. Did they think I was being taken again?

"Cover-up, flower." Hades pulled the comforter off the bed to wipe away any remnants of himself and his lower half while I took the sheet. Hades' hand waved again, and the door burst open.

He. Did. Not.

I screamed in my head while Elea was laughing hysterically. I could see her wiggling her butt in glee while my angry father and my inconsolable mother crying. Covering up my breasts, I looked at the two of them.

Mom dried her face with the palms of her hands. "Oh," she said as she sniffed. "You were just messing around. I'm sorry, come on, Babe." Mom grabbed Dad's hand, but he didn't move. His fists were clenched as he stared at Hades with the most hatred I had ever recalled seeing.

"What were you doing?" he growled as Hades kept the comforter wrapped around his waist. Hades sat beside me and put his arm around me.

"Do you really want a play-by-play?" Hades kissed my cheek while my face flushed with embarrassment. My dad just caught me messing around; I'm going to die before I even shift. He is my mate though, so it is OK, right? The panic didn't leave me even when Hades' put his arm around me. "We are mates, and you said we couldn't mate yet, so we were just relieving some tension."

"Chocolate snickers, shut up, Hades." Hades threw his head back to laugh as I covered my mouth. This was the worst thing that could have ever happened. What would have happened if there wasn't a ward on the door!? They would have seen us ALMOST going at it!

Dad grunted as he crossed his arms. "Get dressed. It's Sunday. Just you. Hades, can wait here." Dad took another glance at Hades before he stomped down the stairs.

Hades wanted to protest, but I grabbed his arm. "Blaze is out in the woods somewhere. He can come with me."

"Then I'm left here with your mother," Hades sighed as he ran his hand through his blonde hair. How could that be so bad? Mom was great. She loved having guests over. Anytime there was a new pack member, she would have them over for dinner and get to know them. Dad hated it. He just wanted them to move into their own house or the packhouse and leave him alone.

Then I remembered, the last time my mom and Hades were in the same room, he was thanking her for the big mistake he basically created. Trixen made my mom's life a living hell for years before she had dad. Mom didn't seem mad or hold a grudge over it; she was happy when she saw Hades and me at the tree line.

"It will be all right; she's forgiven you just like I have. She's probably making you cookies. Mom loves making cookies when guests come over."

"You act like you never left." Hades petted my hair. I hummed as he stroked it.

"There are still some things I can't remember like I feel like I should, though. Ever have that feeling where you lost something and can't find it? That's what I'm feeling. We do need to check my treehouse, and I'm hoping that will lead us to the Sphere of Souls," I said determinedly.

"One step at a time," Hades warned. "You are getting close to shifting. I don't want to add extra pressure on you."

"Ember!" my dad yelled from downstairs. "Let's go!" I groaned and got up, realizing I had no clothes to wear. Of course, Hades willed clothes on me, some from the Underworld, and I was in basic black skinny jeans and a white cashmere sweater.

"Stay warm, my mate."

Wesley

Not a day ago, I was still hunting for my daughter. My firstborn child and the first Alpha Female to the Black Claw pack. At a young age, she was strong, she was more substantial than most of the boys five years her senior, but Charlotte wouldn't let her train early. Charlotte wanted her to have a childhood before I started making her physically strong.

Charlotte did grant me time once a week to pass along wisdom to Ember. We would take our two fishing poles and head down to the giant lake on the territory that I had constructed. It was just a pond, but with a bit of human help and a wad of cash, we were able to create a paradise that everyone could enjoy. No one hardly uses the indoor swimming pool in the packhouse anymore; they run to the lake and become one with nature.

Sundays, however, were off-limits to the pack. That was the time Ember, starting at age four, we would go fishing. Taking the boat out in the middle of the lake, we would fish all day long. Having our lunch in the boat, talking about random things four-year-old's do until she started understanding the real reason we were out there. Her future.

It is expected the firstborn child will take over the pack. Never in the pack's history had there been a female, and I wasn't about to change tradition over a gender issue. Charlotte wouldn't have that either.

As we walked through the forest that had grown considerably since Ember was gone, she grabbed my hand. It was another tradition we would hold hands as we walked down, and my heart started to stutter as she remembered. Remus had missed her. He had kept quiet for many years, upset at the prospect of never finding her. We knew she was alive, but the hunt for her was always never-ending.

"I'm sorry I yelled," I broke the silence as she looked up at me. Ember should have been taller, almost as tall as me, for being an Alpha's child. She was so small, didn't even look like the age fifteen. I could hardly believe she was twenty. Ember waved her hand dismissively.

"You haven't seen me in so long, and then I come back home with my mate and did stuff in my childhood room. I think it is understandable. Mom already told me you would come around before I left the house." I chuckled and rolled my eyes.

"She did now? Did she also tell you why we are out here today?" Ember shook her head as we came upon our boat. It was still usable. I had started taking Dante after two years of looking for Ember. The idea that he would take over the pack had come to light after two years of searching. I had to train a replacement. Dante was hesitant about it; he wanted to wait longer for her to come back, but it had to be done. We had to look after the pack.

"Looks the same," she mused as she hopped in the boat. "Did Dante enjoy fishing with you?" I stepped back a bit in the realization of what she said. She knew I took him out? "Well, obviously, you didn't know I was coming back, Dad, so you had to train Dante." I nodded and pushed the boat out in the water.

"This is a quick trip, no long talks today." We pulled out our poles and hooked them with worms. We were basic while we fished, with no fancy bait or funny bobbers. Just us and nature and the fish we barely caught.

"I'm so happy you are back." I held back the tears. "I blamed myself every day. Hell, we all blamed ourselves." Ember grabbed my hand.

"Dad, it couldn't have been helped. Something compelling got through. At the time, I was scared, but I'm fine now. Hades found me, my mate. It was supposed to be this way." Ember smiled, but the sob escaped me. There had been only a few times I had cried, and they had all been with Charlotte. Now I look at her carbon copy and realize those were the only two women I would ever cry for.

"Everyone keeps blaming themselves." Ember looked out into the distance. "But I wouldn't change it. Sure, it sucked living like that. Wondering if I would be sold, beaten, or raped, but it made me thankful for the smaller things. The grass, the flowers, the friends I've made. I just appreciate everything all the more." Ember smiled up at me. Her identical strawberry blonde locks of her mother blew in the wind. "You all have to give me some credit. I'm pretty strong, you know." she winked.

Chuckling, I threw my line in while I sat beside her in the boat. "And there is something I want to bring up," Ember spoke as she pulled her line in. Taking off the small fish, she threw it back in and put on a worm. "I'm giving up the Alpha Title."

This had crossed my mind since she would be mated to Hades. Goddess of the Underworld was a high position. She needed to be with her mate, who couldn't leave his own position.

"I'm not doing it for Hades; I'm doing it for the greater good of the pack," she added. "Sure, I could spend more time training to be an Alpha." Ember shrugged her shoulders. "But I think I was meant to do something more outside the pack."

How did my little girl become so thoughtful and intelligent? Ember has seen things I had never thought about being a problem. She'd experienced what it was like to be helpless.

"What things are you wanting to change?" I asked thoughtfully as she threw her line back out.

"There are a lot of girls and maybe some guys that are being sold into trafficking. I want to stop it. I want to stop humans and other supernaturals from doing it. Heck, even some angels and demons, not all of them are good, you know that." I nodded in understanding.

"If that is what you want to do, I won't stop you. You will always be wanted here; I hope you know that. Your brother Dante doesn't have to take the position." She smiled.

"I know that, but he would be better at leading wolves than I would. Hades is a handful enough and adding my own conquests to save those who are suffering is enough. Hades had already started something similar. I'm just expanding it. I think I am suited there. Dante was a good brother. I'm sure he still is and is capable of taking over the pack." She smiled, tracing her finger on the old boat.

Dante had been a good son, dare I say, almost too perfect. Anytime his mother or I asked for help, he jumped right in with no hesitation. He never went through the playboy alpha stage that was commonly strong in his adolescent years. He stuck to the high road and picked up extra scouting and border patrol when he could. He never sat down to rest. When he wasn't hunting for Ember or helping the pack, he trained, and he trained hard. In a few years, I wouldn't be surprised if he passed my strength in human form.

"He has." I looked off across the lake.

"You think there is a motive," Ember spoke. "Remember what Hades said. I can read your emotions loud and clear, and you question him."

"Can't get past you, fire, huh?"

"Nope!"

Chapter 44

Hades

"Talk to the covens in Bergarian that you trust. Let them know three gods are missing and watch out for any abnormalities in magic casting, especially in the dark kingdom of Vermillion." Cyrene wrote down a few notes on her scroll. "Not to say the kingdom will go back to its old ways, but it would be better to check."

"I'll be sure to go there myself. I can't trust the communications spells, especially knowing that the Underworld was compromised after all those years. Who knows who could be listening."? I nodded as I took a bite of one of the Luna's cookies.

"I will send you there myself. Just send a nudge when you want to return. If I do not reply, you will have to get back on your own."

Cyrene sat across from me at Alpha Wesley's dining room table. Ember had gone with her father, much to my distaste, but I had to play nice. She hadn't seen him in so long, and the topic of her becoming Alpha of the Black Claw Pack was going to come up. Did she want to be the Alpha? If she did, we would make it work. I already had plans in the works for a portal to be erected here in her parent's home so she could come to and from the Underworld without the help of my magic. I just needed Hecate to help prepare the spell. I wasn't great at essential magic, but she would need my source of power, which was in the Underworld, to procure it.

Hell, this is based on if we can even retrieve Hecate, Selene, and Hermes. Keeping Ember calm was the goal, but the tensions I could feel from Zeus were becoming overpowering. I could feel his struggle as he tried to keep himself together. He wasn't used to the stress; he just tried to help micromanage brawls between gods, and even then, Athena and Hera helped him.

Zeus isn't evil. He just has his head in the wrong places and doesn't know what he wants. A mate would do him some good and knock some sense into him. I prayed to the fates it wasn't Hera. That woman had been through too much.

"I'm ready when you are, my Lord." Cyrene stood up with her robes wrapped around her and hood over her face. I waved my hand non-ceremoniously as she disappeared, and Charlotte walked through the door with some milk and more cookies. Damn, she can cook.

"I thought you would like some milk," she trailed off as she set it on the table. Sitting down, she twiddled with her thumbs while staring intently at them. "Thank you, Hades. For saving her." Charlotte's eyes glazed over as she wiped back a trailing tear. "When I told you that your mate was out there waiting for you, I didn't realize it would be my own daughter."

After Charlotte single-handedly destroyed my self-made mate, she instantly forgave me and felt sorry for me. Me, the God of the Underworld, and she took pity on me. Her little speech didn't give me the hope I needed; after all, her daughter did suffer because of my hardened heart.

"It is funny how the goddess works, huh? Now that you are back here, I wouldn't be surprised if your friends find a few mates. She does have a way with mates meeting each other."

The thought crossed my mind that Ares could find his mate. This was a large pack, and he had desires to find a mate in a Wolf. However, with the Sphere of Souls missing, no one was going to be finding their mates. Selene needed her Sphere to conduct a small ritual to bind them together once their eyes met.

"Ares, Hermes and Vulcan would wish to find mates. More so than I did," I trailed off. "Perhaps one day they will find what they are looking for once this is all over." Charlotte nodded.

"I've got a new bed being brought up to Ember's room. I don't think sleeping on a double bed will fit the both of you." She winked. "Just know that Wesley won't be happy about it. He still sees her as a little girl." I bit my lip, thinking of how my feet hung off the bed as

I pleasured Ember. Her eyes were glowing with lust and desire to complete the bond. We couldn't, not yet. Selene thankfully confirmed our bond before she went missing. In this period, we were the only couple that could be bonded together.

"Thank you, I appreciate it."

"Just be good to her," Charlotte growled. "Otherwise, I won't be so nice." Her claws lengthened around her coffee mug, and her fangs grew while she laughed. I laughed along with her, something I hadn't done with anyone else but Ember. Having Ember's parents in her life wouldn't be so bad. Wesley will be tough to crack, but we have a long time to come with that odd relationship.

Ares

Dante, Hunter, and Steven led Vulcan and I out of the house and through the pack territory. They showed their defenses, the cameras Charlotte had set up as well as the training fields. Many Wolves were shifting, fighting, and sparring. Some were even using older weapons I had used in many battles with humans thousands of years ago.

My heart started pumping; the adrenaline was ripping through my veins. "Lord Ares, would you like to train us? It would be an honor." Dante threw off his shirt as well as Hunter.

"Yes, please, show us your ways!" Steven went to sit on the sidelines. He was only eleven, and his own group of beginners wasn't on the field. The Alpha had strategically set up times for warriors based on age and ability. Right now, the strongest were on the field due to the protection of Ember, the supposed new Alpha. Extra training and extra patrolling were scheduled for the night and especially around the Alpha's home.

"Sounds like a good idea." I ripped my shirt off as I stomped onto the field. The Wolves stopped what they were doing as soon as I stepped foot on the massive training arena. It was in the shape of a football field with obstacle courses, weights, and weapons. Many gave wide eyes as I ripped my human disguise from my body and stomped one foot on the ground, instantly turning the churned-up mud into sand. The sand was a great way to help train your legs and learn to keep your balance; this would help them later but kill their hamstrings now. I also willed massive stands such as the Greek colosseum on a much smaller scale, so those who were not training could watch. Watching was also an effective way of training. Learn from others' mistakes and take in what you should do on your own time.

"It's Ares!" A Wolf yelled from the sideline. My leather coverings on my calves and forearms twinkled in the sun against the bronzed threading. The leather straps on my back donned my sword and shield. Reaching behind me, I pulled my sword and, at my side, my battle-ax. "Who would like to train with the God of War?" I yelled across the field. Wolves came running and screaming in cheers as they approached.

I lived for this, for the blood on my enemies' bodies on the ground and on my sword. These wolves' ancestors were created with such a purpose. To destroy the out-of-control evils that many gods had formed out of experiments. Many humans were taken and given abilities that didn't change just their bodies but also their minds.

Werewolves had the perfect balance because they had a shared soul of both wolf and human. They were two separate entities, and once the wars and battles with the evil rejected beings were created, they were lost. Their wolves craved war while their human side craved emotion. With Selene's help, she created soul mates, which sated both sides of the Werewolves.

Never knew that one day Selene could turn it so both Werewolves, supernatural, and even the gods would be blessed with such a gift.

I had set groups up, some sparing with weapons, others in Wolf forms, and some doing conditioning work. The men and women warriors were in top condition; Alpha had done his part keeping his pack strong. No wonder it was the strongest in North America. I would have to see if they could be in legion with me and part of my war stronghold.

When I am called upon in times of war, it is rare, but it does happen. I bring with me my own army. Once I have appraised both sides, I choose what side I should side with. Hades was the best at the judge of character; he would help often. Those with legion would fight for me, and in repayment, their warriors were given double the strength and training with me.

I swelled my chest at the pride of how hard these Wolves were willing to work. It isn't often that wolves train themselves like this. It reminded me of the Crimson Shadow's in Bergarian. Many packs on Earth had become lazy. It doesn't matter the size of the pack, but its strength. If they are not training and not patrolling their territory, I cannot help when their cries come. It is a two-way street, and unfortunately, I cannot come to save everyone.

My hands were behind my back as I walked by weightlifting stations. Wolves were eager to show off in front of me. She-wolves winked and waved, and I had to do a wink here or there. However, training was the target for the day. Besides, I wanted to have what Hades had. My dick was under wraps for a while.

As I continued to walk down the field, I found one she-wolf working on a punching bag. Her legs were long, lean, and muscular. Her hair was pulled back in a braid that reached her waist. With bare fists, she slammed her arms into the bag without a flinch. Hints of blood flicked off her knuckles as she barreled into it with full strength. Her lips were set in a stiff line as her top stretched tight across her chest. Her ass had to be sculpted from stone; it was muscular perfection. This girl, she got my attention.

As I stood there, watching this woman of at least 6'5" beat the shit out of a bag, Dante walked up to me. "Everything pleasing to you, Lord Ares? The Wolves are eager to make you proud." I smiled back at Dante. He was a good Wolf, always eager to please.

"None of that Lord shit." I elbowed him. "Just Ares." Glancing back at the woman, now using her legs to hit either side of the bag, Dante smirked. "That's Mariah; she's our packs' strongest female. She's been given guard duty to Ember until she shifts." I hummed while listening.

"Is she your mate? You keep looking at her weird." I shook my head.

"I can't smell her. I just think she's beautiful." I frowned.

Mariah continued to strike the bag until it finally burst and sand poured from a hole. Her lips never went to a smile as I approached her.

"Your form is a bit off," I said grimly.

Mariah's eyes trailed to the sand falling out of the back and gave a hard, "What the fuc-" until she turned, and her eyes widened as she saw me approach. "My Lord Ares, I am so sorry for my words." She took a knee immediately as she lowered her head. "I apologize profusely!" I laughed as I put my hand out towards her. Glancing up and placing her hand in mine, I felt the deep disappointment in my heart. She wasn't my mate. A sliver of me had really hoped she was, despite not being able to smell a sweet smell from her.

"Just Ares, and don't worry. You were running on adrenaline." Mariah stood up and dusted the sand away from her knees. Dirty thoughts entered my head as she had kneeled, but I pushed the idea away. Her eyes were a deep purple, a rare color for a Wolf, and they captured me. If I could touch her lips with mine, it would b be all the sweeter. Shaking my head, I cleared my throat.

"If you would like, I could help. It is just a small modification." Mariah nodded as I showed her various techniques to strike an opponent from front to back. Her eyes never left my body, and I found myself trying to show off as much of my muscles and form as I could. I never wanted to please a woman as much as I did her, and I couldn't figure out why.

Mariah's forms matched mine perfectly. I only had to show her once, and she immediately took the forms to memory. The length of her long legs and torso twisting to various degrees had me imagining her in sexual positions that would break a human. I growl left my throat, but I rubbed my neck to act as if it were easing away from pain.

"Excellent," I clapped a few times as she finished. Dante continued to watch both of us. Could the little prick not take a hint?

Mariah smiled up at me; yeah, she was still short in my standards. I was close to 7'5," and even if she was the tallest female, I still towered over her. "Mariah, I heard you will be watching Ember this evening. I would like you to show me in detail what you have planned." This didn't look too obvious, did it? I wanted to spend more time with her, and my hands were aching to touch her. Mariah stood her ground with her hands on her hips. "No funny business, Ares. I'm waiting for my mate." I pulled my hands up in surrender.

"I wouldn't dream." Guess I was a bit obvious. "Since Hades has found his mate, I am on the search for my own, and I intend to wait until I find her. There will be no 'funny business.'" Mariah blushed in embarrassment, which I found adorable on her olive skin.

"Right," she said as she motioned for me to follow.

"Dante, keep up the good work," I yelled over my shoulder. "Make sure your father has enough guards by the lake. Hades wouldn't be too happy if he found his mate all alone with only one Wolf protecting her." Dante's eyes widened in realization as he scampered off to gather some Wolves.

Now I had all the time to get to know this creature in front of me. I wouldn't seduce her, but I wanted to know Mariah, and while I was here, I planned to do just that and why she intrigues me.

Chapter 45

Ember

My father talked for a few hours longer about changes in the pack, and my eyes started to feel heavy. The past few days had been both emotionally as well as physically draining. The thought of shifting now seemed daunting, and I wasn't sure if I would survive even though Hades thought otherwise.

The pills had done wonders, much better than the terrible pokes and prods of an IV twice a day. My bones felt more substantial, and my skin felt more of armor than weak, pliable paper. Dad had hooked up the boat to the dock and grabbed my hand again as we walked away from the lake. Not one fish worthy of taking back home to mom, but that was understandable. We didn't fish for long, and our thoughts didn't go into hunting fish, more of getting to know each other again and dad's intruding questions about how I survived all these years.

I didn't have the thoughts of my family to reel me back to go home. I had wondered if I had the memories of my family if I would have tried harder to go fight my way back, and the answer was yes. I would have fought tooth and nail to get back, and knowing I was a Wolf would have made me fight. The magic was just too strong, and the burden of feeling alone and no one wanting me weighed too heavy. What mind trickery there was and the pain of being alone could do to someone. What about these girls that really did not have anyone? No family? Just plucked from the streets and never to be seen again? Not on my watch, I'd figure something, so this wouldn't be an everyday thing anymore.

Dad took me up to the packhouse, it looked the same after all these years, yet the vines on the northern side of the house had taken root and climbed up the lattice mom had installed. Mom always had a green thumb, and the territory had grown in beautiful plant life filled for all seasons of the year.

"We have a new pack doctor; she's human," Dad mentioned as he opened the front doors of the packhouse. "Her name is Tamera; please don't be startled by her appearance." Before I was able to ask why, a woman in a long white coat stepped out. Her face was thin, and her hands trembled as she opened the door to let us in. Her eyes were sunken, and she looked like she had lost a good amount of weight. One significant scar tore into the side of her neck that had recently healed.

"Good afternoon, Alpha. Is this Alpha Ember?" Tamera looked me up and down and gave a wide smile. The extra collagen that should have covered her beautiful face gave her wrinkles and a sullen look as she beckoned us in.

"*Her mate rejected her after marking her,*" dad mind-linked me. "*It took a toll on her being rejected like that, but at least she didn't change to a werewolf; otherwise, she would not be here with us.*" My heart felt pain that Tamera was still in. Nothing but sorrow and regret radiated off her body.

"Tamera came here about two months ago; she came from a pack in Colorado." Tamera nodded as I sat up on the examining table. "My mother was mated to a Werewolf after she had me." Tamera started taking out syringes to poke my skin to take blood. "I was mated to the Alpha, but when I refused the idea of becoming a Werewolf, he thought it would be best to reject me." Her sad tone didn't go unnoticed as my father gripped the table. "It was for the best. He needed someone strong. I just was too afraid to go through the change at the time."

I touched her hand, and she calmed. "He should have waited," I whispered. Tamera smiled as she wrapped a tourniquet around my arm. "What's done is done," she whispered as she drew the blood from my arm.

"Now I can do what I really enjoy, and that is practicing medicine on supernaturals. I wouldn't have been able to do that as Luna." The regret in her voice filled the room. This wasn't her first choice, but once you have entered a supernatural world, it is hard to leave. To forget what you saw to protect those you loved. Tamera couldn't even stay in the same pack as her mother because her ex-mate was there.

The guilt of not changing was ruining her, and her aura had become weak. I could feel her soul fading through my empath abilities, and the worry I sent to my dad only confirmed that she didn't have long left to live.

"He hasn't found his second chance mate, but my best friend is helping out. She'll be good for him. Keep him in line." She laughed. "Now, have you had any symptoms?

For the next half hour, we talked about my fangs, claws, and even Elea being more and more present in my head. I could feel Blaze in the distance now; he stayed in the woods nearby. Blaze said too many Wolf spirits wanted his help to break through their own barriers too soon for the adolescent children. It was best he stayed behind and watched from the shadows.

"You are ready, little Alpha." Tamera smiled as she patted my arm. "Any hour you could start. Stay by the family since they will be the closest to you. I heard your mate is around; you should stay near him too." Tanya's breath hitched as she said the word mate.

Vulcan walked into the room before I jumped off the table, and his eyes landed on me. "There you are, Ember. Hades has been getting worried." Vulcan closed the door. He had stripped himself of his human form; the rest of the pack must realize that three gods were on the premises. Tamara cleaned up and put the vials of blood in their respected testing tubes and threw away syringes when Vulcan glanced over at the frail human.

"Hello," Vulcan almost stuttered as he held out his hand. "I'm Vulcan; you must be the pack doctor?" Tamera nodded as she put her hand out to him to shake. As they touched, Vulcan's face fell, but he stepped closer to her. His eyes never left her hands until she finally turned around, and their eyes met.

"I've been partly in charge of her medical care; if you would like to go over what we have been giving her, I'd be happy to speak with you about it." I had already told Tamera what I had been given, but the way her eyes looked Vulcan up and down let me know to keep my mouth shut. She was assessing him, but her head shook as she finally looked away.

"Ember gave me good detail. Thank you for offering, though." Vulcan slumped his shoulders, and my dad and I slipped out of the room. On the outside of the room, I couldn't help but listen. I had to use my new hearing.

"Well, maybe we could have dinner together. I don't know anyone around here, and it would be great to talk to a fellow person that has an interest in supernatural medicine." Tamera tutted as she put the last tray on the table.

"I'm not sure that's a good idea. I'm not the sociable type, really." Peeking in, I saw Vulcan grab her hands, the disappointment still there as he held her. "You look in pain; I've been in pain as well. Maybe we could comfort each other." Before I could listen anymore, my dad pulled me down the hall.

"Just because you have good hearing doesn't mean you can listen," he scolded.

"Come on, aren't you a bit curious?"

"I am, but Tamera has been through a lot. She was marked then discarded like trash. He had to get a powerful coven Witch to break the bond, all without Tamera's knowledge because the Alpha couldn't face her. Tamera wants nothing to do with a second chance. Just leave her be. Besides, they aren't mates."

"They could be-" I interjected. "The Sphere of Souls is missing; nobody are getting mates right now until it's found. They could be mates, and Vulcan would be a perfect mate for her. They both have been through rejection. Vulcan has always had a soft spot for humans too."

"Selene messed up her mate," Dad scolded again. I removed my hand from his grip.

"No, she doesn't make mistakes; it's just that people and supernaturals have their agency to accept or reject the bond. He chose to reject it; worthy people can take a second chance if they want it. Did this Alpha get a second chance mate?" Dad stopped in his tracks and turned back to me.

"No, he is doing just as bad as Tamera. The pack is failing because of the rejection." I scoffed.

"He made the wrong choice; he won't get a second chance, but Tamera will. I wouldn't be surprised if this so-called Alpha came back to try and claim her. It will be too late because I see the sparks flying between Vulcan and Tamera even if they can't feel it!"

Father's shoulders slumped. "I forget you have that empath ability. Do you think they would be mates?" I nodded my head in certainty.

"I really do. It isn't infatuation. The souls call to each other." I gasped. Could I really see if people could be matched or mated without them knowing? I felt a tightening in my chest as I scratched it with an extended claw. "Grah!" I yelled out while I fell to my knees. The pain radiated from my chest through the limbs of my arms. My breathing became rapid growls as I involuntary began to scratch the ground.

"It's happening!" I heard my father yell while pack members surrounded me in the foyer.

"Hades!" I half screamed with a painful growl.

The noises around me began to fade as I felt myself being lifted from the cold marble. The cool fall air felt comforting as someone ran me through the central courtyard of the neighborhood of homes. Howls left my mouth as I felt my bones break. The back was the worst; I felt the vertebrae move into different places as the heat extended to my legs.

"*We got this,*" Elea howled as I felt my body was set in a large pile of leaves. Faces of my family had come to hover around me. Clothes were being torn from my body by my family, and I lay there stark naked, shaking and shivering as small bits of fur started to sprout on my arms.

"It's going to be slow," I heard my father say. "She's a full-grown, adult Wolf; it's going to be a process." I heard elders rushing to my side, one my father kept pleading to give me some sort of healing agent.

"No, no, not for an adult." The words became a dull, harsh whisper as my face started to crack. My cheeks flared with heat, and the pull of my bones to create a maw pulled at my brain. If I thought I had experienced pain at the strip club, this was a whole different kind of pain.

"Make it stop!" I howled as I felt a comforting hand touch my shoulder. "Hades!" I whined as I felt him pet my cheek.

"You can do this, flower, you can do this." His touches made the pain lessen but not enough to stop the screaming. Father was pushing people away as I felt the closeness of my family and Hades' warmth fill me. My empath abilities were also out of control. I didn't know what emotion was coming from where. Sadness, helplessness, guilt, and pain all flowed through me, but the one emotion I felt the most was love. My family loved me, and if I concentrated hard enough, I could push through. I felt Hades' worry and love flow through the blood of my veins. My heart exploded inside me, feeling his undying love for me. His worry and thoughts of taking away all the pain so he could have it to himself touched me.

"You are doing so good, so good." I heard his whispers in my now furry ear.

It turned to listen to his voice as I whispered, "More." I wanted more encouraging words to get through it all. My back cracked again as Hades hovered over me, petting the top of my head.

"You are so strong, my Ember. So strong. You were made for this; you are my Alpha. My Alpha, you can beat this."

The encouraging words melted on my new fur as the breaking started to cease. The bones in my toes were now just small breaks that no longer bothered me. The heavy panting slowed, but I kept my eyes shut. I didn't want to see the large crowd over me as I rolled over to see what audience I had procured.

Chapter 46

Hades

Charlotte put a strawberry cheesecake on the table and filled up my coffee mug again. Being the Luna of a bunch of hungry Wolves must have made her think she would have to feed me like one. "I'm actually pretty full, thank you though."

"Nonsense, you should eat more. Especially once Ember shifts, you may not get a chance to eat much for a while." I took a small bite of cheesecake, forcing it down. With a large gulp, I looked up at her concerned.

"Why do you say that?" Charlotte smiled as she plated herself a piece.

"Once I shifted, let's just say I was a bit ravenous." My eyes widened. I could remember all too well what Elea was trying to talk Ember into. Sure, Ember said she was ready now, but I didn't to force it on her either. My cock was dying to be buried deep in her, but I can't just tell that to her mother who is trying to fatten me up for a good mating. I pulled on the collar of my dress shirt as I cleared my throat.

"There is mating cabin, a few miles up Paradise Path. Some Wolves get a little carried away before their bonding, so I had Wesley and his father Odin build a house up the trail. No one would be able to hear you guys." Charlotte snickered. My face automatically blushed thinking that that Ember's own mother was not shy about talking about her daughter being deflowered.

"It's natural; took me awhile to get used to the idea of being so open but it is what the goddess wanted right?" She chuckled. "Plus, you are mated to an Alpha Wolf. Who knows how long you will stay in that cabin."

I internally groaned, I needed to get out of this house. This was too much to talk with the in-laws with no matter how grateful I would be towards her. Charlotte's eyes darkened as she looked straight through me; she was being mind-linked.

"It's started, she's started shifting." We both stood up, our chairs hitting the floor as we bolted out the door. I raced with Charlotte as she knew where they would be. I couldn't automatically transport where Ember was since we haven't bonded yet. Not running for long I saw Wesley hovering over Ember's body who was seizing on the pack house steps.

"She's moving too much; my touch is hurting her. Hades, get over here!"

I raced to the top of the steps and scooped her up in my arms. "It's alright," I cooed. Her back cracked as she let out a horrible cry. My own body began to hurt to see her in so much pain. "Pack doctor?" Panicked as I shifted my body back towards the pack house.

"No, she needs to be in nature," Wesley spoke quickly. "Come we have a designated area for first time shifters, come." Charlotte and Wesley grabbed hands and raced towards the woods while I gently rocked her in my arms. Her moans and whimpers didn't go unnoticed as I tried to keep my lips to her forehead. The tingles still radiated on my face, and I prayed to Selene that Ember could feel them too.

Once we arrived, Ember's brothers Dante, Hunter, and Steven stood in a circle. Steven looked uncomfortable while Dante watched as other Wolves approached. He let out a low growl and shifted while his clothes were still on.

"Son," Wesley exclaimed as he put his hand on Dante's large form. "It's all right, she's safe." Dante's wolf still didn't cease as his hair stood up on end. "Get back," Wesley yelled. "This will be a family affair. We appreciate the support, but this will be a tough shift." Many Wolves nodded and kept their distance. Elders looked on in worry as they stayed behind the tree line.

Another crack of her thigh bone echoed through the forest as she screamed. Charlotte went to Ember's side, cooing at her as she began to take off her clothes. My fingers wanted to rip Charlotte away, to keep her clothes on but shifting the first time, it would be best if she was bare. Dante growled at an unmated male that was late to the shifting and began to bark. "Leave us!" Wesley growled out and he left without as much as a whimper.

"It hurts!" Ember cried as she shielded her breasts from her family. My hand went to her face as I peppered small kisses on her cheeks. "You are so good, such a big Alpha. You can do this; you are going to shift into a beautiful Wolf." I couldn't help but let a few tears shed through lashes as I saw her spasm again. Her back was on the forest floor, her body exposed to the setting sun.

The first shift could last for hours, and it did just that for Ember. Once we approached the third hour, Wesley began to pace frantically. "Get the elders," he begged Steven who laid next to Ember. Bones were breaking, fur was sprouting but only at a snail's pace. Steven scampered off.

"Why not mind link, Wesley?" Charlotte asked worriedly.

"I can't think straight." Wesley pulled his hair as his hand went to Ember's forehead. "Damnit!" He punched a tree next to him while splinters went flying. I hovered over Ember's body. She was deathly still as the bones in her toes and fingers began to pop. "Ember," I called for her, but she didn't respond.

"You listen here, you don't give up," I yelled at her. "You push through that last barrier, and you will shift, do you hear me!? Elea! Do you hear me?" I yelled again as I shook her still body. White fur sprouted as she laid still. All over her body the snow white hair covered her. More bones popped, all the popping made me think there wasn't anything left to break.

Ember's jaw elongated; her ears stood on the top of her head. A tail emerged from behind her, and paws replaced her hands. The slow breathing became pants as a tongue lopped from her mouth. With eyes still shut, her eyebrows moved. A beautiful white wolf laid beneath me. Touching her fur I could still feel the sparks, knowing she was still mine.

Rolling off her, her family and I stood back to give her room to stand. "Ember, open your eyes," I begged. Charlotte and Wesley held onto each other while slowly, her wolf's body came to life. Bright mint-colored eyes looked around as her head perked up.

Standing on all fours, she was a large, and majestic animal. Her tail was fluffed to a perfect white as her eyes looked at the both of us. "Ember?" I whispered as I grew closer. Using her four limbs at the same time she walked towards me, and her head buried into my chest after I lowered myself to the ground. Rubbing her head all over me and licking up my neck I couldn't help but sigh in relief.

"That's our girl." Wesley patted Charlotte's back as he smiled. "You scared us there, Ember." Ember looked at her family and back at me.

"Ember says she's all right, just scared to turn back into a human." Charlotte laughed as she held tightly onto Wesley. Ember licked me back and nuzzled into my neck.

"You did so good. I thought I lost you." Ember snuffed and shook her head.

"It's tradition for her to run with the pack after a shift, if you will allow it, Hades," Wesley spoke. I laughed and gave Ember a rub on the head.

"Can't mess with tradition now, can I?" Ember continued to nuzzle into me while Dante let out an enormous howl.

"They're coming." Hunter spoke and watched his parents go behind a tree to strip. Steven came up with the elders, but relief flooded their faces. "We were so worried," one of the men spoke. "I'm glad she's all right." Everyone was taking the clothes. I was the most clothed guy here while I stood back and watched everyone shift. Ares and Vulcan had gathered as well to watch the spectacle.

Wolves ranging in various colors of tan, black, grey, brown and some had a hint of gold in their fur circled Ember. She was the only white wolf and the only one with beautiful mint colored eyes and she was mine. Ember took one last glance as me and I nodded my head for her to go.

A large howl ripped from her throat as the fellow Wolves howled in unison. With a few hops, Ember dashed at the front of the pack, leading them on her shifted run.

Ember

Four extra limbs to be in control was difficult, but Elea took over and had no problem adjusting to our new form. Hundreds of Wolves dashed through the thickets, the bushes and jumped over streams to keep up. The wind was blowing in my fur as I let out yips and howls of excitement. My heart was racing, and my mind was running a mile a minute. I wanted to feel nature, run through the forest until I could no longer breathe.

We circled the territory, which was large in itself. We took a stop to drink from nearby springs, but we never stopped for long. Everyone was as equally excited, welcoming me as we sprinted under logs. The mind-link was clear as day now, I could hear mom and dad no problem as well as Dante. In fact, I couldn't just hear their voices but feel them too. Whether that was a normal part of the bond with a pack, I wasn't sure. However, the guilt and worry poured off my brother Michael heavily. I felt the sickness of his heart. It was stronger than I ever felt when we told my family about the empath ability. Does my Wolf make this gift stronger, or did I break down another barrier?

Dante stayed by my side the entire run. As we ran, my heart couldn't handle the heaviness that Dante was carrying. How could he live with this pain? Mom and dad had already trailed off halfway through the run to stay with Steven and Hunter. They were both close to shifting but not there yet and didn't want to leave him alone with Ares. Ares could be a trip sometimes.

"Dante, come with me." I nudged him as we walked towards the pack lake. The sun had set long ago, and the crickets were out in full force getting ready for the upcoming snow. They would bury themselves deep into the soil to get away from the frost and come out when spring had finally started to thaw the ground again.

I sat on a nearby rock; it was flat so the heat from the mid-day sun still radiated from it as we looked over the lake. *"What's wrong, Dante?"* I said flatly. *"Don't lie to me."*

Dante's Wolf paws shifted as he whined. *"Don't fight your Wolf. He wants to tell me something too."* I glanced at my brother, my younger brother by just that of a year and few months. I no longer needed an empath ability to know he was hiding something from me, his body language said it all. Ears back, nose pointe down, fur was flat on the top of his head.

"I've cried every single day you have been taken, Ember." Elea in my head was intently listening, as was I. His words were genuine, and I hoped he continued to tell us the truth.

"You were my best friend, you kept my secrets, you wanted me as your Beta, we had it all. I couldn't imagine living my life without you. You are my sister and you protected me even when I deserved to get punished. Like the time I broke mom's favorite succulent plant?" I laughed, remembering Dante throwing a ball and it ricocheted off the table and right in the kitchen window ledge.

"Yeah, I remember. I opened the window and told mom a blue jay flew in and knocked it over." I snorted as I shook my fur.

"We still got caught, but you tried to help me out." Dad could figure out a lie in a second. He had trained his ears to catch lies through heart beats and both of our hearts raced wildly as we repeated the story. There was no way out of it, you just can't lie to an alpha.

"*Anyway, it was the day before Mom's birthday and you always made these cards and colored these pretty drawings. I didn't have anything.*" Dante's head lowered. "*I wanted to give Mom something equally as amazing as your drawing so I made a deal with someone to help get me the perfect present.*" I looked at Dante, whose Wolf began to whimper uncontrollably.

"*Ember, I'm the reason you got taken from us.*"

Chapter 47

Ember

I blinked.

I blinked a few times more as Elea and I stared into my brother's Wolf's eyes. *"What?"* I whispered through the link. *"That isn't true."* I went to stand up, but Dante whined for me to say back down on the flat rock.

"Just listen, and I'll tell you. I'll tell you every bit of it." I could hear Dante silently crying; the remorse dripped from him as I tried to shield myself from the many emotions swirling in him.

"You never told our parents, did you? That's why you have been extra helpful, the guilt. It has plagued you through so many years." I kept my voice quiet, even though I didn't have to. This conversation was linked to just the two of us, and no one could come in unless our father used his power.

"I was so scared, so scared they would cast me out. Apart of me died that day you were taken. The screams, the crying I could hear from your room... I tried to get out; I banged on the door until my own fists bled to get out, but all the house doors were locked from the outside. Dad couldn't get out of his room either; there were vines everywhere pushing against the doors as everyone in the house tried to get you."

They did hear me; when I cried and screamed, they did listen and didn't just leave me. The thought never crossed my mind that they would just let me be taken, but I had wondered why my family didn't come. *"Once the doors were set free, we ran to your room, and you were gone. Nothing but vines littered the hallway, strong ones, and they led all the way out the door and into mom's garden."* More questions plagued me as he told me about the massive amount of growing mom's garden did in a short time. The tomato vines had grown and slithered in each window on the upper floor, besides my bedroom, of course. Persephone was the daughter of Demeter. Could Persephone have procured the vines to grow and control them?

"From the beginning, Dante. I need it from the very beginning because I don't see how this links up to you being involved at all." Dante let out a huff and closed his eyes as he spoke. Remembering just twelve years ago.

"Like I said, it was the day before Mom's birthday. You always could make amazing cards, and I wanted something as equally as good. Uncle Evan told me there was a time when Moon Orchids grew on the territory. They are native to Bergarian and when mom and dad came back from visiting before we were born, some seeds caught in someone's clothing. They sprouted around the property, and for a few autumns, they flourished, that is until humans started spraying for mosquitoes fifty miles away from here. The Moon Orchids are fickle plants, so they started to die. Evan mentioned how much mom liked them. They only bloomed on the week of the full moon, and the white flower would glow purple as the moonlight settled on its petals. "I stared at Dante in awe as he explained. I had heard of the flower only in passing but never gave it much attention because they didn't grow here anymore.

"So, I set off to scout the territory. I went south, where a lot of Wolves didn't trample the ground. I was hoping to find at least one, so I brought a bucket and a shovel, and I was going to bring it back, and mom could take care of it. You know how she likes plants." I nodded. *"I got to the edge of the southern border, no other wolves were around, and the cameras weren't blinking. Sensing someone was there, I turned to leave, but I heard a small voice. It was a tiny Fairy, I had never seen one before, so I walked up. It sat just on the other side of the border. The Fairy said she was looking for safe passage but needed permission from the Alpha to cross. I told her I would have to go get my father, and she shook her head, saying I could tell her it was all right to cross. Repeatedly telling her no, I wasn't acting Alpha, just the Alpha's second-born. She sat down but sprung out an idea.*

"She wanted to give me something for trade. I asked if she knew what a Moon Orchid was and where I could find one. She laughed and said, 'Of course I do; there is one right over there!' Looking over her shoulder, there was one! It was just over the log, but it was on the other side of the border, and I couldn't

grab it. Dad always told us he couldn't protect us if we crossed because of the ward." My heart began to sink as I continued to listen.

"A trade, a deal, that is what we did. Besides, it was just a Fairy. The Fairy was so small. She brought me the Orchid, and I took her across the pack lands to the northern side and dropped her off," Dante sighed.

"Since you are an alpha and brought her on the territory, the ward thought she wasn't a threat," I breathed. *"That's how someone got in."*

"I didn't mean for any of this to happen! I swear it! I just wanted the Orchid, a stupid flower! That flower took you from us; you had to suffer because of me!" My Wolf's body jumped over to Dante's, and I nuzzled into his neck.

"It was not your fault you were tricked and coerced. You cannot blame yourself for something this stupid!" I argued. *"Not your fault, none of it is! It is just a series of unfortunate events!"* I spoke harshly. While consoling him, I couldn't help thinking that everyone's choices affected me so intensely and for the worse. Shaking my head, I nudged him.

"Not your fault, now suck it up, Alpha." Dante shook his head. *"I'm only mad you didn't tell dad, our Alpha who protects his pack, that a Fairy crossed the border. Alphas can't protect if they don't know what is going on, even if you thought it was harmless."* Dante hung his head in shame. *"A child, you were only a child. You can't blame yourself for this mess. There are so many other factors that played into this."* My body started to shake, I felt not just my emotions but Dante's hitting at me in full force. Trying to concentrate on my body, I scooted closer to him, so our fur was touching each other. Laying my head on top of his, I purred in my chest.

"I am not blaming you, never will. Please forgive yourself because I already forgave you. We were so young," I breathed deeply. *"Just tell dad and mom Okay? They won't be mad about that, just the fact you didn't tell them and kept a secret after all these years. That is what they will be mad about. It will work out in time..."* I paused. *"Promise me you will tell them. Tell dad and Mom what happened. I'm not going to tell them for you and get you out of it like some stupid vase on Mom's window,"* I laughed. *"Find courage and be the Alpha. Stop the guilt. What's done is done."* I huffed.

"I can do that, just know-"

"That you are sorry, yeah, yeah." Feeling a smile on my maw, I began to fit my own puzzle together. Vines, plants, wildly growing nature, and even a Fairy had something in common. They all pointed to Persephone, but how far does Persephone's power go? Could her own power be able to do all of this herself?

Malachi was an angel; he was limited to fighting and helping humans. Was he the one who took me while Persephone used her magic? There was a burn in my chest that I tried to scratch, but it proved to be difficult with paws. Dante nuzzled me in my neck as I felt a terrible burn where he touched me.

My body felt a jolt as I whimpered and rolled off Dante. Heat radiated through my body as I tried to pull in all the emotions I was feeling. I felt hot, horny, lustful, excited, and scared all at the same time, and I couldn't block my own emotions, let alone Dante's, who was now freaking out.

"Ember!" he yelled as he hovered over me. My fur retracted as I felt my body's bones breaking. It wasn't as painful as the first time, but it was still uncomfortable. *"You're shifting back; it's all right."* Dante shifted in a blink of an eye and ran to the trees. I whimpered for him to come back, but he brought an oversized shirt for me and shorts for himself.

Pain wracked through my body again as he touched me, putting on the shirt. "What is wrong?" he growled out. Howls were heard in the distance, and Dante tried to pick me up, but the burn of his fingers left hot spots in its wake.

"Don't' touch me!" I screamed as he laid me back down.

"I need to get you back!!" he growled out. "Fuck, Ember, I'm taking you." Dante tucked me in his arms as I screamed, trying to get away. His footsteps were heard as he trampled through the line of trees, coming back into the shifting area where we started. Males growled, pacing in their Wolf forms while other men gathered closer. That were NAKED!

"Dante put her down!" Dad growled as I continued spurting profanities. Rubbing my skin where he held me, I curled into a ball, not caring if my butt was half hanging out. Where the hell was Hades?!

"Hades!" I cried. He was the only one I wanted as Elea howled in my head. She paced the back of my mind while scratching the dirt. *"Hades,"* she moaned as she laid down. "Get them away!" I heard Dad growling and mom ran to my side. "Oh, honey, I'm so sorry." She kept her hands away from my body as she tried to comfort me. My hand jutted out to touch her; I needed contact, but even her touch hurt.

"What's wrong with me?" I stuttered as I wiped tears from my eyes. "Hades!" I cried again, and he rushed towards me.

"The fuck is wrong with her!?" Hades growled out as his hand slung to the side. Wolves fell backward, and whimpers and yelps left them.

"I'm here, Ember, I'm here." I flinched before Hades touched my head, but the coolness of his palm relaxed me. The burn didn't feel as awful as it had been, and for a moment, I felt relief. "Why are those naked fuckers trying to come over here? They are looking at what's MINE!" Hades yelled again, going to stand up, but I grabbed his hand.

"Don't leave," I cried as I felt the cool hand touch my forehead.

"Get back!" I heard Dante shift into their Wolves. Ares pounced in his massive form from the other side of the clearing. A loud roar that sounded ancient and ferocious as he was bellowed through the forest. "Back!" he bellowed in his Wolf form, stunning the crowd. Mariah stood beside him and took a battle stance next to him in her much smaller form.

Blaze came out in like a lion. His fire tail swayed as the Wolves cowered back, not enough to keep anyone in my family comfortable, however. Wolves kept approaching, and my dad was getting restless. Feeling the conflict in his heart to protect me and keep his pack safe was causing him to second guess himself as Alpha.

"Hades, you need to take Ember and go to the cabin I told you about...." Mom looked behind her as she saw male Wolves trying to find an opening. "You can't leave the territory, she's still healing, and Elea still needs the assurance from the pack. Put a ward around your cabin, and don't come out until her heat is over." Hades darted his head to my mom with his mouth agape.

"Her heat?!" Mom nodded her head frantically.

"You wanted to bond with her. You got it, both of you LEAVE!" Ember's Alpha Blood is ten times stronger than that of a normal Wolf in heat! Even Wesley's Alpha voice can't keep them at bay for long!" Hades gripped me in his arms as the smoke came around us as he stood. Smoke tendrils lit fire to the dried leaves that had circled us as the tornado-like smoke hid us from the now ravaging Wolves that were considered my family and friends.

Dante

That wasn't how I planned for everything to go.

I wanted to tell Ember in a more secluded setting and not in our Wolf form. She had other ideas; she always did. When Hades explained her empath abilities, I knew I was screwed; she felt it on me this very day when I led them here.

The heavy guilt and sadness weighed on me for years while she was gone. I led most of the expeditions to surrounding packs and states trying to find her. Her smell was gone; without a trace, no one could track her. At eight years old, I couldn't connect the dots while my family ran around frantically looking for her.

There were no footprints or smells that could help us. Just the twisty vines that had taken over the house and climbed into our rooms, shutting doors that could lead to Ember's escape. The flower that I had gotten for my mother had been hidden in Ember's room, just like the fairy told me I needed to do. My instructions were for me to put it at the top of her closet, it would be the perfect hiding spot, and with her Alpha blood, mom wouldn't be able to smell it. Even though om was strong, she had been Wolfless for so long and only gained some of dad's alpha abilities.

Omegas came by and helped cleaned Ember's room while I sat staring at the window. I was just across the hall, and I heard nothing until her screams echoed through the halls. Replaying it over in my head as an eight-year-old, the thought of a flower bringing the destruction of a happy family never occurred to me.

Once cleaned, I dragged my feet to the closet to see the Moon Orchid not only wilted but crushed. Nothing else in the cabinet had been harmed, just the flower.

My tiny gears turned in my head, and that was when I realized the Fairy had tricked me. She was able to get on the territory and take my sister. I howled for hours after finding the flower; my mother found me clutching it as she tried to console me.

Mom certainly thought it was because of my sister being gone and her birthday being ruined. "It was a beautiful flower, Dante." She kissed my head. "We will celebrate my birthday again when your sister comes home." Her breath deepened as she carried me back to her bed. Mom laid with me that night, as well as my brothers in their large bedroom. We all slept in mom and dad's room for at least two months after Ember was gone.

My mother slept with her monster child that led an evil entity to her innocent daughter.

That moment on, I swore to find her. I couldn't bear losing my parents, too, so I never told them what had happened with the tiny Fairy. Now was the time to come clean, and I wasn't going to hold it in anymore.

Ember knew the truth, and she says she forgives me because, let's face it, she's like mom. Mom always had a heart of gold. I thanked the goddess that Ember was gifted with empath abilities because I could not put into words the feelings I had for Ember and the sorrow I carried with me for years.

Wolves dispersed as Ares turned back into his god form. I heard Ember call the little fireball, Blaze, and he shot back down to his petite size and hopped on my shoulder. His head rubbed against my cheek while I stood in shock. "He likes you," Ares spoke. "You have a strong Wolf too that's in distress. Blaze is trying to comfort him," he chided. "Anything on your mind?" I looked away from him. Hell yeah, I've got a lot on my mind.

My family walked up to me, concerned as they waved for me to follow them.

"Maybe it's best we all go inside. Everyone is going to need to hear what I have to say." Dad nodded as he patted my shoulder as he led us back to our home.

Chapter 48

Hades

I pulled Ember's body close to mine as I lifted her off the ground. The surrounding area was covered in Wolves, more than had run earlier. Wolves were turning into men with a sickening reaction to Ember's smell. Snarling, I covered her body with my cloak from the sick bastards. I was not a Wolf, but I could smell the desire and heat from her body when Dante came running back to us.

How could such a short amount of time from shifting to going into heat could there be?! Ember's body was trying to catch up on all the milestones she had missed in her adolescence, and it hit like a freight train. It made me wonder if all the barriers had been pulled down once she shifted.

Ember groaned as I tucked her body into my cloak tightly. Not one piece of her skin did I want to be exposed to the air. The shirt that had kept her covered during the first few hours of her shift had been ruined. Holes from her claws and teeth had ripped it straight through. I settled for my black robes after she took off, feeling more comfortable.

My mind still was not at ease as she left me standing in the clearing with those who could not shift. Many pregnant women and children were scattered about, making themselves occupied while their parents ran. I did nothing but pace and left my own trenches in the damp soil as I heard her howl through the setting sun.

After three hours of her bones breaking, she still had the energy to go for a run. I hoped she had energy for something else later. I bit my bottom lip hard, thinking I could have her tonight.

The minutes passed by, and an hour had approached of no return. I was filled with worry; my fingers anxiously twitched, waiting for Ember. Could she not feel my nervousness? She had been gone too long, and I wanted to be by her side. I found myself in a dead sprint until I reached the woods and heard women snicker and coo while I waited. "He's so smitten," one heavily pregnant woman spoke. "Who knew the god everyone was so afraid of would be so deeply in love?" Red rose to my cheeks as I tried to hide my face.

The bond had been stretched thin far too long. While the only way to calm my lustful side was to be fully bonded to her, I had to be patient. I didn't want to wait any longer, but I wasn't sure if Ember felt the same. The last thing I wanted to do was force her into something she wasn't ready for, despite the many pleas from her Wolf. With the Sphere of Souls still missing, I wondered if our bond would be fully completed once we became one in body and soul. Only one way to find out.

"You need to leave now!" Charlotte spoke harshly; luckily for her, I didn't mind her talking that way because she only thought of her daughter's safety. Ember's body was drenched in sweat as I put my lips to her forehead and willed us to the trail that Charlotte had spoken of. I had never been to the cabin, so I couldn't myself to it if I was uncertain of the specific location.

Howls came from the distance as I ran down the heavily wooded trail. Ember clutched my shirt as the small dark cabin came into view. Stopping before the steps, I waved my hand to create a ward; no one would be able to cross, and no one would sense her here unless she was seen. With luck not on our side, Wolves stopped abruptly as they tried to pass but were immediately halted by the burn of the ward. If they crossed, they would disintegrate in an instant.

Anger burned through me as I watched them pace around the entire cabin. What kind of idiots do they think they are? I'm a fucking god, and they dare believe there would be an opening anywhere?

"Hades?" Ember whimpered. "I don't think they can help it; mom is telling me dad is sending in the mated males to pull them away and guard us. Please don't hurt them. Their Wolves can't be controlled right now." A growl left my throat. I wanted nothing more than to watch them instantly combust. However, this was her family, her pack; I couldn't do anything but heed to her wishes.

Destroying was all I knew what to do, and right now, I wanted nothing more than to watch the life leave their eyes for staring at what was mine. My beautiful sweet Ember. Ember was bare from the waist down, and her shirt could only cover so much.

"If they somehow cross the ward, I can't promise anything," I whispered as I kicked in the cabin door. With my other foot, it slammed shut, causing the small pictures and tickets on tables to rattle.

It was a small cabin, like a studio apartment. A small kitchenette was in the corner with baskets of fruit, pastries, and drinks. My only concern was the bed; Ember's spasms and jerks had only increased as I took long strides and laid her down. Her shirt and ridden up past her thighs, and her pussy had already leaked her essence on her thighs.

"Fuck," I whispered as I tore the cloak from me. My pants were painfully tight as her hooded eyes dared look into mine.

"Take it off," she moaned as I ripped her shirt down the middle. Her breasts spilled out before me as my mouth attacked her pebbled nipples. Her hands went through my hair. "Bite harder," she whispered as her legs wrapped around my torso. A gust of wind blew by, and I engulfed her scent. Fuck, how could I have ever thought having a mate was revolting? This was sweeter than any heaven I could have dreamed.

Kissing down her stomach, I came to her perfectly shaved pussy. Her pink and puffy lips beckoned me as my tongue stretched her hole. My hands held her hips as she tried to move. Growling into her, she spasmed, and I felt the inner walls of her slick tighten. A moan left her mouth as chills ran down her legs.

Resting wasn't an option; I would have her now and give her the most pleasure she could handle. I need her core soaked to take my large cock.

Biting her nipples, her hips ground into my erection. Her pussy was so close to me, my heavy balls pulled against her to feel her heat. My pants holding me back, I willed them off in an instant as her warmth touched my most intimate places. Her wetness soaked me as I felt my skin jump with sparks. "Please," she groaned while I attacked her pouty lips. My cock rubbed her entrance once more, only for her to growl.

"Don't play with me." Ember's eyes flashed their mint green color as I lined up to thrust into her. My legs were firmly planted on the floor; her ass was cupped in my hands as the tip slowly entered her.

She was unbelievably tight as I inched forward; Ember's mewls and cries for me to hurry made me growl as I finally pushed into her. A cry left her as her breast heaved forward while her back arched, causing me to slip deeper into her core. My hands landed on her lower back as I left my cock all the way to the hilt while my face buried into her breasts.

"I'm sorry, I got carried away." I let out a heavy breath as her hands knotted in my hair. Keeping still so her body would adjust to my size, Ember moved her hips. "Move," her throaty voice caressed me. I slipped out only to admire her cum around my cock. Something about seeing my dick disappear gave me more power than I could ever imagine. I was the only male that would enter this woman.

Thrusting back in, her tightened cavern held onto me like I was retreating and not coming back. Rocking in and out of her, I felt my own soul dislodge from my being; it was beyond my control as I felt it detach from me. Hovering over my body, I watched as my physical self-roll her into the bed.

Ember's soul came up to meet me as her hands cupped my face, her hair floating beside her plump cheeks. We kissed with wild abandon, using our tongues to feel every crevice in each other's mouths. No one could have prepared me for such a feeling, our bodies becoming one while our souls danced above. The ghost of us had hands on each other bodies as my chest melted into hers. Ember's head was thrown back as the burn from my chest latched onto her own heart. We were not one in body but as spirit as well. Heat covered us as our hearts burned together, leaving a burned tattoo in the middle of her chest.

My symbol was the cross with the upturned moon and a bright red jewel in the middle, and it was now forever touching her skin. I kissed her chest as her eyes began to flutter back open.

"Now mark me," I heaved as her fangs protruded from her mouth. Ember bit into my shoulder while my soul shattered. Below us, our physical bodies mimicked our souls as we both seized in pleasure. I had no control of what was happening to us, but we both laid gently back into bodies once Ember's fangs dislodged from my shoulder. Both of us were sweating, still feeling the aftershocks of our orgasms. Lifting my hand, I realized we had both come back to our physical selves and had control of our bodies.

"What was that?" Ember's eyes were still closed, but her hands never left my face. Droplets of my blood still lay on her lips as I kissed her clean.

"That was a soul-bonding; it only happens with gods." I pushed a few locks from Ember's forehead as her eyes fluttered open. "We are the first to experience it; I wasn't sure what was going to happen." I felt my cock twitch inside her; I didn't want to leave her body just yet. "Are you all right?"

"Yes," she croaked. "I feel different." My mark began to glow on her chest as she held onto my biceps tightly. Supernaturals mated to different species tend to take on each other's traits; I wonder if she would be more like me? Cast protection wards or even play with fire in her hands?

"Rest, sleep while you can. I'm here." I rubbed my nose along Ember's neck as she buried her face into my chest. If Ember was changing, she needed to sleep. Hell, I didn't know how she was still going. Finding your parents, shifting, going into heat, and being bonded was far more than I could have ever handled myself in one day. My mate was a strong one and would be a fierce queen once we could go to go home.

Ember

I stirred, feeling delightfully sore. My face was buried into the pillow, and the smell of smores let me know that my mate was near. Turning over, I felt my body heat again. The second wave was near, and I knew I couldn't go long without becoming a horny mess. It wasn't just my body that felt sore, but something inside me. I ached pleasantly. A slight hum came from my extremities and intensified around my heart.

Elea had walked me through what a Werewolf has to do when it comes to being bonded to your mate. A simple bite on the shoulder that marks your mate for all the world to see. My soul leaving my body wasn't something I was prepared for, but I wasn't scared when it happened. Hades' soul beckoned mine as I had left my physical self on the bed. It was certainly an experience I would compare to if someone was dying and looking over the world before they departed to a better place. This, though, was just heaven mere inches from my physical body.

Instead of feeling pleasure between my legs, I felt it in my heart. Waves and waves of love, passion, deep feeling of gratefulness, and understanding had flooded me. It gave all the same result, which was a mind-blowing orgasm. Once our hearts collided together, we were more than just one person in the physical sense but also in soul. Our hearts were beating as one now. I no longer felt out of rhythm with Hades.

I wondered if we could do that again and not just during the bonding?

Hades was standing in the small kitchen nook. A single burner, a small fridge, and a microwave took up just the corner of the sizeable one-room cabin. Hades was wearing black joggers; his strong back muscles tantalizingly moved under his skin. He was exceedingly handsome, and I was lucky enough to have him as a mate.

King of the Underworld, I shook my head. I never would have thought this at a young age that my fascination with Hades would end up getting me here in his bed. I threw the covers off my body and felt the tingle in my chest as I touched between my breasts. Hades' mark looked burned into my skin, but no pain came from it, only tiny sparks of pleasure.

"Oh shit." Hades dropped a cut-up orange and bent down to pick it up. "You need to be careful touching that. I think I just about spewed in my pants." I snorted and pulled the sheet back up.

"Nothing I haven't seen before." Hades eyes darkened as his dark form stalked me across the room. "It's starting again, isn't it?" My breasts felt heavier under his gaze as he went to pull down the sheet.

"Let me take care of you then." His mouth entangled in mine as he dropped the tray full of fruit he had cut on the floor. So much for a snack. Hades threw the sheet off the bed. I was completely bare, but the heat of my body kept me warm enough. His hands trailed to my ass as he squeezed one cheek tightly, and my claws extended to scratch his back. Hades' blonde hair stood up on his arms as a trickle of blood dripped down between the strands. His kiss stopped as he nipped my lip one more time.

"Ride me," he commanded as he flipped us over. Hades put his back to the padded headboard and lined my pussy up with his cock. The heat pulsed through me as I felt the heat engulf my body. My pussy automatically dripped while Hades took a large breath. Rolling his eyes back gently sat me on his cock while he hissed.

Feeling scratching in the back of my head, Elea was throwing a temper tantrum to take control. "*Lemmie out, this is mine.*" I felt her surge forward. My eyes glowed a beautiful mint color in Hades.

"Mate," Elea purred as she remained on Hades' cock. Hissing, Hades grabbed my hips and began to drag us up and down. Elea's arms wrapped around Hades' neck, and my breasts were pushed up in his face. Humming in excitement, Elea jostled up and down, riding Hades until the bed was squeaking uncontrollably. Hickeys and love bites littered my breasts as Hades met thrust for thrust.

"Damnit," Hades growled as his thumb went straight for my clit. Rubbing it while bouncing recklessly, I quickly met my high, and I swore I pissed myself. Cum slid down his cock and onto the sheets while my head was thrown back. Keeping his dick in, he pushed me back on the mattress and pounded into me. Elea slung our legs around Hades' neck as he lifted our ass up and pile drove into my body.

"Mine," Hades fucked me as my heat intensified.

"Yours," Elea growled. "Make me never forget," Hades smirked as he flipped us over and got us on all fours. Who knew there were so many positions?!

Without warning, Hades' cock tickled my pussy while he spread my ass cheeks apart. I popped my head up as Elea shifted back into my mind. "Relax, I just wanted to see." Relaxing, he sped up again as I felt his balls contract against my thigh. Gripping the sheets, I moaned.

"Come now, flower," Hades grunted as I felt ropes of his seed run through me. There was so much, I felt liquid dripping down my leg as we both continued to breathe hard. His torso lined up with my back as he spooned me, pulling me in closer as we fell to our sides.

After a few minutes, his dick still inside me, he peppered kisses on my neck. The coolness of his touch relaxed me as I held onto his arm next to my breast.

"I'm sorry it wasn't more romantic. Your heat threw me off; I promise to give you a romantic getaway." Hades' minty breath tickled my ear.

"This was perfect; I wouldn't change it." My chest let out a continuous purr as Hades pulled up the sheets.

"I'll make sure you have the most beautiful mating ceremony for your people. I want to brag of what a wonderful, beautiful, and intelligent mate and let them know that you are all mine," he hummed.

"Anything for you, my King of the Underworld," I smiled contently.

"And I love you, the queen of my heart."

Chapter 49

Vulcan

"Well, maybe we could have dinner together. I don't know anyone around here, and it would be great to talk to a fellow person that has an interest in supernatural medicine." Tamera tutted as she put the last tray on the table.

"I'm not sure that's a good idea. I'm not the sociable type, really." Touching Tamera's hand again, I was disappointed I didn't feel sparks fly through my skin. Everything about this woman drew me in. It wasn't the permanent pained look on her face or the nasty scar that rode up her shoulder and neck; it was just her. Her brown eyes that looked to have a spark in them at one point in her made me want to ignite them again.

"You look in pain; I've been in pain as well. Maybe we could comfort each other." My thumb rubbed over her knuckles as she pulled away without looking at me.

"There is nothing that would comfort me; I'm a lost cause." Tamara took the tray full of blood samples and walked down the hall to her small office, including a laboratory. Several vials of blood, plasma, and herbal medicine riddled her desk.

"I don't believe that. No one is a lost cause," I almost growled. How could this intelligent woman think she could be lost? Not worth living or being happy? I needed to know more, and I wouldn't leave until I got the answers I sought. Stroking my long beard, the thought of not looking good enough crossed my mind. I wasn't the best-looking god. In fact, I was considered ugly, especially with the limp I held. What sort of god would have a limp? Me. Because lousy luck liked to follow me.

I used to hide the limp the best I could, but I stopped as the years went on. I didn't care what the Olympian gods thought of me, so I left and made friends with Hades. He was the one that didn't care how I looked but how I contributed to society and my loyalty.

Finding myself a bit out of sorts, I tried to straighten my clothes, so they weren't as wrinkled and brushed my beard that trailed down my chest a bit too far for most women's liking. I smelled my underarms, ensuring I wasn't giving off an odor. I had just watched Wolves sparring; maybe I smelled terrible to her?

I looked up, and I saw Tamera with a faint smile on her face as she tried to cover it with her mouth. The little twinkle I was looking for was there as I took a few steps forward. "I'm not the most handsome man-"

"God, you mean?" she mused as she organized her lab area.

"Right, god," I sniffed. "But I am an honest one, and I want you to know my intentions." Tamera slammed the tray down, causing several vials to tip over.

"I don't believe in bonds; they are worthless," she snapped. "Bonds are nothing but physical attraction to make you have sex with your mate, and then you get thrown away." My breath hitched.

"This isn't a bond," I corrected her. "You would have felt sparks, heat, or something; I want nothing but to get to know you. You draw me in, and I want to know why. Just let me get to know you, two damaged souls that need the support of one another. I've been through some shit, and it looks like you have too. Please, just let me be your friend." I stepped back to give her some space.

Her statement about bonds irked me. Leaving it alone for now would be best; besides, we weren't even bonded anyway.

Tamera's shoulders slumped as she crossed her arms. Her eyes still didn't meet mine. "I don't have much longer, Vulcan. I can't promise you a friendship that may only last for a month or so. My soul is broken, and Sorceress Cyrene has already said my time is limited. I don't have much to live for." She was rejected by someone. I growled silently. What person would dare deny a mate? They are precious and a gift.

"Let me be the one to change that." I retook her hand. "Let me give you something to live for while you do the same for me." Her eyes watered, and I pulled her into a hug. She struggled at first but slowly relaxed into me. I don't like using force, but damn it felt good to hold her. I don't remember the last time I had hugged anyone besides Ember when she needed comfort when she first came out of that club.

Tamera let out a breath and put her arms on my chest. "Thank you," she sobbed. "I can't promise anything but thank you for pushing to be a friend." I smiled as I petted her hair. "I-I just don't want to hurt anymore. I am tired of being alone and I guess, you do seem genuine." I sighed, that's all I wanted.

"How about that dinner then?" Tamera was quiet as she finally nodded. We stepped outside the clinic area of the packhouse and heard howls outside. They were so loud one would think they were in the packhouse.

"Someone is shifting; it must be Ember since there are no other Wolves expected to shift for a few more months." Her voice trailed off. "You must go watch your friend." I shook my head. This was Hades' time.

"If you aren't going, I'm not. I say let's get that dinner." Tamara smiled as I held my arm out for her to link arms with me. Her smile was no longer hidden as I saw the faint pearls of her teeth.

"I'll cook; no one will be at the packhouse with a new Alpha shifting."

Tamera led me to her cabin; she didn't stay in the packhouse despite being a single woman. Most of the single Wolves lived in the packhouse or one of the several dormitories around the territory. She wanted her own space, and that was what Alpha Wesley had provided her.

As we walked Tamera explained how she arrived here. She had reached out through a North American Werewolf pack online message board created by Earth supernaturals. Charlotte actually helped run the site so packs could stay in touch better than old fashion snail mail.

Tamera put the message board that she was a pack doctor, and due to unfortunate circumstances, she had to leave her pack. Tamera had trained in both human and Werewolf anatomy. Pack doctors were on-demand, and she was given several options, but Wesley's offer stood out the most. Tamera explained that Wesley had offered her the one thing she wanted, and that was her own living accommodations.

"Why did you want to move packs?" I took a bite of the salmon she had just grilled on her small patio. I had prepared tea and coffee despite her explaining that she was the host, and I didn't have to do anything. Her heavy sigh let me know it was the reason why her body and soul were just twinkling.

"My mate, my ex-mate is why I am here." She placed her plate down and loaded roasted vegetables on the table. "My mother was mated to a Werewolf after I was born. My real father was gone; he wanted nothing to do with a baby anyway. We moved into the Cool Springs Pack when I was only three years old, and my mom was mated to the gamma. She became a Werewolf when I was eight so she could help protect the pack and me." Tamera's eyes glistened in the setting sun.

"I didn't think I would find a mate, that my mom was just one of the lucky humans that got one. I went off to college at eighteen and came back once I had finished my residency at twenty-five. I was pretty smart and jumped ahead a bit," she chuckled. "Anyway, my first night back, I was claimed by Alpha Santos. There were sparks, the whole good smell, and stuff, yadda, yadda." She waved her hands around as she rolled her eyes.

"He claimed me that night because that is what you do, right? Werewolves take their mates then and there. Santos didn't leave room for discussion." Her eyes softened. "We were together for about a month, and he continued to ask me when I would want to be changed into a Werewolf, but I said I wasn't ready, I wasn't sure if I ever would be ready." Her eyes shifted to the woods. "I was scared; mom said it was painful, and technically I didn't have to do it. I thought I had other qualities that made me strong besides becoming a Wolf. Then I told Santos I didn't want to." I took my chair and placed it right beside her as I rubbed her back.

"Without telling me, he went to a witch in a nearby coven and dissolved our bond. I didn't even know that could happen." Tamera began to sob as I pulled her to me. "I felt terrible pain through my neck, fire that burned deep into my shoulder. By the time Santos came back, the bond had dissolved." I grabbed the table with one hand as I heard it crack. What kind of asshole dissolves a bond?

"He told me he needed someone physically strong and that he was sorry, he couldn't make this work. I told my mother, who told the pack, and everyone was upset, but they can't go against their Alpha. I lived with my mother for a few months before I couldn't take seeing him anymore. He had a different she-wolf every night in his room. I started to waste away, and he became intolerable."

I pulled Tamera into me; I didn't care if she only wanted to be friends. I would be her friend if she needed it, but I would hold the shit out of her. Tamera didn't protest as she put her arms around my neck. "And that is how I'm here," she finished.

Stroking her hair a few times, I let out a sigh. "I know you don't want to hear this," I began. "A bond is there to help along with something that is already there. A person can reject it because we all still have our free will. However, that dick head did it the wrong way." I growled. "I swear to Selene that if I ever see him, I'll dismember him myself."

Tamera chuckled. "You do that and let me watch." She fake pouted while she started to laugh. Her laughter caught the attention of a few kids who started pointing in our direction. My hand went through her hair as I saw the sparkle begin to come back.

"See, it isn't that hard to laugh now, is it?" I felt her body perk up as she shook her head.

"You make me laugh; I don't remember the last time I did that." She smiled.

"Something else that might brighten your day, Santos won't get a second chance since he rejected you." Tamera's eyes widened.

"Really?" I nodded.

"Yeah, Selena made those bonds for a reason; you can reject it, but if you do, you have to find someone on your own. He did it for selfish reasons so Selene will not grant him another. Really, you could still have a second chance mate. You didn't initiate the rejection first." Tamera scrunched her button nose.

"Nah, I'm good. I don't need a second chance as long as you'll be my friend." As much as I wanted to be more, a friend was what she needed. One day she could find comfort in me of something more, as long as she didn't friend zone me. I couldn't stand for that.

We finished dinner in comfortable silence. She would try and act like she wasn't staring, but she was. Was this what was Hades felt when Ember first looked at him? I had some damn eagles in my stomach watching her eat. I picked up on every single mannerism she had. The way Tamera closed her eyes as she would eat but scrunched her nose as she forced herself to eat the roasted broccoli.

I was supposed to wait for my mate, which was what I really wanted, but the feeling of just being with her was enough. It was comforting, domestic, and dare I say calming? What if I stayed with Tamera? What would my future mate say? The food I was eating became less appetizing as I tried to stomach it. Could Selene alter a bond, so I was no longer soul-bound to another? I didn't want to put the woman that was destined to be mine in pain.

But what if I was in pain? The thought of leaving Tamera once we have found the gods and the Sphere of Souls was painful. I didn't want to leave her. I wanted to stay.

I felt giddy since Tamera was warming up to me while we sat together watching the sunset. Caressing her arm, holding her hand, she was letting me do it all when just a few hours ago she wanted nothing to do with me. I'd trade any moment of my life to continue this bliss.

"I'm glad there isn't a bond between us," she spoke up as her finger touched my palm. "If there was, I think I would have immediately told you to go away." I squeezed her a bit tighter. "Then I would have chased you," I jokingly spoke. "Not everyone is like that asshole; I would never do what Santos did. I'll prove it to you if you let me? There isn't even a bond involved here, Tamera."

Tamera blushed as I played with her hands. They were so small, just skin and bone from not eating and the broken bond that still pulled her down. "If I'm still around for you to show me," she whispered; I grabbed her chin to look up at me.

"You will be around because I will fix you, just like you are fixing me." Her deep eyes caressed my face as she continued to stare. Little freckles were painted on her cheeks, her brown eyes had flecks of gold. She was like a little pixie. My little pixie.

I'd give up any bond to be with Tamera. We could have a life together. We both had been hurt by people meant for us; we understood each other and know how it felt to be rejected.

"Aphrodite was arranged to be with me by my parents, but we all know what happened there...." I smiled as my finger traced her cheek. "Aphrodite left when I said she couldn't walk all over me and sleep with others. I tried to make it work, and since that day, I have been broken too. After all, she was supposed to be the most beautiful, and I am the worst at the physical appearances of the gods. She couldn't stand to look at me." I blinked back tears.

"That's a lie. You are good-looking! Handsome and sexy even!" Tamera burst out while her face flushed red. I laughed as she put her fingers through my beard. "You are you are insanely good-looking; when you walked in the clinic today to check for Alpha Ember, it was all I could do to look away." Her face looked away, covering her mouth.

Fuck yes, she thought I was handsome. Tamera was the one for me; I didn't care what Selena had prepared for either of us. Once we find her, I'll make sure Tamera will never hurt again and belong to me. It would be a slow, grueling process, but she was worth it.

After a few more hours of talking on the patio, sitting on her comfortable outdoor couch, we talked about our lives. I had become engrossed in her tales of residency of trauma and ER work. Anything to do with battle wounds fascinated her, which was great since she worked in a packhouse full of fighting ready wolves. Tamera's head began to nod off as she leaned against my chest.

This was what I always wanted. Someone to share a life with, and she felt something too, without a bond.

Closing my eyes and leaning my head back, the usual howls and barks turned into growls. Tamera immediately woke up and grabbed my hand. "Heat, someone is in heat," she repeated. "Ember," she whispered again. "Her body must be reacting all at once." Tamera tried to get up, but I held her back down to me.

"Hades is with her; she will be fine." Tamera nodded reluctantly as she put her head back on my chest. Not one peep did I hear from her until Steven, Ember's brother, came running.

"Come to the packhouse; Dad wants your help with something important!" Steven said out of breath. "We think we know who took Ember."

Chapter 50

Charlotte

"Dante!" Wesley rubbed his hand through his hair as he paced by the fireplace.

We had just come back to our home after a long ceremonial first shift run. Normally we would spend time together as a family after the first shift. Ember starting her heat just after threw that idea out the window.

I would have called you a liar if I had woken up this morning and someone told me my daughter was coming home. Now she was home, and I wanted my daughter all to myself, but fate had a funny way of being cruel. Ember was home; my first baby was home. Unfortunately, she wasn't my baby any longer.

Ember wasn't my little girl anymore. Time moved slowly over the years, and now that she was no longer a child, I could no longer enjoy her growing up. Ember was an adult and thankfully grew up so much stronger than I ever was at her age. Now Dante stands before his family and tells us he was the one responsible for his sister's disappearance.

"Hear me out and let me tell you!" he demanded. Wesley wasn't having any of it, he was pissed, and Remus was not going to tolerate it. Remus had been a terrible mess when Ember was gone, and just today, Remus's inner light finally sparked back to life.

"Let's hear it!" Wesley growled out. "You've kept enough secrets; you fucking lied to us for years! You knew something that could have helped us find her, and yet you said nothing!" I rushed to Wesley and tried to get him to sit down.

"Come on, sweetheart, let's hear Dante out. He did not do this on purpose, I'm sure. Please?" Wesley eyed me as he sat in his oversized rocking chair while pulling me in his lap. His nose went straight to my neck as he inhaled deeply. This action usually made the boys gag, but they knew they needed to steer clear when their father was angry.

I had anger built up in myself for Dante; he kept something regarding Ember for years and never spoke up. Unfortunately, I had to be the merciful one of the family full of testosterone. I would keep my feelings at bay until I knew what to do with them.

"Right." Dante stood up, pacing the floor. Blaze, Ember's little pet, had not left Dante's side. He sat perched on his shoulder and constantly stroked his cheek with his little head. I would dare say it was cute, but my worries of that tail catching my house of fire was something fierce.

Dante spilled his heart out as everyone in the room waited for him to finish. Ares and Mariah, who had joined us earlier, sat in the corner together. I was surprised Mariah had taken this opportunity to get to know the God of War, despite wanting to wait for her mate. Wesley had always preached to our pack about the importance of finding your mate and waiting. Mariah had been a strong advocate for that, and now she sits with Ares, taking glances at him when he isn't looking. She's not his, and he will leave when this all blows over, and I will need to be there to pull the pieces together. Being a Luna is exhausting.

They are not mates; otherwise, they wouldn't be able to keep their hands off each other, but there is an attraction there. While still listening to Dante about the southern border and the mysterious Fairy, I see Ares glance down at Mariah's hand. He took it in his and laced her fingers together and gave a brief kiss to her hand.

The God of War had a soft side, or was it just to get in her pants? Mariah blushed as Ares's forehead touched hers. A hot sticky mess this was going to be when he left her in the dust.

"*He isn't your mate is he?*" I mind-linked Mariah, causing her to look at me.

"*No,*" she said quietly. "*I just feel comfortable with him. He makes me laugh, and he treats me softly, unlike everyone else.*" I nodded my head.

"Just be careful. I know how you wish to find your mate." Mariah's eyes softened but didn't let go of Ares's hand. I sighed as I turned my attention back to Dante. Wesley's fists were shaking as he continued to listen.

"You mean to tell me that you helped a Forest Fairy across the border, and you didn't tell me, the Alpha?" Wesley growled out.

"Wesley! He was only a child! He didn't know any better!" I pulled on his arm as he stood up.

"He did know better! He is an Alpha's son! Every pup has been told repeatedly no one is allowed to enter the territory unless I allow it!" Wesley stomped around the room, waving his hands about and muttering under his breath.

Dante stood silent while Blaze chattered in his ear. Who knows what that thing was saying, but it was keeping Dante calm. Walking over to Dante, I put my arms around him. "You were only eight and trying to do something good. Ember has already forgiven you, and so have I." I kissed his cheek, but the tears didn't stop. Dante's eyes wouldn't meet mine as Wesley growled on the other side of the room.

"Dante, you are to be the next Alpha." Dante and my head shot up; the whole room was perfectly still as Hunter and Steven had their mouths hang open. Nodding his head, Wesley continued, "That's right. Ember has passed on her right to be Alpha. Dante is next in line, but I don't know if that would be wise, especially in just a short six years." A growl grew in my chest towards Wesley as I left Dante's side.

"You dare punish our son because of an innocent mistake? He was a child. If it was anyone else's…."

"Then they would receive a punishment. Dante's mistake cost us 12 years of our daughter missing, and who knows what else could have happened during that time! That Fairy could have come back and stolen more children. Ember could have been sold, raped, and killed!" Wesley turned and pointed a heavy finger towards our son. "Dante, you will not inherit the pack at twenty-five. You will only gain it when you have found your mate and have finished Harvard Business school like we talked about. You are lucky you are not receiving harsher punishment being the Alpha's son!"

Wesley had been begging Dante to go to college just as he had to take over the several businesses that kept our large pack running. With Ember still missing and our hearts knowing she was still alive, Dante quickly dismissed the idea. Dante wouldn't rest until Ember was found, and now that she was, this would just revert to the plan Wesley had set Dante out for.

Wesley was hurt that his son didn't feel like he could confide in his own father. I felt the disappointment radiating through our bond. The doubt that he raised a son who felt like he would be cast away for his honesty pulled sadness straight to his heart.

Finding a mate could take years for Dante. Wesley didn't find me for the longest time; who knows how long it would take Dante or how quickly? My heart skipped at that notion. Maybe he could find his mate and take over the pack sooner rather than later. My heart went out to both of my men. Both hurting for different reasons, and now was a complete spectacle with Ares, Mariah, and now Cyrene that had watched all on the sidelines.

Cyrene was always the silent watcher, and yet I never felt judged by her. She was old, ancient, yet her youthful appearance denied any part of the wisdom she carried. Cyrene came forward and handed me the small plate of cookies I had made. If a coven Witch said it was time for a snack, then by the will of the goddess, we would have a snack.

Wesley slumped in the chair and took a cookie begrudgingly; he knew not to refuse my food. The one time he did, he didn't get his favorite steak for weeks. Dante took a seat without saying a word, just nodding and whispering he was sorry under his breath.

"I know this has to be difficult for both sides of this situation," I began. "Babe, I know you had wished Dante had come to you after this all transpired, but what's done is done. He was just a boy; you can't have such high expectations for just a young pup who had yet to even receive his Wolf. And Dante?" I walked to him and kneeled down to see the beautiful green eyes he inherited from his father.

"You didn't know better, but as you grew, you had to have known we would never send you away or cast you out of our family. I thought I taught you we loved you no matter what." Dante's lone tear was wiped away by my finger as he sighed. "Ember has forgiven Dante, and that is all that matters. We will figure out together what we can do now. We have a lead, a Fairy we can…." I paused.

The Fairy was seen on the southern border of the territory. The cameras I used were constantly running, recording everything on that side of the property. The night Ember was taken we only checked the cameras that went off that had the motion sensor detection go off. If Dante could tell us the exact time we could run through the footage.

"Goddess," I breathed as Wesley came to my side on the floor. "Those cameras, that was around the time I was testing out that new technology. Where it constantly records rather than turning on when motion is detected." Cyrene stepped forward, clutching her cloak.

"Do you still have the footage? Do you hold onto that much video streaming?" I smiled, almost evil-like.

"Of course, I do; what kind of Luna would I be if I didn't? I need to get to the packhouse; I have some digging to do." Dante and Wesley grabbed my hand gratefully.

"Kitten, you are so sexy when you are thinking up a plan," Wesley purred in my head.

"You can thank me later if you stop being a grump to our son." I winked as we all raced to the packhouse.

***

The surveillance room had grown since the first time I had worked in here. There were more cameras, more Wolves that had become the eyes of the forest. Primarily pregnant women operated the surveillance room, and several adolescents who had received their wolves yet had not shifted. This taught them the area, along with learning to keep their eyes open for anything unusual. Security had tightened since Ember left, especially since we didn't know if Hades' ward worked anymore.

"You are relieved for the day everyone. Wesley will mind link the backup warriors to patrol today." Everyone in the room looked up confused, but Wesley's look let them know not to ask any questions. As they shuffled out, I sat at my desk, one that I had spent countless nights when I couldn't sleep thinking of my daughter.

I typed in the date she was missing, November 15, along with the year, and pressed enter. The modem riled to life as the computer searched for all videos for that day. I will never regret the time I spent hiding in libraries and earning my technology degrees as a young woman. It has helped the pack and me in far too many ways.

Filtering through the southern border cameras, I find my eight-year-old son, Dante, with his shaggy blonde hair standing on the edge of the territory. The Fairy had wheat-colored hair, a tiny face, and wings that didn't look like a Forest Fairy. They were slightly gold with hints of green on them. Fairies usually held a more translucent look such as a bee or dragonfly's wings. "Weird," Cyrene mentioned as she leaned over the computer. "She looks like a Forest Fairy, but those wings don't confirm it."

"A hybrid, maybe?" I whispered.

Ares and Mariah whispered in the corner, and I swear I saw him peck her forehead. I rubbed my temples as I let out a frustrated sigh. This was too much to deal with right now. Mariah was a big girl, and if she wanted to mess up her first time with some god, she would deal with the consequences.

"Would Vulcan know what kind of Fairy this is?" I asked the room as Wesley continued to stare at the screen. He wasn't staring at the Fairy but that of Dante. Dante was uncomfortable as he shifted from side to side. My baby was all upset, and the tension between him and his father was unbearable. Nudging Wesley, I mind-linked him, *"Go talk to your son."* I glared at him while he whimpered. *"Tell him you love him, and you aren't mad anymore. You knew you blew up, and your anger got the best of you. Now go, or you can't make it up to me tonight."* Wesley's eyes widened as he stood up and walked across the room to Dante. He kept his head low until Wesley cleared his throat.

"Let's take this outside." Wesley led Dante out of the room while I dealt with the problem before me. This stupid Fairy, which couldn't be a Forest Fairy.

"Steven, go get Vulcan, please, dear." Steven stood up and walked out of the room while Hunter tried to follow. "Hunter?" I snapped. He groaned as he turned around.

"Go check on the mated warriors that are watching the mating cabin. Make sure they are fed, and the next shift will be ready to go when it is time." Hunter did an exaggerated bow as he left the room while I laughed. That boy could make anyone laugh besides Tamera. Tamera never laughed or smiled.

I had worried for her. When she first showed up, she was nothing but a shell of a woman. As the months progressed, she opened up to me, and now she was more willing to talk about what happened to her. That reckless Alpha from Cool Springs had lost our alliance with us once I told Wesley what he did. Rumor was he has women in and out of his room every night and has felt the effects of a bond he stripped. Luckily, Tamera was human and has been able to last longer than a Werewolf would. Death would have been immediate, but thankfully Selene was gracious to humans thrust into a world of supernaturals. However, Tamera's time was short, and I didn't know how much longer she wanted to hang on.

Cyrene had mentioned her soul was just down to a dwindle. Her physical features were sunken, and her skin had turned ashy. Tamera was such a sweet girl, I couldn't imagine how a wolf taught the significance and the importance of a bond would throw her away. Tamera reminded me so much of myself, her desire to learn, and the craving she had to be wanted.

My heavy sigh didn't go unnoticed as Cyrene touched my shoulder. "Everything will work out. Whether it be for or against our favor, the strings will begin to unravel." I nodded my head while we heard the door to the surveillance room open.

Vulcan walked in with a smile on his face as he held Tamera's arm in the crook of his own, rubbing her hand calmly. Tamera glanced at his face, and a blush of color painted her face.

"Goddess," I breathed as I gripped my chair. That was the first smile I had seen cross her beautiful face.

"They're not mates," Cyrene whispered as we both stared. "There isn't a bond there."

"I don't care." I shook my head. "That look says it all."

Chapter 51

Ember

The bathroom was massive; it was half the size of the large studio room we were staying in and held both a jacuzzi tub and a large walk-in shower. The entire room was tan with hints of small succulent plants and hanging eucalyptus over the shower. The smell opened my lungs as the steam filled the room with its healing properties.

Steam showers were my new favorite, better than the cold showers I had to deal with for many years. I never wanted to be without one. Breathing in the intoxicating scent the eucalyptus was radiating, I felt the heat begin to rise again. Does it ever really stop? My breaths became heavy; I just wanted a shower to feel a bit normal, but the sex goddess in me had woken up. I couldn't get enough of my mate.

"I knew you would see it my way," Elea joked. *"All this, 'I'm scared,' and junk was just in your insecurities to perform correctly and not thinking you were good enough."*

"Oh, so you are a psychiatrist now? Anything else you want to tell me?" I scoffed while I rinsed my hair.

"Yeah, our mate has been staring at your ass for the past five minutes, and you haven't even once noticed."

I flinched as Hades' hand curved around my waist and made its way down south. His finger cupped my mound as he rubbed it slowly. "My mate is feeling her heat again, hm?" His nose trailed up my neck as I rolled my head back on his chest. Nipples pebbling under his touch, I reached my hand lower to force him to put two fingers into me.

"Getting bold, aren't we?" Fingers pumped into me as he held onto my breast for grip. My hips automatically bucked into his palm as I wanted more. The shower continued to roll down our bodies, and his joggers got wet. He came in the shower with pants?

"I couldn't stand it anymore, I felt you in the other room, and then I got distracted; who wouldn't with a body like this?" Hades hissed as he ground his erection into my ass. My body spasmed; cum going down my leg. I didn't know where the water began or where my slick ended. Taking Hades' hands off me, I felt my inner animal come to the surface. Elea kept whispering what I should do to him, and I wanted nothing more than to make him feel like he makes me feel.

My claws extracted as I ripped his joggers; by the time this heat was over, neither of us would have any clothes left. His dick sprang free and hit his stomach. Fully erected, I still can't imagine him being inside me; he could tickle my belly button with that thing.

"Like what you see?" huskily, he spoke as he stroked it a few times. Hades' touching himself made me wet with need; my heart could be felt straight between my thighs as he tickled my stomach with it. My claws grabbed his hips as I knelt and sucked him right into my mouth. Hades hissed and leaned back on the cold shower wall that caused chills to run down his leg.

Many women felt powerless as they would kneel in front of men, which may be so in most situations, but at this moment, I felt like the one with the power. I could suck him dry in a matter of seconds, prolong his pleasure or not give him anything at all. I could give or take everything away from him. What I wanted most was to give him pleasure; he had taken care of me multiple times and always made sure I felt nothing but heaven before he even thought of himself.

I took his entire length and hit the back of my throat. My knees felt the burn on the cold shower floor as they ached. The ache only gave me the drive to push forward and have my tongue enter part of his slit that gave me his salty snack.

Hades' hands gripped my wet hair tightly as I took him out of my mouth. Something else was calling me, something a bit more daring, and Elea was scratching at me to complete the task. "Spread your legs," I growled out; Hades stiffened as his grip gently let go. "Do it, mate," I growled out again, and his legs widened just enough to do what I wanted.

Sucking in one of his balls in my mouth, Hades' back arched. He was blinded by pleasure as my tongue slipped beneath his balls and licked his taint. Hades yelled as he grabbed his dick and my hair as I continued to lick this forbidden zone.

"Ember," he hissed. "Mother fucking," he growled out as his balls tightened. My body stopped as Hades pulled me up under my arms. "I can't come that quickly, my flower, not when it isn't anywhere near your pussy."

He was right; I didn't want his seed to spill out anywhere else; I wanted in my body. It didn't matter that I knew we couldn't have pups; I just wanted him. All the essence of him inside me. Hades slapped my ass to make me jump and wrap my legs around his waist. Opened mouth kisses marked my neck as I turned off the shower and he led me to the large fluffy rug in the middle of the bathroom.

My back hit the softness of the rug while my cavern was pounded by his enormous shaft. Hades grunted as his muscles gripped my shoulders to thrust himself harder. My body continued to move along the carpet as he watched his dick disappear inside me.

"Bite him," Elea pressured me as I took his cock. *"Bite him harder!"* A growl ripped through my throat as I sprung up as I felt Hades release his pressure. My fangs grew, and I bit Hades harder than I did during our bonding while we both fell over the edge. Hades roared loudly as his seed shot into me; he continued to spurt his hot cum until it overflowed until my body couldn't take it anymore. Blood seeped through his shoulder as I tasted him on his lips.

"Shit," he whispered as he fell to the side. His hard erection still looked angry as it fell from my body. Pulling me close, he wrapped his arms around me. "It just gets better and better, doesn't it?" he chuckled as he kissed my forehead. Our heavy breaths intermingled with each other as I laid my head on his chest.

I hummed in agreement as I listened to his heart. My heart had the same rhythm as his as we lay on the fluffy floor. "They beat together?" I whispered. Hades' eyes were closed as he rolled over to tuck my head under his neck.

"They do, don't they?" Hades was fading fast, his heart slowing, and mine followed suit. My eyes grew heavy as Hades' breath evened out. Before I could ask him why we were so tired, we both fell into a heavy sleep.

Wesley

I took Dante to the pack office. He slumped up the stairs while that stupid animal chatted in his ear. What the hell was that thing anyway? It always hopped out when someone was all disturbed or distressed.

Opening the large mahogany doors, I see the desk that has been replaced far too many times. This whole room had to be redone after Charlotte dealt with her own kidnappings, and Remus decided to trash the place. After the mating and Luna ceremony, Charlotte had the whole room cemented down to the floor so I couldn't throw things; it didn't help with the desk at home; I've broken that one too many times since Ember's disappearance.

I resisted the urge to sit behind my desk and just sat across from Dante on the other couch. Kitten said it was too intimidating for our own children, and I needed to take a more fatherly, subtle approach when talking to our children. She really did run the pants in the family. I rubbed my hand down my face as Dante stared at the floor.

"An alpha does not stare at the floor; he faces his fears. Now, look me in the eye." Dante's face held no tears, thank goddess. I can't handle a crying alpha right now. His back straightened up, and he looked me in the eye. His Wolf was tense; I could feel it.

I growled out as I slapped my knee. "I know I yelled at you; I told your mother I wouldn't be that kind of father, but damnit Dante, I thought you would think of us as better parents." Dante didn't say anything as he shifted his body on the couch. "If you did tell us about this Fairy, I don't think it would have done any good. We would have looked for this Fairy for ages and never found her. Fairies can hide well, and if they don't want to be found, they won't. Still, I need you to tell me these kinds of things. Tell me what is going on in our territory for the sake of others."

"I understand." Dante's voice became stronger than earlier. "I did make a mistake, and I agree with your punishment. I think I should have a greater punishment actually."

"Dante, you were eight," I sighed as I got up to sit beside him. "Today has been exhausting. Your sister is back now, and that is all that matters. She is safe. Ember found her mate even." I gritted my teeth. She was my daughter, and the last time I saw her, she was but a little girl; hell, she still looked like a little girl. Now she is over at the mating cabin getting it on with God of the Underworld; how the hell can Charlotte take this?

Dante and I did our usual side pat on the shoulders; we weren't much for hugs. Charlotte always made us do a mandatory hug when everyone in the family fought, but she wasn't here now, was she? Gods, I love Charlotte; she really pulls our family together. She made sure that our family was everything she ever wanted.

Most of the time, she put her emotions on the backburner so her children could see her happy while they were awake. Charlotte had always been my tiny solid human turned Werewolf.

Dante had agreed to go to business school, which was the plan for the children in the very beginning. The businesses I ran to keep the pack strong financially were necessary. I wasn't going to let my father and I's hard work go to waste. I'll have a few more years as Alpha, but that was fine; with Charlotte, she did half of the job anyway.

We both walked back into the surveillance room with Vulcan holding Tamera's hand. Dante and I looked at each other and back at Charlotte, who quickly shook her head to make sure I didn't blab out something ridiculous.

"Anyway, Vulcan, can you come to take a look at this?" Charlotte announced as he walked over, along with Tamera.

"A Fairy!" Tamera gasped. "I've never seen one moving before, only in pictures." Vulcan stared at the fairy and back at Charlotte. "This isn't a fairy," Vulcan's face scrunched. "That's Demeter. Disguised as a Fairy." Cyrene and Charlotte gasped while we heard sucking noises in the corner.

We all bolted our heads to the sound to find Ares and Mariah making out on the couch. Ares' tongue was halfway down her throat. I'd give anything to be doing that with my Kitten right now. "Mariah!" Charlotte gasped. Ares and Mariah stopped while both blushed. What the hell have I been missing? Are they mates?

"Take that somewhere else!" Charlotte's eyes bulged out of her head as Mariah giggled and pulling a thrilled Ares out of the room. Someone needs to make him wear some sort of support underneath that leather smock he wears.

Charlotte sighed as she rubbed her temples. Going behind the chair, I started to massage her shoulders and kiss the top of her head.

"Great job, Kitten. We are another step closer."

"Closer? We just added another person to the list of suspects and nothing else! Why would Demeter want to get involved now!?"

Vulcan pulled Tamera's waist closer to him as she laid her head on his chest. "We need to find the Sphere; that is the step we need. After that, I think things will fall into place. That was Selene's first request before we found her, Hecate and now Hermes." Charlotte nodded.

"That means we wait for Ember's heat to be over so she can find the sphere." Charlotte muttered. There may be three or four days before we can get Ember and Hades' opinion on the matter, so now we must sit and wait.

***

Charlotte had just put on her favorite fuzzy pair of shorts with a tank top. Her strawberry blonde hair cascaded down her back that touched just above her lower back. She had been mumbling random to-do lists all the way home from the packhouse. Ever since becoming Luna, she put this mental checklist in her head as she spoke aloud.

"I need to make sure the cooks make extra food; the gods probably eat more than we do," she mused to herself. Then her mouth would open again, and more thoughts poured from her peachy lips. "I need to make sure that Ember and Hades have food just outside the ward he created." Before I could comment, she was on to another subject about starting the mating ceremony that now includes a god; how she would have to do some research with Cyrene.

"It's fall, so we could incorporate some of those cornucopia baskets. Have fall foliage decorations, you think?" I had heard enough about everyone else, and my cock was strained as it was watching her bend over to place clean clothes into the dresser drawers. Her breasts were practically begging me to fondle them as she pulled the sheets back on the bed.

I pushed her to the wall next to the bed. I rolled my erection into her hips as her eyes shot up in surprise. "I don't want to talk about anyone else," I nibbled on her ear. Charlotte relaxed as she tangled her fingers in my hair and her hips moved against mine. How does she do these things to make me go crazy?

"Did I not give puppy enough attention today?" Charlotte's put her lips in a pout as her eyes became hooded. As she rolled her hips into me again, I groaned.

"Remus, not puppy," we growled out as I picked her up by her fuzzy ass shorts as I threw her on the bed. She giggled frantically as I pulled her clothes off of her. She'd kill me if I ripped those damn fuzzy shorts; they're her favorite.

"Good boy," she purred as I flicked them to the other side of the room. Fuck, the things she says to rile Remus up could be damn sexy.

I pecked her lips and inhaled her scent. I had been away from her too much today between taking Ember to the lake and dealing with

Dante; I wanted to have my fill. We didn't even have our wake-up sex because she felt like something was going to happen today.

I should trust her intuition more.

"Wesley," she whined as I gripped her breasts harshly. "I want more." Her lip went into a pout as I sucked it into my mouth. What my Kitten wants, Kitten will get. My face went directly between her thighs, licking and nipping her soft spot. Burying my nose in her heat, I could smell her arousal hit the air. Sticking two fingers into her cavern and licking her precious nub, she began to squeal as she rode my face.

"Ahh!" Charlotte yipped as her fingers tightened in my hair. That was my favorite thing, how she pulled my face closer to her heat so I could submerge my tongue as deep as it would go as my fingers massaged her walls.

Charlotte fell apart as she squirted into my mouth. Holy fuck, when was the last time she did that? She had more tension than I thought. I licked her thighs, cleaned her from her pleasure, and rolled her on her back. Remus was still pissed about being called puppy, and he wanted to put her in her place.

Groaning, Charlotte fisted the sheets as she crawled up on all fours. My dick prodded her slick opening as I eased into her; that was all I could promise her that would be easy. Sex right now was going to be up to Remus. Watching my dick disappear, I felt my grip on Charlotte's hips tighten. Thrusting forward, I hit her hard in her cervix.

Her cries only urged me to continue. Charlotte's moans were loud, and I was thankful our boys were out of the house.

As enticing as her ass was, I wanted to see her face as I cummed inside her, so I pulled out while my dick was screaming at me for stopping. "Wesley? What are you-?" Her question fell silent as I continued to sit on my knees while putting her pussy over my shaft. This gave Charlotte the perfect leverage as both her legs flanked either side of my hips like sitting on a damn chair.

"Fucking ride me," I growled as her mouth parted. With hair in her face, she used the bed to bounce up and down on my cock. Charlotte's pants grew faster; my balls were screaming to release my seed into her.

How fucking amazing she looked pregnant; I wanted to put another pup in her. Would she give us another one day now that Ember was home? Charlotte's walls clenched as I spurt my pleasure into her. We both growled into each other's shoulders before biting each other again. Blood dripped from our bites as we licked each other clean. Fuck, I'll never get used to this. Legs shaking, I pulled us down to the bed gently; I could feel my cock still twitching as Charlotte snuggled into me. Her hands started stroking my hair as I felt myself purr.

"You are always so vigorous," Charlotte teased as her finger trailed my tattoos.

"You were poking fun at Remus; you knew what you got yourself into." She laughed. She damn well knew it too. We both tried to close our eyes, but Charlotte shot up out of bed. Her heart was pounding as she muttered to herself.

"I can't believe we forgot!" She squealed.

"Forgot what, Kitten?"

"Wesley! We haven't told your parents that Ember is home!"

Chapter 52

Ember

"Are you sure that it's over? I don't mind spending a few more days here." Hades wrapped his arm around me with one hand as the other cupped my face. Hades had his demon servants summoned and brought us clothes. There were none left after the constant ripping and clawing. The thought of any male coming within 100 yards of the mating cabin made Hades sprout his infamous smoke tendrils.

"Yes, it's over." I straightened out the white blouse over my dark jeans. Hades had the servants bring clothes that were light in color, telling me I was his light to his darkness and that I looked like his very own angel. Can we say swoon?

"We really need to get back; we have a mission to accomplish, right?" Hades nodded his head solemnly as he kissed my forehead.

"I'm not ready to share you." He nuzzled in my ear. His hot breath sent waves of heat down to my core as his arms pulled me into his body. His shoulder now bore my mark; no woman could ever dare come near him, not that they would. I didn't have to worry about Hades ever straying from me; his temperament for anyone else but me had proven that.

"You've had me for four days; once we find the Sphere, I hope we will find Selene and the others. I've missed Hermes." My voice trailed off as I looked out the window. "Do you think they are all right?" Hade's warm touch on my skin calmed me as his heartbeat beat with mine, something that felt indescribable.

"They are gods, they won't die, but they can be weakened. The emotional battle they will struggle with is what I worry about. Who knows where they are, but Selene, Hecate, and Hermes are strong. They will be fine, I'm sure of it. Don't you worry your pretty little self so." Burning my nose into his chest, I felt him chuckle. "They will come back to us, and once I find out who took them and you… it will be my turn to play."

I wasn't as forgiving as my mother; I hoped that whoever was responsible should pay. In fact, I hope Hades locked them up with the Titans and let them have some fun.

Walking back to the center of the territory that held the packhouse along with my family home, we heard squeals of laughter. "Again, again!" Little Wolves ran past us as they ran to the center of town; not noticing Hades, one bumped into his leg as he fell.

"Ouchie!" The little girl rubbed her knee. Ready for an outburst, I go to hold Hades' arm as he bent forward and picked up the little girl. My eyes widened in shock.

"I'm sorry, did I get in your way?" Hades chuckled as he looked at her knee. "Sorry, mister Hades." Her big wet lashes fluttered as Hades wiped a tear away.

"Just be a little more careful, hmm?" The little girl nodded her head as she ran off to the series of laughs and screams. I wanted to coo at Hades but him being so nice to someone other than me was a huge milestone. I couldn't ruin the moment.

He would be a wonderful father if we could have our own. Many packs have orphaned pups that we could adopt. When the time was right, I could have Father ask around and see if we could raise one. The thought of Hades putting a diaper on a little baby made me feel giddy. God of the Underworld changing diapers, rocking babies, and putting them to bed had to be the sexist idea.

There was a deeper voice that sounded vaguely familiar as we walked hand in hand. The laugh was contagious, and I wanted nothing more than to find out who it was. "What is it?" Hades squeezed my hand as I pulled him closer. Giant shrills of a child being thrown up in the air by an unknown Wolf. He was tall, reminding me of my father except with dark hair. His green eyes sparkled as the other children continued to ask him to throw them.

It couldn't be!? Could it!? "Ember!" I heard mom yell from the front porch; I waved, letting her know I heard her until I felt the breeze brush my hair harshly. Hades had let go of my hand and was now pinning the large Wolf up by his neck. His green flannel and khaki pants were covered in mud as Hades gripped him harder.

"You dare try to approach my mate?" Great, Hades was back to the signature choking. Running up to Hades, dad and Dante came to help pry Hades off, which was no use. While they pulled, Hades' eyes lit up like fire. The Wolf looked down at me as I screamed.

"ERIK! Hades!! Let go! It's my uncle!!" Hades let go, but his stare never left Erik as he rubbed his neck. I pounced on Erik while Hades started grumbling and pulling me off.

"Erik!" I cried as I wrestled closer and hugged him close. Erik's voice was raspy as he chanted my name while swaying us on the ground. "You're here, you are really here! I've been in Bergarian with mom and dad looking for you!"

"Shit, more family," Hades cursed as he helped us both up. "Sorry about that. I don't like anyone near my mate." Erik glanced at me and then back at Hades. The power Hades was radiating on purpose was making Erik confused. Hades was more robust than any Alpha or supernatural, so of course, Erik's curiosity was peaked.

"I'm Hades, God of the Underworld. And you are?" I nudged Hades to be polite, but he pulled me in by my waist while kissing my forehead. "Be nice," I whispered. "We are blood-related; he isn't some random Wolf."

"Don't care," he mumbled into my temple.

"Holy, oh, wow," Erik couldn't form words as he stared. After a moment, I felt Hades' patience dwindling.

"Hades, this is my Uncle Erik. My dad's parents' son. We are only three years apart. Once mom and dad got together, Grandpa Odin and Grama Astrid got 'busy.'" I giggled. "We were practically playmates." Hades nodded his head and understood as they shook hands.

"Pleasure," Hades choked as Erik pulled him in for a hug. "Thanks for finding her man. She's basically my sister." Erik sniffed while Hades reluctantly patted him on the back.

"Ember!" We heard another shrill of a scream as Grandma Astrid came running.

"How many family members do you have?" Hades groaned again while Grandma gripped me tightly. Grandpa Odin with his overly large beard and Viking style hair cut came running up to greet us as we were all pulled back to my parents' home.

The rest of the day was spent inside the house, which I thought to be large when I was younger. It was now cramped as Mom and Ashley made fresh food filled with pies, roasts, steaks, spaghetti, and tons of cookies throughout the day. Poor Steven was being rushed to the packhouse every hour to grab more drinks and alcohol as they celebrated my return.

Even with all the food being consumed, there was another celebration tonight with the pack since my unscheduled shift and heat messed everything up. The large bonfire party was to commence just hours from now, but the current private party continued to rage on in the house.

Hades had willed demons to be present to help serve food; everyone was taken aback at their natural forms but quickly took a liking to the men and now women that were serving. Hades and I had a talk that he should hire at least a few women; he couldn't prevent catfights in the demon world, and I knew he would never stray. Besides, we were bonded now; if he did anything, I would know and then rip his eyes out and tear out the guts of any female that dared touch what was mine.

As much as I enjoyed being with my family, the itching feeling in my head came back from trying to find the Sphere. Was I the only one worried for the gods' return? I tapped the glass of apple juice that I drank, not wanting to drink any alcohol until the party tonight. My thoughts of the many places that Sphere could be invaded my mind.

The treehouse, my mind kept going to the treehouse. Everyone was talking, having fun, and even Hades joined in on a game of chess that Erik and Dante had pulled out. Everyone was trying extra hard to break Hades' tough exterior, but he only smiled when he glanced at me. Butterflies erupted in my stomach as I felt my heart pound my chest.

I wanted Hades to have a good time but knowing his heart and smile were only meant for me made us want to take him away and have our own time together. Holding down my desire, I made the decision to go to my treehouse. This mystery needed to come to an end and fast.

Slipping out the front door, without anyone noticing, I lightly pranced down the steps. The sun had begun to set, and the cooks had roasting pits filled with boar for tonight's dinner. As a child, Dante and I would steal hunks of meat while they cooked. We would get scolded every time, but it was worth seeing the cooks waving their tongs around. Like that would stop us.

I hit the tree line in less than five minutes and was about to climb the abandoned treehouse when I heard soft moans. *"Someone is getting frisky,"* Elea laughed. *"Let's go find out."* I snorted quietly as my curiosity increased. Who the heck was messing around in the woods? My feet carried me deeper into the wood. The moans came out again as I peeked over and found none other than Ares and Mariah. Both had a glow where their bodies touched. It was barely a glow, but it was there. Both of their emotions were so strong, it was pungent, stifling. The passion that they had for each other was that of what I felt with Hades. Wait? Ares and Mariah? What the heck happened in four days?

I let out a large gasp as I saw Ares reach his hand up Mariah's shirt.

"The fuck!" Ares took his hand away while Mariah pulled down her shirt. The glow instantly disappeared as their lusty haze faded.

"I'm so sorry!" I put my hand over my mouth. "You were just glowing!" Ares and Mariah looked at each other confused; her body was still pinned on the ground as she stared up at me.

"Touch her again," I pleaded.

Ares smirked. "I didn't think you were into that kind of thing." Ares wiggled his eyebrows while hovering over the top of Mariah as she blushed scarlet.

"Just touch her hand, not her boob!" Ares shrugged her shoulders as he reached for her hand, looking into Mariah's eyes. The glow stood out again. I had never seen a glow like this, it was heaven, almost sacred sort of look.

"Are you mates?" My question seemed to strike a nerve with Ares as Mariah's face went crestfallen.

"You shouldn't ask that; I've had enough of people asking us that," he snapped. "If I care about her, I'll be with her. Mate or not, she is who I want to be with." Stepping back, I saw a small tear leave Mariah's eye.

"Do you really mean that?" she whispered. Ares stilled as he pulled her hand to his chest.

"With all my heart, my little warrior." The softness, the love that was in Ares's eyes, confirmed it. Could they? They might be mates. I had to find that Sphere. Who knows how long people were going without their mates? What if they had already crossed paths and missed their chance?

My body blocked out all sounds of the forest; Mariah was confessing her undying love for Ares as they both held each other and dove in for another passionate kiss. Pushing the bushes back, I ran to the treehouse, hoping that was where the stupid little ball that was the key to everyone's happiness.

The rickety board leading up the treehouse creaked, and planks fell, but my claws caught me before I could do any damage. The door was bolted shut, probably to keep small Wolves from climbing into the playhouse. Dante had mentioned it had become a shrine, and people would leave flowers at the tree's trunk on my birthday.

Biting my lip, I used my Werewolf strength for the first time to rip the door open from the seams and throw the door to the floor.

The air was musty, even with the open windows of the house. Mold and moss had grown up the sides; small mushrooms even took root on the floor. The limbs of the tree had cracked a few boards while one limb had grown out of the window entirely.

It wasn't a giant treehouse, though I could still have a large chest that served as a table when I brought friends in. Kneeling, I felt for the trunk's latch and wiggled the rust to open the latch. With a giant whine of the hinges creaking, I flipped the top over on itself to see nothing but old drawings.

My shoulders slumped, hoping the Sphere would be here. That would have been too easy. Selene wouldn't hide it there. Rustling through, I pulled out all my drawings. Drawings of a large bonfire, family portraits, Mom defeating her demon, and Wolves were held in my hand. I laid them all out like they were a puzzle. There could be no connection to these pictures at all, but this was all I had.

"My favorite place," I whispered again as I touched each picture. Family, fire, demons, and a treehouse. None of these things wrung a bell as I traced each one. One picture laid in the box, a man in the fire. He had blonde hair, but his clothes were black as the fire engulfed him and a little girl that held his hand.

"Oh my gosh." I chuckled out loud. Did I dream of him as a kid? It had been so many years since I'd been here, I couldn't possibly remember every detail about my life. How could I forget this? Especially since my dreams had come true. The wind let in a warm gush of air, and darkness fell around the treehouse; I was about to stand when a warm cloak danced around me, holding me to the floor of the house. I struggled to get free until I felt his raging heartbeat with mine.

"Damnit, Ember," the husky voice pulled me in as I wrapped my arms around his muscular torso. "You can't leave! You cannot leave my sight!" Hades growled out. "What if something happened to you? Took you? I wouldn't be able to live with myself!" Hades' grip went tighter as I felt the terror around him. Fear enveloped my heart of the thought of being taken away from him.

"I'm sorry, Hades, I was just trying to find the Sphere," I whispered.

"Flower, you can't leave me." His hands engulfed my face. "I mean it, you cannot leave my side until we find whoever took you. Please don't do it again."

"I'm not helpless," I bit back. "I have a Wolf now."

"That doesn't mean anything," he argued back. "Gods and angels are out to get you, not supernaturals. They are stronger than them. Now promise me you won't leave again!" Hades growled.

"I promise," I said, whispering in his shoulder.

"Not weak," Elea growled in my head.

"No, we're not. And we will prove it." I replied.

Chapter 53

Ember

"You will not," Hades growled into my hair.

"*Oh shit,*" Elea whispered through me.

"Did, did you just hear me speak to Elea?" My head reared back, looking into Hades. His head tilted to the side.

"What?" He shook his head. "I heard you clear as day, Ember. You will not prove anything. I will keep you safe and you will not have to bring one claw out to protect yourself." My mouth hung open as I took in his words.

"I spoke to Elea in my head. Can you mind-link now?!" I squealed. Hades shook his head as I slumped my shoulders. "*Can you hear me now?*" I concentrated on speaking to him. My lips did not move, while the light bulb went off in his head.

"Kronos, I can hear you," he breathed. My heart leaped for joy that we could mind-link each other. Bonds were as new to me as they were to him; we could speak to one another and have no problem.

"I didn't even have to create one. It happened on its own," he mused as his thumb trailed my cheek. "This is amazing. What a gift this is."

"You mean you can talk to others through a mind-link?"

"Only if I have created them, and even then, it takes a lot of time to secure the bond. It's also one way with demons; they cannot summon me. The only exception is Cerberus because he could keep my secrets." I clapped my hands in excitement while he pulled me closer. "That doesn't excuse that you think you will prove your strength. I know you are strong, Ember, but don't go looking for it. I am a full-blooded god, and nothing is as strong as that."

I grunted as I nodded my head. He was technically correct, but if I had to show my strength, I would. Elea and I haven't trained like the other Wolves in our pack. They have eleven or so years on us, Wolves my age, and just being an Alpha doesn't mean I'm a great fighter. I needed to learn the technicalities of it all. Weapons, dodging using my Wolf skills such a hearing, taste, and smell. I had no training; it was like I was human turned Werewolf -like my mom.

"Alright, I won't go looking for it." I laughed as his cloak hide me from the night air. The air temperature had dropped considerably while we talked. The sun was just on the horizon, about to dip for her slumber, meaning that dinner would be ready soon, along with the giant bonfire and thousands of Wolves prepared to gather.

Our pack was large, the biggest in North America, and also the strongest. If there was a Werewolf king of Earth, dad would be such a king. Everyone wanted alliances with dad, but he was picky. He would often choose smaller packs over the larger ones because of how an Alpha ran his pack. Dad only accepted Alphas with their true mate or second chance; he wouldn't accept a pack that would mate outside of a bond.

Howls were heard in the distance. A tiny ember glowed a thousand yards away. I could smell the fire burning and the pigs being cut into. "I guess we need to make an appearance," I sighed as my thoughts went back to the Sphere.

"We will find it when the time is right. Selene is all about time; you should know this when you grew up and saw people find their mates. As long as the fates play their part, mates will find each other, even with the Sphere being gone." The thick cloud that hung over my heart started to lift. If fate played a role in all of this, this was all supposed to happen. Meaning, people are not missing their mates just yet?

I shook my head; it was all too confusing. If that were the case, I should act as if nothing was wrong, and things should fall in my lap. Something I was not willing to do. "You are certainly more stubborn since we have mated." Hades kissed my temple as he willed us to the bottom of the tree.

"Maybe I got it from you." I poked his chest. "You are leaking all that 'I'm the bad guy, fear me, I do what I want, bishh.'" Throwing his head back and laughing, he willed his cloak off to show nothing but his black dress pants and a deep crimson dress shirt. The first few buttons were unbuttoned, showing off his godly glow.

"And so sassy too," he nipped my ear while my breasts pebbled.

The short distance to the bonfire was met with comfortable silence. His arm was tight around my waist, fearing I would run away from him. That was far from the truth; I wanted nothing more to be by his side. However, these were the people I grew up with.

Familiar faces came to view as I saw my classmates. Many mates beside them while others were still without. The large group came charging towards me, and I stepped forward to speak, but of course, Hades had to go 'Dark Lord' mode.

"Stop," Hades growled while everyone stiffened. One girl dropped her drink in a red cup and splashed a few drops on Hades Italian leather shoes. Her face became beat red as she kneeled to the ground.

"I'm so sorry, forgive me!" Darting away from Hades, I go to help pick her up.

"Sorry, we just mated. He's a bit tense. How are you, Tina?" Tina's eyes brightened as she gave me a hug. I felt Hades' worry through our bond but quickly soothed him with my calming words.

"They are friends, Hades. These Wolves are my family."

"Does not make me any less protective of you, my flower." Hades grabbed my hand and pulled me back to him. My grade school friends had only changed in appearance and not in their humor. Dirty jokes of mating filled the area. Even though my dad made it perfectly clear you should wait to mate, some wolves couldn't. Their animal drive to have pleasure was too intense, especially if a she-wolf was in heat. These were all friends, though, and did it in good fun to help the women out if they wanted it. I personally found it repulsive, but everyone is entitled to their own opinions.

One Wolf my mother warned me about and wanted me to stay away from was Lyle. He was the pack DJ. He was always adorned in black clothing, chains, and piercings. As a child, I found him scary, so I had no desire to talk to him. From the looks of it, Lyle was still mateless and talking up a few of the unmated she-Wolves. He could sniff out a woman that was in heat before she even realized it.

Dad was walking towards Lyle with a determined look and pulled him to his side to speak with him. "Your father said he was going to speak with him; he's the head tracker as of ten years ago. We have come to light that Demeter is the one that took you. If you hadn't wandered off without me, you would have known this." I gasped at the new information.

"Demeter!? Why would she-" Hade's finger came up to my lips.

"Not tonight, flower. We will be having a meeting tomorrow about it. That is all I know, and we aren't doing anything about it tonight." The no-nonsense tone let me know he wasn't kidding. Even I knew when to back off on that tone.

"Your father mentioned he was a bit different. Is he trying to have the Underworld vibe?"

"Did you just say vibe?" I joked.

"Maybe, the slang I have picked up just in this pack alone is deafening." He scoffed.

"I could see that coming; Lyle is said to have a strong nose. He can tell a she-Wolf is about to go in heat." Hades growled as he pulled me closer. "I just finished my heat!"

"I know, but he can probably smell the remnants of it." Lyle looked over and gave a wink while I cupped my mouth with my hand.

"Oops, think he heard you," I said in a sing-song voice while Hades pulled me away.

✳✳✳

The party was in full swing; many drunk wolves and even demons who ended up coming to the party. Hades thought it would be good to bring both Ares and his own demon warriors to surround both the party and the large territory. No one was going to be getting in or out of the area. While the warriors watched, the others drank until their bellies couldn't hold anymore.

Ares danced with Mariah; they both looked ethereal as Ares twirled her in her red dress. Ares was dressed the most casual I had ever seen him. Grey muscle shirt with dark-colored jeans. They both had smiles, and the flickers of light every time they touched could still be seen. I had asked Hades several times if he could see the light around Ares and Mariah, but he just shook his head as he drank his whisky.

At one of the outlying tables, I saw Vulcan tapping his finger on the tablecloth. Vulcan was a god, so of course, he looked handsome but had a rugged look to him. He had one of the longest beards of any god I had seen, and his clothing matched his ruggedness. Tonight, he looked completely different.

His hair was combed back, his beard was trimmed and oiled, making him look nicely groomed. He had taken a razor and cut away stray hairs around his face. Clothing was that of dress pants and a dark brown blazer. He looked like a hot lumber jack! Why was he dressed like that?

Vulcan's eyebrows flew up as he looked through the crowd; the pack doctor, dressed in a jean dress with a black cardigan, was walking up to Vulcan. The look in Vulcan's eyes softened as he stood up from the table and buttoned his blazer. His hand went out to take Tamera's and pulled her close into his chest. The same flickering of light when their skins touched brightened and dimmed all the same when they lost touch.

I stuttered.

"Are you all right?" Hades linked me. I nodded as I held his hand.

"Yes, I think so. I think... I think Vulcan found his mate." Looking up at Hades, he frowned.

"No one can find their mates right now, not with the Sphere missing and away from Selene. Why would you think Vulcan found his mate?"

"I think Ares has found his mate too. When their hands touch they glow. I see it. Then when I reach out to feel their emotions, it is so strong. It's overwhelming. I have to block it off." Hades tapped his glass with his finger as he stared at Vulcan. His eyes never left Tamera's as he grabbed food from the buffet table.

"Do you think you can sense a bond between people?"

"I'm not sure. Their emotions are just strong. It is the same when I think of us. Overwhelming, and I can handle ours. Theirs, I cannot. Maybe it is because it is not meant for me to know."

Hades and I both sat at our table. Wolves and demons were too engrossed in the party to realize who the party was for. The intermingling of laughs and applause while demons did tricks for small audiences made me smile as they all stayed in this little bubble of happiness.

My own parents had taken me to the dance floor several times to dance with them, even with their lack of alcohol. They were so in love, and their worries about me had faded away now that I was back home.

The danger was still around us, but it felt good that we were in a small bubble of time where nothing else mattered. My family was here, my pack and my mate.

Dante hovered around the buffet table, never joining in on the fun. His eyes were distant as I felt his emotions. He was still wracked with guilt, but now there was something else he was longing for. A mate. Seeing his older sister had to strike a spark in him. Now that I was home, he could go do that. His eyes darted from our parents to

Vulcan and Ares and their partners, who all held each other as a slow song had started.

Lyle played his DJ equipment, shooting glances at the new couples dancing. Demons had caught the eyes of the she-Wolves, but the hesitation was there. Demons looked menacing; they had tales, red skin, and horns that grew out of their head. The attraction was still there, though; I saw it in at least two she-wolves' eyes.

One Wolf stepped forward, walking towards a tall demon. He had to be 7 feet tall. Her eyes fluttered as I saw her lips move. The music was too loud, and my hearing wasn't trained, but I swore I heard her ask for a dance. The demon's tail swayed quickly, and his hand extended as that light glowed between their palms.

"GODS!" I whispered yelled as Hades pulled me tighter.

"What is it?" Hades panicked as he looked over the crowd.

"That demon! That she-wolf, her name is...." I hit my head a few times with my palm. "Laura! That's it, Laura! Their hands, Hades! They glow when they touch too!" Hades let out a breath as his hand ran down his face.

"Maybe you are just seeing things," he muttered, and I shot an evil look.

"They are mates, I feel it. Are there others? Come on!" I pulled Hades through the crowd while he mumbled under his breath. Several more demons were becoming bolder in asking the opposite species to dance. Some cowered away while others hesitantly took their hands. Ten couples, there were ten that had the glow. The emotions were as powerful as Ares and Vulcans.

"Mates," I whispered again. "Mates!"

We have to find the Sphere, all these pairs. They were all here because I was taken. The fates had a funny way of having soulmates meet. My short time of suffering led to all these couples finding each other. They could have met another way; it was possible. Still, destiny had a way of working it all out.

"My flower, will you forget about everyone else and just think of me?" Hades eyes traveled to my mark that was poking through my white blouse. I had been worried all this time about everyone else; I had ignored my mate during the whole party.

I noticed he had been clingy since I left to go to the treehouse alone. I didn't mean to upset him, just wanted to help. Hades had saved me, and I wanted to help him. "I'm sorry, Hades." I laid my head on his chest. "I just want everyone to be happy." Hades' chuckle sounded of gravel as he held me close.

"And I only want one person happy, that is you." He tipped my chin to his lips as he kissed me softly. "Now, dance with me." Hades gripped my lower back with both his hands. My arms automatically wrapped around his neck as he swayed with me. The whites of his eyes blackened as he ground his erection into me. "You are too worried about everyone around you; why not worry about me?" His graveled voice let me know he was not playing around; he was upset.

"I'm just trying to help," Hades growled again, his blonde hair darkening while his facial features changed. He had turned back into his human-like form with his dark hair, dark stubble, and pointed features. As much as I loved his true self, this form would still give me shivers of the memory of our first time meeting each other.

He was frightening-looking, yet peace had surrounded me at the same time. The menacing look he gave Malachi, the angel that tried to buy me. The resounding number he placed on my head to take me home from danger made me shiver. Now, it made me feel light with butterflies to waste such money on some lonely soul like mine.

"What are you thinking?" Hades' finger traced my temple with his index finger. It swept down to my jaw to my neck and straight down the scepter tattoo on my chest. The jolt that shook my heart as he touched it made my insides quiver.

"The first time we met, how scared yet, intrigued I was." Hades chuckled as his erection swept past my hip. The height difference was humorous.

"I remember." His lips kissed my forehead as he ducked down lower to meet my lips. "You were as frightened as a lamb." The music must have sped up because Wolves around us were moving their bodies faster. However, the only music I heard was the whispers of Hades' words.

"And you were the hunter, seeking out its prey." Hades' hands traveled down my side as his body dipped lower, making sure to touch every part as his hips rode past my core.

"I got my prey. I conquered it in just a fortnight with my tongue, and then again with my cock just four nights ago." My fingers gripped his shoulders as his lips trailed my neck. My legs wanted nothing but to part for him, have himself sink his body into mine as we made love under the stars. I craved him like the cat craves the saucer of milk. Hades' smile was felt as he buried his mouth into my shoulder.

"Your wish is my command." As the smoke covered us, keeping out the remaining light of the fire.

Vera Foxx

Chapter 54

Hades

I was angry.

More than angry, I was furious.

I wanted nothing more than to destroy every living thing in this pack. Still, it would only bring unhappiness to Ember, my mate. I kept it in; I reined in all my fury for her. Her family was tolerable. They were happy to see her. Who wouldn't be? She was a delicate flower, my flower that I didn't want to share and only hide her in my darkness where only she would shine for me.

But that is selfish. I was selfish.

After finishing a chess game with Dante, her brother, who was now on my "don't fuck up again" list, Wesley pulled me to the side while the others went to refill their glasses. I shouldn't be a damn hypocrite about Dante messing up. It was a terrible domino effect that affected my mate. Every decision everyone else made, made her suffer. It all angered me to no end. I wanted to curse the fates.

"Listen, Hades. We found out some crucial information about the fairy that Dante told us about. We didn't mention it earlier since Ember didn't look to be in the mood to listen." Ember had been squirming in my lap the entire time we had visited with her extended family. There was an itch she wanted to scratch, and I didn't know what it was. She didn't want to talk about Dante's poor decision of not telling his parents of the woodland Fairy. She tried to move on, and her parents gladly did so when her nose scrunched up in disgust as Dante showed his guilt yet again. She was doing it for his sake, but the conversation wasn't nearly over, just over for her.

"We know who the Fairy is."

I narrowed my eyes as I pulled Wesley by his collar closer to me. "And you are just now telling me? You should have said something sooner." Wesley gulped, trying to pull my hands away, but I was a ticking time bomb. Ember and I were recently mated, and now I had to deal with her family. I was used to being alone. Even while alone in a cabin with Ember for a few fantastic days, I wanted more. In fact, I needed her now. Letting go of Wesley, he rubbed his neck.

"I'm sorry, Hades. Ember looked overwhelmed, and I'm looking out for my daughter," Wesley growled. "She's been through enough, and if she didn't want to talk about it right then, I wasn't going to." I nodded my head.

"Your right," I mumbled. Wesley stood back with his eyes furrowed.

"Ember has been through a lot. We will discuss it tomorrow. Just give me the name," I prodded. Wesley sighed and ran his hand through his messy hair.

"Demeter." My eyes whipped to Wesley's. I looked him up and down to see if he was lying, but he only shook his head. "Vulcan confirmed it." The black smoke started to flow through me, and the fire in my eyes reflected into Wesley's.

That snake of a woman. She chose a Fairy form as not to alert me of her presence. The ward protected the pack, it kept the lesser supernaturals out, but it did not keep out gods if they were invited into the territory. I'm going to kill her.

"Anyone want some cheesecake?" Charlotte walked in with a large platter of various flavors while she looked around. "Where is Ember?" The smoke stopped flowing from me as I turned to look at Charlotte. My eyes still glowed red as Ember's family shook in fear.

"Where. Is. She?" I growled out. My breath began to heave as I closed my eyes to find her. She wasn't far, near the woods; I felt her through the bond. In a flash, I had transported myself to her side.

She had been searching in the treehouse.

That damn Sphere, I sighed as I pulled my platinum hair. It was going to be the death of me. Even during her heat, she would bring it up. I didn't give a damn about it right now. All my thoughts and cravings were her and her alone. We would find it in time. I knew we would.

When she spoke to her Wolf proving herself, I wanted to show her that I was all she needed. Not one claw did I want her to lift to protect herself. She suffered enough, and I wanted to be her everything; I wanted to make those who try and take her away from me pay, just like Malachi, Persephone, and Demeter.

As the party continued, Ember continued talking about mates and some glow she saw. I had no doubt she was seeing something, but I saw nothing. Nothing but serving demons now dancing amongst the party. I should command them to get back to what they were meant for, but Ember was too engrossed in how both Wolves and demons intermingled with each other.

That damn glow. Could Ember see a mate bond, a thread of something that should be there? Her empath abilities could help her see if the emotion is strong enough. But hell, I didn't care about that.

Ember's mind wandered again as she pulled me through the crowds. I was happy she was at least pulling me through the crowd and not leaving me. Jealousy swelled in my chest as I saw Lyle. He was constantly staring at Ember, whether she knew or not, but it was enough to make my blood boil. On top of others seeking her attention, I had enough.

Asking her to dance, pulling her close to me had only sated some of my possessiveness over her. Her heat against my upper thigh had pulled me into a trance. I wanted nothing more than to sink myself into her cavern. To taste her, to make her feel like she was in the high heavens all over again.

Then her thoughts came to me; they were there so loud it made me want to chuckle. Ember really did not have any control over her mind-linking; it was almost adorable. Once dirty thoughts entered her mind, my cock twitched, already painfully hard, as I felt the swell of her breasts brush against my body.

How mad would she be if I did her right here, in front of the massive fire around her family and friends? To let them know that a god had her, that she would always be mine and I would never allow her to go? My grip on her waist tightened as I bent lower, deliberately rubbing my cock against her core. With the rhythm of the music, no one would have seen this as obscene.

Blackness evaded her eyes as I felt her lust through our bond. No more playing, no more sharing, for right now, I wanted nothing but her. The smoke gathered around us as I placed my lips on hers. Her lips parted, letting me taste the sweet taste of the strawberries she had just eaten. Her strawberry blonde hair swirled around us as I saw several onlookers peering on in fright.

I willed us to a small clearing in the forest, a queen-sized mattress with blankets, pillows, and nothing but the stars to watch what wicked things I would do to her. Creating a ward, so no man, Wolf, or demon could see us, I continued to kiss her as I backed her up to a nearby tree. The bark was smooth, nothing that would catch her clothes, not that it would matter because I would rip them to pieces anyway.

"Hades," she moaned as my open-mouth kisses went down her neck. My gods' mark, the scepter, glowed as I licked between her breasts. Her nipples pebbled underneath her white laced bra. I groaned, appreciating her reaction to my touch. This would never get old; this would always be the high I was seeking.

Wrapping my hand around her neck, I gave it a slight squeeze while her breasts curved out, begging for me to take them in my mouth. Pulling her right leg up to my thigh and digging my erection into her pussy I growled. "You will not go looking for trouble, will you, Ember?" She squirmed as my cock rubbed her clit between our clothes. "I will always look after you; I will kill whoever dare touches what is mine."

Ember's breath hitched as I pushed her hands above her head and locked both wrists in place. My mouth ripped her lace bra down as I captured her nipple. "Mine," I mumbled. "Not any male or female; you are mine just as I am yours."

Thoughts of Wolves staring at her, staring at what was given to me by Selene made my blood curdle in my veins. Lyle was one of them, the way he slinked his eyes over her body as Ember talked with her friends. She didn't see it, but I did. The lip licking, the adjustment of his pants that he made, infuriated me, and I could do nothing.

Because a pack is a family.

I bit down on Ember's nipple, and she let out a sweet cry of pleasure and pain. Letting her hands go, I swept her to the mattress. We both landed with blankets and pillows falling off to the ground. My shirt was willed off before she could touch me as I pulled down her jeans. Her pussy was glistening with the dew of a morning flower. Its sweetness was begging for me to lick its petals as I rubbed my nose in her pollen exotic pollen.

Taking a large breath and parting her thighs to where I could see every part of her. Licking her honeysuckle, I flicked her nub as her hands came to my hair. Pulsing my face further into her cavern. I slapped her thigh that caused her to whimper.

"Don't make me tie you up," I rumbled through my chest. "What if I wanted you to?" Her voice was breathy as I smelled more of her scent invade my nose. Her essence glistened on my face as my eyes met hers.

"Fuck, Ember," I growled as I willed ropes to her wrists, planted firmly above her head. My cock strained again through my pants as my face dove back down to her pussy. Her hips continued to rock as she broke through her pleasure. Her scream would have driven out every forest animal in the area if there had not been a ward over us.

Licking her thighs clean, her breaths slowed. Once finished, Ember kept the ropes on her wrists and pinned me to the bed in one swift motion. She captured my own wrists with her hands still roped together as she sat on my cock. The jolt of pleasure was felt between my toes as she began to rock me slowly. Her hips played a dance as she ground herself into me. Ember was listening to the beat of her own music as she rounded my cock with her hips. The sweet torture was killing me as she let go of my wrists and began to play with her breasts. The rope scraped her breasts, leaving tiny scratches on her skin.

"Sensational," I whispered as I tried to guide my hand to touch her glorious globes. Slapping my hands, she giggled. "No touching." I groaned as I palmed her ass, moving her slightly faster. Her body began to quicken and slow down, teasing the life out of me. Breasts were bouncing as I tried to keep my hands off them.

"Enough," I growled. As I flipped Ember over with my cock still buried inside her. I would explode any minute, and I didn't want any of my essence to be spilled from her body. My muscles in my back tightened as Ember's legs pulled me impossibly closer. My dick disappeared and reappeared only slightly as she pulled me back in.

A roar left my throat; I felt my fangs itch, a feeling I had never felt before. My body wanted me to bite her, but I wasn't even a Wolf. It wasn't something gods do. Sensing my turmoil, Ember pulled on my neck. "Bite me," without a second thought, my teeth bit into her tender flesh as we both spasmed.

Claws extended from my fingers without warning; I felt the hair stand up on my neck as I felt the meat of my mate in my jaws. "Ohhh," Ember moaned as her legs dropped beside my hips. My dick throbbed a few times before spreading more of my seed into her.

"Did I hurt you?" I panted. Ember's eyes were half hooded as she looked up to me.

"Just the opposite," she giggled as she pushed back some of the hair on my forehead. "That was something else. I didn't know sex could be this satisfying."

"Only with me," purred in my throat.

"Did you just purr?" Ember smiled as she caressed my chest. I tried to make the sound again, but it never showed.

"Must be involuntary; I can't do it again." Ember sighed as I pulled out and lay next to her.

"It was sexy. If you can figure out to do it again, I won't mind." Ember's body cuddled up to me. I felt the cum leaking from her body as she did so. The only thing that would make it more satisfying is that my seed would take root to give her our child.

"Hades, your thoughts are loud too," Ember's finger tickled my chest as my breathing slowed. "We can work on it together. Please stop thinking about children. We have Blaze and Cerberus to look after. If we want, we can adopt. I love you, and I will never want anything more than you." I leaned over to kiss her forehead tenderly. Only she knew of the right things to say. Only she could make me feel like a true King to a world that was full of darkness. Only Ember could be my light to my world.

"I just want you happy. Just don't defy me and look for trouble." Ember gasped as she held her hand to her chest.

"Me! Never!" Mockingly, she hit me on the chest as we both laughed, staring at the stars.

It was a crisp night, not a cloud in the sky. If one went to the highest mountain in the area, one could see for hundreds of miles. The one thing that would make this night better would be the light sprites that Bergarian has. They look like little lights that hang around the forest to light the way for small woodland creatures.

I would take her there, have a long vacation with just me and her. Ember snuggled up next to me as she hummed in contentment. As we were about to fall asleep, she jolted awake and groaned.

"Mom wants us to come back," she slapped her hand down her face. "People are looking for us," I growled out again as Ember laughed again. "Sorry, I've been gone a while. They just miss me and are curious about you. Most of them are afraid-"

"They should be afraid, terrified, and leave me the fuck alone." I growled.

"Hades!" she squealed. "Just be nice to my parents, alright? That's all I ask." My face reddened as I nodded. "You have been nice, haven't you?" I nodded my head again as I got up to will us some new clothes.

"You are lying! I can feel it! And the guilt! What did you do?" She hissed.

"Nothing! I did nothing." I willed Ember a beautiful blue dress with a matching cardigan, but that didn't deter the questioning.

"I might have grabbed your dad by the collar to question him about a few things." Ember rolled her eyes while I stood back. I hadn't seen Ember mad before, and she was as terrifying as me. Her cheeks reddened, and I swear I saw steam seep into the ground.

"You will apologize!" She snapped.

"I already did!" I pleaded. Ember sat back a moment to contemplate my words. The cute curl of her smile had me melting over again.

"Aw, I'm proud of you!" She cooed as she twirled in her dress. "Thank you for the dress!"

Kronos, what the hell was that?

Chapter 55

Ember

Hades willed us back to the bonfire, just by the tree line. Mom had her arms crossed as she scanned the crowd. Hades put his hand on my lower back as we walked closer to her, and as soon as she saw us, she came in for a death hug.

"Ember, you can't just leave like that." Mom's shoulder sagged as her grip loosened.

"I was with Hades, Mom. I won't wander off. Besides, I think there is enough protection with Wolves, demons, and Ares' men, don't you think?" Mom let out a sigh as she rubbed my arms. Mom had been through a lot. She had her own struggles when she was younger, and she was worried about me. I just wanted her to be happy now that I was home and safe.

"You're right, I just... I just... can't bear to keep you out of my sight. Not that we just got you back." Mom petted my hair and gave Hades a grateful nod.

"I'll often be visiting. Mom don't worry. When all this 'missing god' stuff is over, I'll spend two weeks with you, and then we can catch up on everything!" Hades groaned as he pinched his nose. Mom laughed at Hades while patting my hand.

"We will see; Hades looks like he needs to get back to his duties as well. Besides the first few years with your mate is very important. The bond strengthens every day, and neither of you will want to be apart from each other for too long. I now realize that; the rest of your siblings will understand too."

A loud roar came from the fire as one of the Witches threw in some exploding dust. As a child, I remembered the different magical clouds of dust they had provided for parties. Some would turn the fire purple, blue, and gold, while other dust would make music sounds from the land in Bergarian. It was a sound portal, and we could hear the laughter on the other side as people played their own music in their realm. Young pups went closer to the fire to listen to the whispers of the different domain; they talked frantically as they heard the talk about the benevolent Clara and her beast of a mate.

Rumors spread quickly that he could form a half beast and held it for days on end while he went to rescue the future queen. A feat no Werewolf could do except if they were destined to be royal.

As the dust settled and the children departed, I saw a blue glow in the center of the fire. It was small, almost too small to see, but it was there. Dad talked to Hades, no doubt about tomorrow's meeting, to discuss finding Demeter and questioning her. Still, my eyes continued to gaze deeper into the fire.

The round ball glistened as the red and orange flames consumed it. Large flames protruded from the area, flames that reached as high as the tallest trees. Bonfires were not to be taken lightly around these parts. Whole trees would be cut to maintain an intense glow.

Curiosity was getting the best of me as I dropped Hades' hand. His eyebrow raised in question, and when I pointed to the fire, he nodded to finish his conversation as I crept closer. The heat of the fire was intense; if a pup got too close, they would burn their hair. I didn't feel the burn like I used to as a child; in fact, it felt incredible. My hand reached out to try and grab the blue glow in the middle of the fire. However, it was further in the ashes than I thought. A flame whipped by my hair, which should have caught ablaze itself, but it didn't.

The wind blew again, causing the flames to touch my skin; all that was felt was the breeze and not the warmth of the flame. A tapping on my shoulder broke me from my thoughts as Blaze looked up with his bright eyes. His wings fluttered as he sat on my shoulder. "It won't hurt you," Blaze purred. I went to question, but he nodded towards the fire and flew off to sit with Dante.

The blue sparkle shimmered again. It beckoned me once more as it flashed its true brilliance. I felt like a crow who wanted to collect the shiny things and put them in a collection. Glancing over my shoulder Hades wasn't far, just speaking with my parents as I acted like the curious child.

Placing one step into the ashes, I felt my foot aglow with tiny prickles. There was no pain, no burning, just the wind the flames created. Stepping another foot into the circle just past the rocks that contained the fire, the wind engulfed my body as the fire tickled my skin. Taking a large breath, my hands began to reach inside the center of the fire. A few muted screams were heard, but that did not deter me from my mission. To find the flickering blue amongst the orange flames.

Five steps inward, I saw a small pebble, odd in shape, as I bent to pick it up. Beneath the ash, it gave it a blue-like appearance. Still, on close inspection, it had sparkles inside along with tiny movements of grey and deep blue matter.

Standing up, I saw Wolves and demons standing in front of the fire, all horrified and looking on in shock. A hand trailed around my waist, and his sparks filled my very soul. "My flower, are we trying to show off today? What gave you the urge to come in here?" I looked back down at the pebble in my hand; it was misshapen and deformed. Something so beautiful you would think would be a gem.

Hades lifted it from my hand and studied it carefully. His eyes narrowed as he looked closely at the small movements inside. "Kronos," he breathed as his head whipped back to mine. "You found it," he whispered again as the fire around us ceased to exist. The sudden extinction of the fire granted everyone a shiver.

Hades led me out of the ash, arm firmly planted on my waist, and shoved the pebble in his pocket. *"Breathe no word of this,"* he mind-linked me. *"It is of the utmost importance."* I gripped his cloak as we stepped over the stones that contained the fire. His one hand raised, and the flames came to a roar again while the music began to play.

"What were you thinking?" Dad ran up to me. Before he could reach me, a loud crack came from the DJ stand, and a spear came howling through the flames, hitting Hades in the shoulder. Hades fell backward but caught himself as he pulled the spear from his shoulder quickly. Black liquid fell from his wound as I began to panic.

Another loud howl came through the fire again, this time aiming straight towards me. Hades tried to pull me aside, but the shock of his own wound left him confused. A red-skinned demon darted right in front of me as Hades finally pulled me away. The demon fell to the ground, gasping for air, holding the spear that was directly in his chest.

Warriors scrambled to the noise source; the growls and roars of Wolves were heard on the other side of the large fire. Dad had already shifted while Mom got in front of Hades and me. Hades grasped his shoulder and pulled me close. "Get her out of here," Mom screamed until the gasping from the demon who saved my life said my name. "Ember!" The gurgle of blood sputtered as he reached for me. It was Loukas.

"Loukas!" I screamed for him as I fell to the ground. Hades fingers turned bright white as he began to cauterize his wound.

"I.. tried..." Loukas sputtered again. "I tried to get here...fast." The panic in his voice and the fading of light in his eyes gripped me. I pulled him closer to hug him, to let him know everything was going to be okay. His blood stained the royal blue dress that I wore.

"It's Okay! You are going to be okay!" I petted his dark hair between his horns. "You saved my life, Loukas," I whispered. Loukas gently shook his head. The panic ensued as the Wolves transformed, children running to the hidden safe zones of the territory.

Hades grasped my shoulder. "We must go. Say what you need to say, Loukas." Hades' voice was harsh as he glared into Loukas's black eyes. Blood continued to pool from his wound.

"Malachi was in the Underworld. He entered using the helm. He's looking for Ember. She's key to the Sphere," Loukas's voice was fading as he continued to spit out blood. My hand was clutching Loukas's, but it was loosening; his fear became peace as he slowly slipped from my grasp.

"Loukas!" I screamed. Hades picked me up and covered me in his cloak as his hands turned black as fire raised from his fingertips.

"Enough!" Hades roared as the bonfire was extinguished once again, and a fire prison was extended over the DJ stand with Lyle. The Wolves trapping Lyle behind the table transformed back into their human forms.

"What is this?!" my dad roared as he approached Lyle. His slicked-back hair was now a mess, but the devilish smirk didn't evade him.

"I don't know what you are talking about, Alpha? His voice went smooth.

"Don't play games, Lyle. Did you throw the spears?" Mom walked up to my father and gripped Dad's arm. She gave a disappointed glance while Lyle shrugged his shoulders.

"I did. And for a good reason!" He pointed his finger at Dad, who only used his Alpha growl to make him submit. Lyle was now face down in the dirt with his neck bared. My cries were drowning out the gasps as people gathered around Lyle; he had been with the pack for many years, and this sudden outburst of betrayal hurt many.

"Loukas," I whispered as I tried to grab his hand. Hades pulled me up and pushed me to his chest.

"My Little Flower, always one for the dramatics? Hmm?" He chuckled. I sniffed while looking up at him. Petting my hair, he kissed my forehead. "He's one of my demons; I can regenerate him if I so choose, remember? He's just a drama queen, putting on some show to make you like him."

I dried my tears with the back of my hand. "That's mean!" I grumbled. Loukas' body stilled and suddenly reduced to nothing but ash. I sighed, at least he was Okay.

"Yes, well, if you think that's mean, just wait what I'm going to do now." Hades sauntered over to my dad holding me tightly. Dad was still nude after his shift, so I adverted my eyes while my mom pulled me close to her. Hade glades glared at Lyle.

"May I?" The question hung in the air as Hades spoke to dad. It wasn't a question if Hades could do anything; it was a statement. Hades was being polite in his own way standing in front of dad's pack. Dad only growled in agreement, stepping way.

The fiery cage that was around Lyle was waved away as Hades snapped his fingers. Three demons, giant demons that were as scary as the palace dungeon keepers, held onto him. Lyle was a tracker, not the strongest in the pack but more substantial than your average human. The demons didn't flinch as they held him on either side of Lyle's arms. The third demon stood behind him with one hand around his neck.

"Speak, for it may be your last time in doing so." Hades' darkness filled the air with tension. The once clear sky clouded with darkness. Wolves were waved to go home while the warriors stayed and gathered around the area. Lyle only gave half a smile, and the demon behind him instantly adjusted his grip.

Lyles' face turned red as the lack of oxygen wrecked his body. Hades held in his hand the spear that was thrown. It was small, three feet long, with a sharp, black metal at its end. Red markings were written on the most vital point.

"Do tell me, what is this? You have my full attention." Hades' voice boomed. Cyrene neared our group as she held the other spear in her hand where Loukas had fallen.

"Strong, new magic," Cyrene whispered.

"New?" I questioned.

"Magic evolves just as life does. It grows, evolves to adapt just like life. Animals evolve to work with their surroundings, just like the birds of the Galapagos Islands. This magic has evolved to deal with higher beings, that of gods."

Hades turned to Cyrene as his cloak moved along the ground. His fists tightened. "Your spear may have wounded me but a moment, but it did not stop me. What magic was placed on the point?" Lyle continued to shake his hung head as the demon's grip loosened for him to talk.

Hades chuckled as he stepped forward. His fingers pulled up Lyle's chin as he bent forward to inspect his face. "You like the darkness? The blackness that you wish that would surround you?" Lyle's chains clanked together as the demons held a better stance.

"Then you shall have it." Hades stood back up, hands behind his back. "I'm not a patient god. Alpha Wesley, may I use your dungeons?" Again, it wasn't a question, just a formality for Hades to play nice.

"Of course, Hades. Anything that you may need on this territory is at your discretion." Hades chuckled as he grabbed my hand while we walked to the packhouse dungeons.

Chapter 56

Hades

I gripped Ember's hand tighter as I led her close to me, side by side, where she would be on our thrones. Forever we would be equals, and I planned to show her that as soon as the threat had passed. Hypocritical? Maybe. I wasn't going to take chances and test the fates right now. I'm going to make sure she is safe, as well as her pack that she is so fond of. I internally sighed at the thought of that.

Ember gripped me tighter as three of my guards ruffed up Lyle. Their massive stature stunned the Wolves of the group surrounding us, never seeing such a sight. Maybe some of the unmated Wolves would keep the grubby paws and perverted eyes away from my mate. I didn't care they were looking; I would burn their eyes right from the sockets.

The heaviness in Luna Charlotte's heart was evident; this Wolf, Lyle, had been a part of the pack for a long while, even when Charlotte first joined the pack. From Alpha Wesley's explanation earlier, he was promoted to lead tracker not but a few days before Ember's disappearance, something that perked my interest. The weapon throwing, which was an awful shot, by the way, and his duty as a lead tracker to find Ember was almost too much. The evidence stacked against him; if only with his puny throw of a spear, he had a death warrant.

He wouldn't survive this night.

The spear that had struck me, just a mere six inches from my queen, was constructed of both dogwood and black metal I had never seen. A red inscription was written on the arrow, most likely Latin that I would have Cyrene figure out. Many believe there is but one type of Latin, but there are several dialects that help you summon. Latin was originated in Rome, and as it spread through different countries, its words became branched, creating their own magical language. Latium Malifecia was thus then created. Imagine those who spoke Latin every day calling upon demons and deities in their everyday life. It would be almost comical.

I was not familiar with this Malifecia, this Latium dialect, because I don't deal with the magic of this kind. Of course, the one person I needed was Hecate, and she was still missing. I rubbed my chin at the thought if she might have any part of this. Not willingly, of course, but that of force.

Hecate doesn't create the magic; she just handles it justly. If magic deems too strong, she shelters it, conceals it for a better time, but this magic has gotten out of control. With just a fraction of a second of it being pierced into my hide, I felt its power. It was more potent than any power that I had felt previously in all my awakened days.

My power weakened in an instant as I felt the burn in my shoulder. Pulling it out only caused a black sludge to pour from the wound. My power completely regenerated as the rest of the sludge leaked from it. I can heal quickly, but this took me a good ten seconds, which is highly rare for me, a god. I was the strongest yet; could it be possible this was how both Selene, Hecate, and Hermes had been captured?

Gritting my teeth, we all formed a small train to the packhouse; Wesley led the caravan as my demons continued to prod their claws into Lyle. I could smell their want to spill his blood; they never get to torture many of that of the living. I internally smirked, not to offend Charlotte, who was rubbing her hands in worry.

Ember continued to walk with me, head held high while her brother, Dante, was on her side. His anger towards the tracker was compelling, almost heroic; he was the first to pounce the bastard before I willed the cage around him. He may be of some good to this pack after all.

"It's down this way," Wesley spoke sternly as he opened the double doors. The stagnant air blew outward, causing the greasy hair of Lyle to flip to its side.

"I'll stay out here," Charlotte stuttered. She rubbed her ribcage, no doubt feeling the phantom scar from her tortured days due to my insolence.

"It would be for the best, Luna." I nodded toward her. "In fact, if you would be so kind, I am summoning Loukas as we speak. He will need a room, and Cyrene will need to cast a boundary spell for him. I don't want him to be able to leave the room. Can you have her find out the meaning of the words on the spear. Would that be doable?"

Charlotte sighed in relief. "It would be my pleasure, more up to my speed." She bowed as she nodded to Ember.

My eyes glanced down at my mate, who was already looking up at me with a determined look in her eyes. "I'm coming with you," she demanded. Opening my mouth to speak, she stomped her foot as if she was a child.

"I am your mate; I have been made for this. Alpha blood runs through my veins, and I will come down there." As hard as she may, her bottom lip jutted out. I wanted nothing more than to kiss her maliciously, but with her father just beside me, I doubt he would appreciate it.

"*I will not be merciful,*" I mind linked. "*Lyle will be tortured, and he will die.*" Ember relaxed her shoulders as she held firm.

"*You are God of the Underworld; would I expect anything less?*" Her eyes held playfulness while she folded her arms, raising her breasts. I knew what I would rather be doing right now, but I would have to settle on my second favorite thing to do.

Ares and Vulcan stood by the doorway, both with their 'mates,' as Ember called them. I had yet to fully believe this notion but would play along with the idea. "Ares, Vulcan, be sure we are not disturbed. Have our warriors work with the Wolves, secure the border and be on high alert. This could just be a distraction." Ares bowed his head as he motioned for Mariah, who was still in her Wolf form, to follow. The strongest female warrior and the God of War, I suppose it makes sense.

Wesley's dungeons were utterly bare; not one prisoner, alive, was there. The only thing left was a pile of bones in the first cell. The skull had missing fangs that were now lying beside it. "Roman, Charlotte's foster father," Wesley grunted. "A reminder to keep my family safe. Obviously, it wasn't enough for Ember." His head pointed towards Ember, who was still staring at the empty cells, not paying attention.

Lyle growled, trying to escape the demons. Forcing a shift with demons would be suicide. My warriors were equipped to deal with supernaturals. The bones in their hands were partly made of silver and metal, while the blood that flows through them held hints of dogwood oil. Enough to maim a Wolf and kill a vampire.

Lyle was thrown into the last cell. It was large enough for both Wesley and me to stand in. My guards picked him back up to set him on the table that kept Lyle at a 45-degree angle. I brushed my hands together as the excitement flowed through my veins. This was it; this was my time to shine. Show just how powerful I really am to this pathetic Wolf that eyed my mate.

Unfortunately, I needed answers, and the answers I sought meant he would have to remain alive a bit longer.

Wesley tightened the restraints; the silver hardly burned his skin as he latched the fourth one around Lyle's ankle. They burned Lyle's skin with blisters and burning flesh. Ember and her brother stood just outside of the cell, both stoic as they held onto each other.

"This will be a good lesson," Wesley spoke to no one in particular. "To show my children how cruel the world can be, and those evils will be caught and punished." I hummed in agreement as I let one giant claw extend from my index finger. Quickly ripping his black mesh shirt in half, his white skin was sickly, especially for a Wolf. Does he track anything with skin so pale? Not once has his skin seen the sun. Wesley must have been thinking the same thing as he growled within his chest.

"I want everything," I bent down to whisper in his ear. The darkness of the cell to loomed with a dark haze. Ember and Dante faded far into the background; no one was here but Wesley, Lyle, and I. I could not let my feelings for my mate get in the way. Her life was in danger, and I wasn't about to lose my mate.

My claw scraped across his chest, deep enough for the blood to pebble around the wound. "And I mean, everything." The fire burned bright in my eyes, and the cocky attitude that was once fierce in his spirit died right then. Did he not think the Dark Lord would do nothing?

"I... I'm sorry!" Lyle stuttered. "I thought I was helping!" My eyebrow raised as I pulled a bit of my blonde hair. Wesley's Wolf came to the surface as his own eyes turned a bright amber.

"Pray tell, what do you even mean?" I growled lowly. "That I would want you to spear me in my damn chest!" I yelled in his face. Small bits of lightning came from the smoke surrounding us. My fury had been held back, and I was losing every bit of myself.

"She told me you didn't want her anyway. That you refused her when she was born! She said you would appreciate it if I concealed it, and you would reward me handsomely by making me one of your own guards." My jaw ticked.

"What?" I whispered. My hand reached for his neck as I clutched it tightly. "Who spoke this to you? Whose lips and tongue will I cut out with a dull blade and put on the hot plate of desolation?" Lyle shivered as my hot breath bathed over his face.

"She came to me...in the woods." Wesley gripped onto the table. My guards wanted to restrain him, but this was his Wolf. A Wolf that betrayed his own pack, over what? To try and be one of my guards? Pathetic.

"Name," I growled again as my grip loosened. Lyle shook his head quickly, and my hand gripped his wrist, breaking it instantly. His scream filled the cell while Wesley grabbed the other, and the same snap echoed through the hallway. Hmm, I might like this game.

"Demeter!" he cried. "Demeter!"

Ahh, and the name comes up again. "Were you trying to hit Ember or me?" My hand gripped his upper arm and squeezed; another crack ripped through the cell as Wesley did the same to the other arm.

"EMBER!" he yelled out again; his chest was heaving. Four broken bones, rather significant, and he couldn't even heal himself with the silver.

Pity.

"I took you in as a pup, and this is how you repay your Alpha?!" Wesley's Wolf let out a roar as his claws gripped Lyle's neck. The grip tightened, nails puncturing the back of Lyle's neck as blood dripped down the back of the table.

"Enough, Remus," I hissed. "We still need more information, then you can have some fun with your traitor." As much as I wanted to torture this pup, Wesley needed his time. I would get Lyle in the Underworld, and I had much more range of torture down there than up here. Wesley looked like he needed a good release.

"You tell me everything. Start to finish. Leave one thing out, and well, you know what will happen." Ember could tell a lie when she heard one; she would let me know if he was or not. Lyle nodded his head frantically as Remus raised a brow. I waved my hand for him to calm down. Remus would have his revenge.

The tears left Lyle's face, and his black eyeliner pooled on his collarbone. The chains that he hung with pride around his pants now pooled at the bottom of his ankles. My guards took no chances; they ripped him of anything that he could use as a weapon or a means of escape.

"Alpha was talking about making me lead tracker," he breathed. "The night Ember was taken, Demeter came to me. I didn't know who she was at first, but she wore a lot of green, blonde hair, brown eyes, but I knew she was a god, she glowed. She had this dominating aura that had me on my knees." Wesley paced around Lyle like a predator to prey.

"She told me her name, that Ember was Hades' mate. Demeter said Hades didn't want Ember. You found out early who your mate was because Selene was being gracious. You flat out refused your mate, so Demeter wanted to eliminate any signs of Ember finding out and searching for you. Demeter wanted to be a 'good friend' to you, which meant she would take her away. If I made sure that our pack didn't find her that I would be rewarded. I would become one of Hades' guards. I just had to lead everyone the opposite way." Lyle panted again.

Remus ground his teeth and glared at me. "Did you try to reject my pup?"

Well, this turned around into something shitty.

Chapter 57

Ember

Uh oh.

I wasn't expecting this turn of events.

Dad growled as his claws extended. Remus was in control, and I didn't quite understand Remus like I did dad. Mom was the one who calmed him down, and she was far from here. The thought of her coming down here was out of my mind; she hates basements, and for a good reason.

"Dad!" I yelled, but his shorts ripped as his hindquarters sprouted hair. Dad was trying to hold Remus back but to no avail. Hades was a god; I wasn't worried for Hades, just dad's sake. Hades wouldn't really hurt him, rough him up a bit, maybe, but who wants to bring that up at the next holiday party?

"Dad!" I pulled on the silver bars; even if they weren't burning me like an average Wolf, it was still strong. Dante's eyes narrowed at Hades; he was pissed too. I didn't need my empath abilities to tell me that.

"Did you know? Did you know he wanted to reject you?" Dante's voice was stiff, ridged as he bore his judging eyes into Hades.

"I did," I spoke. "And that is something that is between him and me, no one else. Get these bars open now before things are said or done that can't be reversed." Dante's jaw tightened.

"He could have prevented it." Dante waved his hands around. "All of this. If he had just accepted you in the beginning! None of this would have happened!" I shook my head.

"Now is not the time; get these bars open! I swear I'll explain! Now! Please," I begged. I pleaded and even gave him the 'I'm your sister, please help me for once' eyes. Dante's face softened as he glanced back at Hades and Dad.

"Hades would win anyway; it's just a small brawl. I get it though." He took the key from his pocket and unlocked the door. Dad was entirely shifted, in a crouching position to attack. His sandy blond wolf, Remus, bared his teeth, salivating for a bite. Hades wasn't afraid; his posture wasn't even stiff. The sorrow, regret already filled him. Memories of his past caught up with him again. He would let my dad do whatever he wanted to remove the mental anguish and feel the physical pain.

Jumping in front of Hades, I latched onto his waist. "Stop!" I yelled again; my dad paused his steps, surprised to see me stand in front of my mate. Why would I not stand in front of him?

"You still want mate?" Remus mind-linked in his caveman's voice. I gripped onto Hades' torso more.

"More than anything," I replied out loud. "He's already told me we've worked on it on our own. We worked on this. This is between Hades and me, no one else." I felt Hades grip me tight.

"I wronged Ember in the beginning. I know that, and I will always bear the guilt. Ember is too good for me, and yet she decided to stay." Hades' voice was low, unable to hear with human ears. "I'll spend the rest of eternity proving to her how sorry I am. How she suffered because of me, the terrible domino effect it had on her. I'll do anything." Hades took a deep breath as he pulled me close. "Do anything to show her how much I love her."

My eyes pricked with tears; reaching both my arms up around his neck, I pecked the side of his neck. "I love you too, Hades."

Dad stood just feet away. No longer showing his fierce teeth, he backed away slowly, changing instantly back into his human form. "Finish this." Dad waved to Lyle, who had almost been forgotten. Dad opened the cell door and walked alone down the basement hallway.

"Wasn't expecting that bit of information to pop out," I joked.

Hades brushed my hair to the side and kissed my cheek. "Neither was I."

Dante stood leaning on the cell door frame; arms crossed while shaking his head. "I can't say much," he sighed. "I made the wrong decision too, so I can't say much at all. I'm glad you came clean and were honest too." We all stood in silence as we heard Lyle groan.

"I guess we should interrogate him further?" I muttered. Hades gave me a quick peck on the lips and had me stand outside the cell. If he thinks he is hiding the whole torture thing, it doesn't work. I've seen every bit of what he's done; it's not like there is a vast difference between standing beside the whole thing or being on the outside.

Dante and I watched as Hades and his demons extracted every bit of information out of Lyle. He became difficult after spilling Hades' own personal details about a rejection. It must have been a ploy to deter the torturing or bade time for what is yet to come.

The torturing and screaming lasted for hours, and once it was all said and done, you couldn't recognize Lyle. Blood seeped from his head, his fingers were broken, and his toenails were ripped out. A horror movie couldn't do justice as Hades did to this Wolf.

"Let's go upstairs, relay what we know." Hades willed the last bit of blood off his body. It's handy when you are the god of the dead and can take away all remnants of his victims' blood.

Loukas sat upstairs on the sizeable decorative chair in the living room. A purple glow stood out from the seat. Cyrene must have cast a small binding spell to keep him seated. Loukas rubbed his chin with those manicured fingers, and his tail flicked side to side as we walked into the room.

"Welcome back." Hades sauntered up to Loukas. "Ember enjoyed your show," he mocked.

"I'm sorry, Ember, I couldn't help myself." He winked. "What did you think of my acting skills?" I walked straight up to him and slapped him in the face. He chuckled while he rubbed the burn of my hand.

"Don't ever do that again! You had me so worried!" Loukas frowned and grabbed my hand. "I'm sorry, I thought you would have remembered after a few minutes. Then I died and couldn't say, 'gotcha!'" I smiled and punched him in the shoulder.

"Just don't do it again." Hades came forward and pulled me in by the waist.

"There better be a good explanation as to why you got out and to why Malachi was in my palace."

Dad and mom sat in the comfort of a love seat next to Loukas. Dad kept his glare away from Hades; he didn't want anything to do with my mate now. I felt his confusion, anger, and contemplative feelings about the situation. Mom must not know because she was too busy talking to Blaze, who had become a chatterbox with all the Wolves in my family.

"Master, you gave me free rein over the prison demons in the year 324AD, so they were under my command. I just had them release me and went to my room." Hades rolled his eyes and slapped his hand on his face.

"I meant to change that," he grumbled.

"Anyway, Malachi came in with the helm; of course, he came in undetected while using it. He brought in dark Witches, Sorcerers, and even some Vampires," Loukas mused. Mom growled in the corner. She has always said to treat everyone equally because not everyone is evil. Yet, Mom still had trouble shaking the thoughts of Vampires. All the ones she had met brought nothing but pain.

"Excuse me." She rubbed her throat. "Please continue." Dad rubbed mom's shoulders as she grew quiet.

"Malachi came in undetected and opened a portal. I tried contacting you through your office Fire Portal to speak to you, but nothing would go through. It was nothing but static, silence. I haven't used it in centuries, so maybe the spell had been broken."

"There's a disconnection," Cyrene walked into the room. "There is a ward around the Underworld, a powerful one." Cyrene brought in a glass ball and waved her hand across it. "Using a detection spell, I was able to find it; it has weakened me severely." Everyone glanced at Cyrene, who indeed looked worse for wear. Her eyes were sunken, and her fingers trembled. "It is a basic spell, one any Witch can do, but it is enhanced, enhanced so much I could barely find it with my own detection spell. The aura that was consumed to procure it was arduous."

The ball showed the Underworld in an entire glass dome. "This is where the barrier resides. How did you not notice that you were not receiving messages?"

Hades rubbed the back of his head. "Past thousand years, I've been a bit of a recluse. Besides, who wants to spend time with a god in a foul mood." My dad rolled his eyes while I pulled Hades down to a seat. He placed me on his lap while I cuddled closer to him.

"That barrier and your reclusiveness were used to their advantage. No one can contact you within unless it was with one of your own demons that you had frequent contact with." Cyrene leaned back on the couch. "You can send messages out yourself, just not receive. It was just enough for you to believe that there was no such ward," Cyrene concluded. "As for the writing on this spear, it is a basic poisoning spell. A lethal one to any supernatural. What the spell was laced with it is what is frightening." Cyrene clutched her fists. The room grew silent as Dante watched from the corner of the room. His fingers tapped on his arm.

"Dragon shifter blood."

"Dragon's blood? That's it?" Dad spoke out loud. "That type of blood magic was taken care of years ago!"

"A Shifter Dragon, big difference. Witches and Vampires have gone rogue in Bergarian again, and they have been hunting and it appears they have found a few vials. Remember all those years ago? The land of Vermillion was unsettled with their new Queen Diana taking on the throne. She was a hybrid, the first of her kind. Some are still fighting for their cause to rid her of the new heir, and it appears they found some leftover vials from the Dark War years ago."

The Wolf warriors guarding the room growled out. "More of it? We were in that war and saw the head warlock fall along with those bastards! "Father spat. "It was all disposed of!"

Cyrene shook her head. "This is just a small militia. There are small groups, and they plan to join forces once enough blood is found and take up arms again. They have experimented with the magic of pure virgin vampire blood in the past. That alone has made their magic stronger and helped regenerate their auras to fight longer. They must have finally got ahold of dragon's blood again to be able to hit and maim Hades for a good thirty seconds."

"More like ten seconds," Hades mumbled. "If it hit a lesser god, say someone, not of the first twelve, it would do damage," he stated. "It was intense, most potent I've ever had to deal with."

"Regardless, Dragon Shifter blood is hard to come by. They don't just bleed on a whim. Their skin is tough even in their human forms, and they must give it willingly. No dragon in their right mind would do that," Cyrene stressed. "Especially not after the Dark War; that is why I believe they are running low on supplies. They are trying to get rid of Ember for good if Lyle throws spears left and right. One shot of this dark magic with dragon shifter blood, and she would suffer."

Loukas tried to get up from his chair but was quickly sucked back down. "Can I at least move? My butt is numb." Cyrene waved her hand, and he was released rapidly. Her weariness was happy she didn't have to worry about keeping him to the chair.

"What we extracted from Lyle makes me think that Demeter is hiding in Bergarian and not on Earth where she normally likes to dwell. If we are talking Witches and Vampires, then Vermillion is where we must go." Hades played with my hair. Hades raised his hand and pointed to Loukas. "What else? Anything said that would be of use to us?"

"They want her, Master. Ember. Whoever is controlling Malachi thinks Ember can find the Sphere. I don't think they are trying to kill her. I think they want to use her."

"They are right." Hades stood. "In fact, Ember already found it." Everyone in the room gasped.

"The fire," Dad said. "That's why you stepped in."

I laced my hands with Hades. "It almost called to me. I felt very drawn to it." Hades pulled out the pebble; it was still misshapen, in no way was it a sphere. How could something so small be so important, to hold all of the world's matching souls in it? To see every single one and to watch them become one with one another.

Hades flipped the pebble over a few times. "I still don't believe it, all of this." He waved his hand at me. "I never thought a mate would be so precious. I was blind; I was blind for so long. And after finding her...." Hades pulled me in tight. "To know she is mine, and I couldn't ask for anything better." Hades eyes glistened while I nuzzled into his chest. The room stood silent as I put my hand up to touch the pebble.

My middle finger grazed the smooth surface. I felt the warmth in Hades' heart for me; the devotion had had to keep me protected and care for me hit me with all its might. My empath ability wall I had learned to create with Athena fell in an instant. With a flash of brilliant light, the room was engulfed in rays as white as the stars. Blinded by its brilliance, we all looked away until the warmth ceased to be felt on our faces.

Glancing back, Hades held the sizeable midnight-blue Sphere in his hand with tiny specks of grey and white silhouettes floating inside.

How did all these jumbled pieces come together? Being taken from Hades, missing gods, Dragon's blood, and the Sphere were all different, yet they all fit right in the same puzzle. We had our work cut out for us and looking into this Sphere was the first thing we had to do to find Selene.

Chapter 58

Ember

The Sphere had finally appeared, and everyone in the room had stilled. I mean, who wouldn't when that blinding light came from such a tiny pebble? Hades let go of my hand as he cradled it to his chest. Hades began cursing under this breath; I saw his face pale more than his original skin color for the first time.

No one said a word for a few minutes, just stared at the midnight glow along with swirls of grey and speckled light. Cyrene had approached and conjured a box to fit the Sphere inside. Hades gently placed the Sphere of Souls in the darkened box and put the lid on securely, taking the box from Cyrene. Cyrene gave a small smile, her legs weakened as I gripped her by her arms.

"We need to get her to Tamera." I held her and her head and cradled it to my chest. Dante came forward and picked her up, one arm under her legs and the other around he back.

"I'll see to it," Dante mumbled as he left the living room.

"She is weak; it will take time to regain her strength." Hades patted the box like a precious gift it was. "Once she is healed, we will devise a plan. We need to travel to Bergarian, and it won't be a fun holiday."

My grip tightened around Hades' arm. In our many nights falling asleep in bed, he brought up Bergarian and how beautiful it was, the magical wonders of the place compared to Earth. Fairies, Elves, Faes, and even the Wisps that like to toy with a woman's hair. A small smile graced my lips at the thought of finally visiting; even so, this wouldn't be a place for pleasantries.

Mom and dad had fought in the Dark War before I was born, during their "honeymoon" phase, mom calls it. It was a war full of blood; many had died and suffered. Families were broken, and sorrow swept through all the nations. After the war, Queen Clara took the throne along with her mate. They were the real heroes of the war; Clara's quick thinking saved thousands.

After the war, my parents' views were tainted. It had no longer been the magical place they had thought it to be. Too much death, blood, and destruction ruined them, and they had stayed away ever since. Only Grandpa and Grandma would go to visit our distant relatives, along with my uncle.

Dad suggested we retire for the day, which wasn't a bad idea. Lyle's screams and the heavy atmosphere my dad was creating wasn't helping. Dad continued to glare at Hades with nothing but disgust. I couldn't necessarily blame him, but Hades was my mate, and he made the right choice in the end. Did I suffer from it? I did, but I felt Hades' genuine emotion. He deeply regretted it, and I firmly believed his words that he would spend eternity making it up to me. The subject was getting old anyway; I was over this, and dad should be too.

I snickered as Mom asked Hades if he would join them for breakfast in a few hours. Feeling his reluctance was almost comical. *"Please save me,"* Hades begged through the mind link. *"Your father hates me; I can't have your mother too."*

"Mom, we are exhausted. We are going to sleep in." I butted in. "But you must be getting hungry again; you need your strength. You haven't had a proper meal..."

"Mom," I groaned dramatically. My eyes rolled back so far I thought I saw Elea wagging her tail. "Please, we'll come to you when we are hungry, I promise."

"There's the attitude I haven't seen in so long!" Mom approached me and kissed me on the cheek. "Good to see you haven't grown too much." Mom retreated to the door as Blaze followed.

The burn I felt in my chest became stronger. Dad's pine smell wrapped around me as I turned to meet him in the eyes.

"Hi, dad." His eyes were filled with hurt as he scooped my small form in his arms. A deep sigh escaped him, and I heard the big, bad

Alpha sniffle. "I'm Okay, and I'm Okay with Hades. We all make mistakes. I'm here, and I have my mate with me now." I petted his hair, something men liked in general; I've picked up on as dad picked up more of my scent.

"I'm just glad you are here. We knew you were alive; we knew you were somewhere." Dad's voice cracked. "You can't blame me for being angry, that all of this could have been prevented."

"It is how the fates had planned it," I spoke firmly. Looking over Dad's shoulder, I gave Hades a reassuring smile. "Don't ever leave anyone's sight until we've caught Demeter, Malachi and whoever else poses as a threat, do you understand?" he growled as his gripped tightened.

"Promise," I patted his back. Feeling Hades' desperate need to touch me, to be held in cage-like arms, I stepped away from Dad, my childhood, and went to Hades.

***

We didn't wake up until noon the following day. Coming home at three in the morning and the exciting events of yesterday wore heavy on us both. Hades had been awake for hours; I felt him as I tried to sleep. His movements, his worry, anger, and love towards me radiated. The god was thinking up a storm, and it was loud enough for me to feel all of it.

As I finally started to stir, my cheek rubbed up against his slightly hairy chest. "Morning," his deep voice grumbled as he petted my hair. I loved his morning voice, it was sexy and deep, and I wanted nothing more than to hear his voice deep into my…"Someone is happy to feel me this morning," he spoke again, and I realized my hand was right on his happy place.

"I am so sorry!" I squealed. "I didn't realize I was even holding it!"

"You crave me even in your sleep, means I'm doing something right," he chuckled. Hades rubbed his member on my thigh, in which I returned with squeezing them together. How can we both be so turned on in the morning? He was hard, stiff, and was already leaking his cum onto my bare thigh. Taking a sharp breath, I slung my leg over his hip and ground my pussy against him. His whole body was warm, but my bare pussy touching his cock felt extremely hot, just as the fire of Tartarus itself. Hades moved his hips as his length rubbed against my slit. My nipples hardened as his hand went up to grab one harshly.

"These are so damn perfect." His face was immediately buried in my breasts as he nipped and sucked them relentlessly. My back arched as he prodded his dick near my entrance. I was still laying on my side with my leg draped over his hip; it was too tempting for him, too much of an invite to bury himself inside me.

His lips rose up my chest and to my mouth as his tongue powered over me. His dick, wet with my slick, was pushed through, squeezing him as he entered my quivering cavern. Hades, hovering over me while still on my side, moved my leg, so he was hugging it to his torso. The new position, the way his cock entered me, was a whole new feeling. It hit walls that had never felt the ridge of his cock.

Gripping the sheets to hold myself steady, I could feel the powerful push of his hip rocking me into the bed. One hand raked my thigh while the other clawed my ass. His gaze wandered over my opened parts while fucking my scissored legs.

Another moan was going to part my lips until I felt his thumb graze my backside, going to a place I found to be nothing but a forbidden area. My pussy wettened further, feeling his nails dig into my thigh despite his wandering thumb.

A thumb pricked my puckered hole as I gasped. "Shh, just relax." Hades' cock twitched as he continued to rock his muscular hips. His strong abs and lower torso flexed as his dancing hips swiveled to use his cock into every crevice. Becoming lost at the feeling, my body spasmed, ripping my orgasm through me as I felt his thumb enter my ass. It was a full feeling as my body tried to get rid of the foreign object. The fullness of my ass and pussy made me yell out in pleasure and confusion.

This wasn't supposed to be happening; why was I becoming so turned on? Gripping the sheets, Hades let out a sigh of content as he put his thumb in and out. My body shook at the aftershocks of my orgasm. There was no time to stop; Hades had yet to find his release, which was soon. Feeling his balls tighten on my inner thigh, I reached my hand around to fondle his large balls, only to be curious all the same about his wandering finger. Unfortunately, my body could not stretch enough, but another thought entered me.

Taking my wet essence from my pussy I trailed my finger just under his balls and massaged the area next to his own forbidden zone. His thrusts stopped as he let out a war cry that could be heard to the territory border. Thick ropes of seed spilled into me. My body was full; he had filled me in both love and his own body fluids that now dripped from me. I continued to rub him as his orgasm progressed and more and more of his seed continued to flow. The tight jaw, his flexed arm, and chest muscles stirred nothing but want and love. He was by far the most beautiful man, god, being I had ever met, and he was just for me.

Hades' breath heaved as his seed continued to be milked by my by quaking core; his dick never became flaccid as he reluctantly pulled from me. Falling to my backside, he wrapped his arms around me. Minty breath fanned my hair while his harsh breaths flowed.

"Now that was something to wake up to," Elea spoke up. *"What happened to the innocent little angel he always talked about?"* I snickered and waited for Hades to catch his breath, only to find him already asleep. Pulling out of his hold, I rolled over to pet his face. This beautiful face could be of an angel, but he was far from it. He was my devil, my Satan. All these names were to evoke fear in those around him. Hades was to make people fear him because of what he controlled, the dead. The taker of life. The Underworld and all that dwelled within it were under his control.

Hades sleeps, and when he sleeps, he looks nothing short of the handsome mate of mine. Petting his brilliant blonde hair, I ease up out of bed, Hoping to catch a shower before I am pounced on again.

The wood floor was cold, and a few splinters still rose from the boards. The cabin was made in haste when mom had it built, she said. It was all for mating Wolves anyway and had to make not one of these cabins but ten. Luckily we were given the larger, sturdier ones.

Glancing at the kitchen table, the black box sat still. I wanted nothing more than to touch the Sphere again, hold it in my own hands like I had done in the fire. It still beckoned me to grab it, or was it my own selfish desires? Gripping my hands tightly, I remembered the extra something falling between my legs. I chuckled a bit as I entered the large bathroom to shower the mess away.

✳✳✳

Hades still slept in the bed, exhausted. This wasn't like him to be so tired, but we have been busy for the past week. Never thought gods would sleep, but maybe they were more like us than we realized. They ate, slept, and had sex; we were made in their image for the most part.

We were just a step closer. Soon we would be able to relax and be with each other. Start a whole new life. I had been granted a gift, several actually. The ten or so years being locked away and being a slave was just a small price to pay by gaining such a large family. Not just my pack but the gods as well.

Not wanting to disturb Hades or anger him by leaving the cabin, I sat in front of the black box, palms down on either side. Such an ordinary-looking thing to be harboring the famous Sphere that helps match all the souls. My fingers itched, itched to open it. I felt like

Pandora getting ready to open the box of monsters, yet I knew what was inside. It was the Sphere, the one I was supposed to find. Surely that meant I was to touch it too? Why shouldn't I touch it?

"*Just touch the damn thing,*" Elea spat as she rolled her eyes. "*I swear you ask more questions than any other human I've heard talking. Just open it.*"

Rolling my eyes rather dramatically, I inched forward. "Can't help but question everything," I muttered.

Taking the tip of my index finger, I pushed up on the lid. Barely opening it, I peeked inside. It still had the dark, blue glow and the beautiful marbling of souls dancing around it. The bioluminescent inside it did nothing for my empathy ability but strengthen it. My heart strummed to its own tune as I saw several silhouettes come to one side of the Sphere. Lifting the lid more until I finally took it off, I put both my eyes on the two figures. They glowed when they touched each other, just the hint of glow that made them barely there. My emotions felt it, however. Felt not only the love but the connection when the two figures touched.

Fingers trembling, I took my index finger to touch the outside of the Sphere; the closer I got, the closer their soul touched mine. Concentrating, I squinted my eyes to see who it might be. Finger grazing one ghost, I saw Vulcan in my mind. He's smiling, but he is also urging. Urging for me to move me to find his missing pieces. He glanced at the figure that was being held in his hand. Taking my other index finger, I put it on the figure next to him and find none other than Tamara smiling back at me.

Chapter 59

Under the Moon

The stagnant air hit Selene's nostrils; it was a smell she had grown used to. The fire that barely reached the tops of the logs was almost down to a smolder. It kept the room scarcely warm enough to feel her fingers. Normal humans would have frozen to death; thankfully, she was no human. The two others that huddled in the corner for warmth rubbed their hands together. Their faces were a bit brighter than hers.

Selene tried to lay by the fire, the flicker of the flames made her wish she could one day feel the warmth of the blaze and heat of a significant other, but that wasn't in the cards for her. To feel the fiery touches of the warmth of a soul mate that she had granted to so many, yet she could not give herself that.

Hermes held Hecate close. There was no glow between their touches; they were not mates. Selene sighed as she tried to recall her Sphere, the one that helped her match souls from afar. She wondered what their mates were like; the two gods were closer to her than any other.

Selene was able to wield such a device, helping distance souls connect to each other while she stayed in the solace of her home.

Had Ember found it yet? Many were looking for it, for the Sphere and Ember. The evils knew of her mission; the one dream she had sent to Ember had been infiltrated for information. Now Ember was in just as much danger as her. Selene huffed, causing the fire to hiccup and blowing the smoke back to the edge of the chimney wall.

"Selene, come here." Hecate's voice beckoned her. The three gods had one large blanket to share between them. Their captors were not merciful, especially since they dared not cooperate fully. Only when the evils started abusing the gods in different ways caused them to crack under pressure. The dragon shifter blood was enough to keep their powers at bay and trap them in this hovel of a prison.

Hecate was forced to calm her compelling powers among the magic deemed too strong for its time. The Shifter Dragon blood had reached its full potential, able to significantly hurt the gods even among the original twelve. Especially the second generation. Hermes was one of those gods; he could be killed, but neither Selene nor Hecate would allow it.

"Ember has to find it soon," Selene spoke solemnly. "So many souls to match." Selene crawled to the other two; they quickly engulfed her inside their blanket. Hecate's own powers, who helped suppressed with the Dragon's blood, were now as helpless as the others, especially against the binding spell cast on the hovel.

"She will find it," Hermes spoke. "Ember is a strong one; if she could calm the storm in Hades, she can do anything," he chuckled. Selene hummed as she buried herself closer. The yells and roars outside invaded their tender ears. Vampires, Witches, Warlocks, and Sorcerers had been dancing by the fire. Their victory would soon be theirs and rise from the ashes from where they came all because of a promise that had been granted to them.

The damp, musky room was breeding nothing but mold with the barely-there fire. Shivering against each other, they heard a click on the large wooden door. It creaked and whined as it opened. A figure, ever so graceful, walked through. Green and light brown robes of tulle floated inward as she closed the door. Her wheat-colored hair and those brown eyes scanned the room until they landed in the corner of shivering, starving gods.

"Demeter," Hermes hissed. Demeter all but smiled as she approached the table and sat down in front of the shivering trio.

"I've come to ask for today's request," she purred as her chin rested on her thumb, her index finger ran up the side of her face. Leaning on the table, one would think she was the confident, alluring God of Harvest and Grain. One with grace, poise that enhances the beauty of the Earth and of Bergarian. That had all but changed. The area surrounding them was now dank, dark, and desolate. No sun to beckon the crops and no green to soothe the soul.

"You won't get it," Hecate shrilled. "You hurt your own kind and beg to hurt others, and for what? Just so your daughter won't ever leave your side? You need to learn to let go."

Demeter's mannerisms changed in the blink of an eye, her eyes narrowed, and her hand slammed on the table. "Don't tell me how to treat my daughter." Vines from the outside of the window slithered through the cracked window; its tendrils slithered through and round tables and chairs. Finally reaching its intended target, its grip wrapped around Hecate. "Don't forget your powers are substantially weakened with the Dragon's Blood. I could choke you now, and you would fade into nothingness."

"Enough," Selene pleaded. "What do you want?" The vines retracted, and Demeter's face became softened.

"Good girl," Demeter purred. "I need Hecate to strengthen the bond between Malachi and Persephone one more time."

"You are playing with fire!" Selene yelled. "You cannot force a bond with magic! It won't last, and your daughter will suffer!" Demeter stood up and sauntered over to the group on the floor. Bending low and pulling Selene's jaw tight.

"It is only for a while until I find the Sphere," she sang. "Then I will force you to bind Persephone's soul with Malachi. They will then live on Earth with me, and I will never have to be without her. Always living in my home while she helps me tend to the seasons." Demeter bit her cheek to withhold a smile.

"Then I will have you sever Hades and Ember's bond, killing them both." She let go of her cheek and began to laugh maniacally. Holding her stomach in, she glared at Hecate. "Now get up, or Hermes will get a good dose of poison, and this time he won't wake up."

Hermes grabbed Hecate. "Don't, I'll be fine."

Hecate shook her head. "No, you won't be. Let's just hope help is on the way." Hermes' grip tightened as his head lowered, and Hecate walked out the door with Demeter.

"What do we do?" Selene almost sobbed. Her head rested on Hermes, who continued to console Selene. His hands rubbed up and down her arms as he stared at the door.

"The fates are in control now, Selene. All we could do is wait and hope that Ember will find it soon." Selene nodded silently as she gripped Hermes' cloak. The moon that sat in the middle of Selene's forehead began to glow; the light blue lit up the dark blanket that covered them. Hermes pulled Selene back, mouth agape.

"What happened? It's glowing brighter?" Selene touched her forehead.

"Kronos," she whispered as she felt the tingle in her forehead. "A match, a match has been made." Hermes shook his head.

"How can that be possible?" Selene sat back on the wall as she continued to massage her forehead.

"She found it; she found the sphere." Hermes let out a chuckled sigh as he grabbed Selene to hug her. They held each other's embrace for a few moments until she pulled back. "Not only that, but she can match souls."

Hermes let out a single laugh. "What does that mean?"

"She, she can pair them like I can." Selene's heart jumped inside her chest. Taking her hand and rubbing her chest, tears pricked her eyes. Could it be? Could Ember match souls as well as her? Split between the two, they could help more supernaturals and gods be matched more quickly.

And maybe, Ember could find a match for her.

Ember

I stared at the couple in my mind. Their hands were joined together, a bright glow in between their intertwined fingers. Both my fingers twitched as I continued to touch the two figures on the Sphere.

"Now what?" I muttered again. Elea cocked her head to the side, letting me know of her confusion. My index fingers had a mind of their own, and they traveled together, coming to meet in the middle. A bright glow came from the Sphere, as bright as the night before. It was blinding but silent as I closed my eyes. Opening them, the room was still quiet, and Hade's soft snores were still heard from his side of the bed. The ball no longer held their figures, but two more were in their place. Touching the ball again, I saw Ares in my mind's eye, and the other figure came together, Mariah. I pulled my fingers together, doing the same I did with Vulcan and Tamera, but I kept my eyes open this time.

The bright light around the room grew white while my eyes fixated on Ares and Mariah in my mind. Their hands intertwined; their bodies merged as their souls molded with one another. I felt the love, their passion and desires, the moment that their bodies collided, joy, happiness, and eternal gratefulness as they held each other's embrace.

As quick as the soul collision appeared, it was gone in an instant. The Sphere was blank; no figures or souls appeared. Getting ready to close the box, another bit of grey matter floated to the side of the darkened orb. "They just keep coming, don't they?"

"*Touch it again,*" Elea whispered; all her jest was gone, and curiosity had now taken over. My finger brushed the side of the Sphere, and another soul stood in my mind. A she-wolf, the one that asked the demon to dance. The first she-wolf dared break the species barrier and caused a domino effect of others following her lead. Could the demon she danced with be her mate? Their hands glowed, and so far, my suspicions had been correct. My finger was about to touch the grey figure until I felt a warm hand on my shoulder. "Ember?" My finger left the Sphere and closed the box with a slam as my heartbeat rapidly.

"Ember, what are you doing? Are you all right?" Hades stood above me, squeezing my shoulder. "What were you doing?"

That was the real question, what exactly had I been doing? "I was curious and wanted to look?" Hades laughed and sat in the chair next to me.

"I don't think you will break it; I'm not going to scold you for looking." He chuckled.

"W-what if I was more than looking?" Hades narrowed his eyes as he glanced back at the box. "I might have paired some people together?" My voice became high-pitched while his eyes widened.

"You did what?" The sexy grumble in his voice didn't sound sexy at all right now; he sounded mad. Hades had never been mad at me; my heart clenched as his hands gripped the table.

"What do you mean? What did you do? Do you know the consequences of pairing the wrong people, Ember?!" Hades pulled the box from me and looked inside, not that he would know exactly what was happening. If Hades couldn't see when two people glowed when they touched, then he wouldn't understand any of this, would he?

"Show me," he demanded. "What did you do?" he snapped. I ground my teeth together and let out a growl. Elea was not liking this attitude. Hades leaned back in his chair as he took in my stance. I was pissed; I didn't break anything and for him to get mad at me was unreasonable.

Hades' sighed. "I'm sorry, Ember." He rubbed as he pinched his nose. "Selene just entrusted us with her Sphere. It is powerful, able to combine souls to one if accepted on a physical level, like us." He smiled as he caressed my knuckles. "Powerful enough to break a soul-bonding once the physical bond is in place." My breath hitched as I covered my mouth.

"Can you please show me what you have done?"

Pulling the Sphere entirely out of the box, I gently put it on the table. "What do you see?" I asked. Hades looked at it; from afar, it looked like a giant marble with grey swirls around it, but if you looked closely, the swirls became figures. Hades folded his arms, looking at it.

"I see nothing but the fog that spreads thick and thin all over it." I tutted at his response. He couldn't see.

"You see no figures, the outlines of people?" I waved my hand over the Sphere. He shook his head.

"Well, I do." Staring into his eyes, his complexion softened. "There are two, here and here. When I press my finger here." I demonstrated and investigated my mind. I felt Hade's hand wave in front of my face, but I no longer saw him.

"Your eyes are white," Hades muttered contemplatively.

I saw the she-wolf. Her hand was reaching out, begging for the other figure. Taking my other finger, I touched the other floating fog, and immediately, the demon appeared.

"I see both, the she-Wolf and one of your demons."

"Shit." Hades' bare arm brushed with mine, and his body went still. "I see them," he whispered. His touch was recognized by my body, and his hand went over my arm. "He is one of my older demons." His body went still. "They are glowing." He sat amazed.

"I've seen those glow before, during the bonfire that you thought was all silly," I joked. "Now watch, I can pair them." I moved my fingers together, guiding the two souls. Their bodies tangled with one another, forming into one perfect soul. The bright light flashed, and they were gone in an instant. More and more started to appear; Hades watched me guide nine more pairs of souls together with his hand on my arm. The longer I paired, the more tired I became until Hades told me to stop.

My hands shook as I opened my eyes. From inside the Sphere, I had paired them together. Does that mean they are officially mates here in the 'real world?'

The adoring look as Hades glanced at me sent my heart flying. His emotions were gentle, filled with awe. Hades took his hand and guided my head into his chest. My legs found their way into Hades' lap as he cradled me. "I'm sorry I doubted." He kissed the top of my head.

"This,...this is unheard of," Hades mumbled into my hair. "You must have gained god-like qualities or have become a god and are now able to wield for Selene." I tightened my hold around his torso. "I just wanted you, that's all."

Hades laughed. "And all I wanted was you." Indeed, this was a dream. All I wanted was to live in Hades' arms and help him with his duties in Hell, maybe assist demons tracking down sex-trafficking victims and set them free. Now, I was not only a queen of the Underworld, but my god-like powers granted me a responsibility I would have never fathomed. Every god had an influence. Every god had a job. Being a Queen at Hades' side wasn't enough; now, I was Selene's apprentice.

A thrum went through our bodies as we relaxed. The content moment we shared, the joy that others will be coupled and paired gave light at the end of the tunnel. Once Selene was found, she would hopefully tell me what all of this could mean.

"So this means." Hades lifted his head from atop of mine. His statement was cut short as a thunderous growl ripped through the woods to our cabin. It echoed with such ferocity the dead leaves began to fall from the top of the highest trees.

"Ares," I whispered.

Chapter 60

Ares

Growling, I flipped over another young pup on the mat. He sputtered as blood dribbled from the corner of his tanned mouth. "Again," I barked. My body was nothing but sweat, blood, dirt, and muscles spasming from the heavy lifting I had done just an hour before.

I was sexually and mentally frustrated. I've never had to think so much in all my life. Hades helped me with that; he helped me figure out stupid problems regarding war tactics. I liked the fight; point me in the right direction, and I'll spill the blood. The whole mind game was confusing, and I wanted no part of it.

Mariah, sexy, talented Mariah had flooded my head. No woman in my life have I ever thought about more than her. The countless conquests to kill a beast just to have a taste of some pussy was my calling. I liked the challenge; it combined my two favorite things, beating shit up and sex.

Not with Mariah, no, not with her. She had been so reluctant to come near me in the beginning. Her eyes were wary as I stared at her ass, but it wasn't just her ass that had the appeal; it was her stature. Mariah was strong, muscular and could kill any of the male warriors in the pack with her pinky if she wanted to. Taking her training seriously and her future mate even more earnestly. As we walked together while she showed me the perimeter that first day, I knew she was different. Not once did she eye me like a piece of meat like some women do. They wanted the muscles and the dick; that wasn't going to fly with me for a long-term relationship. Then again, none of them interested me like Mariah did.

She asked me about my hobbies, favorite weapons, wars, and a bit of the history of the gods. None had been so curious to ask me about any of that. Mariah was different, she made me think, and I usually hated thinking. With her, I wanted to do more of it.

One brush of her hand against mine, and I was severely disappointed. I had hoped she would have been my mate, but the rush of fire didn't invade my arms. That didn't matter to me, and Mariah didn't seem to mind it either.

We had spent more time together, and the inevitable happened. I damn kissed her. Those lips beckoned my name as we had towered in one of the tallest trees to gain a better vision of the grounds. At the top of the platform, high above the ground, the moon shown right down on us. I silently prayed to Selene that Mariah would be my mate, as she was the most perfect she-Wolf I had ever encountered. She saw me as wise, a warrior, a person she could confide in, and I felt nothing but the same to her.

One kiss was all it took until we kissed every chance we got. It didn't matter where or when, I wanted to massage my tongue with hers until the end of time. Too many nosey Wolves got involved and gave hard looks. This pack was pro-mate, and relationships before mates were frowned upon, but I didn't care. We were in our own time and place; we would enjoy each other's company.

Once we found the Sphere and the gods, I would personally ask Selene to be paired with Mariah. I don't know who her mate is or who mine will be, but I know I had to be with Mariah and her only. My mate could not be better than her.

Knowing she wanted me made it that much harder. However, the thought lingered in my head that Mariah may still want her mate, and she may regret us; what if she met him before I could get to Selene? Mariah said she wanted to save herself for her mate at the beginning of this relationship, which I had to honor.

Ha, me, honor? I wanted to honor her. I wanted to make sure she was given that chance.

I restrained myself from taking her last night. Ember's questions about us being mates rang through my head; even with my confession to Mariah, I couldn't go through with it. I couldn't make her mine; I needed to honor her wishes to make sure she saved her virginity to her mate.

Fuck, I hate thinking. I want to be her mate. More than to spill the blood of my enemies.

Hitting the punching bag, clearing it off the chain, the wolves stopped and stared. I had worked nonstop this morning, and now the younger wolves were running off watching my fit of rage.

"You alright, man?" Dante runs up. "Where's Mariah?"

I growled, setting up another punching bag, and Dante went behind it to hold it steady. I had sent Mariah away so I could think.

"Girl trouble?" He smirked as I hit the bag hard, causing Dante to fly off. "All right, I guess so." He rubbed his ass and went back to holding the bag tighter. Throwing punches, Dante continued to spout off nonsense about girls and what he thinkss he knows.

Seriously?

"But have you done relationships?" I stopped punching and glared at the Wolf.

"Well, obviously you haven't, virgin." Dante laughed as he scratched the back of his head.

"I'm just staying; just wait until this whole Sphere starts working again. I'm sure if you are having these strong feelings, Selene will take that into account..." Droning on, Dante began to lecture me on waiting for your mate; it only fuels my fire until I smell hints of oranges and cranberries. Wind picking up the breeze floated straight to my nose as I paused my hits to the sandbag.

"Shut up," I snapped at Dante, who began to look around. The Wolves sparring, the howls heard in the distance all began to fade. The trees, the ground, my vision only consisted of smelling and seeing the aroma trail to my nose. One step at a time wasn't enough; my nose led me through the thickest part of the wood. The smell grew more substantial, and my heartbeat faster. Could it be? Could it be a mate? Hades said the scent is intoxicating, mouth-watering, and more complex than any smell to resist.

Mariah couldn't possibly be at the end of this path. She wouldn't be the one standing in front of me once I reached my destination. Panging with guilt, I had to see who this person was. I had to confess my heart belonged to another and that I wasn't sure I could ever love them because I had made up my mind. If Mariah didn't reject her mate to be with me, I would suffer alone. The few days she gave me were better than I would have dreamed, and hell, we didn't even have sex.

Her smile, laugh, and ability to keep up with me while sparring was the best gift she was to the Earth, to Bergarian. Repeating those days over and over in my head was enough.

My run was now a walk as I hit the edge of the stream. The woman was wearing a long cloak with a white flower in her hand. Dropping it in the stream, she watched it as it floated away. Smelling the several tears that I knew were falling from this maiden, I stepped forward. "Excuse me?"

The citrus cranberry was stronger now, overpowering. My heart stuttered as the woman turns around in her cloak and slowly pulls off the hood. My breath caught to see none other than Mariah. Her eyes sparkled with remnants of her tears. Cheeks and nose as bright as a cherry. She took a breath and clutches her chest. "Ares?" she spoke with the wind.

"Ares!" Running to her, I lift her in the air by her hips and twirl her around. Mariah squealed and screamed until all the woodland animals had run from the area. She screamed again as I placed her back on the ground, only to assault her lips. She's hungry, feral, and she was all mine!

The fire burned with our touches. Mariah's face lit up in excitement while I cradled her face.

Mariah moaned into my lips as I gripped her ass. All fucking mine.

"Now, I'm marking you now." Mariah gripped my shoulders; I was still covered in sweat, dirt, and blood. She looks at her hands with the dirty mess, only for me to find that her arousal has been heightened. She loves it; she loves the animal in me. Her mouth goes straight to my neck and sucks on it fiercely. As much I as would fuck her on the forest floor, I'm scared nosey Ember will come to find us.

I have her straddle my waist as we run back to the center of the territory. "Where do I go?" I rasp. Wolves are staring as she openly pulls on my hair as my tongue goes down her throat.

"Mmhmm, pack, house," she murmured, and I took off. Faster than any Wolf in the pack, I jutted up the packhouse stairs, taking three or four at a time. "Third floor," she groans again as I feel her pussy rub up against my leather cloth.

"Fuck, have mercy," I growled. Mariah's lips were swollen as she felt up and down the walls of the hallways, trying to find her door.

Her cloak came off, and my sandals unraveled themselves, leaving nothing but trailing clothes to her door. When we reach it, I bang on it once with my shoulder and shut it with my foot. Throwing her on the bed, I pull her dresser to block the door make sure no one comes in. No one is to disturb us, not now and not for at least a few days.

I have my mate, the one I have wanted for many lifetimes and the perfect one for me. Her eyes were hooded, her tank top and black leggings were a barrier that I meant to destroy. I ripped my leather belts from shoulders and waist, weapons dropping to the floor with my breath ragged. Barely containing myself, I pulled my leather cloth from my body while Mariah's mouth hit the floor. My cock sprung free, whacking my stomach as my eleven-inch monster was ready to explore her cave.

"Oh goddess," she panted as she licked her lips. I heavily walked to the bed, my cock rubbing up against her warm pussy. Groaning, the tank top was ripped from her body, along with her bra, and her glorious globes fell into my hand. Kneading them, touching them, and finally being able to suck them harshly made cum leak from the tip of my cock. Her hands were in my hair as she growled for me to be rough. Fuck, I like it rough.

My claws dug into her ass and ripped her leggings straight down; I wanted to taste her; I wanted her scent to be all over me. Before her leggings reached her ankles, my face was in her pussy. Digging deep and lapping up the freshness of her arousal made my dick strain. I could damn near hump the bed right now. However, my thoughts were on her; if she was going to take this cock she needed to be well prepared.

"Ares!" she half growled and screamed. Fingers pulled my hair and hips, rocking into my face; I sucked her nub until she shattered. Squirt after squirt fell into my mouth; her fingers began to pinch her nipples while her hips still rocked into my face. This was better than the nectar of the gods, better than any ambrosia I have ever tasted.

"Fuck me, Ares," Mariah growled. "Fuck me into oblivion," Mariah rasped as she held her pussy up for me. Two of my fingers wiggled into her tight cavern, and fuck, she was tight. Mariah was going to hurt when I thrust myself into this heaven.

My damn warrior, my goddess, my mate, she was truly made for me. "Ugh, Ares, I need it!" While she begged, I lined up my cock, to ease myself in since it was her first time. She growled. She damn growled at me. Her legs wrapped around my back as she pushed herself with enough force it rolled me over. My back was now to the mattress. Mariah took my cock, and she pushed my entire length in her pussy in one swift motion.

I roared until the house shook, small nick knacks fell from the side tables, books fell off shelves, and I'm sure everyone in the damn territory knew what was happening. Mariah caught her breath; a tiny bit of blood tainted my cock. Determination in her eyes, she grunted as she gracefully bounced up and down my straining cock.

Her breasts bounced, and my hand immediately went to cup one of them while the other hand helped guide her hips. Fucking fantastic, she knew how to ride me just the way I liked it, but I liked it because it was her.

Mariah's hair swayed with every movement until she started to swivel her hips in a figure-eight and put my cock in all the right places on her pussy. Her aroma was killing me; her wet pussy was causing the slapping of our skin to be that much louder.

Music to my ears.

Her head rolled back, and her breasts stuck out as her nipples hardened even more; sitting up, I latched onto one of her pebbles with my teeth, biting as she cummed again. Moans like these were meant for everyone to hear because my cock was that damn good.

Mariah came down from her orgasm, but I wasn't done. Flipping her over, so we were faced to face, I rammed my cock into her. Sure, she felt amazing being in charge, but now I could throw my hips into her pussy so hard she would feel it in her throat. "More," she rasped. My face buried into her shoulder, my canines lengthening.

"You are mine, Mariah. Mine." The sparks flew across my shoulder as Mariah's fangs lengthened too.

"Together, my mate, together," I rasped with one more large thrust; I sunk my fangs into her shoulder; not a second later, she pierced through my tough skin. Impressing me even more that my mate could cut through my leathery skin. My hips gyrated a few more times before finally stopping.

Not wanting to let go of this moment, I kept my teeth and cock buried deep within her. "Selene, don't let this be a dream," I begged. With Mariah's deep sigh, her teeth let go and licked my skin to heal it. I chuckled as she did so while kissing hers.

"Wow," she whispered. My cock twitched inside her. "Yeah." I nuzzled into her neck. Her hand came up and drew circles around my back as my body began to relax.

"Mariah?"

"Hmm?" Her eyes were closed; she was falling asleep.

"Why were you at the stream with a rose?" A faint smile played on her lips.

"I-I was telling sorry to my mother, she died a long time ago, in the Dark War." I kissed her cheek and ran my nose along her neck. "Telling her sorry because I wouldn't meet my mate. That I found someone worth more than anything I could ever imagine." Lifting my head and staring into her eyes, she smiled back at me. "I wanted you to be my mate, but we already were." I kissed her lips again and rolled to the side.

"Why now, though? Why didn't we know before?" I scratched my head.

"Let's not think, just be with me." I ground my hips into her thigh. "All that matters is that you're mine, and I am yours."

Chapter 61

Ember

"So this means." Hades lifted his head from atop of mine. His statement was cut short as a thunderous growl ripped through the woods to our cabin. It echoed with such ferocity the dead leaves began to fall from the top of the highest trees.

"Ares," I whispered.

"Um, I think he found his mate." I giggled as Hades willed some clothes on his body.

"Come on." He pulled my arm as we raced outside. The sun was high in the sky, almost past mid-day as we ran down the path to the central courtyard. The warriors had ceased their sparring and were all looking at each other in bewilderment as Dante ran up to us.

"Ares just took Mariah to the packhouse; he kept mumbling 'mine,' and that is the last we saw of them until we felt the ground shake." Dante continued to look at everyone, but the rest of the Wolves were heading back home.

"That's because they are mates!" I gushed as I jumped up and down. Hades gave me a toothy grin as he pulled me by his side.

"How can that be? I thought pairings couldn't happen right now, not without Selene?" Dante's eyes widened. "Did you have something to do with this, Ember?" I nodded my head frantically as I clutched Hades' arm. "Eeeek! Yes!"

"I think because Hades and I have mated, I might have gained some god-like powers." I waved my hands in the air frantically while I spoke. Dante glanced at Hades and back to me.

"It's true, we've soul bonded. She is like me; she didn't just gain god-like powers. She is a god." My eyes took a few big blinks as I felt the color drain from my face. "Ember, not only did we mate in the physical sense, but also with our souls. That can only be done as a god; you are like the rest of the gods of Olympus and me. I don't know why it didn't come to me sooner. You being able to wield the Sphere of Souls proves it. You have a gift, a gift that can help Selene with her work. More souls can be bonded quickly, and maybe she won't have to work as hard." My mouth dropped.

"Are you Okay with this?" Hades held both of my hands as I thought it over. This was a big responsibility, huge. Selene has been the one to pair souls for thousands of years. Of all Wolves, I was to be the one to help her? This is insane; I was not worthy of any of this.

"You are worthy." Hades kissed my lips. "It makes sense actually; your empath ability gives you the gift of sight. To see emotions, specifically the emotion of love and deep connection."

"Holy cow, my sister is a goddess." Dante laughed.

Several screams and howls came from the distance. The forest, sensing the disturbance in the air, began to sway, pushing around smells that had become overwhelming. Wolves ran out of their homes while demons crashed into doors, and Wolves jumped out windows running randomly throughout the territory.

"What's going on?" Dante stared at the chaos.

"I might have paired eleven other souls…." I meekly spoke as Hades pulled me close. "Oh shit," Dante deadpanned as mom and dad ran up to us.

"What is going on?" Mom huffed as Wesley pulled her in to protect her. Demons and Wolves ran wild as they ran to each other, sucking face and groping out in the open. Dante palmed his face with a hard slap as it ran down his fuzzy cheek. "Ember can control the Sphere of Souls; she paired souls together."

"The right ones, right?" Dad spat out. Offended, I stomped my foot and put my fists on my hips.

"Of course, I did! They were all glowing when they touched each other, and their souls were satisfied once I combined them."

My family stared at me with wide eyes; Hades bent over to whisper in my ear. "They have no idea what you are talking about. Besides, you may need to have all the pups leave the packhouse."

My attention was brought to the large packhouse with screaming Wolves running in and out. Some children were wide-eyed as they walked out, confused. Some were crying, clutching to one another as demons ran full force up the steps with their mates in tow.

"Mom." I slapped her arm. Gasping, she sent out a mind-link letting all the parents know that pups needed to leave the recreation area. Too many paired Wolves and too many innocent eyes staring at what could be nothing but emotional trauma later.

The heat houses may have to be put to good use; demons had a robust sexual appetite, maybe more so than Wolves. Mom and I led the children out while parents came to pull them into their embrace. All of them ran back to their respective homes. This may be a pack of thousands of Wolves, but ten or eleven pairs finding each other simultaneously was terrifying.

The screaming died down after a few hours in the packhouse. Many even came down to grab drinks and food and headed back up to their rooms. Hair was disheveled, bite marks were all over their bodies. They were all thoroughly happy with their mates. None of the Wolves were hesitant mating with demons, which was a relief, especially after the bonfire where they were reluctant. It did prove that there was a connection before Selene would connect their souls before they were soul mates. They recognized each other even before joining.

It wasn't just the bond that kept them together; Selene used her blessing to cement a firm foundation of their love. It strengthened not only their souls but their bodies as well. Both are stronger, healthier, heal faster, and not to mention their sex drives were strong. Two souls could find each other much easier in a sea of souls with a connection. Selene made the process easier. She eliminated any doubt if one was your soulmate by feeling fiery touches, looking into their eyes, and aphrodisiac smells. No one should argue that they didn't have a choice in their love for their mate because it would be there whether the bond was there or not.

My thoughts drift to Tamera and to any that are rejected by their mate. Were they soulmates to begin with if they accepted their second chance mate, instead? Many more questions bloomed as the first question haunted me. Could one be soulmates with two? Even if they are not twins?

Identical twins were shared; that was a given. They were conceived in the same egg that the mother produces, only split into two once fertilized. Their souls were shared along with their bodies.

"You are thinking awfully hard," Hades whispered in my ear. We were all gathered in the living room, me in Hades' lap getting updates on Cyrene. Cyrene was healing, but her aura had been sucked dry; it made her weak and defenseless. It would be days before we could plan a search party or attack in Bergarian.

"I'm just thinking about Tamera. Was the first mate that rejected her, was that her mate or is Vulcan her true mate?" Hades hummed while stroking his chin.

"That will be something to learn with Selene when we get her back."

"What do you mean? Vulcan is her mate?" Dad's eyes widened in curiosity while the rest of the room went quiet.

"I don't know," I mumbled, hiding my head in Hades' chest. Selene doesn't go around telling who is mated to who. It is supposed to be a big surprise for the couple; I didn't want to ruin it.

"Aw, come on, I wanna hear!" Hunter shouted until Vulcan came into the room. Mom gave Hunter a stern look to be quiet, and he settled down.

"Nothing," Dad spoke. "Just surprised about all these mates popping up out of nowhere." He chuckled while still glaring at Hades. I guess he still isn't over Hades' almost rejection towards his daughter.

"Oh, yeah." Vulcan looked sad as he played with his beard. "Anyway, I was looking for Tamera. Has anyone seen her?" My eyes lit up while I jumped out of my seat. Hades tried to grab my hand, but I ran to Vulcan too quickly.

"Come with me! She's tending to Cyrene in the clinic!" I pulled Vulcan towards the medical wing, only to be stopped by Hades pulling on my other arm.

"Let them be," he glared. I wobbled my lip in protest, trying to pull away from him. "Not now, Ember." I stuck out my lip some more, and he only sighed with a growl. Picking me up and throwing me over his shoulder, I squealed in laughter as he put me back on the couch.

"But I wanna watch," I whispered as Vulcan made his way down to the clinic.

"I didn't think you were into that," Hades whispered in my ear. "Not that!" I squealed as embarrassment flooded me.

Vulcan

Many had found their mates today, which is surprising since I didn't think anyone could discover mates without Selene. My heart sank thinking that Tamera did not have much time; her bonding with Alpha Santos had depressed her almost beyond repair. I had hoped I would be her second chance because she fit in my life like a ray of hope.

Hope that I will have a mate one day, one that would understand me and I to her. I've wanted nothing than to take care of the one I would be destined with and have waited since the day I split with Aphrodite. We were not bonded, just a marriage of guilt from my father, Zeus. He never listened to my pleas not to marry her, yet I did anyway, and my heart was broken by her constant betrayals. A mate was my second chance. A second chance at love and hopefully would be fruitful. Someone I could spoil and protect. I'd give anything for that, anything.

Until she came. Until Tamera came into my life. We weren't mates, but my feelings have grown for her each day. She's kind, loving, and selfless. Even with her failing health, she takes care of others, not thinking of herself and her rejection.

The hall was long; several exam rooms held empty beds as I approached the nurses' station. She-wolves were cleaning, putting up charts, and typing on the computer until they saw me. One of them smiled and pointed to a door. She had seen me far too many times the past few days to know exactly who I was looking for.

I closed in on the last examination room when I smelled something floral. It was robust, feminine, but not overpowering. Hints of sugar cubes hung in the air as my hand trembled at the door. Could the fates be so cruel to have Tamera and my future mate in the same room? Who was in there with her?

My heart trembled; afraid it would jump out of my throat if I dared open my mouth. My hand hovered the door handle, do I dare? Gritting my teeth, I stepped back. My body wouldn't be able to take it; I'd be crushed into a million pieces. I cannot know who my mate is because I all wanted was Tamera. I turn my back to the door; the coward in me rears its ugly head until I hear the examination room door creak open. "Vulcan?" Tamara's whimpered voice halted me in my heavy steps.

Turning, I see her hands clutching her chest as her eyes flood over her eyes. "Vulcan?" she says again, knocking me out of my stupor. She was just so damn beautiful; my body wanted her, my mind, and I didn't have the heart to reject her. I couldn't deny her for someone else I did not know.

Tamera walked silently up to me; my body stiffened on the contact as her hand trailed up my hairy arm. My body reacted to the tingles. Her touch was fire, radiating up my body and straight to my loins. "Mate," I breathed as I engulfed her into my plaid-covered chest. My neatly trimmed beard gets caught in her bracelet and pulled my chin tight, but I didn't care. The pain of her not being my mate would have been greater. I'll take any sort of pain.

Tamera breathed in, and her worried stance grew into a gentle sigh as she leaned forward. Picking her up, her legs wrapped around my torso, face buried into my neck. Wetness filled my shoulder; small sobs shook her body to the core. Petting her hair, touching her, feeling her, it was better than it was before but all so familiar.

Tamera was my mate, she was mine, and I was hers.

Cyrene, lying in bed, did a silent clap as she smiles. Making a shooing motion, she beckons us to leave while we talk about this miraculous discovery. A nurse nearby saw the entire scene and opened the Luna hospital room for me to duck into. Nodding my head in thanks, I lock the door, but Tamera doesn't let go.

"My mate, my sweet mate," my voice choked, brushing her hair behind her ears. A giant sob racks her body as I sit in the oversized rocking chair. Her face was wet, her hair a mess, and it was all mine. We could be messy together for the rest of eternity.

Tamera rubbed her eyes with the back of her hand as she petted my beard. "How can this be?" she hiccuped. "How did we not know?"

Thinking back to Ember, her eagerness was quite intriguing, wanting to lead me to Tamera. With the Sphere found and an overly curious Goddess of the Underworld, I could piece it together. "We've been paired; that's all that matters." My face goes stoic.

Tamera had been through a lot with her first mate. Alpha Santos mated her the same day, claimed her, and not a month later decided to rid her since she did not want to become a werewolf. His mistake would be the most significant victory for me.

"Will you have me?" My voice shook. Not once had I been afraid; I took my challenges head-on, but this, this challenge was the greatest of them all. She could reject me, throw me aside. Tamera quickly nodded her head and grabbed my shoulders.

"I will have you, I wanted you before the bond, and now I can have you after. I chose you before the bond chose us. As long as you don't ever break my heart," Tamera whispered as her nose went into my neck. I growled.

"I would do no such thing." My voice rumbled in my chest. "Anyone that dares to hurt you will have a death wish. And I know people who specialize in torturing." Tamera laughed as her grip became impossibly tight. We held each other for hours. Breathing each other's scent, touching each other's hair, talking, listening. It was far more intimate than that I ever could imagine. It was something we both needed to mend our hearts, so they were no longer broken. Thanks to the fates, we both had been healed.

Tracing my calloused finger around her jaw, I dared to do the unthinkable. I leaned in closer, only halfway to give her the space if she so desired. To my surprise, she leaned forward and planted her puffy lips on mine. My hands wrapped around her back while hers dug into my hair; I moaned in her lips.

This kiss would be written down for all the gods in history. I poured my love into her mouth as she drank it willingly. Gulping it down to give her life and hope. To fill her empty heart. Her skin instantly brightened as we stopped to catch our breath. She no longer looked like the broken woman I met just a week ago.

"I know you have been wronged before, beautiful. I will wait to solidify our bond until you are ready."

Tamera twiddled her fingers and thought contemplatively. "Thank you," she whispered. "But I... it sounds strange, but I feel closer to you than I ever did with Santos."

"Because we spent time together, we fell for each other without a bond. Bonds are blessings, and it enhances our love. Makes us stronger, dependent on each other, and so much more." Tamera smiled, and a blush tainted her cheeks. A playful smile greeted me.

"Then, do you want to go back to my place?" She winked as her hand rubbed the top of mine.

"Is that code for something?" Tamera winked again as she pulled my arm from my chair.

Chapter 62

Vulcan

Tamera led me up the porch steps to her home, her hand continuing to pull mine. The warmth of her home and the smell of vanilla burning candles made my heart skip. It felt like a home, a home I could see myself living in with her. If she will have me.

Thoughts wracked my brain, what if she changes her mind? What if I'm not good enough for her? Tamera was the perfect woman for me. Leading me to the bedroom, she shut the door, not that it mattered living alone. The lights were dimmed and for once in my life I had no idea what I was doing.

"Vulcan," she whispered as she cupped my cheeks. "Are you nervous?" Her sweet breath beckoned me as she gently pulled me to the bed. Falling backwards, slowly, kissing her lips, I hummed into her mouth. I wish I had something to say, something that could make the moment that much sweeter but what words could I form to make this moment more perfect?

Her leg wound around my waist as my hips rubbed her core. Fuck, I was so damn hard I might explode before I see her. "Vulcan don't be scared. I'm not." Her fingers tangled through my hair. Tamera was comforting me, not the other way around. I liked this, I liked she was telling me it was alright because fuck, she went through hell and back and she is this bold to have me now.

My hand slid under her black turtleneck sweater, palming her breast I felt the silk that covered her pointed peeks. Her chest rose upwards, making my hand grab her harshly and our tongues collided. My hips moved on their own accord and felt the heat beneath her clothes.

She scratched at my flannel shirt, straddling her I removed it only to find she had removed her own clothing from the waist up. Her bra was dangling by her finger, her pink lips swollen from my scratchy beard. "Fates guide me," I almost cried while her hand trailed up my hairy chest.

"You are beautiful, Vulcan." Words failed me yet again. I wasn't considered beautiful, good looking or the like. Not on Olympus, not on any god-like status. No one looked to me, but Tamera did. She looked at me as if I was the only one. Who was trying to care for who here?

My lips brushed her collar bone while she wiggled out of her pants. It was an exhausting task, not wanting my skin to leave her body too long. It became heated quickly as both of our naked bodies felt each other with our hands. Breaking kisses to stare at our bodies, her eyes grew wide at my situation. Gods were big, that's just how we were, and worry set in her eyes.

"I won't hurt you, ever," I declared as my fingers traced the inside of her leg. Her body relaxed. Trailing down the bed, I kissed her chest, nipples and down to her hip bone.

"W-what are you doing?" she gasped while her hips moved away from my lips.

"Tasting your nectar… have you never-?"

"No," she breathed. "Please touch me, I can't stand it." My smile widened, getting ready to pleasure my mate in ways she had never felt. My tongue slipped into her slit; her lips were puffy, engorged with want while my tongue massaged her walls. Moans ripped through her, fingers getting tangled in the sheets. "Vulcan," Tamera cursed my name.

Sticking two fingers into her, I curved to find her g-spot. It was rough to the touch as she spasmed in my hand. Her liquids pooled into my hand as I began to suck on her clit. A sharp intake of breath with her body stiffening. A large moan left her while her pussy clamped onto my fingers. I had subconsciously rubbed my dick on the bed, imagining me inside her.

I growled internally until she sat up and held my face in her hands, something she enjoyed doing to make sure I had her full attention.

"Please be inside me." Heat went straight to my cock at her words; the hunger in her eyes left me no doubt she wanted this.

"I'm going to soul bind-us mate." Few tears rimmed Tamera's eyes while my face followed her back on the pillow. "You are mine, forever. Nothing will bring us apart. Mine."

"Please," she breathed. "Make me yours."

My cock twitched and part of my seed ran down my dick. Entering her slowly, I filled her to the brim with my cock. Large breaths left her until I reached the end of her cavern. My body couldn't wait; my hips jerked at the touch of her cervix. Gasping, her nails gripped into my back. The burn only enhanced me to force the seed from me. I couldn't stop, I had to push through.

Allowing my soul to leave my body, Tamera's left too, we held onto each other as we hovered above our bodies. Both in body and in spirit we had combined with each other. Her head was thrown back as I held her soul close to my body. I came with a roar as I felt her chest heat up as my symbol appeared on her chest. The anvil and the hammer. It glowed brightly as I held onto her before our souls lowered and entered back into our bodies.

Both of us, drenched in sweat and seed her hazy eyes bore into mine.

"I love you." She petted the side of my face.

"And I love you, my Tamera."

Hades

Ember sat with a pout on her face. Not only did I, but her mother also scolded her for wanting to watch Vulcan and Tamera discover each other. After a bit of coaxing, she realized she was being foolish, and she cuddled up next to me.

Her family wasn't all that terrible. They were close and they were happy for her to be home. Thoughts of her leaving so soon after rescuing our friends did hold heavy over the minds. Charlotte still hung onto the hope that the portal that Hecate and I would create was the only relieving thing in her mind.

Wesley certainly hated me. He glared at me with more fire than that of Tartarus. There would be a day of reckoning coming my way, but I would cross that bridge when it comes to it. He can't harm me, but he can make my life miserable for the rest of his days.

"Oh, here is the party!" Ares walks in with Mariah clung to his waist as he sat down in the oversized chair that was meant for maybe three people. Mariah snuggled up to him, both bearing their marks.

"Have fun?" Dante spoke as Ares glared.

"Yes, very much so. My mate can keep up with me, and now she is mine forever. I'll be sure to test her strength." Mariah slapped Ares' bare chest as winked at him. Noticing just the marks, I didn't see Tamera's soul bonding mark the gods give.

"Where is her soul bonding mark?" I asked. Something that I should have done in private, but Ares' wasn't really one to be humiliated.

"What? I marked her right here, damn Hades, get some glasses." Mariah pulled down her sweater to show a large bite mark in her neck. A rather angry mark.

"You haven't soul bonded. Her chest is bare." Ares growled, pulling Mariah closer.

"Stop looking at her!" I raised a brow as I hung my head on my hand that was propped up on the sofa.

"You've mated with her, but you haven't soul bonded. Gods are supposed to soul bond, you twit." Ares looked at her chest and into the air like the answer was there waiting for him to appear. He mumbled a few words to himself while Mariah stared at him blankly.

"Oh shit." He jumped over the couch and threw Mariah over his shoulder. "Be right back!" he yelled as he ran up the stairs with Mariah.

***

Several days had passed since the massive mating party. Ember had spent most of the time resting, matching souls or spending lost time with her family. I hadn't mind in the slightest. I stayed in the shadows or right by her side the entire time.

Ember's face grew brighter by the day, like she glowed in an other-worldly sense. Her eyes were soft, warm, and held the most love I had ever seen. Her appetite had grown and was finally eating the normal caloric intake a powerful Wolf like her should be eating. Charlotte and Wesley hardly left her side unless I took her back to our cabin and forced her to sleep.

Many Werewolves came to visit her, catching up on old times and even discussed if she needed to graduate high school. She was a goddess now, none of that mattered unless she really wanted it. The future didn't need a human diploma for her; it just needed her and her skills once Selene was returned.

It was a waiting game until Cyrene had completely healed. She was stronger each day and with the help of Tamera, it had proved most fruitful. Many days we gathered by Cyrene's bedside, discussing the plan of action.

Scouting demons had already infiltrated Vermillion and found on the outskirts a band of rogue Witches, Vampires and Sorcerers. My demons camouflaged themselves and had picked up that the gods were taken to a secluded cabin, deep into the Bloodied Forest near the Forbidden Forest. Lost spirits, those that were unable to descend into the depths of the Underworld resided there. These spirits were too stubborn to descend so they remained on the dirt of Bergarian. Spirits feel scorching pain through their spirited bodies and the only relief is to put their pain on others, possessing travelers, haunting them, and running them out of the Bloodied Forest until they can no longer relieve the pain once they had left.

Ember shivered at the thought of going into the forest; my stubborn self didn't want her to go. However, I didn't trust anyone with her. She would be the safest with me, by my side, as I shield her from the spirits while I cast them down into the Underworld once and for all. I'm not going to deal with a bunch of whining spirits.

"I have the location. Just southwest of the Ichabod Tree in the Bloodied Forest. There should be one small cabin and several tents set up." Loukas threw the map on the makeshift table over Cyrene's bed.

"There are traps, here, here and here," Loukas circled around each area of the supposed traps while Ember stared. "There's a rough head count, about one-hundred and fifty persons. The demons you sent aren't for sure of the Witch, Vampire and even Demon count." My head whipped around.

"Demon?" I growled.

Loukas nodded as he rolled up the parchment. "Dragon's blood can ruin the bond you hold on them. For sure, four of them." I growled, smoke trailing from my feet, but Ember grabbed my arm.

"You will make them pay, don't worry." That's my little fighter.

"We are bringing four-hundred Wolves. I've talked to the Crimson Shadows Pack, and they have been notified. They will be back up if we need it. I'm hoping this will be a clean sweep; we outnumber them greatly." Wesley pulled Charlotte in tightly. "Then again, we are dealing with that magic we fought so long ago it may not even matter."

"Right, we should all be prepared," Ares spoke. "This time you have the gods on your side. You have good warriors, Alpha. I've picked the ones I found the most experienced and strong. My suggestion is they take the night off from practicing and spend time with their loved ones."

Ember's shoulders slumped. There was a high probability we would lose tomorrow. I could smell her salty tears, threatening to fall. "It will be all right; we are going to protect them the best we can." Ember sniffled, laying her head on my shoulder.

About to scoop Ember up in my arms and take her back to our cabin, I felt a pang in my chest. My ward was trying to be broken, and it was not killing whoever was trying to get in. That only meant one thing, a god was trying to break the barrier around our cabin.

"Get to the cabin," knowing Vulcan and Ares would be right behind me, I willed Ember and I to the border of the cabin's ward. Keeping Ember close, I eyed the area, only to find no in sight. Keeping her glued to my side, we trudged forward. Ember's low growl alerted me that she either heard or smelled something.

"I can feel their emotions, so evil, so much hate," Ember whispered. "It's overpowering." Her claws began to lengthen, and her arms were becoming her stark white fur. Before I could stop her, she had shifted in a blink of an eye and bolted into the house. Her mind was muffled with screams while I was trying to link her. Sounds of babies and children crying flooded her ears as I listened in her mind.

"Ember!" I yelled, willing myself to enter just as she put her front paw in the doorway. However, she wasn't there. "Ember!" I growled out, checking the bed, the bathroom, and even the kitchen. Not even her scent lingered in the doorway. I let out a roar and slammed my fists on the table that broke into splinters of wood.

Heaving, the fire burned through my throat as I looked around the dark, vast room one more time. Ares and Vulcan walked in, eyes bulging out of their heads. Smoke had taken over the room, the fire burned at my fingertips, and red was the only color I could perceive.

"The Sphere," Vulcan glanced to the floor where an empty box lay. I ran my hand through my hair, the soot on my fingers rubbed into the white waves.

Fangs grew, but they were not the same as before; they itched with a mighty fury, thicker, longer. Dark hair sprouted from my body. My figure hunched over into the fetal position, but I still stood. I was not going to give up; some damn curse that Demeter had cast on me would not slow me down. What else could it possibly be?

I would find Demeter and give her the worst torment that any parent could ever endure. Watching her beloved child burn in front of her eyes through all eternity. While she will be helpless, tied, and gagged to a stone pillar only to watch repeatedly.

Chapter 63

Vulcan

Hades' bones cracked, and hair protruded from every pore. His screams turned into growls, groans, and grunts until finally, he howled louder than Ares in his Wolf form. Black majestic fur flowed from his body, and red eyes pierced us all. Each wary step that Hades took left burned paw prints into the wooden floors. Smoke steamed, and the more he walked, the hotter his paws became. Flickers of flames came from his claws while he salivated.

Hades had turned into a hell hound. Hell hounds were something else; I hadn't seen them in many years living in the Underworld. They lived in packs at the furthest region from the palace. They were dangerous, brutal, and most of all, unforgiving. When provoked, they could set ablaze an entire forest. Hades created them as guards to protect his home, but he told us he had nothing to protect once Persephone was taken. If anyone dared to enter his palace, he would see to it himself to destroy all who enters.

Thus the hellhounds were then banished since no demon could control them. Now, we have a hellhound in our midst, unsure how not to provoke the God of the Underworld.

Each pant blew cinder, ash, and smoke while his eyes burned brightly. Pawing the cabin floor, it burned holes beneath his paws. Stalking towards us, I pulled Tamera behind me and elbowed Ares to do something. He was a damn Wolf; he would indeed have something to do or say to calm the beast.

"Ares! Do something!" I whispered harshly. Ares was beside himself as he looked on in horror.

"That isn't an ordinary Wolf. It's a damn hellhound. What do you want me to do with it?" Wolves outside gathered, hearing the unfamiliar cries. Alpha Wesley ran up and pushed us aside to see the commotion but immediately took a few steps back.

"Goddess almighty," he whispered. "What is that?"

"Hades," I gritted my teeth. "Your daughter has been taken, and Hades' emotions got the best of him. Looks like your daughter's Alpha bite gave him the ability to change." I spat.

"I don't know which statement to acknowledge first," he growled. "Where is my daughter?" Wesley roared, no longer concerned with the hellhound. Wesley began to lose himself as Charlotte stepped up to pull Wesley back outside. A large owl flew in through the opened door and landed on the bed railing. I sighed in relief as I saw the glimmering white feathers with gold tips.

"Athena." I grabbed hold of Tamera, keeping her out of sight of Hades. His black saliva dripped on the floor, sizzling.

With a few flutters of her wings, Athena stood before us in human attire of brown pleated pants and a tan blazer. Her hair pulled up in a tight bun as her thick-rimmed glasses sat on her face. "Well, isn't this a sight?" Her finger brushed her lips as she approached Hades. His head snapped in her direction while cinder flew out of his nose. "Didn't expect that. Little Ember packed a punch now, didn't she?"

Ares tightened his jaw, no doubt either jealous or upset of his inability to control a creature before us. Sensing Ares' turmoil, Athena approached while Mariah growled at Athena, not caring if she was a god.

"It's all right, Mariah. I don't want him; men don't do it for me." She chuckled. "No one does it for me," she whispered again. "Now, Ares, treat him like any other rogue Wolf. Just because he looks worse for wear doesn't mean you can't help him." Ares blew out his nose as his back stood up straight to approach.

Hades didn't show any sign of giving up, firing off a couple warning barks. Ares didn't relent, not wanting to step down from a fight. "Fight it, Hades." The hell hound shook his head as the black saliva slung across the room. A rabid beast might have been a better fit than a Wolf.

"I command you, let go of your anger. Let go of the inner beast and get control over the animal. The human controls the Wolf; beasts do not." Hades shook his head again, howling in pain as his paws pulled strips of wood from the floor. Ember wasn't going to like the new look to their home away from home.

Ares lunged forward and grabbed Hades by the neck, wrestling him until Ares had pinned him in one swift swoop. Hades was on the floor, paws in the air, trying to nip at Ares' ear. "Submit!" Ares used his brute strength and was being tested. Drips of condensation tickled his brow while his biceps crushed the windpipe. Hades began to still as the breath was taken from his lungs. "That's it," Ares encouraged. "Take back control of your body, calm your anger. We will get her back." Hades whined and whimpered until his body went limp on the floor.

Tamera gripped my arm, a stray tear running down her face. Hades was hurt, devastated above all else, he was angry. Ember was the only thing that held him together, and now she was gone. Hades stilled, and Ares let up on the massive hellhound.

"Now think of your human form," Ares commanded. "Think of your skin, your hair, then feel of the clothes on your body." Hade's bones cracked again as he turned back into his body; his black robes covered him while smoke continued to rise from the ashes he had left. Grunting, he stood up, but his fire was still there.

Hades nodded to Ares in thanks, his mouth in a thin line. Howling, growling was heard from outside; no doubt the news of the female Alpha been taken. "We leave at midnight," Hades' voice was tight.

Athena glanced on at Hades, a small smile on her lips. "Well done, Hades. Maybe you do have some self-control."

Hades' breath deepened while the smoke continued to flow through his limbs.

"Let's get our fellow god and goddesses back."

Ember

"Let me go!" I screamed into the blackened night air. It was musty, stagnant, and worst of all, it smelled of death. If I could use my hands, I'm sure my hand would land on a corpse beneath my feet. However, I was unable to use my hands because they were bound to my back. With my newfound strength, I tried to burst free, but the tightness only worsened while trying. Dragon's blood must have been coated on each twine of the rope.

I screamed again, but a slap stopped me from continuing. Hisses came from the lips of the two holding me by my biceps. My enhanced vision wouldn't even let me see through the darkness. I grit my teeth, trying to extend my fangs, but that too came up short.

"Elea, you still there?" I whispered.

"*Yes, but something is holding me back, like the time I tried to get free. This one is so much stronger.*" Her voice was weak as Elea tried to talk.

"*Sleep. I'll need you later. We will get out of this.*" Elea didn't speak again; I knew we were in some deep poo.

"Take her with the rest," the snarl rung through my ear. The breath was cold and stunk of old blood. Vampire, it had to be a Vampire. At least my smell hadn't been taken from me. Internally rolling my eyes, their grip tightened as their claws gripped me tighter, piercing my naked skin.

No doubt, Hades was pissed. The worry about myself was thrown into the back of my mind. Hades was going to burn this place up, innocent people here or not. The site would look like a nuclear bomb hit; it would be ash by morning. Trying to rip my arm away again, it only angered my captor, who hissed again.

"Can I at least have a shirt or something?" My body was completely naked, and I hadn't felt this exposed since the club. Something else Hades was going to be mad about, me being naked around a bunch of creepy Vampires. "When Hades gets here, he is gonna kick your sorry butt!" Another shove, and I fell flat on my face. My arms were still behind me; I ate nothing but dirt. The grittiness of the soil must have blackened my teeth; the taste was of rich decaying leaves.

"My mate will make you suffer," I whispered. A cloak was thrown over me, and I was thrown over someone's shoulders.

"Wet dog," the Vampire grumbled, the creaking door was opened, and my body was dropped hard on the floor. My butt was broken; it was officially broken. I rubbed it harshly while glaring at my captor. Fangs stuck out of his mouth, his eyes red with pinched eyebrows. He glanced at me with such disgust it made me feel dirty when I knew I wasn't. Pulling the cloak tighter to my body, he slammed the door to the poorly lit cabin. A small fire glowed lowly, the embers nearly out. I wish I had Hades' fire summoning ability; that would have been fun.

"Ember?" a male voice spoke softly from the darkened corner. Crawling across the floor and finally standing, Hermes stood in the light of the candle. His brightly colored skin had turned grey, and his hair no longer shimmered.

"Hermes?" I cried. Keeping the cloak wrapped tight, I fell into his arms as we held onto each other.

"You are the last person I thought I would see." He heaved a breath of relief. "I see that Hades has lost his touch." Chuckling, two more figures stood up to join us. Selene, the woman in my dreams, touched my hand that was still wrapped around Hermes' torso. The bright moon that shone on her forehead didn't glow as bright, and dark circles tainted her face. Hecate, the 'doctor' that saw me from so long ago, was also here. They were all here, all the missing gods.

"How did you get here?" Selene spoke calmly. "Where is Hades?" I bit my lip while looking everywhere but her eyes.

"Someone was trying to break the ward of our cabin, then I heard a baby cry and thought someone was hurting a pup, so I rushed into the house, but I ended up somewhere, in the dark. Naked. I couldn't shift back into my wolf." I grit my teeth in frustration.

"Demeter has cursed this area with Dragon blood; since you are mated to a god, it affects you too," Hecate brushed my hair back from my muddy face. Sighing heavily, I sat by the nearby table.

"She has the Sphere," I choked. "Demeter must have it; what are we going to do?" Selene shook her head as she kneeled before me.

"It will all work out; Hades will come for you, and that puts everything on our side. How much do you all know?"

Everyone sat in a circle around me. I explained everything I knew. From the Shifter Dragon's blood to Demeter taking me when I was a child, to Malachi who had the Helm and someone breaking the ward. My chest continued to tighten, and my fingers balled into fists. Everything had been against me from the very beginning. All the emotions of being away from my family, suffering, having no one to lean on for so many years came flooding back. I thought I had been through this, went through the motions of forgiving Hades, Dante, my family. Why is this coming back now?

I broke into a sob. So close to having everything back for it just to slip away through my fingers. Was I not allowed to be happy? Were the fates that cruel to me? To give me a life that made me so happy to strip it away so suddenly?

"It's all my fault. I shouldn't have ran. The darkness I felt, the worry, I thought someone was in danger, and I couldn't just let it go." I rubbed a tear from my cheek.

"Oh little flame," Hermes cooed. "Demeter would have gotten the Sphere with or without you. She has too much on her side right now, but your mate is going to make her pay. The Dragon's blood is almost gone," he whispered slowly. "Demeter has just enough for what she wants to accomplish, and that's it." Hermes eyes went to the window, listening to the cheers outside.

"What does she want to do?" Glancing at the three of them, they frowned. Hecate stepped forward, holding my hands in hers. "Break the bond between Persephone and Gabriel and have Selene create a new one with Malachi. Malachi has promised Demeter he would remain in Demeter's home so she could always have her daughter." I gasped. How cruel of a mother to break a bond of her child of her true mate?

"That's terrible," I spoke.

"She's sick," Hermes spat. "A sick woman that is too attached to her daughter. Won't let the girl grow up." Hermes shook his head.

"What does that have to do with Hades and me, though?" Hermes lowered his head as his dirty hair fell into his face.

"Demeter hates Hades for keeping Persephone; Demeter only accepted the deal of six months out of the year with her daughter because that was the only way to have her. Now she wants revenge; she wants to break your bond with Hades as well. If it breaks, your goddess powers will be taken away, and it will kill you." Hermes gripped my hands tightly.

Anger filled me. I was not the one for violence, Hades was, but this was unacceptable. I growled as I threw back the table. The candle blew out as I huffed in annoyance. No one was going to take our bond; I'd make sure of it.

"Well then," Hermes laughed. "You've got a bit of Hades' anger in you." I sat back in the chair, feeling utterly defeated. Hades was coming, I had to remind myself. He would come; he would rescue all of us.

Hecate petted my hair, pushing it back behind my ear. Her touch was calming as I tried to rein my emotions in. My empath abilities had not weakened as much as I thought they would. Maybe I could use it to my advantage later.

"I'm sorry to change the subject so quickly. Most of my powers have weakened significantly and I cannot do much." Hecate lowered her voice as her fingers trailed to my abdomen. "However, there is some good news that I can tell you, Ember." My heart stopped as Hecate squeezed my hand.

"My dear, you are with child."

Chapter 64

Ember

"Wait, what?" My eyes bulged. Hecate wasn't joking; her small smile gave her a bit of twinkle in her dull eyes. There wasn't a possible way I could be pregnant. Hades said so himself. He was sterile.

"Oh, how little Hades' knows," Selene giggled. Her moon glowed a bit. "You are his little light, his little mate. Bonds help balance one another out, and with that, healing takes place. Your Alpha bite is strong, and one of the advantages of the bite you gave him helped him heal himself. Even with his godlike powers, he couldn't help his fertility due to his long-suffering in Kronos. However, your ability to heal, your Wolf, helped him with his. Not to mention, he may turn into a Wolf," she muttered.

My mouth dropped. Feeling my lip wobble, I put my hands to cover my gaping mouth. Warmth in my eyes overflowed, and tears began to tickle my cheeks. "Hades is going to be a daddy?" I almost cried. Hermes slapped his hands together as his teeth sparkled with mirth.

"And you are going to be a mother," Hecate cooed while I rubbed my belly. We were going to be parents! I wanted to tell Hades right away, tell him he was going to have a child. I couldn't wait to see the look on his face! I couldn't wait to...

"We have to get out of here," I said, determined. "We can't wait." Hecate frowned while I stood up. "Who knows how long we will be here, what spells are cast on this place. We can't let Demeter know I'm pregnant either! She would use it against me." I cradled my stomach while Selene held onto my shoulders.

"There isn't a way out; all our powers are suppressed, Ember. I can't even communicate outside the damn ward," Hermes hissed. I narrowed my brows as I concentrated on my empath abilities. It was there with my Wolf, before Hades and I mated; I just didn't know what they were at the time. Using those abilities, if I could determine what Demeter was feeling, it could give us an idea if she was nervous at all. Detect for lies and so forth.

"Does Persephone know what her mother is doing?" I asked.

Hermes shook his head. "Persephone thinks that Malachi really is her mate. They can't feel sparks, and Persephone is getting suspicious from what we have been told. She hasn't been around the encampment, but Malachi comes to do Demeter's bidding." Hermes rolled his eyes as he slumped in the chair. "She's great keeping her daughter in the dark."

"Wait, who told you? How do you know so much?" Hermes' little smile didn't go unnoticed.

"Some little Vampire has a crush." Selene eyed Hermes. "She has snuck us food and information. She wants to get out as well."

Speaking of the little wussy angel from earlier, Malachi opened the door with food in his hand. It contained nothing but bread and water, not even enough to sustain one person. "Here you go." He cheerfully put it on the table. Turning to leave, I walked up to him and pulled his arm back, throwing him to the wall. My grip tightened. A newfound ferocity grew in my body, I had a baby to protect and a mate to tell the good news. I was tired of this and was going to end it.

"Listen here, Malachi," I spat. Trying to pull my nails from my body, they grew ever so slightly, piercing his heavenly skin.

"W-what are you doing?" he stuttered. Trying to get a good look at my hands, I forced my fangs to descend, just enough to show. Malachi's emotions went to annoyance, to fear, to downright petrified.

"If you think you can keep me here, you have another thing coming," I growled. "I'm going to have fun watching you suffer." The door slammed open again, vines gripping my limbs and pinning me to the floor. The goddess' robes swept the floor elegantly as she shut the door, locking it before another word was spoken.

"So feisty you are, much more than you were so many years ago. Maybe another frightful scare and a bash to your head might calm you a bit." Demeter's lips smacked together. "That Helm is dreadfully heavy; however, I could skip scaring you entirely and hit you with more Dragon's blood spells." it is mighty powerful." She hummed. A faint hint of worry hit her emotions; it was a lie. She wouldn't waste that Dragon's blood. Pearly white teeth parted her lips, cackling into the fire. Her hand threw dust that roared it to life, warming the room.

Demeter began walking meticulously around the room, studying each god in a judging manner. Her stature meant seriousness, cold and brutal. However, the underlying emotions were there. I felt her fear, anxiousness, and discomfort.

"It's time to do your part, Selene. Erase the bond of Gabriel and Persephone or have one of your friends here suffer the consequences. I've waited long enough." Another wave of her hand, she sat in the chair, unmoving, staring into Selene. Selene's head dipped in despair while Hermes shook his head.

"Don't do it, Selene," Hermes whispered.

"I could make him suffer then, only if you want, Selene." Demeter tutted and pulled a small spear from her side. Standing, walking closer to Hermes, he flinched, seeing the black liquid at its end.

Clenching my fist, I kept the low growl in my chest. Selene stood with her hands placed in front of her. Looking at Hermes, she gave a small smile and walked with Demeter out the door.

"Malachi, have some of our friends tie our prisoners to the poles outside. This is something I want them to see." Malachi glanced at me while I showed him my pearly whites. Lucky that Demeter had been oblivious to the change as we walked single file outside.

The bonfire stood in the middle of the area. Poles stood in a row for Hecate, Hermes, and I. "Don't get too comfortable, Ember. Breaking your bond with Hades will be the grand finale." While the Vampire holding me tied me down, I was sure to struggle to not get it as tight. Hermes, who was being led to his pole, had a woman, tall, slender with violet eyes, guide him. She wasn't rough, her touch was gentle. Then I saw it, a glimmer of light between their skin. Selene must be too weak to even know the bond between them.

"She's the one that has been our friend here," Hecate whispered. "She snuck us extra rations of food and let us know what has been going on."

"Mates," I whispered to Hecate. "They are mates." Hecate's eyes darted to Hermes, who didn't struggle against her. As she tied the ropes, she kept them loose so Hermes could break free. Giving him a wink, she came by each of our ropes to check their sturdiness. Once she reached me, she sighed and loosened mine as well. I grabbed her hand from behind and gave her a squeeze. I'd get her out too.

"Now then, Selene." Demeter pulled a vile from her robes. There were all but two drops of blood inside. Her jaw tightened as she dropped the slightest amount on the Sphere. There it sat, an orb that could change the destinies of two couples. Persephone and mine. Two souls approached, most likely, they were that of Persephone and Gabriel. Selene flinched as she saw the two souls together, tied together through their bond.

"Malachi, bring in Persephone." Laying on a small cot, with flowers in her hair, Persephone laid asleep. Her lashes were full of dew, and spring flowers wafted through the death of the air. "Good work on the tea." Malachi dropped his head as his smile went wicked, holding onto her hand.

"Begin, Selene, I don't have all day." Selene's hand moved to touch the Sphere. Her shoulders slumped while her other delicate fingers reached for the Sphere.

"What have you promised the Vampires' for their loyalty?" I interrupted. The large group gathered stood still. Not a sound was made as they looked at one another. Candles blew in the gentle wind, and the fire sparked lightly. Demeter's footsteps faltered as she walked towards me, no doubt to silence me.

"Do they know there is no more dragon blood? That it will all be gone by the time you create these next two spells?" Whispers and gasps came from the darkness, and Demeter slammed her hand on my mouth. "You know nothing," Demeter screamed. "I have the blood and can get more!" Lies, all lies.

Biting her hand that dared to grip my neck, she screamed and ripped it away. "Really now? Because Cyrene, the powerful Sorceress, has told me no Shifter Dragon blood will be given to anyone. That most had been destroyed in the Dark War! I yelled again.

"I will get them their blood." Demeter's emotions ran wild with fear. "I have my ways. You should hold your tongue!" Trying to slap my face again, the ropes dropped, and I grabbed her wrist, sinking my claws into her delicate skin.

"If you have more dragon's blood, please, use it on me to tie me back to the pole. For I know is this, the magic is weakening, my fangs are already itching, my claws are lengthening. It will only be a small amount of time until Hades and the entire Black Claw Pack will

invade this forest and send you and the rogues straight to Tartarus."
My grip tightened on Demeter. By her outward appearance, you
wouldn't think she believed me, but I knew. I knew her fear and the
helplessness she was feeling.

Whispers came from the crowd again. "Is it true, there is no more
Dragon Shifter blood in storage? All of it gone? That wasn't written
in the history texts of the war. The history books said it was all buried
into the ground!" One Vampire hissed towards Demeter. I huffed.
Demeter went to extra lengths to hide the history of the Dark War?
How low could she possibly be?

"You changed the history books for your favor. Too bad you
couldn't change the God's history; the fates couldn't allow that. Then
we wouldn't have had a clue that Gabriel was Persephone's mate!" I
squealed in laugher. "You are just full of plot holes, aren't you,
Demeter?" Demeter's confidence wavered, and doubt settled into
her mind.

More time, more time. I needed more time for Hades to get here.
He wouldn't stay away for long, he wouldn't, he couldn't.

Demeter's vines tried to wrap around my ankle, but I swiped
them away. Panic had risen her heartbeat while Vampires and
Witches screamed from the darkness. The light kept them hiding in
the tree line.

"Is it true?" another yelled. Demeter's head darted to the voice.
Running to Hermes and Hecate, I pulled them from their poles.

"Look! Their strength is returning! How are you going to hold us
back now, Demeter?" Demeter darted towards Selene, and a
prolonged fingernail ran over Selene's pale neck. Standing frozen, I
waited for Demeter's next move.

"Come here, mate of Hades," she cackled. "It doesn't matter if
the magic is wearing off because Selene is the weakest; it will take her
time to heal. You don't want her blood on her hands, do you?"
Demeter's eyes grew fire, her white teeth glimmered with the wetness
of her mouth. "Get over here and finish it, or I will finish her. I saw
your little show on your territory. Demons and Wolves, a perfect
combination, hmm? Now separate the goddess from the damn angel
Gabriel who is too busy to move into my domain so I may have my
daughter." Demeter turned to the unsettled crowd.

"I will get you your blood. Have I not delivered my promises so
far? Three goddesses for you to feast on their blood and Dragon
magic that I pull from my cloak when needed? I do have more, and
it is for you if my tasks are completed!" Demeter pulled Selene away,
heels dragging into the dirt.

Demeter had become dirty, nasty, vile. Her emotions had polluted Earth and Bergarian soil. Her reign as a goddess will be put to an end. If not done by me, but by Hades himself. Hades' powers were more robust than any others. He withstood Kronos. He could fight this easily.

Bright red blood dripped from Selene's neck. Not a sound escaped her lips as she shook her head. "Don't." Her hands held onto Demeter, trying to pull her away. Hermes and Hecate could only stand back and watch. The vampire that had helped with my façade stood near Hermes, who only eyed her longingly.

My body was aware of the nature around me. The brisk breeze picked up as my body drew closer. The Sphere shimmered in the firelight, and my fingers pricked with unease. Demeter's emotions grew impatient while she gripped Selene tighter. "Get on with it!" she growled. For a moment, I thought I saw Persephone's finger twitch. Her golden hair dropped to the dirty forest floor.

In front of the Sphere, I stood. No one knows what Selene and I could see in front of us. Just smoke rolling around the ball.

Persephone and Gabriel stood in front as I pictured them in my mind. Their bond was strong; even with the fake bond created for Malachi and Persephone, it held true. I was sure that breaking their bond would cause both of them to die, two strong beings like these. Demeter had no clue what she was asking for.

My finger flung them back into the Sphere as I searched for two more. Hermes and his vampire companion. Hecate was muttering under her breath; Persephone moved her hand, and I found the two I was looking for.

A distraction is what I needed and what I was going to get.

Chapter 65

Hades

Storming out of the cabin, I find nothing but Wolves lined in their military pattern. Many with the desire of death covering their senses. Not once but twice, my Ember was taken from this pack. It took everything within my bones not to strike every one of them.

Wesley, looking equally displeased, was in his human form staring them down with the ferocity I had never seen before from the docile Alpha. He had not been the most aggressive among his fellow Alphas in the Earth realm. He was the peacemaker, but when war threatened his pack, he took with an iron fist. Now, he would be put to the test. Seeing his outrage over the disappearance of his daughter gave me hope his warriors would prevail. They will prevail; there was no if because there was not one but three gods, and one of them is the god of death that will manage the small militia that took my mate.

Demeter was foolish, blinded by the love of her daughter, to think she would get away with any of this. Her years hiding in the dark, perfect planning, and timing had yielded well. However, time was up, and we were coming for her.

Ares, ever so brooding, walked up to Wesley, who only nodded his head in submission to the God of War, letting Ares take control.

Barking orders and having Wolves grab weapons, some were ordered to fight in human form while others remained with their Wolf.

Loukas's body flickered in the distance; his apparition needed some heavy overhaul. I had ripped most of his powers once he had returned to the territory. Not wanting him to try and take my Ember away, not that he would succeed anyway. "Loukas, what are you doing?" I barked. He was supposed to be in the confines of the packhouse, but the damn demon was like a cockroach.

"Forgive me, master." He bowed his head slowly. Finally, some submission from him, if it wasn't for Ember's friendship with the little fire demon, I would have gotten rid him long ago. "I went to gather a much-needed ally." Loukas pointed to the roof of the packhouse. Bright light descended on the roof, revealing a short tunic covering one side of his chest and shoulder with gold armor as well as a breastplate. A long sword in hand, wielded by Vulcan himself, one of the last magical metals he had created before his hiatus from his magical forging position.

Gabriel.

Gabriel's wings were tall and wide; tiny tendrils of gold shimmered in the light as he floated down from the rooftop. The leaves shied away from the swoop. Stepping lightly with his sandals, he approached, wings slightly dragging on the fall ground. "I take it you are here to fight for your mate," I said with a clipped tone. Gabriel looked to Athena, who only smiled in return.

"I'm glad you have come to your senses, Gabriel. Your mate will be pleased once she remembers you." Gabriel's chest tightened. The distant look in his eye gave confirmation that he had felt the bond, yet Persephone had not. The years apart, must have been quite the turmoil.

Gabriel mentioned his heart knew that Persephone was all innocent in this. That she felt the longing many times as they both glanced at each other from afar. However, Malachi was said to be her mate. "Persephone couldn't leave her mate because she trusted Selene," Gabriel spoke. "No matter how much she felt for me, she stayed with an angel she had no love for because of a damn fake mark," he hissed. "Persephone said she had to stay with Malachi because 'Selene doesn't make mistakes. I must make this work,'" he mocked. "But I knew better. I knew there had to be something wrong. Malachi's touches didn't light her fire like mine did." Gabriel looked along the army lines. "For years, I watched her from afar. Yearning for her. Now that I have the evidence it was all a lie, I will kill Malachi." Gabriel stood behind the Wolf lines, along with the warriors, ready for his commands.

"We are nearing midnight; I'd like to get to the Dark Forest before," I gritted my teeth while everyone watched. Charlotte held onto her youngest, Steven, who had tears in his eyes. "He'll bring her back, right Mom?"

"Ember will come back." I stared at the boy. Kneeling, I put my hand on his shoulder. Squeezing it lightly, I spoke softly to him, "She will not evade me again." A glimpse of a smile came to his face as I stood up. Charlotte gripped him tighter while silently begging me to bring her daughter home.

Athena, now donned in her warrior attire, sheets of metal armor all encrusted with her owls and love of books and scrolls decorated on her breastplate. "Four, there will be four of us. To ensure that Demeter is put into place. Zeus has granted you to do as you will to our sister for betraying you and your mate. There will be no trial because the evidence is stacked against her. All that Zeus asks is that you bring home the gods safely and that he wishes he be invited to your mating ceremony." Athena winked as she walked away, her purple cloak brushing my legs.

Of course, Zeus would want to attend a party. I groaned and turned to our small army. We would undoubtedly win, but the cost would be high if there was more Dragon blood found. Losing mated couples would be devastating to Ember and to the rest of the pack.

"Protect yourselves," I warned. The Wolves calmed down as they looked towards Athena, Ares, Vulcan, and me. "Most of all, protect each other. Ember, your Alpha, would not be happy to find that Wolves were slain due to her being kidnapped. This is my order to you, come back alive. Fight fiercely, honorably, but do not sacrifice yourself to gain anyone's favor. Live to fight another day, live for your families, live for your Alpha."

A roar of howls, cheers, and screams filled the air. The trees bowed in the large gust of winds that surrounded us. Leaves scattered and danced around our feet until the wind blew upward. The hordes of Wolves and demons gathered closer together; Athena's tight bun was ripped from her band and flew up as her eyes pointed to the sky.

In an enormous gulf of light, we were all transported, transported to the land where we would fight for my mate and the safety of the gods. One god will lose its status as one of the twelve, the first to so. She will suffer at my hands through all eternity.

Once the wind had died, we found ourselves on the outside of the Dark Forest. No doubt these woods would scare the Wolves who had not been to the realm of Bergarian. These trees were tall, wide, and branches that hung over like thin monster's hands that would pull at your cloak. Instead of feeling a soft breeze from the darkened leaves, they were silent, stagnant, and full of death.

Gabriel immediately took to the sky; glancing at us, he was engulfed in the fog. Gabriel's mission was Persephone. He was to grab and take her away from the fighting.

Spirits floated through the trees, looking on with curiosity, some with malicious intent. One with an evil glint in his eye saw me and immediately alerted the others; they wouldn't bother me, but those who accompanied me would be at risk. Waving my hand, sending a wind that pushed through the first one hundred yards, those spirits were sent straight to hell, waiting to be judged. My time away from the Underworld was going to make my time much more difficult when I returned. So many souls to judge and torment. A faint smile reached the corner of my mouth as Athena acknowledged my act.

"Move out." Athena swung her sword as we marched into the woods. Wesley led the first group; they were to run clear around the other side of the encampment, making sure no soul would escape. Ares led us forward, ready to take the first wave of rogues head-on. Ares' cocky stride let me know we would have no trouble fighting off the first wave.

A few unfamiliar sounds came from the trees. Goblin-like creatures jumped to the ground and hissed. Dark skinned with damaged scales, salivating while licking their fangs. Ares chuckled and swung his ax, and their heads rolled to the forest floor. Younger Wolves came to sniff and acknowledged the new species. These were just the forest creatures that played in the forest, none tied to Demeter.

A glow in the distance, a bonfire that had to be at least two stories tall, lit the way. Hand signals were thrown by Ares and Athena, both flanking my sides and allowing me to approach head-on. I would be the one that talked to Demeter, trying to persuade her to let my mate go. If a battle could be prevented, then so be it. I would still take her by her skinny neck and rip her to shreds once my mate was in my arms.

Walking closer, you could hear a loud hiss and Hermes screaming. There would be no first wave of attacking rogues because they were all retreating. Running towards the commotion, I found Hermes sucking face with a vampire as Ember grips Demeter by the throat.

Ember

I licked my lips gently. The first finger finally touched the midnight blue sphere; Hermes' soul twitched as I commenced to glide him across the curvature of the glass. The vampire woman, the woman that had chosen to betray Demeter and loosen the ropes of my friends, stood there. She smiled as my finger touched her torso. Harlow came to my mind. Her name was Harlow; nodding at me, she reached for Hermes, who did the same in return. Glancing at Demeter one more time, knowing that this union was going to be harsh, fast, and possibly a show with the Dragon's blood dripping down the side, I braced myself.

Touching their souls and merging them into one, Hermes let out a war cry. Harlow let out a loud hiss as everyone began to scramble towards the noise. Vampires tried to reel in their own kind, but Harlow was more robust, faster with the bond pulling them together. Their bond would be the strongest until its magic had worn off. Hermes's dirty blonde hair flipped to the side as he punched one of the Witches square in the nose, blood draining into her lips. The struggle continued until my feet had me charge Demeter.

My claws extended more than earlier, and the warmth spread through my chest. Hades was nearby. I felt his presence and my heartbeat out of my chest. His heart was slow, solid, and steady as I felt him watch the chaos unfold.

From the corner of my eye, Malachi grabbed Persephone and held her to his chest. Her head fell backward, hanging from his arm. A bright light came from the heavens, a stark difference from the dark that had rained down on us for the past few hours. So bright that I became blind, and Demeter's vines grabbed my neck, beginning to squeeze. Her body toppled onto mine and pushed her knee into my stomach.

Remembering the child in my body, I slung my leg around, and my thigh knocked her torso flat on the ground. Before I could throw my claws into her, I was pulled up in a warm embrace. His campfire and s'more smell invaded my nose. My mate, my mate, was here.

"Go hide," he ordered into my ear. I gripped his hand and pulled him to my face; one peck on the lips was all it took for him to pull me to him and his tongue invaded my mouth. Time stopped in those three seconds. Hades' eyes full of fire and passion released me reluctantly as Demeter's thorns shot her vines, ripping him away from me.

I growled in frustration, but Hades took the lead. His cloak had fallen to reveal leather bindings around his torso, corset-like, and wielded a black sword with ember glowing into the darkened night. The tight leather pants showed his extraordinary behind that only made me hot.

"Damn," I whispered, but a blood-curdling howl from Remus, my father's Wolf, made me falter. Across the clearing, my father was battling a demon, so large that its horns curved around his head and straight to the back of its body. Hooves stomped the ground as they dug its blackened hooves into my father's hind leg for a second time.

Remus's howl ripped through me. My make-shift cloak dress was torn from my body as I shifted. The gentle air of white wings blew past me, but I dared not stop. Paws gripping the decaying leaves, I leaped into the air, higher than I had ever jumped. My claws ripped into the biceps of the demon quick enough so my jaws could clamp down on its thick neck. The only hair on its head was in a small ponytail with long strands down his back. The rest was bald and containing only its horns.

It roared in aggravation while my maw clamped harder. Black blood pooled into my mouth; the taste of death came along with it. Holding back a gag, I let go once more to gain more traction with my claws. Large hands came behind his head, dirtying my white fur with its black blood. My grip was tight, and little did this demon know, I was a goddess now and healed faster than an ordinary Wolf. Elea took control, and with one twist of her neck, the monster succumbed to a neck-breaking bite, surrendering to its injuries. Dust filled my lungs; the demon had now returned to the pool of demonic souls.

Elea spat out the remaining blood while glancing at Dad. His leg was a mess, black tar-like substance pouring from his side. Switching to human form, I leaped to his side, holding his wound.

"Dad?!" I breathed helplessly. The fight was still going, Wolves were winning by a landslide, but my father, the Alpha, was dying in my arms. His heart rate weakened while trying to remain his grip on my arm holding his wound. "It's all right, Ember," he heaved.

Everything was not all right. My father was lying on his back, a vulnerable position for a Wolf. "We have to get this magic off of you," I cried. My eyes darted to Hades, who was still dealing with Demeter. Dad coughed again. I bellowed for Hecate, who felt my desperate plea from her hiding position. Kneeling into the dirt, examining his wound, I silently pleaded.

Hecate's eyes held no hope as her fingers dipped into his wound. My own father's blood had begun to turn into a black like-tar, thick and sticky. "What hurt you?" Hecate whispered. Dad coughed again, bits of blood-spitting from his mouth.

"A-a spear, like the one that pierced Hades."

My stomach dropped.

Chapter 66

Hades

Ordering Ember away, Demeter's vines gripped around my neck, razor-sharp thorns ripping through my skin. Growling, my sword cut through the air, cutting the vines with a slight hissing sound from the blazing hot iron. Demeter drew back, bending her knees, about to launch towards me again. "Let's end this, Demeter. You are outnumbered. This is only going to lead to innocent lives lost." Demeter let out a mocking laugh to my face.

"I will never give up, never give up on seeing you suffer and being able to see my child every day! Do you know what torment you put me through?" Demeter hissed as her nails scratched across my leather vest. A mistake in not moving away will only deem her sentence more fruitful.

"A child is to grow and let go, You can't hold onto her forever!" I yelled; my sword being pulled by the roots of a nearby tree. Slinging my hand, the roots died in an instant, cracking as I drew my sword. Fire struck at the dry roots, and flames roared to life.

Gabriel's long wings stretched out, hovering above. The brief breeze sent our way made the flames fly higher up the rotting tree. "You help things grow, and all you are doing is suffocating the one life that really mattered." Demeter stumbled and fell backward, landing on her ass. Scooting back, her head hit the back of the tree. Heavy pants left her lips while she glanced at the steaming sword and my eyes.

"You've done enough damage, Demeter. Zeus has given me permission for punishment."

"Mom?" The weak voice came from the other side of the bonfire. Malachi was nowhere to be found, and Gabriel put Persephone's feet to the ground. Her eyes were glazed with unshed tears looking at her broken mother and her mate. "Did you try to separate me from my mate?" Persephone's whispers were low, clinging to a shawl Gabriel draped over her.

"Malachi is your mate!" Demeter spat while on the ground. Covered in dirt, leaves, and soot, she stood up, trying to dust herself off. "Not this angel. He was trying to keep you from me!" Her hands were thrown in the air, trying to march up to Persephone, but I stopped her with my sword.

"You don't go near her," I growled. "Gabriel is her true mate. You poisoned her with lies, magic and tried to have Selene force a bond." My eyes glanced to the Sphere of Souls, still sitting out in the open with all the fighting. Several warriors brought dead Vampires, Demons, and Witches and threw them into the large fire. Shit, things were going to be busy for a while.

"Persephone," Demeter cooed. "I am only doing what is best for you. You need your mother, don't you? I know how you like your tea. You love to hear those funny fairy stories I used to tell, right?"

Persephone scrunched her nose. "For a while, I did, but then I met Gabriel. Gabriel completes me, and you wanted to take it away. Sure, Hades keeping me was wrong, but he was lonely. He gave me pretty things and made sure I was taken care of, but my heart didn't belong to him." Persephone gave me a small smile.

"I'm sorry I got angry with you towards the end of my stay. I just knew I was missing something and that something just wasn't you." I chuckled. "Yeah, I wasn't. I was just mad I couldn't find my missing something either. I'm sorry I kept you." Persephone nodded, and Gabriel pulled her closer to him, her arms wrapping around his neck.

"No!" Demeter screamed as her claws went to Gabriel. Jumping in front of the couple, my sword's hot blade slid through the skin like butter, coming clear out the other side. Demeter's screams softened, and her arms slumped. Light leaving her eyes, but not wholly going out. My blade was able to render gods helpless once impaled or cut severe enough. Their bodies would vanish into thin air and will assemble on the edge of Tartarus. Her powers won't manifest again until her body reaches the sunlight, and I had no plans of letting that happen ever again.

Persephone's head was buried in Gabriel's chest, gripping his tunic. "I'm sorry you had to see that," I said, bowing to both. "Your mother did commit many crimes, and I was given permission-" Persephone waved his hand to silence me.

"It is better this way," she whispered. Light tears trailed down her face. "She liked to be in control, and it is best for everyone this way." Gabriel wrapped Persephone in his wings. The two had been reunited, and now it was time for me to be reunited with my mate. Glancing across the clearing, most of the Wolves had finished fighting, now surrounding one lone Wolf on the ground.

Only a few trailed in, bringing bodies to the fire. We had been lucky there had been no more Dragon's blood to enhance any sort of abilities for their fighting. Demeter really was foolish. A large cry left my mate's lips. Darting to the noise, I saw Wesley lying in a pool of black matter and Ember clinging to his chest.

"What happened?" I ran over and fell to my knees. Trying to pull Ember from her death grip, she wailed again. Hecate looked longingly as Ember cried into a barely breathing Alpha Wesley.

"He is the only one that has been struck. A spear had some dragon's blood on it, just like the one that speared you." My heart gripped tight into my chest. Wesley wasn't going to survive this. Hecate was weak, still struggling to hold herself up; she had no power until we got her out of this ward.

"Could we move you and him? Maybe your magic will come back stronger?" Hecate shook her head and patted Wesley's arm. "It will take me weeks to be back at full strength."

"Hades, please," Ember cried. "Don't let them take his soul! Don't let them!" Grim Reapers came out of the forest. They were tasked to hold the strongest of Alphas because alphas did not cooperate reasonably to leave their bodies. Wesley was strong, so two came, and my little mate saw them. I gripped my fist in anger. I couldn't bring Wesley back, they had to take his soul, or he would be doomed to wander all Bergarian for his mate who did not even reside in this realm.

"Ember, I can't," I whispered. Both of her hands went to her father's face.

"You cannot give up, Daddy, you can't! You have to take me down the mating aisle! Do you hear me! You can't!" Tears fell onto Wesley's face, several into his eye as her father gave a faint smile.

Too weak to hold his hand up to his daughter, he mouthed to her, "I love you. It will be all right." A cough broke up the words, but Ember understood.

"What about Mom, Daddy? What about Mom? She won't live without you!" Another howl wrecked through Ember, my hand rubbing her bareback. Ember would have to live without Wesley and now her mother. Any bond, especially with an Alpha bond, holds them together. If one dies, the other parts too. Ember's parents would both go to the Underworld. Leaving that bit of information out of the moment, the disturbance in the trees grabbed our attention.

Ember covered her father's body with her own. Protecting him of any threat that remained. She growled as her fur sprouted from her body again.

Ares, in battle stance, waited until the trees parted. A giant partially shifted Werewolf strode out along with a small Wolf about the size of a fox. "Too late," the animal growled, but the foxlike Wolf only barked at the massive beast in scolding. Bones breaking, a woman appeared in the fox Wolf's stead. A blanket was put around her by supposedly her mate. The half-human beast stayed in his form, only one step behind her in a protective stance.

The light in my head shone my idiot ways and realized it was none other than King and Queen of the Cerulean Kingdom, Kane and Clara. "I'm sorry we are late, but it looks like most of you are Okay," she spoke softly. "Except this Wolf right here?" Clara pointed to the labored breathing of Wesley. Her knees are planted firmly into the ground as she pets his forehead. Ember gripped Wesley tighter, only for Clara to rub her hand.

"My mother said your father fought valiantly but would succumb to a nasty stab." Clara glanced over his naked torso and touched the tar-like blood. "That's why I came. She said the fates had more work for Alpha Wesley in the Earth Realm." The former Queen Eden had been given the gift of foresight; the older a Wolf and of higher rank, you were bestowed a god-like gift. Even though Clara was a young Wolf, she was forced to open her powers early and was blessed by the goddess Charis with the ability to heal.

Kronos, she was going to heal him. My body vibrated with anticipation. Ember's eyes held confusion.

Clara put her forehead to Wesley in an upside-down manner. A light went from her forehead to his, and a large breath was sucked in through Wesley's mouth. Clara sat up, smiled, and returned to her mate. "Tell him to take it easy a couple days." Clara stood up, keeping the cloak wrapped tight. "Oh, and congratulations, Ember." Clara winked and walked off into the forest, holding the beast Kane's claws.

That woman should be a goddess to put up with a wolf like Kane. The Grim Reapers had departed, and Ember held her father's head in her lap; he was smiling back at his daughter, crying and thankful for another day of life.

"What was that about?" I asked. Ember shook her head and stared down at her father. His eyes flew open as the last bit of blood spat out from his mouth.

"Ember!" Wesley sat up suddenly, hugging his daughter. "You are all right, you are Okay!" He rocked her back and forth like a father to a baby.

"I don't care about me. I care about you!" she cried. Standing up, I walked to Ares to give them their moment. Reluctantly, but I did so.

"All is accounted for," Ares boasted. "Demeter really wasn't prepared, was she?" I scoffed as I threw my sword to my hip. "So, when do I get a sword like that? Pretty badass."

"Do you rule the Underworld?"

"Well, no."

"Then never." Throwing a big grin his way, I gave him a hug, one that was well deserved. Patting his back heavily, we saw Vulcan in his war attire, swinging his ax and strapping it to his waist.

"Glad that's over," Vulcan shuttered. "I was never one for violence. Those Vampires give me the heebie-jeebies." Glancing over Vulcan's shoulder, I see Hermes and some vampire woman kissing.

"Well, get used to it. I think Ember paired them together," I said, nodding in their direction. Hermes' hand slipped up the woman's shirt and caressed her breast out in the open. We all turned away as we winced at the sight.

"That's gross," Ares gagged and walked away. Feeling a significant push to my body, I look down to see my little mate with her arms around me.

"Kronos, you are naked," I growled and switched to my robes, engulfing her into them.

"That's what you say when you first see me?" Ember winked. Pushing up on her toes, she gave me a peck on the lips. My hands reached around, grabbing her ass, making sure no one saw her white globes, of course. Moaning into her mouth, a throat-clearing interrupted us, I scowled.

Wesley was standing, his leg only had remnants of the blood that left his body, and he was leaning on Dante. "Thank you, Hades. For getting my daughter back." Wesley's hand went out for a handshake.

I was reluctant at first but let my hand slide away from Ember's ass and gripped his tightly. "You've saved her twice, and I know you love her. Keep her safe."

"I certainly will." Wesley gripped Ember's shoulder and patted her back lightly.

"How about we all get home before my mate dies of stress?" Wesley boomed in laughter. Ember's lip wobbled, and Wesley's face softened.

"Don't say that" she whispered. "Don't say anything about anyone dying; I can't take it." Wesley pulled Ember in for a hug as I willed a sizeable black shirt to cover her body. These Wolves and nudity, I swear I don't understand it.

"Back to the territory, then?" Gabriel walked up with Persephone looking longingly into Gabriel's eyes. Shit, we have guests now?

Athena's held her spear tightly, hair a mess and blood under her right cheek. "Yes, I agree. A shower would be nice."

"This is going to be a hell of a victory party!" Ares cheered, and all the Wolves all howled in excitement.

Chapter 67

Hermes

She tasted so damn sweet. Her puffy lips caressed mine again as I sucked her tongue into my mouth. The skin beneath those tattered rags was cool and soothing on my hot skin. Relishing in the coolness of her body, I felt my cock strain to life. It was rigid, harder than I ever thought possible while I rubbed it close to her core. She was tall, almost my height which gave me perfect leverage to shove my rigid member into the only warm spot in her body, her pussy.

Feeling a slight tapping on my shoulder, I groaned grudgingly, pulling away from her hot cinnamon mouth. "What?" I groaned as my hand thrust under her shirt, feeling her pointed peaks. This fire between us was unmistakable; she was my mate. Ember pulled one over on Demeter and matched the two of us. Kronos, I swear I hope she is my mate and not done to gain a distraction.

I wasn't going to give this vampire up. Her eyes radiated red, as red as my lust for her. "I'm sorry to intrude," Selene's soft voice lamented. "But you are making Ares uncomfortable, and that in itself says something." My mouth was already back on my mate. Sucking in those flavorful cinnamon lips.

"Sorry," I mumbled as I sucked her top lip. Slapping my mate's ass, she jumped and straddled her long legs around me, whining my name while pressing her breasts against me. My eyes glanced at Selene, the color already returning to her face and the moon shining brightly. A smile slipped to her lips while shaking her head.

"The Dragon's blood makes the bond almost too intense. I suggest you mark her and join the festivities." Selene rubbed her neck where Demeter had cut her, already healing from the claw scratch. Bits of mud scattered her face when she was thrown down on the ground by Ember, who scarcely saved Selene's life.

I groaned again, pushing my mate to the stone wall of the cottage. Rubbing my erection on her core, she cried out. "Come with me," I tried to pull her away from my body.

"I can't. You keep moving away." Her husky voice was music to my ears. Pulling her inside, I shut the door with a slam, and a bright light invaded the cottage. The noise from the outside had vanished; all was silent. My mate leapt onto me, pulling at her rags. I did the same, removing the dirty cloth from my body. All that was left in the cold cabin were embers, a broken table, and a makeshift mattress made of straw and blankets. It would have to do because my cock and her pussy couldn't stand it any longer.

My mate sucked on my neck, leaving little nibbles in its wake. Smelling the bits of blood left behind from her bites had me gripping her ass like a vice. "Name," I panted as I pulled her pussy closer to my dick. I didn't even know her name. How the hell was I to scream it when I climaxed into her sweet cavern?

Whining my name into my ear, I chuckled, palming her tantalizing pebbles stroking my chest. "What's your name,?" I complained. "I need yours so I can scream it when I fuck you senseless."

Her core clenched, and her bundle of nerves rubbed my cock in such a way it made her come undone. "Ahhh!" Her head flew back while I gripped her ass to rub my cock more. Her sweet essence dripped onto me, and the smell of her honey leaking on me made my nose flare.

Mouthwatering, I flipped her over to lay her on the hay mattress. Spreading her legs wide for all of her glorious body to see, her clit glistened into the low light. "Name," I snarled again while I flicked her nub. "Ahh!" Again, she pushed, trying to get her pussy into my face. "I won't touch you unless I know your name!" Gripping her inner thigh with a tight squeeze, her eyes darted open and stared at my tongue while I licked my chapped lips.

"H-Harlow," she finally breathed.

"Harlow." I purred, Harlow. My sweet vampire Harlow was my mate. This day I never saw coming. I was not worthy of having a mate, not after my years using Hades' concubines, but all my confessions to my mate would have to wait because I was going to claim her as mine. The bond was too strong and my body too weak to fight it.

My mouth descended on her clit, flicking it ever so lightly while she wiggled in my arms. Throwing her thighs over my shoulder, I feasted and filled my hunger for food and drink with her essence. My tongue rubbed inside her pussy lips as her cum filled my mouth. "Mmm, Harlow, you taste divine." Gripping my dirty curls on my head, she cried out my name like angels sing during the birth of a god.

My member throbbed, dripping with my own seed. I needed to bury myself into my mate, claim her as mine, and the only way I could do that was to shove it in like no tomorrow. I didn't care if she was a virgin or had lovers before me; all I cared about was that this cock would be the last to fill her.

"Are you a virgin?" I whispered as the tip of my shaft tickled her clit. Her breathing stopped while glancing at my eyes.

"I'm sorry, no." Her voice was low with disappointment. Grinning, I shoved myself right into her core. My body hovered over hers, my lips tickled her cheek.

"Good," I whispered in her ear. "Then I can fuck you as hard as I want." The light in her eyes brightened; wrapping her arms around my neck and her legs around my torso, I continued my vigorous assault. I rutted her, pulling my dick out far enough only to shove it right into her core.

"Hermes!" Harlow screamed. Her breasts bounced while I sucked them to a pointed peak.

"This is mine forever, Harlow. No one else can touch this sacred temple." I bit down on the side of her breast hard while her chest heaved upward. Crying out my name again, I thrust my hips at a different angle, feeling each part of her tight core. "All mine, and this dick is yours. Do with it what you will." I pounded harder into her cervix. I wanted her to feel every damn part of me.

"I'm going to bind your soul to mine, Harlow. Do you understand?" Nodding her head, I slapped her thigh sharply. "Words!" I yelled out.

"Yes, Sir!"

Holy, mother flipping shit. Mine.

My chest became closer to hers as I slowed down my thrusts, my body willing itself to release my soul, pulling Harlow's with it. Her soul melted into mine as our bodies continued to fuck each other below us. A burn in my chest, a glow in hers, my symbol, the petasos or winged helmet, appeared on her chest. "Yes," I moaned while kissing her again. Our souls merged back together, Harlow withering under me.

"I need to come." I put my hand between us and pinched her clit as we both fell apart. My breath fanned her neck, but she pushed me forward. Feeling a sharp sting in my neck, I felt her fangs sink in. I orgasmed again, and by God, it was a blinding light to my eyes. The world had gone so bright my senses faded out while we both fell asleep in each other's arms.

***

I groaned, my body was stiff, and my dick was even more rigid. It was still buried in Harlow's body as she began wake. As much as I enjoyed our mating, I couldn't help but feel inadequate in myself. I barely knew her name and claimed to mark her before knowing anything about her. Did I give her much of choice?

We were both under the blood magic of the Shifter Dragon, enhancing our bond to make our bodies even more in tune with each other. What was she going to think? That I couldn't control myself?

Harlow's eyes fluttered open. I raised my arms to sit my elbows and began to pull away, but her hands went around my back and pulled me closer. "I'm sorry," I started. Harlow's brows furrowed into confusion as her nails gripped my back.

"I should have at least gotten to know you first; make sure you still wanted me."

Harlow's eyes blinked in amusement, and her puffy red lips went to a smile. "I thought you would have known I would have wanted you." Her hand went to brush my curl away from my face. "I was already attracted to you before I knew you were my mate. This was more than all right." Breathing a sigh of relief, I pecked her lips and slowly pulled out of her. If having a mate meant a raging boner most of the time, I hope she gets used to me being buried inside of her.

Rolling over and pulling her to my body, I tangled my fingers into her hair. Her face buried into the crook of my neck, and we both sighed in relief. My mark was on her body, and that was the most glorious satisfaction I could revel in right now.

"I'm sorry I couldn't save you sooner," she said, laced with sorrow. "My small coven wanted to be a part of Demeter's small army. She promised Dragon's blood, it would enhance the strength of our small coven and make us more powerful." I rubbed my thumb on her lips. She shivered while I kissed her forehead tenderly.

"It's all right. I'm not mad at you. It doesn't look like they treated you well anyway." Shaking her head, she cuddled close.

"I lost my parents to the Dark War; they fought for the Cerulean Moon Kingdom," she added. "Once I lost them, I went to whatever coven would take me; the smaller covens needed slaves. I did the grunt work most of the time."

"Never again will you have to do that. Did they not feed you much either?" I could feel her tiny body; now, it was nothing but skin and bones. Shaking her head again, I sighed and pulled her back. "Can you feed on me?" A blush tinted her pale cheeks, and she looked away. Pulling her chin back to me, I kissed her nose.

"Tell me, I don't know much about your kind." Harlow opened her mouth to speak but closed it as fast as she opened it. Kissing her again, this time on the lips, she sighed into me.

"Yes, mates feed off each other," she whispered.

"Then I will be able to as well, once my fangs come in," I laughed. Harlow's confused look made me laugh more, and I held her tight.

"A mated pair gain the strengths of each other's species. I'll be able to drink blood like you, and you will become a goddess. Of what particular strength for a goddess, we won't know for a while. Just don't feel guilty having to feed on me." Harlow giggled. In all seriousness, I was fucking turned on as hell her wanting to bite me. I've always liked to mix pain and pleasure.

Harlow crept closer; my head automatically leaned to the side. Her heartbeat rapidly while her fangs descended; my own heartbeat matched hers as she hastily pierced my skin. The pain I had hoped for turned out to be straight euphoria. I couldn't cum right now, not while she's drinking. My grip clenched on her body, encouraging her to drink, my hips began to rock against her, and her fingers threaded through my dirty hair.

Groaning, I couldn't help it. I fisted my cock as I opened her legs. Plunging into her, I rolled her over while she sucked. The more she sucked, the more turned on I got, and I rolled my hips into her. The humming, the small gulps in her pretty little neck urged me to fuck her long and slow. Feeling her fangs pull out of my neck, I moaned her name while she came around me.

Chapter 68

Ember

"Hades, babe, you are squishing me." Hades' firm grip around my shoulders was cutting off the blood supply to my head. The large flash of white light that transported the warriors and us back to the Black Claw Pack made me squeamish. The warriors were cheering, howling, and screaming at the top of their lungs as they ran back to their mates and families.

We were transported in the middle of the forest clearing, right where I had shifted for the first time. Hades turned me quickly and engulfed me in an enormous hug. "You are never to leave my side again. Always be an arm's length away from me," he commanded into my ear. A shiver spread through my arms while we held each other.

"That's a little unreasonable," I joked; however, he didn't understand the joke.

"I mean it, never." His nose dove right into my neck, inhaling the dirt and filth, but he didn't seem to mind.

"Hades," I whined while sticking out my bottom lip. The lip, it will work. That or he'll do me in the forest. He took my lip and sucked it into his mouth while I squeaked.

"Fine, first thousand years you cannot leave my side, then we will talk," he muttered while leading me back to the center of the pack. Dad was limping and leaning on Dante. Dante's jaw was rigid as he held my father; his hair was on end and eyes darting between the forest and the center of the pack.

"*What's wrong?*" I mind-linked Dante. His eyes glanced back to mine only to grip further onto father's torso to hold him straight.

"*Malachi is unaccounted for, so is the Helm. None of the warriors had seen him, and I fear he may have transported with us. I don't want to sound the alarm too soon because I can't be for sure. I don't need Hades blowing up the place looking for him.*" He muttered under his breath.

"*Hades wouldn't blow up anything.*" Dante glared at me. I shrunk back.

"*Just keep it quiet. I'll speak to Ares and Vulcan about it.*" He mumbled.

"*I can't keep secrets from my mate, Dante,*" I growled back at him.

"*Oh no? What about the baby you are carrying?*" I gasped internally while he gave me a smirk.

"*Alpha blood, you are still early, but I smell your change. Better tell him sooner than later.*" Dante pulled Father closer to his body and sped up. Mom was calling for him; I could hear her frantic footsteps approaching.

"*Congratulations, sis,*" Dante said again as Dad leapt from his arms. Mom came running with tears in her eyes. Gracefully landing in dad's arms, he spun her around like they had only been together months. A hot, searing kiss was pressed to each other as they openly made out in front of the pack.

"Ew," I heard Steven groan in the background, who was following behind Mom.

Hunter approached and gave me a bone gripping hug. "Welcome back. Stop making habits of disappearing, you hear? Mom can't take it anymore." I chuckled.

"Sure, I'll make sure of that." Hades pulled me back beside him until mom and dad had their moment.

"I thought I lost you, I felt it, I felt your pain," she gasped while she peppered more kisses on his cheek. Letting go, his arms fell around me and pulled me into a death grip. "Gods, you are all right. Bless Hades, bless the gods."

The rest of the gods gathered, minus Hermes and his mate. Scratching my head, I looked to Selene, and she made a circle with one hand and another finger going through it. Winking at me, I laughed hysterically until she put her hand down, and I looked like the fool of the group.

"It's over, for now," Ares spoke valiantly. Mariah huddled closer to him while he smiled down at her blood-stained face. "I'm sure in a few hundred years, some other god might pull a Demeter."

"Where is she now?" Mom asked.

"In hell, on the outskirts of Tartarus awaiting the punishment. Hades gritted his teeth. "She will suffer greatly." Dad nodded and pulled Mom closer. His lips traced the temple of her forehead while nuzzling closer.

"Dawn is approaching; I suggest we get the weaker gods to the hospital to heal and plan for a mating ceremony," Dad announced.

Mom beamed as her hands clapped together. "It will be perfect to celebrate a glorious victory with a binding!" One of the omegas approached Mom while she spouted off a list for Wolves to do.

I yawned heavily and leaned into Hades. The fighting, the worrying, the whole ordeal was enough, not to mention growing a pup inside me. My hands automatically went to my stomach to caress it. Realizing what I was doing, I dropped my hand and peeped at Hades. "Let's go clean up; I think I need a nap." Hades pulled me close, and before I could say goodnight to my family, we blinked right into an unknown room.

The walls were painted navy blue, while the furniture was a classic French white. Small fur rugs scattered the light-colored wood floor. It was a stark difference from the primitive mating cabin that mom had built for the pack. Everything here looked brand new with actual rooms instead of a studio like our previous stay.

Flowers decorated end tables, the couches pristine tans with decorative pillows and girly frills. If I had any say in decorating, I would have picked this exact room. Walking into the next room, it was a bedroom. California-sized king bed with a white comforter, more pillows, and even a sheer tulle canopy that encompassed the whole bed. It reminded me of the clouds in the Celestial Kingdom.

"Hades, this is beautiful, but where are we?" My eyes continued to dart around the room. Large windows and a walk-out porch with a hot tub in place. Mind wondering what kind of dirty things we could do in there, Hade's arms wrapped around my waist.

"It's for you. Our home away from home. I can add or take away anything you like. It is just one bedroom, so your parents must go back once they are done visiting." His dirty chuckle brushed my ear, causing ripples of pleasure to race down to my heart.

"But what if I wanted a second bedroom?" Hades' hand went up the front of my shirt, exposing my thighs and exposed pussy. One finger traced my nipple while I gasped.

"One for Cerberus and Blaze? Fine, I'll create another bedroom for them." His nose traced my collar bone, and my knees almost buckled.

"No, for someone else," I whispered. Hades' fingers tickled my sides and started to rub the folds of my lower lips.

"Then for who?" Nipping my shoulder, I grabbed his hand away from my pussy; as hard as it was to make him stop, I had to tell him. Moving his hand to my belly, I caressed his hand as it laid flat against it.

"For him... or her..." My voice faded, Hades' body stiffened.

"Ember, I thought you understood?" He tried to turn around, but I cupped his cheek.

"Hades, you are going to be a father." His eyes widened, shocked, he pulled back from me. The rush of hurt flooded my face while he stood to look at me. I cradled the non-existent bump with both hands. "Hecate confirmed it. I'm still early. I'm sure if you put your ear up to my stomach you could hear it."

"That isn't possible," he shook his head.

"It is, when I bit you, you took on some of my healing ability, a part of me. You aren't sterile anymore."

Hades

Were my ears deceiving me? Did she just say she was pregnant and with my child? Of course, it would be my child; she would never stray. But I am sterile; I cannot have children. Hecate said so herself so long ago when we were still young.

My time simmering in Kronos' stomach had ruined my chances to conceive. Besides, I was the bringer of death, the King of the tortured souls. I shouldn't have been granted to have such a precious thing. To help bear life and to pass my seed onto the next generation of gods. Yet here I stand, my mate in front of me, cradling the invisible bump that will soon be heavy with child. My mate was carrying a child I never thought to ever exist.

Ember's eyes filled with sadness as I stepped away, but this was something to process. Was I going to be a good father? What would the child say when it went to school and their friends found out I was death? The one who punishes and gives no mercy. Would my child still love me?

Would my child still love me knowing that I almost betrayed their mother, that I was the epitome of evil for so many years and kidnapped an innocent god and tried to force her to love me? My own sins and torment flooded my mind. All I could see was the blackness, the terrible things I had done. But the gentle hand that caressed my arm was none other than my mate. My mate held onto me like a lifeline; her thoughts, feelings, and projections of love to my soul pulled me from the darkness.

"Hades," she cooed. Her hand grazed the stubble on my still bloodied chin. "You will be a wonderful father; your doubt is your only downfall. You are fierce in your own right, and you will protect your child with all the ferocity as you protect me. You have not failed this child or me; you and I made this child out of love and devotion for one another. Amazing, talented, and my wonderful devil, you will be a father. You will not be known as just King of the Underworld but a protective parental figure to your children."

My heart damn near exploded.

Pulling Ember close to me, my lips found her in an instant, and my mouth engulfed hers. Her warm body, her intoxicating scent dove into my nose, we became lost in each other.

My body slid down hers, my ear rubbing against her womb. Hearing not only my Ember's heart but a tiny flutter that flew in the background. Our baby.

Pulling her to the master shower, I threw on the water, crashing my mouth to hers. Our bodies were wet with the pouring water; our clothes were drenched. The outline in her black shirt enhanced her nipples and hips that had me screaming to take her.

"Is it safe to?" My voice trailed while I waited for permission to fuck her. I needed to be closer, in her and with her, but I dare not hurt my future child. Ember giggled and ripped my leather vest with a claw.

"Their head my get poked but nothing major." Her head was thrown back with laughter, tears sprouting her eyes as my face turned white.

"I'm kidding." Ember's hand went straight to my dick, still as hard as a rod of steel. "No harm would come to our child, Hades. I promise. "You can bend me over and have me any way you want." The blood, dirt, and grim slid off our bodies while I washed her.

Taking it slow, my hand trailed up and down each arm, leg, and torso. Exerting my fingers, I trailed down to her pussy; the arousal hit the air, and with the extra moisture in the shower, it only engulfed my senses into complete euphoria. Two fingers slipped between her folds; her core was wet, spilling onto my fingers as the rest of the shampoo rinsed from my hair. Ember's nails scratched my scalp when I thrust another finger up her pussy. The carnal desire to lick between her small folds was heavy as she withered beneath me.

My opened mouth came down to hers as she yearned for more of my touch. Hands reached around, arching her back while my fingers thrust so hard, it put her on her toes. The large shower bench was begging me to bend her over. Her ample cleavage brushed against me, second-guessing me bending her over, wanting to test the weight of her swollen breasts.

Dick decided for me, we wanted her ass. She crashed before I slipped my fingers from her cavern; before she could come down from her high of her climax, I bent her over, her nubs scraping the cold marble of the bench.

"Hades," rasping heavily, I lined my cock to her pussy. I entered my aching bulge into her; her whine filled the heated room. Taking my right hand, I put it around her neck, giving a gentle squeeze, and my other hand rubbed her clit while my hips charged her. Immediately, Ember's ass tilted upward, giving me ample room to plunge right into her g-spot. Crying out in ecstasy, her hair flew back and hit me in the face. Long strands decorated her back and my face while I smelled her essence.

My thrusts became frantic, reaching my peak. Squeezing her neck tighter, Ember's hand came around to grab my balls, milking them at the moment they tried to retract into my body; my seed came forth and buried deep within her womb. A womb that carried my child, our child.

Pride radiated from my chest. My body had finally done something I've always wanted. Give my mate pleasure and give us both a child made by both of our love.

Chapter 69

Ember

Groaning, I rolled over into the bed. The fluffy covers felt soft on my appearance until I felt a hard rock chest pull me upwards and bury me in its chest. Hades sighed heavily as he stroked my naked back with his hand. "Soon," he grumbled into my hair while he kissed it softly. "You won't be able to lay on your stomach; I'll have to spoon you and make love to you from behind." Giggling in his chest, my face looked up at his.

He was happy, genuinely happy. The boyish glint in his smile hinted at his delirious high of becoming a father. "I still can't believe it. Do you think it will be a boy or a girl?" His hand rubbed my stomach longingly while I glanced at his delectable torso. No signs of scratches, scars, or wounds from the previous day's fight.

"I don't know; it is still so early. I don't even feel sick."

"You may not." Hades' hand wrapped around my lower back and pulled me close to his groin. "You're a goddess now. Such small trivial annoyances of what supernatural women have to face won't be in your favor." Excitement ran through me at the thought of not being sick. I had remembered mom being unhappy with each child

467

after me. She ate everything she could get her hands on just to calm her stomach.

"I think I can live with that." Rubbing my finger over Hades' mark, we stayed in better for a few more hours. It was the first time we could relish in each other's touch without worry. My mind did wander to Malachi, but Hades' bliss of fatherdom had overshadowed that little detail.

I trusted my brother and my family to keep an eye out for the rogue angel, and I had hoped even Gabriel was let on to know of the missing suspect. One of the head angels would surely want a piece of the traitor.

We stayed in the cabin for the rest of the day; I heard my mother's mind-linking making sure I was alright. Mom mentioned the mating and binding ceremony was tomorrow. The reality was, we were already mates, and this was a formality. It was just important to Werewolf customs, a tradition mom wanted to skip initially as well. Since I was bound to a god, it was more of a massive deal for the pack. That one of our own had taken flight up to the Celestial heavens and will now be helping Selene find mates for wolves.

Ares and Vulcan took it upon themselves to invite the gods of the Celestial Kingdom. Zeus, Hera, and many more planned to stand in attendance to witness the significant mark in the center of my chest glow for all to see once our vows were complete.

Selene was going to be the officiator. Her power had grown overnight, and she had already started matching more souls together, complaining how far behind she was. Tamera had to take the Sphere away from her and lock it in a safe at the hospital wing, not that it would keep Selene from her work. Hecate had healed as well, mom explained. Hecate worked with Cyrene and planned how the ceremony would be over the top, bigger and better than any mating ceremony she had ever seen. My opinion was asked multiple times throughout the evening while Hades grumbled, listening in. He couldn't understand how women could talk about such things; it was just a ceremony.

I only agreed. I only cared about Hades by my side and was perfectly happy having something small. Hades, me, my family, and of course Vulcan, Ares, Blaze, and Cerberus, who had already been summoned and played at the foot of the bed. His soft snores radiated the room while Hades groaned in annoyance.

In light of Hades' good attitude, he still had his dark side to him. It was funny and enlightening as he would complain about sharing me. Still, he would eventually give in when I gave him the pout. It worked so well that he even went with me to the packhouse to eat our dinner with the warriors and give thanks for a job well done. Without them, I'm sure Hades could have taken on the whole area blowing it up until he found me. Accidentally taking casualties was not something I would have been too happy about. He respected me and my wishes and brought as many as possible to keep the cost of lives down.

Many warriors gave high fives to both Ares and Vulcan, who took them gladly. They were seen as war heroes, and this pack would forever spread history from generation to generation. Vulcan's eyes glittered with love for his mate as well as Ares, both receiving a gift I was so happy to give. They had been my caregivers for a while as Hades learned to control his anger, and the gift of a mate was the perfect solution.

Loukas was in his human form, crossing his arms, but his tail still swaying in a tantalizing motion. His ears and eyes were alert as he scanned the room. No doubt that Dante had briefed him on the circumstances with Malachi. Squeezing Hades' hand, I walked over to Loukas; the burn on the back of my head was felt from across the room as I approached him. Hades and his jealous ways would have to sit on the back burner until I found Loukas's mate.

"Loukas?" I looked up at his tall form. His chiseled face and beard that had grown far too much for my own liking of his human form smiled down at me.

"Queen Ember, what do I owe the pleasure?" My arms engulfed his torso, and his arms went above his head. Hades' growl inflicted through my thoughts, but I shoved them down.

"Thank you, Loukas, for all you have done for me. I know Hades doesn't want to admit it, but you led him to me, and without you, I wouldn't have all this." I waved my hand over the indoor cafeteria. Wolves were smiling, holding each other's mates, and several demons pruned and preened their mates beside them. Loukas's half-smile was sad as he glanced forward through the crowd.

"I'm just glad you are happy," he announced. "You have been a true friend, and you are perfect for Hades. Of course, you and Selene knew that already." His elbow nudged me. I looked over my shoulder, nodding my head, seeing Hades occupied with Gabriel, talking in hushed tones.

"Come with me," I whispered to Loukas. We both headed to the kitchen. Since arriving, several Celestial Fairies came to help with the preparations for tomorrow. Zeus had ordered them to support the Wolves with decorations and cooking and preparing food for the gods that they believed more appropriate for a proper binding ceremony. I had only seen them in a more diminutive form, but this one I saw in the kitchen was tall, as tall as Loukas.

Her wings glittered gold with hints of pale pinks; her outfit was far too short and covered just the curve of her rear end. The thin straps covered her average-sized chest as she stirred a sweet-smelling frosting that was being used to decorate the cake.

"Goddess Ember." Her head bowed low with the bowl in her hand. "I'm sorry for disturbing you." She put the bowl down to leave, but I grabbed her hand.

"No, please stay, I came in here just to talk to Loukas, but I don't want to stop you from your work. Thank you, it looks so beautiful!" The cake was white, and the small intricate details at the base showed Hades and me in different periods. One where we shared our first kiss and another where he had brought be back from the club. My unease was apparent looking at that, but the Celestial Fairy rubbed my hand.

"The Greeks would often time put stories on jars and pottery. This cake represents you and Hades' story. If you would like me to remove this section, I can." I smiled at her thoughtfulness to explain, but I shook my head. "No, it's beautiful. It's a beautiful story that should be shared." Her eyes brightened and bowed as she continued.

Before talking to Loukas about Malachi, a small omega came into the kitchen carrying a bowl full of fruit. Several of the Celestial fairies, also in their larger form, came to help her, but they were too late. Strawberries, grapes, and blueberries littered the kitchen floors. She tripped on a stray spoon. The small omega almost burst into tears. "I'm so sorry! I'm so clumsy!" Her hands went to her knees, picking up every last piece of fruit.

Loukas and I got on our knees as well to help her pick up the remaining fruit. "I'm Nora. I'm sorry, Alpha Ember." Shaking my head, I laughed.

"You have no idea how many messes I have made; please don't worry." Loukas picked up fruit absentmindedly without looking at the ground, his face still on Nora, who concentrated elsewhere. I narrowed my eyes, dropping the fruit I was holding, and grabbed both of their index fingers.

"What are you doing?" Loukas grumbled while Nora tried to pull her finger back.

"Hang on a second," I ordered, and immediately their fingers glowed under my vision. I was getting better at this match-making stuff.

Both of them pulled their hands away. Loukas sighed frustratedly and sat back on his legs. "What was that all about?" Letting out a chuckle, I waved for Nora to come closer while Loukas reluctantly followed. Holding out both of their palms, I placed them together. Did I need a Sphere to do this? Or could I do this on my own?

Suspicions started to arise within me as I closed my eyes. Both of their souls appeared right before me. Taking my hands, I placed one on the bottom and one on the top, making the perfect hand sandwich.

Imagining their souls pulling out of their bodies and touching one another, intermingling their lives and their bodies and heart, I felt the warmth of my hands around them. Once the warmth started to fade, glancing at my friend, Loukas's eyes widened in hysteria. His toothy grin landed on Nora, who was only blushing furiously.

"Mate," he panted. Nora bit her lower lip and could only spout out a single word.

"Hi." She gave a little wave while I stood up to provide them with their time. Hades said I was too nosey, and I needed to provide mates their space. I would want the same, I suppose. It appears the Sphere is to be used for long distances, so Selene does not have to travel.

My bare feet bounded across the floor as I entered the cafeteria. Most of the Wolves had departed, and Hades sat waiting patiently with his body leaning on the cafeteria tables with his elbows. "Have a nice chat?" His voice was annoyed, and I squinted my eyes in complaint.

"What is that supposed to mean?" I questioned.

"Have fun chatting with Loukas? Alone?" I gritted my teeth, I wasn't one to get mad at the God of the Underworld, but if he was going to be this possessive all the time, then he had another thing coming.

"You listen here, devil!" I waved my finger in front of his face. "I was working. I matched Loukas with another Wolf. Their souls must have subconsciously led me right in there. Now you don't have to worry anymore about Loukas. You don't have to figure out some lame mission for him to run away and never come back to the Underworld. You act as if I would leave you for a demon. Do you not trust me?" Hades sat back with his mouth agape.

"I don't trust him!" he retorted back. His hand trembled to the kitchen door. "He has acted like he has wanted you since the first day!" He rebuked.

"And what did I tell you since I knew about mates and our bond? That I would only want you!" My face filled with rage while I stomped my foot. "I think some time alone will do us good before the binding ceremony tomorrow. You have to realize that I do have a job too, you know. I'll be helping Selene, and I'm a goddess now. I can overpower any demon or angel. Once you get it through your thick skull, you wouldn't act like a cattle prod was up your ass!" I snapped.

Mom and dad were staring me down at the doorway. Dad had dropped his werewine on the floor. "I'm going to sleep in my old room. By the time I see you down that aisle, your possessiveness, and untrustworthiness of me better improve."

"Ember, please." Hades' hand went out to grab mine. "Don't leave me tonight." I growled. Elea was on my side with this one. Just because he was the male, some god didn't mean I had to agree with everything he said. This would be good for him.

"Goodnight, Hades." I gave him a kiss on the forehead and sashayed out the door as I felt the hurt and disdain in his emotions. My heart shriveled as the weight of his sadness fell on me.

This might be harder than I thought. Who was I kidding? I couldn't last a whole night. The anger in his soul thickened around mind each step I stepped away from him. Pricks of fire tickled my arms like he was trying to pull me back.

"Are you sure you should do that?" Mom's voice cooed at me. "Maybe the hormones are pushing you a little far." Her fingers went around my shoulders to pull me close. "Hades is reacting to the bond, the pregnancy, and all the stress that comes along with it. It isn't wise to provoke a god."

Growling, defeated, I folded my arms. "I know Hades, he won't stay away. I just needed an hour to myself," I mumbled and walked to my childhood home. God or not, that shouldn't be a reason why I shouldn't voice my opinion or have to explain every move that I make.

Chapter 70

Hades

Ember left the room in a rage. Her hips swayed with the conviction that she would not give in to my minor begging. There wasn't anyone I would beg for except her. Dismissing me, I felt my anger seep into the chair where I still sat, waiting for me to hear the door slam to the Alpha's home. Luckily, no one was here to witness my ugly defeat to become back in my mates' good graces.

Jaw tightening, I slung the chair away from me, flipping over a table in my wake. I felt the smoke tendrils reach out of my clothes as I slammed the door open. Willing a fireball in my hand, I threw it as far as I could, which was the middle of the dense forest to the east. Screams and howls heard, I stomped to where I will feel the burn and let off some fumes. Tartarus was too far; I wasn't willing to leave my mate here on Earth just to torture Demeter. That would have to wait, unfortunately.

Wolves, including Wesley's beta, Evan, yelled for the Wolves to stand clear. He was unreasonably loud and thunderous in his call; I wasn't about to kill anyone in this pack unless they got in my way. My skin and my fangs itched. Hair was sprouting on my body. Ares and his mate ran up to me while my feet scorch the ground.

"Hades, what the hell?" The fire was roaring, trees were toppling to the ground, and the fire would be unbearably hot for a mere mortal; only the gods would be able to withstand it. Cerberus pranced up to me and sat down as I stomped the ground and large pillars of jagged rock erupted from the ground. Loukas had brought back Cerberus when he returned from bringing Gabriel. The mutt had been playing with the smaller wolves ever since.

I could bring Demeter here. I threw the thought away by scratching my chin. The chances were too great to have her powers spring back to life touching the soil.

"Oh, he's gotten in a little tiff with his mate." Athena walked up casually in her dark blazer. "He's gone all 'Alpha male' on her when she left to go have Loukas and Nora mated." Ares let out a scoff and put his arm around Mariah.

"Well, I wouldn't want my mate around Loukas the way he acted around Ember. I say he has a right to be mad." I didn't need anyone vouching for me; I knew I was right. Summoning another fireball, as large as a basketball, I threw it in the air only for it to explode over the lake where Ember liked to fish with her father.

"Hey, hey, hey," I heard Persephone's voice coming closer. Great, now everyone is going to get in on this. I cannot be left alone for one damn minute.

"I can repair the forest, but I can't bring back the fish. Wolves must live here, you know?" Gabriel put a possessive hand around Persephone while his wing shielded her from me. Fuck if I care, I didn't want her, but in the back of Gabriel's mind, I was going to be the dick that hid her all those years.

"Cerberus, why are you not with Ember? You need to protect her." Cerberus scratched the back of his ear with his rear foot. The young pups in the pack had decorated all three heads with flower collars, making him look like a pussy.

"*She said I remind her too much of you. Ember has Blaze, though,*" he whined and laid his head in the still flaming grass. "*Stupid Blaze,*" he growled. "*He's become some damn therapist to all the Wolves. He's been talking to Remus, Wesley's Wolf. Blaze was trying to figure out why Remus insists on talking like a caveman instead of like the other Wolves. Then we found out he only does it because it turns on Victoria and Charlotte, his mate.*" Cerberus made a gagging noise, and Persephone giggled into Gabriel's feathers. "He used to gag like that when I made parsnip soup."

"You need to stop this, Hades. You are scaring everyone." Ares looked out on the mass chaos that I had erupted. It looked like I brought the Underworld to the surface. If I could, I would set the lake on fire and have the apocalypse right now.

"Think Hecate can bring back the fish?" I growled again, feeling the slight sting on the back of my head.

"No, I cannot bring fish back to life, you idiot. Now put it all out so we can fix this. All this mess is going to make Ember mad and the pack more scared of you."

I didn't want to.

I'm angry.

I wanted my mate.

The fire burned hotter, gasping with the intensity of the fire now turning blue; everyone stood back. My chest heaved, feeling Ember's sorrow through our bond. Was I acting like an Alpha dick? I trusted her, not that damn demon, but he shouldn't be a problem anymore. Having her out of my sight was torture. Our child was nestled into her womb, and I have everything at my fingertips, ready for it to be taken away because of Malachi.

Ember thought I had forgotten that little detail. She kept it nestled in the back of her mind, putting up walls and barriers from Elea. I had known that Malachi was still out there and held it to myself. She thought I would blow up the entire pack and destroy everything in sight. He could have traveled back with us just as easily if he still had the Helm.

Proved her wrong. I only set the forest aflame.

Persephone could fix that; she was now taking Demeter's place.

Problem solved.

Screaming was heard in the distance. All of our eyes went to the woods, the portion that hadn't been turned into a raging inferno. There was no sight of where the screams came, only the sound of screams coming closer to us.

"Malachi," I growled. Vulcan laughed from behind, holding his mate tight.

"Stupid angel didn't realize he could catch fire even with the Helm. What an idiot." Gabriel stiffened behind me, wanting to go forth and find the fucker. Hell, I did too.

The voice became louder, passing us. Unfortunately, my arms went to grip the sound only to find I was hugging myself. The Helm could grant invisibility, and smells were nearly neutral, but not completely. My white teeth gleamed in the flame before me; stripping of my robes, I focused on shifting in the beast that my mate had made me to be.

Fur sprouted from my back, flames engulfed my eyes, paws lit to scorch the ground. Using my nose enhanced with the god's abilities,

I caught his dirty scent. The smell of betrayal, sin, and torment. My favorite to skewer in the bowels of hell. Springing forth, my nails curved into the dirt, Ares not far behind. He would not smell Malachi because only I could smell the evil.

Malachi had stopped at the lake that was surrounded by fire. The choice was his to make, jump through the flames to quench the thirst or continue to burn. Not giving him time to think, my jaws clamped on soft feathers. Ripping him back from the water, his screams ripped my ears, feeling like they had been pierced through my own sword.

Shaking him violently, the Helm fell from his feeble head, exposing his fire covered feathers. "Would you look at that," Vulcan spoke from a distance. "It was almost too easy." Kicking the Helm with my hind leg, Vulcan picked it up and handed it to Hecate, who quickly made it vanish to land right where it belonged, behind closed doors of my prized possessions. It would not remain for long; it would be destroyed with Hell's fire and never to be used again.

Dragging Malachi from the flames, his white-covered wings were reduced to nothing but broken feathers, dirt, and grime. Feathers missing, falling to the ground like the useless leaves in the fall.

My Wolf craved the blood from his wings, wanting more than a bite, but this wasn't just my time to torment this soul. I would have him in his afterlife. As much as I wanted to sink my claws in one at a time into his throat, I drug him to Persephone and Gabriel.

Malachi's body, nearly naked, tried to stand, but only his elbows could support him on the ash-ridden ground. Pushing him forward with my snout, I nodded at Gabriel to do what he will. Once he was finished, he would await his fate along with Demeter.

Transforming back into my robes, standing tall, waiting for one of the finest warriors of the Celestial Heavens, I waited to see what he would do. This could be interesting.

"Why?" Gabriel's voice proclaimed as a valiant trumpet. "Why would you agree to take someone else's' mate? Let alone from the angel that could have your head with just a flick of my finger?"

Malachi leaned back. The front of his chest exposed to the setting sun. Boils and burns littered his body. I wanted nothing more than to rip into them and watch the blood pool to the floor. Ares put his shoulder on me, understanding the anguish.

"It was a proposition proposed by her mother, Demeter." Malachi took in a large breath and held his wounds. "I had often gone to Demeter to help with nymphs that would get too handsy with her foliage on her land. Demeter was funny when growing her own flowers and shrubs, but the nymphs would laugh and make them grow too large or not at all. It irritated her, and she only trusted me to take care of it since I wouldn't harm her plants in the process."

"Yawwwwwn," Ares put his hand up to his mouth. "Hurry up with it," he growled.

"Anyway, Demeter took a liking to me. She asked if I would want Persephone as my mate. Persephone was beautiful, but I knew she wasn't mine. Demeter said she would make it happen if I did what I was asked. I got greedy. I didn't want to wait, and Demeter had always been kind to me. If I stayed in the area which she lived and kept Persephone close, I was allowed to have her. Then, I became obsessed." He chuckled.

Persephone stepped behind Gabriel, who puffed out his chest. His white tunic barely held in his heart while his breathing deepened. Dagger in hand, his knuckles popped in retaliation.

"Persephone, I was a good mate when we were together!" Gabriel bent down and pulled Malachi up by the neck.

"You were never her mate, you fool. Never." Gabriel's grip tightened while his sword pierced between his collar bones. Gabriel sliced through the chest cavity down to his bowels with one swift motion. Blood poured from Malachi's torso, and soon his intestines hit Gabriel's feet.

Malachi's mouth hung open, heart still beating in his chest, falling to the ground, unable to move. "You've caused a lot of headaches, Malachi." I growled. "For something so stupid as not being patient. You helped kidnap gods, sent my mate into a sex trafficking ring, gave the Helm to a human, and dared try to bond to Persephone. Your punishment is death, given order by the high God Zeus himself. You are in my dominion now, you insufferable being. Be prepared to suffer."

Wielding my sword from beneath my robes, the black iron steamed while it sliced through the air and plummeted into the angel's black heart. Since made from the heavens, Malachi's body disintegrated into a puff of sparkle that immediately descended beneath the ground where he would stay. Straightening my back, hearing it pop a few times, Gabriel lent out his arm. I took his forearm as we both shook as a sign of unity and no hard feelings.

"Phew, glad that's over." Hermes walked up to the group, his vampire mate by his side. Both sporting new marks on their bodies while his smug smile punched the tense ambiance.

"Now we won't have to worry about him crashing the party!" Hermes does a little dance with his mate, being the annoying little fucker he can be, while everyone joins in on the laughter as if they didn't even witness an angel falling to the depths of Hell.

Having Malachi captured and the probable harm of my mate sated my anger, but my body and soul craved Ember. I didn't have the strength in me to stay away. Looking at the burning forest and shrugging my shoulders, I waved my hand to put out the hot flames. "About time," Persephone chirped as she began to regrow the forest.

First, the lush grass sprouted beneath the ash, shrubs, and small trees grew into wide trunks. Vulcan tracked close to a tree and used his power to build a massive three-story treehouse that expanded through ten trees. Rubbing my eyes, grateful to have gods on my side for once, I gave them a genuine smile.

"I did get carried away, didn't I?" I chuckled while the rest joined in agreement. "Just don't piss me off," I grunted, back to the stoic face, and more laughs and cheers exploded while I walked back through the crowd, to where my mate was no doubt still steaming.

"I expect to see everyone at the celebration," I huffed again, only to be pushed to the ground by a heavyweight sitting on my back. Several times I tried to move upwards, only failing.

"Did someone say party!?" The booming voice and joyous cheer could have only come from one person.

"Get the fuck off me!" Igniting my hands, I put it right on the fool's ass, eliciting a scream of pain.

"Dionysus!" Ares cheered. "I was wondering when you would show up! Come here, my man!"

The God of Celebration and Wine. Great.

Chapter 71

Loukas

Feeling Ember's presents leaving the room, it became much warmer. I never thought finding my mate would be this fast and finding my mate in the craziest of places. A Wolf, and a beautiful one at that. My heart may have known I would have fallen for a Wolf and in Ember's pack, no doubt. Maybe that was the connection I felt for Ember because all Wolves consider each other family within a pack.

"I'm Loukas." My hand went out to touch her fingers that lay damp on the floor with the strawberry and blueberry juices. The jolts of sparks traveled up my arm as Nora's arm chilled with goosebumps.

"I know," she blushed, her chin resting on her shoulder to look away from me. "I noticed when you came back to tell Hades about Malachi invading the Underworld. That was very brave of you to come back, even though he could have burned you to a crisp." Her eyes still cast downward made my breath hitch. Was she scared of me?

Both of us were still sitting on the floor, unable to move from our sudden shock of discovery. Taking my hand, I turned her to face me, and those thick lashes fluttered. Golden brown eyes with flecks of gold glistened in the harsh fluorescent light.

"Are you scared of me? Little Wolf?" A sigh left her lips while biting her cheek.

"N-no. I'm just scared you may not want me. You are very handsome, and I'm just an omega. Nothing special." Her voice trailed off to silence. A blaze burned in me of the thought of ever rejecting her. Why on the gods' green Earth would I ever do such a thing? Pushing the large stainless steel bowl away, causing a large crash, the other Celestial Fairies in the room squealed and ran out of the room. My face formed into disgust while pulling Nora into my lap.

"You should never say such a thing," I scolded. "I would never reject my mate. And you are something special because you are mine." Holy shit balls, I could claim her right now. The overwhelming desire to take her over the kitchen counter was heightened while her plump ass sat right on my erection. The image fell into my mind. She may not want me. I was completely different than her. I was red in complexion, horns on my head, and I had a tail that often escaped and had a mind of its own. Had she seen me in my proper form?

"Have you seen my true form? Little Wolf? This is but an illusion to keep the pack calm. I know other demons have shown theirs, but I look different. Master made me a lot different." Nora's little head tilted to the side in confusion.

"You will still be handsome," she chirped. "Can I see?" Her fingers brushed my lips. Temptation rocked through me as I leaned down and touched hers. If she would dismiss me after seeing my form, at least I had a small taste of her. Lips departing, not even wiggling my tongue to invade her mouth, she smiled. The large sigh that left me, full of anguish, if she couldn't bear my face, would shred me apart.

In the blink of an eye, I lifted my illusion. Nora's eyes didn't even widen, looking at my reddened skin. My facial hair was mostly the same, just the scruff from the lack of shaving the past few days. My hair slicked back with a few unruly strands in my face. My horns, gods, the horns worried me. What if she thought I would impale her? The tiny hand lifted, her finger brushing the base of my horn. My horns were smaller than those of other demons but still menacing, nonetheless. If I could spike my hair high enough, one would think I didn't have them. Nora continued to trace the base of the horn, and my cocked filled with desire. Fuck, no one has touched me like that, not even the concubines of Hades. Fingers so gentle traced my face, my tail swaying like the curious Cheshire cat.

Tracing my jaw and finally, to my lips, I got the smile I craved. "You are still handsome," her whisper was small. "Just as your human form. I like this better, though." My mouth plummeted into hers. The brief shock caught her off guard, but she quickly returned the kiss.

Nora's hands were in my hair while I wrapped my hands around her back. We made our kisses hot and passionate on the kitchen floor. Her sweet moan filled me to the brim with lust. I needed to claim her before she changed her mind and get rid of a filthy demon like me. The question was, would she accept?

"Loukas?" she breathed as I let go of her mouth. Her lips parted, red from my teeth pulling at the sweet petals of her mouth. "Will you accept me?" My forehead touched hers. "Be my mate? Let me have you now?" Nora blushed, hiding her hands behind her face.

Giggling, she nodded her head frantically until I pulled her tiny hands away. "Yes, I will!" she squealed.

My fanged grin grew wide while I pulled her into my chest. She was a small omega, and she was mine. I'd protect her with all my being. Kissing her temple, she held onto my hand and pulled me off the floor. Two of her steps equaled one to mine racing up the stairs. "My room." She pushed the door open to the second floor. Instead of seeing bright pinks, purples, and whites that I thought, her room surprised me. Deep purple, almost black with hints of gold nick knacks scattered the shelves. Geodes of bright luminous colors decorated a desk along with several fossilized relics. The low light hid small pictures on the wall of famous places in Bergarian. Mystic Falls, Dragon's Island, the Fortus Mountains, and the Dark Forest. I had wanted to go to all sites but was too busy dealing with my master.

"I like things within the soil; even though it may be dark and deep beautiful things can be found, don't you think?"

Not answering, I captured her lips again, my tail automatically wrapped around her ankle and up her thigh. The sweet squeaks from pushing her to the bed turned me on the more. Withering under me, her free leg wrapped around the back of my hips, giving me ample access to grind my erection next to her throbbing core.

"Loukas," she breathed. "I've dreamed of meeting my mate, for this moment." Breathing heavily, the clothes between our pleasure centers were driving me mad.

"How can I make your dreams come true, Nora? What can I do to please you?" I grit my teeth in anticipation of her answer. Wanting nothing more than to taste her, to smell her and bathe in her essence.

"Just make me yours." Whining, her chest thrust upward, back coming off the bed. One of my hands wrapped around her lower back, the other ripped her shirt to the side. Her breasts were confined to a sports bra, no doubt from this morning's training. I pulled it off with ease by one single claw. The confines of her chest only surprised me; her breasts were larger than expected. Groaning, I took one into my mouth while my other hand gripped her pants, pulling them down in a swipe.

I don't know how my clothes disappeared; the throws of passion had my mind in a fog. All I wanted was to touch, suck and cause nothing but pleasure to her body.

"Goddess," Nora cried while I palmed her pussy. It was hot, wet, and dripping with the orgasm that fell from her lower lips. My tail whipped around me, gently poking her hole while my mouth descended on her clit. She tasted of the strawberry and blueberry juices from when we first met. "Ahh!" Her legs quivered when my tail inserted into her pussy.

Nora's hand went for my horns, gripping them while my tongue lapped soothed her nub of nerves. Hips thrusting forward, grinding my face to her pussy, her thumbs rubbed the base of my horns. A chill ran through my back, feeling the erotic touches. My cock was bobbing on the side of the bed, begging for friction.

My tail probed her insides, ensuring she was stretched enough to insert my cock. My balls tightened, ready to release. I couldn't hold it in any longer. "Mate," I gritted my teeth. My tail pulled out from her pussy, soaked with her wetness. She watched as I brought it to my mouth, licking the drip of her last orgasm. My clawed hands pulled her hips closer to me, legs going over my shoulders as I lined my cock to her core.

"Please, Loukas," she urged. Her hips thrust closer to my cock. The tip of my cock was black, angry as the veins protruded heavily down my shaft for her pleasure. The stark color difference caught Nora off guard as she gulped at the dripping head. Nora's eyes, full of desire, tickled her body sensually down her body as she caught the drip of my pre-cum falling from the tip with her fingers. Leaning forward, taking me off guard she took my erection to her mouth, she sucked it down, staring into my eyes.

I wasn't going to last. I pushed her back to the bed. Shoving the head of my cock in her body, a burst of light came through the windows. Too busy to look, I thrust forward again, not giving time for my mate to adjust to my size. Nora didn't mind while her legs gripped my head like a vice. My tail tickled her puckered hole, swiping it delicately.

"Loukas! Oh, my gods!" Adjusting the angle, I hit another spot. "What are you doing?"

"Trust me," I grunted, thrusting further into her, my tail gently prying the rosette gently open. A groan of pleasure left her lips. I barely had my tail inside, but it tightened around me.

"So full." Her breasts continued to bounce. Lowering my torso, touching hers, I took both my hands and intertwined them with her fingers above her head, continuing to pound into her. My fangs lengthened.

"Mate," I groaned. "Mine." My fangs bit into her shoulder, blood spurt into my mouth. At the same time, I felt her fangs break into my tough skin.

Nora's pussy clamped on my dick, holding me in, milking me of my seed. Mumbling into her shoulder, licking her wound, I kissed every part of her shoulder, her neck, cheek, ear, and lips. My mate, I had my mate. No one would ever come between us, and I would treat her as my queen. Wherever we may live, I would give her the home she desired. Nora would no longer serve as an omega, waiting on some wolves. Each evening, she would be ready to take her pleasure from me, burying my seed deep inside her.

Chapter 72

Ember

Slamming the door to my old room I fell on the bed with a large "umph." Mom harassed me all the way home. Saying I needed to be more sensitive to Hades, that he was a god on top of that dealing with his new Wolf. Sure, that was true but think of all the crap I have been through. I went from knowing nothing about myself to knowing everything, being mated to the god of the Underworld. I grit my teeth again and slammed my hand on the fluffy comforter.

Who was I kidding? I already missed him and the disappointment and guilt in his feelings didn't help me walk away. Pushing off the bed, I hear a roar and Evan yelling a mass mind-link for everyone to get out of the forest. Running to the window, my hands land on either side of the windowpane. Fire erupted around the forest. Heat could almost be felt right up to the glass.

"Immature dummy," I whispered until mom pushed the door open.

"You get down there and tell him to stop. Your ancestors spent a lot of time putting that forest together! Now look at it!" Mom was almost in sobs, but I didn't want to relent, just yet. The gods walked to Hades from behind, keeping their distance but trying to sooth the fiery attitude.

"He has to learn, mom. He needs to know he can't get jealous all the time, not when I'm pairing other people to help Selene." Dad walks up the stairs wrapping his hand around her waist and whispers in her ear.

"If you are that worried, I'm sure Persephone will rebuild the forest," dad comforted her. He was right, she could rebuild the forest. Not only that, her and Gabriel were amongst the others trying to talk him down. My claws extended and pierced my skin of my palms while I gripped tightly into fists. Why the hell was she there?

Cerberus made a gagging noise and Persephone started giggling frantically. Hades was still a few feet away but too close for my liking. He tried to get in her pants for a long time. Thank Selene that it never happened. All that time he obsessed over her, for over a thousand years. My mind clouded with an emotion I had never felt before. Jealousy.

Is that the feeling? Dad snickered from the doorway, knowing exactly the turmoil going through my head. The gears turning and the emotion had to of been readable on my face. My tears welled into my eyes. I'm a jealous pregnant Wolf, goddess, and I'm doing the exact same thing Hades was doing. I'm such a hypocrite. Covering my mouth, heavy sobs left my mouth while mom came to comfort me.

"Honey, it's all right," she rubbed my arms together. "Wesley, please go get her some of that chamomile tea. It will help her and the baby."

"Hades won't want me anymore because I'm going to be fat!" I wailed again, flopping to the bed. "He is going to go back to Persephone and try and get her back once I'm ugly!" My tears stained the pillow while mom wiped the tears out of my hair.

I don't know how long mom stayed there, cooed me and even spooned me in the bed telling me the tales of how dad had made mom fall in love with him. "He fell even more in love when you came into the world, sweet child. You are his first daughter. You will always have a special place in his heart. It isn't often an Alpha male has a daughter for an heir." Sniffing lightly, mom kissed my forehead and I felt her leave the bed.

The lights dimmed and mom's comforting emotion turned to guilt, love and sorrow. "Mom?" I whispered, but instead I felt the bed dip and warm body, much larger than hers engulf me. Now this was a big spoon. The smell of smoke, burned smores and musk filled my nostrils.

Rolling over immediately, I swung my arms around his neck. "I'm sorry," I cried, Hades petted my hair with one hand while pulling me impossibly closer to the other. "I got mad that you were jealous and then I turned around and got mad because I was jealous." Hades laughed out loud and pulled my head from his neck.

"What do you mean you got jealous?" he asked incredulously.

"I saw Persephone laughing with you when Cerberus was gagging. You both looked happy," I sobbed. "You are going to want her when I'm all fat!" I cried again.

"Oh, oh, Ember." A smile appeared on his face, but he ducked my head back into his chest while continuing is comforting rubs on my back. "I would never, ever want her. You are the only woman I will ever want, ever. You are mine and I will never give you up. I'm sorry I got jealous too, I want you to myself and I know that cannot be all the time. You being pregnant makes it extremely difficult."

I inhaled a large breath of his scent, instantly calming me. "We are both experiencing a bond so strong, we both will get carried away sometimes. That's normal, it's normal to have disagreements. Otherwise our relationship would be insanely boring. Besides, the makeup sex is going to be awesome." I giggled, his fingers detangling my hair while he breathed me in.

"For now, though, let us rest. We have a busy day tomorrow, hmm?" I couldn't even answer, as my eye lids fluttered shut on their own accord as Hades hummed some ancient lullaby for me to sleep.

***

"Stand here," mom had me on a stool, three dresses hung over the door of my bathroom. They were a gorgeous cream colored designs of a mating ceremony dresses. They were all equally beautiful and I couldn't pick just one. Mom fluffed one. It was more of a ball gown with a wide bustle and a huge train. It was a bit much for me, but mom was insistent I at least try it. "It just accentuates your waist so well, but I do understand you have to go what you like best."

Dante was dozing in the corner. He had guard duty since Hades wasn't allowed in my room while I tried on the dresses. Most of the men, gods, goddess were downstairs in the living room eating food brought in by the Celestial Fairies. Dionysus was discussing the preparations and taking the job of the catering, food, wine and even games he had planned. What kind of games do you even play at a mating ceremony? Was it a god thing?

Dionysus was in and out of the house, I could see him running back and forth. For a god that constantly had a drink in his hand, he could walk a strangely straight line. "I don't know." Mom leaned back on the stool she was sitting in. "Please tell me what do you like best?"

"I'm just happy to get the ceremony over with, to be honest." I played with the tulle that laid at my hips. "You can pick." Mom groaned again until Hecate and Selene walked in.

"Need some help?" Hecate walked around the dress, while I smiled at Selene. Her color was back and even the moon glowed brightly, more so than I had ever seen.

"I think something simpler might be for our Ember, what do you think?" Hecate nodded, pulling up a thick amount of tulle.

"I agree. There isn't a special significance to this dress is there?" Mom shook her head. Her body was overwhelmed by the presence of the gods, all the Wolves felt it. The power, the overwhelming energy that eludes them. "Right then." Hecate waved her hand, instantly turning the tulle to a delicate lace with gold threads. The pattern was of delicate flowers, leaves and hints of small bees around the lace. One would have to be close to see it, but it was there.

An off-the shoulder, clear lace hugged my shoulders, and my hair was swirled into loose curls and a braided crown. "Let me try!" Persephone hopped into the door and her fingers traced my crown braid that now held small white roses and baby's breath.

"Goddess," mom breathed, holding her hands to her mouth. "You are gorgeous. This dress looks perfect." The dress held every curve, flaring at the knees with a small train that could be easily buttoned behind the dress during the reception.

"Make up!" Selene scolded.

Selene's hand waved once over my skin. I couldn't feel any change but the hand mirror Selene conjured into her hand told a different story. Smokey eye, long lashes and a touch of pink to my cheeks. My lips were left with pale pink lip gloss. A small moon, that matched Selene's was placed in the middle of my forehead.

"Wow," I breathed. "I don't know what to say." I choked a sob down, not wanting to ruin the makeup.

"A thank you?" Dante roused from the corner, winking at me.

"Y-yes, thank you." Touching my face, I felt the warmth of love and affection from every person in the room. We were all happy, all at peace and this celebration would mark a new era for the gods and to any supernatural, maybe even human. That everyone would be mated, everyone had a soul mate, and every person would find their happily ever after.

"Hades is getting antsy," Dante warned. "Everyone else is dressed ready to go and take him to the ceremony, but he demands to see you first."

"But that will spoil the surprise!" I whined. "I wanna see him cry when he first sees me," I snickered but the goddesses groaned.

"He's god of the Underworld, he won't cry." Persephone rolled her eyes.

Selene's evil glint gave way to my curiosity. "What are you thinking?"

"Oh, you know that mark on your chest there?" Her finger circled around the scepter tattoo on my chest.

"Yes? What about it?" I rubbed it gently. A shock of pleasure hit me hard making me fall off the pedestal.

"That," Selene laughed. "Go to the bathroom and rub on it. He'll be messing his pants and keep his mind off of coming up here to see you." Hecate cackled in the corner, hands on her knees trying to catch her breath.

"Oh, you can do that?" Persephone's smile turned deadly pulling the front of her pale pink dress down. "Everyone out so we can play with our men!" Mom laughed and ran downstairs to watch the fun unfold.

Closing the bathroom door, I felt a bit weird having Persephone just on the other side of the door, but I guess it would have to do. I stripped my dress from my body, not wanting to be too messy. I wasn't sure what was going to happen when I continually stroked the mark on my chest.

Taking my finger, I traced it gently on my chest, the sparks went straight to my clit while my head threw back in ecstasy. Thinking of Hades, the intense pressure became stronger.

"*What are you doing?*" I heard through the mind link. It was Hades and his breathing was labored even in the mind link.

"Playing a game," I whispered back.

"*Fuck, Ember, there is a room full of people.*" He groaned appreciatively.

"Aren't you adventurous?" My finger touched my mark again and my pussy spasmed causing me to instantly climax. I had hoped to last a little longer but that what's done is done. Growling came from the mind link, and I touched myself again, this time, touching my clit at the same time.

"*Kronos, Ember.*" His breath was panting, strong with a heavy lust lacing his voice. "*I can't, can't hold on.*" Smiling to myself I inserted my finger into my pussy, imagining it was his cock.

"Hades." My breath was heavy until I felt his own release. His climax wrecked my own body; it almost felt his come had entered my cavern while I panted. "*How was that, think that can last you until the ceremony?*"

"*If anything, it makes me want you more.*" The growl I heard in my ear wasn't from a mind-link but from the lips of the devil himself. Hades' hand gripped my naked breast harshly, his hot breath leaking down my neck. "*Did you like putting on that little demonstration of your mark? To make me come right in front of your parents?*"

I should be a little worried, but instead I was turned on. "Yes." I bit my lips and giggled.

"Is that so?" His graveled voice shook the apex of my thighs until we heard a harsh knock at the door.

"Hades, you get out. You can't see her until the ceremony!" The banging continued. "Get out!" Hades gripped my ear with his teeth, the stinging sensation made my nipples pebble.

"Later then," he growled. He pushed his pants into my naked behind and I felt the damn spot where he had released. Giggling again, he disappears leaving me to finish getting ready.

Chapter 73

Hades

I trudged back down the stairs. My cock was sticking to my leg because of the little stunt Ember pulled. It was a good one. I'd give her that. She is full of surprises, and I can't wait to take her on a trip away from everyone after the ceremony.

Gabriel grumbled in the corner. He had a great 'O' face. Charlotte was laughing hysterically at our misfortunes, along with several other gods that have been slowly showing up. Willing myself a new black Armani suit because I sweat through the other one through sheer embarrassment, I willed Gabriel new decorative robes. His forehead was still sweaty, and his crazy mop of blonde curls were wet.

"Thanks," he huffed while straightening his belt. "I think she is going to be the death of me." I chuckled, heading out the door while the others followed.

Dionysus took control of the ceremony planning, and Charlotte was all too happy to let him. Charlotte had stressed herself straight sickly, and Wesley was getting perturbed by it. Having gods visiting a Werewolf pack would worry any Luna since she didn't know what to expect of us. We were the legends and stories everyone had heard about, not just your usual extra Wolf pack.

This wouldn't be anything like a normal Werewolf bonding; this was a God bonding. Technically, we were bonded, but gods like a show. If it were up to me, I would have whisked her away a long time ago and said to be done with it. Zeus wouldn't have any of it.

Zeus stood by the edge of the lake, where the ceremony was to be held. Instead of heading to the back of the packhouse where Charlotte had spent hours having flowers decorated over a white arch, Dionysus got to work. The entire lake was transformed into a floating gazebo party boat. Large lily pads with the ability to walk on with ease were placed on the water. Along the edges of the pads held large bushels of flowers that smelled of vanilla and lavender.

In the middle of the lake, a giant golden archway decorated in deep reds scattered throughout the intricate designs of the arch. One person stood in the middle of the archway, the one responsible for my mate and I's paring, Selene. Her moon showed brightly, bright enough that the Wolves on one side of the congregation glowed brightly on their faces. They sat in awe as the gods began to take their own places on the opposite side. Wide eyes and little pointing from the smaller pups had shimmering eyes of wonder and beauty as the gods sat down.

Standing beside Selene, she nudged me and gave a beautiful, red-lipped smile. "I bet you never thought you would be here," she whispered smugly. "I told you she was a perfect match." I sighed heavily, reining my anger in. I knew she was right; most of the unfortunate events would have been prevented, but we are here now, and that was all that mattered.

Selene held her Sphere. Well, it levitated above her hands while we waited. We had only been here five minutes waiting, and I was already ready for my sweet mate to walk down the floating green pads that held a deep red carpet and come to me.

Hera and Michael sat in the front row, holding each other's hands, ogling at each other. Aphrodite flirted with a Wolf across the aisle, blowing kisses while the Wolf threw out some terrible pickup lines. Gripping my fists, I felt the smoke already unleashing from my feet.

"Calm yourself." Selene put a hand on my shoulder. Zeus, my youngest brother, sauntered and put another hand on the other shoulder.

"Congratulations are in order," he held out his hand, and I shook it warningly.

"No tricks today, brother. No fights. This is my mate's day." Zeus feigned innocence as he rubbed his robed chest.

"Never! I would never do that to your mate." He winked and stood beside Selene since he was to be the witness. Supposedly a great honor, but who cares.

Dionysus smacked a few of the instrument players and began whispering harshly for them to play. The angels sat upright and began the flutes and harps while white doves came out of a hidden cage. What the fuck is he doing? This is the cheesiest shit I had ever seen. Before I could protest any more of the nonsense, my mate came into view.

Her ivory lace dress covered her curves and was low enough so all could see the mark on her chest. It glowed a deep red as her bare foot gently tested the lily pad. Though I never cared to look at them, her parents were by her side. It was tunnel vision, and all I could see was my sweet mate. Her hair that I overlooked before was done in a braided crown, flowers adorned, and wisps of curls floated in front of her face.

Kronos, she was beautiful. More beautiful than all the angels in the Celestial Kingdom and more radiant than the sun of Earth and Light Sources of Bergarian. Her eyes set on mine and the brightest white smile gleamed at me. My love, my life, and my light was walking toward me in a torturous manner; I wanted nothing more than to scoop her up in my arms and kiss her senseless.

My eyes grew blurry, and the spit in my mouth choked at my throat. My mate bit her bottom lip and glanced down at her stomach; her hand reached and rubbed her womb just to let me know that we were going to be a family. We would have a beautiful family, and I would never let anything happen to either of them.

Cerberus nudged my side, his head full of flower crowns. It broke my stare with Ember, and a dangerous black tear ran down my cold face.

Fuck.

"We have come to bring you our daughter, first heir to the Black Claw Pack and Alpha," Wesley announced pridefully. "Please take care of her as your mate." His eyes narrowed and his voice deep.

"Through heaven and both the realms, I would fight to keep her safe." Wesley nodded, and Charlotte's tears were wiped away by Ember's finger.

"We are gathered here today to join a special union," Selene announced. Her blue moon showed brighter, lighting up the setting sun. The candles paled in comparison while Selene's hands traced the Sphere. "It is special because not only can supernaturals be paired with other supernaturals and humans, but now the original twelve gods can be paired with anyone." Many wolves and gods whispered among themselves; some were excited while Aphrodite folded her arms in a huff. Whore.

"This will be the first ceremonial bonding of a god to a supernatural now turned goddess through the bond they have created. They have accepted each other through physical and spiritual beings. If that a time ever comes, Ember's change will give her the ability to be my predecessor. She will continue to help me pair mates more quickly as well." Ember squeezed my hand worriedly, but I only kissed her hands.

"Let us begin." Selene chanted a few words in Latin around the Sphere. It raised up into the air so all could see. Granting the Sphere's will, the whole area could finally see the souls that swam in the orb. "As you see, all unmatched souls are collected into the Sphere. Once souls have found each other in a sea of millions, they come to me, and I bind them permanently. God's souls have not been able to be seen in the Sphere, but after many years of trial and error, the Sphere has shown me their souls." Souls of the gods lined up in a line around the sphere.

"Hades' soul is missing because he is now bonded to Ember." Ember smiled at me, and my mouth couldn't stay away as I kissed her quickly on the mouth. Many awed at the motion, but a quick glance into the crowd shut them up. "Hades," Ember rubbed my arm. "Be nice."

"Do you, Hades, God of the Underworld swear to me, the witnesses of the Werewolf pack, Black Claw and that of the entire Celestial Kingdom that you take Ember as your mate, your light to your darkness? To have her throughout eternity to love, to cherish, and complete your soul?" Selene pulled a black onyx ring from the Sphere. It had intricate carvings in Latin spelling out 'love eternal.'

"I do," I roared for all to hear. Taking the ring, I slid it onto Ember's ring finger on her left hand. Cheers came from the Celestial Kingdom's side.

"And do you, Ember, Goddess of Empathy and Soul Binding, swear to me, the witness, the Werewolf pack of the Black Claw and the entire Celestial Kingdom that you take Hades, God of the Underworld, the darkness to your light? To have him throughout eternity to love, to cherish and complete your soul?" Another ring was pulled from the Sphere, gold with intricate designs spelling with the same inscription as hers. The gold ring would always remind me that she was my light.

"I do!" she yelled for everyone in the back to hear. Wolves howled while the gods began clapping frantically. Probably because I'd stop being a pain in their ass.

"With the power granted in me, I pronounce you officially mated and bonded for eternity!"

I didn't wait for Selene to grant me permission; I pulled her by her waist and placed a searing kiss on her mouth. The fire and urgency were real. Her fingers trailed into my hair with one hand while pulling on my black suit collar with the other. Pulling her beautiful lips, I slipped my tongue into her mouth. Her moans filled my throat.

No one bothered to stop us. Why the hell would they? This was my mate, my one and only. I was death. They would have a death sentence if they even tried. Hearing Dionysus yelling some sort of nonsense, large whistles flew and began booming up above.

Ember pulled from the kiss while I whined at the loss of her pouty lips. "Hades look," Ember awed while large white fireworks thundered into the sky. Blue whisps surrounded Ember and began pulling her hair out of her braided crown. Flowers fell all around her, and if she couldn't look more stunning, she surprised me again. Her laugh filled my ears while pulling me closer to her. Her chest pressed to mine while pulling her closer.

My hand willed her a dark crown, full of deep red rubies and diamonds. It was constructed of the finest platinum, hard as steel and unable to be destroyed by the power I invested into it. I willed my crown above my head, black with onyx diamonds in its center. Skulls decorated mine instead of the hell flowers that were on Embers'.

Ember pulled the crown from her head; her mouth hung open in amazement. "Oh my gosh, this is beautiful." Her fingers traced the outside, looking at each jewel. "This is too much," she whispered. Taking the crown from her hands and placing it back where it belonged, I put a hair strand behind her ear.

"It belongs there, it belongs to you, just as my heart belongs to you, my sweet Ember." My mouth descended again to capture her lips.

"So pretty!" I heard the younger pups yell. Screaming, shouting, and even some jumping into the water.

Ember came back up for air while I held her close. "You are mine," I growled, putting a hand around the back of her neck, my thumb tickling her chin. "Mine to love, mine to fuck, my everything." Ember giggled again and grabbed my dick while the congregation started the party without us.

"And this is mine to ride, huh?" Ember smiled while nipping my bottom lip.

Chapter 74

Ember

That was incredible. The decorations, the ceremony, the lights, oh my gosh, the lights! The fireworks weren't really fireworks at all. They stood still in the sky like our own mini galaxy full of twinkling stars.

Hades and I held each other as everyone began to disperse. Dionysus was leading people away from the lily pad holding ceremony. They were all running to the back of the packhouse.

I could smell the roasted boars and some other foods I was unfamiliar with. Celestial fairies flew above us, putting out the candles leaving Hades and me under the pseudo stars above the ceremony ground.

"Now everyone knows you are mine." Hades nipped at my ear while pulling me in by my waist. "No one will ever dare take you away from me.

"Not that they would dare," I snickered. Hades swooped down to kiss me again, but my stomach growled in protest. Getting ready all day was hard work, not to mention the several climaxes before the ceremony even started.

"Let's get you and the little one fed." My face heated up, our little one. Rubbing my belly absentmindedly, Hades led me to the back of the packhouse. Giant balloons of white and red lights glowed over the dance floor. Wolves intermingling with demons, angels, and Celestial Fairies. Gods were also talking to other pack Wolves like they were just one of the group. The stark difference of power was noticeable, but the gods didn't want to overpower them at all. They wanted to celebrate just as much as the others.

There will be several more ceremonies in our future. Vulcan, Ares, and Hermes were all huddled together with their mates. They weren't partying at all. Well, I guess they were drinking with their mates, if that counts. Their mates sat on their laps like little trophies while they fed each other. Many would find it sickening, but I found it adorable.

Peeping around the room, I wanted to see if there were any more mates to be had. The giddiness of finding out that I could mate souls in person reminded me quickly when I glanced at Hera and Michael. My heart almost throbbed with excitement.

Squeezing Hade's hand, I knew this was our moment, and he wasn't going to want to share. I had to be cool, calm, and collected about this. I wanted him to feel as much in the spotlight as possible and that I found him my number one. Biting my lip and bouncing on my toes, Hades quickly caught on that something was bothering me. He sighed heavily and pinched his nose. "Who do you see?" he complained. Kissing his cheek, I pointed to Hera and Michael.

"That might start some drama," he spoke lowly. "Zeus was hoping to get her back." I twisted my mouth in displeasure.

"He wouldn't dare take her, would he?"

Hades shook his head, pulling me close. "Not after what Demeter pulled. Besides, I'd overpower him and take his powers like Demeter." I felt Selene's presence behind me, her soft fingers brushing my bareback.

"What do you see, Ember? I see that gleam in your eye." Tittering, I turned to her and pointed to the couple.

"Hera and Michael," I whispered. "Don't you see it?" Selene tilted her head, looking between the couple and me.

"See what?" She bit her red lips as she stared at the couple slow dancing together.

"The glow, they are supposed to be soul mates, right?" I questioned. Selene gasped in realization.

"You have the empathy gift; you can see the love of their souls just as you can read anyone and their emotions. I can see through the Sphere; you can see with your own eyes." She smiled brightly at me. "This could be a gift or a curse to you," she warned Hades.

"How so?" Hades grumbled. Gripping my waist tightly.

"Because your Ember is a caring soul and might get carried away wanting to pair too many," she laughed. Selene wandered through the crowd, watching the mated couples while I gave my most enormous puppy eyes to my mate.

"Just one couple tonight." I raised my finger. "Just one and then no more. It is all about us." Hades smirked and kissed the side of my mouth.

"One," he growled. "Then you are mine for a few weeks." I went to protest until his finger traced my lips. "Mine." I squealed and pulled Hades with me, wanting him to watch what I could do.

Hera and Gabriel's eyes widened, hands sandwiched together; they both glanced at each other, wondering what I was doing. They dared not tell me no, because Hades stood behind me brooding with his arms crossed raising a brow. He was still mad I had decided to pair a couple, but he could get over it. Hera had deserved it after the many years she put up with Zeus and his douchebaginess.

My eyes closed, and pulling them together, their hands both vibrated and warmed. Hera gasped first while the Arch Angel Michael followed. His large wings, the largest that I had ever seen amongst all the angels, pulled Hera into her as soon as I let go. They were in their own little feather pod while Hades pulled me back.

"Okay, they are done. Now you are mine." Laughing, Hades pulled me to the buffet table and filled my plate full of the most delicious food. Food ranging from my pack's specialties, sweet Bergarian flower salads, Ambrosian Sponge Cakes, and skewers of roasted falcon and vegetables filled my nose. I ate a ridiculous amount of food while Hades had me on his lap. I was too hungry to care, so happy to be in my mate's arms, and finally no more drama. All the drama had slipped away.

Hades kissed my forehead and moved me to my own padded chair he had willed for the both of us. "I need to speak to Ares about the safety of your pack once we leave. I'll be back shortly." I nodded my head, too engrossed in the food, and licked my fingers delicately. I couldn't remember the last time I ate so much food. My stomach was going to be too distended to dance later.

"Ember," a smooth voice spoke until I looked up. Loukas and Nora stood hand in hand, both sporting fresh marks. I popped another grape in my mouth and clapped my hands like a child.

"Oh, you both look adorable!" I squealed, and Loukas blushed a bright shake of deep blue. Nora giggled, looking up at him adoringly. I was so happy for Nora. I had remembered she had always been at the bottom of the pack but a dutiful worker. Her times in the kitchen had made everything so pleasant growing up. Almost like a second mother to me. She was at least sixty years old in human years but with the Werewolf blood, looked not a day over 30.

"We just wanted to say thank you," Nora spoke for Loukas, who was still uncomfortable. His tail was securely wrapped around Nora's other arm. I bit my lip, trying not to laugh at the silliness of it all. "And that, we were wondering if I could live with Loukas in the Underworld and work for you. He has a high position with Hades, and I don't want him to give that up." Nora was such a doll thinking of her mate.

"We don't have to," Loukas babbled. "We can be wherever you want."

Nora shook her head and laid it on the side of his arm. "I would like a change of scenery and helping in the kitchen in the Underworld sounds lovely. I heard they have amazing stone fruits that I'm dying to work with."

Could they be any cuter!?

Oh gosh, they can't. I want to make little dolls out of them and put them on my bed and play with them!

"Duh, you can come to the Underworld! Mates are protected, and you are part demon, too, right? It isn't a problem at all. You can also remain dual citizenship within the Black Claw Pack, too," I chirped. "I am. That way, I always have a mind-link with my family."

Nora grabbed Loukas's face and kissed him repeatedly. "Thank you, Alpha, er Goddess Ember!" I waved longingly as I watched them go to the overcrowded dance floor. They were adorable. Leaning on my fist and watching the others dance, I felt a nudge at my shoulder. Blaze was sitting beside my plate in his tiny form. His tail waved in the wind with little smoke tendrils waving.

"You abandoned me once we got back to the pack. What happened?" I joked.

Blaze chirped before speaking. "You have a lot of Wolves here that need some talking to. A lot of your wolves could shift earlier if given the confidence," he scolded. I shrugged my shoulders. I didn't know Wolves needed a pep talk.

"Most don't need it, but there are some that need some coaxing," his voice trailed off. Was he asking to stay? I hummed in agreement with him while scratching under his chin.

"Do you wanna stay?" I cooed. "Do you want to remain here and be a guardian to the Wolves instead of returning back with us?" Blaze snuffed, his tail withering away. Aw, he's shy too! "Blaze, you can go wherever you want. You helped me, and you are welcome to help others here in the Black Claw Pack. If it's Okay with my dad," I warned.

"Remus said I could." His mood became cheery. "Remus needs some lessons to talk normally." I shook my head. Mom liked it when Remus talked like a cave man.

"Good luck with that," I hummed.

Blaze sat with me while we watched. Many come to congratulate me, some to coax me into dancing, but Hades would have set them ablaze or pulled their heart out and stomped on it, or both. I laughed internally at the thought of him getting all jealous. I couldn't say much now, could I? I would rip Persephone's eyes out if she even joked about it, even if she was pleasant to me.

A heated gaze fell upon me. It felt like flames tickling my cheeks until I turned to see none other than the Devil himself across the dance floor. The sexual tension pulled at me between my legs while Hades' dark gaze continued to assault me. Even though I was sitting at our private table, I could almost feel him touch me.

Taking my eyes away from his gaze, the floor where people danced was covered in smoke. Many thought it was for the party as Dionysus started a keg stand on the other side of the floor. Cheers, loud music continued, but Hades was the only attention I sought.

A tickle at my ankle threw a chill up my leg. The very little hair I had left on my body from a previous waxing stood on end. The tickle wrapped around both legs and pried my legs wide. Trying to shut them, the strength of the force was too much. My throat gasped when my dress had been unceremoniously thrown above my thighs. My white lace thong was pushed to one side of my thigh.

Hades continued to stare from the opposite side of the dance floor, his eyes dark, full of lust, and mischief. Holding a glass of whisky in his hand, he smirked into his drink. Pulling the tablecloth up so I could see what was going on, his whisps of smoke had traveled up my leg and had turned into Hades' own hand. The gold-colored ring could be seen on his smokey ring finger.

Holy Fudge Balls. He wouldn't dare.

Pushing the tablecloth down, I shook my head at a distance, but his white fangs brightened at the site of my nervousness.

"Honey," mom cooed at me. Dad was holding mom by the waist, both blocking my view of my mate. "Aren't you haven't fun? Don't you want to get up and dance? I think Hades is done talking to Ares now." Mom's curled hair was flung over her shoulder.

The tickle in my inner thigh moved to my pussy lips and fingered the folds to my cavern. Biting my lip until it bled, I shook my head. "My flame, what's wrong?" My dad looked me over, concerned. I shook my head again.

"Go dance, I'll be out in a minute," I said strained.

"Is it the baby?" Mom began to pry. Her words were falling on deaf ears because that smoke tendril just brushed my pussy. A loud moan escaped my lips. I couldn't hold it. Slapping my hand over my mouth, my face turned beat red.

"Are you sick?" Dad pushed again, but I felt the flick of a rough finger on my clit again. My achy body shook while I held onto the table with my hands. Two fingers thrust into me while I felt a thumb rub quickly on my bundle of nerves.

"Fine, Dad, might need some ginger ale," I lied, gritting my teeth. My nipples pebbled. They were going to rip through my dress. Smoke trailed up dress and on my hips, feeling nothing but small suction-like kisses.

"*Hades,*" I whispered in the mind-link.

"*Yes, my love?*" His snicker could be felt in my ear.

"*My p-parents,*" I groaned internally.

"*Payback, darling.*"

Hades thrust another finger into me, pushing me back into my seat. Mom came around the table to hold me back up while I fell apart. Hiding my face in my hands, Mom sniffed the air and quickly and raised her hands away from me.

"Wesley, let's go..." her voice trailed off and looked everywhere but where I was sitting. "There..." she pointed to a random spot on the dance floor.

"What for? Ember is sick, we need to..." His nose flared, and his fist tightened. "We are in public," he growled.

"They are playing a game. Let them." Mom gave me a wink, and push dad away. "Remember the time I pleasured you under the desk when your mother was in the office?" Dad's face turned red, and he pulled her away. Grumbling he pulled mom away.

If I wasn't in a haze of bliss, I would have laughed.

Hades' long strides came up to the table, his black suit covered his muscles, and the tight vest he wore outlined his perfectly tight hips. "Have fun?" he cooed in my ear while pulling me up.

His fingers, entangled with the smoke that just left my dress. Sticking them in his mouth he whispered seductively, "Mm, delicious."

I playfully pushed him while his hand pulled me to the dance floor. "You're so evil." It would be our first dance together, and I wanted it to be a good one. Trailing his hands around my waist and pulling my hands around his neck, he placed a tender kiss on my forehead.

"Never thought I'd be here with you," he muttered. "Never thought I would have a mate let alone the most beautiful she-wolf.

His nose traced my neck, moaning at the tickle his hot breath left on my skin.

Zeus sulked unhappily in the corner, his arms crossed, and the bright glow that usually surrounded him was missing. He looked genuinely sad as he watched the other gods dance, drink and be merry. Before I could mention it to Hades, small sparkles exploded from his body and left the party entirely.

"I wouldn't change anything," I whispered. "Not a thing." I hummed, laying my head to his broad chest. Closing my eyes, I didn't realize how tired I had become.

"Enjoy having your eyes closed now my goddess. You won't be closing your eyes for a while," he growled playfully in my ear.

"Oh really," I said seductively. "Pray tell, what will we be doing?"

"Take a wild guess." His nose traced up my neck.

Before I could ask any more questions, the floor cleared, and smoke and fire engulfed us in Hades' tornado. Cheers erupted in the crowd while the fire tornado engulfed us as we left ceremoniously for our friends and family to party into the night.

.

Epilogue

The Underworld was more relaxed than its usual raging inferno. The green undergrowth even dared to pop through the blackened soil of Tartarus. Dark clouds confidently blew over the River of Styx, threatening the sky with rain. The pack of Hell Hounds that had hidden in the farthest region of the Underworld were welcomed back into the Hades' Palace grounds.

The pack of Hell Hounds now had a home. Large barns and kennels resided at the back of the palace property, where they ferociously protected the precious inhabitants of the palace. Phantomtails danced on the front lawn, helping to keep the wild beasts at bay, and not only did Blaze come to help his fellow Phantomtails calm the beasts, but he was here for another particular reason.

The children of the numerous visitors played outside. They ran around The Gods Garden where structures of playhouses and swings built into the trees resided. They had not a care in the world, just the fun of playing with the other species of supernaturals. Demons, Celestial Fairies, Angels, Werewolves, and Vampires played with no animosity towards another, just pure joy and bliss.

The foyer was bright and crowded with both gods of the Celestial Kingdom and of the Black Claw Pack. Ember's family stood at the forefront, all drinking the sweet ambrosia nectar that was once reserved for the gods themselves. Everyone gathered today as an equal as long as no threat was posed to each other.

Mates crowded together on one side of the room while the unmated sighed in jealousy of the love that blossomed. The unmated had hoped to help celebrate a newborn babe, but also if Ember could see the potential in a mated pair since the Goddess Selene was on a hiatus for the unseeable future.

Meanwhile, upstairs, Ember was humming gently while Nora braided her hair. Ember held dark circles, but the faint smile remained because the people had gathered from afar. Seeing them would brighten her spirits. A considerable yawn came from her plump lips, and Hades walked towards her, holding the newborn baby.

"I can send them away," he grunted. "They can come another time when you are feeling better." Ember shook her head at Hades' antics. She didn't want to seem ungrateful to those who wanted to see the newborn that was just born yesterday. She had just hoped they would wait a few more days. Just because it was her third child didn't mean she had the whole motherhood deal in 'the bag.'"

"No, no." She waved as another yawn escaped her. "I don't want them to be disappointed. Besides, it isn't every day you have a baby with the Devil." Ember chortled as she stood up. Nora pulled back the black, slim-fitting gown with dark red rubies adorning the waist. Being a goddess had its perks. She didn't even look pregnant just the day before.

"We have two others," Hades said, disgruntled. "It isn't even like it is the first." Their eldest son walked in, looking ever so much like his father in a dark black suit. He pulled at his sleeves at the especially fit suit. A habit he liked to exhibit when he was nervous.

"Aw, Luci, what's wrong?" Lucifer was 25 years old; unlike his father and mother, he was born with wispy brown hair. He inherited his father's dominance of the room and not to mention the sexual allure he had when he walked. If there could have been a God of beauty, it would have been him. However, he was not.

After thirteen, they quickly figured out what he was the God of Destruction.

The fates had let the power seep through Hades' genes and passed it along to his son. If he wasn't raised right by his parents, who knows what type of destruction he would bring.

Ember worried every day for her son. She had hoped he would have inherited her empath abilities or something of the sort, but that wish didn't happen. "Come here, Lucifer." Ember held out her arms to her son, who towered over her just like his father. He embraced the only woman he swore to himself he would ever touch or love.

Lucifer loved his mother and would do anything to please her, yet the hatred in his heart for others grew. He hated women that came on to him the most. Demon women of hell had tried to lure their way to his bed. Lucifer had killed so many demon women his poor father would spend days by the Soul Pool and revive them. A mate was not in the cards for him, he thought. Even though his mother would do her best to give him the perfect match, she worried he might be mateless.

"Cheer up, baby." Ember kissed his hand since she couldn't reach his cheek. "They will be gone after they see your sister." Ember looked around the room. Hades was cradling his daughter, cooing at her, not looking like the Devil. "Where is your brother?" Lucifer rolled his eyes. His younger brother, Loki, was the mischief-maker. That was apparent when he was just three years old.

Loki squealed and ran into the room. The 10-year-old had whipped cream on his hand and licked it quickly so his parents couldn't see.

"Hi, Luci!" Loki yelled, sliding effortlessly under his mother's vanity. Lucifer gritted his teeth. He hated that name. If Loki wasn't ten years old, he would have socked him in the face.

"What are you doing!?" Ember snapped. "Get up here and look presentable." Loki straightened his suit, licking the remaining bit of whipped cream from his fingers. "The cake is good," he chirped. "Nora might be mad, though."

Hades lifted Loki with a wave of his hand. He now hovered in front of Hades with an evil smirk. "Do you need to spend some time with your aunt Demeter in Tartarus?" Hades warned.

Loki shook his head frantically. Hades had already taken Loki to Tartarus for a field trip of sorts. He had to show his son what exactly his father did and what he was capable of. Since that day, Loki stayed clear of any of the judgment chairs or the grounds of the west that held the land of screams.

Lucifer grinned, fisting his hand with his palm. He liked the souls screaming for mercy, for he knew those evils deserved it. It had become his new playground, testing new and merciless tortures that involved physical pain and mental. Demeter was especially his favorite, dangling a life-like vision of Persephone in front of her over and over. Only for Demeter to wail in despair that she could no longer touch her beloved daughter. It served her right to try and separate his parents. Ember was the best mother he could have ever prayed for.

"Now that's enough. Let's go to the entrance. People are waiting on us." Hades continued to carry the baby girl, their last child. Hades was tired of sharing his mate, but Ember wanted a daughter so badly and he couldn't give up until his mate was sated. Even with his jealousy, he was happy to have his children. After all, he thought there would be no little spawns of the Devil for most of his life.

Ember had an arm linked with Hades while the two boys followed. Loki smirked at Lucifer. Lucifer knew that look, he had something planned, and it wasn't going to be good. Lucifer entered Loki's mind and pried to see what he was up to. That was something Lucifer was quite good at. Finding the fears of others but another treasure he unlocked was finding the sins they were about to commit.

Lucifer narrowed his eyes at Loki. Once Loki realized what his brother was going to do he willed his plan away. If Lucifer was looking he would rat him out like he always does when he is near. Loki knowing the Wolves' favorite part of a boar was the leg. He had planned to snatch them all and hide them under cushions of couches to make them hunt for their food. That plan was now rubbish.

The prideful couple walked to the large balcony, overlooking the gods, goddesses, and the rest of the hand-picked supernaturals invited to the announcement. The quiet stillness fell over the entire crowd while they looked up to the King and Queen of the Underworld. Ember nudged Hades to say something, but he only rolled his eyes.

"You announce it, Flower." He tried to bat his eyes to get her to listen, but she huffed in disagreement.

"You are king! Why should I do it?" she hissed.

"I'm holding the baby. I don't want to wake her." The baby purred in his chest. Ember instantly cooed at the thought that she could have Werewolf blood in her daughter's body. However, this would never happen because Gods blood was too strong. She would more than likely become the goddess of animals or the sorts.

"Fine," she huffed. "But you will rub my feet in the tub tonight."

Hades grinned, thinking he won the argument. "But no funsies until it's completed." Hades scowled again while the crowd took a few steps back.

"Thank you all for coming," Ember announced as queenly as she should. "It is an honor to have you all in our presence as we announce the birth of our…." Ember paused for effect. "Daughter."

The crowd oohed and awed over the baby, making sure to be extra quiet when Hades put his finger to his lips. The baby gripped hold of Hades' jacket and snuggled deeper. "Our daughter will now be known as Lilith, princess of the Underworld." Light claps paraded around.

Ember glanced at the couples, Vulcan, Ares, Hermes, her parents, and even Dante, her brother, present with his mate. The warm feeling, she felt from her empath abilities revitalized her soul. The circles under her eyes instantly vanished, feeling energized. Before she could continue with her speech, she saw a girl, maybe a woman who was as short as her, out of the corner of her eye. It captured her attention since most of the magical creatures were tall. Her wings were small, white, with hints of gold on the tips. The chestnut hair flowed effortlessly down her back, curling at the ends. A small, tiny golden string attached to the front of her dress was gliding upward.

Ember clutched the railing, watching where the golden string would land. Ember's powers had grown over the past twenty-five years. Mates no longer had to touch each other to find out if they were a match. She could now follow the tiny string with her eyes and find the other person's mate if they were in the room. Ember's eyes widened. The string-led up the stairs and straight onto her son Lucifer's heart.

"Oh, ship," she muttered under her breath. Hades' eyebrow raised in confusion. "Please, everyone, enjoy the food. Everyone will be able to gaze at Lilith when we come down," Ember announced. Pulling on Hades' arm, she hurried down the stairs to find this hybrid mate that Ember had seen for her son. Hades only grunted at his mate's antics. He knew exactly what she was doing. Only this time, he didn't think it would be for his son.

On further inspection, Ember strolled up to the girl who was picking up small pieces of shrimp and honeydew flowers. Drizzling everything in honey. How peculiar. "Excuse me," Ember tapped gently on the woman's shoulder. The girl's eyes glittered with excitement turning around quickly. Her eyes were bright gold, matching the smaller wings on her back.

"I don't believe I have met you before; what is your name?" Ember held out her hand to shake. They were both the same size and gave Ember a more welcoming feeling, not the only short goddess in the room.

"My name is Uriel," her sweet voice sang. "I've never been to one of these functions before, so I'm sorry I don't know anyone." Her voice dipped lower, indicating her disappointment. Uriel quickly cheered up and smiled. "But I'm here now, and that's great." Ember liked her already for her cheery attitude, but who was she really?

"Who are your parents? Surely we know them?" Hades wasn't paying attention. He was giving Lilith a bottle of pumped breast milk to his daughter and swaying her back and forth. "The Goddess Hera and Head Angel Michael." Her voice returned with excitement. "They weren't able to come, so they sent me."

"That's a shame." Ember shook her head, showing slight displeasure. She was distraught that Hera and Michael never told anyone she had a daughter. Uriel's presence was indeed a surprise, especially to Ember, who is to mate everyone. Why would they have hidden her for so long?

"How old are you, dear?" Ember pried again.

"Twenty five." Uriel popped a gooey flower in her mouth. "Mother and Father are at home, waiting for a baby." Uriel filled her plate with more honey. Twenty-five years, hiding their child from everyone. What the heck for?

"Oh, I didn't know they were pregnant," Ember added quickly.

"Pregnant?" Uriel tilted her head, not understanding the word. "No, no, they are waiting for the stork to bring me a new brother or sister. They said it could be months, but they didn't want to leave and sent me out because they said my presence might scare the stork off."

Hades turned his head in astonishment while Ember stopped breathing. "*Who is this woman's mate? I feel sorry for him,*" Hades mind-linked Ember.

"*Our son, Lucifer.*" Ember swallowed the wad of spit that gathered in her throat.

"*Fuck.*" Hades' eyes didn't leave the innocent eyes of the girl. "What did you say you are the goddess of?" Hades' gruff voice startled Uriel, who looked she was about to cry.

"Innocence and grace?" Uriel questioned herself.

Lucifer, the God of Destruction, was now paired with the Goddess of Innocence. No wonder her wings were tiny, and she had child-like features. What a pair this would make.

Ember shrugged her shoulders and tugged on the string. Hades grabbed her arm quickly, leaving the baby bottle to float in the air. "Don't do this," Hades whispered harshly. "This will be nothing but a mess."

"I have to do my job. I don't go to your work and tell you how to judge people. Besides, no funsies if you don't let me." Ember gave the lip that Hades couldn't say no to. Sighing and pinching his nose, he nodded. "This will be a shit show."

"Shh, don't talk like that around the baby," Ember scolded him again. Uriel continued to eat and wiggle her wings every time she took a bite of the honey-drenched anything. Shaking her head, she pulled at the string connected to Lucifer.

Lucifer's head shook with annoyance. He was still standing on the large landing at the top of the stairs. He had the sudden urge to mingle among the guests. Rolling his eyes, he followed his intuition. His feet landed in front of his mother, who was smiling brightly at a small girl facing her. Lucifer's annoyance was already building while stepping closer to his mother and father. They were intently speaking with this new annoyance.

"Mother," Lucifer spoke in his deep velvet voice. Ember looked upward and smiled brightly at her son. "Honey, I would like to introduce you to someone." Lucifer's jaw ticked. He knew his mother understood of his reluctance to women. He had not touched one in all the twenty five years of his life, and she knew his wishes. However, if his mother wanted to introduce him to a girl for the first time, it must be important.

The girl's hair flung behind her, gardenia aroma swirling around his nose. Her small stature didn't allow her to even see his face until she looked upward. Eyes gold and full of sparkle, she gave the brightest smile she could give. "Hi, I'm Uriel. What's your name?" Her voice was out of a cartoon princess movie. It was calming, and his shoulders automatically relaxed, his breath evened out, and his facial features were softened.

Ember and Hades looked on intently. Reaching into her mind, he found no future acts of sin and no evil intentions. This intrigued him.

"I'm Lucifer." The voice made Uriel shutter involuntary. It was then, Lucifer realized who she might be to him. Glancing back at his mother and Ember nodded her head frantically, but there was no smile, just one of worry.

"I'm the goddess of Innocence. What are you? Everyone has been asking me mine. I think I should ask you too!" Uriel giggled.

For once, Lucifer felt embarrassed. He wanted nothing more than to strike fear in those around him, but with this small woman, he didn't want to tell her. "It isn't important," he adjusted his collar. Uriel stared back blankly for a moment until her head popped up.

"Ok!" Putting her empty plate down with extra honey, she took his hand and shook it frantically. "Nice to meet you! I'm going to see what the kids are doing outside! Oh, you tickle!" She almost snorted and left without a care in the world.

Lucifer was left standing in shock. Those tickles were the tingles his mother warned him about. No doubt in his mind that the innocent goddess was his mate.

Ember and Hades gripped each other, waiting for Lucifer to say something, anything. A good minute passed by until the uneasy crowd parted, and Lucifer walked out the door and into the garden.

"That went well," Ember chirped back at Hades. "It will be fine. You and I did great!" Hades smiled down at his mate and kissed her forehead.

"You're right. We did. I just worry about Hera and Michael," he grunted.

The party went on well, and the large foyer was now empty. All that was left was Hades, Ember, Loki, and Lilith gazing at the mess. Lucifer was nowhere to be found, and no one wanted to know.

"This was nice, the whole kid thing." Hades pressed a tender kiss to the baby's forehead that had nestled into her mother. Lilith began rooting to be fed again.

"But I think I want to take care of my mate for the rest of eternity." Loki made a gagging noise and ran off with a male guard that was supposed to keep him out of trouble. Loki had already been through five the past year, and each time the demons had been revived, they screamed in fear not to be around the troublemaker.

"Maybe later I can have a turn," Hades growled. Ember hummed, gently exposing her breast to feed and walking the baby upstairs. Hades nipped at her ear.

"Oh certainly." Ember purred back. "Right after my foot rub."

If you want to read more about female lead's parents, you can check out *The Alpha's Kitten* available on Kindle Unlimited and Amazon.

Printed in Great Britain
by Amazon

81065477R00295